Jack London's Tales of Adventure

Jack London's
Tales of Adventure

Edited by Irving Shepard

Hanover House, Garden City, New York

Printed in the United States of America

Library of Congress Catalog Card Number 56–5714

CONTENTS

The Short Story Writer

A Photographic Album

INTRODUCTION

"I would rather be ashes than dust! I would rather that my spark should burn out in a brilliant blaze than it should be stifled by dry-rot. I would rather be a superb meteor, every atom of me in magnificent glow, than a sleepy and permanent planet. The proper function of man is to live, not to exist. I shall not waste my days in trying to prolong them. I shall use my time."

Only the brilliant, restless personality who was Jack London could have conceived of such a dynamic and challenging credo as this. And only he, with his great physical strength, his intense intellect, and his turbulent spirit, could have successfully lived up to it.

Jack London was only forty when he died, but in his time he had lived life to its fullest. He accomplished more and experienced more in his brief existence than most men could in a dozen lifetimes. He was, first of all, a man of extravagance. He plunged into everything with supercharged energy. As Van Wyck Brooks observed, "Veritable waves of force seemed to rush out of him." If his untempered enthusiasm sometimes seemed to lead him astray and to excesses it was only the natural consequence of an exuberant, unfettered imagination and a boundless lust for life.

The world was still knee-deep in Victorian morals, traditions, and ideals when Jack London burst upon the literary scene. To the generations exposed to the sentimental pap of the popular writers of the day, his stories of savage realism and heroic conflict had the effect of a tidal wave, sweeping before them the false, romantic idealism that was the vogue. The world as he saw it (as reflected in his writings) was hostile and cruel, with only the brave and the strong having any chance for survival. He refused to shrink from life's unpleasant and brutal side, yet his work retained more than a good measure of romanticism. He bridged the gap between the nineteenth and twentieth centuries and blazed the trail for a new, more realistic school of writing. Within three years after the publication of his first story by a national magazine (*Atlantic Monthly*) Jack had had five books published and two more were in preparation. In his brief writing career he had published eighteen novels, twenty volumes of short stories, seven non-fiction books, three plays, and hundreds of newspaper and magazine articles, essays, and reviews. What a tremendous intellectual accomplishment!

The passage of almost half a century has had little effect on the dramatic, forceful, unique character of Jack London's work; it retains its ability to enthrall, excite, and entertain. He remains one of the most successful writers in the history of American letters. As recently as 1952, as a result of a world-wide survey, the United Nations agency Unesco reported that Jack London was the most popular, most widely translated American author in Europe, Russia, and the Iron Curtain countries.

Time often plays strange tricks to the reputation of a man. As the years pass the critics become increasingly disposed to search for new angles, new points for interpretation in their attempts to evaluate a man's accomplishments. They tend to go to extremes—attempting either to idolize or to destroy, to praise or to damn. My uncle has been a controversial figure in death, as well as in life. The critics still violently disagree over the place he occupies in American letters. As his nephew it would be both improper and unwise for me to enter the controversy; my views would naturally be prejudiced in his favor. I should rather leave such a decision to posterity which, after all, is the severest yet the truest critic of all. I do believe, however, that much of the confusion that exists is the result of failure to consider Jack London a product of his times. Only by studying the forces that molded his character can we fully appreciate the works of this extraordinary man.

Born in San Francisco in 1876 Jack London grew up in a world witnessing the settlement of the last frontier. Gone forever were the proud days of the pioneer. The country was beset with economic and cultural changes that for decades were to play havoc with the traditional American way of life. It was a world in transition. The easygoing days of an economy dominated by agriculture were being replaced by the world of the machine, the factory, and the financial titan. America in the late 1800s was a battleground for unscrupulous tycoons and robber barons. The Far West was torn apart by the struggles of the big railroad interests. Financial panics followed one after the other as the "Big Four" plotted and conspired to gain more money and power. The economy remained in a state of flux. And the people were the pawns.

The memory of Jack London's early life was etched and scarred by the bitterness of poverty. His family was continually on the move to find subsistence. At the age of ten the boy was on the street selling newspapers to supplement the family's meager income. For fourteen years thereafter—until his first writing success at twenty-four—life was one vicious, downward cycle of toil, escape, toil, escape, toil. He became a "work beast" laboring in a cannery, a jute mill, a laundry, and shoveling coal in a power station. He worked for ten cents an hour, thirteen to fourteen hours a day, six and seven days a week. Is it any wonder that he saw life in terms of man's unending struggle against a ruthless nature? Is it any wonder that he saw in socialism a chance for the salvation of others as lost as he had once been? Is it any wonder that he hungered for knowledge and success that would lift him above the degrading plain of poverty? Look, then, to the formative years for a clue to the life and works of Jack London. There you will see the hunger and want that drove him to become a socialist. There you will see the birth of that indomitable spirit which could eventually lead him only to a philosophy of individualism. In his heart and sympathies Jack London was a socialist; he could not forget the sufferings of his past. But in his mind and actions he was an individualist; he could not forget his achievements. Throughout his life he struggled valiantly to reconcile these conflicting philosophies.

I believe that it was the noted critic, Alfred Kazin, who stated that the greatest story Jack London ever wrote was the story he lived. After reading the first section of this volume, entitled "The Young Man," I feel that you will not only find this to be true, but that you will have gained a valuable insight into the character of a truly remarkable man.

While he did not live long enough to begin the autobiography his notes indicate he planned to write, we are fortunate that so much of my uncle's writing is autobiographical in nature. "The Young Man" is the story of his childhood and youth, composed of autobiographical material gathered from many sources, integrated and arranged in chronological order. Oyster pirate, deep-sea sailor, hobo, Alaskan prospector, all these incidents in his life make fascinating reading. But most important of all Jack London's adventures was his struggle to become a writer. Without guidance, writing under almost impossible circumstances, for the most part educating himself, and faced with continual economic hardship, he stumbled and groped for three long years in the literary wilderness. In the beginning the rejection slips followed one another with monotonous regularity. Had he been a weaker man he might have succumbed. Certainly the odds were against him. But at the end of his three-year travail success was his. He had conquered his Everest; the world was at his feet!

Success was a stimulant to the vivid imagination of the young author. Each new idea that flashed into consciousness soon became father to a dozen more. Jack drove himself at a furious, strenuous pace, writing one to two to three thousand words a day, while devoting the few remaining hours to research and study. He was an avid reader and took voluminous notes for future reference. As his stories and articles became increasingly popular they also became less of a challenge to him. And when he realized that a great many of his ideas could not be fully and effectively developed within the limitations of the short-story form he began to write a novel. He realized before it was finished that this first attempt was a disappointment. The experience it provided, however, proved to be invaluable. The second novel, *The Call of the Wild*, was a tremendous success. A year later this triumph was followed by the dramatic, powerful *The Sea Wolf*, and in subsequent years by *White Fang*, *Martin Eden*, *The Iron Heel*, and *The Valley of the Moon*—all best sellers in the most extravagant sense of the word.

But writing short stories, articles, and novels was still not enough to occupy Jack London fully in these early days. When in 1902 the Hearst Syndicate offered to send him to Africa to report on the Boer War, he readily accepted. Before he reached Europe, however, the Dutch settlers had capitulated. Instead of returning home he went on to London and "disappeared" in the East End slums. In the role of a stranded American sailor the self-trained sociologist moved freely among the impoverished, pitiful inhabitants, observing firsthand the harsh realities of life among the poor of Great Britain. On his return to the States he related his experiences in *The People of the Abyss*. This book remains, over fifty years later, a masterpiece of human interest reporting and a unique sociological document.

As his reputation grew *Harper's*, *Collier's*, *Cosmopolitan*, the Hearst Syndicate, and other leading magazines and newspapers deluged Jack with offers of assignments. He accepted only those that interested him most. In 1904, just two years after his sojourn in the London slums he left for Korea, via Japan, to cover the Russo-Japanese War. Upon his arrival in Tokyo he found that the imperial government had restricted all foreign correspondents to Japan. Jack had come too far to be held back, and he managed to slip through to Fusan before the Japanese seized the boat on which he had sailed. In desperation he hired a junk, picked up a native crew, and sailed for Chemulpo, Korea. In the middle of the Yellow Sea they were engulfed by a howling gale. Half drowned and nearly frozen, Jack brought the boat to safety on the rugged Korean coast. Because of his daring he became one of only seven correspondents to reach the front lines, and his photographs were the first to be received in America. A number of these historic prints appear in this volume, as well as selections from his on-the-spot reports.

A few months after his return home from the war *The Sea Wolf* was published to wildly enthusiastic popular and critical acclaim. The subsequent years were to be filled with many golden days for Jack London. His coffers were never empty and his material wealth mounted. His first marriage had ended in an unhappy divorce, but in 1905 he married Charmian Kittredge, who proved to be the perfect mate for him. Vivacious, indefatigable, unconventional, she shared in all of his adventures and followed him to all corners of the world.

Adventure and excitement were as essential to my uncle's life as were food and water. Whenever the strain of writing became too great the wanderlust of his youth would return. Often he would find release from his problems aboard his boat, the *Spray* (and later, the *Roamer*), as he cruised about San Francisco Bay. It was in February 1906, after a four-month lecture tour from which he returned ill, exhausted, and discouraged, that he began to make plans for his long-dreamed-of world cruise. Inspired by the adventure of Captain Joshua Slocum who single-handedly had sailed around the world in a small boat, Jack began to build a boat to his own design and specifications. This boat, "for the want of a better name," was to be called the *Snark*. Money was no object. Only the best materials were to be used in its construction. To obtain them he literally chained himself to his desk and increased the load of his already staggering work schedule. The building of the *Snark* as related in "The Inconceivable and the Monstrous" turned out to be a heartbreaking farce. Originally estimated at seven thousand dollars, the *Snark* cost over thirty thousand dollars. When, in desperation, Jack put out to sea the boat proved to be "an unfinished, internal wreck." For all of its shortcomings, however, the *Snark* safely carried the Londons and her small crew across the Pacific to Hawaii, Tahiti, Samoa, and the Solomons. When a severe case of tropical sun poisoning forced Jack to terminate the voyage in Australia and to desert the *Snark* he and Charmian were truly heartbroken. Their "little boat" had brought them safely through a superb adventure.

The cruise of the *Snark* had lasted twenty-seven months. Jack was sick and weary as he arrived in San Francisco in July of 1909. Once home, however, he regained his health and soon fell into the familiar pattern of work hard and play hard. In 1905 he had purchased 129 acres of ranch land in the Sonoma valley, and as time went by he continued to add adjoining acreage. While writing remained his vocation, farming became his avocation. As an enthusiast of scientific farming, he set out to make his "Beauty Ranch" the most modern in the West. Among the innovations he built was the first concrete-block silo in California and a stone piggery. He ardently advocated the scientific breeding of animals and imported many European Purebreds to improve his stock. After years of wandering Jack London was finally planting his roots in the "Valley of the Moon." In a letter to his good friend, George Sterling, he wrote, "I am going to throw out an anchor so big and so heavy that all hell could never get it up again." He also began the construction of "Wolf House," a magnificent structure to be built of the giant redwoods and the massive red stones found in abundance on the ranch; a house that was to last "a thousand years." As in the construction of the *Snark* no expense was spared in making this the most perfect house that could be erected. Jack had spent over eighty thousand dollars to accomplish his goal when tragedy struck. The finishing touches were put on the big house on August 18, 1913, and the Londons prepared to move in as soon as possible. Shortly after midnight "Wolf House" mysteriously burst into flame and quickly became a roaring inferno. In only a few moments the results of three years' labor were reduced to a smoking, hollow ruin. The cause of the conflagration was never determined. Jack promised he would rebuild his house but he never did.

He continued to travel extensively all the while he was building his house and developing his ranch. In 1910 he covered the world's heavyweight championship fight between Johnson and Jeffries in Reno, Nevada, for the New York *Herald*. A few years later (1912) Charmian accompanied him on a trip around Cape Horn, from New York to California. In 1914 he went with the American expeditionary force that sailed into Vera Cruz to put down the Mexican insurrection that was endangering American lives and property. This show of force was successful, the revolt was squelched, and Jack's only rewards were five or six inconsequential articles for *Collier's* and a severe case of dysentery.

From this point on his good health began to desert him; his strenuous living had taken its toll. He suffered from severe mental fatigue and depression. A trip to Hawaii in 1915 served to improve his condition only temporarily, for within a few months the uremia that had been plaguing him became acute and fatal. He died on November 22,1916.

Jack London, in truth, had used his time well.

In preparing this anthology I had two goals in mind. I wanted first to compile a collection of Jack London's most entertaining, absorbing stories. My second aim, but perhaps the more important one, was to present for the first time in one volume a representative selection from *all* phases of this author's diverse literary career. Short stories, novels, sociological and political essays, sports and war reporting, autobiography, travel—Jack London was at home in all these media. Everything he wrote was imbued with all of the movement, color, and excitement found in his famous short stories. When I had made my selection I found that, different though they may seem, all of the articles and stories have a common denominator—all are tales of adventure.

While it is not my intent to comment on each of the selections to be found in this volume, there are a number that do merit special notice. One of these is "Typhoon off the Coast of Japan," the first article Jack London wrote for publication. It won first prize in a contest for local authors run by the San Francisco *Call*. The success of this first article was to be the spark which eventually ignited all of Jack's latent creative genius. Other unusual pieces are "The Run Across" and "Bonin Islands," both of which appeared in 1895 in the Oakland High School magazine, *The Aegis*. They are based on his experiences aboard the *Sophie Sutherland*. These two articles, as well as the Russo-Japanese War dispatches, the Johnson-Jeffries fight, "Through the Rapids on the Way to Klondike," and "From Dawson to the Sea" have never before appeared in book form.

For this literary sampler selections have been made from seven of Jack's most popular novels. These selections range from a single chapter to excerpts from several chapters. The longer pieces from *The Iron Heel*, *Martin Eden*, and *The Sea Wolf*, his major literary efforts, reveal the depth and dramatic sweep of his brilliant creative powers. Much of the popularity of these novels may be traced to Jack London's unique talent for dramatizing serious scientific, economic, and philosophical ideas. He took the theories of such men as Darwin, Spencer, and Huxley and wove them into the fabric that clothed each novel's plot. As Van Wyck Brooks so aptly stated, "He made battles of the mind as actual and thrilling as prize-fights, adventures in the gold fields, or scenes of war." In *The Iron Heel* we witness the conflict between the theories of Nietzsche and Marx; in *The Sea Wolf* it is the clash of the "spiritual versus the materialistic"; and in *Martin Eden* it is the death struggle between individualism and socialism. Here is adventure on an unusual level—the adventure of great ideas expressed in the terms of human emotion and conflict.

Anticipating the possible raising of eyebrows at the omission of *The Call of the Wild,* I hasten to make the following explanation. At last count about half a dozen editions of that popular novel were still in print. After much deliberation I decided to forsake this readily available book in favor of other not so well known or accessible articles and stories.

One final comment should be made in reference to the "Photographic Album." The photographs in this thirty-two-page signature were selected from over one hundred albums personally assembled by my aunt and uncle. Most of these pictures (such as those of the Russo-Japanese War and the cruise of the *Snark*) were taken by Jack himself. The balance are photographs taken of him at various times during his life. I think that you will find these photographs of great interest, for they are a pictorial record of many of the events which figure so prominently in Jack London's writings.

IRVING SHEPARD

The Valley of the Moon
Glen Ellen, California

The Young Man

The following section is Jack London's own story of his youth as pieced together from numerous sources. These selections do not pretend to tell the whole story, but are merely highlights of a fantastic childhood and youth. These were the formative years for Jack London, the author, for he was to draw upon their happenings and influences for much of his inspiration. Here are the childhood experiences that shaped the mind and molded the character of a truly remarkable man. ED.

The childhood shows the man,
As morning shows the day.

MILTON

THE CHILD

My father was Pennsylvania-born, a soldier, scout, backwoodsman, trapper, and wanderer. My mother was born in Ohio. Both came west independently, meeting and marrying in San Francisco, where I was born January 12, 1876 . . . My life, from my fourth to my ninth years, was spent upon Californian ranches. I learned to read and write about my fifth year, though I do not remember anything about it. I always could read and write, and have no recollection antedating such a condition. Folks say I simply insisted upon being taught. I was an omniverous reader, principally because reading matter was scarce and I had to be grateful for whatever fell into my hands.[1]

I know that my first school was in Alameda . . . The second school where I tried to pick up a little learning was an irregular hit or miss affair at San Mateo. Each class sat in a separate desk, but there were days when we did not sit at all, for the master used to get drunk very often, and then one of the older boys would thrash him. To even things up, the master would then thrash the younger lads, so you can think what sort of school it was. There was no one belonging to me, or associated with me in any way, who had literary tastes or ideas; the nearest I can make to it is that my grandfather was a circuit rider, a Welshman, known as

"Priest" Jones in the backwoods, where his enthusiasm led him to scatter the Gospel.

One of my earliest and strongest impressions was of the ignorance of other people. I had read and absorbed Washington Irving's "Alhambra" before I was nine, but could never understand how it was that the other ranchers knew nothing about it. Later I concluded that this ignorance was peculiar to the country, and felt that those who lived in cities would not be so dense. One day a man from the city came to the ranch; he wore shiny shoes and a cloth coat, and I felt that here was a good chance for me to exchange thoughts with an enlightened mind. From the bricks of an old fallen chimney I had built an Alhambra of my own; towers, terraces, and all were complete, and chalk inscriptions marked the different sections. Here I led the city man and questioned him about "The Alhambra," but he was as ignorant as the men on the ranch, and then I consoled myself with the thought that there were only two clever people in the world—Washington Irving and myself.

My other reading-matter at that time consisted mainly of dime novels, borrowed from the hired men, and newspapers in which the servants gloated over the adventures of poor but virtuous shopgirls.

Through reading such stuff my mind was necessarily conventional, but being very lonely, I read everything that came my way, and was greatly impressed by Ouida's story, "Signa," which I devoured regularly for a couple of years. I never knew the finish until I grew up, for the closing chapters were missing from my copy, so I kept on dreaming with the hero, like him, unable to see the Nemesis at the end. My work on the ranch at one time was to watch the bees, and as I sat under a tree from sunrise till late in the afternoon, waiting for the swarming, I had plenty of time to read and dream. Livermore Valley was very flat, and even the hills around were then to me devoid of interest, and the only incident to break in on my visions was when I gave the alarm of swarming, and the ranch folk rushed out with pots, pans, and buckets of water. I think the opening line of "Signa" was, "It was only a little lad, yet he had dreams of becoming a great musician, and having all Europe at his feet." Well, I was only a little lad, too, but why could not I become what "Signa" dreamed of being?

Life on a California ranch was then to me the dullest possible existence, and every day I thought of going out beyond the sky-line to see the world. Even then there were whispers, art promptings; my mind inclined to things beautiful, although my environment was unbeautiful. The hills and valleys around were eyesores and aching pits, and I never loved them till I left them.[5]

And then came the city of Oakland, and on the shelves of that Free Library I discovered all the great world beyond the skyline. Here were thousands of books as good as my four wonder-books, and some were even better. Libraries were not concerned with children in those days, and I had strange adventures. I remember, in the catalogue, being impressed by the title, "The Adventures of Peregrine Pickle." I filled an application blank and the librarian handed me the collected and entirely unexpurgated works of Smollet in one huge volume. I read everything, but principally history and adventure, and all the old travels and voyages. I read mornings, afternoons, and nights. I read in bed, I read at table, I read as I walked to and from school, and I read at recess while the other boys were playing. I began to get the "jerks." To everybody I replied: "Go away you make me nervous."

. . . I was eight years old when I wore my first little undershirt actually sold in a store across the counter. And then it had been only one little undershirt. When it was soiled I had to return to the awful home-made things until it was washed. I had been so proud of it that I insisted on wearing it without any outer garment. For the first time I mutinied against my mother—mutinied myself into hysteria, until she let me wear the store undershirt so all the world could see.

By the time I was ten years old, my family had abandoned ranching and gone to live in the city. And here, at ten, I began on the streets as a newsboy. One of the reasons was that we needed money.[2]

Every cent was turned over to my people, and I went to school in constant shame of the hats, shoes, clothes I wore. Duty—from then on, I had no childhood. Up at three o'clock in the morning to carry papers. When that was finished I did not go home but continued on to school. School out, my evening papers. Saturday I worked on an ice wagon. Sunday I went to a bowling alley and set up pins for drunken Dutchmen. Duty—I turned over every cent and went dressed like a scarecrow.[3]

Only a man who has undergone famine can properly value food; only sailors and desert-dwellers know the meaning of fresh water. And only a child, with a child's imagination, can come to know the meaning of things it has been long denied. I early discovered that the only things I could have were those I got for myself.

. . . My first memories of life were pinched by poverty. The pinch of poverty had been chronic.[2]

. . . When I was seven years old, at the country school of San Pedro, this happened. Meat, I was that hungry for it I once opened a girl's basket and stole a piece of meat—a little piece the size of my two fingers. I ate it but I never repeated it. In those days, like Esau, I would have literally sold my birthright for a mess of pottage, a piece of meat. Great God, when those youngsters threw chunks of meat on the ground because of surfeit, I could have dragged it from the dirt and eaten it; but I did not. Just imagine the development of my mind, my soul, under such material conditions.[3]

I was barely turned fifteen, and working long hours in a cannery. Month in and month out, the shortest day I ever worked was ten hours. When to ten hours of actual work at a machine is added the noon hour; the walking to work and walking home from work; the getting up in the morning, dressing, and eating; the eating at night, undressing, and going to bed, there remains no more than the nine hours out of the twenty-four required by a healthy youngster for sleep. Out of those nine hours, after I was in bed and ere my eyes drowsed shut, I managed to steal a little time for reading.[2]

. . . For months at a time, during that year, I was up and at work at six in the morning. I took half an hour for dinner. I took half an hour for supper. I worked every night till ten, eleven and twelve o'clock. My wages were small, but I worked such long hours that I sometimes made as high as fifty dollars a month. Duty—I turned every cent over. Duty—I have worked in that hell hole for thirty-six straight hours, at a machine, and I was only a child. I remember how I was trying to save the money to buy a skiff—eight dollars. All that summer I saved and scraped. In the fall I had five dollars as a result of absolutely doing without all pleasure. My mother came to the machine where I worked and asked for it. I could have killed myself that night. After a year of hell to have that pitiful—to be robbed of that petty joy.[3]

. . . I asked myself if this were the meaning of life—to be a work-beast? I knew of no horse in the city of Oakland that worked the hours I worked. If this were living, I was entirely unenamored of it . . . I remembered the wind that blew every day on the bay, the sunrises and sunsets I never saw; the bite of the salt air in my nostrils, the bite of the salt water on my flesh . . . I remembered all the beauty and the wonder and the sense-delights of the world denied me. There was only one way to escape my deadening toil. I must get out and away on the water. I must earn my bread on the water . . .

I wanted to be where the winds of adventure blew. And the winds of adventure blew the oyster pirate sloops up and down San Francisco Bay, from raided oyster-beds and fights at night on shoal and flat, to markets in the morning against city wharves, where peddlers and saloonkeepers came down to buy. Every raid on an oyster-bed was a felony. The penalty was state imprisonment, the stripes and the lockstep. And what of that? The men in stripes worked a shorter day than I at my machine. And there was vastly more romance in being an oyster pirate or a convict than in being a machine slave. And behind it all, behind all of me with youth a-bubble, whispered Romance, Adventure.

So I interviewed my Mammy Jennie, my old nurse at whose black breast I had suckled. She was more prosperous than my folks. She was nursing sick people at a good weekly wage. Would she lend her "white child" the money? *Would she?* What she had was mine.

Then I sought out French Frank, the oyster pirate, who wanted to sell, I had heard, his sloop, the *Razzle Dazzle*. I found him lying at anchor on the Alameda side of the estuary, near the Webster Street bridge, with visitors aboard, whom he was entertaining with afternoon wine. He came on deck to talk business. He was willing to sell. But it was Sunday. Besides, he had guests. On the morrow he would make out the bill of sale and I could enter into possession. And in the meantime I must come below and meet his friends. They were two sisters, Mamie and Tess; a Mrs. Hadley, who chaperoned them; "Whisky" Bob, a youthful oyster pirate of sixteen; and "Spider" Healey, a black-whiskered wharf-rat of twenty. Mamie, who was Spider's niece, was called the Queen of the Oyster Pirates, and, on occasion, presided at their revels. French Frank was in love with her, though I did not know it at the time; and she steadfastly refused to marry him.

French Frank was elated by the sale, which I had bound with a twenty-dollar goldpiece. He poured more wine. I had learned my strong head and stomach, and I was certain I could drink with them in a temperate way and not poison myself for a week to come. I could stand as much as they; and besides, they had already been drinking for some time.

We got to singing. Spider sang "The Boston Burglar" and "Black Lulu." The Queen sang "Then I Wisht I were a Little Bird." And her sister Tess sang "Oh, Treat My Daughter Kind-i-ly." The fun grew fast and furious. I found myself able to miss drinks without being noticed or called to account. Also, standing in the companionway, head and shoulders out and glass in hand, I could fling the wine overboard.

I reasoned something like this: It is a queerness of these people that they like this vile-tasting wine. Well, let them. I cannot quarrel with their tastes. My manhood, according to their queer notions, must compel me to appear to like this wine. Very well. I shall so appear. But I shall drink no more than is unavoidable.

And the Queen began to make love to me, the latest recruit to the oyster pirate fleet, and no mere hand, but a master and owner. She went upon deck to take the air, and took me with her. She knew, of course, but I never dreamed, how French Frank was raging down below. Then Tess joined us, sitting on the cabin; and Spider, and Bob; and at the last, Mrs. Hadley and French Frank. And we sat there, glasses in hand, and sang, while the big demijohn went around; and I was the only strictly sober one.

And I enjoyed it as no one of them was able to enjoy it. Here, in this atmosphere of bohemianism, I could not but contrast the scene with my scene of the day before, sitting at my machine, in the stifling, shut-in air, repeating, endlessly repeating, at top speed, my series of mechanical motions. And here I sat now, glass in hand, in warm-glowing camaraderie, with the oyster pirates, adventurers who refused to be slaves to petty routine, who flouted restrictions and the law, who carried their lives and their liberty in their hands. And it was through John Barleycorn that I came to join this glorious company of free souls, unashamed and unafraid.

And the afternoon sea breeze blew its tang into my lungs, and curled the waves in mid-channel. Before it came the scow schooners, wing-and-wing, blowing their horns for the drawbridges to open. Red-stacked tugs tore by, rocking the *Razzle Dazzle* in the waves of their wake. A sugar bark towed from the "boneyard" to sea. The sun-wash was on the crisping water, and life was big. And Spider sang:

Oh, it's Lulu, black Lulu, my darling,
Oh, it's where have you been so long?
Been layin' in jail,
A-waitin' for bail,
Till my bully comes rollin' along."

There it was, the smack and slap of the spirit of revolt, of adventure, of romance, of the things forbidden and done defiantly and grandly. And I knew that on the morrow I would not go back to my machine at the cannery. To-morrow I would be an oyster pirate, as free a freebooter as the century and the waters of San Francisco Bay would permit. Spider had already agreed to sail with me as my crew of one, and, also, as cook while I did the deck work. We would outfit our grub and water in the morning, hoist the big mainsail (which was a bigger piece of canvas than any I had ever sailed under), and beat our way out the estuary on the first of the sea breeze and the last of the ebb. Then we would slack sheets, and on the first of the flood run down the bay to the Asparagus Islands, where we would anchor miles off shore. And at last my dream would be realized: I would sleep upon the water. And next morning I would wake upon the water; and thereafter all my days and nights would be on the water.[2]

THE OYSTER PIRATE

The more I saw of the life, the more I was enamored of it. I can never forget my thrills, the first night I took part in a concerted raid, when we assembled on board the *Annie*—rough men, big and unafraid, and weazened wharf rats, some of them ex-convicts, all of them enemies of the law and meriting jail, in sea-boots and sea-gear, talking in gruff, low voices, and "Big" George with revolvers strapped about his waist to show that he meant business.

Oh, I know, looking back, that the whole thing was sordid and silly. But I was not looking back in those days . . . The life was brave and wild, and I was living the adventure I had read so much about.[2]

. . . when I, the youngest of the pirates, commanded my own *Razzle Dazzle*, the Queen went along with me! I was the only skipper in the fleet sailing with a woman aboard, and it made a sensation . . . Why did I take her? It would be hard to say it all. I was making a career for myself, after a picture I had always created out of the books I always kept exchanging at the old library. I was in revolt from the beastly hopelessness of the labor I had been performing and had not yet seen ahead to the other kinds of beastly consequences of the life I was entering—inescapable to anyone who stayed in it. All I saw was glamor of conquest, of scarlet adventure and yellow gold. Men did these reckless things; only I would do them better . . . And then you must take into account I was a husky man at sixteen, and already knew girls—my first wondering knowledge had been presented to me by one much older than myself; and the Queen met more than one need I had come to recognize.[4]

So completely did I break with my parsimonious past that I sent word home to my mother to call in the boys of the neighborhood and give to them all my collections. I never even cared to learn what boys got what collections. I was a man, now, and I made a clean sweep of everything that bound me to my boyhood.

My reputation grew. When the story went around the water-front of how French Frank had tried to run me down with his schooner, and of how I had stood on the deck of the *Razzle Dazzle*, a cocked double-barreled shotgun in my hands, steering with my feet and holding her to her course, and compelled him to put up his wheel and keep away, the water-front decided that there was something to me despite my youth. And I continued to show what was in me. There were the times I brought the *Razzle Dazzle* in with a bigger load of oysters than any other two-man craft; there was the time when we raided far down in Lower Bay and mine was the only craft back at daylight to the anchorage off Asparagus Island; there was the Thursday night we raced for market and I brought the *Razzle Dazzle* in without a rudder, first of the fleet, and skimmed the cream of the Friday morning trade; and there was the time I brought her in from Upper Bay under a jib, when Scotty burned my mainsail.

But the things I did on the water only partly counted. What completed everything and won for me the title of "Prince of the Oyster Beds," was that I was a good fellow ashore with my money, buying drinks like a man. I little dreamed that the time would come when the Oakland water-front, which had shocked me at first, would be shocked and annoyed by the deviltry of the things I did.

But always the life was tied up with drinking. The saloons are poor men's clubs. Saloons are congregating places. We engaged to meet one another in saloons. We celebrated our good fortune or wept our grief in saloons. We got acquainted in saloons.

. . . Drinking was the way of the life I led, the way of the men with whom I lived. While away on my cruises on the bay, I took no drink along; and while out on the bay the thought of the desirableness of a drink never crossed my mind. It was not until I tied the *Razzle Dazzle* up to the wharf and got ashore in the congregating places of men, where drink flowed, that the buying of drinks for other men, and the accepting of drinks from other men, devolved upon me as a social duty and a manhood rite.

Then, too, there were the times, lying at the city wharf or across the estuary on the sandpit, when the Queen, and her sister, and her brother Pat, and Mrs. Hadley came aboard. It was my boat. I was host, and I could only dispense hospitality in the terms of their understanding of it. So I would rush Spider, or Irish, or Scotty, or whoever was my crew, with the can for beer and the demijohn for red wine. And again, lying at the wharf disposing of my oysters, there were dusky twilights when big policemen and plain-clothes men stole on board. And because we lived in the shadow of the police, we opened oysters and fed them to them with squirts of pepper sauce, and rushed the growler or got stronger stuff in bottles.

Drink as I would, I couldn't come to like John Barleycorn. I valued him extremely well for his associations, but not for the taste of him. All the time I was striving to be a man amongst men, and all the time I nursed secret and shameful desires for candy. But I would have died before I'd let anybody guess it. I used to indulge in lonely debauches, on nights when I knew my crew was going to sleep ashore. I would go up to the Free Library, exchange my books, buy a quarter's worth of all sorts of candy that chewed and lasted, sneak aboard the *Razzle Dazzle,* lock myself in the cabin, go to bed, and lie there long hours of bliss, reading and chewing candy. And those were the only times I felt that I got my real money's worth. Dollars and dollars, across the bar, couldn't buy the satisfaction that twenty-five cents did in a candy store. As my drinking grew heavier, I began to note more and more that it was in the drinking bouts the purple passages occurred. Drunks were always memorable. At such times things happened. Men like Joe Goose dated existence from drunk to drunk. The longshoremen all looked forward to their Saturday night drunk. We of the oyster boats waited until we had disposed of our cargoes before we got really started, though a scattering of drinks and a meeting of a chance friend sometimes precipitated an accidental drunk.

And now, of all this that is squalid, and ridiculous, and bestial, try to think what it meant to me, a youth not yet sixteen, burning with the spirit of adventure, fancy-filled with tales of buccaneers and sea-rovers, sacks of cities and conflicts of armed men, and imagination-maddened by the stuff I had drunk. It was life raw and naked, wild and free—the only life of that sort which my birth in time and space permitted me to attain. And more than that. It carried a promise. It was the beginning. From the sandpit the way led out through the Golden Gate to the vastness of adventure of all the world, where battles would be fought, not for old shirts and over stolen salmon boats, but for high purposes and romantic ends.

I abandoned myself to the life, and developed the misconception that the secret of John Barleycorn lay in going on mad drunks, rising through the successive stages that only an iron constitution could endure to final stupefaction and swinish unconsciousness. I did not like the taste, so I drank for the sole purpose of getting drunk, of getting hopelessly, helplessly drunk. And I, who had saved and scraped, traded like a Shylock and made junkmen weep; I, who had stood aghast when French Frank, at a single stroke, spent eighty cents for whisky for eight men; I turned myself loose with a more lavish disregard for money than any of them.

And I had no regrets. I was proud. I had shown them I could spend with the rest of them. Amongst strong men I had proved myself strong. I had clinched again, as I had often clinched, my right to the title of "Prince." Also, my attitude may be considered, in part, as a reaction from my childhood's meagerness and my childhood's excessive toil.

Possibly my inchoate thought was: Better to reign among booze-fighters, a prince, than to toil twelve hours a day at a machine for ten cents an hour. There are no purple passages in machine toil. But if the spending of one hundred and eighty dollars in twelve hours isn't a purple passage, then I'd like to know what is.

And when I never drew a sober breath, on one stretch, for three solid weeks, I was certain I had reached the top. Surely, in that direction, one could go no farther. It was time for me to move on. For always, drunk or sober, at the back of my consciousness something whispered that this carousing and bay-adventuring was not all of life. This whisper was my good fortune. I happened to be so made that I could hear it calling, always calling, out and away over the world. It was not canniness on my part. It was curiosity, desire to know, an unrest and a seeking for things wonderful that I seemed somehow to have glimpsed or guessed. What was this life for, I demanded, if this were all? No; there was something more, away and beyond . . .

But what gave immediacy to my decision to move on, was a trick John Barleycorn played me—a monstrous, incredible trick that showed abysses of intoxication hitherto undreamed. At one o'clock in the morning, after a prodigious drunk, I was tottering aboard a sloop at the end of the wharf, intending to go to sleep. The tides sweep through Carquinez Straits as in a mill-race, and the full ebb was on when I stumbled overboard. There was nobody on the wharf, nobody on the sloop. I was borne away by the current. I was not startled. I thought the misadventure delightful. I was a good swimmer, and in my inflamed condition the contact of the water with my skin soothed me like cool linen.

And then John Barleycorn played me his maniacal trick. Some maundering fancy of going out with the tide suddenly obsessed me. I had never been morbid. Thoughts of suicide had never entered my head. And now that they entered, I thought it fine, a splendid culmination, a perfect rounding off of my short but exciting career. I, who had never known girl's love, nor woman's love, nor the love of children; who had never played in the wide joy-fields of art, nor climbed the star-cool heights of philosophy, nor seen with my eyes more than a pin-point's surface of the gorgeous world; I decided that this was all, that I had seen all, lived all, been all, that was worth while, and that now was the time to cease. This was the trick of John Barleycorn, laying me by the heels of my imagination and in a drug-dream dragging me to death.

Oh, he was convincing. I had really experienced all of life, and it didn't amount to much. The swinish drunkenness in which I had lived for months (this was accompanied by the sense of degradation and the old feeling of conviction of sin) was the last and best, and I could see for myself what it was worth. There were all the broken-down old bums and loafers I had bought drinks for. That was what remained of life. Did I want to become like them? A thousand times no; and I wept tears of sweet sadness over my glorious youth going out with the tide. (And who has not seen the weeping-drunk, the melancholic drunk? They are to be found in all the barrooms, if they can find no other listener, telling their sorrows to the barkeeper, who is paid to listen.)

The water was delicious. It was a man's way to die. John Barleycorn changed the tune he played in my drink-maddened brain. Away with tears and regret. It was a hero's death, and by the hero's own hand and will. So I struck up my death-chant and was singing it lustily, when the gurgle and splash of the current-riffles in my ears reminded me of my more immediate situation.

Below the town of Benicia, where the *Solano* wharf projects, the straits widen out into what bay-farers call the "Bight of Turner's Shipyard." I was in the shore-tide that swept under the *Solano* wharf and on into the bight. I knew of old the power of the suck which developed when the tide swung around the end of Dead Man's Island and drove straight for the wharf. I didn't want to go through those piles. It wouldn't be nice, and I might lose an hour in the bight on my way out with the tide.

I undressed in the water and struck out with a strong, single-overhand stroke, crossing the current at right angles. Nor did I cease until, by the wharf-lights, I knew I was safe to sweep by the end. Then I turned over and rested. The stroke had been a telling one, and I was a little time in recovering my breath.

I was elated, for I had succeeded in avoiding the suck. I started to raise my death-chant again—a purely extemporized farrago of a drug-crazed youth. "Don't sing . . . yet," whispered John Barleycorn. "The *Solano* runs all night. There are railroad men on the wharf. They will hear you, and come out in a boat and rescue you, and you don't want to be rescued." I certainly didn't. What? Be robbed of my hero's death? Never. And I lay on my back in the starlight, watching the familiar wharf-lights go by, red and green and white, and bidding sad, sentimental farewell to them, each and all.

When I was well clear, in mid-channel, I sang again. Sometimes I swam a few strokes, but in the main I contented myself with floating and dreaming long drunken dreams. Before daylight, the chill of the water and the passage of the hours had sobered me sufficiently to make me wonder what portion of the Straits I was in, and also to wonder if the turn of the tide wouldn't catch me and take me back ere I had drifted out into San Pablo Bay.

Next I discovered that I was very weary and very cold, and quite sober, and that I didn't in the least want to be drowned. I could make out the Selby Smelter on the Contra Costa shore and the Mare Island lighthouse. I started to swim for the Solano shore, but was too weak and chilled, and made so little headway, and at the cost of so painful effort that I gave it up and contented myself with floating, now and then giving a stroke to keep my balance in the tide-rips which were increasing their commotion on the surface of the water. And I knew fear. I was sober, now, and I didn't want to die. I discovered scores of reasons for living. And the more reasons I discovered, the more liable it seemed that I was going to drown anyway.

Daylight, after I had been four hours in the water, found me in a parlous condition in the tide-rips off Mare Island light, where the swift ebbs from Vallejo Straits and Carquinez Straits were fighting with each other, and where, at that particular moment, they were fighting the flood tide setting up against them from San Pablo Bay. A stiff breeze had sprung up, and the crisp little waves were persistently lapping into my mouth, and I was beginning to swallow salt water. With my swimmer's knowledge, I knew the end was near. And then the boat came—a Greek fisherman running in for Vallejo; and again I had been saved from John Barleycorn by my constitution and physical vigor.

Back in Oakland from my wanderings, I returned to the water front and renewed my comradeship with Nelson, who was now on shore all the time and living more madly than before. . . . Nelson was a reckless maniac. He was twenty years old, with the body of a Hercules. When he was shot in Benicia, a couple of years later, the coroner said he was the greatest-shouldered man he had ever seen laid on a slab.

Nelson could not read nor write. He had been "dragged" up by his father on San Francisco Bay, and boats were second nature with him. His strength was prodigious, and his reputation along the water front for violence was anything but savory. He had Berserker rages and did mad, terrible things. I made his acquaintance the first cruise of the *Razzle Dazzle*, and saw him sail the *Reindeer* in a blow and dredge oysters all around the rest of us as we lay at two anchors, troubled with fear of going ashore.

He was some man, this Nelson . . . I, too, spent my time on shore with him, only occasionally going for cruises of several days on the bay to help out on short-handed scow-schooners.

The result was that I was no longer reinvigorated by periods of open-air abstinence and healthy toil. I drank every day, and whenever opportunity offered I drank to excess; for I still labored under the misconception that the secret of John Barleycorn lay in drinking to bestiality and unconsciousness. I became pretty thoroughly alcohol-soaked during this period. I practically lived in saloons; became a barroom loafer, and worse.

Nelson and I were sitting in the Overland House. It was early in the evening, and the only reason we were there was because we were broke and it was election time. You see, in election time local politicians, aspirants for office, have a way of making the rounds of the saloons to get votes. One is sitting at a table, in a dry condition, wondering who is going to turn up and buy him a drink, or if his credit is good at some other saloon and if it's worth while to walk that far to find out, when suddenly the saloon doors swing wide and enters a bevy of well-dressed men, themselves usually wide and exhaling an atmosphere of prosperity and fellowship.

They have smiles and greetings for everybody—for you, without the price of a glass of beer in your pocket, for the timid hobo who lurks in the corner and who certainly hasn't a vote but who may establish a lodging-house registration. And do you know, when these politicians swing wide the doors and come in, with their broad shoulders, their deep chests, and their generous stomachs which cannot help making them optimists and masters of life, why, you perk right up. It's going to be a warm evening after all, and you know you'll get a souse started at the very least. And—who knows?—the gods may be kind, other drinks may come, and the night culminate in glorious greatness. And the next thing you know, you are lined up at the bar, pouring drinks down your throat and learning the gentlemen's names and the offices which they hope to fill.

It was during this period, when the politicians went their saloon rounds, that I was getting bitter bits of education and having illusions punctured—I, who had pored and thrilled over "The Rail-Splitter," and "From Canal Boy to President." Yes, I was learning how noble politics and politicians are.

Well, on this night, broke, thirsty, but with the drinker's faith in the unexpected drink, Nelson and I sat in the Overland House waiting for something to turn up, especially politicians. And there entered Joe Goose—he of the unquenchable thirst, the wicked eyes, the crooked nose, the flowered vest.

"Come on, fellows—free booze—all you want of it. I didn't want you to miss it."

"Where?" we wanted to know.

"Come on. I'll tell you as we go along. We haven't a minute to lose." And as we hurried up town, Joe Goose explained. "It's the Hancock Fire Brigade. All you have to do is wear a red shirt and a helmet, and carry a torch. They're going down on a special train to Haywards to parade."

(I think the place was Haywards. It may have been San Leandro or Niles. And, to save me, I can't remember whether the Hancock Fire Brigade was a Republican or a Democratic organization. But anyway, the politicians who ran it were short of torch-bearers, and anybody who would parade could get drunk if he wanted to.)

"The town'll be wide open," Joe Goose went on. "Booze? It'll run like water. The politicians have bought the stocks of the saloons. There'll be no charge. All you got to do is walk right up and call for it. We'll raise hell."

At the hall, on Eighth Street near Broadway, we got into the firemen's shirts and helmets, were equipped with torches, and, growling because we weren't given at least one drink before we started, were herded aboard the train. Oh, those politicians had handled our kind before. At Haywards there were no drinks either. Parade, first, and earn your booze, was the order of the night.

We paraded. Then the saloons were opened. Extra barkeepers had been engaged, and the drinkers jammed six deep before every drink-drenched and unwiped bar. There was no time to wipe the bar, nor wash glasses, nor do anything save fill glasses. The Oakland water front can be real thirsty on occasion.

This method of jamming and struggling in front of the bar was too slow for us. The drink was ours. The politicians had bought it for us. We'd paraded and earned it, hadn't we? So we made a flank attack around the end of the bar, shoved the protesting barkeepers aside, and helped ourselves to bottles.

Outside, we knocked the necks of the bottles off against the concrete curbs, and drank. Now Joe Goose and Nelson had learned discretion with straight whisky, drunk in quantity. I hadn't: I still labored under the misconception that one was to drink all he could get—especially when it didn't cost anything. We shared our bottles with others, and drank a good portion ourselves, while I drank most of all. And I didn't like the stuff. I drank it as I had drunk beer at five, and wine at seven. I mastered my qualms and downed it like so much medicine. And when we wanted more bottles, we went into other saloons where the free drink was flowing, and helped ourselves.

I haven't the slightest idea of how much I drank—whether it was two quarts or five. I do know that I began the orgy with half-pint draughts and with no water afterward to wash the taste away and to dilute the whisky.

Now the politicians were too wise to leave the town filled with drunks from the water front of Oakland. When train time came, there was a round-up of the saloons. Already I was feeling the impact of the whisky. Nelson and I were hustled out of a saloon, and found ourselves in the very last rank of a disorderly parade. I struggled along heroically, my correlations breaking down, my legs tottering under me, my head swimming, my heart pounding, my lungs panting for air.

My helplessness was coming on so rapidly that my reeling brain told me I would go down and out and never reach the train if I remained at the rear of the procession. I left the ranks and ran down a pathway beside the road under broad-spreading trees. Nelson pursued me, laughing. Certain things stand out, as in memories of nightmare. I remember those trees especially, and my desperate running along under them, and how, every time I fell, roars of laughter went up from the other drunks. They thought I was merely antic drunk. They did not dream that John Barleycorn had me by the throat in a death-clutch. But I knew it. And I remember the fleeting bitterness that was mine as I realized that I was in a struggle with death and that these others did not know. It was as if I were drowning before a crowd of spectators who thought I was cutting up tricks for their entertainment.

And running there under the trees, I fell and lost consciousness. What happened afterward, with one glimmering exception, I had to be told. Nelson, with his enormous strength, picked me up and dragged me on and aboard the train. When he had got me into a seat, I fought and panted so terribly for air that even with his obtuseness he knew I was in a bad way. And right there, at any moment, I know now, I might have died. I often think it is the nearest to death I have ever been. I have only Nelson's description of my behavior to go by.

I was scorching up, burning alive internally, in an agony of fire and suffocation, and I wanted air. I madly wanted air. My efforts to raise a window were vain, for all the windows in the car were screwed down. Nelson had seen drink-crazed men, and thought I wanted to throw myself out. He tried to restrain me, but I fought on. I seized some man's torch and smashed the glass.

Now there were pro-Nelson and anti-Nelson factions on the Oakland water front, and men of both factions, with more drink in them than was good, filled the car. My smashing of the window was the signal for the anti's. One of them reached for me, and dropped me, and started the fight, all of which I have no knowledge save what was told me afterward, and a sore jaw next day from the blow that put me out. The man who struck me went down across my body, Nelson followed him, and they say there were few unbroken windows in the wreckage of the car that followed as the free-for-all fight had its course.

This being knocked cold and motionless was perhaps the best thing that could have happened to me. My violent struggles had only accelerated my already dangerously accelerated heart, and increased the need for oxygen in my suffocating lungs.

After the fight was over and I came to, I did not come to myself. I was no more myself than a drowning man is who continues to struggle after he has lost consciousness. I have no memory of my actions, but I cried "Air! Air!" so insistently, that it dawned on Nelson that I did not contemplate self-destruction. So he cleared the jagged glass from the window ledge and let me stick my head and shoulders out. He realized, partially, the seriousness of my condition, and held me by the waist to prevent me from crawling farther out. And for the rest of the run in to Oakland I kept my head and shoulders out, fighting like a maniac whenever he tried to draw me inside.

And here my one glimmering streak of true consciousness came. My sole recollection, from the time I fell under the trees until I awoke the following evening, is of my head out the window, facing the wind caused by the train, cinders striking and burning and blinding me, while I breathed with will. All my will was concentrated on breathing—on breathing the air in the hugest lung-full gulps I could, pumping the greatest amount of air into my lungs in the shortest possible time. It was that or death, and I was a swimmer and diver and I knew it; and in the most intolerable agony of prolonged suffocation, during those moments I was conscious, I faced the wind and the cinders and breathed for life.

All the rest is a blank. I came to the following evening, in a water-front lodging-house. I was alone. No doctor had been called in. And I might well have died there, for Nelson and the others, deeming me merely "sleeping off my drunk," had let me lie there in a comatose condition for seventeen hours. Many a man, as every doctor knows, has died of the sudden impact of a quart or more of whisky. Usually one reads of them so dying, strong drinkers, on account of a wager. But I didn't know . . . then. And so I learned; and by no virtue nor prowess, but simply through good fortune and constitution. Again my constitution had triumphed over John Barleycorn. I had escaped from another death-pit, dragged myself through another morass. . . .[2]

THE "SOPHIE SUTHERLAND"

It was during the early winter of 1892 that I resolved to go to sea. My Hancock Fire Brigade experience was very little responsible for this. I still drank and frequented saloons—practically lived in saloons. Whisky was dangerous, in my opinion, but not wrong. Whisky was dangerous, like other dangerous things in the natural world. Men died of whisky; but then, too, fishermen were capsized and drowned, hoboes fell under trains and were cut to pieces. To cope with winds and waves, railroad trains, and barrooms, one must use judgment. To get drunk after the manner of men was all right, but one must do it with discretion. No more quarts of whisky for me.

What really decided me to go to sea was that I had caught my first vision of the death-road which John Barleycorn maintains for his devotees. It was not a clear vision, however. . . . It struck me, from watching those with whom I associated, that the life we were living was more destructive than that lived by the average man. . . .

So I considered my situation and knew that I was getting into a bad way of living. It made toward death too quickly to suit my youth and vitality. And there was only one way out of this hazardous manner of living and that was to get out. The sealing-fleet was wintering in San Francisco Bay, and in the saloons I met skippers, mates, hunters, boat-steerers, and boat-pullers. I met the seal-hunter, Pete Holt, and agreed to be his boat-puller and to sign on any schooner he signed on. And I had to have half-a-dozen drinks with Pete Holt there and then to seal our agreement.

And at once awoke all my old unrest that John Barleycorn had put to sleep. I found myself actually bored with the saloon-life of the Oakland water front, and wondered what I had ever found fascinating in it. Also, with this death-road concept in my brain, I began to grow afraid that something would happen to me before sailing day, which was set for some time in January. I lived more circumspectly, drank less deeply, and went home more frequently. When drinking grew too wild, I got out. When Nelson was in his maniacal cups, I managed to get separated from him.[2]

THAT DEAD MEN RISE UP NEVER

The month in which my seventeenth birthday arrived I signed on before the mast on the *Sophie Sutherland*, a three-topmast schooner bound on a seven-months' seal-hunting cruise to the coast of Japan. We sailed from San Francisco, and immediately I found confronting me a problem of no inconsiderable proportions.

There were twelve men of us in the forecastle, ten of whom were hardened, tarry-thumbed sailors. Not alone was I a youth and on my first voyage, but I had for shipmates men who had come through the hard school of the merchant service of Europe. As boys, they had had to perform their ship's duty, and, in addition, by immemorial sea custom, they had had to be the slaves of the ordinary and able-bodied seamen. When they became ordinary seamen they were still the slaves of the able-bodied. Thus, in the forecastle, with the watch below, an able seaman, lying in his bunk, will order an ordinary seaman to fetch him his shoes or bring him a drink of water. Now the ordinary seaman may be lying in *his* bunk. He is just as tired as the able seaman. Yet he must get out of his bunk and fetch and carry. If he refuses, he will be beaten. If, perchance, he is so strong that he can whip the able seaman, then all the able seamen, or as many as may be necessary, pitch upon the luckless devil and administer the beating.

My problem now becomes apparent. These hard-bit Scandinavian sailors had come through a hard school. As boys they had served their mates, and as able seamen they looked to be served by other boys. I was a boy—withal with a man's body. I had never been to sea before—withal I was a good sailor and knew my business. It was either a case of holding my own with them or of going under. I had signed on as an equal, and an equal I must maintain myself, or else endure seven months of hell at their hands. And it was this very equality they resented. By what right was I an equal? I had not earned that high privilege. I had not endured the miseries they had endured as maltreated boys or bullied ordinaries. Worse than that, I was a landlubber making his first voyage. And yet, by the injustice of fate, on the ship's articles I was their equal.

My method was deliberate, and simple, and drastic. In the first place, I resolved to do my work, no matter how hard or dangerous it might be, so well that no man would be called upon to do it for me. Further, I put ginger in my muscles. I never malingered when pulling on a rope, for I knew the eagle eyes of my forecastle mates were squinting for just such evidences of my inferiority. I made it a point to be among the first of the watch going on deck, among the last going below, never leaving a sheet or tackle for some one else to coil over a pin. I was always eager for the run aloft for the shifting of topsail sheets and tacks, or for the setting or taking in of topsails; and in these matters I did more than my share.

Furthermore, I was on a hair-trigger of resentment myself. I knew better than to accept any abuse or the slightest patronizing. At the first hint of such, I went off —I exploded. I might be beaten in the subsequent fight, but I left the impression that I was a wild-cat and that I would just as willingly fight again. My intention was to demonstrate that I would tolerate no imposition. I proved that the man who imposed on me must have a fight on his hands. And, doing my work well, the innate justice of the men, assisted by their wholesome dislike for a clawing and rending wild-cat ruction, soon led them to give over their hectoring. After a bit of strife, my attitude was accepted, and it was my pride that I was taken in as an equal in spirit as well as in fact. From then on, everything was beautiful, and the voyage promised to be a happy one.

But there was one other man in the forecastle. Counting the Scandinavians as ten, and myself as the eleventh, this man was the twelfth and last. We never knew his name, contenting ourselves with calling him the "Bricklayer." He was from Missouri—at least he so informed us in the one meagre confidence he was guilty of in the early days of the voyage. Also, at that time, we learned several other things.

He was a bricklayer by trade. He had never even seen salt water until the week before he joined us, at which time he had arrived in San Francisco and looked upon San Francisco Bay. Why he, of all men, at forty years of age, should have felt the prod to go to sea, was beyond all of us; for it was our unanimous conviction that no man less fitted for the sea had ever embarked on it. But to sea he had come. After a week's stay in a sailors' boarding-house, he had been shoved aboard of us as an able seaman.

All hands had to do his work for him. Not only did he know nothing, but he proved himself unable to learn anything. Try as they would, they could never teach him to steer. To him the compass must have been a profound and awful whirligig. He never mastered its cardinal points, much less the checking and steadying of the ship on her course. He never did come to know whether ropes should be coiled from left to right or from right to left. It was mentally impossible for him to learn the easy muscular trick of throwing his weight on a rope in pulling and hauling. The simplest knots and turns were beyond his comprehension, while he was mortally afraid of going aloft. Bullied by captain and mate, he was one day forced aloft. He managed to get underneath the crosstrees, and there he froze to the ratlines. Two sailors had to go after him to help him down.

All of which was bad enough had there been no worse. But he was vicious, malignant, dirty, and without common decency. He was a tall, powerful man, and he fought with everybody. And there was no fairness in his fighting. His first fight on board, the first day out, was with me, when he, desiring to cut a plug of chewing tobacco, took my personal table-knife for the purpose, and whereupon, I, on a hair-trigger, promptly exploded. After that he fought with nearly every member of the crew. When his clothing became too filthy to be bearable by the rest of us, we put it to soak and stood over him while he washed it. In short, the Bricklayer was one of those horrible monstrous things that one must see in order to be convinced that they exist.

I will only say that he was a beast, and that we treated him like a beast. It is only by looking back through the years that I realise how heartless we were to him. He was without sin. He could not, by the very nature of things, have been anything else than he was. He had not made himself, and for his making he was not responsible. Yet we treated him as a free agent and held him personally responsible for all that he was and that he should not have been. As a result, our treatment of him was as terrible as he was himself terrible. Finally we gave him the silent treatment, and for weeks before he died we neither spoke to him nor did he speak to us. And for weeks he moved among us, or lay in his bunk in our crowded house, grinning at us his hatred and malignancy. He was a dying man, and he knew it, and we knew it. And furthermore, he knew that we wanted him to die. He cumbered our life with his presence, and ours was a rough life that made rough men of us. And so he died, in a small space crowded by twelve men and as much alone as if he had died on some desolate mountain peak. No kindly word, no last word, was passed between. He died as he had lived, a beast, and he died hating us and hated by us.

And now I come to the most startling moment of my life. No sooner was he dead than he was flung overboard. He died in a night of wind, drawing his last breath as the men tumbled into their oilskins to the cry of "All hands!" And he was flung overboard, several hours later, on a day of wind. Not even a canvas wrapping graced his mortal remains; nor was he deemed worthy of bars of iron at his feet. We sewed him up in the blankets in which he died and laid him on a hatch-cover for'ard of the main-hatch on the port side. A gunnysack, half-full of galley coal, was fastened to his feet.

It was bitter cold. The weather-side of every rope, spar, and stay was coated with ice, while all the rigging was a harp, singing and shouting under the fierce hand of the wind. The schooner, hove to, lurched and floundered through the sea, rolling her scuppers under and perpetually flooding the deck with icy salt water. We of the forecastle stood in sea-boots and oilskins. Our hands were mittened, but our heads were bared in the presence of the death we did not respect. Our ears stung and numbed and whitened, and we yearned for the body to be gone. But the interminable reading of the burial service went on. The captain had mistaken his place, and while he read on without purpose we froze our ears and resented this final hardship thrust upon us by the helpless cadaver. As from the beginning, so to the end, everything had gone wrong with the Bricklayer. Finally, the captain's son, irritated beyond measure, jerked the book from the palsied fingers of the old man and found the place. Again the quavering voice of the captain arose. Then came the cue: "And the body shall be cast into the sea." We elevated one end of the hatch-cover, and the Bricklayer plunged outboard and was gone.

Back into the forecastle we cleaned house, washing out the dead man's bunk and removing every vestige of him. By sea law and sea custom, we should have gathered his effects together and turned them over to the captain, who, later, would have held an auction in which we should have bid for the various articles. But no man wanted them, so we tossed them up on deck and overboard in the wake of the departed body—the last ill-treatment we could devise to wreak upon the one we had hated so. Oh, it was raw, believe me; but the life we lived was raw, and we were as raw as the life.

The Bricklayer's bunk was better than mine. Less sea water leaked down through the deck into it, and the light was better for lying in bed and reading. Partly for this reason I proceeded to move into his bunk. My other reason was pride. I saw the sailors were superstitious, and by this act I determined to show that I was braver than they. I would cap my proved equality by a deed that would compel their recognition of my superiority. Oh, the arrogance of youth! But let that pass. The sailors were appalled by my intention. One and all, they warned me that in the history of the sea no man had taken a dead man's bunk and lived to the end of the voyage. They instanced case after case in their personal experience. I was obdurate. Then they begged and pleaded with me, and my pride was tickled in that they showed they really liked me and were concerned about me. This but served to confirm me in my madness. I moved in, and, lying in the dead man's bunk, all afternoon and evening listened to dire prophecies of my future. Also were told stories of awful deaths and grewsome ghosts that secretly shivered the hearts of all of us. Saturated with this, yet scoffing at it, I rolled over at the end of the second dog-watch and went to sleep.

At ten minutes to twelve I was called, and at twelve I was dressed and on deck, relieving the man who had called me. On the sealing grounds, when hove to, a watch of only a single man is kept through the night, each man holding the deck for an hour. It was a dark night, though not a black one. The gale was breaking up, and the clouds were thinning. There should have been a moon, and, though invisible, in some way a dim, suffused radiance came from it. I paced back and forth across the deck amidships. My mind was filled with the event of the day and with the horrible tales my shipmates had told, and yet I dare to say, here and now, that I was not afraid. I was a healthy animal, and furthermore, intellectually, I agreed with Swinburne that dead men rise up never. The Bricklayer was dead, and that was the end of it. He would rise up never—at least, never on the deck of the *Sophie Sutherland*. Even then he was in the ocean depths miles to windward of our leeward drift, and the likelihood was that he was already portioned out in the maws of many sharks. Still, my mind pondered on the tales of the ghosts of dead men I had heard, and I speculated on the spirit world. My conclusion was that if the spirits of the dead still roamed the world they carried the goodness or the malignancy of the earth-life with them. Therefore, granting the hypothesis (which I didn't grant at all), the ghost of the Bricklayer was bound to be as hateful and malignant as he in life had been. But there wasn't any Bricklayer's ghost—that I insisted upon.

A few minutes, thinking thus, I paced up and down. Then, glancing casually for'ard, along the port side, I leaped like a startled deer and in a blind madness of terror rushed aft along the poop, heading for the cabin. Gone was all my arrogance of youth and my intellectual calm. I had seen a ghost. There, in the dim light, where we had flung the dead man overboard, I had seen a faint and wavering form. Six feet in length it was, slender, and of substance so attenuated that I had distinctly seen through it the tracery of the fore-rigging.

As for me, I was as panic-stricken as a frightened horse. I, as I, had ceased to exist. Through me were vibrating the fibre-instincts of ten thousand generations of superstitious forebears who had been afraid of the dark and the things of the dark. I was not I. I was, in truth, those ten thousand forebears. I was the race, the whole human race, in its superstitious infancy. Not until part way down the cabin-companionway did my identity return to me. I checked my flight and clung to the steep ladder, suffocating, trembling, and dizzy. Never, before nor since, have I had such a shock. I clung to the ladder and considered. I could not doubt my senses. That I had seen something there was no discussion. But what was it? Either a ghost or a joke. There could be nothing else. If a ghost, the question was: would it appear again? If it did not, and I aroused the ship's officers, I would make myself the laughing stock of all on board. And by the same token, if it were a joke, my position would be still more ridiculous. If I were to retain my hard-won place of equality, it would never do to arouse any one until I ascertained the nature of the thing.

I am a brave man. I dare to say so; for in fear and trembling I crept up the companionway and went back to the spot from which I had first seen the thing. It had vanished. My bravery was qualified, however. Though I could see nothing, I was afraid to go for'ard to the spot where I had seen the thing. I resumed my pacing up and down, and though I cast many an anxious glance toward the dread spot, nothing manifested itself. As my equanimity returned to me, I concluded that the whole affair had been a trick of the imagination and that I had got what I deserved for allowing my mind to dwell on such matters.

Once more my glances for'ard were casual, and not anxious; and then, suddenly, I was a madman, rushing wildly aft. I had seen the thing again, the long, wavering attenuated substance through which could be seen the fore-rigging. This time I had reached only the break of the poop when I checked myself. Again I reasoned over the situation, and it was pride that counselled strongest. I could not afford to make myself a laughing stock. This thing, whatever it was, I must face alone. I must work it out myself. I looked back to the spot where we had tilted the Bricklayer. It was vacant. Nothing moved. And for a third time I resumed my amidships pacing.

In the absence of the thing my fear died away and my intellectual poise returned. Of course it was not a ghost. Dead men did not rise up. It was a joke, a cruel joke. My mates of the forecastle, by some unknown means, were frightening me. Twice already must they have seen me run aft. My cheeks burned with shame. In fancy I could hear the smothered chuckling and laughter even then going on in the forecastle. I began to grow angry. Jokes were all very well, but this was carrying the thing too far. I was the youngest on board, only a youth, and they had no right to play tricks on me of the order that I well knew in the past had made raving maniacs of men and women. I grew angrier and angrier, and resolved to show them that I was made of sterner stuff and at the same time to wreak my resentment upon them. If the thing appeared again, I made my mind up that I would go up to it—furthermore, that I would go up to it knife in hand. When within striking distance, I would strike. If a man, he would get the knife-thrust he deserved. If a ghost, well, it wouldn't hurt the ghost any, while I would have learned that dead men did rise up.

Now I was very angry, and I was quite sure the thing was a trick; but when the thing appeared a third time, in the same spot, long, attenuated, and wavering, fear surged up in me and drove most of my anger away. But I did not run. Nor did I take my eyes from the thing. Both times before, it had vanished while I was running away, so I had not seen the manner of its going. I drew my sheath-knife from my belt and began my advance. Step by step, nearer and nearer, the effort to control myself grew more severe. The struggle was between my will, my identity, my very self, on the one hand, and on the other, the ten thousand ancestors who were twisted into the fibres of me and whose ghostly voices were whispering of the dark and the fear of the dark that had been theirs in the time when the world was dark and full of terror.

I advanced more slowly, and still the thing wavered and flitted with strange eerie lurches. And then, right before my eyes, it vanished. I saw it vanish. Neither to the right nor left did it go, nor backward. Right there, while I gazed upon it, it faded away, ceased to be. I didn't die, but I swear, from what I experienced in those few succeeding moments, that I know full well that men can die of fright. I stood there, knife in hand, swaying automatically to the roll of the ship, paralysed with fear. Had the Bricklayer suddenly seized my throat with corporeal fingers and proceeded to throttle me, it would have been no more than I expected. Dead men did rise up, and that would be the most likely thing the malignant Bricklayer would do.

But he didn't seize my throat. Nothing happened. And, since nature abhors a status, I could not remain there in the one place forever paralysed. I turned and started aft. I did not run. What was the use? What chance had I against the malevolent world of ghosts? Flight, with me, was the swiftness of my legs. But pursuit, with a ghost, was the swiftness of thought. And there were ghosts. I had seen one.

And so, stumbling slowly aft, I discovered the explanation of the seeming. I saw the mizzen-topmast lurching across a faint radiance of cloud behind which was the moon. The idea leaped in my brain. I extended the line between the cloudy radiance and the mizzen-topmast and found that it must strike somewhere near the fore-rigging on the port side. Even as I did this, the radiance vanished. The driving clouds of the breaking gale were alternately thickening and thinning before the face of the moon but never exposing the face of the moon. And when the clouds were at their thinnest, it was a very dim radiance that the moon was able to make. I watched and waited. The next time the clouds thinned I looked for'ard, and there was the shadow of the topmast, long and attenuated, wavering and lurching on the deck and against the rigging.

This was my first ghost. Once again have I seen a ghost. It proved to be a Newfoundland dog, and I don't know which of us was the more frightened, for I hit that Newfoundland a full right-arm swing to the jaw. Regarding the Bricklayer's ghost, I will say that I never mentioned it to a soul on board. Also, I will say that in all my life I never went through more torment and mental suffering than on that lonely night-watch on the *Sophie Sutherland.*[9]

We completed our run across the Pacific, lifted the volcanic peaks, jungle-clad, of the Bonin Islands, sailed in among the reefs to the landlocked harbor, and let our anchor rumble down where lay a score or more of sea-gipsies like ourselves. The scents of strange vegetation blew off the tropic land. Aborigines, in queer outrigger canoes, and Japanese, in queerer sampans, paddled about the bay and came aboard. It was my first foreign land; I had won to the other side of the world, and I would see all I had read in the books come true. I was wild to get ashore.

Victor and Axel, a Swede and a Norwegian, and I planned to keep together. (And so well did we, that for the rest of the cruise we were known as the "Three Sports.") Victor pointed out a pathway that disappeared up a wild canyon, emerged on a steep, bare lava-slope, and thereafter appeared and disappeared, ever climbing, among the palms and flowers. We would go over that path, he said, and we agreed, and we would see beautiful scenery, and strange native villages, and find Heaven alone knew what adventure at the end. And Axel was keen to go fishing. The three of us agreed to that, too. We would get a sampan, and a couple of Japanese fishermen who knew the fishing grounds, and we would have great sport. As for me, I was keen for anything.

And then, our plans made, we rowed ashore over the banks of living coral and pulled our boat up the white beach of coral sand. We walked across the fringe of beach under the cocoanut palms and into the little town, and found several hundred riotous seamen from all the world, drinking prodigiously, singing prodigiously, dancing prodigiously—and all on the main street to the scandal of a helpless handful of Japanese police.

Victor and Axel said we'd have a drink before we started on our long walk. Could I decline to drink with these two chesty shipmates? Drinking together, glass in hand, put the seal on comradeship. It was the way of life. . . .

Queer, fierce, alcoholic stuff it was that we drank. There was no telling where or how it had been manufactured—some native concoction, most likely. But it was hot as fire, pale as water, and quick as death with its kick. It had been filled into empty "square-face" bottles which had once contained Holland gin and which still bore the fitting legend: "Anchor Brand." It certainly anchored us. We never got out of the town. We never went fishing in the sampan. And though we were there ten days, we never trod that wild path along the lava-cliffs and among the flowers.

We met old acquaintances from other schooners, fellows we had met in the saloons of San Francisco before we sailed. And each meeting meant a drink; and

A PHOTOGRAPHIC ALBUM

PORTRAITS OF THE ARTIST

RIGHT: Jack London, circa 1886

BELOW: At Mammy Jennie's, the home of Jack's old nurse.

ABOVE: The young socialist with Alexander Irvine at Yale University, 1906.

RIGHT: Jack aboard the *Roamer*, 1914.

LEFT: Charmian Kittredge married Jack London on November 20, 1905. Jack's "woman in a million" followed him all over the world.

BELOW: 1916, a few months before his death.

The Skipper and his wife aboard the *Snark*, in the harbor at Samoa.

THE VALLEY OF THE MOON

ABOVE: The building of Wolf House. "My house will be standing, Act of God permitting, for a thousand years." Jack's Ranch, Glen Ellen, California.
BELOW: On August 18, 1913, shortly before the Londons were to move in, Wolf House burned to the ground. Cause unknown.

ABOVE: "I am the sailor on horseback! Watch my dust!"
BELOW: The mountain meadows of the Valley of the Moon.

RIGHT: As a friend of Luther Burbank, Jack London became a leading exponent of scientific agriculture. His concrete block silo was the first built in California.

BELOW: November 22, 1916. "And roll over me a red boulder from the ruins of the Big House."

there was much to talk about; and more drinks; and songs to be sung; and pranks and antics to be performed; until the maggots of imagination began to crawl, and it all seemed great and wonderful to me, these lusty, hard-bitten sea-rovers, of whom I made one, gathered in wassail on a coral strand. Old lines about knights at table in the great banquet-halls, and of those above the salt and below the salt, and of Vikings feasting fresh from sea and ripe for battle, came to me; and I knew that the old times were not dead and that we belonged to that selfsame ancient breed.

. . . The main street was a madness. Hundreds of sailors rollicked up and down. Because the chief of police with his small force was helpless, the governor of the colony had issued orders to the captains to have all their men on board by sunset.

What! To be treated in such fashion! As the news spread among the schooners, they were emptied. Everybody came ashore. Men who had had no intention of coming ashore, climbed into the boats. The unfortunate governor's *ukase* had precipitated a general debauch for all hands. It was hours after sunset, and the men wanted to see anybody try to put them on board. They went around inviting the authorities to try to put them on board. In front of the governor's house they were gathered thickest, bawling sea-songs, circulating square-faces, and dancing uproarious Virginia reels and old-country dances. The police, including the reserves, stood in little forlorn groups, waiting for the command the governor was too wise to issue. And I thought this saturnalia was great. It was like the old days of the Spanish Main come back. It was license; it was adventure. And I was part of it, a chesty sea-rover along with all these other chesty sea-rovers among the paper houses of Japan.

The governor never issued the order to clear the streets, and Axel and I wandered on from drink to drink. After a time, in some of the antics, getting hazy myself, I lost him. I drifted along, making new acquaintances, downing more drinks, getting hazier and hazier. I remember, somewhere, sitting in a circle with Japanese fishermen, kanaka boat-steerers from our own vessels, and a young Danish sailor fresh from cowboying in the Argentine and with a penchant for native customs and ceremonials. And with due and proper and most intricate Japanese ceremonial, we of the circle drank *sake*, pale, mild, and lukewarm, from tiny porcelain bowls.

And, later, I remember the runaway apprentices—boys of eighteen and twenty, of middle class English families, who had jumped their ships and apprenticeships in various ports of the world and drifted into the forecastles of the sailing schooners. They were healthy, smooth-skinned, clear-eyed, and they were young—youths like me, learning the way of their feet in the world of men. And they *were* men. No mild *sake* for them, but square-faces illicitly refilled with corrosive fire that flamed through their veins and burst into conflagrations in their heads . . . And one last picture I have, standing out very clear and bright in the midst of vagueness before and blackness afterward. We—the apprentices and I—are swaying and clinging to one another under the stars. We are singing a rollicking sea-song, all save one who sits on the ground and weeps; and we are marking the rhythm with waving square-faces. From up and down the street come far choruses of sea-voices similarly singing, and life is great, and beautiful, and romantic, and magnificently mad.

And next, after the blackness, I open my eyes in the early dawn to see a Japanese woman, solicitously anxious, bending over me. She is the port-pilot's wife, and I am lying in her doorway. I am chilled and shivering, sick with the after sickness of debauch. And I feel lightly clad. Those rascals of run-away apprentices! They have acquired the habit of running away. They have run away with my possessions. My watch is gone. My few dollars are gone. My coat is gone. So is my belt. And yes, my shoes.

And the foregoing is a sample of the ten days I spent in the Bonin Islands . . . we never climbed that lava-path among the flowers. The town and the square-faces were all we saw.

North we raced from the Bonin Islands to pick up the seal-herd, and north we hunted it for a hundred days into frosty, wintry weather and into and through vast fogs which hid the sun from us for a week at a time. . . .[2]

The deck was a slaughter-house, week in and week out. There wasn't a malingerer left among us since the Bricklayer slid overside; and we kept up a lively competition to see who would have the biggest number of skins salted down at the close of the season. It was wild, heavy work off the coast of Siberia, with no let-up weeks on end.[4]

Possibly the proudest achievement of my life, my moment of highest living, occurred when . . . we were in a typhoon. All hands had been on deck most of the night. I was called from my bunk at seven in the morning to take the wheel. Not a stitch of canvas was set. We were running before it under bare poles, yet the schooner fairly tore along. The seas were all of an eighth of a mile apart, and the wind snatched the whitecaps from their summits, filling the air so thick with driving spray that it was impossible to see more than two waves at a time. The schooner was almost unmanageable, rolling her rail under to starboard and to port, veering and yawing anywhere between southeast and southwest, and threatening, when the huge seas lifted under her quarter, to broach to. Had she broached to, she would ultimately have been reported lost with all hands and no tidings.

I took the wheel. The sailing-master watched me for a space. He was afraid of my youth, feared that I lacked the strength and the nerve. But when he saw me successfully wrestle the schooner through several bouts, he went below to breakfast. Fore and aft, all hands were below at breakfast. Had she broached to, not one of them would ever have reached the deck. For forty minutes I stood there alone at the wheel, in my grasp the wildly careening schooner and the lives of twenty-two men. Once we were pooped. I saw it coming, and, half-drowned with tons of water crushing me, I checked the schooner's rush to broach to. At the end of the hour, sweating and played out, I was relieved. But I had done it! With my own hands I had done my trick at the wheel and guided a hundred tons of wood and iron through a few million tons of wind and waves.[8]

THE ELECTRICIAN

. . . After sealing for seven months I came back to California, and took odd jobs at coal shoveling and longshoring, and also in a jute factory, where I worked from six in the morning to seven at night.[5]

. . . Despite my increase in strength and general efficiency, I was receiving no more than when I worked in the cannery several years before. But, then, there was a promise of a raise to a dollar and a quarter a day after a few months.[2]

In my fitful schooldays I had written the usual compositions, which had been praised in the usual way, and while working in the jute mills I still made an occasional try. The factory occupied thirteen hours of my days, and being young and husky, I wanted a little time for myself, so there was little left for composition. The *San Francisco Call* offered a prize for a descriptive article. My mother urged me to try for it, and I did, taking for my subject, "Typhoon off the Coast of Japan" (See page 54). Very tired and sleepy, and knowing I had to be up at half-past five, I began the article at midnight and worked straight on until I had written two thousand words, the limit of the article, but with my idea only half worked out. The next night, under the same conditions, I continued, adding another two thousand words before I had finished, and then the third night I spent in cutting out the excess, so as to bring the article within the conditions of the contest. The first prize came to me, and the second and third went to students of the Stanford and Berkeley Universities.

My success in the *San Francisco Call* competition seriously turned my thoughts to writing, but my blood was too hot for a settled routine, so I practically deferred literature, beyond writing a little gush for the *Call*, which that journal promptly rejected.[5]

The jute mills failed its agreement to increase my pay to a dollar and a quarter a day, and I, a free-born American boy whose direct ancestors had fought in all the wars from the old pre-Revolutionary Indian wars down, exercised my sovereign right of free contract by quitting the job.

I was still resolved to settle down, and I looked about me. One thing was clear. Unskilled labor didn't pay. I must learn a trade, and I decided on electricity. The need for electricians was constantly growing. But how to become an electrician? I hadn't the money to go to a technical school or university; besides, I didn't think much of schools. I was a practical man in a practical world. Also, I still believed in the old myths which were the heritage of the American boy when I was a boy.

A canal boy could become a president. Any boy, who took employment with any firm, could, by thrift, energy, and sobriety, learn the business and rise from position to position until he was taken in as a junior partner. After that the senior partnership was only a matter of time. Very often—so ran the myth—the boy, by reason of his steadiness and application, married his employer's daughter. By this time I had been encouraged to such faith in myself in the matter of girls that I was quite certain I would marry my employer's daughter. There wasn't a doubt of it. All the little boys in the myths did it as soon as they were old enough.

So I bade farewell forever to the adventure-path, and went out to the power-plant of one of our Oakland street-railways. I saw the superintendent himself, in a private office so fine that it almost stunned me. But I talked straight up. I told him I wanted to become a practical electrician, that I was unafraid of work, that I was used to hard work, and that all he had to do was look at me to see I was fit and strong. I told him that I wanted to begin right at the bottom and work up, that I wanted to devote my life to this one occupation and this one employment.

The superintendent beamed as he listened. He told me that I was the right stuff for success, and that he believed in encouraging American youth that wanted to rise. Why, employers were always on the lookout for young fellows like me, and alas, they found them all too rarely. My ambition was fine and worthy, and he would see to it that I got my chance. (And as I listened with swelling heart, I wondered if it was his daughter I was to marry.)

"Before you can go out on the road and learn the more complicated and higher details of the profession," he said, "you will, of course, have to work in the car house with the men who install and repair the motors. (By this time I was sure that it was his daughter, and I was wondering how much stock he might own in the company.)

"But," he said, "as you yourself so plainly see, you couldn't expect to begin as a helper to the car house electricians. That will come when you have worked up to it. You will really begin at the bottom. In the car house your first employment will be sweeping up, washing the windows, keeping things clean. And after you have shown yourself satisfactory at that, then you may become a helper to the car house electricians."

I didn't see how sweeping and scrubbing a building was any preparation for the trade of electrician; but I did know that in the books all the boys started with the most menial tasks and by making good ultimately won to the ownership of the whole concern.

"When shall I come to work?" I asked, eager to launch on this dazzling career.

"But," said the superintendent, "as you and I have already agreed, you must begin at the bottom. Not immediately can you in any capacity enter the car house. Before that you must pass through the engine room as an oiler."

My heart went down slightly and for the moment, as I saw the road lengthen between his daughter and me; then it rose again. I would be a better electrician with knowledge of steam engines. As an oiler in the great engine room I was confident that few things concerning steam would escape me. Heavens! My career shone more dazzling than ever.

"When shall I come to work?" I asked gratefully.

"But," said the superintendent, "you could not expect to enter immediately into the engine room. There must be preparation for that. And through the fire room, of course. Come, you see the matter clearly, I know. And you will see that even the mere handling of coal is a scientific matter and not to be sneezed at. Do you know that we weigh every pound of coal we burn? Thus, we learn the value of the coal we buy; we know to a tee the last penny of cost of every item of production, and we learn which firemen are the most wasteful, which firemen, out of stupidity or carelessness, get the least out of the coal they fire." The superintendent beamed again. "You see how very important the little matter of coal is, and by as much as you learn of this little matter you will become that much better a workman—more valuable to us, more valuable to yourself. Now, are you prepared to begin?"

"Any time," I said valiantly. "The sooner the better."

"Very well," he answered. "You will come to-morrow morning at seven o'clock."

I was taken out and shown my duties. Also, I was told the terms of my employment—a ten-hour day, every day in the month including Sundays and holidays, with one day off each month, with a salary of thirty dollars a month. It wasn't exciting. Years before, at the cannery, I had earned a dollar a day for a ten-hour day. I consoled myself with the thought that the reason my earning capacity had not increased with my years and strength was because I had remained an unskilled laborer. But it was different now. I was beginning to work for skill, for a trade, for career and fortune and the superintendent's daughter.

And I was beginning in the right way—right at the beginning. That was the thing. I was passing coal to the firemen, who shoveled it into the furnaces where its energy was transformed into steam, which, in the engine room, was transformed into the electricity with which the electricians worked. This passing of coal was surely the very beginning . . . unless the superintendent should take it into his head to send me to work in the mines from which the coal came in order to get a completer understanding of the genesis of electricity for street railways.

Work! I, who had worked with men, found that I didn't know the first thing about real work. A ten-hour day! I had to pass coal for the day and night shifts, and, despite working through the noon-hour, I never finished my task before eight at night. I was working a twelve- to thirteen-hour day, and I wasn't being paid overtime as in the cannery.

I might as well give the secret away right here. I was doing the work of two men. Before me, one mature able-bodied laborer had done the day shift and another equally mature able-bodied laborer had done the night shift. They had received forty dollars a month each. The superintendent, bent on an economical administration, had persuaded me to do the work of both men for thirty dollars a month. I thought he was making an electrician of me. In truth and fact, he was saving fifty dollars a month operating expenses to the company.

But I didn't know I was displacing two men. Nobody told me. On the contrary, the superintendent warned everybody not to tell me. How valiantly I went at it that first day. I worked at top speed, filling the iron wheelbarrow with coal, running it on the scales and weighing the load, then trundling it into the fire room and dumping it on the plates before the fires.

Work! I did more than the two men whom I had displaced. They had merely wheeled in the coal and dumped it on the plates. But while I did this for the day coal, the night coal I had to pile against the wall of the fire room. Now the fire room was small. It had been planned for a night coal-passer. So I had to pile the night coal higher and higher, buttressing up the heap with stout planks. Toward the top of the heap I had to handle the coal a second time, tossing it up with a shovel.

I dripped with sweat, but I never ceased from my stride, though I could feel exhaustion coming on. By ten o'clock in the morning, so much of my body's energy had I consumed, I felt hungry and snatched a thick double-slice of bread and butter from my dinner pail. This I devoured, standing, grimed with coal dust, my knees trembling under me. By eleven o'clock, in this fashion, I had consumed my whole lunch. But what of it? I realized that it would enable me to continue working through the noon hour. And I worked all afternoon. Darkness came on, and I worked under the electric lights. The day fireman went off and the night fireman came on. I plugged away.

At half-past eight, famished, tottering, I washed up, changed my clothes, and dragged my weary body to the car. It was three miles to where I lived, and I had received a pass with the stipulation that I could sit down as long as there were no paying passengers in need of a seat. As I sank into a corner outside seat I prayed that no passenger might require my seat. But the car filled up, and, half way in, a woman came on board, and there was no seat for her. I started to get up, and to my astonishment found that I could not. With the chill wind blowing on me, my spent body had stiffened into the seat. It took me the rest of the run in to unkink my complaining joints and muscles and get into a standing position on the lower step. And when the car stopped at my corner I nearly fell to the ground when I stepped off.

I hobbled two blocks to the house and limped into the kitchen. While my mother started to cook I plunged into bread and butter; but before my appetite was appeased, or the steak fried, I was sound asleep. In vain my mother strove to shake me awake enough to eat the meat. Failing in this, with the assistance of my father she managed to get me to my room, where I collapsed dead asleep on the bed. They undressed me and covered me up. In the morning came the agony of being awakened. I was terribly sore, and worst of all my wrists were swelling. But I made up for my lost supper, eating an enormous breakfast, and when I hobbled to catch my car I carried a lunch twice as big as the one the day before.

Work! Let any youth just turned eighteen try to out-shovel two man-grown coal-shovelers. Work! Long before midday I had eaten the last scrap of my huge lunch. But I was resolved to show them what a husky young fellow determined to rise could do. The worst of it was that my wrists were swelling and going back on me. There are few who do not know the pain of walking on a sprained ankle. Then imagine the pain of shoveling coal and trundling a loaded wheelbarrow with two sprained wrists.

Work! More than once I sank down on the coal where no one could see me, and cried with rage, and mortification, and exhaustion, and despair. That second day was my hardest, and all that enabled me to survive it and get in the last of the night coal at the end of thirteen hours was the day fireman, who bound both my wrists with broad leather straps. So tightly were they buckled that they were like slightly flexible plaster casts. They took the stresses and pressures which thitherto had been borne by my wrists, and they were so tight that there was no room for the inflammation to rise in the sprains.

And in this fashion I continued to learn to be an electrician. Night after night I limped home, fell asleep before I could eat my supper, and was helped into bed and undressed. Morning after morning, always with huger lunches in my dinner pail, I limped out of the house on my way to work.

I no longer read my library books. I made no dates with the girls. I was a proper work-beast. I worked, and ate, and slept, while my mind slept all the time. The whole thing was a nightmare. I worked every day, including Sunday, and I looked far ahead to my one day off at the end of a month, resolved to lie abed all that day and just sleep and rest up.

I had often noticed the day fireman staring at me in a curious way. At last, one day, he spoke. He began by swearing me to secrecy. He had been warned by the superintendent not to tell me, and in telling me he was risking his job. He told me of the day coal-passer and the night coal-passer, and of the wages they had received. I was doing for thirty dollars a month what they had received eighty dollars for doing. He would have told me sooner, the fireman said, had he not been so certain that I would break down under the work and quit. As it was, I was killing myself, and all to no good purpose. I was merely cheapening the price of labor, he argued, and keeping two men out of a job.

Being an American boy, and a proud American boy, I did not immediately quit. This was foolish of me, I know; but I resolved to continue the work long enough to prove to the superintendent that I could do it without breaking down. Then I would quit, and he would realize what a fine young fellow he had lost.

All of which I faithfully and foolishly did. I worked on until the time came when I got in the last of the night coal by six o'clock. Then I quit the job of learning electricity by doing more than two men's work for a boy's wages, went home, and proceeded to sleep the clock around.

Fortunately, I had not stayed by the job long enough to injure myself—though I was compelled to wear straps on my wrists for a year afterward. But the effect of this work orgy in which I had indulged was to sicken me with work. I just wouldn't work. The thought of work was repulsive. I didn't care if I ever settled down. Learning a trade could go hang. It was a whole lot better to royster and frolic over the world in the way I had previously done. So I headed out on the adventure-path again, starting to tramp East by beating my way on the railroads.[2]

THE TRAMP

Perhaps the greatest charm of tramp-life is the absence of monotony. In Hobo Land the face of life is protean—an ever changing phantasmagoria, where the impossible happens and the unexpected jumps out of the bushes at every turn of the road. The hobo never knows what is going to happen the next moment; hence, he lives only in the present moment. He has learned the futility of telic endeavor, and knows the delight of drifting along with the whimsicalities of Chance.

Often I think over my tramp days, and ever I marvel at the swift succession of pictures that flash up in my memory. It matters not where I begin to think; any day of all the days is a day apart, with a record of swift-moving pictures all its own. . . .[10]

TWO THOUSAND STIFFS

A "stiff" is a tramp. It was once my fortune to travel a few weeks with a "push" that numbered two thousand. This was known as "Kelly's Army." Across the wild and woolly West, clear from California, General Kelly and his heroes had captured trains; but they fell down when they crossed the Missouri and went up against the effete East. The East hadn't the slightest intention of giving free transportation to two thousand hoboes. Kelly's Army lay helplessly for some time at Council Bluffs. The day I joined it, made desperate by delay, it marched out to capture a train.

It was quite an imposing sight. General Kelly sat a magnificent black charger, and with waving banners, to the martial music of fife and drum corps, company by company, in two divisions, his two thousand stiffs countermarched before him and hit the wagon-road to the little burg of Weston, seven miles away. Being the latest recruit, I was in the last company, of the last regiment, of the Second Division, and, furthermore, in the last rank of the rear-guard. The army went into camp at Weston beside the railroad track—beside the tracks, rather, for two roads went through: the Chicago, Milwaukee, and St. Paul, and the Rock Island.

Our intention was to take the first train out, but the railroad officials "coppered" our play—and won. There was no first train. They tied up the two lines and stopped running trains. In the meantime, while we lay by the dead tracks, the good people of Omaha and Council Bluffs were bestirring themselves. Preparations were making to form a mob, capture a train in Council Bluffs, run it down to us, and make us a present of it. The railroad officials coppered that play, too. They didn't wait for the mob. Early in the morning of the second day, an engine, with a single private car attached, arrived at the station and side-tracked. At this sign that life had renewed in the dead roads, the whole army lined up beside the track.

But never did life renew so monstrously on a dead railroad as it did on those two roads. From the west came the whistle of a locomotive. It was coming in our direction, bound east. We were bound east. A stir of preparation ran down our ranks. The whistle tooted fast and furiously, and the train thundered at top speed. The hobo didn't live that could have boarded it. Another locomotive whistled, and another train came through at top speed, and another, and another, train after train, train after train, till toward the last the trains were composed of passenger coaches, box-cars, flat-cars, dead engines, cabooses, mail-cars, wrecking appliances, and all the riff-raff of worn-out and abandoned rolling-stock that collects in the yards of great railways. When the yards at Council Bluffs had been completely cleaned, the private car and engine went east, and the tracks died for keeps.

That day went by, and the next, and nothing moved, and in the meantime, pelted by sleet, and rain, and hail, the two thousand hoboes lay beside the track. But that night the good people of Council Bluffs went the railroad officials one better. A mob formed in Council Bluffs, crossed the river to Omaha, and there joined with another mob in a raid on the Union Pacific yards. First they captured an engine, next they knocked a train together, and then the united mobs piled aboard, crossed the Missouri, and ran down the Rock Island right of way to turn the train over to us. The railway officials tried to copper this play, but fell down, to the mortal terror of the section boss and one member of the section gang at Weston. This pair, under secret telegraphic orders, tried to wreck our train-load of sympathizers by tearing up the track. It happened that we were suspicious and had our patrols out. Caught red-handed at train-wrecking, and surrounded by twenty hundred infuriated hoboes, that section-gang boss and assistant prepared to meet death. I don't remember what saved them, unless it was the arrival of the train.

It was our turn to fall down, and we did, hard. In their haste, the two mobs had neglected to make up a sufficiently long train. There wasn't room for two thousand hoboes to ride. So the mobs and the hoboes had a talkfest, fraternized, sang songs, and parted, the mobs going back on their captured train to Omaha, the hoboes pulling out next morning on a hundred-and-forty-mile march to Des Moines. It was not until Kelly's Army crossed the Missouri that it began to walk, and after that it never rode again. It cost the railroads slathers of money, but they were acting on principle, and they won.

Underwood, Leola, Menden, Avoca, Walnut, Marno, Atlantic, Wyoto, Anita, Adair, Adam, Casey, Stuart, Dexter, Carlham, De Soto, Van Meter, Booneville, Commerce, Valley Junction—how the names of the towns come back to me as I con the map and trace our route through the fat Iowa country! And the hospitable Iowa farmer-folk! They turned out with their wagons and carried our baggage; gave us hot lunches at noon by the wayside; mayors of comfortable little towns made speeches of welcome and hastened us on our way; deputations of little girls and maidens came out to meet us, and the good citizens turned out by hundreds, locked arms, and marched with us down their main streets. It was circus day when we came to town, and every day was circus day, for there were many towns.

In the evenings our camps were invaded by whole populations. Every company had its campfire, and around each fire something was doing. The cooks in my company, Company L, were song-and-dance artists and contributed most of our entertainment. In another part of the encampment the glee club would be singing —one of its star voices was the "Dentist," drawn from Company L, and we were mighty proud of him. Also, he pulled teeth for the whole army, and, since the extractions usually occurred at meal-time, our digestions were stimulated by variety of incident. The Dentist had no anæsthetics, but two or three of us were always on tap to volunteer to hold down the patient. In addition to the stunts of the companies and the glee club, church services were usually held, local preachers officiating, and always there was a great making of political speeches. All these things ran neck and neck; it was a full-blown Midway. A lot of talent can be dug out of two thousand hoboes. I remember we had a picked baseball nine, and on Sundays we made a practice of putting it all over the local nines. Sometimes we did it twice on Sundays.

Last year, while on a lecturing trip, I rode into Des Moines in a Pullman—I don't mean a "side-door Pullman," but the real thing. On the outskirts of the city I saw the old stove-works, and my heart leaped. It was there, at the stove-works, a dozen years before, that the Army lay down and swore a mighty oath that its feet were sore and that it would walk no more. We took possession of the stove-works and told Des Moines that we had come to stay—that we'd walk in, but we'd be blessed if we'd walk out. Des Moines was hospitable, but this was too much of a good thing. Do a little mental arithmetic, gentle reader. Two thousand hoboes, eating three square meals, make six thousand meals per day, forty-two thousand meals per week, or one hundred and sixty-eight thousand meals per shortest month in the calendar. That's going some. We had no money. It was up to Des Moines.

Des Moines was desperate. We lay in camp, made political speeches, held sacred concerts, pulled teeth, played baseball and seven-up, and ate our six thousand meals per day, and Des Moines paid for it. Des Moines pleaded with the railroads, but they were obdurate; they had said we shouldn't ride, and that settled it. To permit us to ride would be to establish a precedent, and there weren't going to be any precedents. And still we went on eating. That was the terrifying factor in the situation. We were bound for Washington, and Des Moines would have had to float municipal bonds to pay all our railroad fares, even at special rates, and if we remained much longer, she'd have to float bonds anyway to feed us.

Then some local genius solved the problem. We wouldn't walk. Very good. We should ride. From Des Moines to Keokuk on the Mississippi flowed the Des Moines River. This particular stretch of river was three hundred miles long. We could ride on it, said the local genius; and, once equipped with floating stock, we could ride on down the Mississippi to the Ohio, and thence up the Ohio, winding up with a short portage over the mountains to Washington.

Des Moines took up a subscription. Public-spirited citizens contributed several thousand dollars. Lumber, rope, nails, and cotton for calking were bought in large quantities, and on the banks of the Des Moines was inaugurated a tremendous era of shipbuilding. Now the Des Moines is a picayune stream, unduly dignified by the appellation of "river." In our spacious western land it would be called a "creek." The oldest inhabitants shook their heads and said we couldn't make it, that there wasn't enough water to float us. Des Moines didn't care, so long as it got rid of us, and we were such well-fed optimists that we didn't care either.

On Wednesday, May 9, 1894, we got under way and started on our colossal picnic. Des Moines had got off pretty easily, and she certainly owes a statue in bronze to the local genius who got her out of her difficulty. True, Des Moines had to pay for our boats; we had eaten sixty-six thousand meals at the stove-works; and we took twelve thousand additional meals along with us in our commissary—as a precaution against famine in the wilds; but then, think what it would have meant if we had remained at Des Moines eleven months instead of eleven days. Also, when we departed, we promised Des Moines we'd come back if the river failed to float us.

It was all very well having twelve thousand meals in the commissary, and no doubt the commissary "ducks" enjoyed them; for the commissary promptly got lost, and my boat, for one, never saw it again. The company formation was hopelessly broken up during the river-trip. In any camp of men there will always be found a certain percentage of shirks, of helpless, of just ordinary, and of hustlers. There were ten men in my boat, and they were the cream of Company L. Every man was a hustler. For two reasons I was included in the ten. First, I was as good a hustler as ever "threw his feet," and next, I was "Sailor Jack." I understood boats and boating. The ten of us forgot the remaining forty men of Company L, and by the time we had missed one meal we promptly forgot the commissary. We were independent. We went down the river "on our own," hustling and "chewin's," beating every boat in the fleet, and, alas that I must say it, sometimes taking possession of the stores the farmer-folk had collected for the Army.

For a good part of the three hundred miles we were from half a day to a day or so in advance of the Army. We had managed to get hold of several American flags. When we approached a small town, or when we saw a group of farmers gathered on the bank, we ran up our flags, called ourselves the "advance boat," and demanded to know what provisions had been collected for the Army. We represented the Army, of course, and the provisions were turned over to us. But there wasn't anything small about us. We never took more than we could get away with. But we did take the cream of everything. For instance, if some philanthropic farmer had donated several dollars' worth of tobacco, we took it. So, also, we took butter and sugar, coffee and canned goods; but when the stores consisted of sacks of beans and flour, or two or three slaughtered steers, we resolutely refrained and went our way, leaving orders to turn such provisions over to the commissary boats whose business was to follow behind us.

My, but the ten of us did live on the fat of the land! For a long time General Kelly vainly tried to head us off. He sent two rowers, in a light, round-bottomed boat, to overtake us and put a stop to our piratical careers. They overtook us all right, but they were two and we were ten. They were empowered by General Kelly to make us prisoners, and they told us so. When we expressed disinclination to become prisoners, they hurried ahead to the next town to invoke the aid of the authorities. We went ashore immediately and cooked an early supper; and under the cloak of darkness we ran by the town and its authorities.

I kept a diary on part of the trip, and as I read it over now I note one persistently recurring phrase, namely, "Living fine." We did live fine. We even disdained to use coffee boiled in water. We made our coffee out of milk, calling the wonderful beverage, if I remember rightly, "pale Vienna."

While we were ahead, skimming the cream, and while the commissary was lost far behind, the main Army, coming along in the middle, starved. This was hard on the Army, I'll allow; but then, the ten of us were individualists. We had initiative and enterprise. We ardently believed that the grub was to the man who got there first, the pale Vienna to the strong. On one stretch the Army went forty-eight hours without grub; and then it arrived at a small village of some three hundred inhabitants, the name of which I do not remember, though I think it was Red Rock. This town, following the practice of all towns through which the Army passed, had appointed a committee of safety. Counting five to a family, Red Rock consisted of sixty households. Her committee of safety was scared stiff by the eruption of two thousand hungry hoboes who lined their boats two and three deep along the river bank. General Kelly was a fair man. He had no intention of working a hardship on the village. He did not expect sixty households to furnish two thousand meals. Besides, the Army had its treasure-chest.

But the committee of safety lost its head. "No encouragement to the invader" was its programme, and when General Kelly wanted to buy food, the committee turned him down. It had nothing to sell; General Kelly's money was "no good" in their burg. And then General Kelly went into action. The bugles blew. The Army left the boats and on top of the bank formed in battle array. The committee was there to see. General Kelly's speech was brief.

"Boys," he said, "when did you eat last?"

"Day before yesterday," they shouted.

"Are you hungry?"

A mighty affirmation from two thousand throats shook the atmosphere. Then General Kelly turned to the committee of safety:—

"You see, gentlemen, the situation. My men have eaten nothing in forty-eight hours. If I turn them loose upon your town, I'll not be responsible for what happens. They are desperate. I offered to buy food for them, but you refused to sell. I now withdraw my offer. Instead, I shall demand. I give you five minutes to decide. Either kill me six steers and give me four thousand rations, or I turn the men loose. Five minutes, gentlemen."

The terrified committee of safety looked at the two thousand hungry hoboes and collapsed. It didn't wait the five minutes. It wasn't going to take any chances. The killing of the steers and the collecting of the requisition began forthwith, and the Army dined.

And still the ten graceless individualists soared along ahead and gathered in everything in sight. But General Kelly fixed us. He sent horsemen down each bank, warning farmers and townspeople against us. They did their work thoroughly, all right. The erstwhile hospitable farmers met us with the icy mit. Also, they summoned the constables when we tied up to the bank, and loosed the dogs. I know. Two of the latter caught me with a barbed-wire fence between me and the river. I was carrying two buckets of milk for the pale Vienna. I didn't damage the fence any; but we drank plebeian coffee boiled with vulgar water, and it was up to me to throw my feet for another pair of trousers. I wonder, gentle reader, if you ever essayed hastily to climb a barbed-wire fence with a bucket of milk in each hand. Ever since that day I have had a prejudice against barbed wire, and I have gathered statistics on the subject.

Unable to make an honest living so long as General Kelly kept his two horsemen ahead of us, we returned to the Army and raised a revolution. It was a small affair, but it devastated Company L of the Second Division. The captain of Company L refused to recognize us; said we were deserters, and traitors, and scalawags; and when he drew rations for Company L from the commissary, he wouldn't give us any. That captain didn't appreciate us, or he wouldn't have refused us grub.

Promptly we intrigued with the first lieutenant. He joined us with the ten men in his boat, and in return we elected him captain of Company M. The Captain of Company L raised a roar. Down upon us came General Kelly, Colonel Speed, and Colonel Baker. The twenty of us stood firm, and our revolution was ratified.

But we never bothered with the commissary. Our hustlers drew better rations from the farmers. Our new captain, however, doubted us. He never knew when he'd see the ten of us again, once we got under way in the morning, so he called in a blacksmith to clinch his captaincy. In the stern of our boat, one on each side, were driven two heavy eye-bolts of iron. Correspondingly, on the bow of his boat, were fastened two huge iron hooks. The boats were brought together, end on, the hooks dropped into the eye-bolts, and there we were, hard and fast. We couldn't lose that captain. But we were irrepressible. Out of our very manacles we wrought an invincible device that enabled us to put it all over every other boat in the fleet.

Like all great inventions, this one of ours was accidental. We discovered it the first time we ran on a snag in a bit of a rapid. The head-boat hung up and anchored, and the tail-boat swung around in the current, pivoting the head-boat on the snag. I was at the stern of the tail-boat, steering. In vain we tried to shove off. Then I ordered the men from the head-boat into the tail-boat. Immediately the head-boat floated clear, and its men returned into it. After that, snags, reefs, shoals, and bars had no terrors for us. The instant the head-boat struck, the men in it leaped into the tail-boat. Of course, the head-boat floated over the obstruction and the tail-boat then struck. Like automatons, the twenty men now in the tail-boat leaped into the head-boat, and the tail-boat floated past.

The boats used by the Army were all alike, made by the mile and sawed off. They were flat-boats, and their lines were rectangles. Each boat was six feet wide, ten feet long, and a foot and a half deep. Thus, when our two boats were hooked together, I sat at the stern steering a craft twenty feet long, containing twenty husky hoboes who "spelled" each other at the oars and paddles, and loaded with blankets, cooking outfit, and our own private commissary.

Still we caused General Kelly trouble. He had called in his horsemen, and substituted three police-boats that travelled in the van and allowed no boats to pass them. The craft containing Company M crowded the police-boats hard. We could have passed them easily, but it was against the rules. So we kept a respectful distance astern and waited. Ahead we knew was virgin farming country, unbegged and generous; but we waited. White water was all we needed, and when we rounded a bend and a rapid showed up we knew what would happen. Smash! Police-boat number one goes on a boulder and hangs up. Bang! Police-boat number two follows suit. Whop! Police-boat number three encounters the common fate of all. Of course our boat does the same things; but one, two, the men are out of the head-boat and into the tail-boat; one, two, they are out of the tail-boat and into the head-boat; and one, two, the men who belong in the tail-boat are back in it and we are dashing on. "Stop! you blankety-blank-blanks!" shriek the police-boats. "How can we?—blank the blankety-blank river, anyway!" we wail plaintively as we surge past, caught in that remorseless current that sweeps us on out of sight and into the hospitable farmer-country that replenishes our private commissary with the cream of its contributions. Again we drink pale Vienna and realize that the grub is to the man who gets there.

Poor General Kelly! He devised another scheme. The whole fleet started ahead of us. Company M of the Second Division started in its proper place in the line, which was last. And it took us only one day to put the "kibosh" on that particular scheme. Twenty-five miles of bad water lay before us—all rapids, shoals, bars, and boulders. It was over that stretch of water that the oldest inhabitants of Des Moines had shaken their heads. Nearly two hundred boats entered the bad water ahead of us, and they piled up in the most astounding manner. We went through that stranded fleet like hemlock through the fire. There was no avoiding the boulders, bars, and snags except by getting out on the bank. We didn't avoid them. We went right over them, one, two, one, two, head-boat, tail-boat, head-boat, tail-boat, all hands back and forth and back again. We camped that night alone, and loafed in camp all of next day while the Army patched and repaired its wrecked boats and straggled up to us.

There was no stopping our cussedness. We rigged up a mast, piled on the canvas (blankets), and travelled short hours while the Army worked over-time to keep us in sight. Then General Kelly had recourse to diplomacy. No boat could touch us in the straight-away. Without discussion, we were the hottest bunch that ever came down the Des Moines. The ban of the police-boats was lifted. Colonel Speed was put aboard, and with this distinguished officer we had the honor of arriving first at Keokuk on the Mississippi. And right here I want to say to General Kelly and Colonel Speed that here's my hand. You were heroes, both of you, and you were men. And I'm sorry for at least ten per cent of the trouble that was given you by the head-boat of Company M.

At Keokuk the whole fleet was lashed together in a huge raft, and, after being wind-bound a day, a steamboat took us in tow down the Mississippi to Quincy, Illinois, where we camped across the river on Goose Island. Here the raft idea was abandoned, the boats being joined together in groups of four and decked over. Somebody told me that Quincy was the richest town of its size in the United States. When I heard this, I was immediately overcome by an irresistible impulse to throw my feet. No "blowed-in-the-glass profesh" could possibly pass up such a promising burg. I crossed the river to Quincy in a small dug-out; but I came back in a large river-boat, down to the gunwales with the results of my thrown feet. Of course I kept all the money I had collected, though I paid the boat-hire; also I took my pick of the underwear, socks, cast-off clothes, shirts, "kicks," and "sky-pieces"; and when Company M had taken all it wanted there was still a respectable heap that was turned over to Company L. Alas, I was young and prodigal in those days! I told a thousand "stories" to the good people of Quincy, and every story was "good"; but since I have come to write for the magazines I have often regretted the wealth of story, the fecundity of fiction, I lavished that day in Quincy, Illinois.

It was at Hannibal, Missouri, that the ten invincibles went to pieces. It was not planned. We just naturally flew apart. The Boiler-Maker and I deserted secretly. On the same day Scotty and Davy made a swift sneak for the Illinois shore; also McAvoy and Fish achieved their get-away. This accounts for six of the ten; what became of the remaining four I do not know. As a sample of life on The Road, I make the following quotation from my diary of the several days following my desertion.

"Friday, May 25th. Boiler-Maker and I left the camp on the island. We went ashore on the Illinois side in a skiff and walked six miles on the C.B. & Q. to Fell Creek. We had gone six miles out of our way, but we got on a hand-car and rode six miles to Hull's, on the Wabash. While there, we met McAvoy, Fish, Scotty, and Davy, who had also pulled out from the Army.

"Saturday, May 26th. At 2:11 A.M. we caught the Cannon-ball as she slowed up at the crossing. Scotty and Davy were ditched. The four of us were ditched at the Bluffs, forty miles farther on. In the afternoon Fish and McAvoy caught a freight while Boiler-Maker and I were away getting something to eat.

"Sunday, May 27th. At 3:21 A.M. we caught the Cannon-ball and found Scotty and Davy on the blind. We were all ditched at daylight at Jacksonville. The C. & A. runs through here, and we're going to take that. Boiler-Maker went off, but didn't return. Guess he caught a freight.

"Monday, May 28th. Boiler-Maker didn't show up. Scotty and Davy went off to sleep somewhere, and didn't get back in time to catch the K.C. passenger at 3.30 A.M. I caught her and rode her till after sunrise to Masson City, 25,000 inhabitants. Caught a cattle train and rode all night.

"Tuesday, May 29th. Arrived in Chicago at 7 A.M. . . ."[10]

. . . On rods and blind baggages I fought my way from the open West, where men bucked big and the job hunted the man, to the congested labor centres of the East, where men were small potatoes and hunted the job for all they were worth. And on this new *blond-beast* adventure I found myself looking upon life from a new and totally different angle. I had dropped down from the proletariat into what sociologists love to call the "submerged tenth," and I was startled to discover the way in which that submerged tenth was recruited.

I found there all sorts of men, many of whom had once been as good as myself and just as *blond-beastly;* sailor-men, soldier-men, labor-men, all wrenched and distorted and twisted out of shape by toil and hardship and accident, and cast adrift by their masters like so many old horses. I battered on the drag and slammed back gates with them, or shivered with them in box cars and city parks, listening the while to life-histories which began under auspices as fair as mine, with digestions and bodies equal to and better than mine, and which ended there before my eyes in the shambles at the bottom of the Social Pit.

And as I listened my brain began to work. The woman of the streets and the man of the gutter drew very close to me. I saw the picture of the Social Pit as vividly as though it were a concrete thing, and at the bottom of the Pit I saw them, myself above them, not far, and hanging on to the slippery wall by main strength and sweat. And I confess a terror seized me. What when my strength failed? when I should be unable to work shoulder to shoulder with the strong men who were as yet babes unborn? And there and then I swore a great oath. It ran something like this: *All my days I have worked hard with my body, and according to the number of days I have worked, by just that much am I nearer the bottom of the Pit. I shall climb out of the Pit, but not by the muscles of my body shall I climb out. I shall do no more hard work, and may God strike me dead if I do another day's hard work with my body more than I absolutely have to do.* And I have been busy ever since running away from hard work.

Incidentally, while tramping some ten thousand miles through the United States and Canada, I strayed into Niagara Falls, was nabbed by a fee-hunting constable, denied the right to plead guilty or not guilty, sentenced out of hand to thirty days' imprisonment for having no fixed abode and no visible means of support, handcuffed and chained to a bunch of men similarly circumstanced, carted down country to Buffalo, registered at the Erie County Penitentiary, had my head clipped and my budding mustache shaved, was dressed in convict stripes, compulsorily vaccinated by a medical student who practised on such as we, made to march the lock-step, and put to work under the eyes of guards armed with Winchester rifles—all for adventuring in *blond-beastly* fashion. Concerning further details deponent sayeth not, though he may hint that some of his plethoric national patriotism simmered down and leaked out of the bottom of his soul somewhere—at least, since that experience he finds that he cares more for men and women and little children than for imaginary geographical lines.

To return to my conversion. I think it is apparent that my rampant individualism was pretty effectively hammered out of me, and something else as effectively hammered in. But, just as I had been an individualist without knowing it, I was now a Socialist without knowing it, withal, an unscientific one. I had been reborn, but not renamed, and I was running around to find out what manner of thing I was. I ran back to California and opened the books. I do not remember which ones I opened first. It is an unimportant detail anyway. I was already It, whatever It was, and by aid of the books I discovered that It was a Socialist. Since that day I have opened many books, but no economic argument, no lucid demonstration of the logic and inevitableness of Socialism affects me as profoundly and convincingly as I was affected on the day when I first saw the walls of the Social Pit rise around me and felt myself slipping down, down, into the shambles at the bottom.[6]

THE BRAIN MERCHANT

So my new concept was that manual labor was undignified, and that it didn't pay. No trade for me, was my decision, and no superintendent's daughter. And no criminality, I also decided. That would be almost as disastrous as to be a laborer. Brains paid, not brawn, and I resolved never again to offer my muscles for sale in the brawn market. Brain, and brain only, would I sell.[2]

In my nineteenth year I returned to Oakland and started at the High School, which ran the usual school magazine. This publication was a weekly—no, I guess a monthly—one, and I wrote stories for it; very little imaginary, just recitals of my sea and tramping experiences.[5]

. . . To pay my way, I worked as a janitor. My sister helped me, too; and I was not above mowing anybody's lawn or taking up and beating carpets when I had half a day to spare . . . I joined the Henry Clay Debating Society. I was received into the homes of some of the members, where I met nice girls whose skirts reached the ground. I dallied with little home clubs wherein we discussed poetry and art and the nuances of grammar. I joined the socialist local, where we studied and orated political economy, philosophy, and politics. I kept half-a-dozen membership cards working in the Free Library and did an immense amount of collateral reading.

. . . At this time my socialistic utterances had attracted considerable attention, and I was known as the "Boy Socialist," a distinction that brought about my arrest for street-talking.

Three years was the time required to go through high school. I grew impatient.

Also, my schooling was becoming financially impossible. At such rate I could not last out, and I did greatly want to go to the state university. When I had done a year of high school, I decided to attempt a short cut. I borrowed the money and paid to enter the senior class of a "cramming joint" or academy. I was scheduled to graduate right into the university at the end of four months, thus saving two years.

And how I did cram! I had two years' new work to do in a third of a year. For five weeks I crammed, until simultaneous quadratic equations and chemical formulas fairly oozed from my ears. And then the master of the academy took me aside. He was very sorry, but he was compelled to give me back my tuition fee and to ask me to leave the school. It wasn't a matter of scholarship. I stood well in my classes, and did he graduate me into the university he was confident that in that institution I would continue to stand well. The trouble was that tongues were gossiping about my case. What! In four months accomplish two years' work! It would be a scandal, and the universities were becoming severer in their treatment of accredited prep schools. He couldn't afford such a scandal, therefore I must gracefully depart.

I did. And I paid back the borrowed money, and gritted my teeth, and started to cram by myself. There were three months yet before the university entrance-examinations. Without laboratories, without coaching, sitting in my bedroom, I proceeded to compress that two years' work into three months and to keep reviewed on the previous year's work.

Nineteen hours a day I studied. For three months I kept this pace, only breaking it on several occasions. My body grew weary, my mind grew weary, but I stayed with it. My eyes grew weary and began to twitch, but they did not break down. Perhaps, toward the last, I got a bit dotty. I know that at the time I was confident I had discovered the formula for squaring the circle; but I resolutely deferred the working of it out until after the examinations. Then I would show them.

Came the several days of the examinations, during which time I scarcely closed my eyes in sleep, devoting every moment to cramming and reviewing. And when I turned in my last examination paper I was in full possession of a splendid case of brain-fag. I didn't want to see a book. I didn't want to think nor to lay eyes on anybody who was liable to think.

There was but one prescription for such a condition, and I gave it to myself—the adventure-path. I didn't wait to learn the result of my examinations. I stowed a roll of blankets and some cold food into a borrowed whitehall boat and set sail. Out of the Oakland Estuary I drifted on the last of an early morning ebb, caught the first of the flood up bay, and raced along with a spanking breeze. San Pablo Bay was smoking, and the Carquinez Straits off the Selby Smelter were smoking, as I picked up ahead and left astern the old landmarks I had first learned with Nelson in the unreefed *Reindeer*.

My cruise in the salmon boat lasted a week and I returned ready to enter the university . . . My tired brain had recuperated . . . I thought no more about it, returning gladly to my books and studies.

I completed the first half of my freshman year, and in January of 1897 took up my course for the second half. But the pressure from lack of money, plus a conviction that the university was not giving me all that I wanted in the time I could spare for it, forced me to leave. I was not very disappointed. For two years I had studied, and in those two years, what was far more valuable, I had done a prodigious amount of reading. Then, too, my grammar had improved. It is true, I had not yet learned that I must say "It is I"; but I no longer was guilty of the double negative in writing, though still prone to that error in excited speech.

I decided immediately to embark on my career. I had four preferences: first, music; second, poetry; third, the writing of philosophic, economic, and political essays; and, fourth, and last, and least, fiction writing. I resolutely cut out music as impossible, settled down in my bedroom, and tackled my second, third and fourth choices simultaneously. Heavens, how I wrote! Never was there a creative fever such as mine from which the patient escaped fatal results. The way I worked was enough to soften my brain and send me to a mad-house. I wrote, I wrote everything . . . On occasion I composed steadily, day after day, for fifteen hours a day. At times I forgot to eat, or refused to tear myself away from my passionate outpouring in order to eat.

And then there was the matter of typewriting. My brother-in-law owned a machine which he used in the daytime. In the night I was free to use it. That machine was a wonder. I could weep now as I recollect my wrestlings with it. It must have been a first model in the year one of the typewriter era. Its alphabet was all capitals. It was informed with an evil spirit. It obeyed no known laws of physics, and overthrew the hoary axiom that like things performed to like things produce like results. I'll swear that machine never did the same thing in the same way twice. Again and again it demonstrated that unlike actions produce like results.

How my back used to ache with it! Prior to that experience, my back had been good for every violent strain put upon it in a none too gentle career. But that typewriter proved to me that I had a pipe-stem for a back. Also, it made me doubt my shoulders. They ached as with rheumatism after every bout. The keys of that machine had to be hit so hard that to one outside the house it sounded like distant thunder or some one breaking up the furniture. I had to hit the keys so hard that I strained my first fingers to the elbows, while the ends of my fingers were blisters burst and blistered again. Had it been my machine I'd have operated it with a carpenter's hammer.

The worst of it was that I was actually typing my manuscripts at the same time I was trying to master that machine. It was a feat of physical endurance and a brain storm combined to type a thousand words, and I was composing thousands of words every day which just had to be typed for the waiting editors.

But the waiting editors elected to keep on waiting. My manuscripts made amazing round-trip records between the Pacific and the Atlantic. It might have been the weirdness of the typewriting that prevented the editors from accepting at least one little offering of mine. I don't know, and goodness knows the stuff I wrote was as weird as its typing. I sold my hard-bought school books for ridiculous sums to second-hand bookmen. I borrowed small sums of money wherever I could, and suffered my old father to feed me with the meager returns of his failing strength.

It didn't last long, only a few weeks, when I had to surrender and go to work . . . I was not disappointed. My career was retarded, that was all. Perhaps I did need further preparation. I had learned enough from the books to realize that I had touched only the hem of knowledge's garment. I still lived on the heights. My waking hours, and most of the hours I should have used for sleep, were spent with the books.

Out in the country, at the Belmont Academy, I went to work in a small, perfectly appointed steam laundry. Another fellow and myself did all the work from sorting and washing to ironing the white shirts, collars and cuffs, and the "fancy starch" of the wives of the professors. We worked like tigers, especially as summer came on and the academy boys took to the wearing of duck trousers. It consumes a dreadful lot of time to iron one pair of duck trousers. And there were so many pairs of them. We sweated our way through long sizzling weeks at a task that was never done; and many a night, while the students snored in bed, my partner and I toiled on under the electric light at steam mangle or ironing board.

The hours were long, the work was arduous, despite the fact that we became past masters in the art of eliminating waste motion. And I was receiving thirty dollars a month and board—a slight increase over my coal-shoveling and cannery days, at least to the extent of board, which cost my employer little (we ate in the kitchen), but which was to me the equivalent of twenty dollars a month. My robuster strength of added years, my increased skill, and all I had learned from the books, were responsible for this increase of twenty dollars. Judging by my rate of development, I might hope before I died to be a night watchman for sixty dollars a month, or a policeman actually receiving a hundred dollars with pickings.

So relentlessly did my partner and I spring into our work throughout the week that by Saturday night we were frazzled wrecks. I found myself in the old familiar work-beast condition, toiling longer hours than the horses toiled, thinking scarcely more frequent thoughts than horses think. The books were closed to me. I had brought a trunkful to the laundry, but found myself unable to read them. I fell asleep the moment I tried to read; and if I did manage to keep my eyes open for several pages, I could not remember the contents of those pages. I gave over attempts on heavy study, such as jurisprudence, political economy, and biology, and tried lighter stuff, such as history. I fell asleep. I tried literature, and fell asleep. And finally, when I fell asleep over lively novels, I gave up. I never succeeded in reading one book in all the time I spent in the laundry.

And when Saturday night came, and the week's work was over until Monday morning, I knew only one desire besides the desire to sleep, and that was to get drunk. This was the second time in my life that I had heard the unmistakable call of John Barleycorn. The first time it had been because of brain-fag. But I had no overworked brain now. On the contrary, all I knew was the dull numbness of a brain that was not worked at all. That was the trouble. My brain had become so alert and eager, so quickened by the wonder of the new world the books had discovered to it, that it now suffered all the misery of stagnancy and inaction.

And I, the long-time intimate of John Barleycorn, knew just what he promised me—maggots of fancy, dreams of power, forgetfulness, anything and everything save whirling washers, revolving mangles, humming centrifugal wringers, and fancy starch and interminable processions of duck trousers moving in steam under my flying iron. And that's it. John Barleycorn makes his appeal to weakness and failure, to weariness and exhaustion. He is the easy way out. And he is lying all the time. He offers false strength to the body, false elevation to the spirit, making things seem what they are not and vastly fairer than what they are.

I didn't get drunk, however, for the simple reason that it was a mile and a half to the nearest saloon. And this, in turn, was because the call to get drunk was not very loud in my ears. Had it been loud, I would have traveled ten times the distance to win to the saloon. On the other hand, had the saloon been just around the corner, I should have got drunk. As it was, I would sprawl out in the shade on my one day of rest and dallv with the Sunday papers. But I was too weary even for their froth. The comic supplement might bring a pallid smile to my face, and then I would fall asleep.[2]

Then I left the laundry and wrote all the time, and lived and dreamed again. After three months' trial I gave up writing, having decided that I was a failure, and left for the Klondike to prospect for gold.[5]

THE PROSPECTOR

After the laundry, my sister and her husband grubstaked me into the Klondike. It was the first gold rush into that region, the early fall rush of 1897. I was twenty-one years old, and in splendid physical condition. I remember, at the end of the twenty-eight-mile portage across Chilkoot from Dyea Beach to Lake Linderman, I was packing up with the Indians and outpacking many an Indian. The last pack into Linderman was three miles. I back-tripped it four times a day, and on each forward trip carried one hundred and fifty pounds. This means that over the worst trails I daily traveled twenty-four miles, twelve of which were under a burden of one hundred and fifty pounds.

Yes, I had let career go hang, and was on the adventure-path again in quest of fortune . . .[2]

THROUGH THE RAPIDS ON THE WAY TO KLONDIKE

We were in a hurry. Every one was in a hurry. This hurry is characteristic of a gold rush, and especially so of the Klondike rush of '97. October was at hand, the land covered with snow, the river threatening to freeze up at any moment, and Dawson still hundreds of miles to the north.

Never in the history of all the Northland had such wild risks been taken, and never had it been penetrated by a more reckless company of men. The Klondike veterans who had come out with glowing accounts and heavy bags of Arctic gold, and who were responsible for the wave of adventure that swept over the land, laughed at us when we said we would pack our outfits over the passes and boat them down to Dawson in the fall of the year. But we did do it, and when we arrived at Dawson, several thousand strong, in the midst of snow storms and ice jams, the resident population was astounded. Conversant as they were with the terrible hardships of such a journey at such a time of the year, they had never dreamed that it would be attempted, much less successfully carried out.

Naturally, some fell by the way, others were frozen in from one end of the river to the other, thousands, worn out and disheartened, turned back from the passes; but our party was numbered among the lucky. And this, by showing how great was the understanding and how pressing the necessity, having once started, of going through, brings me to the narrative proper—the running of the Box Canyon and the White Horse Rapids.

To show the deep respect felt for these places by the Old Timers, I quote from Miner W. Bruce, an Alaskan pioneer, whose book we constantly consulted throughout the trip.

"If a man is a skilful navigator he can run his boat through the canyon and land on the right hand side. If not, he had better make a portage. From this point he should follow the left hand side two miles to the head of White Horse Rapids. Great precaution should be exercised in reaching the point where the landing is made above the White Horse. Through the White Horse, in a low stage of water, the boat can be dropped with a line; but if the water is high, a portage must be made."

The Sixty Mile River, really a head reach of the Yukon, flows out of Marsh Lake with a varying width of from an eighth to a quarter of a mile. As it is deep and swift, an idea may be gained of the quantity of water in transit. Suddenly, it narrows to one hundred yards, rounds a bend where a landing may be made in an eddy, and dashes between towering rock walls, about eighty feet apart. This enormous volume of water, thus contracted to so small a passageway, attains a terrific speed, marked by great boilings and upheavals, and waves which stiffly stand up like walls. By some peculiar action or pressure against the rocky sides, the center of the rapids rises up in the form of a backbone, varying from six to eight feet in height. This is called the "Ridge."

Midway in this mile of canyon, the walls open out on either hand, like an immense circular court. The water dashes into this, forming a mighty maelstrom. It is said that in former years two Swedes were caught in this whirlpool. Their boat was most seaworthy, and at first they tried to get out; but failing in this, they took turns in bailing and praying, and waiting for something to turn up. Round and round they dashed for some four hours, and then, by a peculiar freak of the waters, were whirled on down the canyon, finally escaping with no damage done save to their nerves.

Tying our boat, the *Yukon Belle*, in the eddy above the Box, my three comrades and myself walked ahead to investigate. Hundreds were portaging their outfits on their backs. For us this would mean two days of severest toil, while if we cared to take the chances and run through, it would mean only two minutes. According to our custom, we put it to the vote, and the latter method was unanimously carried.

Lashing the steering oar so that it could not possibly escape, I allotted my comrades their places; for I was captain. Merritt Sloper, direct from adventures in South America and who knew a little of boating, took his position in the bow with a paddle. Thompson and Goodman, landlubbers who had never rowed before this trip, were stationed side by side at the oars. That the run may better be appreciated, it is well to explain that our twenty-seven-foot boat was carrying over five thousand pounds in addition to human freight, and hence did not possess the buoyancy so requisite for such an undertaking.

"Be sure to keep on the Ridge," cried the men on the bank as we cast off.

The water, though swift, had a slick, oily appearance until we dashed into the very jaws of the Box, where it instantly took on the aspect of chaos broken loose. Afraid that the rowers might catch a crab or make some other disastrous fumble, I called the oars in.

Then we met it on the fly. I caught a glimpse of the spectators fringing the brink of the cliffs above, and another glimpse of the rock walls dashing by like twin lightning express trains; then my whole energy was concentrated in keeping to the Ridge. This was serrated with stiff waves, which the boat, dead with weight, could not mount, being forced to jab her nose through at every lunge. For all the peril, I caught myself smiling at the ridiculous capers cut by Sloper, perched in the very bow and working his paddle like mad. Just as he would let drive for a tremendous stroke, the stern would fall in a trough, jerking the bow clear up, and he would miss the water utterly. And at the next stroke, perhaps, the nose would dive clean under, almost sweeping him away—and he only weighed one hundred pounds. But never did he lose his presence of mind or grit. Once, he turned and cried some warning at the top of his lungs, but it was drowned in the pandemonium of sound. The next instant we fell off the Ridge. The water came inboard in all directions, and the boat, caught in a transverse current, threatened to twist broadside. This would mean destruction. I threw myself against the sweep till I could hear it cracking, while Sloper snapped his paddle short off.

And all this time we were flying down the gutter, less than two yards from the wall. Several times it seemed all up with us; but finally, mounting the Ridge almost sidewise, we took a header through a tremendous comber and shot into the whirlpool of the great circular court.

Ordering out the oars for steerage-way, and keeping a close eye on the split currents, I caught one free breath before we flew into the second half of the canyon. Though we crossed the Ridge from left to right and back again, it was merely a repetition of the first half. A moment later the *Yukon Belle* rubbed softly against the bank. We had run the mile of canyon in two minutes by the watch.

Sloper and I walked back by way of the portage and ran a friend's boat through. This was quite ticklish, for the little craft was but twenty-two feet over all, and proportionately heavier loaded than ours. Then we bailed out and ran two miles of ordinary rapids to the head of the White Horse, passing several wrecks in which a number of lives had been lost.

Of the two the White Horse was more dangerous than the Box. Save for a few who had been drowned, it had never been run in previous years. It had been the custom to portage everything around, even to the boats, which were skidded along on spruce tree trunks. But we were in a hurry and rather enthusiastic over our previous good luck; so not a pound was taken from the boats.

The dangerous point in these rapids is at the tail end, called the "Mane of the Horse," from a succession of foamy, mountainous waves. Extending three-quarters of the way across, a rocky reef throws the whole river against the right bank; then comes the jump, and it is thrown back to the left, forming another whirlpool, more risky by far than that of the Box.

When we struck the "Mane," the *Yukon Belle* forgot her heavy load, taking a series of leaps almost clear of the water, alternating with as many burials in the troughs. To this day I cannot see how it happened, but I lost control. A cross current caught our stern and we began to swing broadside. Then we jumped into the whirlpool, though I did not guess it at the time. Sloper snapped a second paddle and received another ducking.

It must be remembered that we were traveling at racehorse speed, and that things happened in a tithe of the time taken to tell them. From every quarter the water came aboard, threatening to swamp us. The *Yukon Belle* headed directly for the jagged left bank, and though I was up against the steering sweep till it cracked, I could not turn her nose downstream. Onlookers from the shore tried to snapshot us, but failed to gauge our speed or get more than a wild view of angry waters and flying foam.

The bank was alarmingly close, but the boat still had the bit in her teeth. It was all happening so quickly, that I for the first time realized I was trying to buck the whirlpool. Like a flash I was bearing against the opposite side of the sweep. The boat answered, at the same time following the bent of the whirlpool, and headed upstream. But the shave was so close that Sloper leaped to the top of a rock. Then, on seeing we had missed by a couple of inches, he pluckily tumbled aboard, all in a heap, like a man boarding a comet.

Though tearing like mad through a whirlpool, we breathed freer. Completing the circle, we were thrown into the "Mane," which we shot a second time and safely landed in a friendly eddy below.[11]

> *It was late fall when Jack London reached the gold fields and he had time to stake out only a few claims when the northern winter closed in. With his friends he moved into an old deserted cabin and settled down to await the coming of spring. Situated as it was on the banks of the Stewart River where a number of trails crossed, this cabin became a meeting place for all those in the vicinity and for all those travelling through. Jack spent his winter reading, talking to the seasoned prospectors, and listening to their stories. When spring came Jack fell ill and was forced to leave for home—without a penny to show for his efforts. A number of years had yet to pass before he would realize just how valuable this Alaskan adventure would be to his literary career.* ED.

. . . At the end of the year, owing to an outbreak of scurvy, I was compelled to come out, and on a homeward journey of 1,900 miles in an open boat, made the only notes of the trip. It was in the Klondike that I found myself. There nobody talks. Everybody thinks. You get your true perspective. I got mine.[5]

FROM DAWSON TO THE SEA

It was well into June when we cast off the boat's painter, and, with the last good-byes ringing in our ears, began the 2,000-mile journey down the Yukon to St. Michael. As the six-mile current took us briskly in tow, we turned about for a final glimpse of Dawson—dreary, desolate Dawson, built in a swamp, flooded to the second story, populated by dogs, mosquitoes and gold-seekers. Our friends attempted a half-hearted cheer, and filled the air with messages for those at home.

Our boat was home-made, weak-kneed and leaky, but in thorough harmony with the wilderness we were traversing. A smooth and polished creation of the boat-builder's art might have been more beautiful, but we were quite agreed that it would have been less comfortable and a positive discord to our rough-hewn environment. In the bow was the woodshed, while amidships, built of pine boughs and blankets, was the bed chamber. Then came the rower's bench, and, jammed between this and the steersman, was our snug little kitchen. It was a veritable home, and we had little need of going ashore, save out of curiosity or to lay in a fresh supply of firewood.

The three of us had sworn to make of this a pleasure trip, in which all labor was to be performed by gravitation, and all profit reaped by ourselves. And what a profit it was to us who had been accustomed to pack great loads on our backs or drag all day at the sleds for a paltry 25 or 30 miles. We now hunted, played cards, smoked, ate and slept, sure of our six miles an hour, of our 144 a day.

Scarcely pausing at the deserted mining camp of Forty-Mile or at Fort Cudahy, we arrived at Eagle City, the first town on the American side of the boundary.

What with the strange actions and heavy exactions of the Northwest Territory officials, we gave vent to a most excessive enthusiasm on once more treading the soil of Uncle Sam. The 50 inhabitants, while waiting for some steamer to bring them food, were engaged in bucking a faro layout. But they were boomers, halting the game in a vain attempt to sell us corner lots.

Three hundred miles below Dawson we encountered Circle City, the largest camp on the Yukon previous to the Klondike discoveries, and so named because of its proximity to the Arctic Circle. It lay on the edge of the great Yukon Flats, a dismal domain, about which little is known. The "Flats" are a vast area of low country, extending for hundreds of miles in every direction, into which the Yukon plunges and is practically lost. The river, hitherto flowing between mountains, rugged and sternly outlined, with few islands on its breast, now begins its heart-breaking dividing and subdividing. One finds himself in a gigantic puzzle, consisting of thousands of miles of territory, and cut up into countless myriads of islands and channels. Men have been known to lose their way and wander for weeks in this perplexing maze. Great "blind" sloughs, on every hand, lie in wait for the unwary. And most exasperating it is to labor several score of miles into one of these, to find that it is "blind" (has no outlet) and that you must retrace your steps. The islands are well wooded, but, having also been well flooded, are miserable to land upon. The region is one of the greatest nesting grounds in the world, abounding with all kinds of ducks, brant, geese and swans. The adventurer who faces this soggy wilderness of water, mud, dank vegetation and mosquitoes, does not care to linger by the way, but, with an intense longing and exceeding haste, keeps to the largest channels and swiftest currents.

Eighty-five miles within the Flats, where the Yukon crosses the Arctic Circle and makes its magnificent bend to the west and south, and the Porcupine threads the lacustrine wilderness and enters from the east, we landed at the old Hudson Bay Company post of Fort Yukon. The North American Trading and Transportation and the Alaska Commercial companies' caches are located here, also an Indian village. During the winter, while Dawson was on the ragged edge of famine, these caches were stocked to overflowing; yet it was impossible to sled the provisions such a distance up the river, while the steamers had found it equally impossible to get up before navigation closed.

The steamer Bella, a year late, was industriously loading up. It was a peculiar scene of animation and excitement. Four o'clock in the morning, under the Arctic Circle, yet the sun was high in the heavens and it was already uncomfortably warm. It seemed more like some festival day at 3 o'clock in the afternoon. All was gaiety, noise and laughter. The bucks were skylarking or flirting with the maidens; the older squaws were gossiping in bunches, while the young ones shrank and giggled in the corners. The children played or squabbled, and the babies rolled in the muck with the tawny wolf-dogs. Fantastic forms, dimly outlined, flitted to and fro, surged together, eddied, parted, in the smoke-laden atmosphere. Only by nosing and poking about could one see anything; for the reeking smoke rose from untold smudges, bringing grief to the mosquito, tears to the soft eyes of the white men and giving to the whole affair a mysterious air of unreality.

Through all this portion of the trip it was hard to realize our far-northerly latitude. It was more like an enchanted land, teeming with paradoxes. For instance, gasping for breath in the noonday heat and sweltering in a tropic temperature under Arctic skies or panting on top of the blankets at midnight, the red-disked sun poised like a ball of blood above the northern horizon. And the strange beauty and charm of the noonday nights—drifting, always drifting with the stream. Now slipping down a narrow channel where the wooded shores seem to meet overhead; now flashing into the open, where a thousand streams converge and form a mighty river; and again the diverging courses, the tiny channel, the overhanging forest, the smell of the land and the damp warmth of the vegetation. And above all, the hum of life, bursting into sudden gushes of song, slowly swelling to a great, dull roar of satisfaction or dying away into sweetly cadenced silence. Not a sound as we round the tail of a bar, disturbing a solitary crane from his ghostly reveries. A partridge drums in the forest, a moose lunges noisily as it takes to the water, and again silence. Then an owl hoots from some gloomy recess or a raven croaks gutturally overhead. Suddenly, the wild cry of a loon sweeps across a glassy stretch of river, awakening myriad answers. The robins open their full, rich throats and the woods burst into music. The tree squirrels play half a dozen instruments at once, while the blackbirds sing shrill choruses to the sharp-marked time of the woodpecker. The pure treble of the songbirds is accompanied by the steady boom boom of the partridge, till all is lost in the general pandemonium. Then the wild fowl of the swamp join the quick crescendo, and the finale, swelled to bursting, slowly dies away. A kildee calls timidly to its mate, and silence falls.

After 300 miles of the Flats, we made Minook, the principal mining camp on the Lower River. It has since received the less euphemistic name of Rampart City. While the news of Dawson was by no means fresh, the men of the Lower River had had none all winter; so we landed amid a bombardment of queries. They were mostly perturbed over the war, the Thanksgiving football game and the execution of Durant. True to Northland tradition, we expanded items into chapters, yet failed utterly in satisfying their unholy lust for news.

Running the rapids below Minook, where the Yukon at some early period cut its way through the Rampart Mountains, we made Tanana station. Here also was the Indian town of Nuklukyeto, while several miles below stood the old mission of St. James. Great was the merrymaking as we arrived in the wee, sma' hours. The spring run of salmon was expected at any moment, and the mission, Tanana and Tozikakats were all assembled, to say nothing of the general sprinkling contributed by the several hundred miles of Yukon on either side the station. We landed our heavy craft amid the litter of flimsy bark canoes which lined the bank, and found ourselves in the great fishing camp. Picking our steps among the tents and wading through the sprawling babies and fighting dogs, we made our way to a large log structure where a dance was in progress. After much pushing and shoving, we forced an entrance through the swarming children. The long, low room was literally packed with dancers. There was no light, no ventilation, save through the crowded doorway, and, in the semi-darkness, strapping bucks and wild-eyed squaws sweated, howled and reveled in a dance which defies description. With the peculiar elation of the traveler who scales the virgin peak, we prepared to enjoy the novelty of the situation; but, imagine our disappointment on discovering that even here, 1,000 miles beyond the uttermost bounds of civilization, the adventurous white man already had penetrated. In the crowded room, dizzy with heat and the smell of bodies, we at last discerned the fair bronzed skin, the blue eyes, the blond mustache of the ubiquitous Anglo-Saxon. A glance demonstrated how thoroughly at home he was.

One hundred miles below Nuklukyeto, our midnight watch was beguiled by a wild chant, which rose and fell uncannily as it floated across the water. An hour later we rounded a bend and landed at a fishing village, so engrossed in its religious rites that our arrival was unnoted. Climbing the bank, we came full upon the weird scene. It brought us back to the orgies of the cavemen and more closely in touch with our common ancestor, probably arboreal, which Mr. Darwin has so fittingly described. Several score of bucks were giving tongue to unwritten music, evidently born when the world was very young, and still apulse with the spirit of primeval man. Urged on by the chief medicine man, the women had abandoned themselves to the religious ecstacy, their raven hair unbound and falling to their hips, while their bodies were swaying and undulating to the swing of the song.

Nor was the ubiquitous Anglo-Saxon absent; for there, between the flaps of a tent, with a nursing child at the breast, we found him staring at us through the eyes of a half-caste woman. Slender-formed, with her Caucasian features and delicate oval face, she seemed as a pearl cast among swine. Lafcadio Hearn had dwelt with great pathos upon the Japanese half-caste; but how much harder the lot of the Yukon Indian half-breed. It is a life of severest toil, coupled with extreme privation and misery. What white woman would care or dare to strap her suckling babe to her back, and, with the temperature ranging from 50 to 70 degrees below zero, travel 40 miles a day with the dogs? Such is but an instance of their continual life, whether at the hunting or the fishing, or when famine pinches or sickness is in the camps. Yet their lot is a common one, from the Coast Indians of the Panhandle to the Esquimaux of the Arctic Ocean, from the Rocky Mountains to the most westerly Aleutian isle.

In the course of trading with the natives, one soon learns much of the sickness and misery with which their lives are girt. From one end of the land to the other, the piteous cry for medicine goes up. In the most cursory intercourse, one stumbles upon pathetic little keynotes that serve as inklings to the solemn chords of heartache with which their lives vibrate. At the mouth of the Koyokuk, I wandered into a summer camp in the hope of picking up some specimens of beadwork. At one of the neatest tents of the encampment, I opened negotiations with a young half-breed woman for some exceptionally fine work, and, when I went away, I was filled with wonder at the bargain she had got. Nor was I at loss, for, before me, on a bearskin mat, had played a most beautiful child—flaxen-haired, blue-eyed and rosy-complexioned, a typical Saxon lass. As often as I stiffened the lines of the barter in accordance with Indian trading, I softened as I rescued my sheathknife or tobacco pouch from the baby fingers, or gazed into the blue eyes of the white father. And, when I hardened my heart for the articles of the final agreement, the mother said, "O you big white man, why so hard? I do much work, Oh, so much work. I get fish and moose and flour for two, and no man to help me."

I pointed to the child with a glance of interrogation, and she answered, "He go way—one—two—three years now."

And the bargain she made caused great envy among her dark sisters huddled in the doorway.

All through the interior, save in the sheltered nooks and on the northern slopes of the loftier peaks, the snow had quite disappeared by the middle of June. But from Tozikakat it began to grow more plentiful, till at Koyokuk, even the southern exposure was no longer bare—a sign that we were approaching the coast, or rather, the coast climate, for we were still 700 miles above the mouth of the river. It is naturally thus with a marine climate, where, because of the great body of water, the heat is neither absorbed nor radiated as rapidly as in the interior. Hence, the winters are much colder and the summers equally warmer at Dawson than at St. Michael. Along the shores of Bering Sea, even a month after the sun has passed its northern solstice, great bodies of snow are to be found lying at the water's edge.

At Nulato, 650 miles above the mouth, we found two small steamers fitting out and extensive preparations being made for the exploration of the Koyokuk, which is looked upon as the coming Alaskan Klondike. We were just in time for service at the Roman Catholic mission, and, strange it was, gazing upon the finely chiseled features of the be-moccasined, black-stoled priest, and listening to the strange unison of the shrill voices of the Indian women and the deep basses of the fathers. Father Monroe, a cultured, and as rumor puts it, a very wealthy Frenchman, has devoted his life to the cause of the missions, and for five long years has labored zealously at Nulato. The Indians are always more energetic, thrifty, and of better appearance at the missions than elsewhere, though Christianity seems never to get a really deep hold on them. Several of my souvenirs will testify to the readiness with which they will trade a crucifix for an old pack of cards.

It has been a very early spring, and the breaking of the Yukon was accompanied by the greatest high-water known for years. From Dawson to Kutlik, every station and long-established village had been severely flooded, many being washed away. If signs are to be trusted, the ice-run for the last 500 miles of river must have been terrific. Many portions of the mainland and whole islands had been swept clear of the timber which always clusters thickly in the bottoms. The large trees are uprooted or literally gnawed in two by the grinding ice, while the smaller ones bend before it and are rubbed clean of bark, reminding one of well-picked bones on some endless battlefield.

Game and fish were quite abundant the whole length of river, and every camp had a fresh bearskin or so stretched on the drying frames. While we did much of our own hunting, we did not waste time in gathering eggs or fishing, preferring to trade for such staples. However, we were usually disappointed in the eggs, not relishing the embryonic diet of ducks and geese which the natives so delight in. But the fish were excellent, especially the salmon. Oh, you, who pay big for the silver salmon of the fish market and then say it is good, come north and buy a great king salmon, weighing from 40 to 50 pounds of clean meat, for a tin cup or so of flour. They are to be found in the pink of condition in the icy waters of the Yukon, cold, firm-fleshed and, above all, delicious. But it takes one quite a time to learn to trade with the Indians. He must have the foresight of Joseph and the patience of Job, else will he be mulcted as the Gentile should be. The practiced hand endeavors to exhibit a well-disguised desire for the article he does not wish, and but ordinary interest in that which he is after. The native will then elevate the price of the former and correspondingly depress that of the latter. When he has thus brought the thing you wish absurdly low, snap it quick and pay on the spot. He will be chagrined, but a bargain's a bargain.

The hunting we could not forego, though the shotgun was old and decrepit, and one trigger persisted in discharging both barrels. Very pleasant it was during midnight lookouts, listening to the comrades snoring beneath the mosquito tent, drifting along the low-flooded banks, watching the sun above the northern horizon and dropping the startled wild fowl as they rose from the river.

By the time we arrived at Anvik, 600 miles from the mouth, we began to realize the mighty river we were voyaging on. At Fort Yukon, 1,300 miles from the mouth, it is 8 miles wide; at the Koyokuk it narrows to 2 or 3 miles; and from Koserefski it maintains a width of from 8 to 10 miles, till it is lost in the Great Delta, where its southern and northern mouths are over 80 miles apart. But at Anvik it is 40 miles wide, with a spring rise of from 30 to 40 feet. This great width is due to a division which makes possible one of the largest inland islands of the world—an island that is not even named.

A totally different native population is encountered from Anvik to the sea. The clean-limbed stalwart Indians disappear, being replaced by the Malemutes, who are a sort of mongrel cross of Thlinket and Esquimau. Poverty-stricken, with little energy and no ambition, they have not furnished much inducement to the white traders; hence, they continue to exist on a straight fish and meat diet, washed down with incalculable quantities of vile-smelling seal oil. Their houses are merely holes in the ground, shored with driftwood timbers. In the center of this they build an open fire, the smoke of which escapes through a venthole in the roof. In the winter time, the men, women and children crowd into these burrows like sardines. The sanitary, social and moral conditions may be conjectured.

They have quite a reverence for their dead, however; their burial places being neat, clean and pleasing to the eye. Rough palings surround the graves, which are usually covered with a rain shed. Fantastic designs are often painted upon them by the means of soot and seal oil. Occasionally, a curiously carved totem pole is raised; but, by the crosses the great majority rest in the consecrated ground of the Catholic Church. It is hard to say what becomes of the Protestant converts, but the more impressive ritual of the Catholic service, opposed to the bare, Puritanical mode of Protestant worship, and so pregnant with mysticism to the barbaric mind, may perhaps explain it.

From the Mission of the Holy Cross to the Russian Mission of Icogmute, we found the mountains dwindling sadly, and at Andrefsky we bade farewell to the last barren hills and plunged into the dismal solitude of the Great Delta of the Yukon. It was a repetition of the Flats, but fraught with more serious consequences. A mistake in this uncharted wilderness and one would blunder into the Southern Channel, wandering no man knows whither, till he emerged, without guide or landmark, on the bleak coast of Bering Sea. Disdaining Malemute guides, we were two days in traveling these 120 miles. We gave vent to much foolish enthusiasm when we felt the first pulse of the tide; and when in Kutlik we slept in sight of open sea, deemed ourselves to be nearly home.

The 80-mile run up the coast was full of excitement. As we skirted dangerous Point Romanoff, we picked up a Jesuit priest who was having a hard time in the surf. And for all the cloth he was a jolly fellow, pulling an oar, smoking a pipe or telling a tale with the next one. He was an illustration of the many strange types to be found in the Northland. An Italian by blood, a Frenchman by birth, a Spaniard by education and an American by residence, he was a marvelous scholar and his whole life was one continuous romance; but sworn to the oaths of his order, he had sacrificed twelve prime years of his life in bleak Alaska, and in all things, even to reducing the Innuit language to a grammar, was happy.

Our last taste of Bering Sea was a fitting close to the trip. Midnight found us wallowing in the sea, a rocky coast to leeward and a dirty sky to windward, with splutters of rain and wind squalls which soon developed into a gale. Removing the sprit and bagging the after-leech, we shortened to storm canvas and ran before it, reaching the harbor of St. Michael just 21 days from the time we cast off the lines at Dawson.[12]

Back in California . . . recovering from scurvy, I found that my father was dead and that I was the head and the sole bread-winner of a household. When I state that I had passed coal on a steamship from Bering Sea to British Columbia, and traveled in the steerage from there to San Francisco, it will be understood that I brought nothing back from the Klondike but my scurvy.

Times were hard. Work of any sort was difficult to get. And work of any sort was what I had to take, for I was still an unskilled laborer. I had no thought of career. That was over and done with. I had to find food for two mouths besides my own and keep a roof over our heads—yes, and buy a winter suit, my one suit being decidedly summery. I had to get some sort of work immediately. After that, when I had caught my breath, I might think about my future.

Unskilled labor is the first to feel the slackness of hard times, and I had no trades save those of sailor and laundryman. With my new responsibilities I didn't dare go to sea, and I failed to find a job at laundrying. I failed to find a job at anything. I had my name down in five employment bureaus. I advertised in three newspapers. I sought out the few friends I knew who might be able to get me work; but they were either uninterested or unable to find anything for me.

The situation was desperate. I pawned my watch, my bicycle, and a mackintosh of which my father had been very proud and which he had left to me. It was and is my sole legacy in this world. It had cost fifteen dollars, and the pawnbroker let me have two dollars on it. And—oh, yes—a water-front comrade of earlier years drifted along one day with a dress suit wrapped in newspapers. He could give no adequate explanation of how he had come to possess it, nor did I press for an explanation. I wanted the suit myself. No; not to wear. I traded him a lot of rubbish which, being unpawnable, was useless to me. He peddled the rubbish for several dollars, while I pledged the dress suit with my pawnbroker for five dollars. And for all I know, the pawnbroker still has the suit. I had never intended to redeem it.

But I couldn't get any work. Yet I was a bargain in the labor market. I was twenty-two years old, weighed one hundred and sixty-five pounds stripped, every pound of which was excellent for toil; and the last traces of my scurvy were vanishing before a treatment of potatoes chewed raw. I tackled every opening for employment. I tried to become a studio model, but there were too many fine-bodied young fellows out of jobs. I answered advertisements of elderly invalids in need of companions. And I almost became a sewing machine agent, on commission, without salary. But poor people don't buy sewing machines in hard times, so I was forced to forego that employment.

Of course, it must be remembered that along with such frivolous occupations, I was trying to get work as wop, lumper, and roustabout. But winter was coming on, and the surplus labor army was pouring into the cities. Also, I, who had romped along carelessly through the countries of the world and the kingdom of the mind, was not a member of any union.

I sought odd jobs. I worked days, and half-days, at anything I could get. I mowed lawns, trimmed hedges, took up carpets, beat them, and laid them again. Further, I took the civil service examinations for mail carrier and passed first. But alas, there was no vacancy, and I must wait. And while I waited, and in between the odd jobs I managed to procure, I started to earn ten dollars by writing a newspaper account of the voyage I had made, in an open boat down the Yukon . . . I didn't know the first thing about the newspaper game, but I was confident I'd get ten dollars for my article.

But I didn't . . .

Sept. 17, 1898
962 E. 16th St.
Oakland, Calif.

Editor of the "Bulletin"

Dear Sir:

I have just returned from a year's residence in the Klondike entering the country by the way of Dyea and Chilcoot Pass. I left by the way of St. Michael, thus making altogether a journey of 2,500 miles on the Yukon in a small boat. I have sailed and traveled quite extensively in other parts of the world and have learned to size upon that which is interesting, to grasp the true romance of things, and to understand the people I may be thrown amongst.

I have just completed an article of 4,000 words, describing the trip from Dawson to St. Michael in a row boat. Kindly let me know if there would be any demand in your columns for it–of course thoroughly understanding that the acceptance of the manuscript is to depend upon its literary and intrinsic value.

Yours very respectfully,
Jack London

[In pencil]
Interest in Alaska has subsided in an amazing degree. Then again so much has been written that I do not think it would pay us to buy your story.
Editor

And here is the funny thing. Some are born to fortune, and some have fortune thrust upon them. But in my case I was clubbed into fortune, and bitter necessity wielded the club. I had long since abandoned all thought of writing as a career. My honest intention in writing that article was to earn ten dollars. And that was the limit of my intention. It would help to tide me along until I got steady employment. Had a vacancy occurred in the post office at that time, I should have jumped at it.

But the vacancy did not occur, nor did a steady job; and I employed the time between odd jobs with writing a twenty-one-thousand-word serial for the "Youth's Companion." I turned it out and typed it in seven days. I fancy that was what was the matter with it, for it came back.

It took some time for it to go and come, and in the meantime I tried my hand at short stories . . .

And just then came the call from the post office to go to work. It placed me in a most trying predicament. The sixty-five dollars I could earn regularly every month was a terrible temptation. I couldn't decide what to do. And I'll never be able to forgive the postmaster of Oakland. I answered the call, and I talked to him like a man. I frankly told him the situation. It looked as if I might win out at writing. The chance was good, but not certain. Now, if he would pass me by and select the next man on the eligible list, and give me a call at the next vacancy–

But he shut me off with: "Then you don't want the position?"

"But I do," I protested. "Don't you see, if you will pass me over this time–"

"If you want it you will take it," he said coldly.

Happily for me, the cursed brutality of the man made me angry.

"Very well," I said. "I won't take it."

My difficulty was that I had no one to advise me. I didn't know a soul who had written or who had ever tried to write. I didn't even know one reporter. Also, to succeed at the writing game, I found I had to unlearn about everything the teachers and professors of literature of the high school and university had taught me. I was very indignant about this at the time; though now I can understand it. They did not know the trick of successful writing in the years of 1895 and 1896. They knew all about "Snow Bound" and "Sartor Resartus"; but the American editors of 1899 did not want such truck. They wanted the 1899 truck, and offered to pay so well for it that the teachers and professors of literature would have quit their jobs could they have supplied it.

I struggled along, stood off the butcher and the grocer, pawned my watch and bicycle and my father's mackintosh, and I worked. I really did work, and went on short commons of sleep.

Having burned my one ship, I plunged into writing. I am afraid I always was an extremist. Early and late I was at it–writing, typing, studying grammar, studying writing and all the forms of writing, and studying the writers who succeeded in order to find out how they succeeded. I managed on five hours' sleep in the twenty-four, and came pretty close to working the nineteen waking hours left to me. My light burned till two and three in the morning . . .

The trouble with the beginner at the writing game is the long, dry spells, when there is never an editor's check and everything pawnable is pawned. I wore my summer suit pretty well through that winter, and the following summer experienced the longest, dryest spell of all, in the period when salaried men are gone on vacation and manuscripts lie in editorial offices until vacation is over.[2]

I had no one to give me tips, no one's experience to profit by. So I sat down and wrote in order to get an experience of my own. I wrote everything–short stories, articles, anecdotes, jokes, essays, sonnets, ballads, vilanelles, triolets, songs, light plays in iambic tetrameter, and heavy tragedies in blank verse. These various creations I stuck into envelopes, enclosed return postage, and dropped into the mail. Oh, I was prolific. Day by day my manuscripts mounted up, till the problem of finding stamps for them became as great as that of making life livable for my widow landlady.

All my manuscripts came back. They continued to come back. The process seemed like the working of a soulless machine. I dropped the manuscript into the mail box. After the lapse of a certain approximate length of time, the manuscript was brought back to me by the postman. Accompanying it was a stereotyped rejection slip. A part of the machine, some cunning arrangement of cogs and cranks at the other end, (it could not have been a living, breathing man with blood in his veins), had transferred the manuscript to another envelope, taken the stamps from the inside and pasted them outside, and added the rejection slip.

This went on for some months. I was still in the dark. I had not yet gained the smallest particle of experience. Concerning which was the more marketable, poetry or prose, jokes or sonnets, short stories or essays, I knew no more than when I began. I had vague ideas, however, dim and hazy ideas to the effect that a minimum rate of ten dollars a thousand words was paid; that if I only published two or three things the editors would clamor for my wares; that a manuscript held in some editor's hands for the small matter of four or five months did not necessarily mean a manuscript that was sold.

Concerning this minimum rate of ten dollars a thousand words, a thing in which I fondly believed, I must confess that I had gleaned it from some Sunday supplement. Likewise I must confess the beautiful and touching modesty with which I aspired. Let other men, thought I, receive the maximum rate, whatever marvelous sum it may be. As for myself, I shall always be content to receive the minimum rate. And, once I get started, I shall do no more than three thousand words a day, five days only in the week. This will give me plenty of recreation, while I shall be earning six hundred dollars a month without overstocking the market.

As I say, the machine worked on for several months, and then, one morning, the postman brought me a letter, mark you, a letter, not a long thick one but a short thin one, and from a magazine. My stamp problem and my landlady problem were pressing me cruelly, and this short, thin letter from a magazine would of a certainty solve both problems in short order.

I could not open the letter right away. It seemed a sacred thing. It contained the written words of an editor. The magazine he represented I imagined ranked in the first class. I knew it held a four-thousand-word story of mine. What will it be? I asked. The minimum rate, I answered, modest as ever; forty dollars of course. Having thus guarded myself against any possible kind of disappointment, I opened the letter and read what I thought would be blazed in letters of fire on my memory for all time. Alas! the years are few, yet I have forgotten. But the gist of the letter was coldly to the effect that my story was available, that they would print it in the next number, and that they would pay me for it the sum of five dollars.

Five dollars! A dollar and a quarter a thousand! That I did not die right there and then convinces me that I am possessed of a singular ruggedness of soul which will permit me to survive and ultimately qualify for the oldest inhabitant.

Five dollars! When? The editor did not state. I didn't have even a stamp with which to convey my acceptation or rejection of his offer. Just then the landlady's little girl knocked at the back door. Both problems were clamoring more compellingly than ever for solution. It was plain there was no such thing as a minimum rate. Nothing remained but to get out and shovel coal. I had done it before and earned more money at it. I resolved to do it again; and I certainly should have, had it not been for the "Black Cat."

Yes, the "Black Cat." The postman brought me an offer from it of forty dollars for a four-thousand-word story, which same was more lengthy than strengthy, if I would grant permission to cut it down half. This was equivalent to a twenty-dollar rate. Grant permission? I told them they could cut it down two-halves if they'd only send the money along, which they did, by return mail. . . . I forgot my coal-shoveling resolution and continued to whang away at the typewriter . . .[7]

. . . Critics have complained about the swift education one of my characters, Martin Eden, achieved. In three years, from a sailor with a common school education, I made a successful writer of him. The critics say this is impossible. Yet I was Martin Eden. At the end of three working years, two of which were spent in high school and the university and one spent at writing, and all three in studying immensely and intensely, I was publishing stories in magazines such as the *Atlantic Monthly*, was correcting proofs of my first book (issued by Houghton, Mifflin Co.), was selling sociological articles to *Cosmopolitan* and *McClure's*, had declined an associate editorship proffered me by telegraph from New York City, and was getting ready to marry.[2]

This, then, was the childhood and youth of an extraordinary man—a childhood of poverty and struggle, yet one brimming with adventure and achievement. The time was 1899, he was twenty-five years old, and because of his tremendous intellectual accomplishment life held great promise. From this vantage point Jack London leaped up the stairway to success. His stories were sought by all the leading magazines. His novels were serialized before publication and sold hundreds of thousands of copies after publication. His name became a household word. Among other things he became a war correspondent, a world traveller, and a rabid socialist. His restless, turbulent spirit kept driving him forward, never giving his fertile, creative mind rest. Sixteen short years later his tiring body broke down, unable to stand the furious, strenuous pace. Jack London was buried on his famous ranch in the Valley of the Moon. He had left to posterity a rich literary heritage. ED.

Sources

1. Biographical letter to the editor of Houghton, Mifflin Co., January 31, 1900.
2. *John Barleycorn*, copyright 1913 by The Century Co.; copyright 1913 by The Curtis Publishing Company.
3. Letter to Mabel Applegarth, November 30, 1898.
4. *The Book of Jack London*, by Charmian London, copyright 1921 by The Century Co.
5. "Jack London by Himself," from *Mainly About People*, The Macmillan Company, New York.
6. "How I Became a Socialist," from *Revolution and Other Essays*, copyright 1910 by The Macmillan Company.
7. "On Getting into Print," *The Editor*, Vol. XVII, No. 3, March 1903, The Editor Publishing Company, Franklin, Ohio.
8. *The Cruise of the Snark*, copyright 1911 by The Macmillan Company.
9. That Dead Men Rise Up Never," from *The Human Drift*, copyright 1917 by The Macmillan Company.
10. "Two Thousand Stiffs," from *The Road*, copyright 1907 by The Macmillan Company.
11. "Through the Rapids on the Way to Klondike," *Home* Magazine, June 1899.
12. "From Dawson to the Sea," Buffalo *Express*, Buffalo, New York, June 4, 1899.

The Adventurer

STORY OF A TYPHOON OFF THE COAST OF JAPAN

(By John London, age 17. Address, 1321 Twenty-second Avenue, Oakland.)

It was four bells in the morning watch. We had just finished breakfast when the order came forward for the watch on deck to stand by to heave her to and all hands stand by the boats.

"Port! hard a port!" cried our sailing-master. "Clew up the topsails! Let the flying jib run down! Back the jib over to windward and run down the foresail!" And so was our schooner *Sophie Sutherland* hove to off the Japan coast, near Cape Jerimo, on April 10, 1893.

Then came moments of bustle and confusion. There were eighteen men to man the six boats. Some were hooking on the falls, others casting off the lashings; boat-steerers appeared with the boat compasses and water breakers and boat-pullers with the lunch boxes. Hunters were staggering under two or three shotguns, a rifle and heavy ammunition box, all of which were soon stowed away with their oilskins and mittens in the boats.

The sailing-master gave his last orders and away we went pulling the three pairs of oars to gain our positions. We were in the weather boat, and so had a longer pull than the others. The first, second and third lee boats soon had all sails set and were running off to the southward and westward with the wind abeam, while the schooner was running off to leeward of them, so that in case of accident the boats would have fair wind home.

It was a glorious morning, but our boat-steerer shook his head ominously as he glanced at the rising sun and prophetically muttered, "Red sun in the morning, sailor 'take warning.'" The sun had an angry look, and a few light, fleecy "nigger-heads" in that quarter seemed abashed and frightened and soon disappeared. Away off to the northwest Cape Jerimo reared its black, forbidding head like some huge monster rising from the deep. The winter's snow, not yet entirely dissipated by the sun, covered it in patches of glistening white, over which the light wind swept on its way out to sea. Huge gunies rose slowly, fluttering their wings in the light breeze and striking their webbed feet on the surface of the water for over half a mile before they could leave it. Hardly had the patter, patter died away when a flock of sea quail rose, and with whistling wings flew away to windward, where members of a large band of whales were disporting themselves, their blowings sounding like the exhaust of steam engines. The harsh, discordant cries of a sea-parrot grated unpleasantly on the ear, and set half a dozen on the alert in a small band of seals that were ahead of us. Away they went, breaching and jumping entirely out of water. A seagull with slow, deliberate flight and long majestic curves, circled round us, and as a reminder of home a little English sparrow perched impudently on the fo'castle head, and cocking his head on one side chirped merrily. The boats were soon among the seals, and the bang! bang! of the guns could be heard from down to leeward.

The wind was slowly rising, and by 3 o'clock as, with a dozen seals in our boat, we were deliberating whether to go on or turn back, the recall flag was run up at the schooner's mizzen—a sure sign that with the rising wind the barometer was falling and that our sailing-master was getting anxious for the welfare of the boats.

Away we went before the wind with a single reef in our sail. With clenched teeth sat the boat-steerer, grasping the steering oar firmly with both hands, his restless eyes on the alert—a glance at the schooner ahead, as we rose on a sea, another at the mainsheet, and then one astern where the dark ripple of the wind on the water told him of a coming puff or a large white cap that threatened to overwhelm us. The waves were holding high carnival, performing the strangest antics, as with wild glee they danced along in fierce pursuit—now up, now down, here, there and everywhere, until some great sea of liquid green with its milk-white crest of foam rose from the ocean's throbbing bosom and drove the others from view. But only for a moment, for again under new forms they reappeared. In the sun's path they wandered, where every ripple great or small, every little spit or spray looked like molten silver; where the water lost its dark green color and became a dazzling silvery flood, only to vanish and become a wild waste of sullen turbulence, each dark foreboding sea rising and breaking, then rolling on again. The dash, the sparkle, the silvery light soon vanished with the sun, which became obscured by black clouds that were rolling swiftly in from the west-northwest; apt heralds of the coming storm.

We soon reached the schooner and found ourselves the last aboard. In a few minutes the seals were skinned, boats and decks washed, and we were down below by the roaring fo'castle fire, with a wash, change of clothes and a hot, substantial supper before us. Sail had been put on the schooner, as we had a run of seventy-five miles to make to the south'ard before morning, so as to get in the midst of the seals, out of which we had strayed during the last two days' hunting.

We had the first watch, from 8 to midnight. The wind was soon blowing half a gale, and our sailing-master expected little sleep that night as he paced up and down the poop. The topsails were soon clewed up and made fast, then the flying jib run down and furled. Quite a sea was rolling by this time, occasionally breaking over the decks, flooding them and threatening to smash the boats. At six bells we were ordered to turn them over and put on storm-lashings. This occupied us till eight bells, when we were relieved by the midwatch. I was the last to go below, doing so just as the watch on deck was furling the spanker.

Below all were asleep except our green hand, the bricklayer, who was dying of consumption. The wildly dancing movements of the sea lamp cast a pale flickering light through the fo'castle and turned to golden honey the drops of water on the yellow oilskins. In all the corners dark shadows seemed to come and go, while up in the eyes of her, beyond the pall bitts descending from deck to deck, where they seemed to lurk like some dragon at the cavern's mouth, it was dark as Erebus. Now and again the light seemed to penetrate for a moment as the schooner rolled heavier than usual, only to recede, leaving it darker and blacker than before. The roar of the wind whistling through the rigging came to the ear muffled like the distant rumble of a train crossing a trestle or the surf on the beach, while the loud crash of the seas on her weather bow seemed almost to rend the beams and planking asunder as it resounded through the fo'castle. The creaking and groaning of the timbers, stanchions and bulkheads, as the strain the vessel was undergoing was felt, served to drown the groans of the dying man as he tossed uneasily in his bunk. The working of the foremast against the deck beams caused a shower of flaky powder to fall and sent another sound mingling with the tumultuous storm. Small cascades of water streamed from the pall bitts from the fo'castle head above, and, joining issue with the streams from the wet oilskins, ran along the floor and disappeared aft into the main hold.

At two bells in the middle watch—that is, in land parlance 1 o'clock in the morning—the order was roared out on the fo'castle: "All hands on deck and shorten sail!"

Then the sleepy sailors tumbled out of their bunks into their clothes, oilskins and sea boots and up on deck. 'Tis when that order comes on cold, blustering nights that "Jack" grimly mutters: "'Who would not sell a farm and go to sea?'"

It was on deck that the force of the wind could be fully appreciated, especially after leaving the stifling fo'castle. It seemed to stand up against you like a wall, making it almost impossible to move on the heaving decks or to breathe as the fierce gusts came dashing by. The schooner was hove to under jib, foresail and mainsail. We proceeded to lower the foresail and make it fast. The night was dark, greatly impeding our labor. Still, though not a star or the moon could pierce the black masses of storm clouds that obscured the sky as they swept along before the gale, nature aided us in a measure. A soft light emanated from the movement of the ocean. Each mighty sea, all phosphorescent and glowing with the tiny lights of myriads of animalculae, threatened to overwhelm us with a deluge of fire. Higher and higher, thinner and thinner the crest grew as it began to curve and overtop preparatory to breaking until with a roar it fell over the bulwarks, a mass of soft, glowing light and of tons of water which sent the sailors sprawling in all directions and left in each nook and cranny little specks of light that glowed and trembled till the next sea washed them away depositing new ones in their places. Sometimes several seas following each other with great rapidity and thundering down on our decks filled them full to the bulwarks, but soon they were discharged through the lee scuppers.

To reef the mainsail we were forced to run off before the gale under the single reefed jib. By the time we had finished the wind had forced up such a tremendous sea that it was impossible to heave her to. Away we dashed on the wings of the storm through the muck and flying spray. A wild sheer to starboard, then another to port, as the enormous seas struck the schooner astern and nearly broached her to.

As day broke we took in the jib, leaving not a sail unfurled. Since we had begun scudding she had ceased to take the seas over the bow, but amidships they broke fast and furious. It was a dry storm in the matter of rain, but the force of the wind filled the air with fine spray, which flew as high as the crosstrees and cut the face like a knife, making it impossible to see over a hundred yards ahead. The sea was a dark lead color, as with long, slow majestic roll it was heaped by the wind into liquid mountains of foam. The wild antics of the schooner were sickening as she forged along. She would almost stop as though climbing a mountain, then rapidly rolling to right and left as she gained the summit of a huge sea, she steadied herself and paused for a moment as though affrighted at the yawning precipice before her. Like an avalanche she shot forward and down as the sea astern struck her with the force of a thousand battering rams, burying her bow to the catheads in the milky foam at the bottom that came on deck in all directions—forward, astern, to right and to left, through the hawse pipes and over the rail.

The wind began to drop and by 10 o'clock we were talking of heaving her to. We passed a ship, two schooners and a four-masted barkentine under the smallest of canvas, and at 11 o'clock, running up the spanker and the jib, we hove her to and in another hour we were beating back against the after sea under full sail to regain the sealing grounds away to the westward.

Below a couple of men were sewing "the bricklayer's" body in canvas, preparatory to the sea burial. And so with the storm passed away "the bricklayer's" soul.

First Prize—San Francisco *Call*
"Best descriptive article" contest,
November 12, 1893

THE RUN ACROSS

San Francisco—Japan—the "run across"—the southern passage—the tropics. What a wealth of significance such phrases convey! What delightful memories are recalled! What pleasant companionships renewed! What happy hours lived over!

Ah! the very remembrance of the glories of such a voyage is intoxicating, as one recalls those long tropic days, when, with every sail drawing and the northeast trades dead astern, hours slip into hours and days slip into days, and are lost, O so quickly. Days, dreamy and bewitching in their sleepy beauty—days, in which the morn breaks with unrivaled tropic splendor, and the evening shades away almost imperceptibly into night—days, each the counterpart of the other, yet each distinguished by something new, something different—a more glorious sunrise, perhaps, or a more vivid coloring at setting; an unusual display of light and shade on the dancing ocean, or a sky, flecked with the specks of fleecy cloud, golden, crimson and purple, a design more gorgeous than those of previous days.

Time drags not on leaden wings. What of a wheel or a watch! With that steady breeze, ever astern, one almost forgets to steer, so lost is he in contemplation. Each moment new beauties dawn, new glories burst upon him, or new surprises startle and amuse. With dreamy eye, he follows the huge gulls, as, solemn, yet graceful, they sail above the bosom of the deep. Round and round, grandly circling, they ever environ the leaping vessel with their spiral flight. Now the glance is drawn aside by a school of porpoises, or attracted by the silvery flight of flying fish, as they skim from sea to sea, windward, in the path of the sun. The fin of a man-eater, astern, a whale blows to leeward; the horizon is broken by a sail; the wind freshens, and the ocean smiles the merrier; it drops, and the ocean nods and dozes; or a dolphin, harpooned from the jibboom-stays, presents a quivering, ever-changing, mingling, intermingling galaxy of colors, as its poor life ebbs out on the burning decks—these, and a thousand like events, attract the attention, divert the mind, and fill one's breast with a peaceful, insidious happiness, perfect in its mild, unconscious sway.

The cards lie unshuffled on the deck, the book is cast aside, the ditty box neglected, and petty tasks forgotten; while the sailors, full of the calm, enervating joy of nature, stroll the decks, loll around in groups, or stud the fok'sle head in full length, pensive attitudes. The sea lawyer is silent, his accustomed trade grown useless. No jangling quarrels, or lie given and blow returned. This is reserved for more tempestuous weather.

And the nights! What a study in light and shadow! The dim form of the helmsman; the bright binnacle light; the sails, lost to view in the black vault, above; the vessel's bow disappears in the night; the vague, almost intuitive, perception of rope, block, boom and tackle; the black forms, now lost in gloom, now emerging, as they take their accustomed pace; the glow of their pipes or the momentary flicker of a match; the stars, bejeweling the heavens; the sea, each wave crested with a glittering coronet of fire—these, all these, are a pleasure to the languid soul, appealing to his artistic sense, perhaps unconsciously, but nevertheless filling him with peaceful joy, unutterable.

Even so with sound. Nothing is harsh or discordant; everything harmonizes. The creaking of a block is music. The groan of the towering canvas; the dash of the water from the dancing stem; the occasional splutter of the adventurous flying-fish against the sails; the dull, indistinguishable mumble of unseen conversation, and the peculiar, almost inaudible, voice of every straining rope, stay, pin and block, form a sleepy symphony that lulls and soothes, and causes one to become dreamy and to sink into reverie.

And again—when the sky is overcast with black storm clouds, fit background for the vivid lightning—the sea a smother of foam, and the air, a howling, unseen demon, the soul finds pleasure. The enervating influence is broken, and fierce joy is taken in the battle of the elements. As the roar of wind and wave, the rumbling thunder, and the battling ship rises, so rises the kindled enthusiasm. The tempestuous play of nature rouses the tumultuous emotions of the breast. The wind stands up against one like a wall; the spray and rain cut face and hand like knives; the decks are a flood of churning waters; but huge delight is taken in each and all. The heart quickens with sympathy as the vessel springs abruptly to the ascent of each mountainous sea, and throbs with delicious apprehension as she pauses with sickening roll on the giddy summit, bow high in air, and then leaps with precipitous force into the frightful vortex of swirling foam below. The bellowed orders of the sailing-master are received with feverish impatience; the joy of combat sends the blood leaping when the bellying sails are overcome or the reluctant rope forced to yield, and with the chants of the seamen breathing sweet music in his ear, he awakens from his happy reminiscence, and renewed, invigorated, returns to the commonplace tasks of everyday, humdrum life.

From Oakland High School *Aegis*,
December 2, 1895

BONIN ISLANDS

AN INCIDENT OF THE SEALING FLEET OF '93

How many beautiful, unfrequented spots there are that are practically unknown and unheard of! Unknown and unheard of, not only by that great class, the "stay-at-home" people, but by the wandering sight-seer.

"Full many a flower is born to blush unseen,
And waste its fragrance on the desert air."

So it is with these glorious garden spots of nature with which the world abounds —perfect paradises, that the curious traveler has never trod. The ignorant, uncouth inhabitants and the crews of an occasional ship, who do not even pause to realize their beauty, alone see them.

The Bonin Islands, situated between the 25th and 27th degrees of north latitude, and east longitude 140 degrees and 23 minutes, are one of these known, yet unknown spots—known to the navigator and chart-maker and almost entirely unknown to the rest of the world. They were discovered two hundred and fifty years ago, tradition says, by a great junk while beating back to Japan, after having been blown off the coast in a typhoon. Soon after, the Japanese government took possession and colonized them; but fifty years later they were deserted. During the next two centuries their few inhabitants, abandoned by their mother country and cut off from all intercourse with the outside world, relapsed into a state of semi-barbarism. This beautiful but remote group of islets was forgotten, actually forgotten. The world knew of them no more. During the middle of this century, however, occasional whale ships ran in for water, and bought onions, sweet potatoes and yams from their half-civilized inhabitants, while the crews disported themselves ashore, hunting the wild hogs and deer with which the hills abounded, and catching fish and great green turtles along the reefs and shores.

But soon Japan, having aroused from her lethargy, began her onward march towards the civilization which at the present time causes the whole world to look upon her with astonishment and admiration, and awoke to the fact that the possession of these islands was not so trivial a matter after all. For the second time she colonized them, but this time on a grander scale. St. John, the principal island of the group, in which there are about forty, alone received between two and three thousand emigrants from the crowded cities of Yokohama and Tokio. With the typical push and energy of modern Japan, they completely revolutionized the existing state of affairs. The 50 or so savage natives did not take kindly to the encroachments of the foreigners, but, like the Red Indians of America, they were pushed ahead of the advancing tide, till now they are as strangers in their own land. Here and there, on some isolated coral beach or in the dark depths of the mighty volcanic gorges, one occasionally stumbles upon a miserable, grass-thatched hut, from which the savage owner peers threateningly with sullen visage at the venturous traveler who has invaded his domain—his last retreat before the progressive Japanese. These people are of doubtful nationality, being a promiscuous mingling of the descendants of the original settlers with Kanakas and the renegades who deserted from the whalers in earlier times.

The little colony now boasts a governor, a police force, several thriving villages, many rich plantations, a handsome stone pier, numerous school houses, and in fact, a civilization in miniature that is on a par with Japan itself. Nevertheless, they are still practically unknown and unvisited. Only twice a year their intercourse with their mother country and the outside world is revived. Every six months a government steamer arrives with additional emigrants, the luxuries and necessities of civilized life and the news from the outside world. Then the pretty islands slumber peacefully in their semi-tropical climate for another half year, when the next "steamer day" is at hand.

To the beholder, the chief and most manifest charm in the scenery of these islands is that of variety—the sharp and telling contrasts which abound on every hand and in such grand magnitude. The group is of volcanic formation. Here high mountains rise perpendicularly from the sea, covered to their very summits by the luxuriant growth of tropical vegetation; there, a little coral beach of purest, dazzling white, reposes at the base of some mighty cliff, ever washed by the ceaseless surf. Now the bold contour of the landscape is smoothed and chastened by the easy rising of a fruitful plain, all verdant with the loholla, mulberry, banana and cabbage tree, or a gentle slope, where the sugar-cane, pine-apple, sweet potato and yam thrive in the rich soil; and again, great bluffs and frightful precipices enhance the weird beauty and add to the diversity of scenery. And over all, the rich vegetation flourishes in every conceivable nook and cranny. In many places it seems to spring out of the solid, volcanic rock, where not an atom of soil is apparent to the eye. Far up among the cliffs at the head of the deep, cavern-like gorges, pure springs of ice-cold water send down sparkling streams and rivulets to meet the fierce surge of the surf far below. Now dashing through some volcanic rupture in the gorge, they become a wild swirl of churning waters; then rushing over a tremendous precipice, they shoot into mid air and descend like a silvery veil of mist in an unbroken fall of hundreds of feet. Sometimes plunging over a succession of cataracts, they leap clear into the sea; or again, traversing the fruitful clearings and plantations of the industrious farmer, they become slow and dignified in their pace and are finally lost to view in the white beaches of pounded coral rock, through which they sink and filter away to the sea.

Such is the view from the harbor, where the vessel lays at anchor, almost overshadowed by the great, volcanic mountains, whose lofty heads seem to disappear and be lost among the mists and clouds above.

The harbor is nearly land-locked, and has good holding ground in anywhere from ten to fifty fathoms. It could accommodate quite a fleet; but the bay is nearly always deserted, except for the pretty out-rigger canoes and *sampans* of the natives. The whalers of olden time visit this beautiful spot no more, and but twice a year the monotony is broken by the arrival of the government steamer.

However, the year I was there (1893), the easy-going, phlegmatic inhabitants received such a thorough awakening, that I hardly know if they have recovered from it yet. It was about the first part of the month of March. The steamer was not expected for another three months. It had been years since the last whale-ship had put in for water—nothing was expected and the little colony slumbered peacefully. Suddenly a sail appears in the offing. Every inhabitant of St. Johns is on the alert. It squares away, and with flowing sheet, runs through the dangerous channel, regardless of the proffered services of the dirty, bewhiskered renegade, who has put off in his canoe to pilot her in, as he did the whale-ships long ago. It is a little schooner, and as she comes up into the wind with her sails a-shivering, the anchor is let go and the stars and stripes flung to the breeze. She is one of those venturous sealing schooners from the American Coast, 5,000 miles away; the fore-runner of the fleet that is to follow.

The Governor, who at the same time is Harbor Master, supreme head of the custom house, Judge and Justice of the Peace, besides filling a dozen other honorable positions, pays his state visit to the Captain and returns to the shore. The population of the island is greatly excited. The bay swarms with canoes and *sampans*, all bound aboard this strange craft, which has come all the way from America, that country of which they have heard so much, and which they so greatly admire.

The next day the surprise is redoubled, for the little schooner now has a companion to keep her company in the lonely bay. The newcomer floats the English flag. She is the herald of the British fleet, that sails yearly out of Victoria. And at dusk that night the eager inhabitants perceive two more sails laying to in the offing waiting for daylight with which to effect the dangerous passage. And by the middle of March, a fleet of fifteen sealers is assembled in the little port.

When the inhabitants recovered from their first surprise at the unexpected invasion, they realized the great possibilities and profits to accrue from their intercourse with the strangers. With the typical energy of their enterprising race, they launched boldly into the hitherto unknown channels of commerce. The plantations were ransacked, and their joyful proprietors came aboard with whole boat-loads of bananas, pine-apples, yams, sweet potatoes, sugar-cane, and all sorts of vegetables, while the fishermen sold large quantities of the fresh fish, with which the reefs and shoals abound, and innumerable great sea turtles. The hogs, cattle and deer were also slaughtered and sold to the Captains of the various schooners. And how these foreigners drank! Why the liquor dealers netted independent fortunes on "square faces" of Holland gin and big bottles of half fermented *saki*, a drink distilled from rice.

Whew! How things boomed! The simple Japanese must have thought that the millenium had come. And how they all scrambled in the mad rush for wealth! To them, it seemed as though these white sea-rovers were made of gold, and even their vessels laden with the precious metal. Prices went up faster than a hot air balloon. Yesterday, fresh beef was three cents a pound; to-day, four; to-morrow, five; the next day, nine; and by Saturday, it had reached the exorbitant price of twenty-two cents and was still rising. When before, for ten cents one could buy a stick of sugar-cane as long as a fishing pole, he now paid twenty-five cents for a single joint, hardly a foot long. A "square face" of Holland gin, which at first had sold for forty cents, went up in a couple of jumps to the astonishing price of six dollars.

The Japanese are shrewd speculators—it seems inherent, but this time they reckoned without their host. Fresh meat became scarce because of the unreasonable price demanded. One day, however, one of the Captains went ashore with a couple of hunters and killed a steer; but they were prevented from taking it aboard by the Governor and the Chief of Police. The foreign "sea pirates" resolved to break the blockade, and next day the grandest battue that had ever occurred in the history of the islands took place.

Scores of seal hunters, the coolest crack shots in the world, and hundreds of hardy, bold-spirited seamen ranged the island from end to end; from the depths of the dark, volcanic gorges to the dizzy heights of the cloud-topped mountains. All day long nothing was to be heard but the loud reports of the guns and the wild shouts of the simple, good-natured fellows, who were as school boys out for a frolic. Now the sharp crack of the rifle and the quick, whistling ping of the bullet came to the ear; and again, the heavier reports of the shotguns. Then a long scattering of shots like an irregular volley, followed by the merry shouts of the hunters. Sometimes the fleeing cattle could be seen tearing through the thick jungles, pursued by a score of agile sailors, who, in turn, were often put to flight and scattered in all directions before the headlong charge of an infuriated boar or steer.

So the merry hunt went on. In vain the Governor tried to stop it. He stormed, prayed, cursed and entreated by turns, but all in vain. The disturbance was beyond his control. His few dozen native police were completely ignored by the "white pirates" and "foreign devils." And when night fell, the slaughter ceased and the boats returned, heavily laden with the day's spoils, to their respective schooners.

Then the Governor issued a manifesto.

Law and order should be restored and maintained. All disturbers of the peace would be punished. All sailors must be aboard their respective craft by ten o'clock every night. The delinquents to be arrested and confined in the guard house. And if the Captains could not or would not control their men, they would be forced to leave the island.

That night every sea-rover was ashore. Ten o'clock was soon passed, but none dreamed of going aboard. Instead, the evening's festivities were just beginning. Right in front of the Governor's mansion, a rousing Virginia Reel was in progress. "Big Oscar," a giant Norwegian, who towered a whole head and shoulders above the throng, played away for the dancers on an accordion, while "square faces" circulated freely through the crowd. Though the entire police force had been massed to clear the streets, the Governor thought discretion the better part of valor and wisely refrained from precipitating affairs.

The next morning the Captains were ordered to sail their schooners hence; which demand was completely ignored. For a navy, the island boasted three uniformed marines and a gig; so the Governor was powerless to enforce his commands. Still, though triumphant, the sailors committed no indignities or outrages, and the natives, finding them to be a peaceable, law-abiding people, became reconciled to their presence and were glad that such good customers still remained. Prices soon dropped to their normal level, and complete serenity was restored.

At last, one morning, unusual activity was observed aboard the different craft. Gaskets were cast off and the sails loosened. Boats were hoisted aboard and everything made shipshape. Then the merry chants of the crews at the windlasses, as singing their inspiriting "shanties," they hoisted the heavy anchors, came to the ears of the wondering natives. Sail after sail was set, and schooner after schooner filled away, and with a leading wind ran through the narrow passage into the open sea. The fleet was bound for the Coast of Japan, where all summer they would follow the migratory seals northward to the rookeries in Behring Sea. Almost before the natives could realize it, not one of the numerous fleet remained in their little Harbor.

And so, the Bonin Islands were left to slumber peacefully on, in their blissful, tropical climate, lapped by the blue waters of the great ocean and waiting for the next "steamer day." But their inhabitants never tire of recounting the invasion of the white sea-rovers, and of telling of their wild doings and strange customs.

"Ah! Life was life, then!" and they smack their lips appreciatively over that by-gone event, and jingle the foreigner's gold in their girdles.

From Oakland High School *Aegis*,
December 1897

HOLDING HER DOWN

Barring accidents, a good hobo, with youth and agility, can hold a train down despite all the efforts of the train-crew to "ditch" him–given, of course, night-time as an essential condition. When such a hobo, under such conditions, makes up his mind that he is going to hold her down, either he does hold her down, or chance trips him up. There is no legitimate way, short of murder, whereby the train-crew can ditch him. That train-crews have not stopped short of murder is a current belief in the tramp world. Not having had that particular experience in my tramp days I cannot vouch for it personally.

But this I have heard of the "bad" roads. When a tramp has "gone underneath," on the rods, and the train is in motion, there is apparently no way of dislodging him until the train stops. The tramp, snugly ensconced inside the truck, with the four wheels and all the framework around him, has the "cinch" on the crew–or so he thinks, until some day he rides the rods on a bad road. A bad road is usually one on which a short time previously one or several trainmen have been killed by tramps. Heaven pity the tramp who is caught "underneath" on such a road–for caught he is, though the train be going sixty miles an hour.

The "shack" (brakeman) takes a coupling-pin and a length of bell-cord to the platform in front of the truck in which the tramp is riding. The shack fastens the coupling-pin to the bell-cord, drops the former down between the platforms, and pays out the latter. The coupling-pin strikes the ties between the rails, rebounds against the bottom of the car, and again strikes the ties. The shack plays it back and forth, now to this side, now to the other, lets it out a bit and hauls it in a bit, giving his weapon opportunity for every variety of impact and rebound. Every blow of that flying coupling-pin is freighted with death, and at sixty miles an hour it beats a veritable tattoo of death. The next day the remains of that tramp are gathered up along the right of way, and a line in the local paper mentions the unknown man, undoubtedly a tramp, assumably drunk, who had probably fallen asleep on the track.

As a characteristic illustration of how a capable hobo can hold her down, I am minded to give the following experience. I was in Ottawa, bound west over the Canadian Pacific. Three thousand miles of that road stretched before me; it was the fall of the year, and I had to cross Manitoba and the Rocky Mountains. I could expect "crimpy" weather, and every moment of delay increased the frigid hardships of the journey. Furthermore, I was disgusted. The distance between Montreal and Ottawa is one hundred and twenty miles. I ought to know, for I had just come over it and it had taken me six days. By mistake I had missed the main line and come over a small "jerk" with only two locals a day on it. And during these six days I had lived on dry crusts, and not enough of them, begged from the French peasants.

Furthermore, my disgust had been heightened by the one day I had spent in Ottawa trying to get an outfit of clothing for my long journey. Let me put it on record right here that Ottawa, with one exception, is the hardest town in the United States and Canada to beg clothes in; the one exception is Washington, D.C. The latter fair city is the limit. I spent two weeks there trying to beg a pair of shoes, and then had to go on to Jersey City before I got them.

But to return to Ottawa. At eight sharp in the morning I started out after clothes. I worked energetically all day. I swear I walked forty miles. I interviewed the housewives of a thousand homes. I did not even knock off work for dinner. And at six in the afternoon, after ten hours of unremitting and depressing toil, I was still shy one shirt, while the pair of trousers I had managed to acquire was tight and, moreover, was showing all the signs of an early disintegration.

At six I quit work and headed for the railroad yards . . .

When I arrived at the depot, I found, much to my disgust, a bunch of at least twenty tramps that were waiting to ride out the blind baggages of the overland. Now two or three tramps on the blind baggage are all right. They are inconspicuous. But a score! That meant trouble. No train-crew would ever let all of us ride.

I may as well explain here what a blind baggage is. Some mail-cars are built without doors in the ends; hence, such a car is "blind." The mail-cars that possess end doors, have those doors always locked. Suppose, after the train has started, that a tramp gets on to the platform of one of these blind cars. There is no door, or the door is locked. No conductor or brakeman can get to him to collect fare or throw him off. It is clear that the tramp is safe until the next time the train stops. Then he must get off, run ahead in the darkness, and when the train pulls by, jump on to the blind again. But there are ways and ways, as you shall see.

When the train pulled out, those twenty tramps swarmed upon the three blinds. Some climbed on before the train had run a car-length. They were awkward dubs, and I saw their speedy finish. Of course, the train-crew was "on," and at the first stop the trouble began. I jumped off and ran forward along the track. I noticed that I was accompanied by a number of the tramps. They evidently knew their business. When one is beating an overland, he must always keep well ahead of the train at the stops. I ran ahead, and as I ran, one by one those that accompanied me dropped out. This dropping out was the measure of their skill and nerve in boarding a train.

For this is the way it works. When the train starts, the shack rides out the blind. There is no way for him to get back into the train proper except by jumping off the blind and catching a platform where the car-ends are not "blind." When the train is going as fast as the shack cares to risk, he therefore jumps off the blind, lets several cars go by, and gets on to the train. So it is up to the tramp to run so far ahead that before the blind is opposite him the shack will have already vacated it.

I dropped the last tramp by about fifty feet, and waited. The train started. I saw the lantern of the shack on the first blind. He was riding her out. And I saw the dubs stand forlornly by the track as the blind went by. They made no attempt to get on. They were beaten by their own inefficiency at the very start. After them, in the line-up, came the tramps that knew a little something about the game. They let the first blind, occupied by the shack, go by, and jumped on the second and third blinds. Of course, the shack jumped off the first and on to the second as it went by, and scrambled around there, throwing off the men who had boarded it. But the point is that I was so far ahead that when the first blind came opposite me, the shack had already left it and was tangled up with the tramps on the second blind. A half dozen of the more skilful tramps, who had run far enough ahead, made the first blind, too.

At the next stop, as we ran forward along the track, I counted but fifteen of us. Five had been ditched. The weeding-out process had begun nobly, and it continued station by station. Now we were fourteen, now twelve, now eleven, now nine, now eight. It reminded me of the ten little niggers of the nursery rhyme. I was resolved that I should be the last little nigger of all. And why not? Was I not blessed with strength, agility, and youth? (I was eighteen, and in perfect condition.) And didn't I have my "nerve" with me? And furthermore, was I not a tramp-royal? Were not these other tramps mere dubs and "gay-cats" and amateurs alongside of me? If I weren't the last little nigger, I might as well quit the game and get a job on an alfalfa farm somewhere.

By the time our number had been reduced to four, the whole train-crew had become interested. From then on it was a contest of skill and wits, with the odds in favor of the crew. One by one the three other survivors turned up missing, until I alone remained. My, but I was proud of myself! No Crœsus was ever prouder of his first million. I was holding her down in spite of two brakemen, a conductor, a fireman, and an engineer.

And here are a few samples of the way I held her down. Out ahead, in the darkness,—so far ahead that the shack riding out the blind must perforce get off before it reaches me,—I get on. Very well. I am good for another station. When that station is reached, I dart ahead again to repeat the manœuvre. The train pulls out. I watch her coming. There is no light of a lantern on the blind. Has the crew abandoned the fight? I do not know. One never knows, and one must be prepared every moment for anything. As the first blind comes opposite me, and I run to leap aboard, I strain my eyes to see if the shack is on the platform. For all I know he may be there, with his lantern doused, and even as I spring upon the steps that lantern may smash down upon my head. I ought to know. I have been hit by lanterns two or three times.

But no, the first blind is empty. The train is gathering speed. I am safe for another station. But am I? I feel the train slacken speed. On the instant I am alert. A manœuvre is being executed against me, and I do not know what it is. I try to watch on both sides at once, not forgetting to keep track of the tender in front of me. From any one, or all, of these three directions, I may be assailed.

Ah, there it comes. The shack has ridden out the engine. My first warning is when his feet strike the steps of the right-hand side of the blind. Like a flash I am off the blind to the left and running ahead past the engine. I lose myself in the darkness. The situation is where it has been ever since the train left Ottawa. I am ahead, and the train must come past me if it is to proceed on its journey. I have as good a chance as ever for boarding her.

I watch carefully. I see a lantern come forward to the engine, and I do not see it go back from the engine. It must therefore be still on the engine, and it is a fair assumption that attached to the handle of that lantern is a shack. That shack was lazy, or else he would have put out his lantern instead of trying to shield it as he came forward. The train pulls out. The first blind is empty, and I gain it. As before, the train slackens, the shack from the engine boards the blind from one side, and I go off the other side and run forward.

As I wait in the darkness I am conscious of a big thrill of pride. The overland has stopped twice for me—for me, a poor hobo on the bum. I alone have twice stopped the overland with its many passengers and coaches, its government mail, and its two thousand steam horses straining in the engine. And I weigh only one hundred and sixty pounds, and I haven't a five-cent piece in my pocket!

Again I see the lantern come forward to the engine. But this time it comes conspicuously. A bit too conspicuously to suit me, and I wonder what is up. At any rate I have something else to be afraid of than the shack on the engine. The train pulls by. Just in time, before I make my spring, I see the dark form of a shack, without a lantern, on the first blind. I let it go by, and prepare to board the second blind. But the shack on the first blind has jumped off and is at my heels. Also, I have a fleeting glimpse of the lantern of the shack who rode out the engine. He has jumped off, and now both shacks are on the ground on the same side with me. The next moment the second blind comes by and I am aboard it. But I do not linger. I have figured out my countermove. As I dash across the platform I hear the impact of the shack's feet against the steps as he boards. I jump off the other side and run forward with the train. My plan is to run forward and get on the first blind. It is nip and tuck, for the train is gathering speed. Also, the shack is behind me and running after me. I guess I am the better sprinter, for I make the first blind. I stand on the steps and watch my pursuer. He is only about ten feet back and running hard; but now the train has approximated his own speed, and, relative to me, he is standing still. I encourage him, hold out my hand to him; but he explodes in a mighty oath, gives up and makes the train several cars back.

The train is speeding along, and I am still chuckling to myself, when, without warning, a spray of water strikes me. The fireman is playing the hose on me from the engine. I step forward from the car-platform to the rear of the tender, where I am sheltered under the overhang. The water flies harmlessly over my head. My fingers itch to climb up on the tender and lam that fireman with a chunk of coal; but I know if I do that, I'll be massacred by him and the engineer, and I refrain.

At the next stop I am off and ahead in the darkness. This time, when the train pulls out, both shacks are on the first blind. I divine their game. They have blocked the repetition of my previous play. I cannot again take the second blind, cross over, and run forward to the first. As soon as the first blind passes and I do not get on, they swing off, one on each side of the train. I board the second blind, and as I do so I know that a moment later, simultaneously, those two shacks will arrive on both sides of me. It is like a trap. Both ways are blocked. Yet there is another way out, and that way is up.

So I do not wait for my pursuers to arrive. I climb upon the upright ironwork of the platform and stand upon the wheel of the hand-brake. This has taken up the moment of grace and I hear the shacks strike the steps on either side. I don't stop to look. I raise my arms overhead until my hands rest against the down-curving ends of the roofs of the two cars. One hand, of course, is on the curved roof of one car, the other hand on the curved roof of the other car. By this time both shacks are coming up the steps. I know it, though I am too busy to see them. All this is happening in the space of only several seconds. I make a spring with my legs and "muscle" myself up with my arms. As I draw up my legs, both shacks reach for me and clutch empty air. I know this, for I look down and see them. Also I hear them swear.

I am now in a precarious position, riding the ends of the down-curving roofs of two cars at the same time. With a quick, tense movement, I transfer both legs to the curve of one roof and both hands to the curve of the other roof. Then, gripping the edge of that curving roof, I climb over the curve to the level roof above, where I sit down to catch my breath, holding on the while to a ventilator that projects above the surface. I am on top of the train—on the "decks," as the tramps call it, and this process I have described is by them called "decking her." And let me say right here that only a young and vigorous tramp is able to deck a passenger train, and also, that the young and vigorous tramp must have his nerve with him as well.

The train goes on gathering speed, and I know I am safe until the next stop—but only until the next stop. If I remain on the roof after the train stops, I know those shacks will fusillade me with rocks. A healthy shack can "dewdrop" a pretty heavy chunk of stone on top of a car—say anywhere from five to twenty pounds. On the other hand, the chances are large that at the next stop the shacks will be waiting for me to descend at the place I climbed up. It is up to me to climb down at some other platform.

Registering a fervent hope that there are no tunnels in the next half mile, I rise to my feet and walk down the train half a dozen cars. And let me say that one must leave timidity behind him on such a *passear*. The roofs of passenger coaches are not made for midnight promenades. And if any one thinks they are, let me advise him to try it. Just let him walk along the roof of a jolting, lurching car, with nothing to hold on to but the black and empty air, and when he comes to the down-curving end of the roof, all wet and slippery with dew, let him accelerate his speed so as to step across to the next roof, down-curving and wet and slippery. Believe me, he will learn whether his heart is weak or his head is giddy.

As the train slows down for a stop, half a dozen platforms from where I had decked her I come down. No one is on the platform. When the train comes to a standstill, I slip off to the ground. Ahead, and between me and the engine, are two moving lanterns. The shacks are looking for me on the roofs of the cars. I note that the car beside which I am standing is a "four-wheeler"—by which is meant that it has only four wheels to each truck. (When you go underneath on the rods, be sure to avoid the "six-wheelers,"—they lead to disasters.)

I duck under the train and make for the rods, and I can tell you I am mighty glad that the train is standing still. It is the first time I have ever gone underneath on the Canadian Pacific, and the internal arrangements are new to me. I try to crawl over the top of the truck, between the truck and the bottom of the car. But the space is not large enough for me to squeeze through. This is new to me. Down in the United States I am accustomed to going underneath on rapidly moving trains, seizing a gunnel and swinging my feet under to the brake-beam, and from there crawling over the top of the truck and down inside the truck to a seat on the cross-rod.

Feeling with my hands in the darkness, I learn that there is room between the brake-beam and the ground. It is a tight squeeze. I have to lie flat and worm my way through. Once inside the truck, I take my seat on the rod and wonder what the shacks are thinking has become of me. The train gets under way. They have given me up at last.

But have they? At the very next stop, I see a lantern thrust under the next truck to mine at the other end of the car. They are searching the rods for me. I must make my get-away pretty lively. I crawl on my stomach under the brake-beam. They see me and run for me, but I crawl on hands and knees across the rail on the opposite side and gain my feet. Then away I go for the head of the train. I run past the engine and hide in the sheltering darkness. It is the same old situation. I am ahead of the train, and the train must go past me.

The train pulls out. There is a lantern on the first blind. I lie low, and see the peering shack go by. But there is also a lantern on the second blind. That shack spots me and calls to the shack who has gone past on the first blind. Both jump off. Never mind, I'll take the third blind and deck her. But heavens, there is a lantern on the third blind, too. It is the conductor. I let it go by. At any rate I have now the full train-crew in front of me. I turn and run back in the opposite direction to what the train is going. I look over my shoulder. All three lanterns are on the ground and wobbling along in pursuit. I sprint. Half the train has gone by, and it is going quite fast, when I spring aboard. I know that the two shacks and the conductor will arrive like ravening wolves in about two seconds. I spring upon the wheel of the hand-brake, get my hands on the curved ends of the roofs, and muscle myself up to the decks; while my disappointed pursuers, clustering on the platform beneath like dogs that have treed a cat, howl curses up at me and say unsocial things about my ancestors.

But what does that matter? It is five to one, including the engineer and fireman, and the majesty of the law and the might of a great corporation are behind them, and I am beating them out. I am too far down the train, and I run ahead over the roofs of the coaches until I am over the fifth or sixth platform from the engine. I peer down cautiously. A shack is on that platform. That he has caught sight of me, I know from the way he makes a swift sneak inside the car; and I know, also, that he is waiting inside the door, all ready to pounce out on me when I climb down. But I make believe that I don't know, and I remain there to encourage him in his error. I do not see him, yet I know that he opens the door once and peeps up to assure himself that I am still there.

The train slows down for a station. I dangle my legs down in a tentative way. The train stops. My legs are still dangling. I hear the door unlatch softly. He is all ready for me. Suddenly I spring up and run forward over the roof. This is right over his head, where he lurks inside the door. The train is standing still; the night is quiet, and I take care to make plenty of noise on the metal roof with my feet. I don't know, but my assumption is that he is now running forward to catch me as I descend at the next platform. But I don't descend there. Halfway along the roof of the coach, I turn, retrace my way softly, and quickly to the platform both the shack and I have just abandoned. The coast is clear. I descend to the ground on the off-side of the train and hide in the darkness. Not a soul has seen me.

I go over to the fence, at the edge of the right of way, and watch. Ah, ha! What's that? I see a lantern on top of the train, moving along from front to rear. They think I haven't come down, and they are searching the roofs for me. And better than that—on the ground on each side of the train, moving abreast with the lantern on top, are two other lanterns. It is a rabbit-drive, and I am the rabbit. When the shack on top flushes me, the ones on each side will nab me. I roll a cigarette and watch the procession go by. Once past me, I am safe to proceed to the front of the train. She pulls out, and I make the front blind without opposition. But before she is fully under way and just as I am lighting my cigarette, I am aware that the fire-

THE CRUISE OF THE SNARK

ABOVE: The building of the *Snark*.
BELOW: The crew—"not one of whom, aside from Jack, knew how to reef a sail or haul up an anchor." L. to r. Herbert Stoltz, engineer; Roscoe Eames, navigator; Charmian; Jack; and Tochigi, cabin boy. Missing is Martin Johnson, cook.

ABOVE: "Roscoe is ay a masterful man."
BELOW: Sailing Day, April 23, 1907, from Oakland City Wharf.

The last line cast off.

man has climbed over the coal to the back of the tender and is looking down at me. I am filled with apprehension. From his position he can mash me to a jelly with lumps of coal. Instead of which he addresses me, and I note with relief the admiration in his voice.

"You son-of-a-gun," is what he says.

It is a high compliment, and I thrill as a schoolboy thrills on receiving a reward of merit.

"Say," I call up to him, "don't you play the hose on me any more."

"All right," he answers, and goes back to his work.

I have made friends with the engineer, but the shacks are still looking for me. At the next stop, the shacks ride out all three blinds, and as before, I let them go by and deck in the middle of the train. The crew is on its mettle by now, and the train stops. The shacks are going to ditch me or know the reason why. Three times the mighty overland stops for me at that station, and each time I elude the shacks and make the decks. But it is hopeless, for they have finally come to an understanding of the situation. I have taught them that they cannot guard the train from me. They must do something else.

And they do it. When the train stops that last time, they take after me hotfooted. Ah, I see their game. They are trying to run me down. At first they herd me back toward the rear of the train. I know my peril. Once to the rear of the train, it will pull out with me left behind. I double, and twist, and turn, dodge through my pursuers, and gain the front of the train. One shack still hangs on after me. All right, I'll give him the run of his life, for my wind is good. I run straight ahead along the track. It doesn't matter. If he chases me ten miles, he'll nevertheless have to catch the train, and I can board her at any speed that he can.

So I run on, keeping just comfortably ahead of him and straining my eyes in the gloom for cattle-guards and switches that may bring me to grief. Alas! I strain my eyes too far ahead, and trip over something just under my feet, I know not what, some little thing, and go down to earth in a long, stumbling fall. The next moment I am on my feet, but the shack has me by the collar. I do not struggle. I am busy with breathing deeply and with sizing him up. He is narrow-shouldered, and I have at least thirty pounds the better of him in weight. Besides, he is just as tired as I am, and if he tries to slug me, I'll teach him a few things.

But he doesn't try to slug me, and that problem is settled. Instead, he starts to lead me back toward the train, and another possible problem arises. I see the lanterns of the conductor and the other shack. We are approaching them. Not for nothing have I made the acquaintance of the New York police. Not for nothing, in box-cars, by water-tanks, and in prison-cells, have I listened to bloody tales of man-handling. What if these three men are about to man-handle me? Heaven knows I have given them provocation enough. I think quickly. We are drawing nearer and nearer to the other two trainmen. I line up the stomach and the jaw of my captor, and plan the right and left I'll give him at the first sign of trouble.

Pshaw! I know another trick I'd like to work on him, and I almost regret that I did not do it at the moment I was captured. I could make him sick, what of his clutch on my collar. His fingers, tight-gripping, are buried inside my collar. My coat is tightly buttoned. Did you ever see a tourniquet? Well, this is one. All I have to do is to duck my head under his arm and begin to twist. I must twist rapidly—very rapidly. I know how to do it; twisting in a violent, jerky way, ducking my head under his arm with each revolution. Before he knows it, those detaining fingers of his will be detained. He will be unable to withdraw them. It is a powerful leverage. Twenty seconds after I have started revolving, the blood will be bursting out of his finger-ends, the delicate tendons will be rupturing, and all the muscles and nerves will be mashing and crushing together in a shrieking mass. Try it sometime when somebody has you by the collar. But be quick—quick as lightning. Also, be sure to hug yourself while you are revolving—hug your face with your left arm and your abdomen with your right. You see, the other fellow might try to stop you with a punch from his free arm. It would be a good idea, too, to revolve away from that free arm rather than toward it. A punch going is never so bad as a punch coming.

That shack will never know how near he was to being made very, very sick. All that saves him is that it is not in their plan to man-handle me. When we draw near enough, he calls out that he has me, and they signal the train to come on. The engine passes us, and the three blinds. After that, the conductor and the other shack swing aboard. But still my captor holds on to me. I see the plan. He is going to hold me until the rear of the train goes by. Then he will hop on, and I shall be left behind—ditched.

But the train has pulled out fast, the engineer trying to make up for lost time. Also, it is a long train. It is going very lively, and I know the shack is measuring its speed with apprehension.

"Think you can make it?" I query innocently.

He releases my collar, makes a quick run, and swings aboard. A number of coaches are yet to pass by. He knows it, and remains on the steps, his head poked out and watching me. In that moment my next move comes to me. I'll make the last platform. I know she's going fast and faster, but I'll only get a roll in the dirt if I fail, and the optimism of youth is mine. I do not give myself away. I stand with a dejected droop of shoulder, advertising that I have abandoned hope. But at the same time I am feeling with my feet the good gravel. It is perfect footing. Also I am watching the poked-out head of the shack. I see it withdrawn. He is confident that the train is going too fast for me ever to make it.

And the train *is* going fast—faster than any train I have ever tackled. As the last coach comes by I sprint in the same direction with it. It is a swift, short sprint. I cannot hope to equal the speed of the train, but I can reduce the difference of our speed to the minimum, and, hence, reduce the shock of impact, when I leap on board. In the fleeting instant of darkness I do not see the iron hand-rail of the last platform; nor is there time for me to locate it. I reach for where I think it ought to be, and at the same instant my feet leave the ground. It is all in the toss. The next moment I may be rolling in the gravel with broken ribs, or arms, or head. But my fingers grip the hand-hold, there is a jerk on my arms that slightly pivots my body, and my feet land on the steps with sharp violence.

I sit down, feeling very proud of myself. In all my hoboing it is the best bit of train-jumping I have done. I know that late at night one is always good for several stations on the last platform, but I do not care to trust myself at the rear of the train. At the first stop I run forward on the off-side of the train, pass the Pullmans, and duck under and take a rod under a day-coach. At the next stop I run forward again and take another rod.

I am now comparatively safe. The shacks think I am ditched. But the long day and the strenuous night are beginning to tell on me. Also, it is not so windy nor cold underneath, and I begin to doze. This will never do. Sleep on the rods spells death, so I crawl out at a station and go forward to the second blind. Here I can lie down and sleep; and here I do sleep—how long I do not know—for I am awakened by a lantern thrust into my face. The two shacks are staring at me. I scramble up on the defensive, wondering as to which one is going to make the first "pass" at me. But slugging is far from their minds.

"I thought you was ditched," says the shack who had held me by the collar.

"If you hadn't let go of me when you did, you'd have been ditched along with me," I answer.

"How's that?" he asks.

"I'd have gone into a clinch with you, that's all," is my reply.

They hold a consultation, and their verdict is summed up in:—

"Well, I guess you can ride, Bo. There's no use trying to keep you off."

And they go away and leave me in peace to the end of their division.

I have given the foregoing as a sample of what "holding her down" means. Of course, I have selected a fortunate night out of my experiences, and said nothing of the nights—and many of them—when I was tripped up by accident and ditched.

In conclusion, I want to tell of what happened when I reached the end of the division. On single-track, transcontinental lines, the freight trains wait at the divisions and follow out after the passenger trains. When the division was reached, I left my train, and looked for the freight that would pull out behind it. I found the freight, made up on a side-track and waiting. I climbed into a box-car half full of coal and lay down. In no time I was asleep.

I was awakened by the sliding open of the door. Day was just dawning, cold and gray, and the freight had not yet started. A "con" (conductor) was poking his head inside the door.

"Get out of that, you blankety-blank-blank!" he roared at me.

I got, and outside I watched him go down the line inspecting every car in the train. When he got out of sight I thought to myself that he would never think I'd have the nerve to climb back into the very car out of which he had fired me. So back I climbed and lay down again.

Now that con's mental processes must have been paralleling mine, for he reasoned that it was the very thing I would do. For back he came and fired me out.

Now, surely, I reasoned, he will never dream that I'd do it a third time. Back I went, into the very same car. But I decided to make sure. Only one side-door could be opened. The other side-door was nailed up. Beginning at the top of the coal, I dug a hole alongside of that door and lay down in it. I heard the other door open. The con climbed up and looked in over the top of the coal. He couldn't see me. He called to me to get out. I tried to fool him by remaining quiet. But when he began tossing chunks of coal into the hole on top of me, I gave up and for the third time was fired out. Also, he informed me in warm terms of what would happen to me if he caught me in there again.

I changed my tactics. When a man is paralleling your mental processes, ditch him. Abruptly break off your line of reasoning, and go off on a new line. This I did. I hid between some cars on an adjacent side-track, and watched. Sure enough, that con came back again to the car. He opened the door, he climbed up, he called, he threw coal into the hole I had made. He even crawled over the coal and looked into the hole. That satisfied him. Five minutes later the freight was pulling out, and he was not in sight. I ran alongside the car, pulled the door open, and climbed in. He never looked for me again, and I rode that coal-car precisely one thousand

and twenty-two miles, sleeping most of the time and getting out at divisions (where the freights always stop for an hour or so) to beg my food. And at the end of the thousand and twenty-two miles I lost that car through a happy incident. I got a "set-down," and the tramp doesn't live who won't miss a train for a set-down any time.

From *The Road*

THE INCONCEIVABLE AND MONSTROUS

"Spare no money," I said to Roscoe. "Let everything on the *Snark* be of the best. And never mind decoration. Plain pine boards is good enough finishing for me. But put the money into the construction. Let the *Snark* be as stanch and strong as any boat afloat. Never mind what it costs to make her stanch and strong; you see that she is made stanch and strong and I'll go on writing and earning the money to pay for it."

And I did . . . as well as I could; for the *Snark* ate up money faster than I could earn it. In fact, every little while I had to borrow money with which to supplement my earnings. Now I borrowed one thousand dollars, now I borrowed two thousand dollars, and now I borrowed five thousand dollars. And all the time I went on working every day and sinking the earnings in the venture. I worked Sundays, as well, and I took no holidays. But it was worth it. Every time I thought of the *Snark* I knew she was worth it.

For know, gentle reader, the stanchness of the *Snark*. She is forty-five feet long on the water-line. Her garboard strake is three inches thick; her planking two and one-half inches thick; her deck-planking two inches thick; and in all her planking there are no butts. I know, for I ordered that planking especially from Puget Sound. Then the *Snark* has four water-tight compartments, which is to say that her length is broken by three water-tight bulkheads. Thus, no matter how large a leak the *Snark* may spring, only one compartment can fill with water. The other three compartments will keep her afloat anyway, and, besides, will enable us to mend the leak. There is another virtue in these bulkheads. The last compartment of all, in the very stern, contains six tanks that carry over one thousand gallons of gasolene. Now gasolene is a very dangerous article to carry in bulk on a small craft far out on the wide ocean. But when the six tanks that do not leak are themselves contained in a compartment hermetically sealed off from the rest of the boat, the danger will be seen to be very small indeed.

The *Snark* is a sail-boat. She was built primarily to sail. But, incidentally, as an auxiliary, a seventy-horse-power engine was installed. This is a good, strong engine. I ought to know. I paid for it to come out all the way from New York City. Then, on deck, above the engine, is a windlass. It is a magnificent affair. It weighs several hundred pounds and takes up no end of deck room. You see, it is ridiculous to hoist up anchor by hand-power when there is a seventy-horse-power engine on board. So we installed the windlass, transmitting power to it from the engine by means of a gear and castings specially made in a San Francisco foundry.

The *Snark* was made for comfort, and no expense was spared in this regard. There is the bathroom, for instance, small and compact, it is true, but containing all the conveniences of any bathroom upon land. The bathroom is a beautiful dream of schemes and devices, pumps, and levers, and sea-valves. Why, in the course of its building, I used to lie awake nights thinking about that bathroom. And next to the bathroom come the lifeboat and the launch. They are carried on deck, and they take up what little space might have been left us for exercise. But then, they beat life insurance; and the prudent man, even if he has built as stanch and strong a craft as the *Snark*, will see to it that he has a good lifeboat as well. And ours is a good one. It is a dandy. It was stipulated to cost one hundred and fifty dollars, and when I came to pay the bill, it turned out to be three hundred and ninety-five dollars. That shows how good a lifeboat it is.

I could go on at great length relating the various virtues and excellences of the *Snark*, but I refrain. I have bragged enough as it is, and I have bragged to a purpose, as will be seen before my tale is ended. And please remember its title, "The Inconceivable and Monstrous." It was planned that the *Snark* should sail on October 1, 1906. That she did not so sail was inconceivable and monstrous. There was no valid reason for not sailing except that she was not ready to sail, and there was no conceivable reason why she was not ready. She was promised on November first, on November fifteenth, on December first; and yet she was never ready. On December first Charmian and I left the sweet, clean Sonoma country and came down to live in the stifling city—but not for long, oh, no, only for two weeks, for we would sail on December fifteenth. And I guess we ought to know, for Roscoe said so, and it was on his advice that we came to the city to stop two weeks. Alas, the two weeks went by, four weeks went by, six weeks went by, eight weeks went by, and we were farther away from sailing than ever. Explain it? Who?—me? I can't. It is the one thing in all my life that I have backed down on. There is no explaining it; if there were, I'd do it. I, who am an artisan of speech, confess my inability to explain why the *Snark* was not ready. As I have said, and as I must repeat, it was inconceivable and monstrous.

The eight weeks became sixteen weeks, and then, one day, Roscoe cheered us up by saying:

"If we don't sail before April first, you can use my head for a football."

Two weeks later he said, "I'm getting my head in training for that match."

"Never mind," Charmian and I said to each other; "think of the wonderful boat it is going to be when it is completed."

Whereat we would rehearse for our mutual encouragement the manifold virtues and excellences of the *Snark*. Also, I would borrow more money, and I would get down closer to my desk and write harder, and I refused heroically to take a Sunday off and go out into the hills with my friends. I was building a boat, and by the eternal it was going to be a boat, and a boat spelled out all in capitals—B–O–A–T; and no matter what it cost I didn't care, so long as it was a B O A T.

And, oh, there is one other excellence of the *Snark*, upon which I must brag, namely, her bow. No sea could ever come over it. It laughs at the sea, that bow does; it challenges the sea; it snorts defiance at the sea. And withal it is a beautiful bow; the lines of it are dreamlike; I doubt if ever a boat was blessed with a more beautiful and at the same time a more capable bow. It was made to punch storms. To touch that bow is to rest one's hand on the cosmic nose of things. To look at it is to realize that expense cut no figure where it was concerned. And every time our sailing was delayed, or a new expense was tacked on, we thought of that wonderful bow and were content.

The *Snark* is a small boat. When I figured seven thousand dollars as her generous cost, I was both generous and correct. I have built barns and houses, and I know the peculiar trait such things have of running past their estimated cost. This knowledge was mine, was already mine, when I estimated the probable cost of the building of the *Snark* at seven thousand dollars. Well, she cost thirty thousand. Now don't ask me, please. It is the truth. I signed the checks and I raised the money. Of course there is no explaining it. Inconceivable and monstrous is what it is, as you will agree, I know, ere my tale is done.

Then there was the matter of delay. I dealt with forty-seven different kinds of union men and with one hundred and fifteen different firms. And not one union man and not one firm of all the union men and all the firms ever delivered anything at the time agreed upon, nor ever was on time for anything except pay-day and bill-collection. Men pledged me their immortal souls that they would deliver a certain thing on a certain date; as a rule, after such pledging, they rarely exceeded being three months late in delivery. And so it went, and Charmian and I consoled each other by saying what a splendid boat the *Snark* was, so stanch and strong; also, we would get into the small boat and row around the *Snark*, and gloat over her unbelievably wonderful bow.

"Think," I would say to Charmian, "of a gale off the China coast, and of the *Snark* hove to, that splendid bow of hers driving into the storm. Not a drop will come over that bow. She'll be as dry as a feather, and we'll be all below playing whist while the gale howls."

And Charmian would press my hand enthusiastically and exclaim:

"It's worth every bit of it—the delay—and expense, and worry, and all the rest. Oh, what a truly wonderful boat!"

Whenever I looked at the bow of the *Snark* or thought of her water-tight compartments, I was encouraged. Nobody else, however, was encouraged. My friends began to make bets against the various sailing dates of the *Snark*. Mr. Wiget, who was left behind in charge of our Sonoma ranch, was the first to cash his bet. He collected on New Year's Day, 1907. After that the bets came fast and furious. My friends surrounded me like a gang of harpies, making bets against every sailing date I set. I was rash, and I was stubborn. I bet, and I bet, and I continued to bet; and I paid them all. Why, the womenkind of my friends grew so brave that those among them who never bet before began to bet with me. And I paid them too.

"Never mind," said Charmian to me; "just think of that bow and of being hove to on the China Seas."

"You see," I said to my friends, when I paid the latest bunch of wagers, "neither trouble nor cash is being spared in making the *Snark* the most seaworthy craft that ever sailed out through the Golden Gate—that is what causes all the delay."

In the meantime editors and publishers with whom I had contracts pestered me with demands for explanations. But how could I explain to them, when I was unable to explain to myself, or when there was nobody, not even Roscoe, to explain to me? The newspapers began to laugh at me, and to publish rhymes anent the *Snark's* departure with refrains like, "Not yet but soon." And Charmian cheered me up by reminding me of the bow, and I went to a banker and borrowed five thousand more. There was one recompense for the delay, however. A friend of mine, who happens to be a critic, wrote a roast of me, of all I had done, and of all I ever was going to do; and he planned to have it published after I was out on the ocean. I was still on shore when it came out, and he has been busy explaining ever since.

And the time continued to go by. One thing was becoming apparent, namely, that it was impossible to finish the *Snark* in San Francisco. She had been so long in the building that she was beginning to break down and wear out. In fact, she had reached the stage where she was breaking down faster than she could be repaired. She had become a joke. Nobody took her seriously; least of all the men who worked on her. I said we would sail just as she was and finish building her in Honolulu. Promptly she sprang a leak that had to be attended to before we could sail. I started her for the boat-ways. Before she got to them she was caught between two huge barges and received a vigorous crushing. We got her on the ways, and, part way along, the ways spread and dropped her through, stern-first, into the mud.

It was a pretty tangle, a job for wreckers, not boat-builders. There are two high tides every twenty-four hours, and at every high tide, night and day, for a week, there were two steam tugs pulling and hauling on the *Snark*. There she was, stuck, fallen between the ways and standing on her stern. Next, and while still in that predicament, we started to use the gears and castings made in the local foundry whereby power was conveyed from the engine to the windlass. It was the first time we ever tried to use that windlass. The castings had flaws; they shattered asunder, the gears ground together, and the windlass was out of commission. Following upon that, the seventy-horse-power engine went out of commission. This engine came from New York; so did its bed-plate; there was a flaw in the bed-plate; there were a lot of flaws in the bed-plate; and the seventy-horse-power engine broke away from its shattered foundations, reared up in the air, smashed all connections and fastenings, and fell over on its side. And the *Snark* continued to stick between the spread ways, and the two tugs continued to haul vainly upon her.

"Never mind," said Charmian, "think of what a stanch, strong boat she is."

"Yes," said I, "and of that beautiful bow."

So we took heart and went at it again. The ruined engine was lashed down on its rotten foundation; the smashed castings and cogs of the power transmission were taken down and stored away—all for the purpose of taking them to Honolulu where repairs and new castings could be made. Somewhere in the dim past the *Snark* had received on the outside one coat of white paint. The intention of the color was still evident, however, when one got it in the right light. The *Snark* had never received any paint on the inside. On the contrary, she was coated inches thick with the grease and tobacco-juice of the multitudinous mechanics who had toiled upon her. Never mind, we said; the grease and filth could be planed off, and later, when we fetched Honolulu, the *Snark* could be painted at the same time she was being rebuilt.

By main strength and sweat we dragged the *Snark* off from the wrecked ways and laid her alongside the Oakland City Wharf. The drays brought all the outfit from home, the books and blankets and personal luggage. Along with this, everything else came on board in a torrent of confusion—wood and coal, water and water-tanks, vegetables, provisions, oil, the life-boat and the launch, all our friends, all the friends of our friends and those who claimed to be their friends, to say nothing of some of the friends of the friends of the friends of our crew. Also there were reporters, and photographers, and strangers, and cranks, and finally, and over all, clouds of coal-dust from the wharf.

We were to sail Sunday at eleven, and Saturday afternoon had arrived. The crowd on the wharf and the coal-dust were thicker than ever. In one pocket I carried a check-book, a fountain pen, a dater, and a blotter; in another pocket I carried between one and two thousand dollars in paper money and gold. I was ready for the creditors, cash for the small ones and checks for the large ones, and was waiting only for Roscoe to arrive with the balances of the accounts of the hundred and fifteen firms who had delayed me so many months. And then——

And then the inconceivable and monstrous happened once more. Before Roscoe could arrive there arrived another man. He was a United States marshal. He tacked a notice on the *Snark's* brave mast so that all on the wharf could read that the *Snark* had been libelled for debt. The marshal left a little old man in charge of the *Snark*, and himself went away. I had no longer any control of the *Snark*, nor of her wonderful bow. The little old man was now her lord and master, and I learned that I was paying him three dollars a day for being lord and master. Also, I learned the name of the man who had libelled the *Snark*. It was Sellers; the debt was two hundred and thirty-two dollars; and the deed was no more than was to be expected from the possessor of such a name. Sellers! Ye gods! Sellers!

But who under the sun was Sellers? I looked in my check-book and saw that two weeks before I had made him out a check for five hundred dollars. Other check-books showed me that during the many months of the building of the *Snark* I had paid him several thousand dollars. Then why in the name of common decency hadn't he tried to collect his miserable little balance instead of libelling the *Snark?* I thrust my hands into my pockets, and in one pocket encountered the check-book and the dater and the pen, and in the other pocket the gold money and the paper money. There was the wherewithal to settle his pitiful account a few score of times and over—why hadn't he given me a chance? There was no explanation; it was merely the inconceivable and monstrous.

To make the matter worse, the *Snark* had been libelled late Saturday afternoon; and though I sent lawyers and agents all over Oakland and San Francisco, neither United States judge, nor United States marshal, nor Mr. Sellers, nor Mr. Sellers' attorney, nor anybody could be found. They were all out of town for the week end. And so the *Snark* did not sail Sunday morning at eleven. The little old man was still in charge, and he said no. And Charmian and I walked out on an opposite wharf and took consolation in the *Snark's* wonderful bow and thought of all the gales and typhoons it would proudly punch.

"A bourgeois trick," I said to Charmian, speaking of Mr. Sellers and his libel; "a petty trader's panic. But never mind; our troubles will cease when once we are away from this and out on the wide ocean."

And in the end we sailed away, on Tuesday morning, April 23, 1907. We started rather lame, I confess. We had to hoist anchor by hand, because the power transmission was a wreck. Also, what remained of our seventy-horse-power engine was lashed down for ballast on the bottom of the *Snark*. But what of such things? They could be fixed in Honolulu, and in the meantime think of the magnificent rest of the boat! It is true, the engine in the launch wouldn't run, and the life-boat leaked like a sieve; but then they weren't the *Snark;* they were mere appurtenances. The things that counted were the water-tight bulkheads, the solid planking without butts, the bath-room devices—they were the *Snark*. And then there was, greatest of all, that noble, wind-punching bow.

We sailed out through the Golden Gate and set our course south toward that part of the Pacific where we could hope to pick up with the northeast trades. And right away things began to happen. I had calculated that youth was the stuff for a voyage like that of the *Snark*, and I had taken three youths—the engineer, the cook, and the cabin-boy. My calculation was only two-thirds off; I had forgotten to calculate on seasick youth, and I had two of them, the cook and the cabin-boy. They immediately took to their bunks, and that was the end of their usefulness for a week to come. It will be understood, from the foregoing, that we did not have the hot meals we might have had, nor were things kept clean and orderly down below. But it did not matter very much anyway, for we quickly discovered that our box of oranges had at some time been frozen; that our box of apples was mushy and spoiling; that the crate of cabbages, spoiled before it was ever delivered to us, had to go overboard instanter; that kerosene had been spilled on the carrots, and that the turnips were woody and the beets rotten, while the kindling was deadwood that wouldn't burn, and the coal, delivered in rotten potato-sacks, had spilled all over the deck and was washing through the scuppers.

But what did it matter? Such things were mere accessories. There was the boat—she was all right, wasn't she? I strolled along the deck and in one minute counted fourteen butts in the beautiful planking ordered specially from Puget Sound in order that there should be no butts in it. Also, that deck leaked, and it leaked badly. It drowned Roscoe out of his bunk and ruined the tools in the engine-room, to say nothing of the provisions it ruined in the galley. Also, the sides of the *Snark* leaked, and the bottom leaked, and we had to pump her every day to keep her afloat. The floor of the galley is a couple of feet above the inside bottom of the *Snark*; and yet I have stood on the floor of the galley, trying to snatch a cold bite, and been wet to the knees by the water churning around inside four hours after the last pumping.

Then those magnificent water-tight compartments that cost so much time and money—well, they weren't water-tight after all. The water moved free as the air from one compartment to another; furthermore, a strong smell of gasolene from the after compartment leads me to suspect that some one or more of the half-dozen tanks there stored have sprung a leak. The tanks leak, and they are not hermetically sealed in their compartment. Then there was the bathroom with its pumps and levers and sea-valves—it went out of commission inside the first twenty hours. Powerful iron levers broke off short in one's hand when one tried to pump with them. The bathroom was the swiftest wreck of any portion of the *Snark*.

And the iron-work on the *Snark*, no matter what its source, proved to be mush. For instance, the bed-plate of the engine came from New York, and it was mush; so were the castings and gears for the windlass that came from San Francisco. And finally, there was the wrought iron used in the rigging, that carried away in all directions when the first strains were put upon it. Wrought iron, mind you, and it snapped like macaroni.

A gooseneck on the gaff of the mainsail broke short off. We replaced it with the gooseneck from the gaff of the storm trysail, and the second gooseneck broke short off inside fifteen minutes of use, and, mind you, it had been taken from the gaff of the storm trysail, upon which we would have depended in time of storm. At the present moment the *Snark* trails her mainsail like a broken wing, the gooseneck being replaced by a rough lashing. We'll see if we can get honest iron in Honolulu.

Man had betrayed us and sent us to sea in a sieve, but the Lord must have loved us, for we had calm weather in which to learn that we must pump every day in order to keep afloat, and that more trust could be placed in a wooden toothpick than in the most massive piece of iron to be found aboard. As the stanchness and the strength of the *Snark* went glimmering, Charmian and I pinned our faith more and more to the *Snark's* wonderful bow. There was nothing else left to pin to. It was all inconceivable and monstrous, we knew, but that bow, at least, was rational. And then, one evening, we started to heave to.

How shall I describe it? First of all, for the benefit of the tyro, let me explain that heaving to is that sea manœuvre which, by means of short and balanced canvas, compels a vessel to ride bow-on to wind and sea. When the wind is too strong, or the sea is too high, a vessel of the size of the *Snark* can heave to with ease, whereupon there is no more work to do on deck. Nobody needs to steer. The lookout is superfluous. All hands can go below and sleep or play whist.

Well, it was blowing half of a small summer gale, when I told Roscoe we'd heave to. Night was coming on. I had been steering nearly all day, and all hands on deck (Roscoe and Bert and Charmian) were tired, while all hands below were seasick. It happened that we had already put two reefs in the big mainsail. The flying-jib and the jib were taken in, and a reef put in the forestaysail. The mizzen was also taken in. About this time the flying jib-boom buried itself in a sea and broke short off. I started to put the wheel down in order to heave to. The *Snark* at the moment was rolling in the trough. She continued rolling in the trough. I put the spokes down harder and harder. She never budged from the trough. (The trough, gentle reader, is the most dangerous position of all in which to lay a vessel.) I put the wheel hard down, and still the *Snark* rolled in the trough. Eight points was the nearest I could get her to the wind. I had Roscoe and Bert come in on the main-sheet. The *Snark* rolled on in the trough, now putting her rail under on one side and now under on the other side.

Again the inconceivable and monstrous was showing its grizzly head. It was grotesque, impossible. I refused to believe it. Under double-reefed mainsail and single-reefed staysail the *Snark* refused to heave to. We flattened the mainsail down. It did not alter the *Snark's* course a tenth of a degree. We slacked the mainsail off with no more result. We set a storm trysail on the mizzen, and took in the mainsail. No change. The *Snark* rolled on in the trough. That beautiful bow of hers refused to come up and face the wind.

Next we took in the reefed staysail. Thus, the only bit of canvas left on her was the storm trysail on the mizzen. If anything would bring her bow up to the wind that would. Maybe you won't believe me when I say it failed, but I do say it failed. And I say it failed because I saw it fail, and not because I believe it failed. I don't believe it did fail. It is unbelievable, and I am not telling you what I believe; I am telling you what I saw.

Now, gentle reader, what would you do if you were on a small boat, rolling in the trough of the sea, a trysail on that small boat's stern that was unable to swing the bow up into the wind? Get out the sea anchor. It's just what we did. We had a patent one, made to order and warranted not to dive. Imagine a hoop of steel that serves to keep open the mouth of a large, conical, canvas bag, and you have a sea-anchor. Well, we made a line fast to the sea-anchor and to the bow of the *Snark*, and then dropped the sea-anchor overboard. It promptly dived. We had a tripping line on it, so we tripped the sea-anchor and hauled it in. We attached a big timber as a float, and dropped the sea-anchor over again. This time it floated. The line to the bow grew taut. The trysail on the mizzen tended to swing the bow into the wind, but, in spite of this tendency, the *Snark* calmly took that sea-anchor in her teeth, and went on ahead, dragging it after her, still in the trough of the sea. And there you are. We even took in the trysail, hoisted the full mizzen in its place, and hauled the full mizzen down flat, and the *Snark* wallowed in the trough and dragged the sea-anchor behind her. Don't believe me. I don't believe it myself. I'm merely telling you what I saw.

Now I leave it to you. Who ever heard of a sailing-boat that wouldn't heave to?—that wouldn't heave to with a sea-anchor to help it? Out of my brief experience with boats I know I never did. And I stood on deck and looked on the naked face of the inconceivable and monstrous—the *Snark* that wouldn't heave to. A stormy night with broken moonlight had come on. There was a splash of wet in the air, and up to windward there was a promise of rain-squalls; and then there was the trough of the sea, cold and cruel in the moonlight, in which the *Snark* complacently rolled. And then we took in the sea-anchor and the mizzen, hoisted the reefed staysail, ran the *Snark* off before it, and went below—not to the hot meal that should have awaited us, but to skate across the slush and slime on the cabin floor, where cook and cabin-boy lay like dead men in their bunks, and to lie down in our own bunks, with our clothes on ready for a call, and to listen to the bilge-water spouting knee-high on the galley floor.

In the Bohemian Club of San Francisco there are some crack sailors. I know, because I heard them pass judgment on the *Snark* during the process of her building. They found only one vital thing the matter with her, and on this they were all agreed, namely, that she could not run. She was all right in every particular, they said, except that I'd never be able to run her before it in a stiff wind and sea. "Her lines," they explained enigmatically, "it is the fault of her lines. She simply cannot be made to run, that is all." Well, I wish I'd only had those crack sailors of the Bohemian Club on board the *Snark* the other night for them to see for themselves their one, vital, unanimous judgment absolutely reversed. Run? It is the one thing the *Snark* does to perfection. Run? She ran with a sea-anchor fast for'ard and a full mizzen flattened down aft. Run? At the present moment, as I write this, we are bowling along before it, at a six-knot clip, in the northeast trades. Quite a tidy bit of sea is running. There is nobody at the wheel, the wheel is not even lashed and is set over a half-spoke weather helm. To be precise, the wind is northeast; the *Snark's* mizzen is furled, her mainsail is over to starboard, her head-sheets are hauled flat; and the *Snark's* course is south-southwest. And yet there are men who have sailed the seas for forty years and who hold that no boat can run before it without being steered. They'll call me a liar when they read this; it's what they called Captain Slocum when he said the same of his *Spray*.

As regards the future of the *Snark* I'm all at sea. I don't know. If I had the money or the credit, I'd build another *Snark* that *would* heave to. But I am at the end of my resources. I've got to put up with the present *Snark* or quit—and I can't quit. So I guess I'll have to try to get along with heaving the *Snark* to stern-first. I am waiting for the next gale to see how it will work. I think it can be done. It all depends on how her stern takes the seas. And who knows but that some wild morning on the China Sea, some gray-beard skipper will stare, rub his incredulous eyes and stare again, at the spectacle of a weird, small craft, very much like the *Snark*, hove to stern-first and riding out the gale?

P.S. On my return to California after the voyage, I learned that the *Snark* was forty-three feet on the water line instead of forty-five. This was due to the fact that the builder was not on speaking terms with the tape-line or two-foot rule.

From *The Cruise of the Snark*

A PACIFIC TRAVERSE

Sandwich Islands to Tahiti.–There is great difficulty in making this passage across the trades. The whalers and all others speak with great doubt of fetching Tahiti from the Sandwich Islands. Capt. Bruce says that a vessel should keep to the northward until she gets a start of wind before bearing for her destination. In his passage between them in November, 1837, he had no variables near the line in coming south, and never could make easting on either tack, though he endeavored by every means to do so.

So says the sailing directions for the South Pacific Ocean; and that is all it says. There is not a word more to help the weary voyager in making this long traverse —nor is there any word at all concerning the passage from Hawaii to the Marquesas, which lie some eight hundred miles to the northeast of Tahiti and which are the more difficult to reach by just that much. The reason for the lack of directions is, I imagine, that no voyager is supposed to make himself weary by attempting so impossible a traverse. But the impossible did not deter the *Snark*,—principally because of the fact that we did not read that particular little paragraph in the sailing directions until after we had started. We sailed from Hilo, Hawaii, on October 7, and arrived at Nuka-hiva, in the Marquesas, on December 6. The distance was two thousand miles as the crow flies, while we actually travelled at least four thousand miles to accomplish it, thus proving for once and forever that the shortest distance between two points is not always a straight line. Had we headed directly for the Marquesas, we might have travelled five or six thousand miles.

Upon one thing we were resolved: we would not cross the Line west of 130° west longitude. For here was the problem. To cross the Line to the west of that point, if the southeast trades were well around to the southeast, would throw us so far to leeward of the Marquesas that a head-beat would be maddeningly impossible. Also, we had to remember the equatorial current, which moves west at a rate of anywhere from twelve to seventy-five miles a day. A pretty pickle, indeed, to be to leeward of our destination with such a current in our teeth. No; not a minute, nor a second, west of 130° west longitude would we cross the Line. But since the southeast trades were to be expected five or six degrees north of the Line (which, if they were well around to the southeast or south-southeast, would necessitate our sliding off toward south-southwest), we should have to hold to the eastward, north of the Line, and north of the southeast trades, until we gained at least 128° west longitude.

I have forgotten to mention that the seventy-horse-power gasolene engine, as usual, was not working, and that we could depend upon wind alone. Neither was the launch engine working. And while I am about it, I may as well confess that the five-horse-power, which ran the lights, fans, and pumps, was also on the sick-list. A striking title for a book haunts me, waking and sleeping. I should like to write that book some day and to call it "Around the World with Three Gasolene Engines and a Wife." But I am afraid I shall not write it, for fear of hurting the feelings of some of the young gentlemen of San Francisco, Honolulu, and Hilo, who learned their trades at the expense of the *Snark's* engines.

It looked easy on paper. Here was Hilo and there was our objective, 128° west longitude. With the northeast trade blowing we could travel a straight line between the two points, and even slack our sheets off a goodly bit. But one of the chief troubles with the trades is that one never knows just where he will pick them up and just in what direction they will be blowing. We picked up the northeast trade right outside of Hilo harbor, but the miserable breeze was away around into the east. Then there was the north equatorial current setting westward like a mighty river. Furthermore, a small boat, by the wind and bucking into a big head-sea, does not work to advantage. She jogs up and down and gets nowhere. Her sails are full and straining, every little while she presses her lee-rail under, she flounders, and bumps, and splashes, and that is all. Whenever she begins to gather way, she runs ker-chug into a big mountain of water and is brought to a standstill. So, with the *Snark,* the resultant of her smallness, of the trade around into the east, and of the strong equatorial current, was a long sag south. Oh, she did not go quite south. But the easting she made was distressing. On October 11, she made forty miles easting; October 12, fifteen miles; October 13, no easting; October 14, thirty miles; October 15, twenty-three miles; October 16, eleven miles; and on October 17, she actually went to the westward four miles. Thus, in a week, she made one hundred and fifteen miles easting, which was equivalent to sixteen miles a day. But between the longitude of Hilo and 128° west longitude is a difference of twenty-seven degrees, or, roughly, sixteen hundred miles. At sixteen miles a day, one hundred days would be required to accomplish this distance. And even then, our objective, 128° west longitude, was five degrees north of the Line, while Nuka-hiva, in the Marquesas, lay nine degrees south of the Line and twelve degrees to the west!

There remained only one thing to do—to work south out of the trade and into the variables. It is true that Captain Bruce found no variables on his traverse, and that he "never could make easting on either tack." It was the variables or nothing with us, and we prayed for better luck than he had had. The variables constitute the belt of ocean lying between the trades and the doldrums, and are conjectured to be the draughts of heated air which rise in the doldrums, flow high in the air counter to the trades, and gradually sink down till they fan the surface of the ocean where they are found. And they are found . . . where they are found; for they are wedged between the trades and the doldrums, which same shift their territory from day to day and month to month.

We found the variables in 11° north latitude, and 11° north latitude we hugged jealously. To the south lay the doldrums. To the north lay the northeast trade that refused to blow from the northeast. The days came and went, and always they found the *Snark* somewhere near the eleventh parallel. The variables were truly variable. A light head-wind would die away and leave us rolling in a calm for forty-eight hours. Then a light head-wind would spring up, blow for three hours, and leave us rolling in another calm for forty-eight hours. Then—hurrah!—the wind would come out of the west, fresh, beautifully fresh, and send the *Snark* along, wing and wing, her wake bubbling, the log-line straight astern. At the end of half an hour, while we were preparing to set the spinnaker, with a few sickly gasps the wind would die away. And so it went. We wagered optimistically on every favorable fan of air that lasted over five minutes; but it never did any good. The fans faded out just the same.

But there were exceptions. In the variables, if you wait long enough, something is bound to happen, and we were so plentifully stocked with food and water that we could afford to wait. On October 26, we actually made one hundred and three miles of easting, and we talked about it for days afterward. Once we caught a moderate gale from the south, which blew itself out in eight hours, but it helped us to seventy-one miles of easting in that particular twenty-four hours. And then, just as it was expiring, the wind came straight out from the north (the directly opposite quarter), and fanned us along over another degree of easting.

In years and years no sailing vessel has attempted this traverse, and we found ourselves in the midst of one of the loneliest of the Pacific solitudes. In the sixty days we were crossing it we sighted no sail, lifted no steamer's smoke above the horizon. A disabled vessel could drift in this deserted expanse for a dozen generations, and there would be no rescue. The only chance of rescue would be from a vessel like the *Snark*, and the *Snark* happened to be there principally because of the fact that the traverse had been begun before the particular paragraph in the sailing directions had been read. Standing upright on deck, a straight line drawn from the eye to the horizon would measure three miles and a half. Thus, seven miles was the diameter of the circle of the sea in which we had our centre. Since we remained always in the centre, and since we constantly were moving in some direction, we looked upon many circles. But all circles looked alike. No tufted islets, gray headlands, nor glistening patches of white canvas ever marred the symmetry of that unbroken curve. Clouds came and went, rising up over the rim of the circle, flowing across the space of it, and spilling away and down across the opposite rim.

The world faded as the procession of the weeks marched by. The world faded until at last there ceased to be any world except the little world of the *Snark*, freighted with her seven souls and floating on the expanse of the waters. Our memories of the world, the great world, became like dreams of former lives we had lived somewhere before we came to be born on the *Snark*. After we had been out of fresh vegetables for some time, we mentioned such things in much the same way I have heard my father mention the vanished apples of his boyhood. Man is a creature of habit, and we on the *Snark* had got the habit of the *Snark*. Everything about her and aboard her was as a matter of course, and anything different would have been an irritation and an offence.

There was no way by which the great world could intrude. Our bell rang the hours, but no caller ever rang it. There were no guests to dinner, no telegrams, no insistent telephone jangles invading our privacy. We had no engagements to keep, no trains to catch, and there were no morning newspapers over which to waste time in learning what was happening to our fifteen hundred million other fellow-creatures.

But it was not dull. The affairs of our little world had to be regulated, and, unlike the great world, our world had to be steered in its journey through space. Also, there were cosmic disturbances to be encountered and baffled, such as do not afflict the big earth in its frictionless orbit through the windless void. And we never knew, from moment to moment, what was going to happen next. There was spice and variety enough and to spare. Thus, at four in the morning, I relieve Hermann at the wheel.

"East-northeast," he gives me the course. "She's eight points off, but she ain't steering."

Small wonder. The vessel does not exist that can be steered in so absolute a calm.

"I had a breeze a little while ago—maybe it will come back again," Hermann says hopefully, ere he starts forward to the cabin and his bunk.

The mizzen is in and fast furled. In the night, what of the roll and the absence of wind, it had made life too hideous to be permitted to go on rasping at the mast, smashing at the tackles, and buffeting the empty air into hollow outbursts of sound. But the big mainsail is still on, and the staysail, jib, and flying-jib are snapping and slashing at their sheets with every roll. Every star is out. Just for luck I put the wheel hard over in the opposite direction to which it had been left by Hermann, and I lean back and gaze up at the stars. There is nothing else for me to do. There is nothing to be done with a sailing vessel rolling in a stark calm.

Then I feel a fan on my cheek, faint, so faint, that I can just sense it ere it is gone. But another comes, and another, until a real and just perceptible breeze is blowing. How the *Snark's* sails manage to feel it is beyond me, but feel it they do, as she does as well, for the compass card begins slowly to revolve in the binnacle. In reality, it is not revolving at all. It is held by terrestrial magnetism in one place, and it is the *Snark* that is revolving, pivoted upon that delicate cardboard device that floats in a closed vessel of alcohol.

So the *Snark* comes back on her course. The breath increases to a tiny puff. The *Snark* feels the weight of it and actually heels over a trifle. There is flying scud overhead, and I notice the stars being blotted out. Walls of darkness close in upon me, so that, when the last star is gone, the darkness is so near that it seems I can reach out and touch it on every side. When I lean toward it, I can feel it loom against my face. Puff follows puff, and I am glad the mizzen is furled. Phew! that was a stiff one! The *Snark* goes over and down until her lee-rail is buried and the whole Pacific Ocean is pouring in. Four or five of these gusts make me wish that the jib and flying-jib were in. The sea is picking up, the gusts are growing stronger and more frequent, and there is a splatter of wet in the air. There is no use in attempting to gaze to windward. The wall of blackness is within arm's length. Yet I cannot help attempting to see and gauge the blows that are being struck at the *Snark*. There is something ominous and menacing up there to windward, and I have a feeling that if I look long enough and strong enough, I shall divine it. Futile feeling. Between two gusts I leave the wheel and run forward to the cabin companionway, where I light matches and consult the barometer. "29-90" it reads. That sensitive instrument refuses to take notice of the disturbance which is humming with a deep, throaty voice in the rigging. I get back to the wheel just in time to meet another gust, the strongest yet. Well, anyway, the wind is abeam and the *Snark* is on her course, eating up easting. That at least is well.

The jib and flying-jib bother me, and I wish they were in. She would make easier weather of it, and less risky weather likewise. The wind snorts, and stray raindrops pelt like birdshot. I shall certainly have to call all hands, I conclude; then conclude the next instant to hang on a little longer. Maybe this is the end of it, and I shall have called them for nothing. It is better to let them sleep. I hold the

Snark down to her task, and from out of the darkness, at right angles, comes a deluge of rain accompanied by shrieking wind. Then everything eases except the blackness, and I rejoice in that I have not called the men.

No sooner does the wind ease than the sea picks up. The combers are breaking now, and the boat is tossing like a cork. Then out of the blackness the gusts come harder and faster than before. If only I knew what was up there to windward in the blackness! The *Snark* is making heavy weather of it, and her lee-rail is buried oftener than not. More shrieks and snorts of wind. Now, if ever, is the time to call the men. I *will* call them, I resolve. Then there is a burst of rain, a slackening of the wind, and I do not call. But it is rather lonely, there at the wheel, steering a little world through howling blackness. It is quite a responsibility to be all alone on the surface of a little world in time of stress, doing the thinking for its sleeping inhabitants. I recoil from the responsibility as more gusts begin to strike and as a sea licks along the weather rail and splashes over into the cockpit. The salt water seems strangely warm to my body and is shot through with ghostly nodules of phosphorescent light. I shall surely call all hands to shorten sail. Why should they sleep? I am a fool to have any compunctions in the matter. My intellect is arrayed against my heart. It was my heart that said, "Let them sleep." Yes, but it was my intellect that backed up my heart in that judgment. Let my intellect then reverse the judgment; and, while I am speculating as to what particular entity issued that command to my intellect, the gusts die away. Solicitude for mere bodily comfort has no place in practical seamanship, I conclude sagely; but study the feel of the next series of gusts and do not call the men. After all, it *is* my intellect, behind everything, procrastinating, measuring its knowledge of what the *Snark* can endure against the blows being struck at her, and waiting the call of all hands against the striking of still severer blows.

Daylight, gray and violent, steals through the cloud-pall and shows a foaming sea that flattens under the weight of recurrent and increasing squalls. Then comes the rain, filling the windy valleys of the sea with milky smoke and further flattening the waves, which but wait for the easement of wind and rain to leap more wildly than before. Come the men on deck, their sleep out, and among them Hermann, his face on the broad grin in appreciation of the breeze of wind I have picked up. I turn the wheel over to Warren and start to go below, pausing on the way to rescue the galley stovepipe which has gone adrift. I am barefooted, and my toes have had an excellent education in the art of clinging; but, as the rail buries itself in a green sea, I suddenly sit down on the streaming deck. Hermann good-naturedly elects to question my selection of such a spot. Then comes the next roll, and he sits down, suddenly, and without premeditation. The *Snark* heels over and down, the rail takes it green, and Hermann and I, clutching the precious stovepipe, are swept down into the leescuppers. After that I finish my journey below, and while changing my clothes grin with satisfaction—the *Snark* is making easting.

No, it is not all monotony. When we had worried along our easting to 126° west longitude, we left the variables and headed south through the doldrums, where was much calm weather and where, taking advantage of every fan of air, we were often glad to make a score of miles in as many hours. And yet, on such a day, we might pass through a dozen squalls and be surrounded by dozens more. And every squall was to be regarded as a bludgeon capable of crushing the *Snark*. We were struck sometimes by the centers and sometimes by the sides of these squalls, and we never knew just where or how we were to be hit. The squall that rose up, covering

ABOVE: Learning to navigate. "So the *Snark* started on her long voyage without a navigator. . . . One whole afternoon I sat in the cockpit, steering with one hand and studying logarithms with the other. Two afternoons . . . I studied the general theory of navigation. . . . Then I took the sextant, worked out the index error, and shot the sun. . . . The mystery was mystery no longer."

RIGHT: "I doubt if ever a boat was blessed with a more beautiful and at the same time a more capable bow. It was made to punch storms."

ABOVE: ". . . on board the *Minota* for a recruiting cruise along the savage coast of Malaita."
BELOW: The *Snark* leaving Honolulu, August 15, 1907.

Tahiti, Papeete, 1907.

ABOVE: "The anchor rumbled down to the blatting of wild goats on the cliffs, and the air we breathed was heavy with the perfume of flowers."
BELOW: Martin Johnson in Tahiti. The cruise of the *Snark* was to be the first of many adventures for this famous explorer.

Charmian at Langa Langa. "Here, surrounded by hundreds of unblushing naked men, women, and children, we wandered about and saw the sights."

ABOVE: The compound at Penduffryn, a copra plantation on Guadalcanal.
BELOW: A native village in the Solomon Islands.

ABOVE: In the bush, Ambrym, New Hebrides.
BELOW: Recruiting native labor on the Malligolo Coast.

". . . sunsets that bathed the purple sea in rivers of rose-colored light, flowing from a sun whose diverging, heaven-climbing rays were of the purest blue."

half the heavens, and swept down upon us, as likely as not split into two squalls which passed us harmlessly on either side; while the tiny, innocent-looking squall that appeared to carry no more than a hogshead of water and a pound of wind, would abruptly assume cyclopean proportions, deluging us with rain and overwhelming us with wind. Then there were treacherous squalls that went boldly astern and sneaked back upon us from a mile to leeward. Again, two squalls would tear along, one on each side of us, and we would get a fillip from each of them. Now a gale certainly grows tiresome after a few hours, but squalls never. The thousandth squall in one's experience is as interesting as the first one, and perhaps a bit more so. It is the tyro who has no apprehension of them. The man of a thousand squalls respects a squall. He knows what they are.

It was in the doldrums that our most exciting event occurred. On November 20, we discovered that through an accident we had lost over one-half of the supply of fresh water that remained to us. Since we were at that time forty-three days out from Hilo, our supply of fresh water was not large. To lose over half of it was a catastrophe. On close allowance, the remnant of water we possessed would last twenty days. But we were in the doldrums; there was no telling where the southeast trades were, nor where we would pick them up.

The handcuffs were promptly put upon the pump, and once a day the water was portioned out. Each of us received a quart for personal use, and eight quarts were given to the cook. Enters now the psychology of the situation. No sooner had the discovery of the water shortage been made than I, for one, was afflicted with a burning thirst. It seemed to me that I had never been so thirsty in my life. My little quart of water I could easily have drunk in one draught, and to refrain from doing so required a severe exertion of will. Nor was I alone in this. All of us talked water, thought water, and dreamed water when we slept. We examined the charts for possible islands to which to run in extremity, but there were no such islands. The Marquesas were the nearest, and they were the other side of the Line, and of the doldrums, too, which made it even worse. We were in 3° north latitude, while the Marquesas were in 9° south latitude—a difference of over a thousand miles. Furthermore, the Marquesas lay some fourteen degrees to the west of our longitude. A pretty pickle for a handful of creatures sweltering on the ocean in the heat of tropic calms.

We rigged lines on either side between the main and mizzen riggings. To these we laced the big deck awning, hoisting it up aft with a sailing pennant so that any rain it might collect would run forward where it could be caught. Here and there squalls passed across the circle of the sea. All day we watched them, now to port or starboard, and again ahead or astern. But never one came near enough to wet us. In the afternoon a big one bore down upon us. It spread out across the ocean as it approached, and we could see it emptying countless thousands of gallons into the salt sea. Extra attention was paid to the awning, and then we waited. Warren, Martin, and Hermann made a vivid picture. Grouped together, holding on to the rigging, swaying to the roll, they were gazing intently at the squall. Strain, anxiety, and yearning were in every posture of their bodies. Beside them was the dry and empty awning. But they seemed to grow limp and to droop as the squall broke in half, one part passing on ahead, the other drawing astern and going to leeward.

But that night came rain. Martin, whose psychological thirst had compelled him to drink his quart of water early, got his mouth down to the lip of the awning and drank the deepest draught I ever have seen drunk. The precious water came down in bucketfuls and tubfuls, and in two hours we caught and stored away in the tanks one hundred and twenty gallons. Strange to say, in all the rest of our voyage to the Marquesas not another drop of rain fell on board. If that squall had missed us, the handcuffs would have remained on the pump, and we would have busied ourselves with utilizing our surplus gasolene for distillation purposes.

Then there was the fishing. One did not have to go in search of it, for it was there at the rail. A three-inch steel hook, on the end of a stout line, with a piece of white rag for bait, was all that was necessary to catch bonitas weighing from ten to twenty-five pounds. Bonitas feed on flying-fish, wherefore they are unaccustomed to nibbling at the hook. They strike as gamely as the gamest fish in the sea, and their first run is something that no man who has ever caught them will forget. Also, bonitas are the veriest cannibals. The instant one is hooked he is attacked by his fellows. Often and often we hauled them on board with fresh, clean-bitten holes in them the size of teacups.

One school of bonitas, numbering many thousands, stayed with us day and night for more than three weeks. Aided by the *Snark*, it was great hunting; for they cut a swath of destruction through the ocean half a mile wide and fifteen hundred miles in length. They ranged along abreast of the *Snark* on either side, pouncing upon the flying-fish her forefoot scared up. Since they were continually pursuing astern the flying-fish that survived for several flights, they were always overtaking the *Snark*, and at any time one could glance astern and on the front of a breaking wave see scores of their silvery forms coasting down just under the surface. When they had eaten their fill, it was their delight to get in the shadows of the boat, or of her sails, and a hundred or so were always to be seen lazily sliding along and keeping cool.

But the poor flying-fish! Pursued and eaten alive by the bonitas and dolphins, they sought flight in the air, where the swooping seabirds drove them back into the water. Under heaven there was no refuge for them. Flying-fish do not play when they essay the air. It is a life-and-death affair with them. A thousand times a day we could lift our eyes and see the tragedy played out. The swift, broken circling of a guny might attract one's attention. A glance beneath shows the back of a dolphin breaking the surface in a wild rush. Just in front of its nose a shimmering palpitant streak of silver shoots from the water into the air—a delicate, organic mechanism of flight, endowed with sensation, power of direction, and love of life. The guny swoops for it and misses, and the flying-fish, gaining its altitude by rising, kite-like, against the wind, turns in a half-circle and skims off to leeward, gliding on the bosom of the wind. Beneath it, the wake of the dolphin shows in churning foam. So he follows, gazing upward with large eyes at the flashing breakfast that navigates an element other than his own. He cannot rise to so lofty occasion, but he is a thorough-going empiricist, and he knows, sooner or later, if not gobbled up by the guny, that the flying-fish must return to the water. And then—breakfast. We used to pity the poor winged fish. It was sad to see such sordid and bloody slaughter. And then, in the night watches, when a forlorn little flying-fish struck the mainsail and fell gasping and splattering on the deck, we would rush for it just as eagerly, just as greedily, just as voraciously, as the dolphins and bonitas. For know that flying-fish are most toothsome for breakfast. It is always a wonder to me that such dainty meat does not build dainty tissue in the bodies of the devourers. Perhaps the dolphins and bonitas are coarser-fibred because of the high speed at which they drive their bodies in order to catch their prey. But then again, the flying-fish drive their bodies at high speed, too.

Sharks we caught occasionally, on large hooks, with chain-swivels, bent on a length of small rope. And sharks meant pilot-fish, and remoras, and various sorts of parasitic creatures. Regular man-eaters some of the sharks proved, tiger-eyed and with twelve rows of teeth, razor-sharp. By the way, we of the *Snark* are agreed that we have eaten many fish that will not compare with baked shark smothered in tomato dressing. In the calms we occasionally caught a fish called "haké" by the Japanese cook. And once, on a spoon-hook trolling a hundred yards astern, we caught a snakelike fish, over three feet in length and not more than three inches in diameter, with four fangs in his jaw. He proved the most delicious fish—delicious in meat and flavor—that we have ever eaten on board.

The most welcome addition to our larder was a green sea-turtle, weighing a full hundred pounds and appearing on the table most appetizingly in steaks, soups, and stews, and finally in a wonderful curry which tempted all hands into eating more rice than was good for them. The turtle was sighted to windward, calmly sleeping on the surface in the midst of a huge school of curious dolphins. It was a deep-sea turtle of a surety, for the nearest land was a thousand miles away. We put the *Snark* about and went back for him, Hermann driving the granes into his head and neck. When hauled aboard, numerous remora were clinging to his shell, and out of the hollows at the roots of his flippers crawled several large crabs. It did not take the crew of the *Snark* longer than the next meal to reach the unanimous conclusion that it would willingly put the *Snark* about any time for a turtle.

But it is the dolphin that is the king of deep-sea fishes. Never is his color twice quite the same. Swimming in the sea, an ethereal creature of palest azure, he displays in that one guise a miracle of color. But it is nothing compared with the displays of which he is capable. At one time he will appear green—pale green, deep green, phosphorescent green; at another time blue—deep blue, electric blue, all the spectrum of blue. Catch him on a hook, and he turns to gold, yellow gold, all gold. Haul him on deck, and he excels the spectrum, passing through inconceivable shades of blues, greens, and yellows, and then, suddenly, turning a ghostly white, in the midst of which are bright blue spots, and you suddenly discover that he is speckled like a trout. Then back from white he goes, through all the range of colors, finally turning to a mother-of-pearl.

For those who are devoted to fishing, I can recommend no finer sport than catching dolphin. Of course, it must be done on a thin line with reel and pole. A No. 7 O'Shaughnessy tarpon hook is just the thing, baited with an entire flying-fish. Like the bonita, the dolphin's fare consists of flying-fish, and he strikes like lightning at the bait. The first warning is when the reel screeches and you see the line smoking out at right angles to the boat. Before you have time to entertain anxiety concerning the length of your line, the fish rises into the air in a succession of leaps. Since he is quite certain to be four feet long or over, the sport of landing so gamey a fish can be realized. When hooked, he invariably turns golden. The idea of the series of leaps is to rid himself of the hook, and the man who has made the strike must be of iron or decadent if his heart does not beat with an extra flutter when he beholds such gorgeous fish, glittering in golden mail and shaking itself like a stallion in each mid-air leap. 'Ware slack! If you don't, on one of those leaps the hook will be flung out and twenty feet away. No slack, and away he will go on another run, culminating in another series of leaps. About this time one begins to worry over the line, and to wish that he had had nine hundred feet on the reel originally instead of six hundred. With careful playing the line can be saved, and after an hour of keen excitement the fish can be brought to gaff. One such dolphin I landed on the *Snark* measured four feet and seven inches.

Hermann caught dolphins more prosaically. A hand-line and a chunk of shark-meat was all he needed. His hand-line was very thick, but on more than one occasion it parted and lost the fish. One day a dolphin got away with a lure of Hermann's manufacture, to which were lashed four O'Shaughnessy hooks. Within an hour the same dolphin was landed with the rod, and on dissecting him the four hooks were recovered. The dolphins, which remained with us over a month, deserted us north of the line, and not one was seen during the remainder of the traverse.

So the days passed. There was so much to be done that time never dragged. Had there been little to do, time could not have dragged with such wonderful seascapes and cloudscapes—dawns that were like burning imperial cities under rainbows that arched nearly to the zenith; sunsets that bathed the purple sea in rivers of rose-colored light, flowing from a sun whose diverging, heaven-climbing rays were of the purest blue. Overside, in the heat of the day, the sea was an azure satiny fabric, in the depths of which the sunshine focussed in funnels of light. Astern, deep down, when there was a breeze, bubbled a procession of milky-turquoise ghosts—the foam flung down by the hull of the *Snark* each time she floundered against a sea. At night the wake was phosphorescent fire, where the medusa slime resented our passing bulk, while far down could be observed the unceasing flight of comets, with long, undulating, nebulous tails—caused by the passage of the bonitas through the resentful medusa slime. And now and again, from out of the darkness on either hand, just under the surface, larger phosphorescent organisms flashed up like electric lights, marking collisions with the careless bonitas skurrying ahead to the good hunting just beyond our bowsprit.

We made our easting, worked down through the doldrums, and caught a fresh breeze out of south-by-west. Hauled up by the wind, on such a slant, we would fetch past the Marquesas far away to the westward. But the next day, on Tuesday, November 26, in the thick of a heavy squall, the wind shifted suddenly to the southeast. It was the trade at last. There were no more squalls, naught but fine weather, a fair wind, and a whirling log, with sheets slacked off and with spinnaker and mainsail swaying and bellying on either side. The trade backed more and more, until it blew out of the northeast, while we steered a steady course to the southwest. Ten days of this, and on the morning of December 6, at five o'clock, we sighted land "just where it ought to have been," dead ahead. We passed to leeward of Ua-huka, skirted the southern edge of Nuka-hiva, and that night, in driving squalls and inky darkness, fought our way in to an anchorage in the narrow bay of Taiohae. The anchor rumbled down to the blatting of wild goats on the cliffs, and the air we breathed was heavy with the perfume of flowers. The traverse was accomplished. Sixty days from land to land, across a lonely sea above whose horizons never rise the straining sails of ships.

From *The Cruise of the Snark*

CRUISING IN THE SOLOMONS

"Why not come along now?" said Captain Jansen to us, at Penduffryn, on the island of Guadalcanar.

Charmian and I looked at each other and debated silently for half a minute. Then we nodded our heads simultaneously. It is a way we have of making up our minds to do things; and a very good way it is when one has no temperamental tears to shed over the last tin of condensed milk when it has capsized. (We are living on tinned goods these days, and since mind is rumored to be an emanation of matter, our similes are naturally of the packing-house variety.)

"You'd better bring your revolvers along, and a couple of rifles," said Captain Jansen. "I've got five rifles aboard, though the one Mauser is without ammunition. Have you a few rounds to spare?"

We brought our rifles on board, several handfuls of Mauser cartridges, and Wada and Nakata, the *Snark's* cook and cabin-boy respectively. Wada and Nakata were in a bit of a funk. To say the least, they were not enthusiastic, though never did Nakata show the white feather in the face of danger. The Solomon Islands had not dealt kindly with them. In the first place, both had suffered from Solomon sores. So had the rest of us (at the time, I was nursing two fresh ones on a diet of corrosive sublimate); but the two Japanese had had more than their share. And the sores are not nice. They may be described as excessively active ulcers. A mosquito bite, a cut, or the slightest abrasion, serves for lodgment of the poison with which the air seems to be filled. Immediately the ulcer commences to eat. It eats in every direction, consuming skin and muscle with astounding rapidity. The pin-point ulcer of the first day is the size of a dime by the second day, and by the end of the week a silver dollar will not cover it.

Worse than the sores, the two Japanese had been afflicted with Solomon Island fever. Each had been down repeatedly with it, and in their weak, convalescent moments they were wont to huddle together on the portion of the *Snark* that happened to be nearest to faraway Japan, and to gaze yearningly in that direction.

But worst of all, they were now brought on board the *Minota* for a recruiting cruise along the savage coast of Malaita. Wada, who had the worse funk, was sure that he would never see Japan again, and with bleak, lack-lustre eyes he watched our rifles and ammunition going on board the *Minota*. He knew about the *Minota* and her Malaita cruises. He knew that she had been captured six months before on the Malaita coast, that her captain had been chopped to pieces with tomahawks, and that, according to the barbarian sense of equity on that sweet isle, she owed two more heads. Also, a laborer on Penduffryn Plantation, a Malaita boy, had just died of dysentery, and Wada knew that Penduffryn had been put in the debt of Malaita by one more head. Furthermore, in stowing our luggage away in the skipper's tiny cabin, he saw the axe gashes on the door where the triumphant bushmen had cut their way in. And, finally, the galley stove was without a pipe—said pipe having been part of the loot.

The *Minota* was a teak-built, Australian yacht, ketch-rigged, long and lean, with a deep fin-keel, and designed for harbor racing rather than for recruiting blacks. When Charmian and I came on board, we found her crowded. Her double boat's crew, including substitutes, was fifteen, and she had a score and more of "return" boys, whose time on the plantations was served and who were bound back to their bush villages. To look at, they were certainly true head-hunting cannibals. Their perforated nostrils were thrust through with bone and wooden bodkins the size of lead-pencils. Numbers of them had punctured the extreme meaty point of the nose, from which protruded straight out, spikes of turtle-shell or of beads strung on stiff wire. A few had further punctured their noses with rows of holes, following the curves of the nostrils from lip to point. Each ear of every man had from two to a dozen holes in it—holes large enough to carry wooden plugs three inches in diameter down to tiny holes in which were carried clay-pipes and similar trifles. In fact, so many holes did they possess that they lacked ornaments to fill them; and when, the following day, as we neared Malaita, we tried out our rifles to see that they were in working order, there was a general scramble for the empty cartridges, which were thrust forthwith into the many aching voids in our passengers' ears.

At the time we tried out our rifles we put up our barbed wire railing. The *Minota*, crown-decked, without any house, and with a rail six inches high, was too accessible to boarders. So brass stanchions were screwed into the rail and a double row of barbed wire stretched around her from stem to stern and back again. Which was all very well as a protection from savages, but it was mighty uncomfortable to those on board when the *Minota* took to jumping and plunging in a sea-way. When one dislikes sliding down upon the lee-rail barbed wire, and when he dares not catch hold of the weather-rail barbed wire to save himself from sliding, and when, with these various disinclinations, he finds himself on a smooth flush-deck that is heeled over at an angle of forty-five degrees, some of the delights of Solomon Islands cruising may be comprehended. Also, it must be remembered, the penalty of a fall into the barbed wire is more than the mere scratches, for each scratch is practically certain to become a venomous ulcer. That caution will not save one from the wire was evidenced one fine morning when we were running along the Malaita coast with the breeze on our quarter. The wind was fresh, and a tidy sea was making. A black boy was at the wheel. Captain Jansen, Mr. Jacobsen (the mate), Charmian, and I had just sat down on deck to breakfast. Three unusually large seas caught us. The boy at the wheel lost his head. Three times the *Minota* was swept. The breakfast was rushed over the lee-rail. The knives and forks went through the scuppers; a boy aft went clean overboard and was dragged back; and our doughty skipper lay half inboard and half out, jammed in the barbed wire. After that, for the rest of the cruise, our joint use of the several remaining eating utensils was a splendid example of primitive communism. On the *Eugenie*, however, it was even worse, for we had but one teaspoon among four of us—but the *Eugenie* is another story.

Our first port was Su'u on the west coast of Malaita. The Solomon Islands are on the fringe of things. It is difficult enough sailing on dark nights through reef-spiked channels and across erratic currents where there are no lights to guide (from northwest to southeast the Solomons extend across a thousand miles of sea, and on all the thousands of miles of coasts there is not one lighthouse); but the difficulty is seriously enhanced by the fact that the land itself is not correctly charted. Su'u is an example. On the Admiralty chart of Malaita the coast at this point runs a straight, unbroken line. Yet across this straight, unbroken line the *Minota* sailed in twenty fathoms of water. Where the land was alleged to be, was a deep indentation. Into this we sailed, the mangroves closing about us, till we dropped anchor in a mirrored pond. Captain Jansen did not like the anchorage. It was the first time he had been there, and Su'u had a bad reputation. There was no wind with which to get away in case of attack, while the crew could be bushwhacked to a man if they attempted to tow out in the whale-boat. It was a pretty trap, if trouble blew up.

"Suppose the *Minota* went ashore—what would you do?" I asked.

"She's not going ashore," was Captain Jansen's answer.

"But just in case she did?" I insisted.

He considered for a moment and shifted his glance from the mate buckling on a revolver to the boat's crew climbing into the whale-boat each man with a rifle.

"We'd get into the whale-boat, and get out of here as fast as a god'd let us," came the skipper's delayed reply.

He explained at length that no white man was sure of his Malaita crew in a tight place; that the bushmen looked upon all wrecks as their personal property; that the bushmen possessed plenty of Snider rifles; and that he had on board a dozen "return" boys for Su'u who were certain to join in with their friends and relatives ashore when it came to looting the *Minota*.

The first work of the whale-boat was to take the return boys and their trade-boxes ashore. Thus one danger was removed. While this was being done, a canoe came alongside manned by three naked savages. And when I say naked, I mean naked. Not one vestige of clothing did they have on, unless nose-rings, ear-plugs, and shell armlets be accounted clothing. The head man in the canoe was an old chief, one-eyed, reputed to be friendly, and so dirty that a boat-scraper would have lost its edge on him. His mission was to warn the skipper against allowing any of his people to go ashore. The old fellow repeated the warning again that night.

In vain did the whale-boat ply about the shores of the bay in quest of recruits. The bush was full of armed natives, all willing enough to talk with the recruiter, but not one would engage to sign on for three years' plantation labor at six pounds per year. Yet they were anxious enough to get our people ashore. On the second day they raised a smoke on the beach at the head of the bay. This being the customary signal of men desiring to recruit, the boat was sent. But nothing resulted. No one recruited, nor were any of our men lured ashore. A little later we caught glimpses of a number of armed natives moving about on the beach.

Outside of these rare glimpses, there was no telling how many might be lurking in the bush. There was no penetrating that primeval jungle with the eye. In the afternoon, Captain Jansen, Charmian, and I went dynamiting fish. Each one of the boat's crew carried a Lee-Enfield. "Johnny," the native recruiter, had a Winchester beside him at the steering sweep. We rowed in close to a portion of the shore that looked deserted. Here the boat was turned around and backed in; in case of attack, the boat would be ready to dash away. In all the time I was on Malaita I never saw a boat land bow on. In fact, the recruiting vessels use two boats—one to go in on the beach, armed, of course, and the other to lie off several hundred feet and "cover" the first boat. The *Minota*, however, being a small vessel, did not carry a covering boat.

We were close in to the shore and working in closer, stern-first, when a school of fish was sighted. The fuse was ignited and the stick of dynamite thrown. With the explosion, the surface of the water was broken by the flash of leaping fish

At the same instant the woods broke into life. A score of naked savages, armed with bows and arrows, spears, and Sniders, burst out upon the shore. At the same moment our boat's crew lifted their rifles. And thus the opposing parties faced each other, while our extra boys dived over after the stunned fish.

Three fruitless days were spent at Su'u. The *Minota* got no recruits from the bush, and the bushmen got no heads from the *Minota*. In fact, the only one who got anything was Wada, and his was a nice dose of fever. We towed out with a whale-boat, and ran along the coast to Langa Langa, a large village of salt-water people, built with prodigious labor on a lagoon sand-bank—literally *built up*, an artificial island reared as a refuge from the blood-thirsty bushmen. Here, also, on the shore side of the lagoon, was Binu, the place where the *Minota* was captured half a year previously and her captain killed by the bushmen. As we sailed in through the narrow entrance, a canoe came alongside with the news that the man-of-war had just left that morning after having burned three villages, killed some thirty pigs, and drowned a baby. This was the *Cambrian*, Captain Lewes commanding. He and I had first met in Korea during the Japanese-Russian War, and we had been crossing each other's trail ever since without ever a meeting. The day the *Snark* sailed into Suva, in the Fijis, we made out the *Cambrian* going out. At Vila, in the New Hebrides, we missed each other by one day. We passed each other in the night-time off the island of Santo. And the day the *Cambrian* arrived at Tulagi, we sailed from Penduffryn, a dozen miles away. And here at Langa Langa we had missed by several hours.

The *Cambrian* had come to punish the murderers of the *Minota's* captain, but what she had succeeded in doing we did not learn until later in the day, when a Mr. Abbot, a missionary, came alongside in his whale-boat. The villages had been burned and the pigs killed. But the natives had escaped personal harm. The murderers had not been captured, though the *Minota's* flag and other of her gear had been recovered. The drowning of the baby had come about through a misunderstanding. Chief Johnny, of Binu, had declined to guide the landing party into the bush, nor could any of his men be induced to perform that office. Whereupon Captain Lewes, righteously indignant, had told Chief Johnny that he deserved to have his village burned. Johnny's *bêche de mer* English did not include the word "deserve." So his understanding of it was that his village was to be burned anyway. The immediate stampede of the inhabitants was so hurried that the baby was dropped into the water. In the meantime Chief Johnny hastened to Mr. Abbot. Into his hand he put fourteen sovereigns and requested him to go on board the *Cambrian* and buy Captain Lewes off. Johnny's village was not burned. Nor did Captain Lewes get the fourteen sovereigns, for I saw them later in Johnny's possession when he boarded the *Minota*. The excuse Johnny gave me for not guiding the landing party was a big boil which he proudly revealed. His real reason, however, and a perfectly valid one, though he did not state it, was fear of revenge on the part of the bushmen. Had he, or any of his men, guided the marines, he could have looked for bloody reprisals as soon as the *Cambrian* weighed anchor.

As an illustration of conditions in the Solomons, Johnny's business on board was to turn over, for a tobacco consideration, the sprit, mainsail, and jib of a whale-boat. Later in the day, a Chief Billy came on board and turned over, for a tobacco consideration, the mast and boom. This gear belonged to a whale-boat which Captain Jansen had recovered the previous trip of the *Minota*. The whale-boat belonged to Meringe Plantation on the island of Ysabel. Eleven contract laborers, Malaita men and bushmen at that, had decided to run away. Being bushmen, they knew nothing of salt water nor of the way of a boat in the sea. So they persuaded two natives of San Cristoval, salt-water men, to run away with them. It served the San Cristoval men right. They should have known better. When they had safely navigated the stolen boat to Malaita, they had their heads hacked off for their pains. It was this boat and gear that Captain Jansen had recovered.

Not for nothing have I journeyed all the way to the Solomons. At last I have seen Charmian's proud spirit humbled and her emperious queendom of femininity dragged in the dust. It happened at Langa Langa, ashore, on the manufactured island which one cannot see for the houses. Here, surrounded by hundreds of unblushing naked men, women, and children, we wandered about and saw the sights. We had our revolvers strapped on, and the boat's crew, fully armed, lay at the oars, stern in; but the lesson of the man-of-war was too recent for us to apprehend trouble. We walked about everywhere and saw everything until at last we approached a large tree trunk that served as a bridge across a shallow estuary. The blacks formed a wall in front of us and refused to let us pass. We wanted to know why we were stopped. The blacks said we could go on. We misunderstood, and started. Explanations became more definite. Captain Jansen and I, being men, could go on. But no Mary was allowed to wade around that bridge, much less cross it. "Mary" is *bêche de mer* for woman. Charmian was a Mary. To her the bridge was *tambo,* which is the native for taboo. Ah, how my chest expanded! At last my manhood was vindicated. In truth I belonged to the lordly sex. Charmian could trapes along at our heels, but we were MEN, and we could go right over that bridge while she would have to go around by whale-boat.

Now I should not care to be misunderstood by what follows; but it is a matter of common knowledge in the Solomons that attacks of fever are often brought on by shock. Inside half an hour after Charmian had been refused the right of way, she was being rushed aboard the *Minota,* packed in blankets, and dosed with quinine. I don't know what kind of shock had happened to Wada and Nakata, but at any rate they were down with fever as well. The Solomons might be healthfuller.

Also, during the attack of fever, Charmian developed a Solomon sore. It was the last straw. Every one on the *Snark* had been afflicted except her. I had thought that I was going to lose my foot at the ankle by one exceptionally malignant boring ulcer. Henry and Tehei, the Tahitian sailors, had had numbers of them. Wada had been able to count his by the score. Nakata had had single ones three inches in length. Martin had been quite certain that necrosis of his shinbone had set in from the roots of the amazing colony he elected to cultivate in that locality. But Charmian had escaped. Out of her long immunity had been bred a contempt for the rest of us. Her ego was flattered to such an extent that one day she shyly informed me that it was all a matter of pureness of blood. Since all the rest of us cultivated the sores, and since she did not—well, anyway, hers was the size of a silver dollar, and the pureness of her blood enabled her to cure it after several weeks of strenuous nursing. She pins her faith to corrosive sublimate. Martin swears by iodoform. Henry uses lime-juice undiluted. And I believe that when corrosive sublimate is slow in taking hold, alternate dressings of peroxide of hydrogen are just the thing. There are white men in the Solomons who stake all upon boracic acid, and others who are prejudiced in favor of lysol. I also have the weakness of a panacea. It is California. I defy any man to get a Solomon Island sore in California.

We ran down the lagoon from Langa Langa, between mangrove swamps, through passages scarcely wider than the *Minota,* and past the reef villages of Kaloka and Auki. Like the founders of Venice, these salt-water men were originally refugees from the mainland. Too weak to hold their own in the bush, survivors of village massacres, they fled to the sand-banks of the lagoon. These sand-banks they built up into islands. They were compelled to seek their provender from the sea, and in time they became salt-water men. They learned the ways of the fish and the shell-fish, and they invented hooks and lines, nets and fish-traps. They developed canoe-bodies. Unable to walk about, spending all their time in the canoes, they became thick-armed and broad-shouldered, with narrow waists and frail spindly legs. Controlling the sea-coast, they became wealthy, trade with the interior passing largely through their hands. But perpetual enmity exists between them and the bushmen. Practically their only truces are on market-days, which occur at stated intervals, usually twice a week. The bushwomen and the salt-water women do the bartering. Back in the bush, a hundred yards away, fully armed, lurk the bushmen, while to seaward, in the canoes, are the salt-water men. There are very rare instances of the market-day truces being broken. The bushmen like their fish too well, while the salt-water men have an organic craving for the vegetables they cannot grow on their crowded islets.

Thirty miles from Langa Langa brought us to the passage between Bassakanna Island and the mainland. Here, at nightfall, the wind left us, and all night, with the whale-boat towing ahead and the crew on board sweating at the sweeps, we strove to win through. But the tide was against us. At midnight, midway in the passage, we came up with the *Eugenie,* a big recruiting schooner, towing with two whale-boats. Her skipper, Captain Keller, a sturdy young German of twenty-two, came on board for a "gam," and the latest news of Malaita was swapped back and forth. He had been in luck, having gathered in twenty recruits at the village of Fiu. While lying there, one of the customary courageous killings had taken place. The murdered boy was what is called a salt-water bushman—that is, a salt-water man who is half bushman and who lives by the sea but does not live on an islet. Three bushmen came down to this man where he was working in his garden. They behaved in friendly fashion, and after a time suggested *kai-kai*. *Kai-kai* means food. He built a fire and started to boil some taro. While bending over the pot, one of the bushmen shot him through the head. He fell into the flames, whereupon they thrust a spear through his stomach, turned it around, and broke it off.

"My word," said Captain Keller, "I don't want ever to be shot with a Snider. Spread! You could drive a horse and carriage through that hole in his head."

Another recent courageous killing I heard of on Malaita was that of an old man. A bush chief had died a natural death. Now the bushmen don't believe in natural deaths. No one was ever known to die a natural death. The only way to die is by bullet, tomahawk, or spear thrust. When a man dies in any other way, it is a clear case of having been charmed to death. When the bush chief died naturally, his tribe placed the guilt on a certain family. Since it did not matter which one of the family was killed, they selected this old man who lived by himself. This would make it easy. Furthermore, he possessed no Snider. Also, he was blind. The old fellow got an inkling of what was coming and laid in a large supply of arrows. Three brave warriors, each with a Snider, came down upon him in the night-time. All night they fought valiantly with him. Whenever they moved in the bush and made a noise or a rustle, he discharged an arrow in that direction. In the morning, when his last arrow was gone, the three heroes crept up to him and blew his brains out.

Morning found us still vainly toiling through the passage. At last, in despair, we turned tail, ran out to sea, and sailed clear round Bassakanna to our objective, Malu. The anchorage at Malu was very good, but it lay between the shore and an ugly reef, and while easy to enter, it was difficult to leave. The direction of the southeast trade necessitated a beat to windward; the point of the reef was widespread and shallow; while a current bore down at all times upon the point.

Mr. Caulfeild, the missionary at Malu, arrived in his whale-boat from a trip down the coast. A slender, delicate man he was, enthusiastic in his work, level-headed and practical, a true twentieth-century soldier of the Lord. When he came down to this station on Malaita, as he said, he agreed to come for six months. He further agreed that if he were alive at the end of that time, he would continue on. Six years had passed and he was still continuing on. Nevertheless he was justified in his doubt as to living longer than six months. Three missionaries had preceded him on Malaita, and in less than that time two had died of fever and the third had gone home a wreck.

"What murder are you talking about?" he asked suddenly, in the midst of a confused conversation with Captain Jansen.

Captain Jansen explained.

"Oh, that's not the one I have reference to," quoth Mr. Caulfeild. "That's old already. It happened two weeks ago."

It was here at Malu that I atoned for all the exulting and gloating I had been guilty of over the Solomon sore Charmian had collected at Langa Langa. Mr. Caulfeild was indirectly responsible for my atonement. He presented us with a chicken, which I pursued into the bush with a rifle. My intention was to clip off its head. I succeeded, but in doing so fell over a log and barked my shin. Result: three Solomon sores. This made five all together that were adorning my person. Also, Captain Jansen and Nakata had caught *gari-gari*. Literally translated, *gari-gari* is scratch-scratch. But translation was not necessary for the rest of us. The skipper's and Nakata's gymnastics served as a translation without words.

(No, the Solomon Islands are not so healthy as they might be. I am writing this article on the island of Ysabel, where we have taken the *Snark* to careen and clean her copper. I got over my last attack of fever this morning, and I have had only one free day between attacks. Charmian's are two weeks apart. Wada is a wreck from fever. Last night he showed all the symptoms of coming down with pneumonia. Henry, a strapping giant of a Tahitian, just up from his last dose of fever, is dragging around the deck like a last year's crab-apple. Both he and Tehei have accumulated a praiseworthy display of Solomon sores. Also, they have caught a new form of *gari-gari*, a sort of vegetable poisoning like poison oak or poison ivy. But they are not unique in this. A number of days ago Charmian, Martin, and I went pigeon-shooting on a small island, and we have had a foretaste of eternal torment ever since. Also, on that small island, Martin cut the soles of his feet to ribbons on the coral while chasing a shark—at least, so he says, but from the glimpse I caught of him I thought it was the other way about. The coral-cuts have all become Solomon sores. Before my last fever I knocked the skin off my knuckles while heaving on a line, and I now have three fresh sores. And poor Nakata! For three weeks he has been unable to sit down. He sat down yesterday for the first time, and managed to stay down for fifteen minutes. He says cheerfully that he expects to be cured of his *gari-gari,* in another month. Furthermore, his *gari-gari,* from too enthusiastic scratch-scratching, has furnished footholds for countless Solomon sores. Still furthermore, he has just come down with his seventh attack of fever. If I were a king, the worst punishment I could inflict on my enemies would be to banish them to the Solomons. On second thought, king or no king, I don't think I'd have the heart to do it.)

Recruiting plantation laborers on a small, narrow yacht, built for harbor sailing, is not any too nice. The decks swarm with recruits and their families. The main cabin is packed with them. At night they sleep there. The only entrance to our tiny cabin is through the main cabin, and we jam our way through them or walk over them. Nor is this nice. One and all, they are afflicted with every form of malignant skin disease. Some have ringworm, others have *bukua.* This latter is caused by a vegetable parasite that invades the skin and eats it away. The itching is intolerable. The afflicted ones scratch until the air is filled with fine dry flakes. Then there are yaws and many other skin ulcerations. Men come aboard with Solomon sores in their feet so large that they can walk only on their toes, or with holes in their legs so terrible that a fist could be thrust in to the bone. Blood-poisoning is very frequent, and Captain Jansen, with sheath-knife and sail needle, operates lavishly on one and all. No matter how desperate the situation, after opening and cleansing, he claps on a poultice of sea-biscuit soaked in water. Whenever we see a particularly horrible case, we retire to a corner and deluge our own sores with corrosive sublimate. And so we live and eat and sleep on the *Minota,* taking our chance and "pretending it is good."

At Suava, another artificial island, I had a second crow over Chairmian. A big fella marster belong Suava (which means the high chief of Suava) came on board. But first he sent an emissary to Captain Jansen for a fathom of calico with which to cover his royal nakedness. Meanwhile he lingered in the canoe alongside. The regal dirt on his chest I swear was half an inch thick, while it was a good wager that the underneath layers were anywhere from ten to twenty years of age. He sent his emissary on board again, who explained that the big fella marster belong Suava was condescendingly willing enough to shake hands with Captain Jansen and me and cadge a stick or so of trade tobacco, but that nevertheless his high-born soul was still at so lofty an altitude that it could not sink itself to such a depth of degradation as to shake hands with a mere female woman. Poor Charmian! Since her Malaita experiences she has become a changed woman. Her meekness and humbleness is appallingly becoming, and I should not be surprised, when we return to civilization and stroll along a sidewalk, to see her take her station, with bowed head, a yard in the rear.

Nothing much happened at Suava. Bichu, the native cook, deserted. The *Minota* dragged anchor. It blew heavy squalls of wind and rain. The mate, Mr. Jacobsen, and Wada were prostrated with fever. Our Solomon sores increased and multiplied. And the cockroaches on board held a combined Fourth of July and Coronation Parade. They selected midnight for the time, and our tiny cabin for the place. They were from two to three inches long; there were hundreds of them, and they walked all over us. When we attempted to pursue them, they left solid footing, rose up in the air, and fluttered about like humming-birds. They were much larger than ours on the *Snark.* But ours are young yet, and haven't had a chance to grow. Also, the *Snark* has centipedes, big ones, six inches long. We kill them occasionally, usually in Charmian's bunk. I've been bitten twice by them, both times foully, while I was asleep. But poor Martin had worse luck. After being sick in bed for three weeks, the first day he sat up he sat down on one. Sometimes I think they are the wisest who never go to Carcassonne.

Later on we returned to Malu, picked up seven recruits, hove up anchor, and started to beat out the treacherous entrance. The wind was chopping about, the current upon the ugly point of reef setting strong. Just as we were on the verge of clearing it and gaining open sea, the wind broke off four points. The *Minota* attempted to go about, but missed stays. Two of her anchors had been lost at Tulagi. Her one remaining anchor was let go. Chain was let out to give it a hold on the coral. Her fin keel struck bottom, and her main topmast lurched and shivered as if about to come down upon our heads. She fetched up on the slack of the anchor at the moment a big comber smashed her shoreward. The chain parted. It was our only anchor. The *Minota* swung around on her heel and drove headlong into the breakers.

Bedlam reigned. All the recruits below, bushmen and afraid of the sea, dashed panic-stricken on deck and got in everybody's way. At the same time the boat's crew made a rush for the rifles. They knew what going ashore on Malaita meant —one hand for the ship and the other hand to fight off the natives. What they held on with I don't know, and they needed to hold on as the *Minota* lifted, rolled, and pounded on the coral. The bushmen clung in the rigging, too witless to watch out for the topmast. The whale-boat was run out with a tow-line endeavoring in a puny way to prevent the *Minota* from being flung farther in toward the reef, while Captain Jansen and the mate, the latter pallid and weak with fever, were resurrecting a scrap-anchor from out the ballast and rigging up a stock for it. Mr. Caulfeild, with his mission boys, arrived in his whale-boat to help.

When the *Minota* first struck, there was not a canoe in sight; but like vultures circling down out of the blue, canoes began to arrive from every quarter. The boat's crew, with rifles at the ready, kept them lined up a hundred feet away with a promise of death if they ventured nearer. And there they clung, a hundred feet away, black and ominous, crowded with men, holding their canoes with their paddles on the perilous edge of the breaking surf. In the meantime the bushmen were flocking down from the hills, armed with spears, Sniders, arrows, and clubs, until the beach was massed with them. To complicate matters, at least ten of our recruits had been enlisted from the very bushmen ashore who were waiting hungrily for the loot of the tobacco and trade goods and all that we had on board.

The *Minota* was honestly built, which is the first essential for any boat that is pounding on a reef. Some idea of what she endured may be gained from the fact that in the first twenty-four hours she parted two anchor-chains and eight hawsers. Our boat's crew was kept busy diving for the anchors and bending new lines. There were times when she parted the chains reënforced with hawsers. And yet she held together. Tree trunks were brought from ashore and worked under her to save her keel and bilges, but the trunks were gnawed and splintered and the ropes that held them frayed to fragments, and still she pounded and held together. But we were luckier than the *Ivanhoe*, a big recruiting schooner, which had gone ashore on Malaita several months previously and been promptly rushed by the natives. The captain and crew succeeded in getting away in the whale-boats, and the bushmen and salt-water men looted her clean of everything portable.

Squall after squall, driving wind and blinding rain, smote the *Minota*, while a heavier sea was making. The *Eugenie* lay at anchor five miles to windward, but she was behind a point of land and could not know of our mishap. At Captain Jansen's suggestion, I wrote a note to Captain Keller, asking him to bring extra anchors and gear to our aid. But not a canoe could be persuaded to carry the letter. I offered half a case of tobacco, but the blacks grinned and held their canoes bow-on to the breaking seas. A half a case of tobacco was worth three pounds. In two hours, even against the strong wind and sea, a man could have carried the letter and received in payment what he would have labored half a year for on a plantation. I managed to get into a canoe and paddle out to where Mr. Caulfeild was running an anchor with his whale-boat. My idea was that he would have more influence over the natives. He called the canoes up to him, and a score of them clustered around and heard the offer of half a case of tobacco. No one spoke.

"I know what you think," the missionary called out to them. "You think plenty tobacco on the schooner and you're going to get it. I tell you plenty rifles on schooner. You no get tobacco, you get bullets."

At last, one man, alone in a small canoe, took the letter and started. Waiting for relief, work went on steadily on the *Minota.* Her water-tanks were emptied, and spars, sails, and ballast started shoreward. There were lively times on board when the *Minota* rolled one bilge down and then the other, a score of men leaping for life and legs as the trade-boxes, booms, and eighty-pound pigs of iron ballast rushed across from rail to rail and back again. The poor pretty harbor yacht! Her decks and running rigging were a raffle. Down below everything was disrupted. The cabin floor had been torn up to get at the ballast, and rusty bilge-water swashed and splashed. A bushel of limes, in a mess of flour and water, charged about like so many sticky dumplings escaped from a half-cooked stew. In the inner cabin, Nakata kept guard over our rifles and ammunition.

Three hours from the time our messenger started, a whale-boat, pressing along under a huge spread of canvas, broke through the thick of a shrieking squall to windward. It was Captain Keller, wet with rain and spray, a revolver in his belt, his boat's crew fully armed, anchors and hawsers heaped high amidships, coming as fast as wind could drive—the white man, the inevitable white man, coming to a white man's rescue.

The vulture line of canoes that had waited so long broke and disappeared as quickly as it had formed. The corpse was not dead after all. We now had three whale-boats, two plying steadily between the vessel and shore, the other kept busy running out anchors, rebending parted hawsers, and recovering the lost anchors. Later in the afternoon, after a consultation, in which we took into consideration that a number of our boat's crew, as well as ten of the recruits, belonged to this place, we disarmed the boat's crew. This, incidently, gave them both hands free to work for the vessel. The rifles were put in the charge of five of Mr. Caulfeild's mission boys. And down below in the wreck of the cabin the missionary and his converts prayed to God to save the *Minota.* It was an impressive scene: the unarmed man of God praying with cloudless faith, his savage followers leaning on their rifles and mumbling amens. The cabin walls reeled about them. The vessel lifted and smashed upon the coral with every sea. From on deck came the shouts of men heaving and toiling, praying, in another fashion, with purposeful will and strength of arm.

That night Mr. Caulfeild brought off a warning. One of our recruits had a price on his head of fifty fathoms of shell-money and forty pigs. Baffled in their desire to capture the vessel, the bushmen decided to get the head of the man. When killing begins, there is no telling where it will end, so Captain Jansen armed a whale-boat and rowed in to the edge of the beach. Ugi, one of his boat's crew, stood up and orated for him. Ugi was excited. Captain Jansen's warning that any canoe sighted that night would be pumped full of lead, Ugi turned into a bellicose declaration of war, which wound up with a peroration somewhat to the following effect: "You kill my captain, I drink his blood and die with him!"

The bushmen contented themselves with burning an unoccupied mission house, and sneaked back to the bush. The next day the *Eugenie* sailed in and dropped anchor. Three days and two nights the *Minota* pounded on the reef; but she held together, and the shell of her was pulled off at last and anchored in smooth water. There we said good-by to her and all on board, and sailed away on the *Eugenie*, bound for Florida Island.[1]

[1] To point out that we of the *Snark* are not a crowd of weaklings, which might be concluded from our divers afflictions, I quote the following, which I gleaned verbatim from the *Eugenie's* log and which may be considered as a sample of Solomon Islands cruising:

Ulava, Thursday, March 12, 1908.
Boat went ashore in the morning. Got two loads ivory nut, 4000 copra. Skipper down with fever.

Ulava, Friday, March 13, 1908.
Buying nuts from bushmen, 1½ ton. Mate and skipper down with fever.

Ulava, Saturday, March 14, 1908.
At noon hove up and proceeded with a very light E.N.E. wind for Ngora-Ngora. Anchored in 8 fathoms—shell and coral. Mate down with fever.

Ngora-Ngora, Sunday, March 15, 1908.
At daybreak found that the boy Bagua had died during the night, on dysentery. He was about 14 days sick. At sunset, big N.W. squall. (Second anchor ready.) Lasting one hour and 30 minutes.

At sea, Monday, March 16, 1908.
Set course for Sikiana at 4 P. M. Wind broke off. Heavy squalls during the night. Skipper down on dysentery, also one man.

At sea, Tuesday, March 17, 1908.
Skipper and 2 crew down on dysentery. Mate fever.

At sea, Wednesday, March 18, 1908.
Big sea. Lee-rail under water all the time. Skip under reefed mainsail, staysail, and inner jib. Skipper and 3 men dysentery. Mate fever.

At sea, Thursday, March 19, 1908.
Too thick to see anything. Blowing a living gale all the time. Pump plugged up and bailing with buckets. Skipper and five boys down on dysentery.

At sea, Friday, March 20, 1908.
During night squalls with hurricane force. Skipper and six men down on dysentery.

At sea, Saturday, March 21, 1908.
Turned back from Sikiana. Squalls all day with heavy rain and sea. Skipper and best part of crew on dysentery. Mate fever.

And so, day by day, with the majority of all on board prostrated, the *Eugenie's* log goes on. The only variety occurred on March 31, when the mate came down with dysentery and the skipper was floored by fever.

From *The Cruise of the Snark*

The Reporter

THE PEOPLE OF THE ABYSS

Selections

PREFACE

The experiences related in this volume fell to me in the summer of 1902. I went down into the under-world of London with an attitude of mind which I may best liken to that of the explorer. I was open to be convinced by the evidence of my eyes, rather than by the teachings of those who had not seen, or by the words of those who had seen and gone before. Further, I took with me certain simple criteria with which to measure the life of the under-world. That which made for more life, for physical and spiritual health, was good; that which made for less life, which hurt, and dwarfed, and distorted life, was bad.

It will be readily apparent to the reader that I saw much that was bad. Yet it must not be forgotten that the time of which I write was considered "good times" in England. The starvation and lack of shelter I encountered constituted a chronic condition of misery which is never wiped out, even in the periods of greatest prosperity.

Following the summer in question came a hard winter. To such an extent did the suffering and positive starvation increase that society was unable to cope with it. Great numbers of the unemployed formed into processions, as many as a dozen at a time, and daily marched through the streets of London crying for bread. Mr. Justin McCarthy, writing in the month of January, 1903, to the New York *Independent*, briefly epitomizes the situation as follows:—

The workhouses have no space left in which to pack the starving crowds who are craving every day and night at their doors for food and shelter. All the charitable institutions have exhausted their means in trying to raise supplies of food for famishing residents of the garrets and cellars of London lanes and alleys. The quarters of the Salvation Army in various parts of London are nightly besieged by hosts of the unemployed and the hungry for whom neither shelter nor the means of sustenance can be provided.

It has been urged that the criticism I have passed on things as they are in England is too pessimistic. I must say, in extenuation, that of optimists I am the most optimistic. But I measure manhood less by political aggregations than by individuals. Society grows, while political machines rack to pieces and become "scrap." For the English, so far as manhood and womanhood and health and happiness go, I see a broad and smiling future. But for a great deal of the political machinery, which at present mismanages for them, I see nothing else than the scrap heap.

THE DESCENT

"But you can't do it, you know," friends said, to whom I applied for assistance in the matter of sinking myself down into the East End of London. "You had better see the police for a guide," they added, on second thought, painfully endeavoring to adjust themselves to the psychological processes of a madman who had come to them with better credentials than brains.

"But I don't want to see the police," I protested. "What I wish to do, is to go down into the East End and see things for myself. I wish to know how those people are living there, and why they are living there, and what they are living for. In short, I am going to live there myself."

"You don't want to live down there!" everybody said, with disapprobation writ large upon their faces. "Why, it is said there are places where a man's life isn't worth tu'pence."

"The very places I wish to see," I broke in.

"But you can't, you know," was the unfailing rejoinder.

"Which is not what I came to see you about," I answered brusquely, somewhat nettled by their incomprehension. "I am a stranger here, and I want you to tell me what you know of the East End, in order that I may have something to start on."

"But we know nothing of the East End. It is over there, somewhere." And they waved their hands vaguely in the direction where the sun on rare occasions may be seen to rise.

"Then I shall go to Cook's," I announced.

"Oh, yes," they said, with relief. "Cook's will be sure to know."

But O Cook, O Thomas Cook & Son, pathfinders and trail-clearers, living signposts to all the world and bestowers of first aid to bewildered travellers—unhesitatingly and instantly, with ease and celerity, could you send me to Darkest Africa or Innermost Thibet, but to the East End of London, barely a stone's throw distant from Ludgate Circus, you know not the way!

"You can't do it, you know," said the human emporium of routes and fares at Cook's Cheapside branch. "It is so—ahem—so unusual."

"Consult the police," he concluded authoritatively, when I persisted. "We are not accustomed to taking travellers to the East End; we receive no call to take them there, and we know nothing whatsoever about the place at all."

"Never mind that," I interposed, to save myself from being swept out of the office by his flood of negations. "Here's something you can do for me. I wish you to understand in advance what I intend doing, so that in case of trouble you may be able to identify me."

"Ah, I see; should you be murdered, we would be in position to identify the corpse."

He said it so cheerfully and cold-bloodedly that on the instant I saw my stark and mutilated cadaver stretched upon a slab where cool waters trickle ceaselessly, and him I saw bending over and sadly and patiently identifying it as the body of the insane American who would see the East End.

"No, no," I answered; "merely to identify me in case I get into a scrape with the 'bobbies.'" This last I said with a thrill; truly, I was gripping hold of the vernacular.

"That," he said, "is a matter for the consideration of the Chief Office.

"It is so unprecedented, you know," he added apologetically.

The man at the Chief Office hemmed and hawed. "We make it a rule," he explained, "to give no information concerning our clients."

"But in this case," I urged, "it is the client who requests you to give the information concerning himself."

Again he hemmed and hawed.

"Of course," I hastily anticipated, "I know it is unprecedented, but–"

"As I was about to remark," he went on steadily, "it is unprecedented, and I don't think we can do anything for you."

However, I departed with the address of a detective who lived in the East End, and took my way to the American consul-general. And here, at last, I found a man with whom I could 'do business.' There was no hemming and hawing, no lifted brows, open incredulity, or blank amazement. In one minute I explained myself and my project, which he accepted as a matter of course. In the second minute he asked my age, height, and weight, and looked me over. And in the third minute, as we shook hands at parting, he said: "All right, Jack. I'll remember you and keep track."

I breathed a sigh of relief. Having built my ships behind me, I was now free to plunge into that human wilderness of which nobody seemed to know anything. But at once I encountered a new difficulty in the shape of my cabby, a gray-whiskered and eminently decorous personage, who had imperturbably driven me for several hours about the 'City.'

"Drive me down to the East End," I ordered, taking my seat.

"Where, sir?" he demanded with frank surprise.

"To the East End, anywhere. Go on."

The hansom pursued an aimless way for several minutes, then came to a puzzled stop. The aperture above my head was uncovered, and the cabman peered down perplexedly at me.

"I say," he said, "wot plyce yer wanter go?"

"East End," I repeated. "Nowhere in particular. Just drive me around, anywhere."

"But wot's the haddress, sir?"

"See here!" I thundered. "Drive me down to the East End, and at once!"

It was evident that he did not understand, but he withdrew his head and grumblingly started his horse.

Nowhere in the streets of London may one escape the sight of abject poverty, while five minutes' walk from almost any point will bring one to a slum; but the region my hansom was now penetrating was one of unending slum. The streets were filled with a new and different race of people, short of stature, and of wretched or beer-sodden appearance. We rolled along through miles of bricks and squalor, and from each cross street and alley flashed long vistas of bricks and misery. Here and there lurched a drunken man or woman, and the air was obscene with sounds of jangling and squabbling. At a market, tottery old men and women were searching in the garbage thrown in the mud for rotten potatoes, beans, and vegetables, while little children clustered like flies around a festering mass of fruit, thrusting their arms to the shoulders into the liquid corruption, and drawing forth morsels, but partially decayed, which they devoured on the spot.

Not a hansom did I meet with in all my drive, while mine was like an apparition from another and better world, the way the children ran after it and alongside. And as far as I could see were the solid walls of brick, the slimy pavements, and the screaming streets; and for the first time in my life the fear of the crowd smote me. It was like the fear of the sea; and the miserable multitudes, street upon street, seemed so many waves of a vast and malodorous sea, lapping about me and threatening to well up and over me.

"Stepney, sir; Stepney Station," the cabby called down.

I looked about. It was really a railroad station, and he had driven desperately to it as the one familiar spot he had ever heard of in all that wilderness.

"Well?" I said.

He spluttered unintelligibly, shook his head, and looked very miserable. "I'm a stryngerʼere," he managed to articulate. "An' if yer don't want Stepney Station, I'm blessed if I know wotcher do want."

"I'll tell you what I want," I said. "You drive along and keep your eye out for a shop where old clothes are sold. Now, when you see such a shop, drive right on till you turn the corner, then stop and let me out."

I could see that he was growing dubious of his fare, but not long afterward he pulled up to the curb and informed me that an old clothes shop was to be found a bit of the way back.

"Won'tcher py me?" he pleaded. "There's seven an' six owin' me."

"Yes," I laughed, "and it would be the last I'd see of you."

"Lord lumme, but it'll be the last I see of you if yer don't py me," he retorted.

But a crowd of ragged onlookers had already gathered around the cab, and I laughed again and walked back to the old clothes shop.

Here the chief difficulty was in making the shop-man understand that I really and truly wanted old clothes. But after fruitless attempts to press upon me new and impossible coats and trousers, he began to bring to light heaps of old ones, looking mysterious the while and hinting darkly. This he did with the palpable intention of letting me know that he had 'piped my lay,' in order to bulldose me, through fear of exposure, into paying heavily for my purchases. A man in trouble, or a high-class criminal from across the water, was what he took my measure for —in either case, a person anxious to avoid the police.

But I disputed with him over the outrageous difference between prices and values, till I quite disabused him of the notion, and he settled down to drive a hard bargain with a hard customer. In the end I selected a pair of stout though well-worn trousers, a frayed jacket with one remaining button, a pair of brogans which had plainly seen service where coal was shovelled, a thin leather belt, and a very dirty cloth cap. My underclothing and socks, however, were new and warm, but of the sort that any American waif, down in his luck, could acquire in the ordinary course of events.

"I must sy yer a sharp 'un," he said, with counterfeit admiration, as I handed over the ten shillings finally agreed upon for the outfit. "Blimey, if you ain't ben up an' down Petticut Lane afore now. Yer trouseys is wuth five bob to hany man, an' a docker 'ud give two an' six for the shoes, to sy nothin' of the coat an' cap an' new stoker's singlet an' hother things."

"How much will you give me for them?" I demanded suddenly. "I paid you ten bob for the lot, and I'll sell them back to you, right now, for eight. Come, it's a go!"

But he grinned and shook his head, and though I had made a good bargain, I was unpleasantly aware that he had made a better one.

I found the cabby and a policeman with their heads together, but the latter, after looking me over sharply and particularly scrutinizing the bundle under my arm, turned away and left the cabby to wax mutinous by himself. And not a step would he budge till I paid him the seven shillings and sixpence owing him. Whereupon he was willing to drive me to the ends of the earth, apologizing profusely for his insistence, and explaining that one ran across queer customers in London Town.

But he drove me only to Highbury Vale, in North London, where my luggage was waiting for me. Here, next day, I took off my shoes (not without regret for their lightness and comfort), and my soft, gray travelling suit, and, in fact, all my clothing; and proceeded to array myself in the clothes of the other and unimaginable men, who must have been indeed unfortunate to have had to part with such rags for the pitiable sums obtainable from a dealer.

Inside my stoker's singlet, in the armpit, I sewed a gold sovereign (an emergency sum certainly of modest proportions); and inside my stoker's singlet I put myself. And then I sat down and moralized upon the fair years and fat, which had made my skin soft and brought the nerves close to the surface; for the singlet was rough and raspy as a hair shirt, and I am confident that the most rigorous of ascetics suffer no more than did I in the ensuing twenty-four hours.

The remainder of my costume was fairly easy to put on, though the brogans, or brogues, were quite a problem. As stiff and hard as if made of wood, it was only after a prolonged pounding of the uppers with my fists that I was able to get my feet into them at all. Then, with a few shillings, a knife, a handkerchief, and some brown papers and flake tobacco stowed away in my pockets, I thumped down the stairs and said good-by to my foreboding friends. As I passed out the door, the 'help,' a comely, middle-aged woman, could not conquer a grin that twisted her lips and separated them till the throat, out of involuntary sympathy, made the uncouth animal noises we are wont to designate as 'laughter.'

No sooner was I out on the streets than I was impressed by the difference in status effected by my clothes. All servility vanished from the demeanor of the common people with whom I came in contact. Presto! in the twinkling of an eye, so to say, I had become one of them. My frayed and out-at-elbows jacket was the badge and advertisement of my class, which was their class. It made me of like kind, and in place of the fawning and too-respectful attention I had hitherto received, I now shared with them a comradeship. The man in corduroy and dirty neckerchief no longer addressed me as 'sir' or 'governor.' It was 'mate,' now—and a fine and hearty word, with a tingle to it, and a warmth and gladness, which the other term does not possess. Governor! It smacks of mastery, and power, and high authority—the tribute of the man who is under to the man on top, delivered in the hope that he will let up a bit and ease his weight. Which is another way of saying that it is an appeal for alms.

This brings me to a delight I experienced in my rags and tatters which is denied the average American abroad. The European traveller from the States, who is not a Croesus, speedily finds himself reduced to a chronic state of self-conscious sordidness by the hordes of cringing robbers who clutter his steps from dawn till dark, and deplete his pocketbook in a way that puts compound interest to the blush.

In my rags and tatters I escaped the pestilence of tipping, and encountered men on a basis of equality, Nay, before the day was out I turned the tables, and said, most gratefully, "Thank you, sir," to a gentleman whose horse I held, and who dropped a penny into my eager palm.

Other changes I discovered were wrought in my condition by my new garb. In crossing crowded thoroughfares I found I had to be, if anything, more lively in avoiding vehicles, and it was strikingly impressed upon me that my life had cheapened in direct ratio with my clothes. When before, I inquired the way of a policeman, I was usually asked, "Bus or 'ansom, sir?" But now the query became, "Walk or ride?" Also, at the railway stations it was the rule to be asked, "First or second, sir?" Now I was asked nothing, a third-class ticket being shoved out to me as a matter of course.

But there was compensation for it all. For the first time I met the English lower classes face to face, and knew them for what they were. When loungers and workmen, on street corners and in public houses, talked with me, they talked as one man to another, and they talked as natural men should talk, without the least idea of getting anything out of me for what they talked, or the way they talked.

And when at last I made into the East End, I was gratified to find that the fear of the crowd no longer haunted me. I had become a part of it. The vast and malodorous sea had welled up and over me, or I had slipped gently into it, and there was nothing fearsome about it—with the one exception of the stoker's singlet.

THE CARTER AND THE CARPENTER

The Carter, with his clean-cut face, chin beard, and shaved upper lip, I should have taken in the United States for anything from a master workman to a well-to-do farmer. The Carpenter—well, I should have taken him for a carpenter. He looked it, lean and wiry, with shrewd, observant eyes, and hands that had grown twisted to the handles of tools through forty-seven years' work at the trade. The chief difficulty with these men was that they were old, and that their children, instead of growing up to take care of them, had died. Their years had told on them, and they had been forced out of the whirl of industry by the younger and stronger competitors who had taken their places.

These two men, turned away from the casual ward of the Whitechapel Workhouse, were bound with me for Poplar Workhouse. Not much of a show, they thought, but to chance it was all that remained to us. It was Poplar, or the streets and night. Both men were anxious for a bed, for they were "about gone," as they phrased it. The Carter, fifty-eight years of age, had spent the last three nights without shelter or sleep, while the Carpenter, sixty-five years of age, had been out five nights.

But, O dear, soft people, full of meat and blood, with white beds and airy rooms waiting for you each night, how can I make you know what it is to suffer as you would suffer if you spent a weary night on London's streets? Believe me, you would think a thousand centuries had come and gone before the east paled into dawn; you would shiver till you were ready to cry aloud with the pain of each aching muscle; and you would marvel that you could endure so much and live. Should you rest upon a bench, and your tired eyes close, depend upon it the policeman would rouse you and gruffly order you to "move on." You may rest upon the bench, and benches are few and far between; but if rest means sleep, on you must go, dragging your tired body through the endless streets. Should you, in desperate slyness, seek some forlorn alley or dark passageway and lie down, the omnipresent policeman will rout you out just the same. It is his business to rout you out. It is a law of the powers that be that you shall be routed out.

But when the dawn came, the nightmare over, you would hie you home to refresh yourself, and until you died you would tell the story of your adventure to groups of admiring friends. It would grow into a mighty story. Your little eight-hour night would become an Odyssey and you a Homer.

Not so with these homeless ones who walked to Poplar Workhouse with me. And there are thirty-five thousand of them, men and women, in London Town this night. Please don't remember it as you go to bed; if you are as soft as you ought to be you may not rest so well as usual. But for old men of sixty, seventy, and eighty, ill-fed, with neither meat nor blood, to greet the dawn unrefreshed, and to stagger through the day in mad search for crusts, with relentless night rushing down upon them again, and to do this five nights and days—O dear, soft people, full of meat and blood, how can you ever understand?

I walked up Mile End Road between the Carter and the Carpenter. Mile End Road is a wide thoroughfare, cutting the heart of East London, and there were tens of thousands of people abroad on it. I tell you this so that you may fully appreciate what I shall describe in the next paragraph. As I say, we walked along, and when they grew bitter and cursed the land, I cursed with them, cursed as an American waif would curse, stranded in a strange and terrible land. And, as I tried to lead them to believe, and succeeded in making them believe, they took me for a "seafaring man," who had spent his money in riotous living, lost his clothes (no unusual occurrence with seafaring men ashore), and was temporarily broke while looking for a ship. This accounted for my ignorance of English ways in general and casual wards in particular, and my curiosity concerning the same.

The Carter was hard put to keep the pace at which we walked (he told me that he had eaten nothing that day), but the Carpenter, lean and hungry, his gray and ragged overcoat flapping mournfully in the breeze, swung on in a long and tireless stride which reminded me strongly of the plains coyote. Both kept their eyes upon the pavement as they walked and talked, and every now and then one or the other would stoop and pick something up, never missing the stride the while. I thought it was cigar and cigarette stumps they were collecting, and for some time took no notice. Then I did notice.

From the slimy, spittle-drenched side-walk, they were picking up bits of orange peel, apple skin, and grape stems, and they were eating them. The pits of green gage plums they cracked between their teeth for the kernels inside. They picked up stray crumbs of bread the size of peas, apple cores so black and dirty one would not take them to be apple cores, and these things these two men took into their mouths, and chewed them, and swallowed them; and this, between six and seven o'clock in the evening of August 20, year of our Lord 1902, in the heart of the greatest, wealthiest, and most powerful empire the world has ever seen.

These two men talked. They were not fools. They were merely old. And, quite naturally, a-reek with pavement offal, they talked of bloody revolution. They talked as anarchists, fanatics, and madmen would talk. And who shall blame them? In spite of my three good meals that day, and the snug bed I could occupy if I wished, and my social philosophy, and my evolutionary belief in the slow development and metamorphosis of things—in spite of all this, I say, I felt impelled to talk rot with them or hold my tongue. Poor fools! Not of their sort are revolutions bred. And when they are dead and dust, which will be shortly, other fools will talk bloody revolution as they gather offal from the spittle-drenched side-walk along Mile End Road to Poplar Workhouse.

Being a foreigner, and a young man, the Carter and the Carpenter explained things to me and advised me. Their advice, by the way, was brief and to the point; it was to get out of the country. "As fast as God'll let me," I assured them; "I'll hit only the high places, till you won't be able to see my trail for smoke." They felt the force of my figures rather than understood them, and they nodded their heads approvingly.

"Actually make a man a criminal against 'is will," said the Carpenter. "'Ere I am, old, younger men takin' my place, my clothes gettin' shabbier an' shabbier, an' makin' it 'arder every day to get a job. I go to the casual ward for a bed. Must be there by two or three in the afternoon or I won't get in. You saw what happened today. What chance does that give me to look for work? S'pose I do get into the casual ward? Keep me in all day tomorrow, let me out mornin' o' next day. What then? The law sez I can't get in another casual ward that night less'n ten miles distant. Have to hurry an' walk to be there in time that day. What chance does that give me to look for a job? S'pose I don't walk. S'pose I look for a job? In no time there's night come, an' no bed. No sleep all night, nothin' to eat, what shape am I in in the mornin' to look for work? Got to make up my sleep in the park somehow" (the vision of Christ's Church, Spitalfield, was strong on me) "an' get something to eat. An' there I am! Old, down, an' no chance to get up."

"Used to be a toll-gate 'ere," said the Carter. "Many's the time I've paid my toll 'ere in my cartin' days."

"I've 'ad three 'a'penny rolls in two days," the Carpenter announced, after a long pause in the conversation.

"Two of them I ate yesterday, an' the third to-day," he concluded, after another long pause.

"I ain't 'ad anything today," said the Carter. "An' I'm fagged out. My legs is hurtin' me somethin' fearful."

"The roll you get in the 'spike' is that 'ard you can't eat it nicely with less than a pint of water," said the Carpenter, for my benefit. And, on asking him what the "spike" was, he answered, "The casual ward. It's a cant word, you know."

But what surprised me was that he should have the word "cant" in his vocabulary that I found was no mean one before we parted.

I asked him what I may expect in the way of treatment, if we succeeded in getting into the Poplar Workhouse, and between them I was supplied with much information. Having taken a cold bath on entering, I would be given for supper six ounces of bread and "three parts of skilly." "Three parts" means three-quarters of a pint, and "skilly" is a fluid concoction of three quarts of oatmeal stirred into three buckets and a half of hot water.

"Milk and sugar, I suppose, and a silver spoon?" I queried.

"No fear. Salt's what you'll get, an' I've seen some places where you'd not get any spoon. 'Old 'er up an' let 'er run down, that's 'ow they do it."

"You do get good skilly at 'Ackney," said the Carter.

"Oh, wonderful skilly, that," praised the Carpenter, and each looked eloquently at the other.

"Flour an' water at St. George's in the East," said the Carter.

The Carpenter nodded. He had tried them all.

"Then what?" I demanded.

And I was informed that I was sent directly to bed. "Call you at half after five in the mornin', an' you get up an' take a 'sluice'—if there's any soap. Then breakfast, same as supper, three parts o' skilly an' a six-ounce loaf."

"'Tisn't always six ounces," corrected the Carter.

"'Tisn't, no; an' often that sour you can 'ardly eat it. When first I started I couldn't eat the skilly nor the bread, but now I can eat my own an' another man's portion."

"I could eat three other men's portions," said the Carter. "I 'aven't 'ad a bit this blessed day."

"Then what?"

"Then you've got to do your task, pick four pounds of oakum, or clean an' scrub, or break ten to eleven hundredweight o' stones. I don't 'ave to break stones; I'm past sixty, you see. They'll make you do it, though. You're young an' strong."

"What I don't like," grumbled the Carter, "is to be locked up in a cell to pick oakum. It's too much like prison."

"But suppose after you've had your night's sleep, you refuse to pick oakum, or break stones, or do any work at all?" I asked.

"No fear you'll refuse the second time; they'll run you in," answered the Carpenter. "Wouldn't advise you to try it on, my lad."

"Then comes dinner," he went on. "Eight ounces of bread, one and a 'arf ounces of cheese, an' cold water. Then you finish your task and 'ave supper, same as before, three parts o' skilly an' six ounces of bread. Then to bed, six o'clock, an' next mornin' you're turned loose, provided you've finished your task."

We had long since left Mile End Road, and after traversing a gloomy maze of narrow, winding streets, we came to Poplar Workhouse. On a low stone wall we spread our handkerchiefs, and each in his handkerchief put all his worldly possessions with the exception of the "bit o' baccy" down his sock. And then, as the last light was fading from the drab-colored sky, the wind blowing cheerless and cold, we stood, with our pitiful little bundles in our hands, a forlorn group at the workhouse door.

Three working girls came along, and one looked pityingly at me; as she passed I followed her with my eyes, and she still looked pityingly back at me. The old men she did not notice, Dear Christ, she pitied me, young and vigorous and strong, but she had no pity for the two old men who stood by my side! She was a young woman, and I was a young man, and what vague sex promptings impelled her to pity me put her sentiment on the lowest plane. Pity for old men is an altruistic feeling, and besides, the workhouse door is the accustomed place for old men. So she showed no pity for them, only for me, who deserved it least or not at all. Not in honor do gray hairs go down to the grave in London Town.

On one side the door was a bell handle, on the other side a press button.

"Ring the bell," said the Carter to me.

And just as I ordinarily would at anybody's door, I pulled out the handle and rang a peal.

"Oh! Oh!" they cried in one terrified voice. "Not so 'ard!"

I let go, and they looked reproachfully at me, as though I had imperilled their chance for a bed and three parts of skilly. Nobody came. Luckily, it was the wrong bell, and I felt better.

"Press the button," I said to the Carpenter.

"No, no, wait a bit," the Carter hurriedly interposed.

From all of which I drew the conclusion that a poorhouse porter, who commonly draws a yearly salary of from thirty to forty dollars, is a very finicky and important personage, and cannot be treated too fastidiously by—paupers.

So we waited, ten times a decent interval, when the Carter stealthily advanced a timid forefinger to the button, and gave it the faintest possible push. I have looked at waiting men where life and death was in the issue; but anxious suspense showed less plainly on their faces than it showed on the faces of these two men as they waited for the coming of the porter.

He came. He barely looked at us. "Full up," he said, and shut the door.

"Another night of it," groaned the Carpenter. In the dim light the Carter looked wan and gray.

Indiscriminate charity is vicious, say the professional philanthropists. Well, I resolved to be vicious.

"Come on; get your knife out and come here," I said to the Carter, drawing him into a dark alley.

He glared at me in a frightened manner, and tried to draw back. Possibly he took me for a latter-day Jack-the-Ripper, with a penchant for elderly male paupers. Or he may have thought I was inveigling him into the commission of some desperate crime. Anyway, he was frightened.

It will be remembered, at the outset, that I sewed a pound inside my stoker's singlet under the arm-pit. This was my emergency fund, and I was now called upon to use it for the first time.

Not until I had gone through the acts of a contortionist, and shown the round coin sewed in, did I succeed in getting the Carter's help. Even then his hand was trembling so that I was afraid he would cut me instead of the stitches, and I was forced to take the knife away and do it myself. Out rolled the gold piece, a fortune in their hungry eyes; and away we stampeded for the nearest coffee-house.

Of course, I had to explain to them that I was merely an investigator, a social student, seeking to find out how the other half lived. And at once they shut up like clams. I was not of their kind; my speech had changed, the tones of my voice were different, in short, I was a superior, and they were superbly class conscious.

"What will you have?" I asked, as the waiter came for the order.

"Two slices an' a cup of tea," meekly said the Carter.

"Two slices an' a cup of tea," meekly said the Carpenter.

Stop a moment, and consider the situation. Here were two men, invited by me into the coffee-house. They had seen my gold piece, and they could understand that I was no pauper. One had eaten a ha'penny roll that day, the other had eaten nothing. And they called for "two slices an' a cup of tea!" Each man had given a tu'penny order. "Two slices," by the way, means two slices of bread and butter.

This was the same degraded humility that had characterized their attitude toward the poorhouse porter. But I wouldn't have it. Step by step I increased their orders—eggs, rashers of bacon, more eggs, more bacon, more tea, more slices, and so forth—they denying wistfully all the while that they cared for anything more, and devouring it ravenously as fast as it arrived.

"First cup o' tea I've 'ad in a fortnight," said the Carter.

"Wonderful tea, that," said the Carpenter.

They each drank two pints of it, and I assure you that it was slops. It resembled tea less than lager beer resembles champagne. Nay, it was "water-bewitched," and did not resemble tea at all.

It was curious, after the first shock, to notice the effect the food had on them. At first they were melancholy, and talked of the divers times they had contemplated suicide. The Carter, not a week before, had stood on the bridge and looked at the water, and pondered the question. Water, the Carpenter insisted with heat, was a bad route. He, for one, he knew, would struggle. A bullet was "'andier," but how under the sun was he to get hold of a revolver? That was the rub.

They grew more cheerful as the hot "tea" soaked in, and talked more about themselves. The Carter had buried his wife and children, with the exception of one son, who grew to manhood and helped him in his little business. Then the thing happened. The son, a man of thirty-one, died of the smallpox. No sooner was this over than the father came down with fever and went to the hospital for three months. Then he was done for. He came out weak, debilitated, no strong young son to stand by him, his little business gone glimmering, and not a farthing. The thing had happened, and the game was up. No chance for an old man to start again. Friends all poor and unable to help. He had tried for work when they were putting up stands for the first Coronation parade. "An' I got fair sick of the answer: 'No! no! no!' It rang in my ears at night when I tried to sleep, always the same, 'No! no! no!'" Only the past week he had answered an advertisement in Hackney, and on giving his age was told, "Oh, too old, too old by far."

The Carpenter had been born in the army, where his father had served twenty-two years. Likewise, his two brothers had gone into the army; one, troop sergeant-major of the Seventh Hussars, dying in India after the Mutiny; the other, after nine years under Roberts in the East, had been lost in Egypt. The Carpenter had not gone into the army, so here he was, still on the planet.

"But 'ere, give me your 'and," he said, ripping open his ragged shirt. "I'm fit for the anatomist, that's all. I'm wastin' away, sir, actually wastin' away for want of food. Feel my ribs an' you'll see."

I put my hand under his shirt and felt. The skin was stretched like parchment over the bones, and the sensation produced was for all the world like running one's hand over a washboard.

"Seven years o' bliss I 'ad," he said. "A good missus and three bonnie lassies. But they all died. Scarlet fever took the girls inside a fortnight."

"After this, sir," said the Carter, indicating the spread, and desiring to turn the conversation into more cheerful channels; "after this, I wouldn't be able to eat a workhouse breakfast in the morning."

"Nor I," agreed the Carpenter, and they fell to discussing stomach delights and the fine dishes their respective wives had cooked in the old days.

"I've gone three days and never broke my fast," said the Carter.

"And I, five," his companion added, turning gloomy with the memory of it. "Five days once, with nothing on my stomach but a bit of orange peel, an' outraged nature wouldn't stand it, sir, an' I near died. Sometimes, walkin' the streets at night, I've been that desperate I've made up my mind to win the horse or lose the saddle. You know what I mean sir—to commit some big robbery. But when mornin' come, there was I, too weak from 'unger an' cold to 'arm a mouse."

As their poor vitals warmed to the food, they began to expand and wax boastful, and to talk politics. I can only say that they talked politics as well as the average middle-class man, and a great deal better than some of the middle-class men I have heard. What surprised me was the hold they had on the world, its geography and peoples, and on recent and contemporaneous history. As I say, they were not fools, these two men. They were merely old, and their children had undutifully failed to grow up and give them a place by the fire.

One last incident, as I bade them good-by on the corner, happy with a couple of shillings in their pockets and the certain prospect of a bed for the night. Lighting a cigarette, I was about to throw away the burning match when the Carter reached for it. I proffered him the box, but he said, "Never mind, won't waste it, sir." And while he lighted the cigarette I had given him, the Carpenter hurried with the filling of his pipe in order to have a go at the same match.

"It's wrong to waste," said he.

"Yes," I said, but I was thinking of the washboard ribs over which I had run my hand.

CARRYING THE BANNER

"To carry the banner" means to walk the streets all night; and I, with the figurative emblem hoisted, went out to see what I could see. Men and women walk the streets at night all over this great city, but I selected the West End, making Leicester Square my base, and scouting about from the Thames Embankment to Hyde Park.

The rain was falling heavily when the theatres let out, and the brilliant throng which poured from the places of amusement was hard put to find cabs. The streets were so many wild rivers of cabs, most of which were engaged, however; and here I saw the desperate attempts of ragged men and boys to get a shelter from the night by procuring cabs for the cabless ladies and gentlemen. I use the word "desperate" advisedly; for these wretched homeless ones were gambling a soaking against a bed; and most of them, I took notice, got the soaking and missed the bed. Now, to go through a stormy night with wet clothes, and, in addition, to be ill nourished and not to have tasted meat for a week or a month, is about as severe a hardship as a man can undergo. Well-fed and well-clad, I have travelled all day with the spirit thermometer down to seventy-four degrees below zero; and though I suffered, it was a mere nothing compared with carrying the banner for a night, ill-fed, ill-clad, and soaking wet.

The streets grew very quiet and lonely after the theatre crowd had gone home. Only were to be seen the ubiquitous policemen, flashing their dark lanterns into doorways and alleys, and men and women and boys taking shelter in the lee of buildings from the wind and rain. Piccadilly, however, was not quite so deserted. Its pavements were brightened by well dressed women without escort, and there was more life and action there than elsewhere, due to the process of finding escort. But by three o'clock the last of them had vanished, and it was then indeed lonely.

At half-past one the steady downpour ceased, and only showers fell thereafter. The homeless folk came away from the protection of the buildings, and slouched up and down and everywhere, in order to rush up the circulation and keep warm.

One old woman, between fifty and sixty, a sheer wreck, I had noticed earlier in the night, standing on Piccadilly, not far from Leicester Square. She seemed to have neither the sense nor the strength to get out of the rain or keep walking, but stood stupidly, whenever she got the chance, meditating on past days, I imagine, when life was young and blood was warm. But she did not get the chance often. She was moved on by every policeman, and it required an average of six moves to send her doddering off one man's beat and on to another's. By three o'clock she had progressed as far as St. James Street, and as the clocks were striking four I saw her sleeping soundly against the iron railings of Green Park. A brisk shower was falling at the time, and she must have been drenched to the skin.

Now, said I, at one o'clock, to myself, consider that you are a poor young man, penniless, in London Town, and that tomorrow you must look for work. It is necessary, therefore, that you get some sleep in order that you may have strength to look for work and to do work in case you find it.

So I sat down on the stone steps of a building. Five minutes later a policeman was looking at me. My eyes were wide open, so he only grunted and passed on. Ten minutes later my head was on my knees, I was dozing, and the same policeman was saying gruffly, "Ere, you, get outa that!"

I got. And, like the old woman, I continued to get; for every time I dozed a policeman was there to rout me along again. Not long after, when I had given this up, I was walking with a young Londoner (who had been out to the colonies and wished he were out to them again) when I noticed an open passage leading under a building and disappearing in darkness. A low iron gate barred the entrance.

"Come on," I said. "Let's climb over and get a good sleep."

"Wot?" he answered, recoiling from me. "An' get run in fer three months! Blimey if I do!"

Later on, I was passing Hyde Park with a young boy of fourteen or fifteen, a most wretched-looking youth, gaunt, and hollow-eyed and sick.

"Let's go over the fence," I proposed, "and crawl into the shrubbery for a sleep. The bobbies couldn't find us there."

"No fear," he answered. "There's the park guardians, and they'd run you in for six months."

Times have changed, alas! When I was a youngster I used to read of homeless boys sleeping in doorways. Already the thing has become a tradition. As a stock situation it will doubtlessly linger in literature for a century to come, but as a cold fact it has ceased to be. Here are the doorways, and here are the boys, but happy conjunctions are no longer effected. The doorways remain empty, and the boys keep awake and carry the banner.

"I was down under the arches," grumbled another young fellow. By "arches" he meant the shore arches where begin the bridges that span the Thames. "I was down under the arches, w'en it was ryning its 'ardest, an' a bobby comes in an' chyses me out. But I come back, an' 'e come too. ' 'Ere,' sez 'e, 'wot you doin' 'ere?' An' out I goes, but I sez, 'Think I want to pinch the bleeding bridge?' "

Among those who carry the banner, Green Park has the reputation of opening its gates earlier than the other parks, and at quarter-past four in the morning, I, and many more, entered Green Park. It was raining again, but they were worn out with the night's walking, and they were down on the benches and asleep at once.

Many of the men stretched out full length on the dripping wet grass, and, with the rain falling steadily upon them, were sleeping the sleep of exhaustion.

And now I wish to criticise the powers that be. They *are* the powers, therefore they may decree whatever they please; so I make bold only to criticise the ridiculousness of their decrees. All night long they make the homeless ones walk up and down. They drive them out of doors and passages, and lock them out of the parks. The evident intention of all this is to deprive them of sleep. Well and good, the powers have the power to deprive them of sleep, or of anything else for that matter; but why under the sun do they open the gates of the parks at five o'clock in the morning and let the homeless ones go inside and sleep? If it is their intention to deprive them of sleep, why do they let them sleep after five in the morning? And if it is not their intention to deprive them of sleep, why don't they let them sleep earlier in the night?

In this connection, I will say that I came by Green Park that same day, at one in the afternoon, and that I counted scores of the ragged wretches asleep in the grass. It was Sunday afternoon, the sun was fitfully appearing, and the well-dressed West Enders, with their wives and progeny, were out by thousands, taking the air. It was not a pleasant sight for them, those horrible, unkempt, sleeping vagabonds; while the vagabonds themselves, I know, would rather have done their sleeping the night before.

And so, dear soft people, should you ever visit London Town, and see these men asleep on the benches and in the grass, please do not think they are lazy creatures, preferring sleep to work. Know that the powers that be have kept them walking all the night long, and that in the day they have nowhere else to sleep.

THE MANAGEMENT

In this final chapter it were well to look at the Social Abyss in its widest aspect, and to put certain questions to Civilization, by the answers to which Civilization must stand or fall. For instance, has Civilization bettered the lot of man? "Man" I use in its democratic sense, meaning the average man. So the question reshapes itself: *Has Civilization bettered the lot of the average man?*

Let us see. In Alaska, along the banks of the Yukon River, near its mouth, live the Innuit folk. They are a very primitive people, manifesting but mere glimmering adumbrations of that tremendous artifice, Civilization. Their capital amounts possibly to $10 per head. They hunt and fish for their food with bone-headed spears and arrows. They never suffer from lack of shelter. Their clothes, largely made from the skins of animals, are warm. They always have fuel for their fires, likewise timber for their houses, which they build partly underground, and in which they lie snugly during the periods of intense cold. In the summer they live in tents, open to every breeze and cool. They are healthy and strong and happy. Their one problem is food. They have their times of plenty and times of famine. In good times they feast; in bad times they die of starvation. But starvation, as a chronic condition, present with a large number of them all the time, is a thing unknown. Further they have no debts.

In the United Kingdom, on the rim of the Western Ocean, live the English folk. They are a consummately civilized people. Their capital amounts to at least $1500 per head. They gain their food, not by hunting and fishing, but by toil at colossal artifices. For the most part they suffer from lack of shelter. The greater number of them are vilely housed, do not have enough fuel to keep them warm, and are insufficiently clothed. A constant number never have any house at all, and sleep shelterless under the stars. Many are to be found, winter and summer, shivering on the streets in their rags. They have good times and bad. In good times most of them manage to get enough to eat, in bad times they die of starvation. They are dying now, they were dying yesterday and last year, they will die tomorrow and next year, of starvation; for they, unlike the Innuit, suffer from a chronic condition of starvation. There are 40,000,000 of the English folk, and 939 out of every 1000 of them die in poverty, while a constant army of 8,000,000 struggle on the ragged edge of starvation. Further, each babe that is born, is born in debt to the sum of $110. This is because of an artifice called the National Debt.

In a fair comparison of the average Innuit and the average Englishman, it will be seen that life is less rigorous for the Innuit; that while the Innuit suffers only during bad times from starvation, the Englishman suffers during good times as well; that no Innuit lacks fuel, clothing or housing, while the Englishman is in perpetual lack of these three essentials. In this connection it is well to instance the judgment of a man such as Huxley. From the knowledge gained as a medical officer in the East End of London, and as a scientist pursuing investigations among the most elemental savages, he concludes, "Were the alternative presented to me I would deliberately prefer the life of a savage to that of those people of Christian London."

The creature comforts man enjoys are the products of man's labor. Since Civilization has failed to give the average Englishman food and shelter equal to that enjoyed by the Innuit, the question arises: *Has Civilization increased the producing power of the average man?* If it has not increased man's producing power, then Civilization cannot stand.

But it will be instantly admitted, Civilization *has* increased man's producing power. Five men can produce bread for a thousand. One man can produce cotton cloth for 250 people, woolens for 300, and boots and shoes for 1000. Yet it has been shown throughout the pages of this book that English folk by the millions do not receive enough food, clothes and boots. Then arises the third and inexorable question: *If Civilization has increased the producing power of the average man, why has it not bettered the lot of the average man?*

There can be one answer only—MISMANAGEMENT. Civilization has made possible all manner of creature comforts and heart's delights. In these the average Englishman does not participate. If he shall be forever unable to participate, then Civilization falls. There is no reason for the continued existence of an artifice so avowed a failure. But it is impossible that men should have reared this tremendous artifice in vain. It stuns the intellect. To acknowledge so crushing a defeat is to give the death-blow to striving and progress.

One other alternative, and one other only, presents itself. *Civilization must be compelled to better the lot of the average man.* This accepted, it becomes at once a question of business management. Things profitable must be continued; things unprofitable must be eliminated. Either the Empire is a profit to England or it is a loss. If it is a loss, it must be done away with. If it is a profit, it must be managed so that the average man comes in for a share of the profit.

If the struggle for commercial supremacy is profitable, continue it. If it is not, if it hurts the worker and makes his lot worse than the lot of a savage, then fling foreign markets and industrial empire overboard. For it is a patent fact that if

ABOVE: "As we were traveling faster than the army, we were continually overtaking the 'sore-feets' who straggled in the rear of every detachment of infantry."
BELOW: A Japanese artillery unit moving into position.

ABOVE: "But no Japanese did they encounter till they reached the ancient walled city of Ping Yang. . . ."
BELOW: ". . . the farriers of the Japanese army seemed to have no luck in shoeing our horses. Every day they were putting on shoes for us, and every day the shoes were coming off."

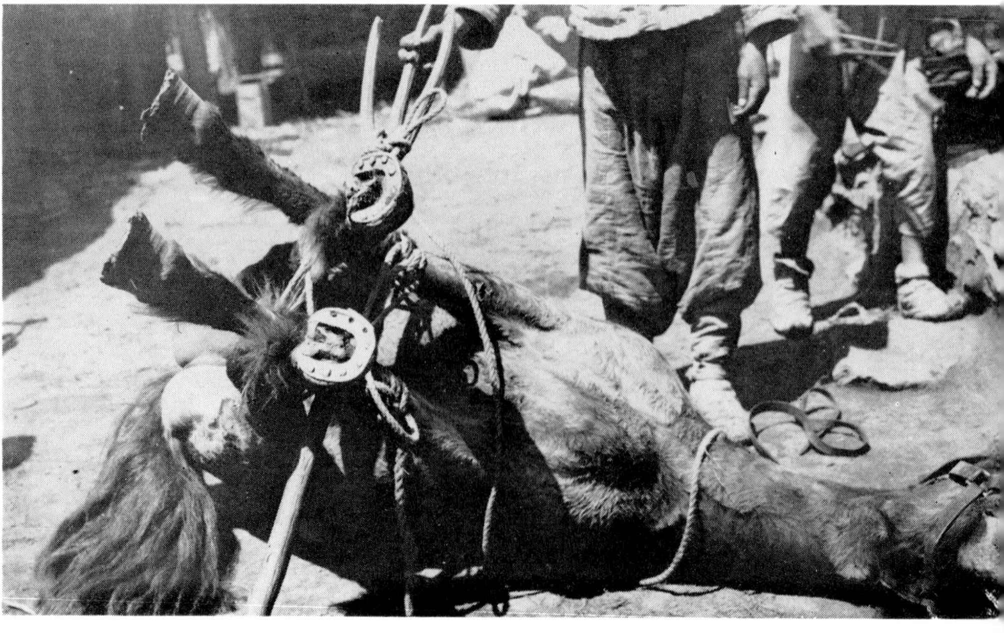

ABOVE: "The first contact of the Japanese and Russians on the land and the first powder actually burned by the land forces occurred at Ping Yang on the morning of February 28th."
BELOW: "The reserves, fresh and chafing from inaction, wild to take part in a glorious day, received the order for general pursuit. Right, left, and center, they took after the Russians."

ABOVE: The harbor at Seoul.
BELOW: Jack London's party headed by his Korean interpreter, Ming-Yang, entering Whang-ju.

ABOVE: "As luck would have it our interpreters were ahead or behind, but we showed our credentials . . . and were most courteously treated by the officers."
BELOW: The jetty at Chemulpo, Korea.

ABOVE: "Opposed to their three divisions on the Yalu was a greatly inferior Russian force, but the Japanese had to cross a river under fire and attack an enemy lying in wait for them."
BELOW: "The night of April 29th and the day of the 30th was an anxious time for the Japanese. Their army was cut in half, and it was no less than the Yalu that divided it."

40,000,000 people, aided by Civilization, possess a greater individual producing power than the Innuit, then those 40,000,000 people should enjoy more creature comforts and heart's delights than the Innuits enjoy.

If the 400,000 English gentlemen, "of no occupation," according to their own statement of the census of 1881, are unprofitable, do away with them. Set them to work ploughing game preserves and planting potatoes. If they are profitable, continue them by all means, but let it be seen to that the average Englishman shares somewhat in the profits they produce by working at no occupation.

In short, society must be reorganized, and a capable management put at the head. That the present management is incapable, there can be no discussion. It has drained the United Kingdom of its life-blood. It had enfeebled the stay-at-home folk till they are unable longer to struggle in the van of the competing nations. It has built up a West End and an East End as large as the Kingdom is large, in which one end is riotous and rotten, the other end sickly and underfed.

A vast empire is foundering on the hands of this incapable management. And by empire is meant the political machinery which holds together the English-speaking people of the world outside of the United States. Nor is this charged in a pessimistic spirit. Blood empire is greater than political empire, and the English of the New World and the Antipodes are strong and vigorous as ever. But the political empire under which they are nominally assembled is perishing. The political machine known as the British Empire is running down. In the hands of its management it is losing momentum every day.

It is inevitable that this management, which has grossly and criminally mismanaged, shall be swept away. Not only has it been wasteful and inefficient, but it has misappropriated the funds. Every worn-out, pasty-faced pauper, every blind man, every prison babe, every man, woman and child whose belly is gnawing with hunger pangs, is hungry because the funds have been misappropriated by the management.

Nor can one member of the managing class plead not guilty before the judgment bar of Man. "The living in their houses, and in the graves the dead," are challenged by every babe that dies of innutrition, by every girl that flees the sweater's den to the nightly promenade of Piccadilly, by every worked-out toiler that plunges into the canal. The food this managing class eats, the wine it drinks, the show it makes, and the fine clothes it wears, are challenged by eight million mouths which have never had enough to fill them, and by twice eight million bodies which have never been sufficiently clothed and housed.

There can be no mistake. Civilization has increased man's producing power an hundred fold, and through mismanagement the men of Civilization live worse than the beasts, and have less to eat and wear and protect them from the elements than the savage Innuit in a frigid climate who lives today as he lived in the stone age ten thousand years ago.

1903

THE RUSSO-JAPANESE WAR

Selected Dispatches

THE TRIP TO PING YANG

February 26th, 1904

"Buy everything in sight and get ready to start for Ping Yang."

Thus was I greeted as I landed at Chemulpo. It was the first mouthful of white-man's speech I had had in eight days, during which time I had been traveling with a native crew up the Korean coast in a sampan, or open fishing boat.

The speaker was one of the two non-local newspapermen on the spot. I made the third. Fifty or more were expected at any moment from Japan, as soon as they could find a ship to carry them—hence the advice.

"I've been here two weeks and am all ready to strike out," he added, "horses, coolies, interpreters, everything."

War had been on for a week, though I learned it now for the first time. I had been badly poisoned with charcoal fumes, and my mind was in a daze. I could scarcely identify myself with people and houses and white-man's chow, yet I proceeded to outfit. The trip had to be performed on horseback. I did not know how to ride. Jones, who had advised me, and Macleod, the second newspaperman, proceeded to teach me.

Their method was illuminating—for the mob of mapus (grooms), rickshawmen, coolies and passersby, before the Grand Hotel. Jones and Macleod were mounted on mild, medium-sized Chinese ponies. For me they procured a stallion. He was splendid-looking. My heart thrilled as I looked at him. I felt very proud. I failed to see anything significant in the fact of the two mapus holding his head. I mounted. The mob laughed and scattered. The mapus loosed their hold, and away I went.

But I did not go like an arrow from a bow. Rather was my course that of a boomerang charged with unlimited energy and speed. I curved back and forth, circled about, plunged into snow banks, knocked other people's horses out of my path (which was a path other people could not divine), and cut up scandalously.

But it was not my fault. All I tried to do was to make the horse go straight ahead, and all I succeeded in doing was to stick on. Other horses bit at mine. He bit back, reared on his hind legs, his teeth snapping, striking with his forelegs and pawing the air.

"Say, old man, do it this way!" Jones shouted at me.

I had no breath left in me to thank him, but my steed responded. His forefeet just missed the small of Jones' back. Jones circled his horse about. Mine followed, striking with his forefeet and biting. Jones beat him over the face and nose with a whip. I hauled with all my strength on the reins. I hauled vainly, for Jones ran away after Macleod. I followed, plunged off the beaten path into the soft snow, and flurried about like a hailstorm. Two mapus made a rush and swung onto my horse's head, and I slipped off and got out of the way. I looked at my watch. The performance had lasted four minutes, yet I could have staked my life that it had lasted twenty minutes. Every bone and muscle was aching and sore. I was breathing heavily. My heart was going like a Waterbury. It was a cold morning—several degrees above zero—yet the sweat was starting from every pore; I could feel it trickling down my back, and my face was wet as from a shower bath.

"You take the horse," suggested Macleod to Jones, "and let him get on your horse."

Jones shook his head, and my stallion pranced back to the hotel between two mapus, who looked anything but happy.

"What you need, old man, is a mild, sweet-tempered animal," said Jones.

The remark was superogatory. It was the thing I had expressly stipulated just previous to beginning the lesson.

And all this preliminary to going off to see the Russians and Japanese fight.

"Anyway," said I, "that horse is one of the things in sight which I shall not buy."

I engaged an interpreter—provisionally. I know not what happy thought led me to make the engagement provisional, for his conversation was excellent. He was a Japanese, and he had memorized it all!

When the bargain was concluded he delivered himself of his last sentence: "I wish to go with you to the war with all my heart."

He had reached the end of his rope, and five minutes later I had to borrow Jones' interpreter in order to understand what my interpreter was talking about.

"You need a mapu," said Jones; "also a boy."

A mapu is a groom, whose ordinary wage is four to six dollars a month and who finds himself.

I declined engaging a mapu until I should find the mild, sweet-tempered horse; but a boy was a necessity, and Mr. Emberly, proprietor of the hotel, said he had just the man. Wanyoungi was his name, and he came to work for me for $17.50 and find himself—a liberal wage.

He dressed in European clothes, with a white shirt, stand-up collar, tie, studs, and all complete, and he talked English better, far better, than my provisional interpreter, and he was Korean. Not only did he know how to work himself and achieve results, but he possessed the miraculous faculty of getting work out of other Koreans. For the first time the hotel boys built a fire in my room and brought hot water before I was dressed and away. And for the first time the fires they built burned.

Having secured me such a gem of a boy, I concluded that Mr. Emberly was just the man to get me a horse—mild and sweet-tempered. So I listened to him and went off with him to see Mr. Brown, chief of the Korean Customs.

Mr. Brown had two horses. We looked at them. One stamped firily. "I need a horse; I shall take that one," said Mr. Emberly. "Of course, he's too lively for you," he added.

I quite agreed. The second horse I fell in love with on first sight. The prettiest head and gentlest eyes I had ever seen in a horse. It allowed me to pet him, rubbed his neck against me, whinnied, and begged for more petting.

"Is he all right?" I asked. "You know I know nothing about horses."

"Just the horse for you," was the reply.

I bought him. Next morning he was brought around to the hotel. Frazier, a gentleman jockey and steeplechase rider, took him for a canter. General Allen looked on.

"Splendid motion," said he. "The easiest riding horse of all, and the hardiest."

"Well set up," said Frazier. "Will endure more than either Macleod's or Jones'."

Again I was proud over a horse. I mounted, and this time rode away. I rode into Seoul, and as I rode I noticed the horse sheered constantly to the right.

"Carries a weather helm," I said to myself, and therefore rode with the helm hard aport. The resulting course was approximately straight ahead, but it struck me that the manner of obtaining it was not precisely the proper thing.

I determined to see how far this predeliction to the right would carry him, so I hauled the helm amidships and waited. At once the sheer to the right began, and to the right yawned a ten-foot ditch.

"Surely he will give over when he gets to the edge," I thought, and steeled my soul to endure his daring. He dared the edge, the very edge. In fact he was falling into the ditch when I luffed him out of it to port.

And with helm to port I navigated the narrow, crowded streets of the capital of Korea. I marvel at it, when I look back upon it—bulls and bullock carts, trains of Korean pack-ponies, soldiers afoot and ahorse, a swarm of children, apathetic Koreans too lazy to get out of the way, blocked traffic, jams, plunging and rearing of many horses—most of them stallions, and never a collision.

It was not till I turned homeward that the first collision occurred. It was on Legation Street, just beyond the Palace, and it was deliberate. To the right, instead of a yawning ditch, was a frowning wall. I put the helm amidships to study the sheer. The horse sheered, plump into the wall, sideways, and brought up with a resounding thump. I passed my hand in front of his eye. It never fluttered. A minute later, walking, he butted head-on into a wall. He was blind, stone blind. I wonder if the derivation of the phrase "stone blind" has anything to do with horses and stone walls?

In the afternoon I rode in a rickshaw. Also I discharged my interpreter, who had become wholly unintelligible, and hired another. His name was Yamada, and he had been Jones' interpreter; but he had resigned because Jones addressed him as "boy." I engaged always to call him "Mr. Yamada," whereupon he looked very pleased and asked me for an advance of two months' salary.

"Macleod and I start on Monday," said Jones. "Will you be ready?"

It was Sunday. Likewise it was Japanese, Chinese and Korean New Year, and shopkeepers and artisans had given over work and were busy with a celebration scheduled to last anywhere between six days and as long as their money held out.

"Impossible," I answered. "I'll meet you in Ping Yang."

"We're all ready, you know," said Jones; "or we wouldn't mind waiting for you."

I saw Macleod. He said he was all ready to start.

I alone was unprepared, so I went off to be vaccinated, and not only was I vaccinated but I bought a horse from the doctor—one of the Russian Minister's horses which he had left behind when he hurriedly departed. It was a splendid animal, had been imported from Australia, and was as cheap as a Chinese pony, while several times as large. In fact, the girths of the saddle which I had bought for my blind horse would not go half way around.

I returned in glee to the hotel to find that three Korean pack-ponies had been purchased for me. But before I ratified the purchase I assured myself that they were at least not blind. Also I learned that Macleod and Jones, who were all ready, would not be ready until Tuesday, whereupon I went out and bought a horse for my interpreter—I beg his pardon, I mean Mr. Yamada.

I was now the owner of five horses, and two mapus were engaged to take care of them. Then came the rush, in which Wanyoungi, the gem of boys, was my savior. He worked like a demon, and had everybody else working. Everything was to be bought—saddles, bridles, blankets, hitching straps, nose bags, rope lashings, spare sets of horseshoes all around, horseshoer's tools, pack-saddles, extra girths, canned goods, rubber boots, mittens, caps, gloves, clothes, flour, cooking utensils, shoes, candles, and all the thousand and one articles necessary for a campaign which might extend into Manchuria. And it was New Year's!

Tuesday found Macleod and Jones not yet ready, and Wednesday found Jones outfitting from canned goods which I was lightening from my packs, and Macleod delayed and unable to start until Thursday. So my pack-ponies were the first to take the highroad north through Peking Pass; and that night, at the end of fifty li, found Jones sans boy, sans mapus, sans everything, and dining with me.

But I am the proud possessor of the horse of horses. It is a little Korean pony scarcely larger than a Newfoundland dog. I verily believe I could tuck it under my arm and walk away with it. The first day I found it loaded with the heaviest pack. Under the mountain of luggage I could see only its tail and its patient little feet which went pit-a-pat, pit-a-pat throughout the day.

"This will never do," I said. "It is cruel. To-morrow, Wanyoungi, you must put a light pack on that little pony (you see it is the smallest of the lot), and ride it yourself."

It is the wise custom for the boy to ride, so that at the end of the day he will be fresh enough to make camp and cook dinner.

Next day Wanyoungi rode the pony. He weighed 120 pounds and he rode on a pack weighing 130 pounds, while the pack saddle weighed at least twenty pounds more—270 pounds in all. The pony weighed possibly 350 pounds, and yet all day it kept up with our riding horses. Whenever we broke into a lope, it loped after us, whinnying all the while. Nor could Wanyoungi hold it back. He tried with the reins and his strength, and he tried with the Korean language and his imagination, but the pony trotted, loped, or walked always at our heels.

Jones and I decided that it would be dead by the time we made camp. But I changed my mind that night at feeding time, when it kicked and plunged and bit the other larger ponies till it had its own food and half their share to boot, to say nothing of the best place to sleep and the most room. Jones is now trying to buy it, and I am trying to decide whether or not I shall ride it if something happens to my own horse. Jones' principal objection to this is that both my feet will drag on the ground, and I half believe him. To-morrow I shall mount it and find out for myself. Perhaps I may be able to tuck my feet up a little.

COSSACKS FIGHT THEN RETREAT

Ping Yang, March 5, 1904—The first land fight!

The first contact of the Japanese and Russians on the land and the first powder actually burned by the land forces occurred at Ping Yang on the morning of February 28th.

A scouting party of Russian Cossacks, crossing the Yalu at Wiju, had ventured 200 miles south into Korea to get in touch with the Japanese and discover how far north they had penetrated.

Three Americans escorting women from the mines of the American concession, fifty miles east of Anjou, encountered the scouting party of Cossacks at Anjou, on the main Pekin road. They traveled with the troop for a day and described the Cossacks as splendid looking soldiers, perfect horsemen and mounted on sturdy Russian ponies.

As an instance of the discipline of the men the following is related: One of the Americans had given a trooper the makings of a cigarette. The soldier, sitting in the saddle, had just begun to roll the cigarette when the command was given for them to break into a gallop. Away fluttered tobacco and rice paper as the soldier instantly obeyed.

The Cossacks had not the slightest idea of where they would pick up with the Japanese, and each village was a possible and probable ambuscade. Approaching a village, they dismounted and spread out, and in this order they entered, with their horses between them and the houses.

But no Japanese did they encounter till they reached the ancient walled city of Ping Yang, the scene of the slaughter of the Chinese by the Japanese in 1894 and a city whose written history leaps boldly back into the centuries before Christ. Here in the pleasant valley beyond the walls of Ping Yang the Cossacks, twenty in number, ran upon five Japanese cavalry. A race resulted, the Cossacks pursuing and only giving over when met with a hot fire from the wall.

To Company 7 of the Forty-sixth regiment of infantry, Twelfth division of the Japanese army, belongs the honor of firing the first shots on the land. Fourteen men of this company, under command of First Lieutenant C. Yoshimura, ensconced upon the crumbling battlement, had watched the chase as it led up to them. At 700 meters (about 2,300 feet) distance, time 9:30 A.M., they opened fire.

The Cossacks promptly whirled their horses and rode away. Thirty shots were fired in all, to which the Cossacks made no reply. They had fulfilled their errand of finding the Japanese and wisely entertained no idea of capturing Ping Yang.

It is remarkable that none was killed or wounded by such short range fire. The Japanese explain it by the fact that they were afraid of hitting their own fleeing cavalry. They aver, however, that two Cossacks were seen to dismount from evidently wounded horses and lead them away. So Russian blood was shed in the first land engagement, even if it was only horse blood.

Lieutenant C. Yoshimura gave the command to fire and was the only officer present, though my first details were obtained from a brother officer, Lieutenant Y. Abe, who called upon me in my quarters in a Japanese hotel, and whom I entertained in the Japanese fashion—the only fashion available.

We sat on the matting floor of my room, shoes off, drinking tea and saki and eating pickled onions with chopsticks. Between us was the customary lulbachi with its few glowing coals, and into it was dropped the ashes from endless cigarettes. The Japanese are inveterate cigarette smokers, and politeness demands that they shall be fed to one's visitors. Which is all very well, but which is rather hard on the poor correspondent, far from his base of supplies.

Lieutenant Abe, by the way, is a typical officer of the new Japan. For all his European uniform and close-cropped beard, he was Oriental. His legs were folded under him to the manner born, and he was very comfortable, while my legs sprawled out awkwardly and required constant shifting to prevent going to sleep, and I was decidedly uncomfortable.

A graduate of the military academy at Tokio, he knew French and English and Chinese, and was studying German at the present moment. After the war was over, he informed me, he was scheduled to return to the academy and take post-graduate courses in military science.

The Japanese are surely a military race. Their men are soldiers, and their officers are soldiers. I called upon Captain Kauchiba of the Pioneers, who lives in the room adjoining mine. He was a very busy man, just now having charge of the construction of the bridge across the Tai-tong river and of the Ping Yang fortifications.

He sat on the floor in the midst of a mass of correspondence, maps and plans. Orderlies came and went with innumerable reports, messengers arrived and were dispatched—all serving to punctuate our brief conversation. Between us was the lulbachi, cigarettes were offered, and tea ordered. The wall was lined with military chests, of a size convenient for pack ponies. Saddle bags, belt and saber hung on the wall. There was no table. All his work was done on the floor.

His men had marched up from Seoul averaging twenty miles a day; and on my inquiring about sore feet he reluctantly admitted that some of his men were suffering, but added immediately that they were so fired with love of country that sore feet would not matter when it came to fighting the Russians. So far as the Russians were concerned, there was no such thing as sore feet, was his way of putting it. Some few of them might be in poor condition for marching, but all were in good condition for fighting.

I was in search of horseshoes and departed after a brief ten minutes with a letter to an officer of cavalry. Also, I carried with me Captain Kauchiba's promise of an additional set of shoes from himself. In all such matters of help and advice the Japanese officers have shown themselves uniformly courteous and kind, and though they are busy men they always have a minute to spare for the stray correspondent seeking help of some sort or other.

OVER THE PEKIN ROAD ON THE WAY TO THE YALU

Ping Yang, March 7, 1904.

The Pekin road has been described as a river of mud. This is not quite correct, for it is true only in the daytime. In the night it turns to a river of ice, while on the north side of every pass the road remains sheeted with ice all day long.

And on these ice-sheets, pitching down at a slope of from 15 to 30 degrees, is where a man loads his horse and prays—first, that the horse will not break its legs, and next, that it will not fall upon him. Not only must the man look out for his horse behind him and above him, and in imminent likelihood of falling upon him and crushing him, but he must look out for his own footing. For it must be borne in mind that it is glare ice, hard as adamant, and that its pitch makes it many times more slippery than a polished floor.

The combination of a slippery man and a slipping horse is not a happy one, while the combination of many slipping horses and men, in a long string, brings out the sweat alike on man and beast. I shall not soon forget such an ice slope we climbed at the rear of a column of infantry. The men were sprawling right and left. Slipping became contagious. Macleod, in front of me, after mad gyrations, went down. A soldier picked him up and promptly went down himself. My feet were inclined to move in divers simultaneous directions, and the resultant was precarious equilibrium maintained at hazard and by miracle. But poor Belle, my horse, had four feet sliding in many simultaneous directions, and behind her and under her was Jones and his horse, both slipping and floundering, the former shouting each time Belle threatened to fall back upon him. As Belle threatened every moment, his shouting was continuous.

"Watch out! Your horse is breaking its legs!" was his burden. Then it changed to, "Look at her shoes!"

I looked. She was pawing and scrambling wildly, and at each impact of a foot with the ice I could see the shoe itself move and slide on the foot as well as on the ice. When we gained the summit—and there was no stopping till we did—all her shoes were loose and two could be pulled off by hand; while Macleod's horse had no shoes at all on its hind feet.

Jones pushed on with the packs, and Macleod and I led our horses. Five li farther on we encountered a village filled with soldiers. As luck would have it our interpreters were ahead or behind, but we showed our credentials; also a letter written in Japanese by Minister Hiyashi, and were most courteously treated by the officers. One trim young lieutenant, astride his horse, unbuckled his saddlebags and drew forth a horseshoe.

"Well, all I can say is that I have learned something about war," said Macleod.

And so had I. G. Bernard Shaw's chocolate cream soldier may be true of Europe, but it is not true of Japan. The officers of Nippon certainly do not carry confectionery in their saddlebags and holsters. But there were no farriers, and while we stamped our feet in the cold for three hours, waiting the arrival of the next detachment of cavalry, we resolved that henceforth we would carry horseshoes in our own saddlebags; also that we would become farriers ourselves.

We started out after dark, the hoofs of our horses ringing out sharply on the frozen roadbed, and at the end of ten li caught up with Jones. He had found quarters in a village of six houses, where 100 soldiers had been billeted, and right valliantly had he held our room. There was just space in it for our three camp cots side by side, yet it would have accommodated a dozen soldiers packed on the floor. He had been ordered by an officer a number of times to vacate, and a number of times all our goods had been carted into the street. The Korean mapus and interpreters, mortally afraid of the "dwarfs," had begged him, after each eviction, to go on to the next village; but Jones figured that the next village was equally crammed with soldiers, and each time our goods were thrown out he had ordered the trembling mapus to carry them back.

And here arises a question of ethics. Was Jones justified, and were we, as sharers in the night's shelter, justified in occupying the house? The house might be called ours by right of possession; it might be called the soldiers' by right of occupation of the country. On the other hand, how about the Korean who owned it? Anyway, Macleod and I were grateful to Jones, and our sleep was sound.

To keep shoes on our horses was the great problem. In the first place, our horseshoes were white man's horseshoes, about which the Korean farriers knew nothing; and as their knowledge of their own kind of shoes was the accumulated wisdom of centuries, it was beyond the wildest flights of imagination to dream that they could learn anything about white man's shoes inside several centuries more. In the meantime we could scarcely afford to wait.

Next, the farriers of the Japanese army seemed to have no luck in shoeing our horses. Every day they were putting on shoes for us, and every day the shoes were coming off. It made us sigh for a good American smithy, and it made us lead our horses into Ping Yang at the end of the first hundred and eighty miles.

Here I bought several pounds of horseshoe nails from Mr. Graham Lee, American missionary. Through the same missionary I managed to get hold of a Korean blacksmith who agreed to make two sets after the pattern of Belle's shoes, and who promptly got drunk upon receipt of so extensive an order. But Mr. Lee wrestled with him, and I ultimately obtained the sets; also a set of ready-made shoes from a Captain of Pioneers, and another set from a cavalry captain, quite fixed me up. Hereafter I travel with a complete set in my saddlebags; likewise with a hammer, pinchers and a wedge of iron for clinching the nails. And if Belle survives the ordeal I shall surely learn something of the farrier's trade.

But horses' feet were not the only feet that suffered on the Pekin road. Sore-footed soldiers were pretty much in evidence. They trailed along for miles behind every marching company and battalion; and few miseries are greater than sore feet of men on the march. Each step is torture, and they must go on, step by step, all day long. If they could only lie down and rest till the sores were healed, all would be well; but on they must go, step by step, each step hurting anew the lacerated flesh.

To them Paradise would sum itself up in cessation of movement, and doubtless they dreamed of their Buddhist Nirvana through the long hours of tramping. At any rate, they dreamed as they marched, for nothing could rouse them. The sound of our flying hoofs made no impression upon them and when we zigzagged through a bunch of "sore-feets" they did not scatter. Not the least effort did they make to get out of the way when our horses came in contact with them thrusting past. They were too far gone, like seasick persons, to care. It was easier to be run down than to make a quick effort to leap aside. We did not run any down, but it was through no virtue of care on their part.

As we were traveling faster than the army, we were continually overtaking the "sore-feets" who straggled in the rear of every detachment of infantry. The majority had discarded their knapsacks, which they heaped upon the backs of coolies impressed for the service. Many of them discarded the army shoe of stiff leather and went back to their native gear, the soft straw sandal. And some I saw with a piece of stiff cloth under the sole of the foot, the foot naked, trudging along through the freezing mud. But this was the breaking-in process; there will be few "sore-feets" after they have marched half a thousand miles.

There were other breaking-in processes along the road, as instance at Whang-ju, where the Korean inhabitants were broken in to the expediency of giving lodgings and horsefood to white men and to the inexpediency of stealing from white men. Whang-ju is an ancient walled city of an estimated population of 30,000, beautifully situated on the right bank of the Namchlion river. Macleod and Jones had traveled 140 li that day, crossed the great Tong-sun pass in the late afternoon, journeyed on in the darkness through twenty li where there were no villages because of fear of the native mountain robbers, and arrived, horses and men exhausted, at Whang-ju. I, as usual, was pushing along behind, delayed by a loose horseshoe.

Whang-ju has 20,000 people who live in houses, yet not one room would they rent to Macleod and Jones, nor one ounce of beans or barley would they sell for the horses. The weary men and jaded horses were led back and forth over the town. There was endless chin-chin, but no chow, while there were frequent invitations to go on to the next village, "ten li more."

This phrase, "ten li more," has a peculiarly irritating effect on Jones. He avers that he has heard nothing else since he entered the country, and that he has heard it so often and under such exasperating circumstances that he is going to write a book on Korea and entitle it "Ten Li More." When he found himself, with Macleod, finally led to the gate and invited, with the objectionable phrase appended, to go on to the next village, he balked.

If 30,000 people would not sell shelter, what was to be expected of a small village? Jones declined to move on. Macleod seconded him. They negligently transferred their revolvers from one pocket to the other, and it would have done Isabella Bird Bishop's heart good to see the transformation. It would have atoned for much which she suffered at the hands of inhospitable and insulting Koreans. At once heads were put together, there was quick whispering, and in two minutes horses and men were in comfortable quarters.

Later in the night I arrived, rousing all Whang-ju with my yells as I rode through its streets seeking my party. Luckily I was without an interpreter, and so escaped knowledge of the many invitations doubtlessly extended to continue on my way "ten li more." So I rode and yelled and woke the town, till I heard the welcome voice of Jones' interpreter and found Jones and Macleod stretched out on the floor of a miserable Korean room and waiting chow.

We had left our packs behind and were making a dash for Ping Yang. Our camp cots were with the packs, and a rug apiece was our portion; and our commissary was exhausted. No milk, little sugar, no bread, a little tea, and dirty, half-cooked native rice was the menu; and the rice was eaten without sugar, which later went into the making of a lot of whisky toddy. And then we had no more whisky.

In the morning we awoke to a still more limited menu and to the fact that two blankets had been stolen off our horses. The housemaster knew nothing. This was ascertained after an eternity of chin-chin. The housemaster was very sorry. A second eternity of chin-chin was required to extract this information, and after a third eternity we learned that the housemaster could do nothing to recover the blankets.

Our horses were saddled. We were ready to start. We expressed our wrath by appropriate vociferation and gesture, and thrust the housemaster out in quest of the stolen property. It was a cold, raw morning, and I do not remember ever seeing a more pitiful and miserable specimen of humanity than that same housemaster as he stood, irresolute and helpless, in the middle of the street, hands thrust for warmth into either voluminous sleeve, shoulders stooped, eyes weazened and appealing and deprecating, his whole bearing and expression that of a man passively and fearfully awaiting death by slow torture.

But the fear of death sprang up in another man's heart. We sent for the headman of the neighborhood, a well-dressed individual with the rotund indications of material prosperity. Him we addressed, through an interpreter, something in this fashion: "Two blankets have been stolen. We hold you responsible. We want, not chin-chin, but blankets. We give you five minutes to find them. If at the end of five minutes they are not forthcoming we will stand you in the corner there, on that heap of refuse, and give your men five additional minutes to find the blankets. And then if they are not found we will take you with us to Ping Yang and—"

We never finished that final sentence, but left what horrid fate awaited him at Ping Yang to his own imagination. His first five minutes were fruitless, and we stood him in a corner on the refuse. Then began the search of his men. Under his direction it was feverish. They turned everything topsy-turvy. All Whang-ju had arrived to look on. I was beginning to wonder how we could possibly back our bluff if it failed, or save our faces, when a shout went up. An enterprising coolie had unearthed the missing blankets from a hiding place not a dozen feet away.

But in Korea it does not pay to be enterprising. For the coolie's discovery was the signal of a general onslaught upon none other than himself. Macleod's interpreter was the first to get him, and he got him by the topknot. Blows and kicks were rained upon him, the while he protested to high heaven and Whang-ju. High heaven did not hear but Whang-ju was delighted.

In the meantime I was busy with the headman. In my innocence I had thought he was rushing to attack the interpreter, and to make life liveable on the Pekin road one must back up his interpreter. So I shoved the headman back into his corner. I shoved a little too sharply, for he lost his footing. Yet I had done his intention, not himself, an injustice. In reality he had leaped forward to join in the beating being given his coolie.

But why under the sun the coolie was beaten passed my comprehension for the moment. It was certainly Asiatic—a conception that the weak, by wreaking hurt upon the weaker, would propitiate the strong. By the time I had got this through my head Ming-Yang, the Korean interpreter, had the headman by the topknot. I was delighted. Assembled Whang-ju was astounded. The state of mind of the headman was something beyond words; so was his topknot when Ming-Yang had done with him.

"Tell him that fifty more white men, just like us, will arrive in half an hour," said Jones, as we mounted our horses.

"If you do, in twenty minutes there won't be a single inhabitant left in Whang-ju," said Macleod.

And, heedful of his warning, we rode away, our consciences salved with the knowledge that we had withheld the full measure of our wrath and not depopulated a flourishing city of 30,000 souls.

BEWARE THE MONKEY CAGE

Antung, Manchuria. May 10th, 1904. The Japanese, following the German model, make every possible preparation, take every possible precaution, and then proceed to act, confident in the belief that nothing short of a miracle can prevent success. Opposed to their three divisions on the Yalu was a greatly inferior Russian force, but the Japanese had to cross a river under fire and attack an enemy lying in wait for them.

By the manipulation of their three divisions, and what of their ruses, they must have sadly befuddled the Russians. At the mouth of the Yalu the Japanese had two small gunboats, two torpedo-boats and four small steamers armed with Hotchkiss-guns. Also they had fifty sampans loaded with bridge materials. These were intended for a permanent bridge across the Yalu at Wiju; but they served another purpose—first, farther down the stream. The presence of the small navy and the loaded sampans led the Russians to believe that right there was where the bridge was to be built. So right there they stationed some three thousand men to prevent the building of the bridge. Thus a handful of Japanese sailors kept 3,000 Russian soldiers occupied in doing nothing and reduced the effectiveness of the Russian strength of that much.

Another ruse was the building of a bridge in front of Wiju. This was in plain view of the Russians on the conical hill opposite just east of Kieu-Liang-Cheng, and they consumed much time and powder in shelling it. This was precisely what the Japanese intended for the bridge. While it held the Russian attention, a little farther down the stream the Japanese were at work on another bridge screened by small willow trees on the intervening island, and which, when completed, had never had a shot fired at it.

Have you ever stood in front of a cage wherein there was a monkey gazing innocently and peaceably into your eyes—so innocent and peaceable the hands grasping the bars and wholly unbelligerent, the eyes that bent with friendly interest on yours, and all the while and unbeknown a foot sliding out to surprise your fancied security and set you shrieking with sudden fright? Beware the monkey cage! You have need of more than eyes; and beware the Japanese. When he sits down stupidly to build a bridge with his two hands before your eyes, have a thought to the quiet place behind the willow-screen where another bridge is being builded by his two feet. He works with hands and feet, he works night and day, and he never does but one thing expected of him, and that is the unexpected thing.

The night of April 29th and the day of the 30th was an anxious time for the Japanese. Their army was cut in half, and it was no less than the Yalu that divided it. One-third of its force, the Z division, had crossed the river to the right and was in Manchuria. They had no very accurate knowledge of the Russian strength, and it was not beyond liability that the Russians might make a counter attack on the Z division and destroy it. So the X and Y divisions on the south bank were in momentary readiness to prevent this by delivering an attack upon the Russians straight across the river. But there was no need for this. The Russians were not in sufficient force to attack a single division, advancing as it was across mountainous country. This, in turn, the Japanese did not know, but they prepared for the possibility as they prepare for everything.

The Ai-ho river flows out of Manchuria and enters the Yalu valley a mile or more above Kieu-Liang-Cheng. It also flows down past that village, close to the Manchurian shore, thus interposing an obstacle to the advance of the whole Japanese army (even the Z division), after it had crossed the Yalu proper. The crossing of the Ai-ho was seriously menaced by the sixteen guns of the Russian right on the conical hill. The day's work for April 30th was to put those sixteen guns out of business. The Japanese bent themselves to the task. It was an exposed position, and a concentrated fire lasting twenty-five minutes and in which time sixty common shells were thrown, did the work. The Russian fire was silenced and the guns were withdrawn that night! Incidentally the Japanese shelled the Russian camp, carelessly situated where it was exposed to view from the Korean hills, and wrought great havoc.

On the night of April 30th the X and Y divisions crossed the main Yalu and rested on the sands, with the Ai-ho between them and the Russians. The X division forming the Japanese left, faced the Russian right on the conical hill, the Y division was extended near the mouth of the Ai-ho; and up the Ai-ho, extended for several miles, lay the Z division. Opposing these three divisions was a Russian actual fighting force of about 4,000 men. The Russian line, extending some six or seven miles, was not intact. In fact, because of the lay of the land, the Russians really occupied two positions—one on and about the conical hill at Kieu-Liang-Cheng, the other on the Ai-ho, from its mouth several miles up.

Against these two positions, each occupied by about 2,000 men, was hurled an army of three divisions (probably 25,000 men actually on the spot), backed by a powerful artillery of field guns and howitzers. Prevented by shell fire and shrapnel from doing their best to repel the general attack, in process of being flanked by the immensely superior force, the Russian left on the Ai-ho broke first and fled in the direction of Hamatan. The Russian right on the conical hill, fought more tenaciously, the survivors in turn fleeing toward Hamatan.

The Japanese understand the utility of things. Reserves they consider should be used, not only to strengthen the line or to protect the repulsed line, but in the moment of victory to clinch victory hard and fast. The reserves, fresh and chafing from inaction wild to take part in a glorious day, received the order for general pursuit. Right, left and center, they took after the Russians. The field guns, delayed by the Ai-ho followed at a gallop.

The retreat became a rout. The Russian reserves, two regiments, had fled without firing a shot—at least the Japanese have no record of these two regiments. Hamatan is at the conjunction of three roads, six miles to the rear of the conical hill. Down these three roads the Russians ran, coming together and passing on to the main road—the Pekin or Mandarin road. And down these three roads, from right, left and center, came the fresh reserves, and after them the artillery.

In the meantime, however, far from the Japanese right and outstripping the rest of the pursuit; arrived one company of men in time to cut off fifteen Russian guns and eight maxims. The remnants of three battalions rallied around the guns. A hasty position was taken. The rest of the pursuing Japanese did not arrive. But one company of men stood between the Russians and the Pekin road. And it stood. Its captain and three lieutenants were killed. One officer only remained alive. The last cartridge was fired. Those that survived fixed their bayonets ready to receive a charge. And in that moment, left, right and center, their pursuing comrades arrived.

The Russians were assailed from three sides. The tables were turned, but they fought with equal courage. The day was lost; they knew it; yet they fought on doggedly. Night was falling. As the Japanese drew closer the Russians turned loose their horses, destroyed or threw away the breechblocks of their guns, smashed the breeches of the maxims and then, as bayonet countered bayonet, drew white handkerchiefs from their pockets in token of surrender.

One other noteworthy thing occurred in the Japanese pursuit. Midway to Hamatan, flying on the heels of a rout, in the very heat and sweep of triumph, they dropped a line of reserves to receive and protect them should they be hurled back broken and crushed by Russian re-inforcements. Hand in hand with terrifying bravery goes this cold-blooded precaution. Verily, nothing short of the miracle can wreck a plan they have once started to put into execution. The men furnish the unfaltering bravery, confident in the knowledge that their officers have furnished the precaution.

Of course the officers are as brave as the men. On the night of the 30th, when the army took up its position on the Ai-ho, it was not known whether that stream was fordable. Officers from each of the three divisions stripped and swam or waded the river at many different points, practically under the rifles of the Russians.

"Men determined to die" is the way one Japanese officer characterized the volunteers who answer in large numbers to every call for dangerous work. Not knowing whether the Ai-ho was fordable, three plans were seriously considered. First, each soldier was to go into action May 1st dressed in a cartridge belt and equipped with a rifle and a board, the latter to be used as a means for paddling across the Ai-ho. Second, same garb and equipment with a tub substituted for the board, and, third, the strongest swimmers to cross over with ropes, along which, when once fast on the other side bank, the weaker swimmers and non-swimmers could make their way. In any case, had the river not proved fordable, Kipling's "Taking of Lung-Tong-Pen" would have been repeated on a most formidable scale. Surely the Russians would have broken and fled precipitately before so terrible a charge.

Every division, every battery was connected with headquarters by field telephone. When the divisions moved forward they dragged their wires after them like spiders drag the silk of their webs. Even the tiny navy at the mouth of the Yalu was in instant communication with headquarters. Thus, on a wide-stretching and largely invisible field, the commander-in-chief was in immediate control of everything. Inventions, weapons, systems (the navy modeled after the English, the army after the German) everything utilized by the Japanese has been supplied by the Western world; but the Japanese have shown themselves the only Eastern people capable of utilizing them.

From The San Francisco *Examiner*

THE STORY OF AN EYE-WITNESS

(The San Francisco Earthquake, 1906)

The earthquake shook down in San Francisco hundreds of thousands of dollars' worth of walls and chimneys. But the conflagration that followed burned up hundreds of millions of dollars' worth of property. There is no estimating within hundreds of millions the actual damage wrought. Not in history has a modern imperial city been so completely destroyed. San Francisco is gone. Nothing remains of it but memories and a fringe of dwelling-houses on its outskirts. Its industrial section is wiped out. Its business section is wiped out. Its social and residential section is wiped out. The factories and warehouses, the great stores and newspaper buildings, the hotels and the palaces of the nabobs, are all gone. Remains only the fringe of dwelling-houses on the outskirts of what was once San Francisco.

Within an hour after the earthquake shock the smoke of San Francisco's burning was a lurid tower visible a hundred miles away. And for three days and nights this lurid tower swayed in the sky, reddening the sun, darkening the day, and filling the land with smoke.

On Wednesday morning at a quarter past five came the earthquake. A minute later the flames were leaping upward. In a dozen different quarters south of Market Street, in the working-class ghetto, and in the factories, fires started. There was no opposing the flames. There was no organization, no communication. All the cunning adjustments of a twentieth century city had been smashed by the earthquake. The streets were humped into ridges and depressions, and piled with the débris of fallen walls. The steel rails were twisted into perpendicular and horizontal angles. The telephone and telegraph systems were disrupted. And the great water-mains had burst. All the shrewd contrivances and safeguards of man had been thrown out of gear by thirty seconds' twitching of the earth-crust.

By Wednesday afternoon, inside of twelve hours, half the heart of the city was gone. At that time I watched the vast conflagration from out on the bay. It was dead calm. Not a flicker of wind stirred. Yet from every side wind was pouring in upon the city. East, west, north, and south, strong winds were blowing upon the doomed city. The heated air rising made an enormous suck. Thus did the fire of itself build its own colossal chimney through the atmosphere. Day and night this dead calm continued, and yet, near to the flames, the wind was often half a gale, so mighty was the suck.

Wednesday night saw the destruction of the very heart of the city. Dynamite was lavishly used, and many of San Francisco's proudest structures were crumbled by man himself into ruins, but there was no withstanding the onrush of the flames. Time and again successful stands were made by the fire-fighters, and every time the flames flanked around on either side, or came up from the rear, and turned to defeat the hard-won victory.

An enumeration of the buildings destroyed would be a directory of San Francisco. An enumeration of the buildings undestroyed would be a line and several addresses. An enumeration of the deeds of heroism would stock a library and bankrupt the Carnegie medal fund. An enumeration of the dead—will never be made. All vestiges of them were destroyed by the flames. The number of the victims of the earthquake will never be known. South of Market Street, where the loss of life was particularly heavy, was the first to catch fire.

Remarkable as it may seem, Wednesday night, while the whole city crashed and roared into ruin, was a quiet night. There were no crowds. There was no shouting and yelling. There was no hysteria, no disorder. I passed Wednesday night in the path of the advancing flames, and in all those terrible hours I saw not one woman who wept, not one man who was excited, not one person who was in the slightest degree panic-stricken.

Before the flames, throughout the night, fled tens of thousands of homeless ones. Some were wrapped in blankets. Others carried bundles of bedding and dear household treasures. Sometimes a whole family was harnessed to a carriage or delivery wagon that was weighted down with their possessions. Baby buggies, toy wagons, and go-carts were used as trucks, while every other person was dragging a trunk. Yet everybody was gracious. The most perfect courtesy obtained. Never, in all San Francisco's history, were her people so kind and courteous as on this night of terror.

All night these tens of thousands fled before the flames. Many of them, the poor people from the labor ghetto, had fled all day as well. They had left their homes burdened with possessions. Now and again they lightened up, flinging out upon the street clothing and treasures they had dragged for miles.

They held on longest to their trunks, and over these trunks many a strong man broke his heart that night. The hills of San Francisco are steep, and up these hills, mile after mile, were the trunks dragged. Everywhere were trunks, with across them lying their exhausted owners, men and women. Before the march of the flames were flung picket lines of soldiers. And a block at a time, as the flames advanced, these pickets retreated. One of their tasks was to keep the trunk-pullers moving. The exhausted creatures, stirred on by the menace of bayonets, would arise and struggle up the steep pavements, pausing from weakness every five or ten feet.

Often, after surmounting a heart-breaking hill, they would find another wall of flame advancing upon them at right angles and be compelled to change anew the line of their retreat. In the end, completely played out, after toiling for a dozen hours like giants, thousands of them were compelled to abandon their trunks. Here the shopkeepers and soft members of the middle class were at a disadvantage. But the working-men dug holes in vacant lots and backyards and buried their trunks.

At nine o'clock Wednesday evening I walked down through the very heart of the city. I walked through miles and miles of magnificent buildings and towering skyscrapers. Here was no fire. All was in perfect order. The police patrolled the streets. Every building had its watchman at the door. And yet it was doomed, all of it. There was no water. The dynamite was giving out. And at right angles two different conflagrations were sweeping down upon it.

At one o'clock in the morning I walked down through the same section. Everything still stood intact. There was no fire. And yet there was a change. A rain of ashes was falling. The watchmen at the doors were gone. The police had been withdrawn. There were no firemen, no fire-engines, no men fighting with dynamite. The district had been absolutely abandoned. I stood at the corner of Kearney and Market, in the very innermost heart of San Francisco. Kearney Street was deserted.

April 18, 1906

ABOVE: "A waste of smoking ruins."
BELOW: "Within an hour after the earthquake shock the smoke of San Francisco's burning was a lurid tower visible a hundred miles away."

ABOVE: ". . . there was no withstanding the onrush of the flames."
BELOW: "The streets were humped into ridges and depressions . . ."

LEFT: "... the shattered dome of the City Hall. Than it there was no better exhibit of the destructive force of the earthquake. Most of the stone had been shaken from the great dome, leaving standing the naked framework of steel."

BELOW: "San Francisco . . . is like the crater of a volcano, around which are camped tens of thousands of refugees."

Half a dozen blocks away it was burning on both sides. The street was a wall of flame. And against this wall of flame, silhouetted sharply, were two United States cavalrymen sitting their horses, calmly watching. That was all. Not another person was in sight. In the intact heart of the city two troopers sat their horses and watched.

Surrender was complete. There was no water. The sewers had long since been pumped dry. There was no dynamite. Another fire had broken out further uptown, and now from three sides conflagrations were sweeping down. The fourth side had been burned earlier in the day. In that direction stood the tottering walls of the Examiner building, the burned-out Call building, the smoldering ruins of the Grand Hotel, and the gutted, devastated, dynamited Palace Hotel.

The following will illustrate the sweep of the flames and the inability of men to calculate their spread. At eight o'clock Wednesday evening I passed through Union Square. It was packed with refugees. Thousands of them had gone to bed on the grass. Government tents had been set up, supper was being cooked, and the refugees were lining up for free meals.

At half-past one in the morning three sides of Union Square were in flames. The fourth side, where stood the great St. Francis Hotel, was still holding out. An hour later, ignited from top and sides, the St. Francis was flaming heavenward. Union Square, heaped high with mountains of trunks, was deserted. Troops, refugees, and all had retreated.

It was at Union Square that I saw a man offering a thousand dollars for a team of horses. He was in charge of a truck piled high with trunks from some hotel. It had been hauled here into what was considered safety, and the horses had been taken out. The flames were on three sides of the Square, and there were no horses.

Also, at this time, standing beside the truck, I urged a man to seek safety in flight. He was all but hemmed in by several conflagrations. He was an old man and he was on crutches. Said he: "To-day is my birthday. Last night I was worth thirty thousand dollars. I bought five bottles of wine, some delicate fish, and other things for my birthday dinner. I have had no dinner, and all I own are these crutches."

I convinced him of his danger and started him limping on his way. An hour later, from a distance, I saw the truck-load of trunks burning merrily in the middle of the street.

On Thursday morning, at a quarter past five, just twenty-four hours after the earthquake, I sat on the steps of a small residence on Nob Hill. With me sat Japanese, Italians, Chinese, and negroes—a bit of the cosmopolitan flotsam of the wreck of the city. All about were the palaces of the nabob pioneers of Forty-nine. To the east and south, at right angles, were advancing two mighty walls of flame.

I went inside with the owner of the house on the steps of which I sat. He was cool and cheerful and hospitable. "Yesterday morning," he said, "I was worth six hundred thousand dollars. This morning this house is all I have left. It will go in fifteen minutes. He pointed to a large cabinet. "That is my wife's collection of china. This rug upon which we stand is a present. It cost fifteen hundred dollars. Try that piano. Listen to its tone. There are few like it. There are no horses. The flames will be here in fifteen minutes."

Outside, the old Mark Hopkins residence, a palace, was just catching fire. The troops were falling back and driving the refugees before them. From every side came the roaring of flames, the crashing of walls, and the detonations of dynamite.

I passed out of the house. Day was trying to dawn through the smoke-pall. A sickly light was creeping over the face of things. Once only the sun broke through the smoke-pall, blood-red, and showing a quarter its usual size. The smoke-pall itself, viewed from beneath, was a rose color that pulsed and fluttered with lavender shades. Then it turned to mauve and yellow and dun. There was no sun. And so dawned the second day on stricken San Francisco.

An hour later I was creeping past the shattered dome of the City Hall. Than it there was no better exhibit of the destructive force of the earthquake. Most of the stone had been shaken from the great dome, leaving standing the naked framework of steel. Market Street was piled high with the wreckage, and across the wreckage lay the overthrown pillars of the City Hall shattered into short crosswise sections.

This section of the city, with the exception of the Mint and the Post-Office, was already a waste of smoking ruins. Here and there through the smoke, creeping warily under the shadows of tottering walls, emerged occasional men and women. It was like the meeting of the handful of survivors after the day of the end of the world.

On Mission Street lay a dozen steers, in a neat row stretching across the street, just as they had been struck down by the flying ruins of the earthquake. The fire had passed through afterward and roasted them. The human dead had been carried away before the fire came. At another place on Mission Street I saw a milk wagon. A steel telegraph pole had smashed down sheer through the driver's seat and crushed the front wheels. The milk cans lay scattered around.

All day Thursday and all Thursday night, all day Friday and Friday night, the flames still raged.

Friday night saw the flames finally conquered, though not until Russian Hill and Telegraph Hill had been swept and three-quarters of a mile of wharves and docks had been licked up.

The great stand of the fire-fighters was made Thursday night on Van Ness Avenue. Had they failed here, the comparatively few remaining houses of the city would have been swept. Here were the magnificent residences of the second generation of San Francisco nabobs, and these, in a solid zone, were dynamited down across the path of the fire. Here and there the flames leaped the zone, but these fires were beaten out, principally by the use of wet blankets and rugs.

San Francisco, at the present time, is like the crater of a volcano, around which are camped tens of thousands of refugees. At the Presidio alone are at least twenty thousand. All the surrounding cities and towns are jammed with the homeless ones, where they are being cared for by the relief committees. The refugees were carried free by the railroads to any point they wished to go, and it is estimated that over one hundred thousand people have left the peninsula on which San Francisco stood. The Government has the situation in hand, and, thanks to the immediate relief given by the whole United States, there is not the slightest possibility of a famine. The bankers and business men have already set about making preparations to rebuild San Francisco.

From *Collier's* May 5, 1906

THE JEFFRIES-JOHNSON FIGHT

Selected Articles

NEVER A MAN SO FIT

Reno, Nevada, Saturday, June 25, 1910—Despite the scribes and sports who accepted the rumor that Jeffries was to box at three o'clock this morning and who journeyed vainly out to Moana Springs at that unearthly time, Jeffries himself selected the perfectly respectable hour of ten. He skipped rope and shadow boxed to the time of many tunes, which he whistled himself instead of panting for air in this high altitude, and the punching bag rat-tatted the lilt of Mendelssohn's "Spring Song."

For another thing he evidenced was a remarkable good temper and cheerfulness. He has passed through the strain and drag of his long and terrific training, and with that far behind him, perforce yields to the good spirits that are the emanation of perfect well being. All through his couple of hours of hard work to-day he was kittenish and frisky in a huge way, full of "joshes" and bubbling with grim laughter. One does not imagine him laughing heartily ever. It is his nature and his make-up to hint of grimness, even when he is jovial to the top of his bent.

For after the rope skipping he stripped and showed the wonderfully built man he is from the ground up. His legs were like columns—not gnarled, knobby columns, but clean, swelling columns, soft lined and in keeping with the soft lined strength of the rest of him. There is little doubt that in the history of the ring there was never a heavyweight so well and symmetrically proportioned.

His thighs are so mighty that they remind one inevitably of the legendary Teutonic warrior who by the grip of his thighs made his war horse groan beneath him. It would have to be an armor plated, steel trussed horse that Jeffries could not make groan. Leanbellied as a Greek athlete, the muscles of his torso begin their long, deep swell outward and upward from the waist. His back muscles play in matted masses, while those of the shoulders and biceps leap into a twisted roll at the slightest uplift of the arms. And they are all the right kind of muscles. They are not hard and knotted, like those of the professional strong men and weight lifters. They do not bind him and hold him by their inflexibility and weight.

And this is something that the uninitiated do not understand. While those that knew looked on and gloried at Jeff's condition some one remarked naïvely that they were surprised at his softness and at the sheath of fat that encased him. Fat! There is not any fat on him. Those soft mounds and ridges and rolls are the finest grade and quality of muscle a man can possess. One might as well call a cat fat because when it is relaxed its muscles become all velvety softness. That may best describe Jeff's muscular condition at the present moment—a velvety softness, splendid and superb.

Take one of those soft pads of Jeff and watch it. Suddenly it leaps and quivers, takes form and bulk, is alive with swift and excessive energy, then relaxes and sinks back and down into the soft pad that it was. Now, that is a muscle. It is the real thing.

And let it be said that Jeff right now is fit and ready to go into the ring. The best thing for him to do from now till the Fourth is to go fishing and to take only moderate exercise. He is at concert pitch and ready for the summons "let her go."

The floor on which he skipped rope was very slippery, and once he went down. But the quick play of those supple, powerful muscles saved him. He is a heavy man, and to fall on his knee cap meant serious injury. You and I and most of all the rest of us under the same circumstances would have received the injury. Not so with Jeffries. Like lightning the foot and leg muscles of the leg that slipped flexed into action, taking the weight of the falling body and saving the knee.

That Jeffries is no mean judge of distance was shown when in the shadow boxing he made occasional passes at the nose and jaws of his training staff. They were stiff and snappy punches and hooks, yet they paused or whistled by the mark with no more than half an inch to an inch to spare.

Out at Rick's it was the same old Arthur Johnson who sparred fast and furiously with three of his sparring partners in rapid succession. I should not like to be a sparring partner in the Johnson camp. Kaufman was glad when his four rounds were ended, and Cotton showed no signs of regret when his turn was finished. Both had been cuffed and pummelled to the queen's taste; both were bleeding profusely from mouth and nose. And Johnson, unconcerned, was taking on a third man and making him look serious as he went after him.

One thing is certain, barring a lucky punch, which is an extremely unlikely happening, the fight on July 4 is not going to be a short one. Johnson is so clever on the defensive that it would take a long time for Jeff to get him, while, on the other hand, Jeff is no slouch at defending himself, and he is such a behemoth that it would not be in two punches nor forty that Johnson could get him. Whoever gets it will have to work for it, and work hard.

It was the same old "Jack" Johnson of a year and a half ago, looking if anything stronger and better than in his Sydney fight. He had his full bag of familiar tricks with him; the old cleverness of defence; the old letting his opponent hit him repeatedly on his unguarded stomach; the old dreaming and sudden awakening to fierce onslaught for three or four seconds; the old placing of his hand on his opponent's biceps to stop a blow; the old smiling into the camera while in a clinch, and the old "rubbering," trance-like, at the audience or passing of facetious remarks while at the same time cuffing his opponent or blocking and withstanding a violent assault.

Johnson seemed to take the altitude well. Beyond profuse sweating under the hot sun, there was no evidence of exertion. When Kaufman sparred with him the former devoted himself almost wholly to ripping at Johnson's stomach. It may be that this is in anticipation of the terrible raps to be expected from Jeff.

Make no mistake, the fight on the Fourth is going to be a great one. There are only two heavyweights that are at the top notch, and they are Jeff and Johnson.

THE "ABYSMAL BRUTE"

Reno, Nevada, Sunday, June 26, 1910—In considering the relative merits of the two big men who are to try conclusions a week from tomorrow it must be remembered that neither man has ever been really extended, and that neither man has ever been compelled to endure to the uttermost. Barring a lucky punch in the opening rounds endurance will play a large part in determining which man is the better. And by endurance is meant the capacity not only to assimilate punishment but the capacity to administer punishment and to keep on administering more and more punishment.

This question of endurance is worthy of analysis. Men are made differently. Some have but a slight life-grip in their bodies and muscles. Others are apparently impossible to kill. One man can walk seventy-five miles in a day and walk a second seventy-five the next day. Another man will collapse at the end of a twenty mile jaunt and be a lame and groaning wreck for a week to come. Yet both these men will be organically sound, of the same size and weight, and their chance of passing a life insurance examination would be equal.

Then what makes the difference? In the fibres of the one reside a primitive vigor and capacity for exertion that the other lacks. Their muscles may look alike, may be of the same size and tensity, yet the protoplasmic, energy-generating quality is different.

Take a professional weight lifter. He may tip the scales at 160 pounds. He can elevate a 200-pound dumbbell with one hand. Another man, tipping the scales at the same mark, cannot elevate 100 pounds. He is as sound and healthy as the other man, yet he cannot do it. He may faithfully train and exercise for five years, or ten, and yet he will be unable to elevate 200 pounds with one hand. Nor has will anything to do with it. He may have ten times more will power than the other, but will power can't lift the 200 pounds for him. He lacks in the quality of his muscle, that is all.

This protoplasmic vigor may be our brute heritage, but whatever it is, it is a good thing to have whether one is a prize fighter or not. It was in describing the fight at Colma with Jimmy Britt that I pointed out the possession of this muscular quality by Battling Nelson. I called him an abysmal brute, and he never forgave me. Yet I meant it as a compliment.

Of two boxers equal to look upon in every way, equally well trained, with equal organs, equal gameness and equal will power, one will reach his limit in five or ten rounds, the other, fighting just as severely, will be able to last thirty or forty rounds, or even fifty. It was this peculiar quality that Battling Nelson possessed to such an extreme degree. Jimmy Britt did not possess it. He could outspar and outpunch Nelson, but he could not keep on sparring and punching as long as Nelson could. At the Colma fight he was not knocked out by Nelson. He was merely exhausted. He had reached his limit. He could not move any more. He lost the fight because he knocked himself out by his own exertions.

Corbett lacked this abysmal brutishness to a considerable degree. Choynski had far more of it. So did Sharkey and Fitzsimmons. But when it comes to Jeffries and Johnson there is no line on them at all. They have never been called upon to demonstrate it. Neither knows that he possesses it. Neither has ever engaged in a long, hard, gruelling fight, round after round, striking and being struck, consuming energy at an enormous rate and still going on fighting furiously, on and on, endlessly.

Of the two men Jeffries has thought more about himself, studied himself more, and he has hinted that he believes he possesses it. He has called it reserve power—a sort of second wind that does not depend on the lungs, but that resides in the muscles themselves. But seeing and believing are different, and he has yet to show it to the world. Nevertheless I venture a shrewd guess that he has it. Also, he may be called upon to show it on July 4.

Nor does the world know that Johnson possesses this abysmal brutishness or lacks it. Johnson does not know himself. He has never had a chance to find out. And in this connection it is not a question of "yellow streak" or will power. No matter to what superlative degree Johnson possesses this protoplasmic vigor it will go for naught if he proves yellow. On the other hand, he has never shown any hints of the yellowness, and, it must be added, he has never been in a fight that forced a test of this particular quality.

There is one quality in which Johnson has the advantage over Jeffries and that is in relaxation. Jeffries, while cool and keen, is always more tense. The tensing of muscle consumes energy. Boxing calls for the use of all the muscles in the body, and five minutes' unnecessary tension of all these muscles out of thirty minutes of fighting means a serious consumption of energy.

This is one of Johnson's great assets. He has the art of relaxing perfectly. His fiercest rallies are always followed by intervals of repose. In a clinch, except when he is punishing, he invariably rests. It is because of this relaxing so continually that he is notorious with the sporting public as a loafing fighter. And he seems to relax in mind as well as in body. He seems to stop thinking and perceiving even, and in a clinch he goes into a sort of resting trance. His very flat footed way of fighting takes off from the tension of the legs. It is far less tiring to shuffle about flat footedly than to spring and poise with the muscles tensed from the hips down.

One thing is certain. A week from to-day Johnson will be compelled to put up the fight of his life. He has never in his career faced so formidable an antagonist. With Jeffries it remains to be seen whether Johnson can make him put up the fight of his life.

THE APE AND THE TIGER

Reno, Nevada, Tuesday, June 28, 1910—Here is the problem. At half-past one in the afternoon of July 4 two men, a white and a black, are going to face each other in a square ring elevated in the centre of a large arena. They are not going to try to kill each other. They are to fight each other, true, but the fighting will be done with natural weapons and according to very rigid and restricted rules.

They are to strike each other with their hands and their hands only. No other blow will be permitted. They cannot wrestle with each other or throw each other down. The very area on which they are allowed to land their blows is limited. It is the upper portion of the body. From the waist down all striking is taboo. Nor may a blow be struck when a man is off his feet.

The fists, which are their only fighting weapons, will be encased in padded gloves that weigh one-third of a pound. A naked knuckle can cut and injure and it is a thing to be avoided.

A third man will be in the ring with them to see that all the rules are observed. He is the referee. His word is law. Whatever he says must be obeyed. If a man strikes a foul blow the referee will immediately disqualify him and award the victory to the other man. The referee will watch closely, circling about the two men, sometimes speaking to them in a low voice, sometimes touching one on the shoulder and sometimes the other.

And what are these two men, with the padded gloves, the rigid rules and the referee in the ring for? What is it they desire to achieve? Simply this:—By means of blows with their gloved hands to see which can put the other down on the ground and put him down so hard that he will stay down for ten consecutive seconds. And why do they want to do this? For honor and fame and a prize of $100,000.

It sounds silly on the face of it, doesn't it? But when it is considered that from fifteen to twenty thousand men, paying each from $10 to $50 for a seat, will be in the arena to watch the two men, that millions of dollars will be spent on this contest, that men will journey from the uttermost parts of the earth to witness it, that the ablest journalists and cartoonists of the country will be present, and that it has been and will be for a week to come the one overshadowing issue of the whole United States, all to see which of the two men can put the other down for ten consecutive seconds—why, it would seem to become a colossal silliness.

But is it such a silliness? Is it a silliness at all, when the pages of all the newspapers are daily filled with it, the only concession that a very large portion of the people of the country are interested in it? There is a reason for their interest, just as there is a reason for my interest—and why am I interested? In the next paragraph let me show you.

But here, let me stand up and announce that I am so keenly interested, so overwhelmingly desirous of witnessing this contest, that there are moments when sudden fears assail me, such as that the fight will not come off, that it may be prevented by some great earthquake or terrific cataclysm of nature. Why, I want to see that fight so bad that it hurts.

This contest of men with padded gloves on their hands is a sport that belongs unequivocally to the English speaking race and that has taken centuries for the race to develop. It is no superficial thing, a fad of a moment or a generation. No genius or philosopher devised it and persuaded the race to adopt it as their racial sport of sports. It is as deep as our consciousness and is woven into the fibres of our being. It grew as our very language grew. It is an instinctive passion of race.

And as men to-day thrill to short Saxon words, just so do they thrill to the thud of blows of a prize fight, to the onslaught and the repulse and to the exhibition of gameness and courage.

This is the ape and tiger in us, granted; but, like the man in jail, it is in us, isn't it? We can't get away from it. It is the fact, the irrefragible fact. We like fighting; it's our nature. We are realities in a real world and we must accept the reality of our nature and all its thrillableness if we are to live in accord with the real world, and those who try to get away from these realities, who, by ukase of the will, deny their existence, succeed only in living in a world of illusion and misunderstanding.

These are the people who compose theatre panics, fire panics and wreck panics. They are so far out of accord with the real world that they can make no adjustment with it when the supreme moment comes. It goes without discussion, so patent is it, that an audience composed wholly of prize fighters would never engage in a theatre panic. They would be too close to the real, too ... clear seeing and cool to stampede like a herd of brute cattle. The fact is they would stay and put out fire.

Another thing that merits pointing out is that our sport of prize fighting is a fair sport. It gives play to our ethical natures. No one can disbelieve this who has ever heard a fighter guilty of a foul blow hooted by indignant and outraged spectators.

Our sport of prize fighting is hedged with ethical restrictions. It is synonymous with fair play. It is different from the fighting of the jungle, of which it is a development. There is absolutely no fair play in the jungle fighting. So has man improved. By that much is he less red of fang and claw. By that much has he climbed up the ladder of life. Don't rush his development too hard. He will climb higher.

In token of this one has but to call attention to the fact that our modern soldiers dislike slaughter as no soldiery has ever disliked it in the world before. And in line with this is the passing of the bare knuckle London prize ring fighting into the fighting with padded gloves. Some day, long and long from now, the ape and the tiger in us will completely die out and our sports will come to consist of forensic, artistic and ethical battles between our chosen champions. But in the meantime we are what we are, and there is no need to be ashamed of ourselves. Only by long and arduous evolution will the ape and tiger go their way.

It is not a matter of legislation nor superrational censure. When we ourselves don't want any more prize fighting the newspapers will cease filling their columns with it, and the very fighters themselves will dwindle and weed out and cease.

JOHNSON WHIPS JEFFRIES

Reno, Nevada, Monday, July 4, 1910—Once again has Johnson sent down to defeat the chosen representative of the white race, and this time the greatest of them. And as of old, it was play for Johnson. From the opening round to the closing round he never ceased from his witty sallies, his exchanges of repartee with his opponent's seconds and with the audience. And, for that matter, Johnson had a funny thing or two to say to Jeffries in every round.

The "golden smile" was as much in evidence as ever and neither did it freeze on his face nor did it vanish. It came and went throughout the fight, spontaneously, naturally.

It was not a great battle after all, save in its setting and its significance. Little "Tommy" Burns, down in far off Australia, put up a faster, quicker, livelier battle than did Jeffries. The fight to-day, and again I repeat, was great only in its significance. In itself it was not great. The issue, after the fiddling of the opening rounds, was never in doubt. In the fiddling of those first rounds the honors lay with Johnson, and for the rounds after the seventh or eighth it was more Johnson, while for the closing rounds it was all Johnson.

Johnson played, as usual. With his opponent not strong in the attack Johnson, blocking and defending in masterly fashion, could afford to play. And he played and fought a white man, in the white man's country, before a white man's audience. And the audience was a Jeffries audience.

When Jeffries sent in that awful rip of his the audience would madly applaud, believing it had gone home to Johnson's stomach, and Johnson, deftly interposing his elbow, would smile in irony at the audience, play acting, making believe he thought the applause was for him—and never believing it at all.

The greatest battle of the century was a monologue delivered to twenty thousand spectators by a smiling negro, who was never in doubt and who was never serious for more than a moment at a time.

As a fighter Johnson did not show himself a wonder. He did not have to. Never once was he extended. There was no need. Jeffries could not make him extend. Jeffries never had him in trouble once. No blow Jeffries ever landed hurt his dusky opponent. Johnson came out of the fight practically undamaged. The blood on his lip was from a recent cut received in the course of training and which Jeffries managed to reopen.

Jeffries failed to lead and land. The quickness he brought into the fight quickly evaporated, and while Jeffries was dead game to the end, he was not so badly punished. What he failed to bring into the ring with him was his stamina, which he lost somewhere in the last seven years. Jeffries failed to come back. That is the whole story. . . .

Johnson is a wonder. No one understands him, this man who smiles. Well, the story of the fight is the story of a smile. If ever man won by nothing more fatiguing than a smile Johnson won to-day.

And where now is the champion who will make Johnson extend himself? Who will glaze those bright eyes, remove that smile and silence that golden repartee?

The Novelist

THE SEA WOLF

Selections

While crossing San Francisco Bay in a dense fog the ferry-steamer "Martinez" collides with another ship and begins to sink. Humphrey Van Weyden, one of the passengers, jumps overboard to save himself and is caught in the swift tide and swept out to sea. Miles from shore he is rescued by the sealing vessel, "Ghost." Van Weyden's relief and happiness at being saved from a watery grave is shortlived, for instead of being taken back to San Francisco he is forced to perform the menial duties of cabin boy on a ship bound for the North Pacific.

In the selections following Van Weyden describes his desperate situation; his first glimpse of Captain Wolf Larsen; and his struggle for survival against the physical and philosophical onslaught of the brutal master of the hell ship "Ghost." ED.

Pacing back and forth the length of the hatchway, and savagely chewing the end of a cigar, was the man whose casual glance had rescued me from the sea. His height was probably five feet ten inches, or ten and a half; but my first impression, or feel of the man, was not of this, but of his strength. And yet, while he was of massive build, with broad shoulders and deep chest, I could not characterize his strength as massive. It was what might be termed a sinewy, knotty strength, of the kind we ascribe to lean and wiry men, but which, in him, because of his heavy build, partook more of the enlarged gorilla order. Not that in appearance he seemed in the least gorilla-like. What I am striving to express is this strength itself, more as a thing apart from his physical semblance. It was a strength we are wont to associate with things primitive, with wild animals, and the creatures we imagine our tree-dwelling prototypes to have been—a strength savage, ferocious, alive in itself, the essence of life in that it is the potency of motion, the elemental stuff itself out of which the many forms of life have been molded; in short, that which writhes in the body of a snake when the head is cut off, and the snake, as a snake, is dead, or which lingers in a shapeless lump of turtle-meat and recoils and quivers from the prod of a finger.

Such was the impression of strength I gathered from this man who paced up and down. He was firmly planted on his legs; his feet struck the deck squarely and with surety; every movement of a muscle, from the heave of the shoulders to the tightening of the lips about the cigar, was decisive, and seemed to come out of a strength that was excessive and overwhelming. In fact, though this strength pervaded every action of his, it seemed but the advertisement of a greater strength that lurked within, that lay dormant and no more than stirred from time to time, but which might arouse, at any moment, terrible and compelling, like the rage of a lion or the wrath of a storm.

As I lay there thinking, I naturally dwelt upon myself in my situation. It was unparalleled, undreamed-of, that I, Humphrey Van Weyden, a scholar and a dilettante, if you please, in things artistic and literary, should be lying here on a Bering Sea seal-hunting schooner. Cabin-boy! I had never done any hard manual labor, or scullion labor, in my life. I had lived a placid, uneventful, sedentary existence all my days—the life of a scholar and a recluse on an assured and comfortable income. Violent life and athletic sports had never appealed to me. I had always been a bookworm; so my sisters and father had called me during my childhood. I had gone camping but once in my life, and then I left the party almost at its start and returned to the comforts and conveniences of a roof. And here I was, with dreary and endless vistas before me of table-setting, potato-peeling, and dish-washing. And I was not strong. The doctors had always said that I had a remarkable constitution, but I had never developed it or my body through exercise. My muscles were small and soft, like a woman's, or so the doctors had said time and again in the course of their attempts to persuade me to go in for physical-culture fads. But I had preferred to use my head, rather than my body; and here I was, in no fit condition for the rough life in prospect.

These are merely a few of the things that went through my mind, and are related for the sake of vindicating myself in advance in the weak and helpless rôle I was destined to play. But I thought, also, of my mother and sisters, and pictured their grief. I was among the missing dead of the *Martinez* disaster, an unrecovered body. I could see the head-lines in the papers; the fellows at the University Club and the Bibelot shaking their heads and saying, "Poor chap!" And I could see Charley Furuseth, as I had said good-by to him that morning, lounging in a dressing-gown on the be-pillowed window couch and delivering himself of oracular and pessimistic epigrams.

And all the while, rolling, plunging, climbing the moving mountains and falling and wallowing in the foaming valleys, the schooner *Ghost* was fighting her way farther and farther into the heart of the Pacific—and I was on her. . . .

Sometimes I think Wolf Larsen mad, or half-mad at least, what of his strange moods and vagaries. At other times I take him for a great man, a genius who has never arrived. And, finally, I am convinced that he is the perfect type of the primitive man, born a thousand years or generations too late and an anachronism in this culminating century of civilization. He is certainly an individualist of the most pronounced type. Not only that, but he is very lonely. There is no congeniality between him and the rest of the men aboard ship. His tremendous virility and mental strength wall him apart. They are more like children to him, even the hunters, and as children he treats them, descending perforce to their level and playing with them as a man plays with puppies. Or else he probes them with the cruel hand of a vivisectionist, groping about in their mental processes and examining their souls as though to see of what soul-stuff is made.

I have seen him a score of times, at table, insulting this hunter or that, with cool and level eyes and, withal, a certain air of interest, pondering their actions or replies or petty rages with a curiosity almost laughable to me who stood onlooker and who understood. Concerning his own rages, I am convinced that they are not real, that they are sometimes experiments, but that in the main they are the habits of a pose or attitude he has seen fit to take toward his fellowmen. I know, with the possible exception of the incident of the dead mate, that I have not seen him really angry; nor do I wish ever to see him in a genuine rage, when all the force of him is called into play.

While on the question of vagaries, I shall tell what befell Thomas Mugridge in the cabin, and at the same time complete an incident upon which I have already touched once or twice. The twelve o'clock dinner was over, one day, and I had just finished putting the cabin in order, when Wolf Larsen and Thomas Mugridge descended the companion stairs. Though the cook had a cubbyhole of a stateroom opening off from the cabin, in the cabin itself he had never dared to linger or to be seen, and he flitted to and fro, once or twice a day, like a timid spectre.

"So you know how to play 'Nap,'" Wolf Larsen was saying in a pleased sort of voice. "I might have guessed an Englishman would know. I learned it myself in English ships."

Thomas Mugridge was beside himself, a blithering imbecile, so pleased was he at chumming thus with the captain. The little airs he put on and the painful striving to assume the easy carriage of a man born to a dignified place in life would have been sickening had they not been ludicrous. He quite ignored my presence, though I credited him with being simply unable to see me. His pale, wishy-washy eyes were swimming like lazy summer seas, though what blissful visions they beheld were beyond my imagination.

"Get the cards, Hump," Wolf Larsen ordered, as they took seats at the table. "And bring out the cigars and the whiskey you'll find in my berth."

I returned with the articles in time to hear the Cockney hinting broadly that there was a mystery about him, that he might be a gentleman's son gone wrong or something or other; also, that he was a remittance man and was paid to keep away from England—"p'yed 'ansomely, sir," was the way he put it; "p'yed 'ansomely to sling my 'ook an' keep slingin' it."

I had brought the customary liquor glasses, but Wolf Larsen frowned, shook his head, and signalled with his hands for me to bring the tumblers. These he filled two-thirds full with undiluted whiskey—"a gentleman's drink," quoth Thomas Mugridge,—and they clinked their glasses to the glorious game of "Nap," lighted cigars, and fell to shuffling and dealing the cards.

They played for money. They increased the amounts of the bets. They drank whiskey, they drank it neat, and I fetched more. I do not know whether Wolf Larsen cheated or not,—a thing he was thoroughly capable of doing,—but he won steadily. The cook made repeated journeys to his bunk for money. Each time he performed the journey with greater swagger, but he never brought more than a few dollars at a time. He grew maudlin, familiar, could hardly see the cards or sit upright. As a preliminary to another journey to his bunk, he hooked Wolf Larsen's buttonhole with a greasy forefinger and vacuously proclaimed and reiterated, "I got money. I got money, I tell yer, an' I'm a gentleman's son."

Wolf Larsen was unaffected by the drink, yet he drank glass for glass, and if anything his glasses were fuller. There was no change in him. He did not appear even amused at the other's antics.

In the end, with loud protestations that he could lose like a gentleman, the cook's last money was staked on the game and lost. Whereupon he leaned his head on his hands and wept. Wolf Larsen looked curiously at him, as though about to probe and vivisect him, then changed his mind, as from the foregone conclusion that there was nothing there to probe.

"Hump," he said to me, elaborately polite, "kindly take Mr. Mugridge's arm and help him up on deck. He is not feeling very well."

"And tell Johnson to douse him with a few buckets of salt water," he added, in a lower tone for my ear alone.

I left Mr. Mugridge on deck, in the hands of a couple of grinning sailors who had been told off for the purpose. Mr. Mugridge was sleepily spluttering that he was a gentleman's son. But as I descended the companion stairs to clear the table I heard him shriek as the first bucket of water struck him.

Wolf Larsen was counting his winnings.

"One hundred and eighty-five dollars even," he said aloud. "Just as I thought. The beggar came aboard without a cent."

"And what you have won is mine, sir," I said boldly.

He favored me with a quizzical smile. "Hump, I have studied some grammar in my time, and I think your tenses are tangled. 'Was mine,' you should have said, not 'is mine.'"

"It is a question, not of grammar, but of ethics," I answered.

It was possibly a minute before he spoke.

"D'ye know, Hump," he said, with a slow seriousness which had in it an indefinable strain of sadness, "that this is the first time I have heard the word 'ethics' in the mouth of a man. You and I are the only men on this ship who know its meaning."

"At one time in my life," he continued, after another pause, "I dreamed that I might some day talk with men who used such language, that I might lift myself out of the place in life in which I had been born, and hold conversation and mingle with men who talked about just such things as ethics. And this is the first time I have ever heard the word pronounced. Which is all by the way, for you are wrong. It is a question, neither of grammar nor ethics, but of fact."

"I understand," I said. "The fact is that you have the money."

His face brightened. He seemed pleased at my perspicacity.

"But it is avoiding the real question," I continued, "which is one of right."

"Ah," he remarked, with a wry pucker of his mouth, "I see you still believe in such things as right and wrong."

"But don't you?—at all?" I demanded.

"Not the least bit. Might is right, and that is all there is to it. Weakness is wrong. Which is a very poor way of saying that it is good for oneself to be strong, and evil for oneself to be weak—or better yet, it is pleasurable to be strong, because of the profits; painful to be weak, because of the penalties. Just now the possession of this money is a pleasurable thing. It is good for one to possess it. Being able to possess it, I wrong myself and the life that is in me if I give it to you and forego the pleasure of possessing it."

"But you wrong me by withholding it," I objected.

"Not at all. One man cannot wrong another man. He can only wrong himself. As I see it, I do wrong always when I consider the interests of others. Don't you see? How can two particles of the yeast wrong each other by striving to devour each other? It is their inborn heritage to strive to devour, and to strive not to be devoured. When they depart from this they sin."

"Then you don't believe in altruism?" I asked.

He received the word as if it had a familiar ring, though he pondered it thoughtfully. "Let me see, it means something about coöperation, doesn't it?"

"Well, in a way there has come to be a sort of connection," I answered, unsurprised by this time at such gaps in his vocabulary, which, like his knowledge, was the acquirement of a self-read, self-educated man, whom no one had directed in his studies, and who had thought much and talked little or not at all. "An altruistic act is an act performed for the welfare of others. It is unselfish, as opposed to an act performed for self, which is selfish."

He nodded his head. "Oh, yes, I remember it now. I ran across it in Spencer."

"Spencer!" I cried. "Have you read him?"

"Not very much," was his confession. "I understood quite a good deal of 'First Principles,' but his 'Biology' took the wind out of my sails, and his 'Psychology' left me butting around in the doldrums for many a day. I honestly could not understand what he was driving at. I put it down to mental deficiency on my part, but since then I have decided that it was for want of preparation. I had no proper basis. Only Spencer and myself know how hard I hammered. But I did get something out of his 'Data of Ethics.' There's where I ran across 'altruism,' and I remember now how it was used."

I wondered what this man could have got from such a work. Spencer I remembered enough to know that altruism was imperative to his ideal of highest conduct. Wolf Larsen, evidently, had sifted the great philosopher's teachings, rejecting and selecting according to his needs and desires.

"What else did you run across?" I asked.

His brows drew in slightly with the mental effort of suitably phrasing thoughts which he had never before put into speech. I felt an elation of spirit. I was groping into his soul-stuff as he made a practice of groping in the soul-stuff of others. I was exploring virgin territory. A strange, a terribly strange, region was unrolling itself before my eyes.

"In as few words as possible," he began, "Spencer puts it something like this: First, a man must act for his own benefit—to do this is to be moral and good. Next, he must act for the benefit of his children. And third, he must act for the benefit of his race."

"And the highest, finest, right conduct," I interjected, "is that act which benefits at the same time the man, his children, and his race."

"I wouldn't stand for that," he replied. "Couldn't see the necessity for it, nor the common sense. I cut out the race and the children. I would sacrifice nothing for them. It's just so much slush and sentiment, and you must see it yourself, at least for one who does not believe in eternal life. With immortality before me, altruism would be a paying business proposition. I might elevate my soul to all kinds of altitudes. But with nothing eternal before me but death, given for a brief spell this yeasty crawling and squirming which is called life, why, it would be immoral for me to perform any act that was a sacrifice. Any sacrifice that makes me lose one crawl or squirm is foolish,—and not only foolish, for it is a wrong against myself and a wicked thing. I must not lose one crawl or squirm if I am to get the most out of the ferment. Nor will the eternal movelessness that is coming to me be made easier or harder by the sacrifices or selfishnesses of the time when I was yeasty and acrawl."

"Then you are an individualist, a materialist, and, logically, a hedonist."

"Big words," he smiled. "But what is a hedonist?"

He nodded agreement when I had given the definition.

"And you are also," I continued, "a man one could not trust in the least thing where it was possible for a selfish interest to intervene?"

"Now you're beginning to understand," he said, brightening.

"You are a man utterly without what the world calls morals?"

"That's it."

"A man of whom to be always afraid—"

"That's the way to put it."

"As one is afraid of a snake, or a tiger, or a shark?"

"Now you know me," he said. "And you know me as I am generally known. Other men call me 'Wolf.' "

"You are a sort of monster," I added audaciously, "a Caliban who has pondered Setebos, and who acts as you act, in idle moments, by whim and fancy."

His brow clouded at the allusion. He did not understand, and I quickly learned that he did not know the poem.

"I'm just reading Browning," he confessed, "and it's pretty tough. I haven't got very far along, and as it is I've about lost my bearings."

Not to be tiresome, I shall say that I fetched the book from his state-room and read "Caliban" aloud. He was delighted. It was a primitive mode of reasoning and of looking at things that he understood thoroughly. He interrupted again and again with comment and criticism. When I finished, he had me read it over a second time, and a third. We fell into discussion—philosophy, science, evolution, religion. He betrayed the inaccuracies of the self-read man, and, it must be granted, the sureness and directness of the primitive mind. The very simplicity of his reasoning was its strength, and his materialism was far more compelling than the subtly complex materialism of Charley Furuseth. Not that I,—a confirmed and, as Furuseth phrased it, a temperamental idealist,—was to be compelled; but that Wolf Larsen stormed the last strongholds of my faith with a vigor that received respect, while not accorded conviction.

Time passed. Supper was at hand and the table not laid. I became restless and anxious, and when Thomas Mugridge glared down the companionway, sick and angry of countenance, I prepared to go about my duties. But Wolf Larsen cried out to him:—

"Cooky, you've got to hustle to-night. I'm busy with Hump, and you'll do the best you can without him."

And again the unprecedented was established. That night I sat at table with the captain and the hunters, while Thomas Mugridge waited on us and washed the dishes afterward—a whim, a Caliban-mood of Wolf Larsen's, and one I foresaw would bring me trouble. In the meantime we talked and talked, much to the disgust of the hunters, who could not understand a word.

Three days of rest, three blessed days of rest, are what I had with Wolf Larsen, eating at the cabin table and doing nothing but discuss life, literature, and the universe, the while Thomas Mugridge fumed and raged and did my work as well as his own.

"Watch out for squalls, is all I can say to you," was Louis's warning, given during a spare half-hour on deck while Wolf Larsen was engaged in straightening out a row among the hunters.

"Ye can't tell what'll be happenin'," Louis went on, in response to my query for more definite information. "The man's as contrary as air currents or water currents. You can never guess the ways iv him. 'Tis just as you're thinkin' you know him and are makin' a favorable slant along him, that he whirls around, dead ahead, and comes howlin' down upon you and a-rippin' all iv your fine-weather sails to rags."

So I was not altogether surprised when the squall foretold by Louis smote me. We had been having a heated discussion,—upon life, of course,—and, grown overbold, I was passing stiff strictures upon Wolf Larsen and the life of Wolf Larsen. In fact, I was vivisecting him and turning over his soul-stuff as keenly and thoroughly as it was his custom to do it to others. It may be a weakness of mine that I have an incisive way of speech; but I threw all restraint to the winds and cut and slashed until the whole man of him was snarling. The dark sun-bronze of his face went black with wrath, his eyes were ablaze. There was no clearness or sanity in them—nothing but the terrific rage of a madman. It was the wolf in him that I saw, and a mad wolf at that.

He sprang for me with a half-roar, gripping my arm. I had steeled myself to brazen it out, though I was trembling inwardly; but the enormous strength of the man was too much for my fortitude. He had gripped me by the biceps with his single hand, and when that grip tightened I wilted and shrieked aloud. My feet went out from under me. I simply could not stand upright and endure the agony. The muscles refused their duty. The pain was too great. My biceps was being crushed to a pulp.

He seemed to recover himself, for a lucid gleam came into his eyes, and he relaxed his hold with a short laugh that was more like a growl. I fell to the floor, feeling very faint, while he sat down, lighted a cigar, and watched me as a cat watches a mouse. As I writhed about I could see in his eyes that curiosity I had so often noted, that wonder and perplexity, that questing, that everlasting query of his as to what it was all about.

I finally crawled to my feet and ascended the companion stairs. Fair weather was over, and there was nothing left but to return to the galley. My left arm was numb, as though paralyzed, and days passed before I could use it, while weeks went by before the last stiffness and pain went out of it. And he had done nothing but put his hand upon my arm and squeeze. There had been no wrenching or jerking. He had just closed his hand with a steady pressure. What he might have done I did not fully realize till next day, when he put his head into the galley, and, as a sign of renewed friendliness, asked me how my arm was getting on.

"It might have been worse," he smiled.

I was peeling potatoes. He picked one up from the pan. It was fair-sized, firm, and unpeeled. He closed his hand upon it, squeezed, and the potato squirted out between his fingers in mushy streams. The pulpy remnant he dropped back into the pan and turned away, and I had a sharp vision of how it might have fared with me had the monster put his real strength upon me.

But the three days' rest was good in spite of it all, for it had given my knee the very chance it needed. It felt much better, the swelling had materially decreased, and the cap seemed descending into its proper place. Also, the three days' rest brought the trouble I had foreseen. It was plainly Thomas Mugridge's intention to make me pay for those three days. He treated me vilely, cursed me continually, and heaped his own work upon me. He even ventured to raise his fist to me, but I was becoming animal-like myself, and I snarled in his face so terribly that it must have frightened him back. It is no pleasant picture I can conjure up of myself, Humphrey Van Weyden, in that noisome ship's galley, crouched in a corner over my task, my face raised to the face of the creature about to strike me, my lips lifted and snarling like a dog's, my eyes gleaming with fear and helplessness and the courage that comes of fear and helplessness. I do not like the picture. It reminds me too strongly of a rat in a trap. I do not care to think of it; but it was effective, for the threatened blow did not descend.

Thomas Mugridge backed away, glaring as hatefully and viciously as I glared. A pair of beasts is what we were, penned together and showing our teeth. He was a coward, afraid to strike me because I had not quailed sufficiently in advance; so he chose a new way to intimidate me. There was only one galley knife that, as a knife, amounted to anything. This, through many years of service and wear, had acquired a long, lean blade. It was unusually cruel-looking, and at first I had shuddered every time I used it. The cook borrowed a stone from Johansen and proceeded to sharpen the knife. He did it with great ostentation, glancing significantly at me the while. He whetted it up and down all day long. Every odd moment he could find he had the knife and stone out and was whetting away. The steel acquired a razor edge. He tried it with the ball of his thumb or across the nail. He shaved hairs from the back of his hand, glanced along the edge with miscroscopic acuteness, and found, or feigned that he found, always, a slight inequality in its edge somewhere. Then he would put it on the stone again and whet, whet, whet, till I could have laughed aloud, it was so very ludicrous.

It was also serious, for I learned that he was capable of using it, that under all his cowardice there was a courage of cowardice, like mine, that would impel him to do the very thing his whole nature protested against doing and was afraid of doing. "Cooky's sharpening his knife for Hump," was being whispered about among the sailors, and some of them twitted him about it. This he took in good part, and was really pleased, nodding his head with direful foreknowledge and mystery, until George Leach, the erstwhile cabin-boy, ventured some rough pleasantry on the subject.

Now it happened that Leach was one of the sailors told off to douse Mugridge after his game of cards with the captain. Leach had evidently done his task with a thoroughness that Mugridge had not forgiven, for words followed and evil names involving smirched ancestries. Mugridge menaced with the knife he was sharpening for me. Leach laughed and hurled more of his Telegraph Hill billingsgate, and before either he or I knew what had happened, his right arm had been ripped open from elbow to wrist by a quick slash of the knife. The cook backed away, a fiendish expression on his face, the knife held before him in a position of defence.

But Leach took it quite calmly, though blood was spouting upon the deck as generously as water from a fountain.

"I'm goin' to get you, Cooky," he said, "and I'll get you hard. And I won't be in no hurry about it. You'll be without that knife when I come for you."

So saying, he turned and walked quietly forward. Mugridge's face was livid with fear at what he had done and at what he might expect sooner or later from the man he had stabbed. But his demeanor toward me was more ferocious than ever. In spite of his fear at the reckoning he must expect to pay for what he had done, he could see that it had been an object-lesson to me, and he became more domineering and exultant. Also there was a lust in him, akin to madness, which had come with sight of the blood he had drawn. He was beginning to see red in whatever direction he looked. The psychology of it is sadly tangled, and yet I could read the workings of his mind as clearly as though it were a printed book.

Several days went by, the *Ghost* still foaming down the trades, and I could swear I saw madness growing in Thomas Mugridge's eyes. And I confess that I became afraid, very much afraid. Whet, whet, whet, it went all day long. The look in his eyes as he felt the keen edge and glared at me was positively carnivorous. I was afraid to turn my shoulder to him, and when I left the galley I went out backwards—to the amusement of the sailors and hunters, who made a point of gathering in groups to witness my exit. The strain was too great. I sometimes thought my mind would give way under it—a meet thing on this ship of madmen and brutes. Every hour, every minute of my existence was in jeopardy. I was a human soul in distress, and yet no soul, fore or aft, betrayed sufficient sympathy to come to my aid. At times I thought of throwing myself on the mercy of Wolf Larsen, but the vision of the mocking devil in his eyes that questioned life and sneered at it would come strong upon me and compel me to refrain. At other times I seriously contemplated suicide, and the whole force of my hopeful philosophy was required to keep me from going over the side in the darkness of night.

Several times Wolf Larsen tried to inveigle me into discussion, but I gave him short answers and eluded him. Finally, he commanded me to resume my seat at the cabin table for a time and let the cook do my work. Then I spoke frankly, telling him what I was enduring from Thomas Mugridge because of the three days of favoritism which had been shown me. Wolf Larsen regarded me with smiling eyes.

"So you're afraid, eh?" he sneered.

"Yes," I said defiantly and honestly, "I am afraid."

"That's the way with you fellows," he cried, half angrily, "sentimentalizing about your immortal souls and afraid to die. At sight of a sharp knife and a cowardly Cockney the clinging of life to life overcomes all your fond foolishness. Why, my dear fellow, you will live forever. You are a god, and God cannot be killed. Cooky cannot hurt you. You are sure of your resurrection. What's there to be afraid of?

"You have eternal life before you. You are a millionnaire in immortality, and a millionnaire whose fortune cannot be lost, whose fortune is less perishable than the stars and as lasting as space or time. It is impossible for you to diminish your principal. Immortality is a thing without beginning or end. Eternity is eternity, and though you die here and now you will go on living somewhere else and hereafter. And it is all very beautiful, this shaking off of the flesh and soaring of the imprisoned spirit. Cooky cannot hurt you. He can only give you a boost on the path you eternally must tread.

"Or, if you do not wish to be boosted just yet, why not boost Cooky? According to your ideas, he, too, must be an immortal millionnaire. You cannot bankrupt him. His paper will always circulate at par. You cannot diminish the length of his living by killing him, for he is without beginning or end. He's bound to go on living, somewhere, somehow. Then boost him. Stick a knife in him and let his spirit free. As it is, it's in a nasty prison, and you'll do him only a kindness by breaking down the door. And who knows?—it may be a very beautiful spirit that will go soaring up into the blue from that ugly carcass. Boost him along, and I'll promote you to his place, and he's getting forty-five dollars a month."

It was plain that I could look for no help or mercy from Wolf Larsen. Whatever was to be done I must do for myself; and out of the courage of fear I evolved the plan of fighting Thomas Mugridge with his own weapons. I borrowed a whetstone from Johansen. Louis, the boat-steerer, had already begged me for condensed milk and sugar. The lazarette, where such delicacies were stored, was situated beneath the cabin floor. Watching my chance, I stole five cans of the milk, and that night, when it was Louis's watch on deck, I traded them with him for a dirk as lean and cruel-looking as Thomas Mugridge's vegetable knife. It was rusty and dull, but I turned the grindstone while Louis gave it an edge. I slept more soundly than usual that night.

Next morning, after breakfast, Thomas Mugridge began his whet, whet, whet. I glanced warily at him, for I was on my knees taking the ashes from the stove. When I returned from throwing them overside, he was talking to Harrison, whose honest yokel's face was filled with fascination and wonder.

"Yes," Mugridge was saying, "an' wot does 'is worship do but give me two years in Reading. But blimey if I cared. The other mug was fixed plenty. Should 'a seen 'im. Knife just like this. I stuck it in, like into soft butter, an' the w'y 'e squealed was better'n a tu-penny gaff." He shot a glance in my direction to see if I was taking it in, and went on. " 'I didn't mean it, Tommy,' 'e was snifflin'; 'so 'elp me Gawd, I didn't mean it!' 'I'll fix yer bloody well right,' I sez, an' kept right after 'im. I cut 'im in ribbons, that's wot I did, an' 'e a-squealin' all the time. Once 'e got 'is 'and on the knife an' tried to 'old it. 'Ad 'is fingers around it, but I pulled it through, cuttin' to the bone. O, 'e was a sight, I can tell yer."

A call from the mate interrupted the gory narrative, and Harrison went aft. Mugridge sat down on the raised threshold to the galley and went on with his knife-sharpening. I put the shovel away and calmly sat down on the coal-box facing him. He favored me with a vicious stare. Still calmly, though my heart was going pitapat, I pulled out Louis's dirk and began to whet it on the stone. I had looked for almost any sort of explosion on the Cockney's part, but to my surprise he did not appear aware of what I was doing. He went on whetting his knife. So did I. And for two hours we sat there, face to face, whet, whet, whet, till the news of it spread abroad and half the ship's company was crowding the galley doors to see the sight.

Encouragement and advice were freely tendered, and Jock Horner, the quiet, self-spoken hunter who looked as though he would not harm a mouse, advised me to leave the ribs alone and to thrust upward for the abdomen, at the same time giving what he called the "Spanish twist" to the blade. Leach, his bandaged arm prominently to the fore, begged me to leave a few remnants of the cook for him; and Wolf Larsen paused once or twice at the break of the poop to glance curiously at what must have been to him a stirring and crawling of the yeasty thing he knew as life.

And I make free to say that for the time being life assumed the same sordid values to me. There was nothing pretty about it, nothing divine—only two cowardly moving things that sat whetting steel upon stone, and a group of other moving things, cowardly and otherwise, that looked on. Half of them, I am sure, were anxious to see us shedding each other's blood. It would have been entertainment. And I do not think there was one who would have interfered had we closed in a death-struggle.

On the other hand, the whole thing was laughable and childish. Whet, whet, whet,—Humphrey Van Weyden sharpening his knife in a ship's galley and trying its edge with his thumb! Of all situations this was the most inconceivable. I know that my own kind could not have believed it possible. I had not been called "Sissy" Van Weyden all my days without reason, and that "Sissy" Van Weyden should be capable of doing this thing was a revelation to Humphrey Van Weyden, who knew not whether to be exultant or ashamed.

But nothing happened. At the end of two hours Thomas Mugridge put away knife and stone and held out his hand.

"Wot's the good of mykin' a 'oly show of ourselves for them mugs?" he demanded. "They don't love us, an' bloody well glad they'd be a-seein' us cuttin' our throats. Yer not 'arf bad, 'Ump! You've got spunk, as you Yanks s'y, an' I like yer in a w'y. So come on an' shyke."

Coward that I might be, I was less a coward than he. It was a distinct victory I had gained, and I refused to forego any of it by shaking his detestable hand.

"All right," he said pridelessly, "tyke it or leave it, I'll like yer none the less for it." And to save his face he turned fiercely upon the onlookers. "Get outa my galley-doors, you bloomin' swabs!"

This command was reinforced by a steaming kettle of water, and at sight of it the sailors scrambled out of the way. This was a sort of victory for Thomas Mugridge, and enabled him to accept more gracefully the defeat I had given him, though, of course, he was too discreet to attempt to drive the hunters away.

"I see Cooky's finish," I heard Smoke say to Horner.

"You bet," was the reply. "Hump runs the galley from now on, and Cooky pulls in his horns."

Mugridge heard and shot a swift glance at me, but I gave no sign that the conversation had reached me. I had not thought my victory was so far-reaching and complete, but I resolved to let go nothing I had gained. As the days went by, Smoke's prophecy was verified. The Cockney became more humble and slavish to me than even to Wolf Larsen. I mistered him and sirred him no longer, washed no more greasy pots, and peeled no more potatoes. I did my own work, and my own work only, and when and in what fashion I saw fit. Also, I carried the dirk in a sheath at my hip, sailor-fashion, and maintained toward Thomas Mugridge a constant attitude which was composed of equal parts of domineering, insult, and contempt.

My intimacy with Wolf Larsen increases—if by intimacy may be denoted those relations which exist between master and man, or, better yet, between king and jester. I am to him no more than a toy, and he values me no more than a child values a toy. My function is to amuse, and so long as I amuse all goes well; but let him become bored, or let him have one of his black moods come upon him, and at once I am relegated from cabin table to galley, while, at the same time, I am fortunate to escape with my life and a whole body.

The loneliness of the man is slowly being borne in upon me. There is not a man aboard but hates or fears him, nor is there a man whom he does not despise. He seems consuming with the tremendous power that is in him and that seems never to have found adequate expression in works. He is as Lucifer would be, were that proud spirit banished to a society of soulless, Tomlinsonian ghosts.

This loneliness is bad enough in itself, but, to make it worse, he is oppressed by the primal melancholy of the race. Knowing him, I review the old Scandinavian myths with clearer understanding. The white-skinned, fair-haired savages who created that terrible pantheon were of the same fibre as he. The frivolity of the laughter-loving Latins is no part of him. When he laughs it is from a humor that is nothing else than ferocious. But he laughs rarely; he is too often sad. And it is a sadness as deep-reaching as the roots of the race. It is the race heritage, the sadness which has made the race sober-minded, clean-lived, and fanatically moral, and which, in this latter connection, has culminated among the English in the Reformed Church and Mrs. Grundy.

In point of fact, the chief vent to this primal melancholy has been religion in its more agonizing forms. But the compensations of such religion are denied Wolf Larsen. His brutal materialism will not permit it. So, when his blue moods come on, nothing remains for him but to be devilish. Were he not so terrible a man, I could sometimes feel sorry for him, as instance three mornings ago, when I went into his state-room to fill his water-bottle and came unexpectedly upon him. He did not see me. His head was buried in his hands, and his shoulders were heaving convulsively as with sobs. He seemed torn by some mighty grief. As I softly withdrew I could hear him groaning, "God! God! God!" Not that he was calling upon God; it was a mere expletive, but it came from his soul.

At dinner he asked the hunters for a remedy for headache, and by evening, strong man that he was, he was half-blind and reeling about the cabin.

"I've never been sick in my life, Hump," he said, as I guided him to his room. "Nor did I ever have a headache except the time my head was healing after having been laid open for six inches by a capstan-bar."

For three days this blinding headache lasted, and he suffered as wild animals suffer, as it seemed the way on ship to suffer, without plaint, without sympathy, utterly alone.

This morning, however, on entering his state-room to make the bed and put things in order, I found him well and hard at work. Table and bunk were littered with designs and calculations. On a large transparent sheet, compass and square in hand, he was copying what appeared to be a scale of some sort or other.

"Hello, Hump," he greeted me genially. "I'm just finishing the finishing touches. Want to see it work?"

"But what is it?" I asked.

"A labor-saving device for mariners, navigation reduced to kindergarten simplicity," he answered gayly. "From to-day a child will be able to navigate a ship. No more long-winded calculations. All you need is one star in the sky on a dirty night to know instantly where you are. Look. I place the transparent scale on this star-map, revolving the scale on the North Pole. On the scale I've worked out the circles of altitude and the lines of bearing. All I do is to put it on a star, revolve the scale till it is opposite those figures on the map underneath, and presto! there you are, the ship's precise location!"

There was a ring of triumph in his voice, and his eyes, clear blue this morning as the sea, were sparkling with light.

"You must be well up in mathematics," I said. "Where did you go to school?"

"Never saw the inside of one, worse luck," was the answer. "I had to dig it out for myself."

"And why do you think I have made this thing?" he demanded, abruptly. "Dreaming to leave footprints on the sands of time?" He laughed one of his horrible mocking laughs. "Not at all. To get it patented, to make money from it, to revel in piggishness with all night in while other men do the work. That's my purpose. Also, I have enjoyed working it out."

"The creative joy," I murmured.

"I guess that's what it ought to be called. Which is another way of expressing the joy of life in that it is alive, the triumph of movement over matter, of the quick over the dead, the pride of the yeast because it is yeast and crawls."

I threw up my hands with helpless disapproval of his inveterate materialism and went about making the bed. He continued copying lines and figures upon the transparent scale. It was a task requiring the utmost nicety and precision, and I could not but admire the way he tempered his strength to the fineness and delicacy of the need.

When I had finished the bed, I caught myself looking at him in a fascinated sort of way. He was certainly a handsome man—beautiful in the masculine sense. And again, with never-failing wonder, I remarked the total lack of viciousness, or wickedness, or sinfulness, in his face. It was the face, I am convinced, of a man who did no wrong. And by this I do not wish to be misunderstood. What I mean is that it was the face of a man who either did nothing contrary to the dictates of his conscience, or who had no conscience. I am inclined to the latter way of accounting for it. He was a magnificent atavism, a man so purely primitive that he was of the type that came into the world before the development of the moral nature. He was not immoral, but merely unmoral.

As I have said, in the masculine sense his was a beautiful face. Smooth-shaven, every line was distinct, and it was cut as clear and sharp as a cameo; while sea and sun had tanned the naturally fair skin to a dark bronze which bespoke struggle and battle and added both to his savagery and his beauty. The lips were full, yet possessed of the firmness, almost harshness, which is characteristic of thin lips. The set of his mouth, his chin, his jaw, was likewise firm or harsh, with all the fierceness and indomitableness of the male—the nose also. It was the nose of a being born to conquer and command. It just hinted of the eagle beak. It might have been Grecian, it might have been Roman, only it was a shade too massive for the one, a shade too delicate for the other. And while the whole face was the incarnation of fierceness and strength, the primal melancholy from which he suffered seemed to greaten the lines of mouth and eye and brow, seemed to give a largeness and completeness which otherwise the face would have lacked.

And so I caught myself standing idly and studying him. I cannot say how greatly the man had come to interest me. Who was he? What was he? How had he happened to be? All powers seemed his, all potentialities,—why, then, was he no more than the obscure master of a seal-hunting schooner with a reputation for frightful brutality amongst the men who hunted seals?

My curiosity burst from me in a flood of speech.

"Why is it that you have not done great things in this world? With the power that is yours you might have risen to any height. Unpossessed of conscience or moral instinct, you might have mastered the world, broken it to your hand. And yet here you are, at the top of your life, where diminishing and dying begin, living an obscure and sordid existence, hunting sea animals for the satisfaction of woman's vanity and love of decoration, revelling in a piggishness, to use your own words, which is anything and everything except splendid. Why, with all that wonderful strength, have you not done something? There was nothing to stop you, nothing that could stop you. What was wrong? Did you lack ambition? Did you fall under temptation? What was the matter? What was the matter?"

He had lifted his eyes to me at the commencement of my outburst, and followed me complacently until I had done and stood before him breathless and dismayed. He waited a moment, as though seeking where to begin, and then said:

"Hump, do you know the parable of the sower who went forth to sow? If you will remember, some of the seed fell upon stony places, where there was not much earth, and forthwith they sprung up because they had no deepness of earth. And when the sun was up they were scorched, and because they had no root they withered away. And some fell among thorns, and the thorns sprung up and choked them."

"Well?" I said.

"Well?" he queried, half petulantly. "It was not well. I was one of those seeds."

He dropped his head to the scale and resumed the copying. I finished my work and had opened the door to leave, when he spoke to me.

"Hump, if you will look on the west coast of the map of Norway you will see an indentation called Romsdal Fiord. I was born within a hundred miles of that stretch of water. But I was not born Norwegian. I am a Dane. My father and mother were Danes, and how they ever came to that bleak bight of land on the west coast I do not know. I never heard. Outside of that there is nothing mysterious. They were poor people and unlettered. They came of generations of poor unlettered people—peasants of the sea who sowed their sons on the waves as has been their custom since time began. There is no more to tell."

"But there is," I objected. "It is still obscure to me."

"What can I tell you?" he demanded, with a recrudescence of fierceness. "Of the meagreness of a child's life? of fish diet and coarse living? of going out with the boats from the time I could crawl? of my brothers, who went away one by one to the deep-sea farming and never came back? of myself, unable to read or write, cabin-boy at the mature age of ten on the coastwise, old-country ships? of the rough fare and rougher usage, where kicks and blows were bed and breakfast and took the place of speech, and fear and hatred and pain were my only soul-experiences? I do not care to remember. A madness comes up in my brain even now as I think of it. But there were coastwise skippers I would have returned and killed when a man's strength came to me, only the lines of my life were cast at the time in other places. I did return, not long ago, but unfortunately the skippers were dead, all but one, a mate in the old days, a skipper when I met him, and when I left him a cripple who would never walk again."

"But you who read Spencer and Darwin and have never seen the inside of a school, how did you learn to read and write?" I queried.

"In the English merchant service. Cabin-boy at twelve, ship's boy at fourteen, ordinary seaman at sixteen, able seaman at seventeen, and cock of the fo'c'sle, infinite ambition and infinite loneliness, receiving neither help nor sympathy, I did it all for myself—navigation, mathematics, science, literature, and what not. And of what use has it been? Master and owner of a ship at the top of my life, as you say, when I am beginning to diminish and die. Paltry, isn't it? And when the sun was up I was scorched, and because I had no root I withered away."

"But history tells of slaves who rose to the purple," I chided.

"And history tells of opportunities that came to the slaves who rose to the purple," he answered grimly. "No man makes opportunity. All the great men ever did was to know it when it came to them. The Corsican knew. I have dreamed as greatly as the Corsican. I should have known the opportunity, but it never came. The thorns sprung up and choked me. And, Hump, I can tell you that you know more about me than any living man, except my own brother."

"And what is he? And where is he?"

"Master of the steamship *Macedonia*, seal-hunter," was the answer. "We will meet him most probably on the Japan coast. Men call him 'Death' Larsen."

"Death Larsen!" I involuntarily cried. "Is he like you?"

"Hardly. He is a lump of an animal without any head. He has all my—my—"

"Brutishness," I suggested.

"Yes,—thank you for the word,—all my brutishness, but he can scarcely read or write."

"And he has never philosophized on life," I added.

"No," Wolf Larsen answered, with an indescribable air of sadness. "And he is all the happier for leaving life alone. He is too busy living it to think about it. My mistake was in ever opening the books."

The *Ghost* has attained the southernmost point of the arc she is describing across the Pacific, and is already beginning to edge away to the west and north toward some lone island, it is rumored, where she will fill her water-casks before proceeding to the season's hunt along the coast of Japan. The hunters have experimented and practised with their rifles and shotguns till they are satisfied, and the boat-pullers and steerers have made their spritsails, bound the oars and rowlocks in leather and sennit so that they will make no noise when creeping on the seals, and put their boats in apple-pie order—to use Leach's homely phrase.

His arm, by the way, has healed nicely, though the scar will remain all his life. Thomas Mugridge lives in mortal fear of him, and is afraid to venture on deck after dark. There are two or three standing quarrels in the forecastle. Louis tells me that the gossip of the sailors finds its way aft, and that two of the telltales have been badly beaten by their mates. He shakes his head dubiously over the outlook for the man Johnson, who is boat-puller in the same boat with him. Johnson has been guilty of speaking his mind too freely, and has collided two or three times with Wolf Larsen over the pronunciation of his name. Johansen he thrashed on the amidships deck the other night, since which time the mate has called him by his proper name. But of course it is out of the question that Johnson should thrash Wolf Larsen.

Louis has also given me additional information about Death Larsen, which tallies with the captain's brief description. We may expect to meet Death Larsen on the Japan coast. "And look out for squalls," is Louis's prophecy, "for they hate one another like the wolf-whelps they are." Death Larsen is in command of the only sealing-steamer in the fleet, the *Macedonia*, which carries fourteen boats, whereas the rest of the schooners carry only six. There is wild talk of cannon aboard, and of strange raids and expeditions she may make, ranging from opium smuggling into the States and arms smuggling into China, to blackbirding and open piracy. Yet I cannot but believe Louis, for I have never yet caught him in a lie, while he has a cyclopædic knowledge of sealing and the men of the sealing fleets.

As it is forward and in the galley, so it is in the steerage and aft, on this veritable hell-ship. Men fight and struggle ferociously for one another's lives. The hunters are looking for a shooting scrape at any moment between Smoke and Henderson, whose old quarrel has not healed, while Wolf Larsen says positively that he will kill the survivor of the affair, if such affair comes off. He frankly states that the position he takes is based on no moral grounds, that all the hunters could kill and eat one another so far as he is concerned, were it not that he needs them alive for the hunting. If they will only hold their hands until the season is over, he promises them a royal carnival, when all grudges can be settled and the survivors may toss the non-survivors overboard and arrange a story as to how the missing men were lost at sea. I think even the hunters are appalled at his cold-bloodedness. Wicked men though they be, they are certainly very much afraid of him.

Thomas Mugridge is cur-like in his subjection to me, while I go about in secret dread of him. His is the courage of fear,—a strange thing I know well of myself,—and at any moment it may master the fear and impel him to the taking of my life. My knee is much better, though it often aches for long periods, and the stiffness is gradually leaving the arm which Wolf Larsen squeezed. Otherwise I am in splendid condition, feel that I am in splendid condition. My muscles are growing harder and increasing in size. My hands, however, are a spectacle for grief. They have a parboiled appearance, are afflicted with hang-nails, while the nails are broken and discolored, and the edges of the quick seem to be assuming a fungoid sort of growth. Also, I am suffering from boils, due to the diet, most likely, for I was never afflicted in this manner before.

I was amused, a couple of evenings back, by seeing Wolf Larsen reading the Bible, a copy of which, after the futile search for one at the beginning of the voyage, had been found in the dead mate's sea-chest. I wondered what Wolf Larsen could get from it, and he read aloud to me from Ecclesiastes. I could imagine he was speaking the thoughts of his own mind as he read to me, and his voice, reverberating deeply and mournfully in the confined cabin, charmed and held me. He may be uneducated, but he certainly knows how to express the significance of the written word. I can hear him now, as I shall always hear him, the primal melancholy vibrant in his voice as he read:

"I gathered me also silver and gold, and the peculiar treasure of kings and of the provinces; I gat me men singers and women singers, and the delights of the sons of men, as musical instruments, and that of all sorts.

"So I was great, and increased more than all that were before me in Jerusalem; also my wisdom remained with me.

"Then I looked on all the works that my hands had wrought and on the labor that I had labored to do; and behold, all was vanity and vexation of spirit, and there was no profit under the sun.

"All things come alike to all; there is one event to the righteous and to the wicked; to the good and to the clean, and to the unclean; to him that sacrificeth, and to him that sacrificeth not; as is the good, so is the sinner; and he that sweareth, as he that feareth an oath.

"This is an evil among all things that are done under the sun, that there is one event unto all; yea, also the heart of the sons of men is full of evil, and madness is in their heart while they live, and after that they go to the dead.

"For to him that is joined to all the living there is hope; for a living dog is better than a dead lion.

"For the living know that they shall die; but the dead know not anything, neither have they any more a reward; for the memory of them is forgotten.

"Also their love, and their hatred, and their envy, is now perished; neither have they any more a portion forever in anything that is done under the sun."

"There you have it, Hump," he said, closing the book upon his finger and looking up at me. "The Preacher who was king over Israel in Jerusalem thought as I think. You call me a pessimist. Is not this pessimism of the blackest?—'All is vanity and vexation of spirit,' 'There is no profit under the sun,' 'There is one event unto all,' to the fool and the wise, the clean and the unclean, the sinner and the saint, and that event is death, and an evil thing, he says. For the Preacher loved life, and did not want to die, saying, 'For a living dog is better than a dead lion.' He preferred the vanity and vexation to the silence and unmovableness of the grave. And so I. To crawl is piggish; but to not crawl, to be as the clod and rock, is loathsome to contemplate. It is loathsome to the life that is in me, the very essence of which is movement, the power of movement, and the consciousness of the power of movement. Life itself is unsatisfaction, but to look ahead to death is greater unsatisfaction."

"You are worse off than Omar," I said. "He, at least, after the customary agonizing of youth, found content and made of his materialism a joyous thing."

"Who was Omar?" Wolf Larsen asked, and I did no more work that day, nor the next, nor the next.

In his random reading he had never chanced upon the Rubáiyát, and it was to him like a great find of treasure. Much I remembered, possibly two-thirds of the quatrains, and I managed to piece out the remainder without difficulty. We talked for hours over single stanzas, and I found him reading into them a wail of regret and a rebellion which, for the life of me, I could not discover myself. Possibly I recited with a certain joyous lilt which was my own, for,—his memory was good, and at a second rendering, very often the first, he made a quatrain his own,—he recited the same lines and invested them with an unrest and passionate revolt that was well-nigh convincing.

I was interested as to which quatrain he would like best, and was not surprised when he hit upon the one born of an instant's irritability, and quite at variance with the Persian's complacent philosophy and genial code of life:—

"*What, without asking, hither hurried* Whence?
And, without asking, Whither *hurried hence!*
Oh, many a Cup of this forbidden Wine
Must drown the memory of that insolence!"

"Great!" Wolf Larsen cried. "Great! That's the keynote. Insolence! He could not have used a better word."

In vain I objected and denied. He deluged me, overwhelmed me with argument.

"It's not the nature of life to be otherwise. Life, when it knows that it must cease living, will always rebel. It cannot help itself. The Preacher found life and the works of life all a vanity and vexation, an evil thing; but death, the ceasing to be able to be vain and vexed, he found an eviler thing. Through chapter after chapter he is worried by the one event that cometh to all alike. So Omar, so I, so you, even you, for you rebelled against dying when Cooky sharpened a knife for you. You were afraid to die; the life that was in you, that composes you, that is greater than you, did not want to die. You have talked of the instinct of immortality. I talk of the instinct of life, which is to live, and which, when death looms near and large, masters the instinct, so called, of immortality. It mastered it in you (you cannot deny it), because a crazy Cockney cook sharpened a knife.

"You are afraid of him now. You are afraid of me. You cannot deny it. If I should catch you by the throat, thus,"—his hand was about my throat and my breath was shut off,—"and began to press the life out of you, thus, and thus, your instinct of immortality will go glimmering, and your instinct of life, which is longing for life, will flutter up, and you will struggle to save yourself. Eh? I see the fear of death in your eyes. You beat the air with your arms. You exert all your puny strength to struggle to live. Your hand is clutching my arm, lightly it feels as a butterfly resting there. Your chest is heaving, your tongue protruding, your skin turning dark, your eyes swimming. 'To live! To live! To live!' you are crying; and you are crying to live here and now, not hereafter. You doubt your immortality, eh? Ha! Ha! You are not sure of it. You won't chance it. This life only you are certain is real. Ah, it is growing dark and darker. It is the darkness of death, the ceasing to be, the ceasing to feel, the ceasing to move, that is gathering about you, descending upon you, rising around you. Your eyes are becoming set. They are glazing. My voice sounds faint and far. You cannot see my face. And still you struggle in my grip. You kick with your legs. Your body draws itself up in knots like a snake's. Your chest heaves and strains. To live! To live! To live—"

I heard no more. Consciousness was blotted out by the darkness he had so graphically described, and when I came to myself I was lying on the floor and he was smoking a cigar and regarding me thoughtfully with that old familiar light of curiosity in his eyes.

"Well, have I convinced you?" he demanded. "Here, take a drink of this. I want to ask you some questions."

I rolled my head negatively on the floor. "Your arguments are too—er—forcible" I managed to articulate, at cost of great pain to my aching throat.

"You'll be all right in half an hour," he assured me. "And I promise I won't use any more physical demonstrations. Get up now. You can sit on a chair."

And, toy that I was of this monster, the discussion of Omar and the Preacher was resumed. And half the night we sat up over it.

The last twenty-four hours have witnessed a carnival of brutality. From cabin to forecastle it seems to have broken out like a contagion. I scarcely know where to begin. Wolf Larsen was really the cause of it. The relations among the men, strained and made tense by feuds, quarrels, and grudges, were in a state of unstable equilibrium, and evil passions flared up in flame like prairie-grass.

Thomas Mugridge is a sneak, a spy, an informer. He has been attempting to curry favor and reinstate himself in the good graces of the captain by carrying tales of the men forward. He it was, I know, that carried some of Johnson's hasty talk to Wolf Larsen. Johnson, it seems, bought a suit of oilskins from the slop-chest and found them to be of greatly inferior quality. Nor was he slow in advertising the fact.

The slop-chest is a sort of miniature dry-goods store which is carried by all sealing schooners and which is stocked with articles peculiar to the needs of the sailors. Whatever a sailor purchases is taken from his subsequent earnings on the sealing grounds; for, as it is with the hunters so it is with the boat-pullers and steerers—in the place of wages they receive a "lay," a rate of so much per skin for every skin captured in their particular boat.

But of Johnson's grumbling at the slop-chest I knew nothing, so that what I witnessed came with the shock of sudden surprise. I had just finished sweeping the cabin, and had been inveigled by Wolf Larsen into a discussion of Hamlet, his favorite Shakesperian character, when Johansen descended the companion stairs followed by Johnson. The latter's cap came off after the custom of the sea, and he stood respectfully in the centre of the cabin, swaying heavily and uneasily to the roll of the schooner and facing the captain.

"Shut the doors and draw the slide," Wolf Larsen said to me.

As I obeyed I noticed an anxious light come into Johnson's eyes, but I did not dream of its cause. I did not dream of what was to occur until it did occur, but he knew from the very first what was coming and awaited it bravely. And in his action I found complete refutation of all Wolf Larsen's materialism. The sailor Johnson was swayed by idea, by principle, and truth, and sincerity. He was right, he knew he was right, and he was unafraid. He would die for the right if needs be, he would be true to himself, sincere with his soul. And in this was portrayed the victory of the spirit over the flesh, the indomitability and moral grandeur of the soul that knows no restriction and rises above time and space and matter with a surety and invincibleness born of nothing else than eternity and immortality.

But to return. I noticed the anxious light in Johnson's eyes, but mistook it for the native shyness and embarrassment of the man. The mate, Johansen, stood away several feet to the side of him, and fully three yards in front of him sat Wolf Larsen on one of the pivotal cabin chairs. An appreciable pause fell after I had closed the doors and drawn the slide, a pause that must have lasted fully a minute. It was broken by Wolf Larsen.

"Yonson," he began.

"My name is Johnson, sir," the sailor boldly corrected.

"Well, Johnson, then, damn you! Can you guess why I have sent for you?"

"Yes, and no, sir," was the slow reply. "My work is done well. The mate knows that, and you know it, sir. So there cannot be any complaint."

"And is that all?" Wolf Larsen queried, his voice soft, and low, and purring.

"I know you have it in for me," Johnson continued with his unalterable and ponderous slowness. "You do not like me. You—You—"

"Go on," Wolf Larsen prompted. "Don't be afraid of my feelings."

"I am not afraid," the sailor retorted, a slight angry flush rising through his sunburn. "If I speak not fast, it is because I have not been from the old country as long as you. You do not like me because I am too much of a man; that is why, sir."

"You are too much of a man for ship discipline, if that is what you mean, and if you know what I mean," was Wolf Larsen's retort.

"I know English, and I know what you mean, sir," Johnson answered, his flush deepening at the slur on his knowledge of the English language.

"Johnson," Wolf Larsen said, with an air of dismissing all that had gone before as introductory to the main business in hand, "I understand you're not quite satisfied with those oilskins?"

"No, I am not. They are no good, sir."

"And you've been shooting off your mouth about them."

"I say what I think, sir," the sailor answered courageously, not failing at the same time in ship courtesy, which demanded that "sir" be appended to each speech he made.

It was at this moment that I chanced to glance at Johansen. His big fists were clenching and unclenching, and his face was positively fiendish, so malignantly did he look at Johnson. I noticed a black discoloration, still faintly visible, under Johansen's eye, a mark of the thrashing he had received a few nights before from the sailor. For the first time I began to divine that something terrible was about to be enacted,—what, I could not imagine.

"Do you know what happens to men who say what you've said about my slop-chest and me?" Wolf Larsen was demanding.

"I know, sir," was the answer.

"What?" Wolf Larsen demanded, sharply and imperatively.

"What you and the mate there are going to do to me, sir."

"Look at him, Hump," Wolf Larsen said to me, "look at this bit of animated dust, this aggregation of matter that moves and breathes and defies me and thoroughly believes itself to be compounded of something good; that is impressed with certain human fictions such as righteousness and honesty, and that will live up to them in spite of all personal discomforts and menaces. What do you think of him, Hump? What do you think of him?"

"I think that he is a better man than you are," I answered, impelled, somehow, with a desire to draw upon myself a portion of the wrath I felt was about to break upon his head. "His human fictions, as you choose to call them, make for nobility and manhood. You have no fictions, no dreams, no ideals. You are a pauper."

He nodded his head with a savage pleasantness. "Quite true, Hump, quite true. I have no fictions that make for nobility and manhood. A living dog is better than a dead lion, say I with the Preacher. My only doctrine is the doctrine of expediency, and it makes for surviving. This bit of the ferment we call 'Johnson,' when he is no longer a bit of the ferment, only dust and ashes, will have no more nobility than any dust and ashes, while I shall still be alive and roaring."

"Do you know what I am going to do?" he questioned.

I shook my head.

"Well, I am going to exercise my prerogative of roaring and show you how fares nobility. Watch me."

Three yards away from Johnson he was, and sitting down. Nine feet! And yet he left the chair in full leap, without first gaining a standing position. He left the chair, just as he sat in it, squarely, springing from the sitting posture like a wild animal, a tiger, and like a tiger covered the intervening space. It was an avalanche of fury that Johnson strove vainly to fend off. He threw one arm down to protect the stomach, the other arm up to protect the head; but Wolf Larsen's fist drove midway between, on the chest, with a crushing, resounding impact. Johnson's breath, suddenly expelled, shot from his mouth and as suddenly checked, with the forced, audible expiration of a man wielding an axe. He almost fell backward, and swayed from side to side in an effort to recover his balance.

I cannot give the further particulars of the horrible scene that followed. It was too revolting. It turns me sick even now when I think of it. Johnson fought bravely enough, but he was no match for Wolf Larsen, much less for Wolf Larsen and the mate. It was frightful. I had not imagined a human being could endure so much and still live and struggle on. And struggle on Johnson did. Of course there was no hope for him, not the slightest, and he knew it as well as I, but by the manhood that was in him he could not cease from fighting for that manhood.

It was too much for me to witness. I felt that I should lose my mind, and I ran up the companion stairs to open the doors and escape on deck. But Wolf Larsen, leaving his victim for the moment, and with one of his tremendous springs, gained my side and flung me into the far corner of the cabin.

"The phenomena of life, Hump," he girded at me. "Stay and watch it. You may gather data on the immortality of the soul. Besides, you know, we can't hurt Johnson's soul. It's only the fleeting form we may demolish."

It seemed centuries—possibly it was no more than ten minutes that the beating continued. Wolf Larsen and Johansen were all about the poor fellow. They struck him with their fists, kicked him with their heavy shoes, knocked him down, and dragged him to his feet to knock him down again. His eyes were blinded so that he could not see, and the blood running from ears and nose and mouth turned the cabin into a shambles. And when he could no longer rise they still continued to beat and kick him where he lay.

"Easy, Johansen; easy as she goes," Wolf Larsen finally said.

But the beast in the mate was up and rampant, and Wolf Larsen was compelled to brush him away with a backhanded sweep of the arm, gentle enough, apparently, but which hurled Johansen back like a cork, driving his head against the wall with a crash. He fell to the floor, half stunned for the moment, breathing heavily and blinking his eyes in a stupid sort of way.

"Jerk open the doors, Hump," I was commanded.

I obeyed, and the two brutes picked up the senseless man like a sack of rubbish and hove him clear up the companion stairs, through the narrow doorway, and out on deck. The blood from his nose gushed in a scarlet stream over the feet of the helmsman, who was none other than Louis, his boat-mate. But Louis took and gave a spoke and gazed imperturbably into the binnacle.

Not so was the conduct of George Leach, the erstwhile cabin-boy. Fore and aft there was nothing that could have surprised us more than his consequent behavior. He it was that came up on the poop without orders and dragged Johnson forward, where he set about dressing his wounds as well as he could and making him comfortable. Johnson, as Johnson, was unrecognizable; and not only that, for his features, as human features at all, were unrecognizable, so discolored and swollen had they become in the few minutes which had elapsed between the beginning of the beating and the dragging forward of the body.

But of Leach's behavior— By the time I had finished cleansing the cabin he had taken care of Johnson. I had come up on deck for a breath of fresh air and to try to get some repose for my overwrought nerves. Wolf Larsen was smoking a cigar and examining the patent log which the *Ghost* usually towed astern but which had been hauled in for some purpose. Suddenly Leach's voice came to my ears. It was tense and hoarse with an overmastering rage. I turned and saw him standing just beneath the break of the poop on the port side of the galley. His face was convulsed and white, his eyes were flashing, his clenched fists raised overhead.

"May God damn your soul to hell, Wolf Larsen, only hell's too good for you, you coward, you murderer, you pig!" was his opening salutation.

I was thunderstruck. I looked for his instant annihilation. But it was not Wolf

Larsen's whim to annihilate him. He sauntered slowly forward to the break of the poop, and, leaning his elbow on the corner of the cabin, gazed down thoughtfully and curiously at the excited boy.

And the boy indicted Wolf Larsen as he had never been indicted before. The sailors assembled in a fearful group just outside the forecastle scuttle and watched and listened. The hunters piled pell-mell out of the steerage, but as Leach's tirade continued I saw that there was no levity in their faces. Even they were frightened, not at the boy's terrible words, but at his terrible audacity. It did not seem possible that any living creature could thus beard Wolf Larsen in his teeth. I know for myself that I was shocked into admiration of the boy, and I saw in him the splendid invincibleness of immortality rising above the flesh and the fears of the flesh, as in the prophets of old, to condemn unrighteousness.

And such condemnation! He hailed forth Wolf Larsen's soul naked to the scorn of men. He rained upon it curses from God and High Heaven, and withered it with a heat of invective that savored of a mediæval excommunication of the Catholic Church. He ran the gamut of denunciation, rising to heights of wrath that were sublime and almost Godlike, and from sheer exhaustion sinking to the vilest and most indecent abuse.

His rage was a madness. His lips were flecked with a soapy froth, and sometimes he choked and gurgled and became inarticulate. And through it all, calm and impassive, leaning on his elbow and gazing down, Wolf Larsen seemed lost in a great curiosity. This wild stirring of yeasty life, this terrific revolt and defiance of matter that moved, perplexed and interested him.

Each moment I looked, and everybody looked, for him to leap upon the boy and destroy him. But it was not his whim. His cigar went out, and he continued to gaze silently and curiously.

Leach had worked himself into an ecstasy of impotent rage.

"Pig! Pig! Pig!" he was reiterating at the top of his lungs. "Why don't you come down and kill me, you murderer? You can do it! I ain't afraid! There's no one to stop you! Damn sight better dead and outa your reach than alive and in your clutches! Come on, you coward! Kill me! Kill me! Kill me!"

It was at this stage that Thomas Mugridge's erratic soul brought him into the scene. He had been listening at the galley door, but he now came out, ostensibly to fling some scraps over the side, but obviously to see the killing he was certain would take place. He smirked greasily up into the face of Wolf Larsen, who seemed not to see him. But the Cockney was unabashed, though mad, stark mad. He turned to Leach, saying:

"Such langwidge! Shockin'!"

Leach's rage was no longer impotent. Here at last was something ready to hand. And for the first time since the stabbing the Cockney had appeared outside the galley without his knife. The words had barely left his mouth when he was knocked down by Leach. Three times he struggled to his feet, striving to gain the galley, and each time was knocked down.

"Oh, Lord!" he cried. "'Elp! 'Elp! Tyke 'im aw'y, carn't yer? Tyke 'im aw'y!"

The hunters laughed from sheer relief. Tragedy had dwindled, the farce had begun. The sailors now crowded boldly aft, grinning and shuffling, to watch the pummelling of the hated Cockney. And even I felt a great joy surge up within me. I confess that I delighted in this beating Leach was giving to Thomas Mugridge, though it was as terrible, almost, as the one Mugridge had caused to be given to

Johnson. But the expression of Wolf Larsen's face never changed. He did not change his position either, but continued to gaze down with a great curiosity. For all his pragmatic certitude, it seemed as if he watched the play and movement of life in the hope of discovering something more about it, of discerning in its maddest writhings a something which had hitherto escaped him,—the key to its mystery, as it were, which would make all clear and plain.

But the beating! It was quite similar to the one I had witnessed in the cabin. The Cockney strove in vain to protect himself from the infuriated boy. And in vain he strove to gain the shelter of the cabin. He rolled toward it, grovelled toward it, fell toward it when he was knocked down. But blow followed blow with bewildering rapidity. He was knocked about like a shuttlecock, until, finally, like Johnson, he was beaten and kicked as he lay helpless on the deck. And no one interfered. Leach could have killed him, but, having evidently filled the measure of his vengeance, he drew away from his prostrate foe, who was whimpering and wailing in a puppyish sort of way, and walked forward.

But these two affairs were only the opening events of the day's programme. In the afternoon Smoke and Henderson fell foul of each other, and a fusillade of shots came up from the steerage, followed by a stampede of the other four hunters for the deck. A column of thick, acrid smoke—the kind always made by black powder—was arising through the open companionway, and down through it leaped Wolf Larsen. The sound of blows and scuffling came to our ears. Both men were wounded, and he was thrashing them both for having disobeyed his orders and crippled themselves in advance of the hunting season. In fact, they were badly wounded, and, having thrashed them, he proceeded to operate upon them in a rough surgical fashion and to dress their wounds. I served as assistant while he probed and cleansed the passages made by the bullets, and I saw the two men endure his crude surgery without anæsthetics and with no more to uphold them than a stiff tumbler of whiskey.

Then, in the first dog-watch, trouble came to a head in the forecastle. It took its rise out of the tittle-tattle and tale-bearing which had been the cause of Johnson's beating, and from the noise we heard, and from the sight of the bruised men next day, it was patent that half the forecastle had soundly drubbed the other half.

The second dog-watch and the day were wound up by a fight between Johansen and the lean, Yankee-looking hunter, Latimer. It was caused by remarks of Latimer's concerning the noises made by the mate in his sleep, and though Johansen was whipped, he kept the steerage awake for the rest of the night while he blissfully slumbered and fought the fight over and over again.

As for myself, I was oppressed with nightmare. The day had been like some horrible dream. Brutality had followed brutality, and flaming passions and cold-blooded cruelty had driven men to seek one another's lives, and to strive to hurt, and maim, and destroy. My nerves were shocked. My mind itself was shocked. All my days had been passed in comparative ignorance of the animality of man. In fact, I had known life only in its intellectual phases. Brutality I had experienced, but it was the brutality of the intellect—the cutting sarcasm of Charley Furuseth, the cruel epigrams and occasional harsh witticisms of the fellows at the Bibelot, and the nasty remarks of some of the professors during my undergraduate days.

That was all. But that men should wreak their anger on others by the bruising of the flesh and the letting of blood was something strangely and fearfully new to me. Not for nothing had I been called "Sissy" Van Weyden, I thought, as I tossed restlessly on my bunk between one nightmare and another. And it seemed to me that my innocence of the realities of life had been complete indeed. I laughed bitterly to myself, and seemed to find in Wolf Larsen's forbidding philosophy a more adequate explanation of life than I found in my own.

And I was frightened when I became conscious of the trend of my thought. The continual brutality around me was degenerative in its effect. It bid fair to destroy for me all that was best and brightest in life. My reason dictated that the beating Thomas Mugridge had received was an ill thing, and yet for the life of me I could not prevent my soul joying in it. And even while I was oppressed by the enormity of my sin,—for sin it was,—I chuckled with an insane delight. I was no longer Humphrey Van Weyden. I was Hump, cabin-boy on the schooner *Ghost.* Wolf Larsen was my captain, Thomas Mugridge and the rest were my companions, and I was receiving repeated impresses from the die which had stamped them all.

1904

THE IRON HEEL

Selections

The Iron Heel *is a novel of conflict and revolution. The following selections open with a stirring speech by Ernest Everhard at the Philomath Club, a social organization of millionaires. In this speech Everhard, a militant socialist leader, berates the Capitalists for their betrayal of the working classes and prophesies how the Socialist party will eventually sieze control of the management of society.*

After this speech events begin to move rapidly. The socialists, unaware of their danger, prefer to gain power by legal means, at the polls. The Capitalists, however, are aroused, and soon, slowly, quietly, momentous events begin to take place. Step by step the Oligarchy (the Capitalists) destroy the democratic institutions of the country and replace the old structure of society with a new caste system governed by a dictatorship.

The Iron Heel *is the diary of Avis Everhard, wife of the socialist leader. Supposedly lost for centuries the diary is discovered, edited, and published when the Socialists have finally triumphed over the Oligarchy.* ED.

THE PHILOMATHS

Ernest was often at the house. Nor was it my father, merely, nor the controversial dinners, that drew him there. Even at that time I flattered myself that I played some part in causing his visits, and it was not long before I learned the correctness of my surmise. For never was there such a lover as Ernest Everhard. His gaze and his hand-clasp grew firmer and steadier, if that were possible; and the question that had grown from the first in his eyes, grew only the more imperative.

My impression of him, the first time I saw him, had been unfavorable. Then I had found myself attracted toward him. Next came my repulsion, when he so savagely attacked my class and me. After that, as I saw that he had not maligned my class, and that the harsh and bitter things he said about it were justified, I had drawn closer to him again. He became my oracle. For me he tore the sham from the face of society and gave me glimpses of reality that were as unpleasant as they were undeniably true.

As I have said, there was never such a lover as he. No girl could live in a university town till she was twenty-four and not have love experiences. I had been made love to by beardless sophomores and gray professors, and by the athletes and the football giants. But not one of them made love to me as Ernest did. His arms were around me before I knew. His lips were on mine before I could protest or resist. Before his earnestness conventional maiden dignity was ridiculous. He swept me off my feet by the splendid invincible rush of him. He did not propose. He put his arms around me and kissed me and took it for granted that we should be married. There was no discussion about it. The only discussion—and that arose afterward—was when we should be married.

It was unprecedented. It was unreal. Yet, in accordance with Ernest's test of truth, it worked. I trusted my life to it. And fortunate was the trust. Yet during those first days of our love, fear of the future came often to me when I thought of the violence and impetuosity of his love-making. Yet such fears were groundless. No woman was ever blessed with a gentler, tenderer husband. This gentleness and violence on his part was a curious blend similar to the one in his carriage of awkwardness and ease. That slight awkwardness! He never got over it, and it was delicious. His behavior in our drawing-room reminded me of a careful bull in a china shop.[1]

It was at this time that vanished my last doubt of the completeness of my love for him (a subconscious doubt, at most). It was at the Philomath Club—a wonderful night of battle, wherein Ernest bearded the masters in their lair. Now the Philomath Club was the most select on the Pacific Coast. It was the creation of Miss Brentwood, an enormously wealthy old maid; and it was her husband, and family, and toy. Its members were the wealthiest in the community, and the strongest-minded of the wealthy, with, of course, a sprinkling of scholars to give it intellectual tone.

The Philomath had no club house. It was not that kind of a club. Once a month its members gathered at some one of their private houses to listen to a lecture. The lecturers were usually, though not always, hired. If a chemist in New York made a new discovery in say radium, all his expenses across the continent were paid, and as well he received a princely fee for his time. The same with a returning explorer from the polar regions, or the latest literary or artistic success. No visitors were allowed, while it was the Philomath's policy to permit none of its discussions to get into the papers. Thus great statesmen—and there had been such occasions—were able fully to speak their minds.

I spread before me a wrinkled letter, written to me by Ernest twenty years ago, and from it I copy the following:

"Your father is a member of the Philomath, so you are able to come. Therefore come next Tuesday night. I promise you that you will have the time of your life. In your recent encounters, you failed to shake the masters. If you come, I'll shake them for you. I'll make them snarl like wolves. You merely questioned their morality. When their morality is questioned, they grow only the more complacent and superior. But I shall menace their money-bags. That will shake them to the roots of their primitive natures. If you can come, you will see the cave-man, in evening dress, snarling and snapping over a bone. I promise you a great caterwauling and an illuminating insight into the nature of the beast.

"They've invited me in order to tear me to pieces. This is the idea of Miss Brentwood. She clumsily hinted as much when she invited me. She's given them that kind of fun before. They delight in getting trustful-souled gentle reformers before them. Miss Brentwood thinks I am as mild as a kitten and as good-natured and stolid as the family cow. I'll not deny that I helped to give her that impression. She was very tentative at first, until she divined my harmlessness. I am to receive a

[1] In those days it was still the custom to fill the living rooms with bric-a-brac. They had not discovered simplicity of living. Such rooms were museums, entailing endless labor to keep clean. The dust-demon was the lord of the household. There were a myriad devices for catching dust, and only a few devices for getting rid of it.

handsome fee—two hundred and fifty dollars—as befits the man who, though a radical, once ran for governor. Also, I am to wear evening dress. This is compulsory. I never was so apparelled in my life. I suppose I'll have to hire one somewhere. But I'd do more than that to get a chance at the Philomaths."

Of all places, the Club gathered that night at the Pertonwaithe house. Extra chairs had been brought into the great drawing room, and in all there must have been two hundred Philomaths that sat down to hear Ernest. They were truly lords of society. I amused myself with running over in my mind the sum of the fortunes represented, and it ran well into the hundreds of millions. And the possessors were not of the idle rich. They were men of affairs who took most active parts in industrial and political life.

We were all seated when Miss Brentwood brought Ernest in. They moved at once to the head of the room, from where he was to speak. He was in evening dress, and, what of his broad shoulders and kingly head he looked magnificent. And then there was that faint and unmistakable touch of awkwardness in his movements. I almost think I could have loved him for that alone. And as I looked at him I was aware of a great joy. I felt again the pulse of his palm on mine, the touch of his lips; and such pride was mine that I felt I must rise up and cry out to the assembled company: "He is mine! He has held me in his arms, and I, mere I, have filled that mind of his to the exclusion of all his multitudinous and kingly thoughts!"

At the head of the room, Miss Brentwood introduced him to Colonel Van Gilbert, and I knew that the latter was to preside. Colonel Van Gilbert was a great corporation lawyer. In addition, he was immensely wealthy. The smallest fee he would deign to notice was a hundred thousand dollars. He was a master of law. The law was a puppet with which he played. He moulded it like clay, twisted and distorted it like a Chinese puzzle into any design he chose. In appearance and rhetoric he was old-fashioned, but in imagination and knowledge and resource he was as young as the latest statute. His first prominence had come when he broke the Shardwell will.[2] His fee for this one act was five hundred thousand dollars. From then on he had risen like a rocket. He was often called the greatest lawyer in the country—corporation lawyer, of course; and no classification of the three greatest lawyers in the United States could have excluded him.

He arose and began, in a few well-chosen phrases that carried an undertone of faint irony, to introduce Ernest. Colonel Van Gilbert was subtly facetious in his introduction of the social reformer and member of the working class, and the audience smiled. It made me angry, and I glanced at Ernest. The sight of him made me doubly angry. He did not seem to resent the delicate slurs. Worse than that, he did not seem to be aware of them. There he sat, gentle, and stolid, and somnolent. He really looked stupid. And for a moment the thought rose in my mind, What if he were overawed by this imposing array of power and brains? Then

[2] This breaking of wills was a peculiar feature of the period. With the accumulation of vast fortunes, the problem of disposing of these fortunes after death was a vexing one to the accumulators. Will-making and will-breaking became complementary trades, like armor-making and gun-making. The shrewdest will-making lawyers were called in to make wills that could not be broken. But these wills were always broken, and very often by the very lawyers that had drawn them up. Nevertheless the delusion persisted in the wealthy class that an absolutely unbreakable will could be cast; and so, through the generations, clients and lawyers pursued the illusion. It was a pursuit like unto that of the Universal Solvent of the mediaeval alchemists.

I smiled. He couldn't fool me. But he fooled the others, just as he had fooled Miss Brentwood. She occupied a chair right up to the front, and several times she turned her head toward one or another of her *confrères* and smiled her appreciation of the remarks.

Colonel Van Gilbert done, Ernest arose and began to speak. He began in a low voice, haltingly and modestly, and with an air of evident embarrassment. He spoke of his birth in the working class, and of the sordidness and wretchedness of his environment, where flesh and spirit were alike starved and tormented. He described his ambitions and ideals, and his conception of the paradise wherein lived the people of the upper classes. As he said:

"Up above me, I knew, were unselfishnesses of the spirit, clean and noble thinking, keen intellectual living. I knew all this because I read 'Seaside Library'[3] novels, in which, with the exception of the villains and adventuresses, all men and women thought beautiful thoughts, spoke a beautiful tongue, and performed glorious deeds. In short, as I accepted the rising of the sun, I accepted that up above me was all that was fine and noble and gracious, all that gave decency and dignity to life, all that made life worth living and that remunerated one for his travail and misery."

He went on and traced his life in the mills, the learning of the horseshoeing trade, and his meeting with the socialists. Among them, he said, he had found keen intellects and brilliant wits, ministers of the Gospel who had been broken because their Christianity was too wide for any congregation of mammon-worshippers, and professors who had been broken on the wheel of university subservience to the ruling class. The socialists were revolutionists, he said, struggling to overthrow the irrational society of the present and out of the material to build the rational society of the future. Much more he said that would take too long to write, but I shall never forget how he described the life among the revolutionists. All halting utterance vanished. His voice grew strong and confident, and it glowed as he glowed, and as the thoughts glowed that poured out from him. He said:

"Amongst the revolutionists I found, also, warm faith in the human, ardent idealism, sweetnesses of unselfishness, renunciation, and martyrdom—all the splendid, stinging things of the spirit. Here life was clean, noble, and alive. I was in touch with great souls who exalted flesh and spirit over dollars and cents, and to whom the thin wail of the starved slum child meant more than all the pomp and circumstance of commercial expansion and world empire. All about me were nobleness of purpose and heroism of effort, and my days and nights were sunshine and starshine, all fire and dew, with before my eyes, ever burning and blazing, the Holy Grail, Christ's own Grail, the warm human, long-suffering and maltreated but to be rescued and saved at the last."

As before I had seen him transfigured, so now he stood transfigured before me. His brows were bright with the divine that was in him, and brighter yet shone his eyes from the midst of the radiance that seemed to envelop him as a mantle. But the others did not see this radiance, and I assumed that it was due to the tears of joy and love that dimmed my vision. At any rate, Mr. Wickson, who sat behind me, was unaffected, for I heard him sneer aloud, "Utopian."[4]

[3] A curious and amazing literature that served to make the working class utterly misapprehend the nature of the leisure class.

[4] The people of that age were phrase slaves. The abjectness of their servitude is incomprehensible to us. There was a magic in words greater than the conjurer's art. So befuddled

Ernest went on to his rise in society, till at last he came in touch with members of the upper classes, and rubbed shoulders with the men who sat in the high places. Then came his disillusionment, and this disillusionment he described in terms that did not flatter his audience. He was surprised at the commonness of the clay. Life proved not to be fine and gracious. He was appalled by the selfishness he encountered, and what had surprised him even more than that was the absence of intellectual life. Fresh from his revolutionists, he was shocked by the intellectual stupidity of the master class. And then, in spite of their magnificent churches and well-paid preachers, he had found the masters, men and women, grossly material. It was true that they prattled sweet little ideals and dear little moralities, but in spite of their prattle the dominant key of the life they lived was materialistic. And they were without real morality—for instance, that which Christ had preached but which was no longer preached.

"I met men," he said, "who invoked the name of the Prince of Peace in their diatribes against war, and who put rifles in the hands of Pinkertons[5] with which to shoot down strikers in their own factories. I met men incoherent with indignation at the brutality of prize-fighting, and who, at the same time, were parties to the adulteration of food that killed each year more babes than even red-handed Herod had killed.

"This delicate, aristocratic-featured gentleman was a dummy director and a tool of corporations that secretly robbed widows and orphans. This gentleman, who collected fine editions and was a patron of literature, paid blackmail to a heavy-jowled, black-browed boss of a municipal machine. This editor, who published patent medicine advertisements, called me a scoundrelly demagogue because I dared him to print in his paper the truth about patent medicines.[6] This man, talking soberly and earnestly about the beauties of idealism and the goodness of God, had just betrayed his comrades in a business deal. This man, a pillar of the church and heavy contributor to foreign missions, worked his shop girls ten hours a day on a starvation wage and thereby directly encouraged prostitution. This man, who endowed chairs in universities and erected magnificent chapels, perjured himself in courts of law over dollars and cents. This railroad magnate broke his word as a citizen, as a gentleman, and as a Christian, when he granted a secret rebate, and he granted many secret rebates. This senator was the tool and the slave, the little puppet, of a brutal uneducated machine boss;[7] so was this governor and this supreme court judge; and all three rode on railroad passes; and, also, this sleek capi-

---

and chaotic were their minds that the utterance of a single word could negate the generalizations of a lifetime of serious research and thought. Such a word was the adjective *Utopian*. The mere utterance of it could damn any scheme, no matter how sanely conceived, of economic amelioration or regeneration. Vast populations grew frenzied over such phrases as "an honest dollar" and "a full dinner pail." The coinage of such phrases was considered strokes of genius.

[5] Originally, they were private detectives; but they quickly became hired fighting men of the capitalists, and ultimately developed into the Mercenaries of the Oligarchy.

[6] *Patent medicines* were patent lies, but, like the charms and indulgences of the Middle Ages, they deceived the people. The only difference lay in that the patent medicines were more harmful and more costly.

[7] Even as late as 1912, A.D., the great mass of the people still persisted in the belief that they ruled the country by virtue of their ballots. In reality, the country was ruled by what were called *political machines*. At first the machine bosses charged the master capitalists extortionate tolls for legislation; but in a short time the master capitalists found it cheaper to own the political machines themselves and to hire the machine bosses.

talist owned the machine, the machine boss, and the railroads that issued the passes.

"And so it was, instead of in paradise, that I found myself in the arid desert of commercialism. I found nothing but stupidity, except for business. I found none clean, noble, and alive, though I found many who were alive—with rottenness. What I did find was monstrous selfishness and heartlessness, and a gross, gluttonous, practised, and practical materialism."

Much more Ernest told them of themselves and of his disillusionment. Intellectually they had bored him; morally and spiritually they had sickened him; so that he was glad to go back to his revolutionists, who were clean, noble, and alive, and all that the capitalists were not.

"And now," he said, "let me tell you about that revolution."

But first I must say that his terrible diatribe had not touched them. I looked about me at their faces and saw that they remained complacently superior to what he had charged. And I remembered what he had told me: that no indictment of their morality could shake them. However, I could see that the boldness of his language had affected Miss Brentwood. She was looking worried and apprehensive.

Ernest began by describing the army of revolution, and as he gave the figures of its strength (the votes cast in the various countries), the assemblage began to grow restless. Concern showed in their faces, and I noticed a tightening of lips. At last the gage of battle had been thrown down. He described the international organization of the socialists that united the million and a half in the United States with the twenty-three millions and a half in the rest of the world.

"Such an army of revolution," he said, "twenty-five million strong, is a thing to make rulers and ruling classes pause and consider. The cry of this army is: 'No quarter! We want all that you possess. We will be content with nothing less than all that you possess. We want in our hands the reins of power and the destiny of mankind. Here are our hands. They are strong hands. We are going to take your governments, your palaces, and all your purpled ease away from you, and in that day you shall work for your bread even as the peasant in the field or the starved and runty clerk in your metropolises. Here are our hands. They are strong hands!' "

And as he spoke he extended from his splendid shoulders his two great arms, and the horseshoer's hands were clutching the air like eagle's talons. He was the spirit of regnant labor as he stood there, his hands outreaching to rend and crush his audience. I was aware of a faintly perceptible shrinking on the part of the listeners before this figure of revolution, concrete, potential, and menacing. That is, the women shrank, and fear was in their faces. Not so with the men. They were of the active rich, and not the idle, and they were fighters. A low, throaty rumble arose, lingered on the air a moment, and ceased. It was the forerunner of the snarl, and I was to hear it many times that night—the token of the brute in man, the earnest of his primitive passions. And they were unconscious that they had made this sound. It was the growl of the pack, mouthed by the pack, and mouthed in all unconsciousness. And in that moment, as I saw the harshness form in their faces and saw the fight-light flashing in their eyes, I realized that not easily would they let their lordship of the world be wrested from them.

Ernest proceeded with his attack. He accounted for the existence of the million and a half of revolutionists in the United States by charging the capitalist class with having mismanaged society. He sketched the economic condition of the caveman and of the savage peoples of to-day, pointing out that they possessed neither tools nor machines, and possessed only a natural efficiency of one in producing power. Then he traced the development of machinery and social organization so that to-day the producing power of civilized man was a thousand times greater than that of the savage.

"Five men," he said, "can produce bread for a thousand. One man can produce cotton cloth for two hundred and fifty people, woollens for three hundred, and boots and shoes for a thousand. One would conclude from this that under a capable management of society modern civilized man would be a great deal better off than the cave-man. But is he? Let us see. In the United States to-day there are fifteen million[8] people living in poverty; and by poverty is meant that condition in life in which, through lack of food and adequate shelter, the mere standard of working efficiency cannot be maintained. In the United States to-day, in spite of all your so-called labor legislation, there are three million child laborers.[9] In twelve years their numbers have been doubled. And in passing I will ask you managers of society why you did not make public the census figures of 1910? And I will answer for you, that you were afraid. The figures of misery would have precipitated the revolution that even now is gathering.

"But to return to my indictment. If modern man's producing power is a thousand times greater than that of the cave-man, why then, in the United States to-day, are there fifteen million people who are not properly sheltered and properly fed? Why then, in the United States to-day, are there three million child laborers? It is a true indictment. The capitalist class has mismanaged. In face of the facts that modern man lives more wretchedly than the cave-man, and that his producing power is a thousand times greater than that of the cave-man, no other conclusion is possible than that the capitalist class has mismanaged, that you have mismanaged, my masters, that you have criminally and selfishly mismanaged. And on this count you cannot answer me here to-night, face to face, any more than can your whole class answer the million and a half of revolutionists in the United States. You cannot answer. I challenge you to answer. And furthermore, I dare to say to you now that when I have finished you will not answer. On that point you will be tongue-tied, though you will talk wordily enough about other things.

"You have failed in your management. You have made a shambles of civilization. You have been blind and greedy. You have risen up (as you to-day rise up), shamelessly, in our legislative halls, and declared that profits were impossible without the toil of children and babes. Don't take my word for it. It is all in the records against you. You have lulled your conscience to sleep with prattle of sweet ideals and dear moralities. You are fat with power and possession, drunken with success; and you have no more hope against us than have the drones, clustered about the honey-vats, when the worker-bees spring upon them to end their rotund existence. You have failed in your management of society, and your management is to be taken away from you. A million and a half of the men of the working class say that they are going to get the rest of the working class to join with them and take the management away from you. This is the revolution, my masters. Stop it if you can."

For an appreciable lapse of time Ernest's voice continued to ring through the

[8] Robert Hunter, in 1906, in a book entitled "Poverty," pointed out that at that time there were ten million in the United States living in poverty.

[9] In the United States Census of 1900 (the last census the figures of which were made public), the number of child laborers was placed at 1,752,187.

great room. Then arose the throaty rumble I had heard before, and a dozen men were on their feet clamoring for recognition from Colonel Van Gilbert. I noticed Miss Brentwood's shoulders moving convulsively, and for the moment I was angry, for I thought that she was laughing at Ernest. And then I discovered that it was not laughter, but hysteria. She was appalled by what she had done in bringing this firebrand before her blessed Philomath Club.

Colonel Van Gilbert did not notice the dozen men, with passion-wrought faces, who strove to get permission from him to speak. His own face was passion-wrought. He sprang to his feet, waving his arms, and for a moment could utter only incoherent sounds. Then speech poured from him. But it was not the speech of a one-hundred-thousand-dollar lawyer, nor was the rhetoric old-fashioned.

"Fallacy upon fallacy!" he cried. "Never in all my life have I heard so many fallacies uttered in one short hour. And besides, young man, I must tell you that you have said nothing new. I learned all that at college before you were born. Jean Jacques Rousseau enunciated your socialistic theory nearly two centuries ago. A return to the soil, forsooth! Reversion! Our biology teaches the absurdity of it. It has been truly said that a little learning is a dangerous thing, and you have exemplified it to-night with your madcap theories. Fallacy upon fallacy! I was never so nauseated in my life with overplus of fallacy. That for your immature generalizations and childish reasonings!"

He snapped his fingers contemptuously and proceeded to sit down. There were lip-exclamations of approval on the part of the women, and hoarser notes of confirmation came from the men. As for the dozen men who were clamoring for the floor, half of them began speaking at once. The confusion and babel was indescribable. Never had Mrs. Pertonwaithe's spacious walls beheld such a spectacle. These, then, were the cool captains of industry and lords of society, these snarling, growling savages in evening clothes. Truly Ernest had shaken them when he stretched out his hands for their money-bags, his hands that had appeared in their eyes as the hands of the fifteen hundred thousand revolutionists.

But Ernest never lost his head in a situation. Before Colonel Van Gilbert had succeeded in sitting down, Ernest was on his feet and had sprung forward.

"One at a time!" he roared at them.

The sound arose from his great lungs and dominated the human tempest. By sheer compulsion of personality he commanded silence.

"One at a time," he repeated softly. "Let me answer Colonel Van Gilbert. After that the rest of you can come at me—but one at a time, remember. No mass-plays here. This is not a football field.

"As for you," he went on, turning toward Colonel Van Gilbert, "you have replied to nothing I have said. You have merely made a few excited and dogmatic assertions about my mental caliber. That may serve you in your business, but you can't talk to me like that. I am not a workingman, cap in hand, asking you to increase my wages or to protect me from the machine at which I work. You cannot be dogmatic with truth when you deal with me. Save that for dealing with your wage-slaves. They will not dare reply to you because you hold their bread and butter, their lives, in your hands.

"As for this return to nature that you say you learned at college before I was born, permit me to point out that on the face of it you cannot have learned anything since. Socialism has no more to do with the state of nature than has differential calculus with a Bible class. I have called your class stupid when outside the realm of business. You, sir, have brilliantly exemplified my statement."

This terrible castigation of her hundred-thousand-dollar lawyer was too much for Miss Brentwood's nerves. Her hysteria became violent, and she was helped, weeping and laughing, out of the room. It was just as well, for there was worse to follow.

"Don't take my word for it," Ernest continued, when the interruption had been led away. "Your own authorities with one unanimous voice will prove you stupid. Your own hired purveyors of knowledge will tell you that you are wrong. Go to your meekest little assistant instructor of sociology and ask him what is the difference between Rousseau's theory of the return to nature and the theory of socialism; ask your greatest orthodox bourgeois political economists and sociologists; question through the pages of every text-book written on the subject and stored on the shelves of your subsidized libraries; and from one and all the answer will be that there is nothing congruous between the return to nature and socialism. On the other hand, the unanimous affirmative answer will be that the return to nature and socialism are diametrically opposed to each other. As I say, don't take my word for it. The record of your stupidity is there in the books, your own books that you never read. And so far as your stupidity is concerned, you are but the exemplar of your class.

"You know law and business, Colonel Van Gilbert. You know how to serve corporations and increase dividends by twisting the law. Very good. Stick to it. You are quite a figure. You are a very good lawyer, but you are a poor historian, you know nothing of sociology, and your biology is contemporaneous with Pliny."

Here Colonel Van Gilbert writhed in his chair. There was perfect quiet in the room. Everybody sat fascinated—paralyzed, I may say. Such fearful treatment of the great Colonel Van Gilbert was unheard of, undreamed of, impossible to believe—the great Colonel Van Gilbert before whom judges trembled when he arose in court. But Ernest never gave quarter to an enemy.

"This is, of course, no reflection on you," Ernest said. "Every man to his trade. Only you stick to your trade, and I'll stick to mine. You have specialized. When it comes to a knowledge of the law, of how best to evade the law or make new law for the benefit of thieving corporations, I am down in the dirt at your feet. But when it comes to sociology—my trade—you are down in the dirt at my feet. Remember that. Remember, also, that your law is the stuff of a day, and that you are not versatile in the stuff of more than a day. Therefore your dogmatic assertions and rash generalizations on things historical and sociological are not worth the breath you waste on them."

Ernest paused for a moment and regarded him thoughtfully, noting his face dark and twisted with anger, his panting chest, his writhing body, and his slim white hands nervously clenching and unclenching.

"But it seems you have breath to use, and I'll give you a chance to use it. I indicted your class. Show me that my indictment is wrong. I pointed out to you the wretchedness of modern man—three million child slaves in the United States, without whose labor profits would not be possible, and fifteen million underfed, ill-clothed, and worse-housed people. I pointed out that modern man's producing power through social organization and the use of machinery was a thousand times greater than that of the cave-man. And I stated that from these two facts no other conclusion was possible than that the capitalist class had mismanaged. This was my indictment, and I specifically and at length challenged you to answer it. Nay, I did more. I prophesied that you would not answer. It remains for your breath to smash my prophecy. You called my speech fallacy. Show the fallacy, Colonel Van Gilbert. Answer the indictment that I and my fifteen hundred thousand comrades have brought against your class and you."

Colonel Van Gilbert quite forgot that he was presiding, and that in courtesy he should permit the other clamorers to speak. He was on his feet, flinging his arms, his rhetoric, and his control to the winds, alternately abusing Ernest for his youth and demagoguery, and savagely attacking the working class, elaborating its inefficiency and worthlessness.

"For a lawyer, you are the hardest man to keep to a point I ever saw," Ernest began his answer to the tirade. "My youth has nothing to do with what I have enunciated. Nor has the worthlessness of the working class. I charged the capitalist class with having mismanaged society. You have not answered. You have made no attempt to answer. Why? Is it because you have no answer? You are the champion of this whole audience. Every one here, except me, is hanging on your lips for that answer. They are hanging on your lips for that answer because they have no answer themselves. As for me, as I said before, I know that you not only cannot answer, but that you will not attempt an answer."

"This is intolerable!" Colonel Van Gilbert cried out. "This is insult!"

"That you should not answer is intolerable," Ernest replied gravely. "No man can be intellectually insulted. Insult, in its very nature, is emotional. Recover yourself. Give me an intellectual answer to my intellectual charge that the capitalist class has mismanaged society."

Colonel Van Gilbert remained silent, a sullen, superior expression on his face, such as will appear on the face of a man who will not bandy words with a ruffian.

"Do not be downcast," Ernest said. "Take consolation in the fact that no member of your class has ever yet answered that charge." He turned to the other men who were anxious to speak. "And now it's your chance. Fire away, and do not forget that I here challenge you to give the answer that Colonel Van Gilbert has failed to give."

It would be impossible for me to write all that was said in the discussion. I never realized before how many words could be spoken in three short hours. At any rate, it was glorious. The more his opponents grew excited, the more Ernest deliberately excited them. He had an encyclopædic command of the field of knowledge, and by a word or a phrase, by delicate rapier thrusts, he punctured them. He named the points of their illogic. This was a false syllogism, that conclusion had no connection with the premise, while the next premise was an impostor because it had cunningly hidden in it the conclusion that was being attempted to be proved. This was an error, that was an assumption, and the next was an assertion contrary to ascertained truth as printed in all the text-books.

And so it went. Sometimes he exchanged the rapier for the club and went smashing amongst their thoughts right and left. And always he demanded facts and refused to discuss theories. And his facts made for them a Waterloo. When they attacked the working class, he always retorted, "The pot calling the kettle black; that is no answer to the charge that your own face is dirty." And to one and all he said: "Why have you not answered the charge that your class has mismanaged? You have talked about other things and things concerning other things, but you have not answered. Is it because you have no answer?"

It was at the end of the discussion that Mr. Wickson spoke. He was the only one that was cool, and Ernest treated him with a respect he had not accorded the others.

"No answer is necessary," Mr. Wickson said with slow deliberation. "I have followed the whole discussion with amazement and disgust. I am disgusted with you, gentlemen, members of my class. You have behaved like foolish little schoolboys, what with intruding ethics and the thunder of the common politician into such a discussion. You have been outgeneralled and outclassed. You have been very wordy, and all you have done is buzz. You have buzzed like gnats about a bear. Gentlemen, there stands the bear" (he pointed at Ernest), "and your buzzing has only tickled his ears.

"Believe me, the situation is serious. That bear reached out his paws to-night to crush us. He has said there are a million and a half of revolutionists in the United States. That is a fact. He has said that it is their intention to take away from us our governments, our palaces, and all our purpled ease. That, also, is a fact. A change, a great change, is coming in society; but, haply, it may not be the change the bear anticipates. The bear has said that he will crush us. What if we crush the bear?"

The throat-rumble arose in the great room, and man nodded to man with indorsement and certitude. Their faces were set hard. They were fighters, that was certain.

"But not by buzzing will we crush the bear," Mr. Wickson went on coldly and dispassionately. "We will hunt the bear. We will not reply to the bear in words. Our reply shall be couched in terms of lead. We are in power. Nobody will deny it. By virtue of that power we shall remain in power."

He turned suddenly upon Ernest. The moment was dramatic.

"This, then, is our answer. We have no words to waste on you. When you reach out your vaunted strong hands for our palaces and purpled ease, we will show you what strength is. In roar of shell and shrapnel and in whine of machine-guns will our answer be couched.[10] We will grind you revolutionists down under our heel, and we shall walk upon your faces. The world is ours, we are its lords, and ours it shall remain. As for the host of labor, it has been in the dirt since history began, and I read history aright. And in the dirt it shall remain so long as I and mine and those that come after us have the power. There is the word. It is the king of words—Power. Not God, not Mammon, but Power. Pour it over your tongue till it tingles with it. Power."

"I am answered," Ernest said quietly. "It is the only answer that could be given. Power. It is what we of the working class preach. We know, and well we know by bitter experience, that no appeal for the right, for justice, for humanity, can ever touch you. Your hearts are hard as your heels with which you tread upon the faces of the poor. So we have preached power. By the power of our ballots on election day will we take your government away from you—"

"What if you do get a majority, a sweeping majority, on election day?" Mr.

[10] To show the tenor of thought, the following definition is quoted from "The Cynic's Word Book" (1906 A.D.), written by one Ambrose Bierce, an avowed and confirmed misanthrope of the period: "Grapeshot, n. *An argument which the future is preparing in answer to the demands of American Socialism.*"

Wickson broke in to demand. "Suppose we refuse to turn the government over to you after you have captured it at the ballot-box?"

"That, also, have we considered," Ernest replied. "And we shall give you an answer in terms of lead. Power, you have proclaimed the king of words. Very good. Power it shall be. And in the day that we sweep to victory at the ballot-box, and you refuse to turn over to us the government we have constitutionally and peacefully captured, and you demand what we are going to do about it—in that day, I say, we shall answer you; and in roar of shell and shrapnel and in whine of machine-guns shall our answer be couched.

"You cannot escape us. It is true that you have read history aright. It is true that labor has from the beginning of history been in the dirt. And it is equally true that so long as you and yours and those that come after you have power, that labor shall remain in the dirt. I agree with you. I agree with all that you have said. Power will be the arbiter, as it always has been the arbiter. It is a struggle of classes. Just as your class dragged down the old feudal nobility, so shall it be dragged down by my class, the working class. If you will read your biology and your sociology as clearly as you do your history, you will see that this end I have described is inevitable. It does not matter whether it is in one year, ten, or a thousand—your class shall be dragged down. And it shall be done by power. We of the labor hosts have conned that word over till our minds are all a-tingle with it. Power. It is a kingly word."

And so ended the night with the Philomaths.

THE VORTEX

. . . Whether it was my love for Ernest, or the clear sight he had given me of the society in which I lived, that made me a revolutionist, I know not; but a revolutionist I became, and I was plunged into a whirl of happenings that would have been inconceivable three short months before.

The crisis in my own fortunes came simultaneously with great crises in society. First of all, father was discharged from the university. Oh, he was not technically discharged. His resignation was demanded, that was all. This, in itself, did not amount to much. Father, in fact, was delighted. He was especially delighted because his discharge had been precipitated by the publication of his book, "Economics and Education." It clinched his argument, he contended. What better evidence could be advanced to prove that education was dominated by the capitalist class?

But this proof never got anywhere. Nobody knew he had been forced to resign from the university. He was so eminent a scientist that such an announcement, coupled with the reason for his enforced resignation, would have created somewhat of a furor all over the world. The newspapers showered him with praise and honor, and commended him for having given up the drudgery of the lecture room in order to devote his whole time to scientific research.

At first father laughed. Then he became angry—tonic angry. Then came the suppression of his book. This suppression was performed secretly, so secretly that at first we could not comprehend. The publication of the book had immediately caused a bit of excitement in the country. Father had been politely abused in the capitalist press, the tone of the abuse being to the effect that it was a pity so great a scientist should leave his field and invade the realm of sociology, about which he knew nothing and wherein he had promptly become lost. This lasted for a week, while father chuckled and said the book had touched a sore spot on capitalism And then, abruptly, the newspapers and the critical magazines ceased saying anything about the book at all. Also, and with equal suddenness, the book disappeared from the market. Not a copy was obtainable from any bookseller. Father wrote to the publishers and was informed that the plates had been accidentally injured. An unsatisfactory correspondence followed. Driven finally to an unequivocal stand, the publishers stated that they could not see their way to putting the book into type again, but that they were quite willing to relinquish their rights in it.

"And you won't find another publishing house in the country to touch it," Ernest said. "And if I were you, I'd hunt cover right now. You've merely got a foretaste of the Iron Heel."

But father was nothing if not a scientist. He never believed in jumping to conclusions. A laboratory experiment was no experiment if it were not carried through in all its details. So he patiently went the round of the publishing houses. They gave a multitude of excuses, but not one house would consider the book.

When father became convinced that the book had actually been suppressed, he tried to get the fact into the newspapers; but his communications were ignored. At a political meeting of the socialists, where many reporters were present, father saw his chance. He arose and related the history of the suppression of the book. He laughed next day when he read the newspapers, and then he grew angry to a degree that eliminated all tonic qualities. The papers made no mention of the book, but they misreported him beautifully. They twisted his words and phrases away from the context, and turned his subdued and controlled remarks into a howling anarchistic speech. It was done artfully. One instance, in particular, I remember. He had used the phrase "social revolution." The reporter merely dropped out "social." This was sent out all over the country in an Associated Press despatch, and from all over the country arose a cry of alarm. Father was branded as a nihilist and an anarchist, and in one cartoon that was copied widely he was portrayed waving a red flag at the head of a mob of long-haired, wild-eyed men who bore in their hands torches, knives, and dynamite bombs.

He was assailed terribly in the press, in long and abusive editorials, for his anarchy, and hints were made of mental breakdown on his part. This behavior, on the part of the capitalist press, was nothing new, Ernest told us. It was the custom, he said, to send reporters to all the socialist meetings for the express purpose of misreporting and distorting what was said, in order to frighten the middle class away from any possible affiliation with the proletariat. And repeatedly Ernest warned father to cease fighting and to take to cover.

The socialist press of the country took up the fight, however, and throughout the reading portion of the working class it was known that the book had been suppressed. But this knowledge stopped with the working class. Next, the "Appeal to Reason," a big socialist publishing house, arranged with father to bring out the book. Father was jubilant, but Ernest was alarmed.

"I tell you we are on the verge of the unknown," he insisted. "Big things are happening secretly all around us. We can feel them. We do not know what they are, but they are there. The whole fabric of society is a-tremble with them. Don't ask me. I don't know myself. But out of this flux of society something is about to crystallize. It is crystallizing now. The suppression of the book is a precipitation. How many books have been suppressed? We haven't the least idea. We are in the dark. We have no way of learning. Watch out next for the suppression of the socialist press and socialist publishing houses. I'm afraid it's coming. We are going to be throttled."

Ernest had his hand on the pulse of events even more closely than the rest of the socialists, and within two days the first blow was struck. The *Appeal to Reason* was a weekly, and its regular circulation amongst the proletariat was seven hundred and fifty thousand. Also, it very frequently got out special editions of from two to five million. These great editions were paid for and distributed by the small army of voluntary workers who had marshalled around the *Appeal*. The first blow was aimed at these special editions, and it was a crushing one. By an arbitrary ruling of the Post Office, these editions were decided to be not the regular circulation of the paper, and for that reason were denied admission to the mails.

A week later the Post Office Department ruled that the paper was seditious, and barred it entirely from the mails. This was a fearful blow to the socialist propaganda. The *Appeal* was desperate. It devised a plan of reaching its subscribers through the express companies, but they declined to handle it. This was the end of the *Appeal*. But not quite. It prepared to go on with its book publishing. Twenty thousand copies of father's book were in the bindery, and the presses were turning off more. And then, without warning, a mob arose one night, and, under a waving American flag, singing patriotic songs, set fire to the great plant of the *Appeal* and totally destroyed it.

Now Girard, Kansas, was a quiet, peaceable town. There had never been any labor troubles there. The *Appeal* paid union wages; and, in fact, was the backbone of the town, giving employment to hundreds of men and women. It was not the citizens of Girard that composed the mob. This mob had risen up out of the earth apparently, and to all intents and purposes, its work done, it had gone back into the earth. Ernest saw in the affair the most sinister import.

"The Black Hundreds[1] are being organized in the United States," he said. "This is the beginning. There will be more of it. The Iron Heel is getting bold."

And so perished father's book. We were to see much of the Black Hundreds as the days went by. Week by week more of the socialist papers were barred from the mails, and in a number of instances the Black Hundreds destroyed the socialist presses. Of course, the newspapers of the land lived up to the reactionary policy of the ruling class, and the destroyed socialist press was misrepresented and vilified, while the Black Hundreds were represented as true patriots and saviours of society. So convincing was all this misrepresentation that even sincere ministers in the pulpit praised the Black Hundreds while regretting the necessity of violence.

History was making fast. The fall elections were soon to occur, and Ernest was nominated by the socialist party to run for Congress. His chance for election was most favorable. The street-car strike in San Francisco had been broken. And following upon it the teamsters' strike had been broken. These two defeats had been very disastrous to organized labor. The whole Water Front Federation, along with its allies in the structural trades, had backed up the teamsters, and all had smashed down ingloriously. It had been a bloody strike. The police had broken countless heads with their riot clubs; and the death list had been augmented by the turning

[1] The Black Hundreds were reactionary mobs organized by the perishing Autocracy in the Russian Revolution. These reactionary groups attacked the revolutionary groups, and also, at needed moments, rioted and destroyed property so as to afford the Autocracy the pretext of calling out the Cossacks.

loose of a machine-gun on the strikers from the barns of the Marsden Special Delivery Company.

In consequence, the men were sullen and vindictive. They wanted blood, and revenge. Beaten on their chosen field, they were ripe to seek revenge by means of political action. They still maintained their labor organizations, and this gave them strength in the political struggle that was on. Ernest's chance for election grew stronger and stronger. Day by day unions and more unions voted their support to the socialists, until even Ernest laughed when the Undertakers' Assistants and the Chicken Pickers fell into line. Labor became mulish. While it packed the socialist meetings with mad enthusiasm, it was impervious to the wiles of the old-party politicians. The old-party orators were usually greeted with empty halls, though occasionally they encountered full halls where they were so roughly handled that more than once it was necessary to call out the police reserves.

History was making fast. The air was vibrant with things happening and impending. The country was on the verge of hard times,[2] caused by a series of prosperous years wherein the difficulty of disposing abroad of the unconsumed surplus had become increasingly difficult. Industries were working short time; many great factories were standing idle against the time when the surplus should be gone; and wages were being cut right and left.

Also, the great machinist strike had been broken. Two hundred thousand machinists, along with their five hundred thousand allies in the metal-working trades, had been defeated in as bloody a strike as had ever marred the United States. Pitched battles had been fought with the small armies of armed strike-breakers[3] put in the field by the employers' associations; the Black Hundreds, appearing in scores of wide-scattered places, had destroyed property; and, in consequence, a hundred thousand regular soldiers of the United States had been called out to put a frightful end to the whole affair. A number of the labor leaders had been executed; many others had been sentenced to prison, while thousands of the rank and file of the strikers had been herded into bull-pens[4] and abominably treated by the soldiers.

The years of prosperity were now to be paid for. All markets were glutted; all markets were falling; and amidst the general crumble of prices the price of labor crumbled fastest of all. The land was convulsed with industrial dissensions. Labor was striking here, there, and everywhere; and where it was not striking, it was being turned out by the capitalists. The papers were filled with tales of violence and

[2] Under the capitalist régime these periods of hard times were as inevitable as they were absurd. Prosperity always brought calamity. This, of course, was due to the excess of unconsumed profits that was piled up.

[3] *Strike-breakers* — these were, in purpose and practice and everything except name, the private soldiers of the capitalists. They were thoroughly organized and well armed, and they were held in readiness to be hurled in special trains to any part of the country where labor went out on strike or was locked out by the employers. Only those curious times could have given rise to the amazing spectacle of one, Farley, a notorious commander of strike-breakers, who, in 1906, swept across the United States in special trains from New York to San Francisco with an army of twenty-five hundred men, fully armed and equipped, to break a strike of the San Francisco street-car men. Such an act was in direct violation of the laws of the land. The fact that this act, and thousands of similar acts, went unpunished, goes to show how completely the judiciary was the creature of the Plutocracy.

[4] *Bull-pen* — in a miners' strike in Idaho, in the latter part of the nineteenth century, it happened that many of the strikers were confined in a bull-pen by the troops. The practice and the name continued in the twentieth century.

blood. And through it all the Black Hundreds played their part. Riot, arson, and wanton destruction of property was their function, and well they performed it. The whole regular army was in the field, called there by the actions of the Black Hundreds.[5] All cities and towns were like armed camps, and laborers were shot down like dogs. Out of the vast army of the unemployed the strike-breakers were recruited; and when the strike-breakers were worsted by the labor unions, the troops always appeared and crushed the unions. Then there was the militia. As yet, it was not necessary to have recourse to the secret militia law. Only the regularly organized militia was out, and it was out everywhere. And in this time of terror, the regular army was increased an additional hundred thousand by the government.

Never had labor received such an all-around beating. The great captains of industry, the oligarchs, had for the first time thrown their full weight into the breach the struggling employers' associations had made. These associations were practically middle-class affairs, and now, compelled by hard times and crashing markets, and aided by the great captains of industry, they gave organized labor an awful and decisive defeat. It was an all-powerful alliance, but it was an alliance of the lion and the lamb, as the middle class was soon to learn.

Labor was bloody and sullen, but crushed. Yet its defeat did not put an end to the hard times. The banks, themselves constituting one of the most important forces of the Oligarchy, continued to call in credits. The Wall Street[6] group turned the stock market into a maelstrom where the values of all the land crumbled away almost to nothingness. And out of all the rack and ruin rose the form of the nascent Oligarchy, imperturbable, indifferent, and sure. Its serenity and certitude was terrifying. Not only did it use its own vast power, but it used all the power of the United States Treasury to carry out its plans.

The captains of industry had turned upon the middle class. The employers' associations, that had helped the captains of industry to tear and rend labor, were now torn and rent by their quondam allies. Amidst the crashing of the middle men, the small business men and manufacturers, the trusts stood firm. Nay, the trusts did more than stand firm. They were active. They sowed wind, and wind, and ever more wind; for they alone knew how to reap the whirlwind and make a profit out of it. And such profits! Colossal profits! Strong enough themselves to weather the storm that was largely their own brewing, they turned loose and plundered the wrecks that floated about them. Values were pitifully and inconceivably shrunken, and the trusts added hugely to their holdings, even extending their enterprises into many new fields—and always at the expense of the middle class.

[5] The name only, and not the idea, was imported from Russia. The Black Hundreds were a development out of the secret agents of the capitalists, and their use arose in the labor struggles of the nineteenth century. There is no discussion of this. No less an authority of the times than Carroll D. Wright, United States Commissioner of Labor, is responsible for the statement. From his book, entitled "The Battles of Labor," is quoted the declaration that "*in some of the great historic strikes the employers themselves have instigated acts of violence;*" that manufacturers have deliberately provoked strikes in order to get rid of surplus stock; and that freight cars have been burned by employers' agents during railroad strikes in order to increase disorder. It was out of these secret agents of the employers that the Black Hundreds arose; and it was they, in turn, that later became that terrible weapon of the Oligarchy, the agents-provocateurs.

[6] *Wall Street* — so named from a street in ancient New York, where was situated the stock exchange, and where the irrational organization of society permitted underhanded manipulation of all the industries of the country.

Thus the summer of 1912 witnessed the virtual death-thrust to the middle class. Even Ernest was astounded at the quickness with which it had been done. He shook his head ominously and looked forward without hope to the fall elections.

"It's no use," he said. "We are beaten. The Iron Heel is here. I had hoped for a peaceable victory at the ballot-box. I was wrong. Wickson was right. We shall be robbed of our few remaining liberties; the Iron Heel will walk upon our faces; nothing remains but a bloody revolution of the working class. Of course we will win, but I shudder to think of it."

And from then on Ernest pinned his faith in revolution. In this he was in advance of his party. His fellow-socialists could not agree with him. They still insisted that victory could be gained through the elections. It was not that they were stunned. They were too cool-headed and courageous for that. They were merely incredulous, that was all. Ernest could not get them seriously to fear the coming of the Oligarchy. They were stirred by him, but they were too sure of their own strength. There was no room in their theoretical social evolution for an oligarchy, therefore the Oligarchy could not be.

"We'll send you to Congress and it will be all right," they told him at one of our secret meetings.

"And when they take me out of Congress," Ernest replied coldly, "and put me against a wall, and blow my brains out—what then?"

"Then we'll rise in our might," a dozen voices answered at once.

"Then you'll welter in your gore," was his retort. "I've heard that song sung by the middle class, and where is it now in its might?"

THE BEGINNING OF THE END

As early as January, 1913, Ernest saw the true trend of affairs, but he could not get his brother leaders to see the vision of the Iron Heel that had arisen in his brain. They were too confident. Events were rushing too rapidly to culmination. A crisis had come in world affairs. The American Oligarchy was practically in possession of the world-market, and scores of countries were flung out of that market with unconsumable and unsalable surpluses on their hands. For such countries nothing remained but reorganization. They could not continue their method of producing surpluses. The capitalistic system, so far as they were concerned, had hopelessly broken down.

The reorganization of these countries took the form of revolution. It was a time of confusion and violence. Everywhere institutions and governments were crashing. Everywhere, with the exception of two or three countries, the erstwhile capitalist masters fought bitterly for their possessions. But the governments were taken away from them by the militant proletariat. At last was being realized Karl Marx's classic: "The knell of private capitalist property sounds. The expropriators are expropriated." And as fast as capitalistic governments crashed, coöperative commonwealths arose in their place.

"Why does the United States lag behind?"; "Get busy, you American revolutionists!"; "What's the matter with America?"—were the messages sent to us by our successful comrades in other lands. But we could not keep up. The Oligarchy stood in the way. Its bulk, like that of some huge monster, blocked our path.

"Wait till we take office in the spring," we answered. "Then you'll see."

Behind this lay our secret. We had won over the Grangers, and in the spring a dozen states would pass into their hands by virtue of the elections of the preceding fall. At once would be instituted a dozen coöperative commonwealth states. After that, the rest would be easy.

"But what if the Grangers fail to get possession?" Ernest demanded. And his comrades called him a calamity howler.

But this failure to get possession was not the chief danger that Ernest had in mind. What he foresaw was the defection of the great labor unions and the rise of the castes.

"Ghent has taught the oligarchs how to do it," Ernest said. "I'll wager they've made a text-book out of his 'Benevolent Feudalism.'"[1]

Never shall I forget the night when, after a hot discussion with half a dozen labor leaders, Ernest turned to me and said quietly: "That settles it. The Iron Heel has won. The end is in sight."

This little conference in our home was unofficial; but Ernest, like the rest of his comrades, was working for assurances from the labor leaders that they would call out their men in the next general strike. O'Connor, the president of the Association of Machinists, had been foremost of the six leaders present in refusing to give such assurance.

"You have seen that you were beaten soundly at your old tactics of strike and boycott," Ernest urged.

O'Connor and the others nodded their heads.

"And you saw what a general strike would do," Ernest went on. "We stopped the war with Germany. Never was there so fine a display of the solidarity and the power of labor. Labor can and will rule the world. If you continue to stand with us, we'll put an end to the reign of capitalism. It is your only hope. And what is more, you know it. There is no other way out. No matter what you do under your old tactics, you are doomed to defeat, if for no other reason because the masters control the courts."[2]

"You run ahead too fast," O'Connor answered. "You don't know all the ways out. There is another way out. We know what we're about. We're sick of strikes.

[1] "Our Benevolent Feudalism," a book published in 1902 A.D., by W. J. Ghent. It has always been insisted that Ghent put the idea of the Oligarchy into the minds of the great capitalists. This belief persists throughout the literature of the three centuries of the Iron Heel, and even in the literature of the first century of the Brotherhood of Man. To-day we know better, but our knowledge does not overcome the fact that Ghent remains the most abused innocent man in all history.

[2] As a sample of the decisions of the courts adverse to labor, the following instances are given. In the coal-mining regions the employment of children was notorious. In 1905 A.D., labor succeeded in getting a law passed in Pennsylvania providing that proof of the age of the child and of certain educational qualifications must accompany the oath of the parent. This was promptly declared unconstitutional by the Luzerne County Court, on the ground that it violated the Fourteenth Amendment in that it discriminated between individuals of the same class — namely, children above fourteen years of age and children below. The state court sustained the decision. The New York Court of Special Sessions, in 1905 A.D., declared unconstitutional the law prohibiting minors and women from working in factories after nine o'clock at night, the ground taken being that such a law was "class legislation." Again, the bakers of that time were terribly overworked. The New York Legislature passed a law restricting work in bakeries to ten hours a day. In 1906 A.D., the Supreme Court of the United States declared this law to be unconstitutional. In part the decision read: "*There is no reasonable ground for interfering with the liberty of persons or the right of free contract by determining the hours of labor in the occupation of a baker.*"

They've got us beaten that way to a frazzle. But I don't think we'll ever need to call our men out again."

"What is your way out?" Ernest demanded bluntly.

O'Connor laughed and shook his head. "I can tell you this much: We've not been asleep. And we're not dreaming now."

"There's nothing to be afraid of, or ashamed of, I hope," Ernest challenged.

"I guess we know our business best," was the retort.

"It's a dark business, from the way you hide it," Ernest said with growing anger.

"We've paid for our experience in sweat and blood, and we've earned all that's coming to us," was the reply. "Charity begins at home."

"If you're afraid to tell me your way out, I'll tell it to you." Ernest's blood was up. "You're going in for grab-sharing. You've made terms with the enemy, that's what you've done. You've sold out the cause of labor, of all labor. You are leaving the battle-field like cowards."

"I'm not saying anything," O'Connor answered sullenly. "Only I guess we know what's best for us a little bit better than you do."

"And you don't care a cent for what is best for the rest of labor. You kick it into the ditch."

"I'm not saying anything," O'Connor replied, "except that I'm president of the Machinists' Association, and it's my business to consider the interests of the men I represent, that's all."

And then, when the labor leaders had left, Ernest, with the calmness of defeat, outlined to me the course of events to come.

"The socialists used to foretell with joy," he said, "the coming of the day when organized labor, defeated on the industrial field, would come over on to the political field. Well, the Iron Heel has defeated the labor unions on the industrial field and driven them over to the political field; and instead of this being joyful for us, it will be a source of grief. The Iron Heel learned its lesson. We showed it our power in the general strike. It has taken steps to prevent another general strike."

"But how?" I asked.

"Simply by subsidizing the great unions. They won't join in the next general strike. Therefore it won't be a general strike."

"But the Iron Heel can't maintain so costly a programme forever," I objected.

"Oh, it hasn't subsidized all of the unions. That's not necessary. Here is what is going to happen. Wages are going to be advanced and hours shortened in the railroad unions, the iron and steel workers unions, and the engineer and machinist unions. In these unions more favorable conditions will continue to prevail. Membership in these unions will become like seats in Paradise."

"Still I don't see," I objected. "What is to become of the other unions? There are far more unions outside of this combination than in it."

"The other unions will be ground out of existence—all of them. For, don't you see, the railway men, machinists and engineers, iron and steel workers, do all of the vitally essential work in our machine civilization. Assured of their faithfulness, the Iron Heel can snap its fingers at all the rest of labor. Iron, steel, coal, machinery, and transportation constitute the backbone of the whole industrial fabric."

"But coal?" I queried. "There are nearly a million coal miners."

"They are practically unskilled labor. They will not count. Their wages will go down and their hours will increase. They will be slaves like all the rest of us, and they will become about the most bestial of all of us. They will be compelled to work, just as the farmers are compelled to work now for the masters who robbed them of their land. And the same with all the other unions outside the combination. Watch them wobble and go to pieces, and their members become slaves driven to toil by empty stomachs and the law of the land.

"Do you know what will happen to Farley[3] and his strike-breakers? I'll tell you. Strike-breaking as an occupation will cease. There won't be any more strikes. In place of strikes will be slave revolts. Farley and his gang will be promoted to slave-driving. Oh, it won't be called that; it will be called enforcing the law of the land that compels the laborers to work. It simply prolongs the fight, this treachery of the big unions. Heaven only knows now where and when the Revolution will triumph."

"But with such a powerful combination as the Oligarchy and the big unions, is there any reason to believe that the Revolution will ever triumph?" I queried. "May not the combination endure forever?"

He shook his head. "One of our generalizations is that every system founded upon class and caste contains within itself the germs of its own decay. When a system is founded upon class, how can caste be prevented? The Iron Heel will not be able to prevent it, and in the end caste will destroy the Iron Heel. The oligarchs have already developed caste among themselves; but wait until the favored unions develop caste. The Iron Heel will use all its power to prevent it, but it will fail.

"In the favored unions are the flower of the American workingmen. They are strong, efficient men. They have become members of those unions through competition for place. Every fit workman in the United States will be possessed by the ambition to become a member of the favored unions. The Oligarchy will encourage such ambition and the consequent competition. Thus will the strong men, who might else be revolutionists, be won away and their strength used to bolster the Oligarchy.

"On the other hand, the labor castes, the members of the favored unions, will strive to make their organizations into close corporations. And they will succeed. Membership in the labor castes will become hereditary. Sons will succeed fathers, and there will be no inflow of new strength from that eternal reservoir of strength, the common people. This will mean deterioration of the labor castes, and in the end they will become weaker and weaker. At the same time, as an institution, they will become temporarily all-powerful. They will be like the guards of the palace in old Rome, and there will be palace revolutions whereby the labor castes will seize the reins of power. And there will be counter-palace revolutions of the oligarchs, and sometimes the one, and sometimes the other, will be in power. And through it all the inevitable caste-weakening will go on, so that in the end the common people will come into their own."

This foreshadowing of a slow social evolution was made when Ernest was first depressed by the defection of the great unions. I never agreed with him in it, and I disagree now, as I write these lines, more heartily than ever; for even now, though Ernest is gone, we are on the verge of the revolt that will sweep all oligarchies away. Yet I have here given Ernest's prophecy because it was his

[3] James Farley — a notorious strike-breaker of the period. A man more courageous than ethical, and of undeniable ability. He rose high under the rule of the Iron Heel and finally was translated into the oligarch class. He was assassinated in 1932 by Sarah Jenkins, whose husband, thirty years before, had been killed by Farley's strike-breakers.

prophecy. In spite of his belief in it, he worked like a giant against it, and he, more than any man, has made possible the revolt that even now waits the signal to burst forth.[4]

"But if the Oligarchy persists," I asked him that evening, "what will become of the great surpluses that will fall to its share every year?"

"The surpluses will have to be expended somehow," he answered; "and trust the oligarchs to find a way. Magnificent roads will be built. There will be great achievements in science, and especially in art. When the oligarchs have completely mastered the people, they will have time to spare for other things. They will become worshippers of beauty. They will become art lovers. And under their direction, and generously rewarded, will toil the artists. The result will be great art; for no longer, as up to yesterday, will the artists pander to the bourgeois taste of the middle class. It will be great art, I tell you, and wonder cities will arise that will make tawdry and cheap the cities of old time. And in these cities will the oligarchs dwell and worship beauty.[5]

"Thus will the surplus be constantly expended while labor does the work. The building of these great works and cities will give a starvation ration to millions of common laborers, for the enormous bulk of the surplus will compel an equally enormous expenditure, and the oligarchs will build for a thousand years—ay, for ten thousand years. They will build as the Egyptians and the Babylonians never dreamed of building; and when the oligarchs have passed away, their great roads and their wonder cities will remain for the brotherhood of labor to tread upon and dwell within.[6]

"These things the oligarchs will do because they cannot help doing them. These great works will be the form their expenditure of the surplus will take, and in the same way that the ruling classes of Egypt of long ago expended the surplus they robbed from the people by the building of temples and pyramids. Under the oligarchs will flourish, not a priest class, but an artist class. And in place of the merchant class of bourgeoisie will be the labor castes. And beneath will be the abyss, wherein will fester and starve and rot, and ever renew itself, the common people, the great bulk of the population. And in the end, who knows in what day, the common people will rise up out of the abyss; the labor castes and the Oligarchy will crumble away, and then, at last, after the travail of the centuries, will it be the day of the common man. I had thought to see that day; but now I know that I shall never see it."

He paused and looked at me, and added:

"Social evolution is exasperatingly slow, isn't it, sweetheart?"

My arms were about him, and his head was on my breast.

[4] Everhard's social foresight was remarkable. As clearly as in the light of past events, he saw the defection of the favored unions, the rise and the slow decay of the labor castes, and the struggle between the decaying oligarchs and labor castes for control of the great governmental machine.

[5] We cannot but marvel at Everhard's foresight. Before even the thought of wonder cities like Ardis and Asgard entered the minds of the oligarchs, Everhard saw those cities and the inevitable necessity for their creation.

[6] And since that day of prophecy, have passed away the three centuries of the Iron Heel and the four centuries of the Brotherhood of Man, and to-day we tread the roads and dwell in the cities that the oligarchs built. It is true, we are even now building still more wonderful wonder cities, but the wonder cities of the oligarchs endure, and I write these lines in Ardis, one of the most wonderful of them all.

"Sing me to sleep," he murmured whimsically. "I have had a visioning, and I wish to forget."

LAST DAYS

It was near the end of January, 1913, that the changed attitude of the Oligarchy toward the favored unions was made public. The newspapers published information of an unprecedented rise in wages and shortening of hours for the railroad employees, the iron and steel workers, and the engineers and machinists. But the whole truth was not told. The oligarchs did not dare permit the telling of the whole truth. In reality, the wages had been raised much higher, and the privileges were correspondingly greater. All this was secret, but secrets will out. Members of the favored unions told their wives, and the wives gossiped, and soon all the labor world knew what had happened.

It was merely the logical development of what in the nineteenth century had been known as grab-sharing. In the industrial warfare of that time, profit-sharing had been tried. That is, the capitalists had striven to placate the workers by interesting them financially in their work. But profit-sharing, as a system, was ridiculous and impossible. Profit-sharing could be successful only in isolated cases in the midst of a system of industrial strife; for if all labor and all capital shared profits, the same conditions would obtain as did obtain when there was no profit-sharing.

So, out of the unpractical idea of profit-sharing, arose the practical idea of grab-sharing. "Give us more pay and charge it to the public," was the slogan of the strong unions. And here and there this selfish policy worked successfully. In charging it to the public, it was charged to the great mass of unorganized labor and of weakly organized labor. These workers actually paid the increasing wages of their stronger brothers who were members of unions that were labor monopolies. This idea, as I say, was merely carried to its logical conclusion, on a large scale, by the combination of the oligarchs and the favored unions.[1]

As soon as the secret of the defection of the favored unions leaked out, there were rumblings and mutterings in the labor world. Next, the favored unions withdrew from the international organizations and broke off all affiliations. Then came trouble and violence. The members of the favored unions were branded as traitors, and in saloons and brothels, on the streets and at work, and, in fact, everywhere, they were assaulted by the comrades they had so treacherously deserted.

Countless heads were broken, and there were many killed. No member of the favored unions was safe. They gathered together in bands in order to go to work or to return from work. They walked always in the middle of the street. On the sidewalk they were liable to have their skulls crushed by bricks and cobblestones

[1] All the railroad unions entered into this combination with the oligarchs, and it is of interest to note that the first definite application of the policy of profit-grabbing was made by a railroad union in the nineteenth century A.D., namely, the Brotherhood of Locomotive Engineers. P. M. Arthur was for twenty years Grand Chief of the Brotherhood. After the strike on the Pennsylvania Railroad in 1877, he broached a scheme to have the Locomotive Engineers make terms with the railroads and to "go it alone" so far as the rest of the labor unions were concerned. This scheme was eminently successful. It was as successful as it was selfish, and out of it was coined the word "arthurization," to denote grab-sharing on the part of labor unions. This word "arthurization" has long puzzled the etymologists, but its derivation, I hope, is now made clear.

thrown from windows and house-tops. They were permitted to carry weapons, and the authorities aided them in every way. Their persecutors were sentenced to long terms in prison, where they were harshly treated; while no man, not a member of the favored unions, was permitted to carry weapons. Violation of this law was made a high misdemeanor and punished accordingly.

Outraged labor continued to wreak vengeance on the traitors. Caste lines formed automatically. The children of the traitors were persecuted by the children of the workers who had been betrayed, until it was impossible for the former to play on the streets or to attend the public schools. Also, the wives and families of the traitors were ostracized, while the corner groceryman who sold provisions to them was boycotted.

As a result, driven back upon themselves from every side, the traitors and their families became clannish. Finding it impossible to dwell in safety in the midst of the betrayed proletariat, they moved into new localities inhabited by themselves alone. In this they were favored by the oligarchs. Good dwellings, modern and sanitary, were built for them, surrounded by spacious yards, and separated here and there by parks and playgrounds. Their children attended schools especially built for them, and in these schools manual training and applied science were specialized upon. Thus, and unavoidably, at the very beginning, out of this segregation arose caste. The members of the favored unions became the aristocracy of labor. They were set apart from the rest of labor. They were better housed, better clothed, better fed, better treated. They were grab-sharing with a vengeance.

In the meantime, the rest of the working class was more harshly treated. Many little privileges were taken away from it, while its wages and its standard of living steadily sank down. Incidentally, its public schools deteriorated, and education slowly ceased to be compulsory. The increase in the younger generation of children who could not read nor write was perilous. . . .

THE END

When it came time for Ernest and me to go to Washington, father did not accompany us. He had become enamoured of proletarian life. He looked upon our slum neighborhood as a great sociological laboratory, and he had embarked upon an apparently endless orgy of investigation. He chummed with the laborers, and was an intimate in scores of homes. Also, he worked at odd jobs, and the work was play as well as learned investigation, for he delighted in it and was always returning home with copious notes and bubbling over with new adventures. He was the perfect scientist.

. . . Contrary to our expectation, no obstacles were raised to prevent the socialist Congressmen from taking their seats. Everything went smoothly, and I laughed at Ernest when he looked upon the very smoothness as something ominous.

We found our socialist comrades confident, optimistic of their strength and of the things they would accomplish. A few Grangers who had been elected to Congress increased our strength, and an elaborate programme of what was to be done was prepared by the united forces. In all of which Ernest joined loyally and energetically, though he could not forbear, now and again, from saying, apropos of nothing in particular, "When it comes to powder, chemical mixtures are better than mechanical mixtures, you take my word."

The trouble arose first with the Grangers in the various states they had captured at the last election. There were a dozen of these states, but the Grangers who had been elected were not permitted to take office. The incumbents refused to get out. It was very simple. They merely charged illegality in the elections and wrapped up the whole situation in the interminable red tape of the law. The Grangers were powerless. The courts were the last recourse, and the courts were in the hands of their enemies.

This was the moment of danger. If the cheated Grangers became violent, all was lost. How we socialists worked to hold them back! There were days and nights when Ernest never closed his eyes in sleep. The big leaders of the Grangers saw the peril and were with us to a man. But it was all of no avail. The Oligarchy wanted violence, and it set its agents-provocateurs to work. Without discussion, it was the agents-provocateurs who caused the Peasant Revolt.

In a dozen states the revolt flared up. The expropriated farmers took forcible possession of the state governments. Of course this was unconstitutional, and of course the United States put its soldiers into the field. Everywhere the agents-provocateurs urged the people on. These emissaries of the Iron Heel disguised themselves as artisans, farmers, and farm laborers. In Sacramento, the capital of California, the Grangers had succeeded in maintaining order. Thousands of secret agents were rushed to the devoted city. In mobs composed wholly of themselves, they fired and looted buildings and factories. They worked the people up until they joined them in the pillage. Liquor in large quantities was distributed among the slum classes further to inflame their minds. And then, when all was ready, appeared upon the scene the soldiers of the United States, who were, in reality, the soldiers of the Iron Heel. Eleven thousand men, women, and children were shot down on the streets of Sacramento or murdered in their houses. The national government took possession of the state government, and all was over for California.

And as with California, so elsewhere. Every Granger state was ravaged with violence and washed in blood. First, disorder was precipitated by the secret agents and the Black Hundreds, then the troops were called out. Rioting and mob-rule reigned throughout the rural districts. Day and night the smoke of burning farms, warehouses, villages, and cities filled the sky. Dynamite appeared. Railroad bridges and tunnels were blown up and trains were wrecked. The poor farmers were shot and hanged in great numbers. Reprisals were bitter, and many plutocrats and army officers were murdered. Blood and vengeance were in men's hearts. The regular troops fought the farmers as savagely as had they been Indians. And the regular troops had cause. Twenty-eight hundred of them had been annihiliated in a tremendous series of dynamite explosions in Oregon, and in a similar manner, a number of train loads, at different times and places had been destroyed. So it was that the regular troops fought for their lives as well as did the farmers.

As for the militia, the militia law of 1903* was put into effect, and the workers of one state were compelled, under pain of death, to shoot down their comrade-workers in other states. Of course, the militia law did not work smoothly at first. Many militia officers were murdered, and many militiamen were executed by drumhead court martial. . . .

* (The Militia Act of 1903 provides that the militia shall consist of every able-bodied male between the ages of eighteen and forty-five. It further provides that anyone who shall refuse or neglect to present himself upon being called forth shall be subject to trial by court martial. Ed.)

Many young men fled into the mountains to escape serving in the militia. There they became outlaws, and it was not until more peaceful times that they received their punishment. It was drastic. The government issued a proclamation for all law-abiding citizens to come in from the mountains for a period of three months. When the proclaimed date arrived, half a million soldiers were sent into the mountainous districts everywhere. There was no investigation, no trial. Wherever a man was encountered, he was shot down on the spot. The troops operated on the basis that no man not an outlaw remained in the mountains. Some bands, in strong positions, fought gallantly, but in the end every deserter from the militia met death.

A more immediate lesson, however, was impressed on the minds of the people by the punishment meted out to the Kansas militia. The great Kansas Mutiny occurred at the very beginning of military operations against the Grangers. Six thousand of the militia mutinied. They had been for several weeks very turbulent and sullen, and for that reason had been kept in camp. Their open mutiny, however, was without doubt precipitated by the agents-provocateurs.

On the night of the 22nd of April they arose and murdered their officers, only a small remnant of the latter escaping. This was beyond the scheme of the Iron Heel, for the agents-provocateurs had done their work too well. But everything was grist to the Iron Heel. It had prepared for the outbreak, and the killing of so many officers gave it justification for what followed. As by magic, forty thousand soldiers of the regular army surrounded the malcontents. It was a trap. The wretched militiamen found that their machine-guns had been tampered with, and that the cartridges from the captured magazines did not fit their rifles. They hoisted the white flag of surrender, but it was ignored. There were no survivors. The entire six thousand were annihilated. Common shell and shrapnel were thrown in upon them from a distance, and, when, in their desperation, they charged the encircling lines, they were mowed down by the machine-guns. I talked with an eye-witness, and he said that the nearest any militiamen approached the machine-guns was a hundred and fifty yards. The earth was carpeted with the slain, and a final charge of cavalry, with trampling of horses' hoofs, revolvers, and sabres, crushed the wounded into the ground.

Simultaneously with the destruction of the Grangers came the revolt of the coal miners. It was the expiring effort of organized labor. Three-quarters of a million of miners went out on strike. But they were too widely scattered over the country to advantage from their own strength. They were segregated in their own districts and beaten into submission. This was the first great slave-drive. Pocock[1] won his spurs as a slave-driver and earned the undying hatred of the proletariat. Countless attempts were made upon his life, but he seemed to bear a charmed existence. It was he who was responsible for the introduction of the Russian passport system

1 Albert Pocock, another of the notorious strike-breakers of earlier years, who, to the day of his death, successfully held all the coal-miners of the country to their task. He was succeeded by his son, Lewis Pocock, and for five generations this remarkable line of slave-drivers handled the coal mines. The elder Pocock, known as Pocock I., has been described as follows: "A long, lean head, semicircled by a fringe of brown and gray hair, with big cheek-bones and a heavy chin, . . . a pale face, lustreless gray eyes, a metallic voice, and a languid manner." He was born of humble parents, and began his career as a bartender. He next became a private detective for a street railway corporation, and by successive steps developed into a professional strike-breaker. Pocock V., the last of the line, was blown up in a pumphouse by a bomb during a petty revolt of the miners in the Indian Territory. This occurred in 2073 A.D.

among the miners, and the denial of their right of removal from one part of the country to another.

In the meantime, the socialists held firm. While the Grangers expired in flame and blood, and organized labor was disrupted, the socialists held their peace and perfected their secret organization. In vain the Grangers pleaded with us. We rightly contended that any revolt on our part was virtually suicide for the whole Revolution. The Iron Heel, at first dubious about dealing with the entire proletariat at one time, had found the work easier than it had expected, and would have asked nothing better than an uprising on our part. But we avoided the issue, in spite of the fact that agents-provocateurs swarmed in our midst. In those early days, the agents of the Iron Heel were clumsy in their methods. They had much to learn and in the meantime our Fighting Groups weeded them out. It was bitter, bloody work, but we were fighting for life and for the Revolution, and we had to fight the enemy with its own weapons. Yet we were fair. No agent of the Iron Heel was executed without a trial. We may have made mistakes, but if so, very rarely. The bravest, and the most combative and self-sacrificing of our comrades went into the Fighting Groups. Once, after ten years had passed, Ernest made a calculation from figures furnished by the chiefs of the Fighting Groups, and his conclusion was that the average life of a man or woman after becoming a member was five years. The comrades of the Fighting Groups were heroes all, and the peculiar thing about it was that they were opposed to the taking of life. They violated their own natures, yet they loved liberty and knew of no sacrifice too great to make for the Cause.[2]

[2] These Fighting groups were modelled somewhat after the Fighting Organization of the Russian Revolution, and, despite the unceasing efforts of the Iron Heel, these groups persisted throughout the three centuries of its existence. Composed of men and women actuated by lofty purpose and unafraid to die, the Fighting Groups exercised tremendous influence and tempered the savage brutality of the rulers. Not alone was their work confined to unseen warfare with the secret agents of the Oligarchy. The oligarchs themselves were compelled to listen to the decrees of the Groups, and often, when they disobeyed, were punished by death — and likewise with the subordinates of the oligarchs, with the officers of the army and the leaders of the labor castes.

Stern justice was meted out by these organized avengers, but most remarkable was their passionless and judicial procedure. There were no snap judgments. When a man was captured he was given fair trial and opportunity for defence. Of necessity, many men were tried and condemned by proxy, as in the case of General Lampton. This occurred in 2138 A.D. Possibly the most bloodthirsty and malignant of all the mercenaries that ever served the Iron Heel, he was informed by the Fighting Groups that they had tried him, found him guilty, and condemned him to death — and this, after three warnings for him to cease from his ferocious treatment of the proletariat. After his condemnation he surrounded himself with a myriad protective devices. Years passed, and in vain the Fighting Groups strove to execute their decree. Comrade after comrade, men and women, failed in their attempts, and were cruelly executed by the Oligarchy. It was the case of General Lampton that revived crucifixion as a legal method of execution. But in the end the condemned man found his executioner in the form of a slender girl of seventeen, Madeline Provence, who, to accomplish her purpose, served two years in his palace as a seamstress to the household. She died in solitary confinement after horrible and prolonged torture; but to-day she stands in imperishable bronze in the Pantheon of Brotherhood in the wonder city of Serles.

We, who by personal experience know nothing of bloodshed, must not judge harshly the heroes of the Fighting Groups. They gave up their lives for humanity, no sacrifice was too great for them to accomplish, while inexorable necessity compelled them to bloody expression in an age of blood. The Fighting Groups constituted the one thorn in the side of the Iron Heel that the Iron Heel could never remove. Everhard was the father of this

The task we set ourselves was threefold. First, the weeding out from our circles of the secret agents of the Oligarchy. Second, the organizing of the Fighting Groups, and, outside of them, of the general secret organization of the Revolution. And third, the introduction of our own secret agents into every branch of the Oligarchy —into the labor castes and especially among the telegraphers and secretaries and clerks, into the army, the agents-provocateurs, and the slave-drivers. It was slow work, and perilous, and often were our efforts rewarded with costly failures.

The Iron Heel had triumphed in open warfare, but we held our own in the new warfare, strange and awful and subterranean, that we instituted. All was unseen, much was unguessed; the blind fought the blind; and yet through it all was order, purpose, control. We permeated the entire organization of the Iron Heel with our agents, while our own organization was permeated with the agents of the Iron Heel. It was warfare dark and devious, replete with intrigue and conspiracy, plot and counterplot. And behind all, ever menacing, was death, violent and terrible. Men and women disappeared, our nearest and dearest comrades. We saw them to-day. To-morrow they were gone; we never saw them again, and we knew that they had died.

There was no trust, no confidence anywhere. The man who plotted beside us, for all we knew, might be an agent of the Iron Heel. We mined the organization of the Iron Heel with our secret agents, and the Iron Heel countermined with its secret agents inside its own organization. And it was the same with our organization. And despite the absence of confidence and trust we were compelled to base our every effort on confidence and trust. Often were we betrayed. Men were weak. The Iron Heel could offer money, leisure, the joys and pleasures that waited in the repose of the wonder cities. We could offer nothing but the satisfaction of being faithful to a noble ideal. As for the rest, the wages of those who were loyal were unceasing peril, torture, and death.

Men were weak, I say, and because of their weakness we were compelled to make the only other reward that was within our power. It was the reward of death. Out of necessity we had to punish our traitors. For every man who betrayed us, from one to a dozen faithful avengers were loosed upon his heels. We might fail to carry out our decrees against our enemies, such as the Pococks, for instance; but the one thing we could not afford to fail in was the punishment of our own traitors. Comrades turned traitor by permission, in order to win to the wonder cities and there execute our sentences on the real traitors. In fact, so terrible did we make ourselves, that it became a greater peril to betray us than to remain loyal to us.

The Revolution took on largely the character of religion. We worshipped at the shrine of the Revolution, which was the shrine of liberty. It was the divine flashing through us. Men and women devoted their lives to the Cause, and new-born babes were sealed to it as of old they had been sealed to the service of God. We were lovers of Humanity.

---

curious army, and its accomplishments and successful persistence for three hundred years bear witness to the wisdom with which he organized and the solid foundation he laid for the succeeding generations to build upon. In some respects, despite his great economic and sociological contributions, and his work as a general leader in the Revolution, his organization of the Fighting Groups must be regarded as his greatest achievement.

THE ROARING ABYSMAL BEAST

. . . Out of the flux of transition the new institutions were forming more definitely and taking on the appearance and attributes of permanence. The oligarchs had succeeded in devising a governmental machine, as intricate as it was vast, that worked—and this despite all our efforts to clog and hamper.

This was a surprise to many of the revolutionists. They had not conceived it possible. Nevertheless the work of the country went on. The men toiled in the mines and fields—perforce they were no more than slaves. As for the vital industries, everything prospered. The members of the great labor castes were contented and worked on merrily. For the first time in their lives they knew industrial peace. No more were they worried by slack times, strike and lockout, and the union label. They lived in more comfortable homes and in delightful cities of their own—delightful compared with the slums and ghettos in which they had formerly dwelt. They had better food to eat, less hours of labor, more holidays, and a greater amount and variety of interests and pleasures. And for their less fortunate brothers and sisters, the unfavored laborers, the driven people of the abyss, they cared nothing. An age of selfishness was dawning upon mankind. And yet this is not altogether true. The labor castes were honeycombed by our agents—men whose eyes saw, beyond the belly-need, the radiant figure of liberty and brotherhood.

Another great institution that had taken form and was working smoothly was the Mercenaries. This body of soldiers had been evolved out of the old regular army and was now a million strong, to say nothing of the colonial forces. The Mercenaries constituted a race apart. They dwelt in cities of their own which were practically self-governed, and they were granted many privileges. By them a large portion of the perplexing surplus was consumed. They were losing all touch and sympathy with the rest of the people, and, in fact, were developing their own class morality and consciousness. And yet we had thousands of our agents among them.[1]

The oligarchs themselves were going through a remarkable and, it must be confessed, unexpected development. As a class, they disciplined themselves. Every member had his work to do in the world, and this work he was compelled to do. There were no more idle-rich young men. Their strength was used to give united strength to the Oligarchy. They served as leaders of troops and as lieutenants and captains of industry. They found careers in applied science, and many of them became great engineers. They went into the multitudinous divisions of the government, took service in the colonial possessions, and by tens of thousands went into the various secret services. They were, I may say, apprenticed to education, to art, to the church, to science, to literature; and in those fields they served the important function of moulding the thought-processes of the nation in the direction of the perpetuity of the Oligarchy.

They were taught, and later they in turn taught, that what they were doing was right. They assimilated the aristocratic idea from the moment they began, as children, to receive impressions of the world. The aristocratic idea was woven into the making of them until it became bone of them and flesh of them. They looked

[1]The Mercenaries, in the last days of the Iron Heel, played an important rôle. They constituted the balance of power in the struggles between the labor castes and the oligarchs, and now to one side and now to the other, threw their strength according to the play of intrigue and conspiracy.

upon themselves as wild-animal trainers, rulers of beasts. From beneath their feet rose always the subterranean rumbles of revolt. Violent death ever stalked in their midst; bomb and knife and bullet were looked upon as so many fangs of the roaring abysmal beast they must dominate if humanity were to persist. They were the saviours of humanity, and they regarded themselves as heroic and sacrificing laborers for the highest good.

They, as a class, believed that they alone maintained civilization. It was their belief that if ever they weakened, the great beast would engulf them and everything of beauty and wonder and joy and good in its cavernous and slime-dripping maw. Without them, anarchy would reign and humanity would drop backward into the primitive night out of which it had so painfully emerged. The horrid picture of anarchy was held always before their child's eyes until they, in turn, obsessed by this cultivated fear, held the picture of anarchy before the eyes of the children that followed them. This was the beast to be stamped upon, and the highest duty of the aristocrat was to stamp upon it. In short, they alone, by their unremitting toil and sacrifice, stood between weak humanity and the all-devouring beast; and they believed it, firmly believed it.

I cannot lay too great stress upon this high ethical righteousness of the whole oligarch class. This has been the strength of the Iron Heel, and too many of the comrades have been slow or loath to realize it. Many of them have ascribed the strength of the Iron Heel to its system of reward and punishment. This is a mistake. Heaven and hell may be the prime factors of zeal in the religion of a fanatic; but for the great majority of the religious, heaven and hell are incidental to right and wrong. Love of the right, desire for the right, unhappiness with anything less than the right–in short, right conduct, is the prime factor of religion. And so with the Oligarchy. Prisons, banishment and degradation, honors and palaces and wonder-cities, are all incidental. The great driving force of the oligarchs is the belief that they are doing right. Never mind the exceptions, and never mind the oppressions and injustice in which the Iron Heel was conceived. All is granted. The point is that the strength of the Oligarchy to-day lies in its satisfied conception of its own righteousness.[2]

. . . The labor castes, the Mercenaries, and the great hordes of secret agents and police of various sorts were all pledged to the Oligarchy. In the main, and ignoring the loss of liberty, they were better off than they had been. On the other hand, the great helpless mass of the population, the people of the abyss, was sinking into a brutish apathy of content with misery. Whenever strong proletarians asserted their strength in the midst of the mass, they were drawn away from the mass by the oligarchs and given better conditions by being made members of the labor castes or of the Mercenaries. Thus discontent was lulled and the proletariat robbed of its natural leaders.

The condition of the people of the abyss was pitiable. Common school education, so far as they were concerned, had ceased. They lived like beasts in great squalid labor-ghettos, festering in misery and degradation. All their old liberties were gone.

[2] Out of the ethical incoherency and inconsistency of capitalism, the oligarchs emerged with a new ethics, coherent and definite, sharp and severe as steel, the most absurd and unscientific and at the same time the most potent ever possessed by any tyrant class. The oligarchs believed their ethics, in spite of the fact that biology and evolution gave them the lie; and, because of their faith, for three centuries they were able to hold back the mighty tide of human progress — a spectacle, profound, tremendous, puzzling to the metaphysical moralist, and one that to the materialist is the cause of many doubts and reconsiderations.

They were labor-slaves. Choice of work was denied them. Likewise was denied them the right to move from place to place, or the right to bear or possess arms. They were not land-serfs like the farmers. They were machine-serfs and labor-serfs. When unusual needs arose for them, such as the building of the great highways and air-lines, of canals, tunnels, subways, and fortifications, levies were made on the labor-ghettos, and tens of thousands of serfs, willy-nilly, were transported to the scene of operations. Great armies of them are toiling now at the building of Ardis, housed in wretched barracks where family life cannot exist, and where decency is displaced by dull bestiality. In all truth, there in the labor-ghettos is the roaring abysmal beast the oligarchs fear so dreadfully—but it is the beast of their own making. In it they will not let the ape and tiger die.

And just now the word has gone forth that new levies are being imposed for the building of Asgard, the projected wonder-city that will far exceed Ardis when the latter is completed.[3] We of the Revolution will go on with that great work, but it will not be done by the miserable serfs. The walls and towers and shafts of that fair city will arise to the sound of singing, and into its beauty and wonder will be woven, not sighs and groans, but music and laughter. . . .

THE SCARLET LIVERY

With the destruction of the Granger states, the Grangers in Congress disappeared. They were being tried for high treason, and their places were taken by the creatures of the Iron Heel. The socialists were in a pitiful minority, and they knew that their end was near. Congress and the Senate were empty pretences, farces. Public questions were gravely debated and passed upon according to the old forms, while in reality all that was done was to give the stamp of constitutional procedure to the mandates of the Oligarchy.

Ernest was in the thick of the fight when the end came. It was in the debate on the bill to assist the unemployed. The hard times of the preceding year had thrust great masses of the proletariat beneath the starvation line, and the continued and wide-reaching disorder had but sunk them deeper. Millions of people were starving, while the oligarchs and their supporters were surfeiting on the surplus.[1] We called these wretched people the people of the abyss,[2] and it was to alleviate their awful

[3] Ardis was completed in 1942 A.D., while Asgard was not completed until 1984 A.D. It was fifty-two years in the building, during which time a permanent army of half a million serfs was employed. At times these numbers swelled to over a million — without any account being taken of the hundreds of thousands of the labor castes and the artists.

[1] The same conditions obtained in the nineteenth century A.D., under British rule in India. The natives died of starvation by the million, while their rulers robbed them of the fruits of their toil and expended it on magnificent pageants and mumbo-jumbo fooleries. Perforce, in this enlightened age, we have much to blush for in the acts of our ancestors. Our only consolation is philosophic. We must accept the capitalistic stage in social evolution as about on a par with the earlier monkey stage. The human had to pass through those stages in its rise from the mire and slime of low organic life. It was inevitable that much of the mire and slime should cling and be not easily shaken off.

[2] *The people of the abyss* — this phrase was struck out by the genius of H. G. Wells in the late nineteenth century A.D. Wells was a sociological seer, sane and normal as well as warmly human. Many fragments of his work have come down to us, while two of his greatest achievements, "Anticipations" and "Mankind in the Making," have come down intact. Before the oligarchs, and before Everhard, Wells speculated upon the building of the wonder cities, though in his writings they are referred to as "pleasure cities."

suffering that the socialists had introduced the unemployed bill. But this was not to the fancy of the Iron Heel. In its own way it was preparing to set these millions to work, but the way was not our way, wherefore it had issued its orders that our bill should be voted down. Ernest and his fellows knew that their effort was futile, but they were tired of the suspense. They wanted something to happen. They were accomplishing nothing, and the best they hoped for was the putting of an end to the legislative farce in which they were unwilling players. They knew not what end would come, but they never anticipated a more disastrous end than the one that did come.

I sat in the gallery that day. We all knew that something terrible was imminent. It was in the air, and its presence was made visible by the armed soldiers drawn up in lines in the corridors, and by the officers grouped in the entrances to the House itself. The Oligarchy was about to strike. Ernest was speaking. He was describing the sufferings of the unemployed, as if with the wild idea of in some way touching their hearts and consciences; but the Republican and Democratic members sneered and jeered at him, and there was uproar and confusion. Ernest abruptly changed front.

"I know nothing that I may say can influence you," he said. "You have no souls to be influenced. You are spineless, flaccid things. You pompously call yourselves Republicans and Democrats. There is no Republican Party. There is no Democratic Party. There are no Republicans nor Democrats in this House. You are lick-spittlers and panderers, the creatures of the Plutocracy. You talk verbosely in antiquated terminology of your love of liberty, and all the while you wear the scarlet livery of the Iron Heel."

Here the shouting and the cries of "Order! order!" drowned his voice, and he stood disdainfully till the din had somewhat subsided. He waved his hand to include all of them, turned to his own comrades, and said:

"Listen to the bellowing of the well-fed beasts."

Pandemonium broke out again. The Speaker rapped for order and glanced expectantly at the officers in the doorways. There were cries of "Sedition!" and a great, rotund New York member began shouting "Anarchist!" at Ernest. And Ernest was not pleasant to look at. Every fighting fibre of him was quivering, and his face was the face of a fighting animal, withal he was cool and collected.

"Remember," he said, in a voice that made itself heard above the din, "that as you show mercy now to the proletariat, some day will that same proletariat show mercy to you."

The cries of "Sedition!" and "Anarchist!" redoubled.

"I know that you will not vote for this bill," Ernest went on. "You have received the command from your masters to vote against it. And yet you call me anarchist. You, who have destroyed the government of the people, and who shamelessly flaunt your scarlet shame in public places, call me anarchist. I do not believe in hell-fire and brimstone; but in moments like this I regret my unbelief. Nay, in moments like this I almost do believe. Surely there must be a hell, for in no less place could it be possible for you to receive punishment adequate to your crimes. So long as you exist, there is a vital need for hell-fire in the Cosmos."

There was movement in the doorways. Ernest, the Speaker, all the members turned to see.

"Why do you not call your soldiers in, Mr. Speaker, and bid them do their work?" Ernest demanded. "They should carry out your plan with expedition."

"There are other plans afoot," was the retort. "That is why the soldiers are present."

"Our plans, I suppose," Ernest sneered. "Assassination or something kindred."

But at the word "assassination" the uproar broke out again. Ernest could not make himself heard, but he remained on his feet waiting for a lull. And then it happened. From my place in the gallery I saw nothing except the flash of the explosion. The roar of it filled my ears and I saw Ernest reeling and falling in a swirl of smoke, and the soldiers rushing up all the aisles. His comrades were on their feet, wild with anger, capable of any violence. But Ernest steadied himself for a moment, and waved his arms for silence.

"It is a plot!" his voice rang out in warning to his comrades. "Do nothing, or you will be destroyed."

Then he slowly sank down, and the soldiers reached him. The next moment soldiers were clearing the galleries and I saw no more.

Though he was my husband, I was not permitted to get to him. When I announced who I was, I was promptly placed under arrest. And at the same time were arrested all socialist Congressmen in Washington, including the unfortunate Simpson, who lay ill with typhoid fever in his hotel.

The trial was prompt and brief. The men were foredoomed. The wonder was that Ernest was not executed. This was a blunder on the part of the Oligarchy, and a costly one. But the Oligarchy was too confident in those days. It was drunk with success, and little did it dream that that small handful of heroes had within them the power to rock it to its foundations. To-morrow, when the Great Revolt breaks out and all the world resounds with the tramp, tramp of the millions, the Oligarchy will realize, and too late, how mightily that band of heroes has grown.

1908

MARTIN EDEN

Selections

Martin Eden *is a story of success—of success that came too late. As a rough, uneducated sailor Martin Eden was quite content with life as he knew it. But an invitation to dinner at the Morses, a moderately wealthy family, changed all that. In that upper middle class home Martin discovered a new world of beauty, culture, and luxury he had never known existed. Life for him after this discovery could never be the same.*

Motivated by the love of Ruth Morse, a highly intelligent ethereal beauty, Martin struggled against great odds to reach, what was to him, "the high plateau of society." The way to accomplish this, he decided, was to become a writer. Without previous training, without encouragement even from the woman he loved, Martin drove himself mercilessly to gain an education and to learn the craft of a writer.

But this plan contained one fatal flaw. Martin was in pursuit of the wrong goals. He wrote not for the love of writing, but for the rewards it would bring him. When at last he had attained success he discovered it was without meaning. The price he had paid was enormous: he had lost his girl; his best friend, Brissenden; and his health.

The selections following take place when, after so much effort and sacrifice, success has come to Martin Eden—and with it disillusionment. ED.

One day Martin became aware that he was lonely. He was healthy and strong, and had nothing to do. The cessation from writing and studying, the death of Brissenden, and the estrangement from Ruth had made a big hole in his life; and his life refused to be pinned down to good living in cafés and the smoking of Egyptian cigarettes. It was true the South Seas were calling to him, but he had a feeling that the game was not yet played out in the United States. Two books were soon to be published, and he had more books that might find publication. Money could be made out of them, and he would wait and take a sackful of it into the South Seas. He knew a valley and a bay in the Marquesas that he could buy for a thousand Chili dollars. The valley ran from the horseshoe, land-locked bay to the tops of the dizzy, cloud-capped peaks and contained perhaps ten thousand acres. It was filled with tropical fruits, wild chickens, and wild pigs, with an occasional herd of wild cattle, while high up among the peaks were herds of wild goats harried by packs of wild dogs. The whole place was wild. Not a human lived in it. And he could buy it and the bay for a thousand Chili dollars.

The bay, as he remembered it, was magnificent, with water deep enough to accommodate the largest vessel afloat, and so safe that the South Pacific Directory recommended it as the best careening place for ships for hundreds of miles around. He would buy a schooner—one of these yacht-like, coppered crafts that sailed like witches—and go trading copra and pearling among the islands. He would make the valley and the bay his headquarters. He would build a patriarchal grass house like Tati's, and have it and the valley and the schooner filled with dark-skinned servitors. He would entertain there the factor of Taiohæ, captains of wandering traders, and all the best of the South Pacific riffraff. He would keep open house and entertain like a prince. And he would forget the books he had opened and the world that had proved an illusion.

To do all this he must wait in California to fill the sack with money. Already it was beginning to flow in. If one of the books made a strike, it might enable him to sell the whole heap of manuscripts. Also he could collect the stories and the poems into books, and make sure of the valley and the bay and the schooner. He would never write again. Upon that he was resolved. But in the meantime, awaiting the publication of the books, he must do something more than live dazed and stupid in the sort of uncaring trance into which he had fallen.

He noted, one Sunday morning, that the Bricklayers' Picnic took place that day at Shell Mound Park, and to Shell Mound Park he went. He had been to the working-class picnics too often in his earlier life not to know what they were like, and as he entered the park he experienced a recrudescence of all the old sensations. After all, they were his kind, these working people. He had been born among them, he had lived among them, and though he had strayed for a time, it was well to come back among them.

"If it ain't Mart!" he heard some one say, and the next moment a hearty hand was on his shoulder. "Where you ben all the time? Off to sea? Come on an' have a drink."

It was the old crowd in which he found himself—the old crowd, with here and there a gap, and here and there a new face. The fellows were not bricklayers, but, as in the old days, they attended all Sunday picnics for the dancing, and the fighting, and the fun. Martin drank with them, and began to feel really human once more. He was a fool to have ever left them, he thought; and he was very certain that his sum of happiness would have been greater had he remained with them and let alone the books and the people who sat in the high places. Yet the beer seemed not so good as of yore. It didn't taste as it used to taste. Brissenden had spoiled him for steam beer, he concluded, and wondered if, after all, the books had spoiled him for companionship with these friends of his youth. He resolved that he would not be so spoiled, and he went on to the dancing pavilion. Jimmy, the plumber, he met there, in the company of a tall, blond girl who promptly forsook him for Martin.

"Gee, it's like old times," Jimmy explained to the gang that gave him the laugh as Martin and the blonde whirled away in a waltz. "An' I don't give a rap. I'm too damned glad to see 'm back. Watch 'm waltz, eh? It's like silk. Who'd blame any girl?"

But Martin restored the blonde to Jimmy, and the three of them, with half a dozen friends, watched the revolving couples and laughed and joked with one another. Everybody was glad to see Martin back. No book of his had been published; he carried no fictitious value in their eyes. They liked him for himself. He felt like a prince returned from exile, and his lonely heart burgeoned in the geniality in which it bathed. He made a mad day of it, and was at his best. Also, he had money in his pockets, and, as in the old days when he returned from sea with a pay-day, he made the money fly.

Once, on the dancing-floor, he saw Lizzie Connolly go by in the arms of a young workingman; and, later, when he made the round of the pavilion, he came upon her sitting by a refreshment table. Surprise and greetings over, he led her away into the grounds, where they could talk without shouting down the music. From the instant he spoke to her, she was his. He knew it. She showed it in the proud humility of her eyes, in every caressing movement of her proudly carried body, and in the way she hung upon his speech. She was not the young girl as he had known her. She was a woman, now, and Martin noted that her wild, defiant beauty had improved, losing none of its wildness, while the defiance and the fire seemed more in control. "A beauty, a perfect beauty," he murmured admiringly under his breath. And he knew she was his, that all he had to do was to say "Come," and she would go with him over the world wherever he led.

Even as the thought flashed through his brain he received a heavy blow on the side of his head that nearly knocked him down. It was a man's fist, directed by a man so angry and in such haste that the fist had missed the jaw for which it was aimed. Martin turned as he staggered, and saw the fist coming at him in a wild swing. Quite as a matter of course he ducked, and the fist flew harmlessly past, pivoting the man who had driven it. Martin hooked with his left, landing on the pivoting man with the weight of his body behind the blow. The man went to the ground sidewise, leaped to his feet, and made a mad rush. Martin saw his passion-distorted face and wondered what could be the cause of the fellow's anger. But while he wondered, he shot in a straight left, the weight of his body behind the blow. The man went over backward and fell in a crumpled heap. Jimmy and others of the gang were running toward them.

Martin was thrilling all over. This was the old days with a vengeance, with their dancing, and their fighting, and their fun. While he kept a wary eye on his antagonist, he glanced at Lizzie. Usually the girls screamed when the fellows got to scrapping, but she had not screamed. She was looking on with bated breath, leaning slightly forward, so keen was her interest, one hand pressed to her breast, her cheek flushed, and in her eyes a great and amazed admiration.

The man had gained his feet and was struggling to escape the restraining arms that were laid on him.

"She was waitin' for me to come back!" he was proclaiming to all and sundry. "She was waitin' for me to come back, an' then that fresh guy comes buttin' in. Let go o' me, I tell yeh. I'm goin' to fix 'm."

"What's eatin' yer?" Jimmy was demanding, as he helped hold the young fellow back. "That guy's Mart Eden. He's nifty with his mits, lemme tell you that, an' he'll eat you alive if you monkey with 'm."

"He can't steal her on me that way," the other interjected.

"He licked the Flyin' Dutchman, an' you know *him*," Jimmy went on expostulating. "An' he did it in five rounds. You couldn't last a minute against him. See?"

This information seemed to have a mollifying effect, and the irate young man favored Martin with a measuring stare.

"He don't look it," he sneered; but the sneer was without passion.

"That's what the Flyin' Dutchman thought," Jimmy assured him. "Come on, now, let's get outa this. There's lots of other girls. Come on."

The young fellow allowed himself to be led away toward the pavilion, and the gang followed after him.

"Who is he?" Martin asked Lizzie. "And what's it all about, anyway?"

Already the zest of combat, which of old had been so keen and lasting, had died down, and he discovered that he was self-analytical, too much so to live, single heart and single hand, so primitive an existence.

Lizzie tossed her head.

"Oh, he's nobody," she said. "He's just ben keepin' company with me.

"I had to, you see," she explained after a pause. "I was gettin' pretty lonesome. But I never forgot." Her voice sank lower, and she looked straight before her. "I'd throw 'm down for you any time."

Martin, looking at her averted face, knowing that all he had to do was to reach out his hand and pluck her, fell to pondering whether, after all, there was any real worth in refined, grammatical English, and, so, forgot to reply to her.

"You put it all over him," she said tentatively, with a laugh.

"He's a husky young fellow, though," he admitted generously. "If they hadn't taken him away, he might have given me my hands full."

"Who was that lady friend I seen you with that night?" she asked abruptly.

"Oh, just a lady friend," was his answer.

"It was a long time ago," she murmured contemplatively. "It seems like a thousand years."

But Martin went no further into the matter. He led the conversation off into other channels. They had lunch in the restaurant, where he ordered wine and expensive delicacies and afterward he danced with her and with no one but her, till she was tired. He was a good dancer, and she whirled around and around with him in a heaven of delight, her head against his shoulder, wishing that it could last forever. Later in the afternoon they strayed off among the trees, where, in the good old fashion, she sat down while he sprawled on his back, his head in her lap. He lay and dozed, while she fondled his hair, looked down on his closed eyes, and loved him without reserve. Looking up suddenly, he read the tender advertisement in her face. Her eyes fluttered down, then they opened and looked into his with soft defiance.

"I've kept straight all these years," she said, her voice so low that it was almost a whisper.

In his heart Martin knew that it was the miraculous truth. And at his heart pleaded a great temptation. It was in his power to make her happy. Denied happiness himself, why should he deny happiness to her? He could marry her and take her down with him to dwell in the grass-walled castle in the Marquesas. The desire to do it was strong, but stronger still was the imperative command of his nature not to do it. In spite of himself he was still faithful to Love. The old days of license and easy living were gone. He could not bring them back, nor could he go back to them. He was changed—how changed he had not realized until now.

"I am not a marrying man, Lizzie," he said lightly.

The hand caressing his hair paused perceptibly, then went on with the same gentle stroke. He noticed her face harden, but it was with the hardness of resolution, for still the soft color was in her cheeks and she was all glowing and melting.

"I did not mean that—" she began, then faltered. "Or anyway I don't care.

"I don't care," she repeated. "I'm proud to be your friend. I'd do anything for you. I'm made that way, I guess."

Martin sat up. He took her hand in his. He did it deliberately, with warmth but without passion; and such warmth chilled her.

"Don't let's talk about it," she said.

"You are a great and noble woman," he said. "And it is I who should be proud to know you. And I am, I am. You are a ray of light to me in a very dark world, and I've got to be straight with you, just as straight as you have been."

"I don't care whether you're straight with me or not. You could do anything with me. You could throw me in the dirt an' walk on me. An' you're the only man in the world that can," she added with a defiant flash. "I ain't taken care of myself ever since I was a kid for nothin'."

"And it's just because of that that I'm not going to," he said gently. "You are so big and generous that you challenge me to equal generousness. I'm not marrying, and I'm not—well, loving without marrying, though I've done my share of that in the past. I'm sorry I came here to-day and met you. But it can't be helped now, and I never expected it would turn out this way.

"But look here, Lizzie. I can't begin to tell you how much I like you. I do more than like you. I admire and respect you. You are magnificent, and you are magnificently good. But what's the use of words? Yet there's something I'd like to do. You've had a hard life; let me make it easy for you." (A joyous light welled into her eyes, then faded out again.) "I'm pretty sure of getting hold of some money soon—lots of it."

In that moment he abandoned the idea of the valley and the bay, the grass-walled castle and the trim, white schooner. After all, what did it matter? He could go away, as he had done so often, before the mast, on any ship bound anywhere.

"I'd like to turn it over to you. There must be something you want—to go to school or business college. You might like to study and be a stenographer. I could fix it for you. Or maybe your father and mother are living—I could set them up in a grocery store or something. Anything you want, just name it, and I can fix it for you."

She made no reply, but sat, gazing straight before her, dry-eyed and motionless, but with an ache in the throat which Martin divined so strongly that it made his own throat ache. He regretted that he had spoken. It seemed so tawdry what he had offered her—mere money—compared with what she offered him. He offered her an extraneous thing with which he could part without a pang, while she offered him herself, along with disgrace and shame, and sin, and all her hopes of heaven.

"Don't let's talk about it," she said with a catch in her voice that she changed to a cough. She stood up. "Come on, let's go home. I'm all tired out."

The day was done, and the merrymakers had nearly all departed. But as Martin and Lizzie emerged from the trees they found the gang waiting for them. Martin knew immediately the meaning of it. Trouble was brewing. The gang was his bodyguard. They passed out through the gates of the park with, straggling in the rear, a second gang, the friends that Lizzie's young man had collected to avenge the loss of his lady. Several constables and special police officers, anticipating trouble, trailed along to prevent it, and herded the two gangs separately aboard the train for San Francisco. Martin told Jimmy that he would get off at Sixteenth Street Station and catch the electric car into Oakland. Lizzie was very quiet and without interest in what was impending. The train pulled in to Sixteenth Street Station, and the waiting electric car could be seen, the conductor of which was impatiently clanging the gong.

"There she is," Jimmy counselled. "Make a run for it, an' we'll hold 'em back. Now you go! Hit her up!"

The hostile gang was temporarily disconcerted by the manœuvre, then it dashed from the train in pursuit. The staid and sober Oakland folk who sat upon the car scarcely noted the young fellow and the girl who ran for it and found a seat in front on the outside. They did not connect the couple with Jimmy, who sprang on the steps, crying to the motorman:—

"Slam on the juice, old man, and beat it outa here!"

The next moment Jimmy whirled about, and the passengers saw him land his fist on the face of a running man who was trying to board the car. But fists were landing on faces the whole length of the car. Thus, Jimmy and his gang, strung out on the long, lower steps, met the attacking gang. The car started with a great clanging of its gong, and, as Jimmy's gang drove off the last assailants, they, too, jumped off to finish the job. The car dashed on, leaving the flurry of combat far behind, and its dumfounded passengers never dreamed that the quiet young man and the pretty working-girl sitting in the corner on the outside seat had been the cause of the row.

Martin had enjoyed the fight, with a recrudescence of the old fighting thrills. But they quickly died away, and he was oppressed by a great sadness. He felt very old—centuries older than those careless, care-free young companions of his other days. He had travelled far, too far to go back. Their mode of life, which had once been his, was now distasteful to him. He was disappointed in it all. He had developed into an alien. As the steam beer had tasted raw, so their companionship seemed raw to him. He was too far removed. Too many thousands of opened books yawned between them and him. He had exiled himself. He had travelled in the vast realm of intellect until he could no longer return home. On the other hand, he was human, and his gregarious need for companionship remained unsatisfied. He had found no new home. As the gang could not understand him, as his own family could not understand him, as the bourgeoisie could not understand him, so this girl beside him, whom he honored high, could not understand him nor the honor he paid her. His sadness was not untouched with bitterness as he thought it over.

"Make it up with him," he advised Lizzie, at parting, as they stood in front of the workingman's shack in which she lived, near Sixth and Market. He referred to the young fellow whose place he had usurped that day.

"I can't—now," she said.

"Oh, go on," he said jovially. "All you have to do is whistle and he'll come running."

"I didn't mean that," she said simply.

And he knew what she had meant.

She leaned toward him as he was about to say good night. But she leaned not imperatively, not seductively, but wistfully and humbly. He was touched to the heart. His large tolerance rose up in him. He put his arms around her, and kissed her, and knew that upon his own lips rested as true a kiss as man ever received.

"My God!" she sobbed. "I could die for you. I could die for you."

She tore herself from him suddenly and ran up the steps. . . .

"The Shame of the Sun" was published in October. As Martin cut the cords of the express package and the half-dozen complimentary copies from the publishers spilled out on the table, a heavy sadness fell upon him. He thought of the wild delight that would have been his had this happened a few short months before, and he contrasted that delight that should have been with his present uncaring coldness. His book, his first book, and his pulse had not gone up a fraction of a beat, and he was only sad. It meant little to him now. The most it meant was that it might bring some money, and little enough did he care for money.

He carried a copy out into the kitchen and presented it to Maria.

"I did it," he explained, in order to clear up her bewilderment. "I wrote it in the room there, and I guess some few quarts of your vegetable soup went into the making of it. Keep it. It's yours. Just to remember me by, you know."

He was not bragging, not showing off. His sole motive was to make her happy, to make her proud of him, to justify her long faith in him. She put the book in the front room on top of the family Bible. A sacred thing was this book her lodger had made, a fetich of friendship. It softened the blow of his having been a laundryman, and though she could not understand a line of it, she knew that every line of it was great. She was a simple, practical, hard-working woman, but she possessed faith in large endowment.

Just as emotionlessly as he had received "The Shame of the Sun" did he read the reviews of it that came in weekly from the clipping bureau. The book was making a hit, that was evident. It meant more gold in the money sack. He could fix up Lizzie, redeem all his promises, and still have enough left to build his grass-walled castle.

Singletree, Darnley & Co. had cautiously brought out an edition of fifteen hundred copies, but the first reviews had started a second edition of twice the size through the presses; and ere this was delivered a third edition of five thousand had been ordered. A London firm made arrangements by cable for an English edition, and hotfooted upon this came the news of French, German, and Scandinavian translations in progress. The attack upon the Maeterlinck school could not have been made at a more opportune moment. A fierce controversy was precipitated. Saleeby and Haeckel indorsed and defended "The Shame of the Sun," for once finding themselves on the same side of a question. Crookes and Wallace ranged up on the opposing side, while Sir Oliver Lodge attempted to formulate a compromise that would jibe with his particular cosmic theories. Maeterlinck's followers rallied around the standard of mysticism. Chesterton set the whole world laughing with a series of alleged non-partisan essays on the subject, and the whole affair, controversy and controversialists, was well-nigh swept into the pit by a thundering broadside from George Bernard Shaw. Needless to say the arena was crowded with hosts of lesser lights, and the dust and sweat and din became terrific.

"It is a most marvellous happening," Singletree, Darnley & Co. wrote Martin, "a critical philosophic essay selling like a novel. You could not have chosen your subject better, and all contributory factors have been unwarrantedly propitious. We need scarcely to assure you that we are making hay while the sun shines. Over forty thousand copies have already been sold in the United States and Canada, and a new edition of twenty thousand is on the presses. We are overworked, trying to supply the demand. Nevertheless we have helped to create that demand. We have already spent five thousand dollars in advertising. The book is bound to be a record-breaker.

"Please find herewith a contract in duplicate for your next book which we have taken the liberty of forwarding to you. You will please note that we have increased your royalties to twenty per cent, which is about as high as a conservative publishing house dares go. If our offer is agreeable to you, please fill in the proper blank space with the title of your book. We make no stipulations concerning its nature. Any book on any subject. If you have one already written, so much the better. Now is the time to strike. The iron could not be hotter.

"On receipt of signed contract we shall be pleased to make you an advance on royalties of five thousand dollars. You see, we have faith in you, and we are going in on this thing big. We should like, also, to discuss with you the drawing up of a contract for a term of years, say ten, during which we shall have the exclusive right of publishing in book-form all that you produce. But more of this anon."

Martin laid down the letter and worked a problem in mental arithmetic, finding the product of fifteen cents times sixty thousand to be nine thousand dollars. He signed the new contract, inserting "The Smoke of Joy" in the blank space, and mailed it back to the publishers along with the twenty storiettes he had written in the days before he discovered the formula for the newspaper storiette. And promptly as the United States mail could deliver and return, came Singletree, Darnley & Co.'s check for five thousand dollars. . . .

In the meantime the world had begun to ask: "Who is this Martin Eden?" He had declined to give any biographical data to his publishers, but the newspapers were not to be denied. Oakland was his own town, and the reporters nosed out scores of individuals who could supply information. All that he was and was not, all that he had done and most of what he had not done, was spread out for the delectation of the public, accompanied by snapshots and photographs—the latter procured from the local photographer who had once taken Martin's picture and who promptly copyrighted it and put it on the market. At first, so great was his disgust with the magazines and all bourgeois society, Martin fought against publicity; but in the end, because it was easier than not to, he surrendered. He found that he could not refuse himself to the special writers who travelled long distances to see him. Then again, each day was so many hours long, and, since he no longer was occupied with writing and studying, those hours had to be occupied somehow; so he yielded to what was to him a whim, permitted interviews, gave his opinions on literature and philosophy, and even accepted invitations of the bourgeoisie. He had settled down into a strange and comfortable state of mind. He no longer cared. He forgave everybody, even the cub reporter who had painted him red and to whom he now granted a full page with specially posed photographs.

He saw Lizzie occasionally, and it was patent that she regretted the greatness that had come to him. It widened the space between them. Perhaps it was with the hope of narrowing it that she yielded to his persuasions to go to night school and business college and to have herself gowned by a wonderful dressmaker who charged outrageous prices. She improved visibly from day to day, until Martin wondered if he was doing right, for he knew that all her compliance and endeavor was for his sake. She was trying to make herself of worth in his eyes—of the sort of worth he seemed to value. Yet he gave her no hope, treating her in brotherly fashion and rarely seeing her.

"Overdue" was rushed upon the market by the Meredith-Lowell Company in the height of his popularity, and being fiction, in point of sales it made even a bigger strike than "The Shame of the Sun." Week after week his was the credit of the unprecedented performance of having two books at the head of the list of best-sellers. Not only did the story take with the fiction-readers, but those who read "The

Shame of the Sun" with avidity were likewise attracted to the sea-story by the cosmic grasp of mastery with which he had handled it. First, he had attacked the literature of mysticism, and had done it exceeding well; and, next, he had successfully supplied the very literature he had exposited, thus proving himself to be that rare genius, a critic and a creator in one.

Money poured in on him, fame poured in on him; he flashed, comet-like, through the world of literature, and he was more amused than interested by the stir he was making. One thing was puzzling him, a little thing that would have puzzled the world had it known. But the world would have puzzled over his bepuzzlement rather than over the little thing that to him loomed gigantic. Judge Blount invited him to dinner. That was the little thing, or the beginning of the little thing, that was soon to become the big thing. He had insulted Judge Blount, treated him abominably, and Judge Blount, meeting him on the street, invited him to dinner. Martin bethought himself of the numerous occasions on which he had met Judge Blount at the Morses' and when Judge Blount had not invited him to dinner. Why had he not invited him to dinner then? he asked himself. He had not changed. He was the same Martin Eden. What made the difference? The fact that the stuff he had written had appeared inside the covers of books? But it was work performed. It was not something he had done since. It was achievement accomplished at the very time Judge Blount was sharing this general view and sneering at his Spencer and his intellect. Therefore it was not for any real value, but for a purely fictitious value that Judge Blount invited him to dinner.

Martin grinned and accepted the invitation, marvelling the while at his complacence. And at the dinner, where, with their womenkind, were half a dozen of those that sat in high places, and where Martin found himself quite the lion, Judge Blount, warmly seconded by Judge Hanwell, urged privately that Martin should permit his name to be put up for the Styx—the ultra-select club to which belonged, not the mere men of wealth, but the men of attainment. And Martin declined, and was more puzzled than ever.

He was kept busy disposing of his heap of manuscripts. He was overwhelmed by requests from editors. It had been discovered that he was a stylist, with meat under his style. *The Northern Review*, after publishing "The Cradle of Beauty," had written him for half a dozen similar essays, which would have been supplied out of the heap, had not *Burton's Magazine*, in a speculative mood, offered him five hundred dollars each for five essays. He wrote back that he would supply the demand, but at a thousand dollars an essay. He remembered that all these manuscripts had been refused by the very magazines that were now clamoring for them. And their refusals had been cold-blooded, automatic, stereotyped. They had made him sweat, and now he intended to make them sweat. *Burton's Magazine* paid his price for five essays, and the remaining four, at the same rate, were snapped up by *Mackintosh's Monthly*, *The Northern Review* being too poor to stand the pace. Thus went out to the world "The High Priests of Mystery," "The Wonder-Dreamers," "The Yardstick of the Ego," "Philosophy of Illusion," "God and Clod," "Art and Biology," "Critics and Test-tubes," "Star-dust," and "The Dignity of Usury,"—to raise storms and rumblings and mutterings that were many a day in dying down.

Editors wrote to him telling him to name his own terms, which he did, but it was always for work performed. He refused resolutely to pledge himself to any new thing. The thought of again setting pen to paper maddened him. He had seen Brissenden torn to pieces by the crowd, and despite the fact that him the crowd acclaimed, he could not get over the shock nor gather any respect for the crowd. His very popularity seemed a disgrace and a treason to Brissenden. It made him wince, but he made up his mind to go on and fill the money-bag.

He received letters from editors like the following: "About a year ago we were unfortunate enough to refuse your collection of love-poems. We were greatly impressed by them at the time, but certain arrangements already entered into prevented our taking them. If you still have them, and if you will be kind enough to forward them, we shall be glad to publish the entire collection on your own terms. We are also prepared to make a most advantageous offer for bringing them out in book-form."

Martin recollected his blank-verse tragedy, and sent it instead. He read it over before mailing, and was particularly impressed by its sophomoric amateurishness and general worthlessness. But he sent it; and it was published, to the everlasting regret of the editor. The public was indignant and incredulous. It was too far a cry from Martin Eden's high standard to that serious bosh. It was asserted that he had never written it, that the magazine had faked it very clumsily, or that Martin Eden was emulating the elder Dumas and at the height of success was hiring his writing done for him. But when he explained that the tragedy was an early effort of his literary childhood, and that the magazine had refused to be happy unless it got it, a great laugh went up at the magazine's expense and a change in the editorship followed. The tragedy was never brought out in book-form, though Martin pocketed the advance royalties that had been paid.

Coleman's Weekly sent Martin a lengthy telegram, costing nearly three hundred dollars, offering him a thousand dollars an article for twenty articles. He was to travel over the United States, with all expenses paid, and select whatever topics interested him. The body of the telegram was devoted to hypothetical topics in order to show him the freedom of range that was to be his. The only restriction placed upon him was that he must confine himself to the United States. Martin sent his inability to accept and his regrets by wire "collect."

"Wiki-Wiki," published in *Warren's Monthly*, was an instantaneous success. It was brought out forward in a wide-margined, beautifully decorated volume that struck the holiday trade and sold like wildfire. The critics were unanimous in the belief that it would take its place with those two classics by two great writers, "The Bottle Imp" and "The Magic Skin."

The public, however, received the "Smoke of Joy" collection rather dubiously and coldly. The audacity and unconventionality of the storiettes was a shock to bourgeois morality and prejudice, but when Paris went mad over the immediate translation that was made, the American and English reading public followed suit and bought so many copies that Martin compelled the conservative house of Singletree, Darnley & Co. to pay a flat royalty of twenty-five per cent for a third book, and thirty per cent flat for a fourth. These two volumes comprised all the short stories he had written and which had received, or were receiving, serial publication. "The Ring of Bells" and his horror stories constituted one collection; the other collection was composed of "Adventure," "The Pot," "The Wine of Life," "The Whirlpool," "The Jostling Street," and four other stories. The Lowell-Meredith Company captured the collection of all his essays, and the Maxmillian Company got his "Sea Lyrics" and the "Love-cycle," the latter receiving serial publication in the *Ladies' Home Companion* after the payment of an extortionate price.

Martin heaved a sigh of relief when he had disposed of the last manuscript. The grass-walled castle and the white, coppered schooner were very near to him. Well, at any rate he had discovered Brissenden's contention that nothing of merit found its way into the magazines. His own success demonstrated that Brissenden had been wrong. And yet, somehow, he had a feeling that Brissenden had been right, after all. "The Shame of the Sun" had been the cause of his success more than the stuff he had written. That stuff had been merely incidental. It had been rejected right and left by the magazines. The publication of "The Shame of the Sun" had started a controversy and precipitated the landslide in his favor. Had there been no "Shame of the Sun" there would have been no landslide, and had there been no miracle in the go of "The Shame of the Sun" there would have been no landslide. Singletree, Darnley & Co. attested that miracle. They had brought out a first edition of fifteen hundred copies and been dubious of selling it. They were experienced publishers and no one had been more astounded than they at the success which had followed. To them it had been in truth a miracle. They never got over it, and every letter they wrote him reflected their reverent awe of that first mysterious happening. They did not attempt to explain it. There was no explaining it. It had happened. In the face of all experience to the contrary, it had happened.

So it was, reasoning thus, that Martin questioned the validity of his popularity. It was the bourgeoisie that bought his books and poured its gold into his money-sack, and from what little he knew of the bourgeoisie it was not clear to him how it could possibly appreciate or comprehend what he had written. His intrinsic beauty and power meant nothing to the hundreds of thousands who were acclaiming him and buying his books. He was the fad of the hour, the adventurer who had stormed Parnassus while the gods nodded. The hundreds of thousands read him and acclaimed him with the same brute non-understanding with which they had flung themselves on Brissenden's "Ephemera" and torn it to pieces—a wolf-rabble that fawned on him instead of fanging him. Fawn or fang, it was all a matter of chance. One thing he knew with absolute certitude: "Ephemera" was infinitely greater than anything he had done. It was infinitely greater than anything he had in him. It was a poem of centuries. Then the tribute the mob paid him was a sorry tribute indeed, for that same mob had wallowed "Ephemera" into the mire. He sighed heavily and with satisfaction. He was glad the last manuscript was sold and that he would soon be done with it all.

Mr. Morse met Martin in the office of the Hotel Metropole. Whether he had happened there just casually, intent on other affairs, or whether he had come there for the direct purpose of inviting him to dinner, Martin never could quite make up his mind, though he inclined toward the second hypothesis. At any rate, invited to dinner he was by Mr. Morse—Ruth's father, who had forbidden him the house and broken off the engagement.

Martin was not angry. He was not even on his dignity. He tolerated Mr. Morse, wondering the while how it felt to eat such humble pie. He did not decline the invitation. Instead, he put it off with vagueness and indefiniteness and inquired after the family, particularly after Mrs. Morse and Ruth. He spoke her name without hesitancy, naturally, though secretly surprised that he had had no inward quiver, no old, familiar increase of pulse and warm surge of blood.

He had many invitations to dinner, some of which he accepted. Persons got themselves introduced to him in order to invite him to dinner. And he went on puzzling over the little thing that was becoming a great thing . . . He remembered the days of his desperate starvation when no one invited him to dinner. That was the time he needed dinners, and went weak and faint for lack of them and lost weight from sheer famine. That was the paradox of it. When he wanted dinners, no one gave them to him, and now that he could buy a hundred thousand dinners and was losing his appetite, dinners were thrust upon him right and left. But why? There was no justice in it, no merit on his part. He was no different. All the work he had done was even at that time work performed. Mr. and Mrs. Morse had condemned him for an idler and a shirk and through Ruth had urged that he take a clerk's position in an office. Furthermore, they had been aware of his work performed. Manuscript after manuscript of his had been turned over to them by Ruth. They had read them. It was the very same work that had put his name in all the papers, and it was his name being in all the papers that led them to invite him.

One thing was certain: the Morses had not cared to have him for himself or for his work. Therefore they could not want him now for himself or for his work, but for the fame that was his, because he was somebody amongst men, and—why not? —because he had a hundred thousand dollars or so. That was the way bourgeois society valued a man, and who was he to expect it otherwise? But he was proud. He disdained such valuation. He desired to be valued for himself, or for his work, which, after all, was an expression of himself. That was the way Lizzie valued him. The work, with her, did not even count. She valued him, himself. That was the way Jimmy, the plumber, and all the old gang valued him. That had been proved often enough in the days when he ran with them; it had been proved that Sunday at Shell Mound Park. His work could go hang. What they liked, and were willing to scrap for, was just Mart Eden, one of the bunch and a pretty good guy.

Then there was Ruth. She had liked him for himself, that was indisputable. And yet, much as she had liked him she had liked the bourgeois standard of valuation more. She had opposed his writing, and principally, it seemed to him, because it did not earn money. That had been her criticism of his "Love-cycle." She, too, had urged him to get a job. It was true, she refined it to "position," but it meant the same thing, and in his own mind the old nomenclature stuck. He had read her all that he wrote—poems, stories, essays—"Wiki-Wiki," "The Shame of the Sun," everything. And she had always and consistently urged him to get a job, to go to work—good God! as if he hadn't been working, robbing sleep, exhausting life, in order to be worthy of her.

So the little thing grew bigger. He was healthy and normal, ate regularly, slept long hours, and yet the growing little thing was becoming an obsession. *Work performed.* The phrase haunted his brain. . . .

Invitations to dinner poured in on Martin; and the more they poured, the more he puzzled. He sat, the guest of honor, at an Arden Club banquet, with men of note whom he had heard about and read about all his life; and they told him how, when they had read "The Ring of Bells" in the *Transcontinental*, and "The Peri and the Pearl" in *The Hornet*, they had immediately picked him for a winner. My God! and I was hungry and in rags, he thought to himself. Why didn't you give me a dinner then? Then was the time. It was work performed. If you are feeding me now for work performed, why did you not feed me then when I needed it? Not one word in "The Ring of Bells," nor in "The Peri and the Pearl" has been changed. No; you're not feeding me now for work performed. You are feeding me because everybody else is feeding me and because it is an honor to feed me. You are feeding me now because you are herd animals; because you are part of the mob; because the one blind, automatic thought in the mob-mind just now is to feed me. And where does Martin Eden and the work Martin Eden performed come in in all this? he asked himself plaintively, then arose to respond cleverly and wittily to a clever and witty toast.

So it went. Wherever he happened to be—at the Press Club, at the Redwood Club, at pink teas and literary gatherings—always were remembered "The Ring of Bells" and "The Peri and the Pearl" when they were first published. And always was Martin's maddening and unuttered demand: Why didn't you feed me then? It was work performed. "The Ring of Bells" and "The Peri and the Pearl" are not changed one iota. They were just as artistic, just as worth while, then as now. But you are not feeding me for their sake, nor for the sake of anything else I have written. You're feeding me because it is the style of feeding just now, because the whole mob is crazy with the idea of feeding Martin Eden.

And often, at such times, he would abruptly see slouch in among the company a young hoodlum in square-cut coat and under a stiff-rim Stetson hat. It happened to him at the Gallina Society in Oakland one afternoon. As he rose from his chair and stepped forward across the platform, he saw stalk through the wide door at the rear of the great room the young hoodlum with the square-cut coat and stiff-rim hat. Five hundred fashionably gowned women turned their heads, so intent and steadfast was Martin's gaze, to see what he was seeing. But they saw only the empty centre aisle. He saw the young tough lurching down that aisle and wondered if he would remove the stiff-rim which never yet had he seen him without. Straight down the aisle he came, and up the platform. Martin could have wept over that youthful shade of himself, when he thought of all that lay before him. Across the platform he swaggered, right up to Martin, and into the foreground of Martin's consciousness disappeared. The five hundred women applauded softly with gloved hands, seeking to encourage the bashful great man who was their guest. And Martin shook the vision from his brain, smiled, and began to speak. . . .

. . . Mrs. Morse drove by Martin on the street one day, and smiled and nodded. He smiled back and lifted his hat. The episode did not affect him. A month before it might have disgusted him, or made him curious and set him to speculating about her state of consciousness at that moment. But now it was not provocative of a second thought. He forgot about it the next moment. He forgot about it as he would have forgotten the Central Bank Building or the City Hall after having walked past them. Yet his mind was preternaturally active. His thoughts went ever around and around in a circle. The centre of that circle was "work performed"; it ate at his brain like a deathless maggot. He awoke to it in the morning. It tormented his dreams at night. Every affair of life around him that penetrated through his senses immediately related itself to "work performed." He drove along the path of relentless logic to the conclusion that he was nobody, nothing. Mart Eden, the hoodlum, and Mart Eden, the sailor, had been real, had been he; but Martin Eden! the famous writer, did not exist. Martin Eden, the famous writer, was a vapor that had arisen in the mob-mind and by the mob-mind had been thrust into the corporeal being of Mart Eden, the hoodlum and sailor. But it couldn't fool him. He was not that sun-myth that the mob was worshipping and sacrificing dinners to. He knew better.

He read the magazines about himself, and pored over portraits of himself published therein until he was unable to associate his identity with those portraits. He was the fellow who had lived and thrilled and loved; who had been easy-going and tolerant of the frailties of life; who had served in the forecastle, wandered in strange lands, and led his gang in the old fighting days. He was the fellow who had been stunned at first by the thousands of books in the free library, and who had afterward learned his way among them and mastered them; he was the fellow who had burned the midnight oil and bedded with a spur and written books himself. But the one thing he was not was that colossal appetite that all the mob was bent upon feeding.

There were things, however, in the magazines that amused him. All the magazines were claiming him. *Warren's Monthly* advertised to its subscribers that it was always on the quest after new writers, and that, among others, it had introduced Martin Eden to the reading public. *The White Mouse* claimed him; so did *The Northern Review* and *Mackintosh's Magazine,* until silenced by *The Globe,* which pointed triumphantly to its files where the mangled "Sea Lyrics" lay buried. *Youth and Age,* which had come to life again after having escaped paying its bills, put in a prior claim, which nobody but farmers' children ever read. The *Transcontinental* made a dignified and convincing statement of how it first discovered Martin Eden, which was warmly disputed by *The Hornet,* with the exhibit of "The Peri and the Pearl." The modest claim of Singletree, Darnley & Co. was lost in the din. Besides, that publishing firm did not own a magazine wherewith to make its claim less modest.

The newspapers calculated Martin's royalties. In some way the magnificent offers certain magazines had made him leaked out, and Oakland ministers called upon him in a friendly way, while professional begging letters began to clutter his mail. But worse than all this were the women. His photographs were published broadcast, and special writers exploited his strong, bronzed face, his scars, his heavy shoulders, his clear, quiet eyes, and the slight hollows in his cheeks like an ascetic's. At this last he remembered his wild youth and smiled. Often, among the women he met, he would see now one, now another, looking at him, appraising him, selecting him. He laughed to himself. He remembered Brissenden's warning and laughed again. The women would never destroy him, that much was certain. He had gone past that stage.

Once, walking with Lizzie toward night school, she caught a glance directed toward him by a well-gowned, handsome woman of the bourgeoisie. The glance was a trifle too long, a shade too considerative. Lizzie knew it for what it was, and her body tensed angrily. Martin noticed, noticed the cause of it, told her how used he was becoming to it and that he did not care anyway.

"You ought to care," she answered with blazing eyes. "You're sick. That's what's the matter."

"Never healthier in my life. I weigh five pounds more than I ever did."

"It ain't your body. It's your head. Something's wrong with your think-machine. Even I can see that, an' I ain't nobody."

He walked on beside her, reflecting.

"I'd give anything to see you get over it," she broke out impulsively. "You ought to care when women look at you that way, a man like you. It's not natural. It's all right enough for sissy-boys. But you ain't made that way. So help me, I'd be willing an' glad if the right woman came along an' made you care."

When he left Lizzie at night school, he returned to the Metropole.

Once in his rooms, he dropped into a Morris chair and sat staring straight before him. He did not doze. Nor did he think. His mind was a blank, save for the intervals when unsummoned memory pictures took form and color and radiance just under his eyelids. He saw these pictures, but he was scarcely conscious of them—no more so than if they had been dreams. Yet he was not asleep. Once, he roused himself and glanced at his watch. It was just eight o'clock. He had nothing to do, and it was too early for bed. Then his mind went blank again, and the pictures began to form and vanish under his eyelids. There was nothing distinctive about the pictures. They were always masses of leaves and shrub-like branches shot through with hot sunshine.

A knock at the door aroused him. He was not asleep, and his mind immediately connected the knock with a telegram, or letter, or perhaps one of the servants bringing back clean clothes from the laundry. He was thinking about Joe and wondering where he was, as he said, "Come in."

He was still thinking about Joe, and did not turn toward the door. He heard it close softly. There was a long silence. He forgot that there had been a knock at the door, and was still staring blankly before him when he heard a woman's sob. It was involuntary, spasmodic, checked, and stifled—he noted that as he turned about. The next instant he was on his feet.

"Ruth!" he said, amazed and bewildered.

Her face was white and strained. She stood just inside the door, one hand against it for support, the other pressed to her side. She extended both hands toward him piteously, and started forward to meet him. As he caught her hands and led her to the Morris chair he noticed how cold they were. He drew up another chair and sat down on the broad arm of it. He was too confused to speak. In his own mind his affair with Ruth was closed and sealed. He felt much in the same way that he would have felt had the Shelly Hot Springs Laundry suddenly invaded the Hotel Metropole with a whole week's washing ready for him to pitch into. Several times he was about to speak, and each time he hesitated.

"No one knows I am here," Ruth said in a faint voice, with an appealing smile.

"What did you say?" he asked.

He was surprised at the sound of his own voice.

She repeated her words.

"Oh," he said, then wondered what more he could possibly say.

"I saw you come in, and I waited a few minutes."

"Oh," he said again.

He had never been so tongue-tied in his life. Positively he did not have an idea in his head. He felt stupid and awkward, but for the life of him he could think of nothing to say. It would have been easier had the intrusion been the Shelly Hot Springs laundry. He could have rolled up his sleeves and gone to work.

"And then you came in," he said finally.

She nodded, with a slightly arch expression, and loosened the scarf at her throat.

"I saw you first from across the street when you were with that girl."

"Oh, yes," he said simply. "I took her down to night school."

"Well, aren't you glad to see me?" she said at the end of another silence.

"Yes, yes." He spoke hastily. "But wasn't it rash of you to come here?"

"I slipped in. Nobody knows I am here. I wanted to see you. I came to tell you I have been very foolish. I came because I could no longer stay away, because my heart compelled me to come, because—because I wanted to come."

She came forward, out of her chair and over to him. She rested her hand on his shoulder a moment, breathing quickly, and then slipped into his arms. And in his large, easy way, desirous of not inflicting hurt, knowing that to repulse this proffer of herself was to inflict the most grievous hurt a woman could receive, he folded his arms around her and held her close. But there was no warmth in the embrace, no caress in the contact. She had come into his arms, and he held her, that was all. She nestled against him, and then, with a change of position, her hands crept up and rested upon his neck. But his flesh was not fire beneath those hands, and he felt awkward and uncomfortable.

"What makes you tremble so?" he asked. "Is it a chill? Shall I light the grate?"

He made a movement to disengage himself, but she clung more closely to him, shivering violently.

"It is merely nervousness," she said with chattering teeth. "I'll control myself in a minute. There, I am better already."

Slowly her shivering died away. He continued to hold her, but he was no longer puzzled. He knew now for what she had come.

"My mother wanted me to marry Charley Hapgood," she announced.

"Charley Hapgood, that fellow who speaks always in platitudes?" Martin groaned. Then he added, "And now, I suppose, your mother wants you to marry me."

He did not put it in the form of a question. He stated it as a certitude, and before his eyes began to dance the rows of figures of his royalties.

"She will not object, I know that much," Ruth said.

"She considers me quite eligible?"

Ruth nodded.

"And yet I am not a bit more eligible now than I was when she broke our engagement," he meditated. "I haven't changed any. I'm the same Martin Eden, though for that matter I'm a bit worse—I smoke now. Don't you smell my breath?"

In reply she pressed her open fingers against his lips, placed them graciously and playfully, and in expectancy of the kiss that of old had always been a consequence. But there was no caressing answer of Martin's lips. He waited until the fingers were removed and then went on.

"I am not changed. I haven't got a job. I'm not looking for a job. Furthermore, I am not going to look for a job. And I still believe that Herbert Spencer is a great and noble man and that Judge Blount is an unmitigated ass. I had dinner with him the other night, so I ought to know."

"But you didn't accept father's invitation," she chided.

"So you know about that? Who sent him? Your mother?"

She remained silent.

"Then she did send him. I thought so. And now I suppose she has sent you."

"No one knows that I am here," she protested. "Do you think my mother would permit this?"

"She'd permit you to marry me, that's certain."

She gave a sharp cry. "Oh, Martin, don't be cruel. You have not kissed me once. You are as unresponsive as a stone. And think what I have dared to do." She looked about her with a shiver, though half the look was curiosity. "Just think of where I am."

"*I could die for you! I could die for you!*"—Lizzie's words were ringing in his ears.

"Why didn't you dare it before?" he asked harshly. "When I hadn't a job? When

I was starving? When I was just as I am now, as a man, as an artist, the same Martin Eden? That's the question I've been propounding to myself for many a day—not concerning you merely, but concerning everybody. You see I have not changed, though my sudden apparent appreciation in value compels me constantly to reassure myself on that point. I've got the same flesh on my bones, the same ten fingers and toes. I am the same. I have not developed any new strength nor virtue. My brain is the same old brain. I haven't made even one new generalization on literature or philosophy. I am personally of the same value that I was when nobody wanted me. And what is puzzling me is why they want me now. Surely they don't want me for myself, for myself is the same old self they did not want. Then they must want me for something else, for something that is outside of me, for something that is not I! Shall I tell you what that something is? It is for the recognition I have received. That recognition is not I. It resides in the minds of others. Then again for the money I have earned and am earning. But that money is not I. It resides in banks and in the pockets of Tom, Dick, and Harry. And is it for that, for the recognition and the money, that you now want me?"

"You are breaking my heart," she sobbed. "You know I love you, that I am here because I love you."

"I am afraid you don't see my point," he said gently. "What I mean is: if you love me, how does it happen that you love me now so much more than you did when your love was weak enough to deny me?"

"Forget and forgive," she cried passionately. "I loved you all the time, remember that, and I am here, now, in your arms."

"I'm afraid I am a shrewd merchant, peering into the scales, trying to weigh your love and find out what manner of thing it is."

She withdrew herself from his arms, sat upright, and looked at him long and searchingly. She was about to speak, then faltered and changed her mind.

"You see, it appears this way to me," he went on. "When I was all that I am now, nobody out of my own class seemed to care for me. When my books were all written, no one who had read the manuscripts seemed to care for them. In point of fact, because of the stuff I had written they seemed to care even less for me. In writing the stuff it seemed that I had committed acts that were, to say the least, derogatory. 'Get a job,' everybody said."

She made a movement of dissent.

"Yes, yes," he said; "except in your case you told me to get a position. The homely word *job*, like much that I have written, offends you. It is brutal. But I assure you it was no less brutal to me when everybody I knew recommended it to me as they would recommend right conduct to an immoral creature. But to return. The publication of what I had written, and the public notice I received, wrought a change in the fibre of your love. Martin Eden, with his work all performed, you would not marry. Your love for him was not strong enough to enable you to marry him. But your love is now strong enough, and I cannot avoid the conclusion that its strength arises from the publication and the public notice. In your case I do not mention royalties, though I am certain that they apply to the change wrought in your mother and father. Of course, all this is not flattering to me. But worst of all, it makes me question love, sacred love. Is love so gross a thing that it must feed upon publication and public notice? It would seem so. I have sat and thought upon it till my head went around."

"Poor, dear head." She reached up a hand and passed the fingers soothingly through his hair. "Let it go around no more. Let us begin anew, now. I loved you all the time. I know that I was weak in yielding to my mother's will. I should not have done so. Yet I have heard you speak so often with broad charity of the fallibility and frailty of humankind. Extend that charity to me. I acted mistakenly. Forgive me."

"Oh, I do forgive," he said impatiently. "It is easy to forgive where there is really nothing to forgive. Nothing that you have done requires forgiveness. One acts according to one's lights, and more than that one cannot do. As well might I ask you to forgive me for my not getting a job."

"I meant well," she protested. "You know that. I could not have loved you and not meant well."

"True; but you would have destroyed me out of your well-meaning.

"Yes, yes," he shut off her attempted objection. "You would have destroyed my writing and my career. Realism is imperative to my nature, and the bourgeois spirit hates realism. The bourgeoisie is cowardly. It is afraid of life. And all your effort was to make me afraid of life. You would have formalized me. You would have compressed me into a two-by-four pigeonhole of life, where all life's values are unreal, and false, and vulgar." He felt her stir protestingly. "Vulgarity—a hearty vulgarity, I'll admit—is the basis of bourgeois refinement and culture. As I say, you wanted to formalize me, to make me over into one of your own class, with your class-ideals, class-values, and class-prejudices." He shook his head sadly. "And you do not understand, even now, what I am saying. My words do not mean to you what I endeavor to make them mean. What I say is so much fantasy to you. Yet to me it is vital reality. At the best you are a trifle puzzled and amused that this raw boy, crawling up out of the mire of the abyss, should pass judgment upon your class and call it vulgar."

She leaned her head wearily against his shoulder, and her body shivered with recurrent nervousness. He waited for a time for her to speak, and then went on.

"And now you want to renew our love. You want us to be married. You want me. And yet, listen—if my books had not been noticed, I'd nevertheless have been just what I am now. And you would have stayed away. It is all those damned books—"

"Don't swear," she interrupted.

Her reproof startled him. He broke into a harsh laugh.

"That's it," he said, "at a high moment, when what seems your life's happiness is at stake, you are afraid of life in the same old way—afraid of life and a healthy oath."

She was stung by his words into realization of the puerility of her act, and yet she felt that he had magnified it unduly and was consequently resentful. They sat in silence for a long time, she thinking desperately and he pondering upon his love which had departed. He knew, now, that he had not really loved her. It was an idealized Ruth he had loved, an ethereal creature of his own creating, the bright and luminous spirit of his love-poems. The real bourgeois Ruth, with all the bourgeois failings and with the hopeless cramp of the bourgeois psychology in her mind, he had never loved.

She suddenly began to speak.

"I know that much you have said is so. I have been afraid of life. I did not love you well enough. I have learned to love better. I love you for what you are, for what you were, for the ways even by which you have become. I love you for the ways wherein you differ from what you call my class, for your beliefs which I do not understand but which I know I can come to understand. I shall devote myself to understanding them. And even your smoking and your swearing—they are part of you and I will love you for them, too. I can still learn. In the last ten minutes I have learned much. That I have dared to come here is a token of what I have already learned. Oh, Martin!—"

She was sobbing and nestling close against him.

For the first time his arms folded her gently and with sympathy, and she acknowledged it with a happy movement and a brightening face.

"It is too late," he said. He remembered Lizzie's words. "I am a sick man—oh, not my body. It is my soul, my brain. I seem to have lost all values. I care for nothing. If you had been this way a few months ago, it would have been different. It is too late, now."

"It is not too late," she cried. "I will show you. I will prove to you that my love has grown, that it is greater to me than my class and all that is dearest to me. All that is dearest to the bourgeoisie I will flout. I am no longer afraid of life. I will leave my father and mother, and let my name become a by-word with my friends. I will come to you here and now, in free love if you will, and I will be proud and glad to be with you. If I have been a traitor to love, I will now, for love's sake, be a traitor to all that made that earlier treason."

She stood before him, with shining eyes.

"I am waiting, Martin," she whispered, "waiting for you to accept me. Look at me."

It was splendid, he thought, looking at her. She had redeemed herself for all that she had lacked, rising up at last, true woman, superior to the iron rule of bourgeois convention. It was splendid, magnificent, desperate. And yet, what was the matter with him? He was not thrilled nor stirred by what she had done. It was splendid and magnificent only intellectually. In what should have been a moment of fire, he coldly appraised her. His heart was untouched. He was unaware of any desire for her. Again he remembered Lizzie's words.

"I am sick, very sick," he said with a despairing gesture. "How sick I did not know till now. Something has gone out of me. I have always been unafraid of life, but I never dreamed of being sated with life. Life has so filled me that I am empty of any desire for anything. If there were room, I should want you, now. You see how sick I am."

He leaned his head back and closed his eyes; and like a child, crying, that forgets its grief in watching the sunlight percolate through the tear-dimmed films over the pupils, so Martin forgot his sickness, the presence of Ruth, everything, in watching the masses of vegetation, shot through hotly with sunshine that took form and blazed against the background of his eyelids. It was not restful, that green foliage. The sunlight was too raw and glaring. It hurt him to look at it, and yet he looked, he knew not why.

He was brought back to himself by the rattle of the door-knob. Ruth was at the door.

"How shall I get out?" she questioned tearfully. "I am afraid."

"Oh, forgive me," he cried, springing to his feet. "I'm not myself, you know. I forgot you were here." He put his hand to his head. "You see, I'm not just right. I'll take you home. We can go out by the servants' entrance. No one will see us. Pull down that veil and everything will be all right."

She clung to his arm through the dim-lighted passages and down the narrow stairs.

"I am safe now," she said, when they emerged on the sidewalk, at the same time starting to take her hand from his arm.

"No, no, I'll see you home," he answered.

"No, please don't," she objected. "It is unnecessary."

Again she started to remove her hand. He felt a momentary curiosity. Now that she was out of danger she was afraid. She was in almost a panic to be quit of him. He could see no reason for it and attributed it to her nervousness. So he restrained her withdrawing hand and started to walk on with her. Halfway down the block, he saw a man in a long overcoat shrink back into a doorway. He shot a glance in as he passed by, and, despite the high turned-up collar, he was certain that he recognized Ruth's brother, Norman.

During the walk Ruth and Martin held little conversation. She was stunned. He was apathetic. Once, he mentioned that he was going away, back to the South Seas, and, once, she asked him to forgive her having come to him. And that was all. The parting at her door was conventional. They shook hands, said good night, and he lifted his hat. The door swung shut, and he lighted a cigarette and turned back for his hotel. When he came to the doorway into which he had seen Norman shrink, he stopped and looked in in a speculative humor.

"She lied," he said aloud. "She made believe to me that she had dared greatly, and all the while she knew the brother that brought her was waiting to take her back." He burst into laughter. "Oh, these bourgeois! When I was broke, I was not fit to be seen with his sister. When I have a bank account, he brings her to me." . . .

Martin . . . went on to the hotel. He paused in the office to look up steamer sailings. The *Mariposa* sailed for Tahiti in five days.

"Telephone over to-morrow and reserve a stateroom for me," he told the clerk. "No deck-stateroom, but down below, on the weather-side,–the port-side, remember that, the port-side. You'd better write it down."

Once in his room he got into bed and slipped off to sleep as gently as a child. The occurrences of the evening had made no impression on him. His mind was dead to impressions. . . . That in five more days he sailed for his loved South Seas meant nothing to him. So he closed his eyes and slept normally and comfortably for eight uninterrupted hours. He was not restless. He did not change his position, nor did he dream. Sleep had become to him oblivion, and each day that he awoke, he awoke with regret. Life worried and bored him, and time was a vexation.

. . . Editors and publishers contributed to the daily heap of letters, the former on their knees for his manuscripts, the latter on their knees for his books–his poor disdained manuscripts that had kept all he possessed in pawn for so many dreary months in order to find them in postage. There were unexpected checks for English serial rights and for advance payments on foreign translations. His English agent announced the sale of German translation rights in three of his books, and informed him that Swedish editions, from which he could expect nothing because Sweden was not a party to the Berne Convention, were already on the market. Then there was a nominal request for his permission for a Russian translation, that country being likewise outside the Berne Convention.

He turned to the huge bundle of clippings which had come in from his press bureau, and read about himself and his vogue, which had become a furore. All his creative output had been flung to the public in one magnificent sweep. That seemed to account for it. He had taken the public off its feet, the way Kipling had, that time when he lay near to death and all the mob, animated by a mob-mind thought, began suddenly to read him. Martin remembered how that same world-mob, having read him and acclaimed him and not understood him in the least, had, abruptly, a few months later, flung itself upon him and torn him to pieces. Martin grinned at the thought. Who was he that he should not be similarly treated in a few more months? Well, he would fool the mob. He would be away, in the South Seas, building his grass house, trading for pearls and copra, jumping reefs in frail outriggers, catching sharks and bonitas, hunting wild goats among the cliffs of the valley that lay next to the valley of Taiohæ.

In the moment of that thought the desperateness of his situation dawned upon him. He saw, clear eyed, that he was in the Valley of the Shadow. All the life that was in him was fading, fainting, making toward death. He realized how much he slept, and how much he desired to sleep. Of old, he had hated sleep. It had robbed him of precious moments of living. Four hours of sleep in the twenty-four had meant being robbed of four hours of life. How he had grudged sleep! Now it was life he grudged. Life was not good; its taste in his mouth was without tang, and bitter. This was his peril. Life that did not yearn toward life was in fair way toward ceasing. Some remote instinct for preservation stirred in him, and he knew he must get away. He glanced about the room, and the thought of packing was burdensome. Perhaps it would be better to leave that to the last. In the meantime he might be getting an outfit.

He put on his hat and went out, stopping in at a gunstore, where he spent the remainder of the morning buying automatic rifles, ammunition, and fishing tackle. Fashions changed in trading, and he knew he would have to wait till he reached Tahiti before ordering his trade-goods. They could come up from Australia, anyway. This solution was a source of pleasure. He had avoided doing something, and the doing of anything just now was unpleasant. He went back to the hotel gladly, with a feeling of satisfaction in that the comfortable Morris chair was waiting for him. . . .

Once, when the instinct of preservation fluttered, he went to a doctor and underwent a searching physical examination. Nothing could be found the matter with him. His heart and lungs were pronounced magnificent. Every organ, so far as the doctor could know, was normal and was working normally.

"There is nothing the matter with you, Mr. Eden," he said, "positively nothing the matter with you. You are in the pink of condition. Candidly, I envy you your health. It is superb. Look at that chest. There, and in your stomach, lies the secret of your remarkable constitution. Physically, you are a man in a thousand—in ten thousand. Barring accidents, you should live to be a hundred."

And Martin knew that Lizzie's diagnosis had been correct. Physically he was all right. It was his "think-machine" that had gone wrong, and there was no cure for that except to get away to the South Seas. The trouble was that now, on the verge of departure, he had no desire to go. The South Seas charmed him no more than did bourgeois civilization. There was no zest in the thought of departure, while the act of departure appalled him as a weariness of the flesh. He would have felt better it he were already on board and gone. . . .

From the deck of the *Mariposa*, at the sailing hour, he saw Lizzie Connolly hiding on the skirts of the crowd on the wharf. Take her with you, came the thought. It is easy to be kind. She will be supremely happy. It was almost a temptation one moment, and the succeeding moment it became a terror. He was in a panic at the thought of it. His tired soul cried out in protest. He turned away from the rail with a groan, muttering, "Man, you are too sick, you are too sick."

He fled to his stateroom, where he lurked until the steamer was clear of the dock. In the dining saloon, at luncheon, he found himself in the place of honor, at the captain's right; and he was not long in discovering that he was the great man on board. But no more unsatisfactory great man ever sailed on a ship. He spent the afternoon in a deck-chair, with closed eyes, dozing brokenly most of the time, and in the evening went early to bed.

After the second day, recovered from seasickness, the full passenger list was in evidence, and the more he saw of the passengers the more he disliked them. Yet he knew that he did them injustice. They were good and kindly people, he forced himself to acknowledge, and in the moment of acknowledgment he qualified—good and kindly like all the bourgeoisie, with all the psychological cramp and intellectual futility of their kind. They bored him when they talked with him, their little superficial minds were so filled with emptiness; while the boisterous high spirits and the excessive energy of the younger people shocked him. They were never quiet, ceaselessly playing deck-quoits, tossing rings, promenading, or rushing to the rail with loud cries to watch the leaping porpoises and the first schools of flying fish.

He slept much. After breakfast he sought his deck-chair with a magazine he never finished. The printed pages tired him. He puzzled that men found so much to write about, and, puzzling, dozed in his chair. When the gong awoke him for luncheon, he was irritated that he must awaken. There was no satisfaction in being awake.

Once, he tried to arouse himself from his lethargy, and went forward into the forecastle with the sailors. But the breed of sailors seemed to have changed since the days he had lived in the forecastle. He could find no kinship with these stolid-faced, ox-minded bestial creatures. He was in despair. Up above nobody had wanted Martin Eden for his own sake, and he could not go back to those of his own class who had wanted him in the past. He did not want them. He could not stand them any more than he could stand the stupid first-cabin passengers and the riotous young people.

Life was to him like strong, white light that hurts the tired eyes of a sick person. During every conscious moment life blazed in a raw glare around him and upon him. It hurt. It hurt intolerably. It was the first time in his life that Martin had travelled first class. On ships at sea he had always been in the forecastle, the steerage, or in the black depths of the coal-hold, passing coal. In those days, climbing up the iron ladders from out the pit of stifling heat, he had often caught glimpses of the passengers, in cool white, doing nothing but enjoying themselves, under awnings spread to keep the sun and wind away from them, with subservient stewards taking care of their every want and whim, and it had seemed to him that the realm in which they moved and had their being was nothing else than paradise. Well, here he was, the great man on board, in the midmost centre of it, sitting at the captain's right hand, and yet vainly harking back to forecastle and stoke-hole in quest of the Paradise he had lost. He had found no new one, and now he could not find the old one.

He strove to stir himself and find something to interest him. He ventured the petty officers' mess, and was glad to get away. He talked with a quartermaster off duty, an intelligent man who promptly prodded him with the socialist propaganda and forced into his hands a bunch of leaflets and pamphlets. He listened to the man expounding the slave-morality, and as he listened, he thought languidly of his own Nietzsche philosophy. But what was it worth, after all? He remembered one of Nietzsche's mad utterances wherein that madman had doubted truth. And who was to say? Perhaps Nietzsche had been right. Perhaps there was no truth in anything, no truth in truth—no such thing as truth. But his mind wearied quickly and he was content to go back to his chair and doze.

Miserable as he was on the steamer, a new misery came upon him. What when the steamer reached Tahiti? He would have to go ashore. He would have to order his trade-goods, to find a passage on a schooner to the Marquesas, to do a thousand and one things that were awful to contemplate. Whenever he steeled himself deliberately to think, he could see the desperate peril in which he stood. In all truth, he was in the Valley of the Shadow, and his danger lay in that he was not afraid. If he were only afraid, he would make toward life. Being unafraid, he was drifting deeper into the shadow. He found no delight in the old familiar things of life. The *Mariposa* was now in the northeast trades, and this wine of wind, surging against him, irritated him. He had his chair moved to escape the embrace of this lusty comrade of old days and nights.

The day the *Mariposa* entered the doldrums, Martin was more miserable than ever. He could no longer sleep. He was soaked with sleep, and perforce he must now stay awake and endure the white glare of life. He moved about restlessly. The air was sticky and humid, and the rain-squalls were unrefreshing. He ached with life. He walked around the deck until that hurt too much, then sat in his chair until he was compelled to walk again. He forced himself at last to finish the magazine, and from the steamer library he culled several volumes of poetry. But they could not hold him, and once more he took to walking.

He stayed late on deck, after dinner, but that did not help him, for when he went below, he could not sleep. This surcease for life had failed him. It was too much. He turned on the electric light and tried to read. One of the volumes was a Swinburne. He lay in bed, glancing through its pages, until suddenly he became aware that he was reading with interest. He finished the stanza, attempted to read on, then came back to it. He rested the book face downward on his breast and fell to thinking. That was it. The very thing. Strange that it had never come to him before. That was the meaning of it all; he had been drifting that way all the time, and now Swinburne showed him that it was the happy way out. He wanted rest, and here was rest awaiting him. He glanced at the open port-hole. Yes, it was large enough. For the first time in weeks he felt happy. At last he had discovered the cure of his ill. He picked up the book and read the stanza slowly aloud:—

"'*From too much love of living,*
From hope and fear set free,
We thank with brief thanksgiving
Whatever gods may be
That no life lives forever;
That dead men rise up never;
That even the weariest river
Winds somewhere safe to sea.'"

He looked again at the open port. Swinburne had furnished the key. Life was ill, or, rather, it had become ill—an unbearable thing. "That dead men rise up never!" That line stirred him with a profound feeling of gratitude. It was the one beneficent thing in the universe. When life became an aching weariness, death was ready to soothe away to everlasting sleep. But what was he waiting for? It was time to go.

He arose and thrust his head out the port-hole, looking down into the milky wash. The *Mariposa* was deeply loaded, and, hanging by his hands, his feet would be in the water. He could slip in noiselessly. No one would hear. A smother of spray dashed up, wetting his face. It tasted salt on his lips, and the taste was good. He wondered if he ought to write a swan-song, but laughed the thought away. There was no time. He was too impatient to be gone.

Turning off the light in his room so that it might not betray him, he went out the port-hole feet first. His shoulders stuck, and he forced himself back so as to try it with one arm down by his side. A roll of the steamer aided him, and he was through, hanging by his hands. When his feet touched the sea, he let go. He was in a milky froth of water. The side of the *Mariposa* rushed past him like a dark wall, broken here and there by lighted ports. She was certainly making time. Almost before he knew it, he was astern, swimming gently on the foam-crackling surface.

A bonita struck at his white body, and he laughed aloud. It had taken a piece out, and the sting of it reminded him of why he was there. In the work to do he had forgotten the purpose of it. The lights of the *Mariposa* were growing dim in the distance, and there he was, swimming confidently, as though it were his intention to make for the nearest land a thousand miles or so away.

It was the automatic instinct to live. He ceased swimming, but the moment he felt the water rising above his mouth the hands struck out sharply with a lifting movement. The will to live, was his thought, and the thought was accompanied by a sneer. Well, he had will,—ay, will strong enough that with one last exertion it could destroy itself and cease to be.

He changed his position to a vertical one. He glanced up at the quiet stars, at the same time emptying his lungs of air. With swift, vigorous propulsion of hands and feet, he lifted his shoulders and half his chest out of water. This was to gain impetus for the descent. Then he let himself go and sank without movement, a white statue, into the sea. He breathed in the water deeply, deliberately, after the manner of a man taking an anæsthetic. When he strangled, quite involuntarily his arms and legs clawed the water and drove him up to the surface and into the clear sight of the stars.

The will to live, he thought disdainfully, vainly endeavoring not to breathe the air into his bursting lungs. Well, he would have to try a new way. He filled his lungs with air, filled them full. This supply would take him far down. He turned over and went down head first, swimming with all his strength and all his will. Deeper and deeper he went. His eyes were open, and he watched the ghostly, phosphorescent trails of the darting bonita. As he swam, he hoped that they would not strike at him, for it might snap the tension of his will. But they did not strike, and he found time to be grateful for this last kindness of life.

Down, down, he swam till his arms and legs grew tired and hardly moved. He knew that he was deep. The pressure on his ear-drums was a pain, and there was a buzzing in his head. His endurance was faltering, but he compelled his arms and legs to drive him deeper until his will snapped and the air drove from his lungs in a great explosive rush. The bubbles rubbed and bounded like tiny balloons against his cheeks and eyes as they took their upward flight. Then came pain and strangulation. This hurt was not death, was the thought that oscillated through his reeling consciousness. Death did not hurt. It was life, the pangs of life, this awful, suffocating feeling; it was the last blow life could deal him.

His wilful hands and feet began to beat and churn about, spasmodically and feebly. But he had fooled them and the will to live that made them beat and churn. He was too deep down. They could never bring him to the surface. He seemed floating languidly in a sea of dreamy vision. Colors and radiances surrounded him and bathed him and pervaded him. What was that? It seemed a lighthouse; but it was inside his brain—a flashing, bright white light. It flashed swifter and swifter. There was a long rumble of sound, and it seemed to him that he was falling down a vast and interminable stairway. And somewhere at the bottom he fell into darkness. That much he knew. He had fallen into darkness. And at the instant he knew, he ceased to know.

1908

THE POKER GAME

From *Burning Daylight*

It was two in the morning when the dancers, bent on getting something to eat, adjourned the dancing for half an hour. And it was at this moment that Jack Kearns suggested poker. Jack Kearns was a big, bluff-featured man, who, along with Bettles, had made the disastrous attempt to found a post on the head-reaches of the Koyokuk, far inside the Arctic Circle. After that, Kearns had fallen back on his posts at Forty Mile and Sixty Mile and changed the direction of his ventures by sending out to the States for a small sawmill and a river steamer. The former was even then being sledded across Chilcoot Pass by Indians and dogs, and would come down the Yukon in the early summer after the ice-run. Later in the summer, when Bering Sea and the mouth of the Yukon cleared of ice, the steamer, put together at St. Michaels, was to be expected up the river loaded to the guards with supplies.

Jack Kearns suggested poker. French Louis, Dan MacDonald, and Hal Campbell (who had made a strike on Moosehide), all three of whom were not dancing because there were not girls enough to go around, inclined to the suggestion. They were looking for a fifth man when Burning Daylight emerged from the rear room, the Virgin on his arm, the train of dancers in his wake. In response to the hail of the poker-players, he came over to their table in the corner.

"Want you to sit in," said Campbell. "How's your luck?"

"I sure got it to-night," Burning Daylight answered with enthusiasm, and at the same time felt the Virgin press his arm warningly. She wanted him for the dancing. "I sure got my luck with me, but I'd sooner dance. I ain't hankerin' to take the money away from you-all."

Nobody urged. They took his refusal as final, and the Virgin was pressing his arm to turn him away in pursuit of the supper-seekers, when he experienced a change of heart. It was not that he did not want to dance, nor that he wanted to hurt her; but that insistent pressure on his arm put his free man-nature in revolt. The thought in his mind was that he did not want any woman running him. Himself a favorite with women, nevertheless they did not bulk big with him. They were toys, playthings, part of the relaxation from the bigger game of life. He met women along with the whiskey and gambling, and from observation he had found that it was far easier to break away from the drink and the cards than from a woman once the man was properly entangled.

He was a slave to himself, which was natural in one with a healthy ego, but he rebelled in ways either murderous or panicky at being a slave to anybody else. Love's sweet servitude was a thing of which he had no comprehension. Men he had seen in love impressed him as lunatics, and lunacy was a thing he had never considered worth analyzing. But comradeship with men was different from love with women. There was no servitude in comradeship. It was a business proposition, a square deal between men who did not pursue each other, but who shared the risks of trail and river and mountain in the pursuit of life and treasure. Men and women pursued each other, and one must needs bend the other to his will or hers. Comradeship was different. There was no slavery about it; and though he, a strong man beyond strength's seeming, gave far more than he received, he gave not something due but in royal largess, his gifts of toil or heroic effort falling generously from his hands. To pack for days over the gale-swept passes or across the mosquito-ridden marshes, and to pack double the weight his comrade packed, did not involve unfairness or compulsion. Each did his best. That was the business essence of it. Some men were stronger than others—true; but so long as each man did his best it was fair exchange, the business spirit was observed, and the square deal obtained.

But with women—no. Women gave little and wanted all. Women had apron-strings and were prone to tie them about any man who looked twice in their direction. There was the Virgin, yawning her head off when he came in and mightily pleased that he asked her to dance. One dance was all very well, but because he danced twice and thrice with her and several times more, she squeezed his arm when they asked him to sit in at poker. It was the obnoxious apron-string, the first of the many compulsions she would exert upon him if he gave in. Not that she was not a nice bit of a woman, healthy and strapping and good to look upon, also a very excellent dancer, but that she was a woman with all a woman's desire to rope him with her apron-strings and tie him hand and foot for the branding. Better poker. Besides, he liked poker as well as he did dancing.

He resisted the pull on his arm by the mere negative mass of him, and said:—

"I sort of feel a hankering to give you-all a flutter."

Again came the pull on his arm. She was trying to pass the apron-string around him. For the fraction of an instant he was a savage, dominated by the wave of fear and murder that rose up in him. For that infinitesimal space of time he was to all purposes a frightened tiger filled with rage and terror at the apprehension of the trap. Had he been no more than a savage, he would have leapt wildly from the place or else sprung upon her and destroyed her. But in that same instant there stirred in him the generations of discipline by which man had become an inadequate social animal. Tact and sympathy strove with him, and he smiled with his eyes into the Virgin's eyes as he said:—

"You-all go and get some grub. I ain't hungry. And we'll dance some more by and by. The night's young yet. Go to it, old girl."

He released his arm and thrust her playfully on the shoulder, at the same time turning to the poker-players.

"Take off the limit and I'll go you-all."

"Limit's the roof," said Jack Kearns.

"Take off the roof."

The players glanced at one another, and Kearns announced, "The roof's off."

Elam Harnish dropped into the waiting chair, started to pull out his gold-sack, and changed his mind. The Virgin pouted a moment, then followed in the wake of the other dancers.

"I'll bring you a sandwich, Daylight," she called back over her shoulder.

He nodded. She was smiling her forgiveness. He had escaped the apron-string, and without hurting her feelings too severely.

"Let's play markers," he suggested. "Chips do everlastingly clutter up the table. . . . If it's agreeable to you-all?"

"I'm willing," answered Hal Campbell. "Let mine run at five hundred."

"Mine, too," answered Harnish, while the others stated the values they put on their own markers, French Louis, the most modest, issuing his at a hundred dollars each.

In Alaska, at that time, there were no rascals and no tin-horn gamblers. Games were conducted honestly, and men trusted one another. A man's word was as good as his gold in the blower. A marker was a flat, oblong composition chip worth, perhaps, a cent. But when a man betted a marker in a game and said it was worth five hundred dollars, it was accepted as worth five hundred dollars. Whoever won it knew that the man who issued it would redeem it with five hundred dollars' worth of dust weighed out on the scales. The markers being of different colors, there was no difficulty in identifying the owners. Also, in that early Yukon day, no one dreamed of playing table-stakes. A man was good in a game for all that he possessed, no matter where his possessions were or what was their nature.

Harnish cut and got the deal. At this good augury, and while shuffling the deck, he called to the barkeepers to set up the drinks for the house. As he dealt the first card to Dan MacDonald, on his left, he called out:—

"Get down to the ground, you-all, Malemutes, huskies, and Siawash purps! Get down and dig in! Tighten up them traces! Put your weight into the harness and bust the breast-bands! Whoop-la! Yow! We're off and bound for Helen Breakfast! And I tell you-all clear and plain there's goin' to be stiff grades and fast goin' to-night before we win to that same lady. And somebody's goin' to bump . . . hard."

Once started, it was a quiet game, with little or no conversation, though all about the players the place was a-roar. Elam Harnish had ignited the spark. More and more miners dropped in to the Tivoli and remained. When Burning Daylight went on the tear, no man cared to miss it. The dancing-floor was full. Owing to the shortage of women, many of the men tied bandanna handkerchiefs around their arms in token of femininity and danced with other men. All the games were crowded, and the voices of the men talking at the long bar and grouped about the stove were accompanied by the steady click of chips and the sharp whir, rising and falling, of the roulette-ball. All the materials of a proper Yukon night were at hand and mixing.

The luck at the table varied monotonously, no big hands being out. As a result, high play went on with small hands, though no play lasted long. A filled straight belonging to French Louis gave him a pot of five thousand against two sets of threes held by Campbell and Kearns. One pot of eight hundred dollars was won by a pair of treys on a showdown. And once Harnish called Kearns for two thousand dollars on a cold steal. When Kearns laid down his hand it showed a bobtail flush, while Harnish's hand proved that he had had the nerve to call on a pair of tens.

But at three in the morning the big combination of hands arrived. It was the moment of moments that men wait weeks for in a poker game. The news of it tingled over the Tivoli. The onlookers became quiet. The men farther away ceased talking and moved over to the table. The players deserted the other games, and the dancing-floor was forsaken, so that all stood at last, fivescore and more, in a compact and silent group, around the poker-table. The high betting had begun before the draw, and still the high betting went on, with the draw not in sight. Kearns had dealt, and French Louis had opened the pot with one marker—in his case one hundred dollars. Campbell had merely "seen" it, but Elam Harnish, coming next, had tossed in five hundred dollars, with the remark to MacDonald that he was letting him in easy.

MacDonald, glancing again at his hand, put in a thousand in markers. Kearns, debating a long time over his hand, finally "saw." It then cost French Louis nine hundred to remain in the game, which he contributed after a similar debate. It cost Campbell likewise nine hundred to remain and draw cards, but to the surprise of all he saw the nine hundred and raised another thousand.

"You-all are on the grade at last," Harnish remarked, as he saw the fifteen hundred and raised a thousand in turn. "Helen Breakfast's sure on top this divide, and you-all had best look out for bustin' harness."

"Me for that same lady," accompanied MacDonald's markers for two thousand and for an additional thousand-dollar raise.

It was at this stage that the players sat up and knew beyond peradventure that big hands were out. Though their features showed nothing, each man was beginning unconsciously to tense. Each man strove to appear his natural self, and each natural self was different. Hal Campbell affected his customary cautiousness. French Louis betrayed interest. MacDonald retained his whole-souled benevolence, though it seemed to take on a slightly exaggerated tone. Kearns was coolly dispassionate and noncommittal, while Elam Harnish appeared as quizzical and jocular as ever. Eleven thousand dollars were already in the pot, and the markers were heaped in a confused pile in the centre of the table.

"I ain't go no more markers," Kearns remarked plaintively. "We'd best begin I.O.U.'s."

"Glad you're going to stay," was MacDonald's cordial response.

"I ain't stayed yet. I've got a thousand in already. How's it stand now?"

"It'll cost you three thousand for a look in, but nobody will stop you from raising."

"Raise—hell. You must think I got a pat like yourself." Kearns looked at his hand. "But I'll tell you what I'll do, Mac. I've got a hunch, and I'll just see that three thousand."

He wrote the sum on a slip of paper, signed his name, and consigned it to the centre of the table.

French Louis became the focus of all eyes. He fingered his cards nervously for a space. Then, with a "By Gar! Ah got not one leetle beet hunch," he regretfully tossed his hand into the discards.

The next moment the hundred and odd pairs of eyes shifted to Campbell.

"I won't hump you, Jack," he said, contenting himself with calling the requisite two thousand.

The eyes shifted to Harnish, who scribbled on a piece of paper and shoved it forward.

"I'll just let you-all know this ain't no Sunday-school society of philanthropy," he said. "I see you, Jack, and I raise you a thousand. Here's where you-all get action on your pat, Mac."

"Action's what I fatten on, and I lift another thousand," was MacDonald's rejoinder. "Still got that hunch, Jack?"

"I still got the hunch." Kearns fingered his cards a long time. "And I'll play it, but you've got to know how I stand. There's my steamer, the *Bella*—worth twenty thousand if she's worth an ounce. There's Sixty Mile with five thousand in stock on the shelves. And you know I got a sawmill coming in. It's at Linderman now, and the scow is building. Am I good?"

"Dig in; you're sure good," was Daylight's answer. "And while we're about it, I may mention casual that I got twenty thousand in Mac's safe, there, and there's twenty thousand more in the ground on Moosehide. You know the ground, Campbell. Is they that-all in the dirt?"

"There sure is, Daylight."

"How much does it cost now?" Kearns asked.

"Two thousand to see."

"We'll sure hump you if you-all come in," Daylight warned him.

"It's an almighty good hunch," Kearns said, adding his slip for two thousand to the growing heap. "I can feel her crawlin' up and down my back."

"I ain't got a hunch, but I got a tolerable likeable hand," Campbell announced, as he slid in his slip; "but it's not a raising hand."

"Mine is," Daylight paused and wrote. "I see that thousand and raise her the same old thousand."

The Virgin, standing behind him, then did what a man's best friend was not privileged to do. Reaching over Daylight's shoulder, she picked up his hand and read it, at the same time shielding the faces of the five cards close to his chest. What she saw were three queens and a pair of eights, but nobody guessed what she saw. Every player's eyes were on her face as she scanned the cards, but no sign did she give. Her features might have been carved from ice, for her expression was precisely the same before, during, and after. Not a muscle quivered; nor was there the slightest dilation of a nostril, nor the slightest increase of light in the eyes. She laid the hand face down again on the table, and slowly the lingering eyes withdrew from her, having learned nothing.

MacDonald smiled benevolently. "I see you, Daylight, and I hump this time for two thousand. How's that hunch, Jack?"

"Still a-crawling, Mac. You got me now, but that hunch is a rip-snorter persuadin' sort of a critter, and it's my plain duty to ride it. I call for three thousand. And I got another hunch: Daylight's going to call, too."

"He sure is," Daylight agreed, after Campbell had thrown up his hand. "He knows when he's up against it, and he plays accordin'. I see that two thousand, and then I'll see the draw."

In a dead silence, save for the low voices of the three players, the draw was made. Thirty-four thousand dollars were already in the pot, and the play possibly not half over. To the Virgin's amazement, Daylight held up his three queens, discarding his eights and calling for two cards. And this time not even she dared look at what he had drawn. She knew her limit of control. Nor did he look. The two new cards lay face down on the table where they had been dealt to him.

"Cards?" Kearns asked of MacDonald.

"Got enough," was the reply.

"You can draw if you want to, you know," Kearns warned him.

"Nope; this'll do me."

Kearns himself drew two cards, but did not look at them.

Still Harnish let his cards lie.

"I never bet in the teeth of a pat hand," he said slowly, looking at the saloon-keeper. "You-all start her rolling, Mac."

MacDonald counted his cards carefully, to make doubly sure it was not a foul hand, wrote a sum on a paper slip, and slid it into the pot, with the simple utterance:—

"Five thousand."

Kearns, with every eye upon him, looked at his two-card draw, counted the other three to dispel any doubt of holding more than five cards, and wrote on a betting slip.

"I see you, Mac," he said, "and I raise her a little thousand just so as not to keep Daylight out."

The concentrated gaze shifted to Daylight. He likewise examined his draw and counted his five cards.

"I see that six thousand, and I raise her five thousand . . . just to try and keep you out, Jack."

"And I raise you five thousand just to lend a hand at keeping Jack out," MacDonald said, in turn.

His voice was slightly husky and strained, and a nervous twitch in the corner of his mouth followed speech.

Kearns was pale, and those who looked on noted that his hand trembled as he wrote his slip. But his voice was unchanged.

"I lift her along for five thousand," he said.

Daylight was now the centre. The kerosene lamps above flung high lights from the rash of sweat on his forehead. The bronze of his cheeks was darkened by the accession of blood. His black eyes glittered, and his nostrils were distended and eager. They were large nostrils, tokening his descent from savage ancestors who had survived by virtue of deep lungs and generous air-passages.

Yet, unlike MacDonald, his voice was firm and customary, and, unlike Kearns, his hand did not tremble when he wrote.

"I call, for ten thousand," he said. "Not that I'm afraid of you-all, Mac. It's that hunch of Jack's."

"I hump his hunch for five thousand just the same," said MacDonald. "I had the best hand before the draw, and I still guess I got it."

"Mebbe this is a case where a hunch after the draw is better'n the hunch before," Kearns remarked; "wherefore duty says, 'Lift her, Jack, lift her,' and so I lift her another five thousand."

Daylight leaned back in his chair and gazed up at the kerosene lamps while he computed aloud.

"I was in nine thousand before the draw, and I saw and raised eleven thousand —that makes thirty. I'm only good for ten more." He leaned forward and looked at Kearns. "So I call that ten thousand."

"You can raise if you want," Kearns answered. "Your dogs are good for five thousand in this game."

"Nary dawg. You-all can win my dust and dirt, but nary one of my dawgs. I just call."

MacDonald considered for a long time. No one moved or whispered. Not a muscle was relaxed on the part of the onlookers. Not the weight of a body shifted from one leg to the other. It was a sacred silence. Only could be heard the roaring draft of the huge stove, and from without, muffled by the log-walls, the howling of dogs. It was not every night that high stakes were played on the Yukon, and for that matter, this was the highest in the history of the country. The saloon-keeper finally spoke.

"If anybody else wins, they'll have to take a mortgage on the Tivoli."

The two other players nodded.

"So I call, too."

MacDonald added his slip for five thousand.

Not one of them claimed the pot, and not one of them called the size of his hand. Simultaneously and in silence they faced their cards on the table, while a general tiptoeing and craning of necks took place among the onlookers. Daylight showed four queens and an ace; MacDonald four jacks and an ace; and Kearns four kings and a trey. Kearns reached forward with an encircling movement of his arm and drew the pot in to him, his arm shaking as he did so.

Daylight picked the ace from his hand and tossed it over alongside MacDonald's ace, saying:—

"That's what cheered me along, Mac. I knowed it was only kings that could beat me, and he had them.

"What did you-all have?" he asked, all interest, turning to Campbell.

"Straight flush of four, open at both ends—a good drawing hand."

"You bet! You could a' made a straight, a straight flush, or a flush out of it."

"That's what I thought," Campbell said sadly. "It cost me six thousand before I quit."

"I wisht you-all'd drawn," Daylight laughed. "Then I wouldn't a' caught that fourth queen. Now I've got to take Billy Rawlins' mail contract and *mush* for Dyea. —What's the size of the killing, Jack?"

Kearns attempted to count the pot, but was too excited. Daylight drew it across to him, with firm fingers separating and stacking the markers and I.O.U.'s and with clear brain adding the sum.

"One hundred and twenty-seven thousand," he announced. "You-all can sell out now, Jack, and head for home."

The winner smiled and nodded, but seemed incapable of speech.

"I'd shout the drinks," MacDonald said, "only the house don't belong to me any more."

"Yes, it does," Kearns replied, first wetting his lips with his tongue. "Your note's good for any length of time. But the drinks are on me."

"Name your snake-juice, you-all—the winner pays!" Daylight called out loudly to all about him, at the same time rising from his chair and catching the Virgin by the arm. "Come on for a reel, you-all dancers. The night's young yet, and it's Helen Breakfast and the mail contract for me in the morning. Here, you-all Rawlins, you—I hereby do take over that same contract, and I start for salt water at nine A.M.—savvee? Come on, you-all! Where's that fiddler?"

1910

THE STRIKE

From *The Valley of the Moon*

Spring was on when the strike came in the railroad shops. The Sunday before it was called, Saxon and Billy had dinner at Bert's house. Saxon's brother came, though he had found it impossible to bring Sarah, who refused to budge from her household rut. Bert was blackly pessimistic, and they found him singing with sardonic glee:

"Nobody loves a mil-yun-aire.
Nobody likes his looks.
Nobody'll share his slightest care,
He classes with thugs and crooks.
Thriftiness has become a crime,
So spend everything you earn;
We're living now in a funny time,
When money is made to burn."

Mary went about the dinner preparation, flaunting unmistakable signals of rebellion; and Saxon, rolling up her sleeves and tying on an apron, washed the breakfast dishes. Bert fetched a pitcher of steaming beer from the corner saloon, and the three men smoked and talked about the coming strike.

"It oughta come years ago," was Bert's dictum. "It can't come any too quick now to suit me, but it's too late. We're beaten thumbs down. Here's where the last of the Mohegans gets theirs, in the neck, ker-whop!"

"Oh, I don't know," Tom, who had been smoking his pipe gravely, began to counsel. "Organized labor's gettin' stronger every day. Why, I can remember when there wasn't any unions in California. Look at us now—wages, an' hours, an' everything."

"You talk like an organizer," Bert sneered, "shovin' one bull con on the boneheads. But we know different. Organized wages won't buy as much now as unorganized wages used to buy. They've got us whipsawed. Look at Frisco, the labor leaders doin' dirtier politics than the old parties, pawin' an' squabblin' over graft, an' goin' to San Quentin, while—what are the Frisco carpenters doin'? Let me tell you one thing, Tom Brown, if you listen to all you hear you'll hear that every Frisco carpenter is union an' gettin' full union wages. Do you believe it? It's a damn lie. There ain't a carpenter that don't rebate his wages Saturday night to the contractor. An' that's your buildin' trades in San Francisco, while the leaders are makin' trips to Europe on the earnings of the tenderloin—when they ain't coughing it up to the lawyers to get out of wearin' stripes."

"That's all right," Tom concurred. "Nobody's denyin' it. The trouble is labor ain't quite got its eyes open. It ought to play politics, but the politics ought to be the right kind."

"Socialism, eh?" Bert caught him up with scorn. "Wouldn't they sell us out just as the Ruefs and Schmidts have?"

"Get men that are honest," Billy said. "That's the whole trouble. ––Not that I stand for socialism. I don't. All our folks was a long time in America, an' I for one won't stand for a lot of fat Germans an' greasy Russian Jews tellin' me how to run my country when they can't speak English yet."

"*Your* country!" Bert cried. "Why, you bonehead, you ain't got a country. That's a fairy story the grafters shove at you every time they want to rob you some more."

"But don't vote for the grafters," Billy contended. "If we selected honest men we'd get honest treatment."

"I wish you'd come to some of our meetings, Billy," Tom said wistfully. "If you would, you'd get your eyes open an' vote the socialist ticket next election."

"Not on your life," Billy declined. "When you catch me in a socialist meeting'll be when they can talk like white men."

Bert was humming:

"We're living now in a funny time,
When money is made to burn."

Mary was too angry with her husband, because of the impending strike and his incendiary utterances, to hold conversation with Saxon, and the latter, bepuzzled, listened to the conflicting opinions of the men.

"Where are we at?" she asked them, with a merriness that concealed her anxiety at heart.

"We ain't at," Bert snarled. "We're gone."

"But meat and oil have gone up again," she chafed. "And Billy's wages have been cut, and the shop men's were cut last year. Something must be done."

"The only thing to do is fight like hell," Bert answered. "Fight, an' go down fightin'. That's all. We're licked anyhow, but we can have a last run for our money."

"That's no way to talk," Tom rebuked.

"The time for talkin' 's past, old cock. The time for fightin' 's come."

"A hell of a chance you'd have against regular troops and machine guns," Billy retorted.

"Oh, not that way. There's such things as greasy sticks that go up with a loud noise and leave holes. There's such things as emery powder––"

"Oh, ho!" Mary burst out upon him, arms akimbo. "So that's what it means. That's what the emery in your vest pocket meant."

Her husband ignored her. Tom smoked with a troubled air. Billy was hurt. It showed plainly in his face.

"You ain't ben doin' that, Bert?" he asked, his manner showing his expectancy of his friend's denial.

"Sure thing, if you want to know. I'd see'm all in hell if I could, before I go."

"He's a bloody-minded anarchist," Mary complained. "Men like him killed McKinley, and Garfield, an'–an'–an' all the rest. He'll be hung. You'll see. Mark my words. I'm glad there's no children in sight, that's all."

"It's hot air," Billy comforted her.

"He's just teasing you," Saxon soothed. "He always was a josher."

But Mary shook her head.

"I know. I hear him talkin' in his sleep. He swears and curses something awful, an' grits his teeth. Listen to him now."

Bert, his handsome face bitter and devil-may-care, had tilted his chair back against the wall and was singing:

"Nobody loves a mil-yun-aire,
Nobody likes his looks,
Nobody'll share his slightest care,
He classes with thugs and crooks."

Tom was saying something about reasonableness and justice, and Bert ceased from singing to catch him up.

"Justice, eh? Another pipe-dream. I'll show you where the working class gets justice. You remember Forbes—J. Alliston Forbes—wrecked the Alta California Trust Company an' salted down two cold millions. I saw him yesterday, in a big hell-bent automobile. What'd he get? Eight years' sentence. How long did he serve? Less'n two years. Pardoned out on account of ill health. Ill hell! We'll be dead an' rotten before he kicks the bucket. Here. Look out this window. You see the back of that house with the broken porch rail. Mrs. Danaker lives there. She takes in washin'. Her old man was killed on the railroad. Nitsky on damages—contributory negligence, or fellow-servant-something-or-other flimflam. That's what the courts handed her. Her boy, Archie, was sixteen. He was on the road, a regular road-kid. He blew into Fresno an' rolled a drunk. Do you want to know how much he got? Two dollars and eighty cents. Get that? ——Two-eighty. And what did the alfalfa judge hand'm? Fifty years. He's served eight of it already in San Quentin. And he'll go on serving it till he croaks. Mrs. Danaker says he's bad with consumption—caught it inside, but she ain't got the pull to get'm pardoned. Archie the Kid steals two dollars an' eighty cents from a drunk and gets fifty years. J. Alliston Forbes sticks up the Alta Trust for two millions an' gets less'n two years. Who's country is this anyway? Yourn an' Archie the Kid's? Guess again. It's J. Alliston Forbes' ——Oh:

"Nobody likes a mil-yun-aire,
Nobody likes his looks,
Nobody'll share his slightest care,
He classes with thugs and crooks."

Mary, at the sink, where Saxon was just finishing the last dish, untied Saxon's apron and kissed her with the sympathy that women alone feel for each other under the shadow of maternity.

"Now you sit down, dear. You mustn't tire yourself, and it's a long way to go yet. I'll get your sewing for you, and you can listen to the men talk. But don't listen to Bert. He's crazy."

Saxon sewed and listened, and Bert's face grew bleak and bitter as he contemplated the baby clothes in her lap.

"There you go," he blurted out, "bringin' kids into the world when you ain't got any guarantee you can feed 'em."

"You must a-had a souse last night," Tom grinned.

Bert shook his head.

"Aw, what's the use of gettin' grouched?" Billy cheered. "It's a pretty good country."

"It *was* a pretty good country," Bert replied, "when we was all Mohegans. But not now. We're jiggerooed. We're hornswoggled. We're backed to a standstill. We're double-crossed to a fare-you-well. My folks fought for this country. So did yourn, all of you. We freed the niggers, killed the Indians, an' starved, an' froze, an' sweat, an' fought. This land looked good to us. We cleared it, an' broke it, an' made the roads, an' built the cities. And there was plenty for everybody. And we went on fightin' for it. I had two uncles killed at Gettysburg. All of us was mixed up in that war. Listen to Saxon talk any time what her folks went through to get out here an' get ranches, an' horses, an' cattle, an' everything. And they got 'em. All our folks got 'em, Mary's, too—"

"And if they'd ben smart they'd a-held on to them," she interpolated.

"Sure thing," Bert continued. "That's the very point. We're the losers. We've ben robbed. We couldn't mark cards, deal from the bottom, an' ring in cold decks like the others. We're the white folks that failed. You see, times changed, and there was two kinds of us, the lions and the plugs. The plugs only worked, the lions only gobbled. They gobbled the farms, the mines, the factories, an' now they've gobbled the government. We're the white folks an' the children of white folks, that was too busy being good to be smart. We're the white folks that lost out. We're the ones that's ben skinned. D'ye get me?"

"You'd make a good soap-boxer," Tom commended, "if only you'd get the kinks straightened out in your reasoning."

"It sounds all right, Bert," Billy said, "only it ain't. Any man can get rich to-day—"

"Or be president of the United States," Bert snapped. "Sure thing—if he's got it in him. Just the same I ain't heard you makin' a noise like a millionaire or a president. Why? You ain't got it in you. You're a bonehead. A plug. That's why. Skiddoo for you. Skiddoo for all of us."

At the table, while they ate, Tom talked of the joys of farm-life he had known as a boy and as a young man, and confided that it was his dream to go and take up government land somewhere as his people had done before him. Unfortunately, as he explained, Sarah was set, so that the dream must remain a dream.

"It's all in the game," Billy sighed. "It's played to rules. Some one has to get knocked out, I suppose." . . .

"Hey, Bill, you seem to think I've got a grouch. Sure thing. I have. You ain't had my experiences. You've always done teamin' an' pulled down easy money prize-fightin'. You ain't known hard times. You ain't ben through strikes. You ain't had to take care of an old mother an' swallow dirt on her account. It wasn't until after she died that I could rip loose an' take or leave as I felt like it.

"Take that time I tackled the Niles Electric an' see what a work-plug gets handed out to him. The Head Cheese sizes me up, pumps me a lot of questions, an' gives me an application blank. I made it out, payin' a dollar to a doctor they sent me to for a health certificate. Then I got to go to a picture garage an' get my mug taken—for the Niles Electric rogues' gallery. And I cough up another dollar for the mug. The Head Squirt takes the blank, the health certificate, and the mug, an' fires more questions. *Did I belong to a labor union?* —ME? Of course I told'm the truth I guess nit. I needed the job. The grocery wouldn't give me any more tick, and there was my mother.

"Huh, thinks I, here's where I'm a real carman. Back platform for me, where I can pick up the fancy skirts. Nitsky. Two dollars, please. Me—my two dollars. All for a pewter badge. Then there was the uniform—nineteen fifty, and get it anywhere else for fifteen. Only that was to be paid out of my first month. And then five dollars in change in my pocket, my own money. That was the rule. —I borrowed that five from Tom Donovan, the policeman. Then what? They worked me for two weeks without pay, breakin' me in."

"Did you pick up any fancy skirts?" Saxon queried teasingly.

Bert shook his head glumly.

"I only worked a month. Then we organized, and they busted our union higher'n a kite."

"And you boobs in the shops will be busted the same way if you go out on strike," Mary informed him.

"That's what I've ben tellin' you all along," Bert replied. "We ain't got a chance to win."

"Then why go out?" was Saxon's question.

He looked at her with lack-luster eyes for a moment, then answered:

"Why did my two uncles get killed at Gettysburg?"

Saxon went about her housework greatly troubled. She no longer devoted herself to the making of pretties. The materials cost money, and she did not dare. Bert's thrust had sunk home. It remained in her quivering consciousness like a shaft of steel that ever turned and rankled. She and Billy were responsible for this coming young life. Could they be sure, after all, that they could adequately feed and clothe it and prepare it for its way in the world? Where was the guaranty? She remembered, dimly, the blight of hard times in the past, and the plaints of fathers and mothers in those days returned to her with a new significance. Almost could she understand Sarah's chronic complaining.

Hard times were already in the neighborhood, where lived the families of the shopmen who had gone out on strike. Among the small storekeepers, Saxon, in the course of the daily marketing, could sense the air of despondency. Light and geniality seemed to have vanished. Gloom pervaded everywhere. The mothers of the children that played in the streets showed the gloom plainly in their faces. When they gossiped in the evenings, over front gates and on door stoops, their voices were subdued and less of laughter rang out.

Mary Donahue, who had taken three pints from the milkman, now took one pint. There were no more family trips to the moving picture shows. Scrap-meat was harder to get from the butcher. Nora Delaney, in the third house, no longer bought fresh fish for Friday. Salted codfish, not of the best quality, was now on her table. The sturdy children that ran out upon the street between meals with huge slices of bread and butter and sugar now came out with no sugar and with thinner slices spread more thinly with butter. The very custom was dying out, and some children already had desisted from piecing between meals.

Everywhere was manifest a pinching and scraping, a tightening and shortening down of expenditure. And everywhere was more irritation. Women became angered with one another, and with the children, more quickly than of yore; and Saxon knew that Bert and Mary bickered incessantly.

"If she'd only realize I've got troubles of my own," Bert complained to Saxon.

She looked at him closely, and felt fear for him in a vague, numb way. His black eyes seemed to burn with a continuous madness. The brown face was leaner, the skin drawn tightly across the cheekbones. A slight twist had come to the mouth, which seemed frozen into bitterness. The very carriage of his body and the way he wore his hat advertised a recklessness more intense than had been his in the past.

Sometimes, in the long afternoons, sitting by the window with idle hands, she caught herself reconstructing in her vision that folk-migration of her people across the plains and mountains and deserts to the sunset land by the Western sea. And often she found herself dreaming of the arcadian days of her people, when they had not lived in cities nor been vexed with labor unions and employers' associations. She would remember the old people's tales of self-sufficingness, when they shot or raised their own meat, grew their own vegetables, were their own blacksmiths and carpenters, made their own shoes—yes, and spun the cloth of the clothes they wore. And something of the wistfulness in Tom's face she could see as she recollected it when he talked of his dream of taking up government land.

A farmer's life must be fine, she thought. Why was it that people had to live in cities? Why had times changed? If there had been enough in the old days, why was there not enough now? Why was it necessary for men to quarrel and jangle, and strike and fight, all about the matter of getting work? Why wasn't there work for all? ——Only that morning, and she shuddered with the recollection, she had seen two scabs, on their way to work, beaten up by the strikers, by men she knew by sight, and some by name, who lived in the neighborhood. It had happened directly across the street. It had been cruel, terrible—a dozen men on two. The children had begun it by throwing rocks at the scabs and cursing them in ways children should not know. Policemen had run upon the scene with drawn revolvers, and the strikers had retreated into the houses and through the narrow alleys between the houses. One of the scabs, unconscious, had been carried away in an ambulance; the other, assisted by special railroad police, had been taken away to the shops. At him, Mary Donahue, standing on her front stoop, her child in her arms, had hurled such vile abuse that it had brought the blush of shame to Saxon's cheeks. On the stoop of the house on the other side, Saxon had noted Mercedes, in the height of the beating up, looking on with a queer smile. She had seemed very eager to witness, her nostrils dilated and swelling like the beat of pulses as she watched. It had struck Saxon at the time that the old woman was quite unalarmed and only curious to see.

To Mercedes, who was so wise in love, Saxon went for explanation of what was the matter with the world. But the old woman's wisdom in affairs industrial and economic was cryptic and unpalatable.

"La la, my dear, it is so simple. Most men are born stupid. They are the slaves. A few are born clever. They are the masters. God made men so, I suppose."

"Then how about God and that terrible beating across the street this morning?"

"I'm afraid he was not interested," Mercedes smiled. "I doubt he even knows that it happened."

"I was frightened to death," Saxon declared. "I was made sick by it. And yet you —I saw you—you looked on as cool as you please, as if it was a show."

"It was a show, my dear."

"Oh, how could you?"

"La la, I have seen men killed. It is nothing strange. All men die. The stupid ones die like oxen, they know not why. It is quite funny to see. They strike each other with fists and clubs, and break each other's heads. It is gross. They are like a lot of animals. They are like dogs wrangling over bones. Jobs are bones, you know. Now, if they fought for women, or ideas, or bars of gold, or fabulous diamonds, it would be splendid. But no; they are only hungry, and fight over scraps for their stomach."

"Oh, if I could only understand!" Saxon murmured, her hands tightly clasped in anguish of incomprehension and vital need to know.

"There is nothing to understand. It is clear as print. There have always been the stupid and the clever, the slave and the master, the peasant and the prince. There always will be."

"But why?"

"Why is a peasant a peasant, my dear? Because he is a peasant. Why is a flea a flea?"

Saxon tossed her head fretfully.

"Oh, but my dear, I have answered. The philosophies of the world can give no better answer. Why do you like your man for a husband rather than any other man? Because you like him that way, that is all. Why do you like? Because you like. Why does fire burn and frost bite? Why are there clever men and stupid men? masters and slaves? employers and workingmen? Why is black black? Answer that and you answer everything."

"But it is not right that men should go hungry and without work when they want to work if only they can get a square deal," Saxon protested.

"Oh, but it is right, just as it is right that stone won't burn like wood, that sea sand isn't sugar, that thorns prick, that water is wet, that smoke rises, that things fall down and not up."

But such doctrine of reality made no impression on Saxon. Frankly, she could not comprehend. It seemed like so much nonsense.

"Then we have no liberty and independence," she cried passionately. "One man is not as good as another. My child has not the right to live that a rich mother's child has."

"Certainly not," Mercedes answered.

"Yet all my people fought for these things," Saxon urged, remembering her school history and the sword of her father.

"Democracy—the dream of the stupid peoples. Oh, la la, my dear, democracy is a lie, an enchantment to keep the work brutes content, just as religion used to keep them content. When they groaned in their misery and toil, they were persuaded to keep on in their misery and toil by pretty tales of a land beyond the skies where they would live famously and fat while the clever ones roasted in everlasting fire. Ah, how the clever ones must have chuckled! And when that lie wore out, and democracy was dreamed, the clever ones saw to it that it should be in truth a dream, nothing but a dream. The world belongs to the great and clever."

"But you are of the working people," Saxon charged.

The old woman drew herself up, and almost was angry.

"I? Of the working people? My dear, because I had misfortune with moneys invested, because I am old and can no longer win the brave young men, because I have outlived the men of my youth and there is no one to go to, because I live here in the ghetto with Barry Higgins and prepare to die—why, my dear, I was born with the masters, and have trod all my days on the necks of the stupid. I have drunk rare wines and sat at feasts that would have supported this neighborhood for a lifetime. Dick Golden and I—it was Dickie's money, but I could have had it—Dick Golden and I dropped four hundred thousand francs in a week's play at Monte Carlo. He was a Jew, but he was a spender. In India I have worn jewels that could have saved the lives of ten thousand families dying before my eyes."

"You saw them die? . . . and did nothing?" Saxon asked aghast.

"I kept my jewels—la la, and was robbed of them by a brute of a Russian officer within the year."

"And you let them die," Saxon reiterated.

"They were cheap spawn. They fester and multiply like maggots. They meant nothing—nothing, my dear, nothing. No more than your work people mean here, whose crowning stupidity is their continuing to beget more stupid spawn for the slavery of the masters."

So it was that while Saxon could get little glimmering of common sense from others, from the terrible old woman she got none at all. Nor could Saxon bring herself to believe much of what she considered Mercedes' romancing. As the weeks passed, the strike in the railroad shops grew bitter and deadly. Billy shook his head and confessed his inability to make head or tail of the troubles that were looming on the labor horizon.

"I don't get the hang of it," he told Saxon. "It's a mix-up. It's like a roughhouse with the lights out. Look at us teamsters. Here we are, the talk just starting of going out on sympathetic strike for the mill-workers. They've ben out a week, most of their places is filled, an' if us teamsters keep on haulin' the mill-work the strike's lost."

"Yet you didn't consider striking for yourselves when your wages were cut," Saxon said with a frown.

"Oh, we wasn't in position then. But now the Frisco teamsters and the whole Frisco Water Front Confederation is liable to back us up. Anyway, we're just talkin' about it, that's all. But if we do go out, we'll try to get back that ten per cent cut."

"It's rotten politics," he said another time. "Everybody's rotten. If we'd only wise up and agree to pick out honest men——"

"But if you, and Bert, and Tom can't agree, how do you expect all the rest to agree?" Saxon asked.

"It gets me," he admitted. "It's enough to give a guy the willies thinkin' about it. And yet it's plain as the nose on your face. Get honest men for politics, an' the whole thing's straightened out. Honest men'd make honest laws, an' then honest men'd get their dues. But Bert wants to smash things, an' Tom smokes his pipe and dreams pipe dreams about by an' by when everybody votes the way he thinks. But this by an' by ain't the point. We want things now. Tom says we can't get them now, an' Bert says we ain't never goin' to get them. What can a fellow do when everybody's of different minds? Look at the socialists themselves. They're always disagreeing, splittin' up, an' firin' each other out of the party. The whole thing's bughouse, that's what, an' I almost get dippy myself thinkin' about it. The point I can't get out of my mind is that we want things now." . . .

It began quietly, as the fateful unexpected so often begins. Children, of all ages and sizes, were playing in the street, and Saxon, by the open front window, was watching them and dreaming day dreams of her child soon to be. The sunshine mellowed peacefully down, and a light wind from the bay cooled the air and gave to it a tang of salt. One of the children pointed up Pine Street toward Seventh. All the children ceased playing, and stared and pointed. They formed into groups, the larger boys, of from ten to twelve, by themselves, the older girls anxiously clutching the small children by the hands or gathering them into their arms.

Saxon could not see the cause of all this, but she could guess when she saw the larger boys rush to the gutter, pick up stones, and sneak into the alleys between the houses. Smaller boys tried to imitate them. The girls, dragging the tots by the arms, banged gates and clattered up the front steps of the small houses. The doors slammed behind them, and the street was deserted, though here and there front shades were drawn aside so that anxious-faced women might peer forth. Saxon heard the uptown train puffing and snorting as it pulled out from Center Street. Then, from the direction of Seventh, came a hoarse, throaty manroar. Still, she could see nothing, and she remembered Mercedes Higgins' words: "*They are like dogs wrangling over bones. Jobs are bones, you know.*"

The roar came closer, and Saxon, leaning out, saw a dozen scabs, conveyed by as many special police and Pinkertons, coming down the sidewalk on her side of the street. They came compactly, as if with discipline, while behind, disorderly, yelling confusedly, stooping to pick up rocks, were seventy-five or a hundred of the striking shopmen. Saxon discovered herself trembling with apprehension, knew that she must not, and controlled herself. She was helped in this by the conduct of Mercedes Higgins. The old woman came out of her front door, dragging a chair, on which she coolly seated herself on the tiny stoop at the top of the steps.

In the hands of the special police were clubs. The Pinkertons carried no visible weapons. The strikers, urging on from behind, seemed content with yelling their rage and threats, and it remained for the children to precipitate the conflict. From across the street, between the Olsen and the Isham houses, came a shower of stones. Most of these fell short, though one struck a scab on the head. The man was no more than twenty feet away from Saxon. He reeled toward her front picket fence, drawing a revolver. With one hand he brushed the blood from his eyes and with the other he discharged the revolver into the Isham house. A Pinkerton seized his arm to prevent a second shot, and dragged him along. At the same instant a wilder roar went up from the strikers, while a volley of stones came from between Saxon's house and Maggie Donahue's. The scabs and their protectors made a stand, drawing revolvers. From their hard, determined faces—fighting men by profession—Saxon could augur nothing but bloodshed and death. An elderly man, evidently the leader, lifted a soft felt hat and mopped the perspiration from the bald top of his head. He was a large man, very rotund of belly and helpless looking. His gray beard was stained with streaks of tobacco juice, and he was smoking a cigar. He was stoop-shouldered, and Saxon noted the dandruff on the collar of his coat.

One of the men pointed into the street, and several of his companions laughed. The cause of it was the little Olsen boy, barely four years old, escaped somehow from his mother and toddling toward his economic enemies. In his right he bore a rock so heavy that he could scarcely lift it. With this he feebly threatened them. His rosy little face was convulsed with rage, and he was screaming over and over: "Dam scabs! Dam scabs! Dam scabs!" The laughter with which they greeted him only increased his fury. He toddled closer, and with a mighty exertion threw the rock. It fell a scant six feet beyond his hand.

This much Saxon saw, and also Mrs. Olsen rushing into the street for her child. A rattling of revolver-shots from the strikers drew Saxon's attention to the men beneath her. One of them cursed sharply and examined the biceps of his left arm, which hung limply by his side. Down the hand she saw the blood beginning to drip. She knew she ought not remain and watch, but the memory of her fighting forefathers was with her, while she possessed no more than normal human fear—if anything, less. She forgot her child in the eruption of battle that had broken upon her quiet street. And she forgot the strikers, and everything else, in amazement at what had happened to the round-bellied, cigar-smoking leader. In some strange way, she knew not how, his head had become wedged at the neck between the tops of the pickets of her fence. His body hung down outside, the knees not quite touching the ground. His hat had fallen off, and the sun was making an astounding high light on his bald spot. The cigar, too, was gone. She saw he was looking at her. One hand, between the pickets, seemed waving at her, and almost he seemed to wink at her jocosely, though she knew it to be the contortion of deadly pain.

Possibly a second, or, at most, two seconds, she gazed at this, when she was aroused by Bert's voice. He was running along the sidewalk, in front of her house, and behind him charged several more strikers, while he shouted: "Come on, you Mohegans! We got 'em nailed to the cross!"

In his left hand he carried a pick-handle, in his right a revolver, already empty, for he clicked the cylinder vainly around as he ran. With an abrupt stop, dropping the pick-handle, he whirled half about, facing Saxon's gate. He was sinking down, when he straightened himself to throw the revolver into the face of a scab who was jumping toward him. Then he began swaying, at the same time sagging at the knees and waist. Slowly, with infinite effort, he caught a gate picket in his right hand, and, still slowly, as if lowering himself, sank down, while past him leaped the crowd of strikers he had led.

It was battle without quarter—a massacre. The scabs and their protectors, surrounded, backed against Saxon's fence, fought like cornered rats, but could not withstand the rush of a hundred men. Clubs and pick-handles were swinging, revolvers were exploding, and cobblestones were flung with crushing effect at arm's distance. Saxon saw young Frank Davis, a friend of Bert's and a father of several months' standing, press the muzzle of his revolver against a scab's stomach and fire. There were curses and snarls of rage, wild cries of terror and pain. Mercedes was right. These things were not men. They were beasts, fighting over bones, destroying one another for bones.

Jobs are bones; jobs are bones. The phrase was an incessant iteration in Saxon's brain. Much as she might have wished it, she was powerless now to withdraw from the window. It was as if she were paralyzed. Her brain no longer worked. She sat numb, staring, incapable of anything save seeing the rapid horror before her eyes that flashed along like a moving picture film gone mad. She saw Pinkertons, special police, and strikers go down. One scab, terribly wounded, on his knees and begging for mercy, was kicked in the face. As he sprawled backward, another striker, standing over him, fired a revolver into his chest, quickly and deliberately, again and again, until the weapon was empty. Another scab, backed over the pickets by a hand clutching his throat, had his face pulped by a revolver butt. Again and again, continually, the revolver rose and fell, and Saxon knew the man who wielded it—Chester Johnson. She had met him at dances and danced with him in the days before she was married. He had always been kind and good natured. She remembered the Friday night, after a City Hall band concert, when he had taken her and two other girls to Tony's Tamale Grotto on Thirteenth street. And after that they had all gone to Pabst's Café and drunk a glass of beer before they went home. It was impossible that this could be the same Chester Johnson. And as she looked, she saw the round-bellied leader, still wedged by the neck between the pickets, draw a revolver with his free hand, and, squinting horribly sidewise, press the muzzle against Chester's side. She tried to scream a warning. She did scream, and Chester looked up and saw her. At that moment the revolver went off, and he collapsed prone upon the body of the scab. And the bodies of three men hung on her picket fence.

Anything could happen now. Quite without surprise, she saw the strikers leaping the fence, trampling her few little geraniums and pansies into the earth as they fled between Mercedes' house and hers. Up Pine street, from the railroad yards, was coming a rush of railroad police and Pinkertons, firing as they ran. While down Pine street, gongs clanging, horses at a gallop, came three patrol wagons packed with police. The strikers were in a trap. The only way out was between the houses and over the back yard fences. The jam in the narrow alley prevented them all from escaping. A dozen were cornered in the angle between the front of her house and the steps. And as they had done, so were they done by. No effort was made to arrest. They were clubbed down and shot down to the last man by the guardians of the peace who were infuriated by what had been wreaked on their brethren.

It was all over, and Saxon, moving as in a dream, clutching the banister tightly, came down the front steps. The round-bellied leader still leered at her and fluttered one hand, though two big policemen were just bending to extricate him. The gate was off its hinges, which seemed strange, for she had been watching all the time and had not seen it happen.

Bert's eyes were closed. His lips were blood-flecked, and there was a gurgling in his throat as if he were trying to say something. As she stooped above him, with her handkerchief brushing the blood from his cheek where some one had stepped on him, his eyes opened. The old defiant light was in them. He did not know her. The lips moved, and faintly, almost reminiscently, he murmured, "The last of the Mohegans, the last of the Mohegans." Then he groaned, and the eyelids drooped down again. He was not dead. She knew that. The chest still rose and fell, and the gurgling still continued in his throat.

She looked up. Mercedes stood beside her. The old woman's eyes were very bright, her withered cheeks flushed.

"Will you help me carry him into the house?" Saxon asked.

Mercedes nodded, turned to a sergeant of police, and made the request to him. The sergeant gave a swift glance at Bert, and his eyes were bitter and ferocious as he refused:

"To hell with 'm. We'll care for our own."

"Maybe you and I can do it," Saxon said.

"Don't be a fool." Mercedes was beckoning to Mrs. Olsen across the street. "You go into the house, little mother that is to be. This is bad for you. We'll carry him in. Mrs. Olsen is coming, and we'll get Maggie Donahue."

Saxon led the way into the back bedroom which Billy had insisted on furnishing. As she opened the door, the carpet seemed to fly up into her face as with the force of a blow, for she remembered Bert had laid that carpet. And as the women placed him on the bed she recalled that it was Bert and she, between them, who had set the bed up one Sunday morning.

And then she felt very queer, and was surprised to see Mercedes regarding her with questioning, searching eyes. After that her queerness came on very fast, and she descended into the hell of pain that is given to women alone to know. She was supported, half-carried, to the front bedroom. Many faces were about her—Mercedes, Mrs. Olsen, Maggie Donahue. It seemed she must ask Mrs. Olsen if she had saved little Emil from the street, but Mercedes cleared Mrs. Olsen out to look after Bert, and Maggie Donahue went to answer a knock at the front door. From the street came a loud hum of voices, punctuated by shouts and commands, and from time to time there was a clanging of the gongs of ambulances and patrol wagons. Then appeared the fat, comfortable face of Martha Skelton, and, later, Doctor Hentley came. Once, in a clear interval, through the thin wall Saxon heard the high opening notes of Mary's hysteria. And, another time, she heard Mary repeating over and over: "I'll never go back to the laundry. Never. Never."

1913

ROUNDING THE CAPE

From *The Mutiny of the Elsinore*

I wonder. I wonder. Did the Samurai [Captain West] make a mistake? Or was it the darkness of oncoming death that chilled and clouded that star-cool brain of his and made a mock of all his wisdom? Or was it the blunder that brought death upon him beforehand? I do not know, I shall never know; for it is a matter no one of us dreams of hinting at, much less discussing.

I shall begin at the beginning—yesterday afternoon. For it was yesterday afternoon, five weeks to a day since we emerged from the Straits of Le Maire into this gray storm-ocean, that once again we found ourselves hove to directly off the Horn. At the changing of the watches at four o'clock, Captain West gave the command to Mr. Pike to wear ship. We were on the starboard tack at the time, making leeway off shore. This maneuver placed us on the port tack, and the consequent leeway, to me, seemed on shore, though at an acute angle, to be sure.

In the chart-room, glancing curiously at the chart, I measured the distance with my eye and decided that we were in the neighborhood of fifteen miles off Cape Horn.

"With our drift we'll be close up under the land by morning, won't we?" I ventured tentatively.

"Yes," Captain West nodded, "and if it weren't for the West Wind Drift, and if the land did not trend to the northeast, we'd be ashore by morning. As it is, we'll be well under it at daylight, ready to steal around if there is a change, ready to wear ship if there is no change."

It did not enter my head to question his judgment. What he said had to be. Was he not the Samurai?

And yet, a few minutes later, when he had gone below, I noticed Mr. Pike enter the chart-house. After several paces up and down and a brief pause to watch Nancy and several men shift the weather-cloth from lee to weather, I strolled aft to the chart-house. Prompted by I know not what, I peeped through one of the glass ports.

There stood Mr. Pike, his sou'wester doffed, his oilskins streaming rivulets to the floor while he, dividers and parallel rulers in hand, bent over the chart. It was the expression of his face that startled me. The habitual sourness had vanished. All that I could see was anxiety and apprehension . . . yes, and age. I had never seen him look so old; for there, at that moment, I beheld the wastage and weariness of all his sixty-nine years of sea-battling and sea-staring.

I slipped away from the port and went along the deck to the break of the poop, where I held on and stood staring through the gray and spray in the conjectural direction of our drift. Somewhere, there, in the northeast and north, I knew was a broken, iron coast of rocks upon which the graybeards thundered. And there, in the chart-room, a redoubtable sailorman bent anxiously over a chart as he measured and calculated, and measured and calculated again, our position and our drift.

And I knew it could not be. It was not the Samurai but the henchman who was weak and wrong. Age was beginning to tell upon him at last, which could not be otherwise than expected when one considered that no man in ten thousand had weathered age so successfully as he.

I laughed at my moment's qualm of foolishness and went below, well content to meet my loved one and to rest secure in her father's wisdom. Of course he was right. He had proved himself right too often already on the long voyage from Baltimore.

At dinner, Mr. Pike was quite distrait. He took no part whatever in the conversation, and seemed always to be listening to something from without—to the vexing clang of taut ropes that came down the hollow jiggermast, to the muffled roar of the gale in the rigging, to the smash and crash of the seas along our decks and against our iron walls.

Again I found myself sharing his apprehension, although I was too discreet to question him then, or afterward alone, about his trouble. At eight he went on deck again to take the watch till midnight, and as I went to bed I dismissed all forebodings and speculated as to how many more voyages he could last after this sudden onslaught of old age.

I fell asleep quickly, and awoke at midnight, my lamp still burning, Conrad's "Mirror of the Sea" on my breast where it had dropped from my hands. I heard the watches change, and was wide awake and reading when Mr. Pike came below by the booby hatch and passed down my hall by my open door, on his way to his room.

In the pause I had long since learned so well, I knew he was rolling a cigarette. Then I heard him cough, as he always did, when the cigarette was lighted and the first inhalation of smoke flushed his lungs.

At twelve-fifteen, in the midst of Conrad's delightful chapter, "The Weight of the Burden," I heard Mr. Pike come along the hall.

Stealing a glance over the top of my book, I saw him go by, sea-booted, oilskinned, sou'westered. It was his watch below, and his sleep was meager in this perpetual bad weather, yet he was going on deck.

I read and waited for an hour, but he did not return; and I knew that somewhere up above he was staring into the driving dark. I dressed fully, in all my heavy storm-gear, from sea-boots and sou'wester to sheepskin under my oilskin coat. At the foot of the stairs I noted along the hall that Margaret's light was burning. I peeped in—she keeps her door open for ventilation—and found her reading.

"Merely not sleepy," she assured me.

Nor in the heart of me do I believe she had any apprehension. She does not know even now, I am confident, the Samurai's blunder—if blunder it was. As she said, she was merely not sleepy, although there is no telling in what occult ways she may have received though not recognized Mr. Pike's anxiety.

At the head of the stairs, passing along the tiny hall to go out the lee door of the chart-house, I glanced into the chart-room. On the couch, lying on his back, his head uncomfortably high I thought, slept Captain West. The room was warm from the ascending heat of the cabin, so that he lay unblanketed, fully dressed save for oilskins and boots. He breathed easily and steadily, and the lean, ascetic lines of his face seemed softened by the light of the low-turned lamp. And that one glance restored to me all my surety and faith in his wisdom, so that I laughed at myself for having left my warm bed for a freezing trip on deck.

Under the weather cloth at the break of the poop, I found Mr. Mellaire. He was wide awake, but under no strain. Evidently it had not entered his mind to consider, much less question, the maneuver of wearing ship the previous afternoon.

"The gale is breaking," he told me, waving his mittened hand at a starry-segment of sky momentarily exposed by the thinning clouds.

But where was Mr. Pike? Did the second mate know he was on deck? I proceeded to feel Mr. Mellaire out as we worked our way aft along the mad poop toward the wheel. I talked about the difficulty of sleeping in stormy weather, stated the restlessness and semi-insomnia that the violent motion of the ship caused in me, and raised the query of how bad weather affected the officers.

"I noticed Captain West, in the chart-room, as I came up, sleeping like a baby," I concluded.

We leaned in the lee of the chart-house and went no further.

"Trust us to sleep just the same way, Mr. Pathurst," the second mate laughed. "The harder the weather the harder the demand on us, and the harder we sleep. I'm dead the moment my head touches the pillow. It takes Mr. Pike longer, because he always finishes his cigarette after he turns in. But he smokes while he's undressing, so that he doesn't require more than a minute to go deado. I'll wager he hasn't moved, right now, since ten minutes after twelve."

So the second mate did not dream the first was even then on deck. I went below to make sure. A small sea-lamp was burning in Mr. Pike's room, and I saw his bunk unoccupied. I went in by the big stove in the dining-room and warmed up, then again came on deck. I did not go near the weather-cloth, where I was certain Mr. Mellaire was; but, keeping along the lee of the poop, I gained the bridge and started for'ard.

I was in no hurry, so I paused often in that cold, wet journey. The gale was breaking, for again and again the stars glimmered through the thinning storm-clouds. On the 'midship house was no Mr. Pike. I crossed it, stung by the freezing, flying spray, and carefully reconnoitered the top of the for'ard house, where, in such bad weather, I knew the lookout was stationed. I was within twenty feet of them, when a wider clearance of starry sky showed me the figures of the lookout, whoever he was, and of Mr. Pike, side by side. Long I watched them, not making my presence known, and I knew that the old mate's eyes were boring like gimlets into the windy darkness that separated the *Elsinore* from the thunder-surfed iron coast he sought to find.

Coming back to the poop, I was caught by the surprised Mr. Mellaire.

"Thought you were asleep, sir," he chided.

"I'm too restless," I explained. "I've read until my eyes are tired, and now I'm trying to get chilled so that I can fall asleep while warming up in my blankets."

"I envy you, sir," he answered. "Think of it! So much of all night in that you cannot sleep. Some day, if ever I make a lucky strike, I shall make a voyage like this as a passenger, and have all watches below. Think of it! All blessed watches below! And I shall, like you, sir, bring a Jap servant along, and I'll make him call me at every changing of the watches, so that, wide awake, I can appreciate my good fortune in the several minutes before I roll over and go to sleep again."

We laughed good night to each other. Another peep into the chart-room showed me Captain West sleeping as before. He had not moved in general, though all his body moved with every roll and fling of the ship. Below, Margaret's light still burned, but a peep showed her asleep, her book fallen from her hands just as was the so frequent case with my books.

And I wondered. Half the souls of us on the *Elsinore* slept. The Samurai slept. Yet the old first mate, who should have slept, kept a bitter watch on the for'ard house. Was his anxiety right? Could it be right? Or was it the crankiness of ultimate age? Were we drifting and leewaying to destruction? Or was it merely an old man being struck down by senility in the midst of his life-task?

Too wide awake to think of sleeping, I ensconced myself with "The Mirror of the Sea" at the dining table. Nor did I remove aught of my storm-gear save the soggy mittens, which I wrung out and hung to dry by the stove. Four bells struck, and six bells, and Mr. Pike had not returned below. At eight bells, with the changing of the watches, it came upon me what a night of hardship the old mate was enduring. Eight to twelve had been his own watch on deck. He had now completed the four hours of the second mate's watch and was beginning his own watch, which would last till eight in the morning—twelve consecutive hours in a Cape Horn gale with the mercury at freezing.

Next—for I had dozed—I heard loud cries above my head that were repeated along the poop. I did not know till afterward that it was Mr. Pike's command to hard-up the helm, passed along from for'ard by the men he had stationed at intervals on the bridge.

All that I knew at this shock of waking was that something was happening above. As I pulled on my steaming mittens and hurried my best up the reeling stairs, I could hear the stamp of men's feet that for once were not lagging. When I was in the chart-house hall I heard Mr. Pike, who had already covered the length of the bridge from the for'ard house, shouting:

"Mizzen braces! Slack, damn you! Slack on the run! But hold a turn! Aft, here, all of you! Jump! Lively, if you don't want to swim! Come in, port braces! Don't let 'em get away! Lee braces!—If you lose that turn I'll split your skull! Lively! Lively!—Is that helm hard over? Why in hell don't you answer?"

All this I heard as I dashed for the lee door and as I wondered why I did not hear the Samurai's voice. Then, as I passed the chart-room door, I saw him. He was sitting on the couch, white-faced, one sea-boot in his hands, and I could have sworn his hands were shaking. That much I saw, and the next moment was out on deck.

At first, just emerged from the light, I could see nothing, although I could hear men at the pin-rails and the mate snarling and shouting commands. But I knew the maneuver. With a weak crew, in the big, tail-end sea of a broken gale, breakers and destruction under her lee, the *Elsinore* was being worn around. We had been under lower topsails and a reefed foresail all night. Mr. Pike's first action, after putting the wheel up, had been to square the mizzen yards. With the wind-pressure thus eased aft, the stern could more easily swing against the wind while the wind pressure on the for'ard sails paid the bow off.

But it takes time to wear a ship, under short canvas, in a big sea. Slowly, very slowly, I could feel the direction of the wind altering against my cheek. The moon, dim at first, showed brighter and brighter as the last shreds of a flying cloud drove away from before it. In vain I looked for any land.

"Main braces!—all of you!—jump!" Mr. Pike shouted, himself leading the rush along the poop. And the men really rushed. Not in all the months I had observed them had I seen such swiftness of energy.

I made my way to the wheel where Tom Spink stood. He did not notice me. With one hand holding the idle wheel, he was leaning out to one side, his eyes fixed in a fascinated stare. I followed its direction, on between the chart-house and the port-jigger shrouds, and on across a mountain sea that was very vague in the moonlight. And then I saw it! The *Elsinore's* stern was flung skyward, and across that cold ocean I saw land—black rocks and snow-covered slopes and crags. And toward this land the *Elsinore,* now almost before the wind, was driving.

From the 'midship house came the snarls of the mate and the cries of the sailors. They were pulling and hauling for very life. Then came Mr. Pike, across the poop, leaping with incredible swiftness, sending his snarl before him.

"Ease that wheel there! What the hell you gawkin' at? Steady her as I tell you! That's all you got to do!"

From for'ard came a cry, and I knew Mr. Mellaire was on top of the for'ard house and managing the fore-yards.

"Now!"—from Mr. Pike. "More spokes! Steady! Steady! And be ready to check her!"

He bounded away along the poop again, shouting for men for the mizzen braces. And the men appeared, some of his watch, others of the second mate's watch, routed from sleep—men coatless, and hatless, and bootless; men ghastly-faced with fear but eager for once to spring to the orders of the man who knew and could save their miserable lives from miserable death. Yes—and I noted the delicate-handed cook, and Yatsuda, the sail-maker, pulling with his one unparalyzed hand. It was all hands to save ship, and all hands knew it. Even Sundry Buyers, who had drifted aft in his stupidity instead of being for'ard with his own officer, forebore to stare about and to press his abdomen. For the nonce he pulled like a youngling of twenty.

The moon covered again, and it was in darkness that the *Elsinore* rounded up on the wind on the starboard tack. This, in her case, under lower topsails only, meant that she lay eight points from the wind, or, in land terms, at right angles to the wind.

Mr. Pike was splendid, marvelous. Even as the *Elsinore* was rounding to on the wind, while the head yards were still being braced, and even as he was watching the ship's behavior and the wheel, in between his commands to Tom Spink of "A spoke! A spoke or two! Another! Steady! Hold her! Ease her!" he was ordering the men aloft to loose sail. I had thought, the maneuver of wearing achieved, that we were saved, but this setting of all three upper topsails unconvinced me.

The moon remained hidden, and to leeward nothing could be seen. As each sail was set, the *Elsinore* was pressed farther and farther over, and I realized that there was plenty of wind left despite the fact that the gale had broken or was breaking. Also, under this additional canvas, I could feel the *Elsinore* moving through the water. Pike now sent the Maltese Cockney to help Tom Spink at the wheel. As for himself, he took his stand beside the booby hatch, where he could gauge the *Elsinore,* gaze to leeward, and keep his eye on the helmsmen.

"Full and by," was his reiterated command. "Keep her a good full—a rap-full; but don't let her fall away. Hold her to it, and drive her."

He took no notice whatever of me, although I, on my way to the lee of the chart-house, stood at his shoulder a full minute, offering him a chance to speak. He knew I was there, for his big shoulder brushed my arm as he swayed and turned to warn the helmsmen in the one breath to hold her up to it but to keep her full. He had neither time nor courtesy for a passenger in such a moment.

Sheltering by the chart-house, I saw the moon appear. It grew brighter and brighter, and I saw the land, dead to leeward of us, not three hundred yards away. It was a cruel sight—black rock and bitter snow, with cliffs so perpendicular that the *Elsinore* could have laid alongside of them in deep water, with great gashes and fissures, and with great surges thundering and spouting along all the length of it.

Our predicament was now clear to me. We had to weather the bight of land and islands into which we had drifted, and sea and wind worked directly on shore. The only way out was to drive through the water, to drive fast and hard, and this was borne in upon me by Mr. Pike bounding past to the break of the poop, where I heard him shout to Mr. Mellaire to set the mainsail.

Evidently the second mate was dubious, for the next cry of Mr. Pike's was:

"Damn the reef! You'd be in hell first! Full mainsail! All hands to it!"

The difference was appreciable at once when that huge spread of canvas opposed the wind. The *Elsinore* fairly leaped and quivered as she sprang to it, and I could feel her eat to windward as she at the same time drove faster ahead. Also, in the rolls and gusts she was forced down till her lee-rail buried and the sea foamed level across to her hatches. Mr. Pike watched her like a hawk, and like certain death he watched the Maltese Cockney and Tom Spink at the wheel.

"Land on the lee bow!" came a cry from for'ard that was carried on from mouth to mouth along the bridge to the poop.

I saw Mr. Pike nod his head grimly and sarcastically. He had already seen it from the lee-poop, and what he had not seen he had guessed. A score of times I saw him test the weight of the gusts on his cheek and with all the brain of him study the *Elsinore's* behavior. And I knew what was in his mind. Could she carry what she had? Could she carry more?

Small wonder, in this tense passage of time, that I had forgotten the Samurai. Nor did I remember him until the chart-house door swung open and I caught him by the arm. He steadied and swayed beside me, while he watched that cruel picture of rock and snow and spouting surf.

"A good full!" Mr. Pike snarled. "Or I'll eat your heart out, God damn you for the farmer's hound you are, Tom Spink! Ease her! Ease her! Ease her into the big ones, damn you! Don't let her head fall off! Steady! Where in hell did you learn to steer? What cow farm was you raised on?"

Here he bounded for'ard past us with those incredible leaps of his.

"It would be good to set the mizzen-topgallant," I heard Captain West mutter in a weak, quavery voice. "Mr. Pathurst, will you please tell Mr. Pike to set the mizzen-topgallant."

And at that very instant Mr. Pike's voice rang out from the break of the poop:

"Mr. Mellaire!—the mizzen-topgallant!"

Captain West's head drooped until his chin rested on his breast, and so low did he mutter that I leaned to hear.

"A very good officer," he said. "An excellent officer. Mr. Pathurst, if you will kindly favor me, I should like to go in. I . . . I haven't got on my boots."

The muscular feat was to open the heavy iron door and hold it open in the rolls and plunges. This I accomplished; but when I had helped Captain West across the high threshold he thanked me and waived further services. And I did not know that even then he was dying.

Never was a Blackwood ship driven as was the *Elsinore* during the next half hour. The full jib was also set, and, as it departed in shreds, the fore-topmast staysail was being hoisted. For'ard of the 'midship house it was made unlivable by the bursting seas. Mr. Mellaire, with half the crew, clung on somehow on top the 'midship house, while the rest of the crew was with us in the comparative safety of the poop. Even Charles Davis, drenched and shivering, hung on beside me to the brass ring-handle of the chart-house door.

Such sailing! It was a madness of speed and motion, for the *Elsinore* drove over and through and under those huge graybeards that thundered shoreward. There were times, when rolls and gusts worked against her at the same moment, when I could have sworn the ends of her lower yard arms swept the sea.

It was one chance in ten that we could claw off. All knew it, and all knew there was nothing more to do but await the issue. And we waited in silence. The only voice was that of the mate, intermittently cursing, threatening, and ordering Tom Spink and the Maltese Cockney at the wheel. Between whiles, and all the while, he gauged the gusts, and ever his eyes lifted to the main-topgallant yard. He wanted to set that one more sail. A dozen times I saw him half open his mouth to give the order he dared not give. And as I watched him, so all watched him. Hard-bitten, bitter-natured, sour-featured, and snarling-mouthed, he was the one man, the henchman of the race, the master of the moment. "And where," was my thought, "O where was the Samurai?"

One chance in ten? It was one in a hundred as we fought to weather the last bold tooth of rock that gashed into sea and tempest between us and open ocean. So close were we that I looked to see our far-reeling skysail yard strike the face of the rock. So close were we, no more than a biscuit toss from its iron buttress, that as we sank down into the last great trough between two seas I can swear every one of us held breath and waited for the *Elsinore* to strike.

Instead, we drove free. And as if in very rage at our escape, the storm took that moment to deal us the mightiest buffet of all. The mate felt that monster sea coming, for he sprang to the wheel ere the blow fell. I looked for'ard, and I saw all for'ard blotted out by the mountain of water that fell aboard. The *Elsinore* righted from the shock and reappeared to the eye, full of water from rail to rail. Then a gust caught her sails and heeled her over, spilling half the enormous burden outboard again.

Along the bridge came the relayed cry of "Man overboard!"

I glanced at the mate, who had just released the wheel to the helmsmen. He shook his head, as if irritated by so trivial a happening, walked to the corner of the half-wheel-house, and stared at the coast he had escaped, white and black and cold in the moonlight.

Mr. Mellaire came aft, and they met beside me in the lee of the chart-house.

"All hands, Mr. Mellaire," the mate said, "and get the mainsail off of her. After that, the mizzen-topgallant."

"Yes, sir," said the second.

"Who was it?" the mate asked, as Mr. Mellaire was turning away.

"Boney—he was no good anyway," came the answer.

That was all. Boney, the Splinter, was gone, and all hands were answering the command of Mr. Mellaire to take in the mainsail. But they never took it in; for at that moment it started to blow away out of the bolt-ropes, and in but few moments all that was left of it were a few short, slatting ribbons.

"Mizzen-topgallantsail!" Mr. Pike ordered.

Then, and for the first time, he recognized my existence.

"Well rid of it," he growled. "It never did set properly. I was always aching to get my hands on the sail-maker that made it."

On my way below, a glance into the chart-room gave me the cue to the Samurai's blunder—if blunder it can be called, for no one will ever know. He lay on the floor in a loose heap, rolling willy-nilly with every roll of the *Elsinore.*

1914

THE MOUNTAIN MEADOW MASSACRE

From *The Star Rover*

The Star Rover *is a novel of prison brutality and reincarnation. Darrell Standing, a condemned murderer, is implicated in an unsuccessful prison break. As punishment he is savagely laced in a straight jacket and thrown into solitary confinement. As the selection opens Standing has just succeeded in escaping the tortures of the jacket through a process of self-hypnosis called "the little death." Once in this condition his body loses all sensation, his spirit soars free into time, and he relives past existences. "The Mountain Meadow Massacre" is one of the prisoner's adventures in transmigration.* ED.

Now that I had learned the trick the way was easy. And I knew the way was bound to become easier the more I travelled it. Once establish a line of least resistance, every succeeding journey along it will find still less resistance. And so, as you shall see, my journeys from San Quentin life into other lives were achieved almost automatically as time went by.

After Warden Atherton and his crew had left me it was a matter of minutes to will the resuscitated portion of my body back into the little death. Death in life it was, but it was only the little death, similar to the temporary death produced by an anæsthetic.

And so, from all that was sordid and vile, from brutal solitary and jacket hell, from acquainted flies and sweats of darkness and the knuckle-talk of the living dead, I was away at a bound into time and space.

Came the duration of darkness, and the slow-growing awareness of other things and of another self. First of all, in this awareness, was dust. It was in my nostrils, dry and acrid. It was on my lips. It coated my face, my hands, and especially was it noticeable on the finger-tips when touched by the ball of my thumb.

Next I was aware of ceaseless movement. All that was about me lurched and oscillated. There was jolt and jar, and I heard what I knew as a matter of course to be the grind of wheels on axles and the grate and clash of iron tyres against rock and sand. And there came to me the jaded voices of men, in curse and snarl of slow-plodding, jaded animals.

I opened my eyes, that were inflamed with dust, and immediately fresh dust bit into them. On the coarse blankets on which I lay the dust was half an inch thick. Above me, through sifting dust, I saw an arched roof of lurching, swaying canvas, and myriads of dust motes descended heavily in the shafts of sunshine that entered through holes in the canvas.

I was a child, a boy of eight or nine, and I was weary, as was the woman, dusty-visaged and haggard, who sat up beside me and soothed a crying babe in her arms.

She was my mother; that I knew as a matter of course, just as I knew, when I glanced along the canvas tunnel of the wagon-top, that the shoulders of the man on the driver's seat were the shoulders of my father.

When I started to crawl along the packed gear with which the wagon was laden my mother said in a tired and querulous voice, "Can't you ever be still a minute, Jesse?"

That was my name, Jesse. I did not know my surname, though I heard my mother call my father John. I have a dim recollection of hearing, at one time or another, the other men address my father as Captain. I knew that he was the leader of this company, and that his orders were obeyed by all.

I crawled out through the opening in the canvas and sat down beside my father on the seat. The air was stifling with the dust that rose from the wagons and the many hoofs of the animals. So thick was the dust that it was like mist or fog in the air, and the low sun shone through it dimly and with a bloody light.

Not alone was the light of this setting sun ominous, but everything about me seemed ominous—the landscape, my father's face, the fret of the babe in my mother's arms that she could not still, the six horses my father drove that had continually to be urged and that were without any sign of colour, so heavily had the dust settled on them.

The landscape was an aching, eye-hurting desolation. Low hills stretched endlessly away on every hand. Here and there only on their slopes were occasional scrub growths of heat-parched brush. For the most part the surface of the hills was naked-dry and composed of sand and rock. Our way followed the sand-bottoms between the hills. And the sand-bottoms were bare, save for spots of scrub, with here and there short tufts of dry and withered grass. Water there was none, nor sign of water, except for washed gullies that told of ancient and torrential rains.

My father was the only one who had horses to his wagon. The wagons went in single file, and as the train wound and curved I saw that the other wagons were drawn by oxen. Three or four yoke of oxen strained and pulled weakly at each wagon, and beside them, in the deep sand, walked men with ox-goads, who prodded the unwilling beasts along. On a curve I counted the wagons ahead and behind. I knew that there were forty of them, including our own; for often I had counted them before. And as I counted them now, as a child will to while away tedium, they were all there, forty of them, all canvas-topped, big and massive, crudely fashioned, pitching and lurching, grinding and jarring over sand and sage-brush and rock.

To right and left of us, scattered along the train, rode a dozen or fifteen men and youths on horses. Across their pommels were long-barrelled rifles. Whenever any of them drew near to our wagon I could see that their faces, under the dust, were drawn and anxious like my father's. And my father, like them, had a long-barrelled rifle close to hand as he drove.

Also, to one side, limped a score or more of footsore, yoke-galled, skeleton oxen, that ever paused to nip at the occasional tufts of withered grass, and that ever were prodded on by the tired-faced youths who herded them. Sometimes one or another of these oxen would pause and low, and such lowing seemed as ominous as all else about me.

Far, far away I have a memory of having lived, a smaller lad, by the tree-lined banks of a stream. And as the wagon jolts along, and I sway on the seat with my father, I continually return and dwell upon that pleasant water flowing between the trees. I have a sense that for an interminable period I have lived in a wagon and travelled on, ever on, with this present company.

But strongest of all upon me is what is strong upon all the company, namely, a sense of drifting to doom. Our way was like a funeral march. Never did a laugh arise. Never did I hear a happy tone of voice. Neither peace nor ease marched with us. The faces of the men and youths who outrode the train were grim, set, hopeless. And as we toiled through the lurid dust of sunset often I scanned my father's face in vain quest of some message of cheer. I will not say that my father's face, in all its dusty haggardness, was hopeless. It was dogged, and oh! so grim and anxious, most anxious.

A thrill seemed to run along the train. My father's head went up. So did mine. And our horses raised their weary heads, scented the air with long-drawn snorts, and for the nonce pulled willingly. The horses of the outriders quickened their pace. And as for the herd of scarecrow oxen, it broke into a forthright gallop. It was almost ludicrous. The poor brutes were so clumsy in their weakness and haste. They were galloping skeletons draped in mangy hide, and they out-distanced the boys who herded them. But this was only for a time. Then they fell back to a walk, a quick, eager, shambling, sore-footed walk; and they no longer were lured aside by the dry bunch-grass.

"What is it?" my mother asked from within the wagon.

"Water," was my father's reply. "It must be Nephi."

And my mother: "Thank God! And perhaps they will sell us food."

And into Nephi, through blood-red dust, with grind and grate and jolt and jar, our great wagons rolled. A dozen scattered dwellings or shanties composed the place. The landscape was much the same as that through which we had passed. There were no trees, only scrub growths and sandy bareness. But here were signs of tilled fields, with here and there a fence. Also there was water. Down the stream ran no current. The bed, however, was damp, with now and again a water-hole into which the loose oxen and the saddle-horses stamped and plunged their muzzles to the eyes. Here, too, grew an occasional small willow.

"That must be Bill Black's mill they told us about," my father said, pointing out a building to my mother, whose anxiousness had drawn her to peer out over our shoulders.

An old man, with buckskin shirt and long, matted, sunburnt hair, rode back to our wagon and talked with father. The signal was given, and the head wagons of the train began to deploy in a circle. The ground favoured the evolution, and, from long practice, it was accomplished without a hitch, so that when the forty wagons were finally halted they formed a circle. All was bustle and orderly confusion. Many women, all tired-faced and dusty like my mother, emerged from the wagons. Also poured forth a very horde of children. There must have been at least fifty children, and it seemed I knew them all of long time; and there were at least two score of women. These went about the preparations for cooking supper.

While some of the men chopped sage-brush and we children carried it to the fires that were kindling, other men unyoked the oxen and let them stampede for water. Next the men, in big squads, moved the wagons snugly into place. The tongue of each wagon was on the inside of the circle, and, front and rear, each wagon was in solid contact with the next wagon before and behind. The great brakes were locked fast; but, not content with this, the wheels of all the wagons were connected with chains. This was nothing new to us children. It was the trouble sign of a camp in hostile country. One wagon only was left out of the circle, so as to form a gate to the corral. Later on, as we knew, ere the camp slept, the animals would be driven inside, and the gate-wagon would be chained like the others in place. In the meanwhile, and for hours, the animals would be herded by men and boys to what scant grass they could find.

While the camp-making went on my father, with several others of the men, including the old man with the long, sunburnt hair, went away on foot in the direction of the mill. I remember that all of us, men, women, and even the children, paused to watch them depart; and it seemed their errand was of grave import.

While they were away other men, strangers, inhabitants of desert Nephi, came into camp and stalked about. They were white men, like us, but they were hard-faced, stern-faced, sombre, and they seemed angry with all our company. Bad feeling was in the air, and they said things calculated to rouse the tempers of our men. But the warning went out from the women, and was passed on everywhere to our men and youths, that there must be no words.

One of the strangers came to our fire, where my mother was alone, cooking. I had just come up with an armful of sage-brush, and I stopped to listen and to stare at the intruder, whom I hated, because it was in the air to hate, because I knew that every last person in our company hated these strangers who were white-skinned like us and because of whom we had been compelled to make our camp in a circle.

This stranger at our fire had blue eyes, hard and cold and piercing. His hair was sandy. His face was shaven to the chin, and from under the chin, covering the neck and extending to the ears, sprouted a sandy fringe of whiskers well-streaked with gray. Mother did not greet him, nor did he greet her. He merely stood and glowered at her for some time. Then he cleared his throat and said with a sneer:

"Wisht you was back in Missouri right now I bet."

I saw mother tighten her lips in self-control ere she answered:

"We are from Arkansas."

"I guess you've got good reasons to deny where you come from," he next said, "you that drove the Lord's chosen people from Missouri."

Mother made no reply.

". . . Seein'," he went on, after the pause accorded her, "as you're now comin' a-whinin' an' a-beggin' bread at our hands that you persecuted."

Whereupon, and instantly, child that I was, I knew anger, the old, red, intolerant wrath, ever unrestrainable and unsubduable.

"You lie!" I piped up. "We ain't Missourians. We ain't whinin'. An' we ain't beggars. We got the money to buy."

"Shut up, Jesse!" my mother cried, landing the back of her hand stingingly on my mouth. And then, to the stranger, "Go away and let the boy alone."

"I'll shoot you full of lead, you damned Mormon!" I screamed and sobbed at him, too quick for my mother this time, and dancing away around the fire from the back-sweep of her hand.

As for the man himself, my conduct had not disturbed him in the slightest. I was prepared for I knew not what violent visitation from this terrible stranger, and I watched him warily while he considered me with the utmost gravity.

At last he spoke, and he spoke solemnly, with solemn shaking of the head, as if delivering a judgment.

"Like fathers like sons," he said. "The young generation is as bad as the elder. The whole breed is unregenerate and damned. There is no saving it, the young or the old. There is no atonement. Not even the blood of Christ can wipe out its iniquities."

"Damned Mormon!" was all I could sob at him. "Damned Mormon! Damned Mormon! Damned Mormon!"

And I continued to damn him and to dance around the fire before my mother's avenging hand, until he strode away.

When my father, and the men who had accompanied him, returned, camp-work ceased, while all crowded anxiously about him. He shook his head.

"They will not sell?" some woman demanded.

Again he shook his head.

A man spoke up, a blue-eyed, blond-whiskered giant of thirty, who abruptly pressed his way into the centre of the crowd.

"They say they have flour and provisions for three years, Captain," he said. "They have always sold to the immigration before. And now they won't sell. And it ain't our quarrel. Their quarrel's with the government, an' they're takin' it out on us. It ain't right, Captain. It ain't right, I say, us with our women an' children, an' California months away, winter comin' on, an' nothin' but desert in between. We ain't got the grub to face the desert."

He broke off for a moment to address the whole crowd.

"Why, you-all don't know what desert is. This around here ain't desert. I tell you it's paradise, and heavenly pasture, an' flowin' with milk an' honey alongside what we're goin' to face."

"I tell you, Captain, we got to get flour first. If they won't sell it, then we must just up an' take it."

Many of the men and women began crying out in approval, but my father hushed them by holding up his hand.

"I agree with everything you say, Hamilton," he began.

But the cries now drowned his voice, and he again held up his hand.

"Except one thing you forgot to take into account, Hamilton—a thing that you and all of us must take into account. Brigham Young has declared martial law, and Brigham Young has an army. We could wipe out Nephi in the shake of a lamb's tail and take all the provisions we can carry. But we wouldn't carry them very far. Brigham's Saints would be down upon us and we would be wiped out in another shake of a lamb's tail. You know it. I know it. We all know it."

His words carried conviction to listeners already convinced. What he had told them was old news. They had merely forgotten it in a flurry of excitement and desperate need.

"Nobody will fight quicker for what is right than I will," father continued. "But it just happens we can't afford to fight now. If ever a ruction starts we haven't a chance. And we've all got our women and children to recollect. We've got to be peaceable at any price, and put up with whatever dirt is heaped on us."

"But what will we do with the desert coming?" cried a woman who nursed a babe at her breast.

"There's several settlements before we come to the desert," father answered. "Fillmore's sixty miles south. Then comes Corn Creek. And Beaver's another fifty miles. Next is Parowan. Then it's twenty miles to Cedar City. The farther we get away from Salt Lake the more likely they'll sell us provisions."

"And if they won't?" the same woman persisted.

"Then we're quit of them," said my father. "Cedar City is the last settlement. We'll have to go on, that's all, and thank our stars we are quit of them. Two days' journey beyond is good pasture and water. They call it Mountain Meadows. Nobody lives there, and that's the place we'll rest our cattle and feed them up before we tackle the desert. Maybe we can shoot some meat. And if the worst comes to the worst, we'll keep going as long as we can, then abandon the wagons, pack what we can on our animals, and make the last stages on foot. We can eat our cattle as we go along. It would be better to arrive in California without a rag to our backs than to leave our bones here; and leave them we will if we start a ruction."

With final reiterated warnings against violence of speech or act, the impromptu meeting broke up. I was slow in falling asleep that night. My rage against the Mormon had left my brain in such a tingle that I was still awake when my father crawled into the wagon after a last round of the night-watch. They thought I slept, but I heard mother ask him if he thought that the Mormons would let us depart peacefully from their land. His face was turned aside from her as he busied himself with pulling off a boot, while he answered her with hearty confidence that he was sure the Mormons would let us go if none of our own company started trouble.

But I saw his face at that moment in the light of a small tallow dip, and in it was none of the confidence that was in his voice. So it was that I fell asleep, oppressed by the dire fate that seemed to overhang us, and pondering upon Brigham Young who bulked in my child imagination as a fearful, malignant being, a very devil with horns and tail and all. . . .

Long before daylight the camp at Nephi was astir. The cattle were driven out to water and pasture. While the men unchained the wheels and drew the wagons apart and clear for yoking in, the women cooked forty breakfasts over forty fires. The children, in the chill of dawn, clustered about the fires, sharing places, here and there, with the last relief of the night-watch waiting sleepily for coffee.

It requires time to get a large train such as ours under way, for its speed is the speed of the slowest. So the sun was an hour high and the day was already uncomfortably hot when we rolled out of Nephi and on into the sandy barrens. No inhabitant of the place saw us off. All chose to remain indoors, thus making our departure as ominous as they had made our arrival the night before.

Again it was long hours of parching heat and biting dust, sage-brush and sand, and a land accursed. No dwellings of men, neither cattle nor fences, nor any sign of human kind, did we encounter all that day; and at night we made our wagon-circle beside an empty stream, in the damp sand of which we dug many holes that filled slowly with water seepage.

Our subsequent journey is always a broken experience to me. We made camp so many times, always with the wagons drawn in circle, that to my child mind a weary long time passed after Nephi. But always, strong upon all of us, was that sense of drifting to an impending and certain doom.

We averaged about fifteen miles a day. I know, for my father had said it was sixty miles to Fillmore, the next Mormon settlement, and we made three camps on the way. This meant four days of travel. From Nephi to the last camp of which I have any memory we must have taken two weeks or a little less.

At Fillmore the inhabitants were hostile, as all had been since Salt Lake. They laughed at us when we tried to buy food, and were not above taunting us with being Missourians.

When we entered the place, hitched before the largest house of the dozen houses that composed the settlement were two saddle-horses, dusty, streaked with sweat, and drooping. The old man I have mentioned, the one with long, sunburnt hair and buckskin shirt and who seemed a sort of aide or lieutenant to father, rode close to our wagon and indicated the jaded saddle-animals with a cock of his head.

"Not sparin' horseflesh, Captain," he muttered in a low voice. "An' what in the name of Sam Hill are they hard-riding for if it ain't for us?"

But my father had already noted the condition of the two animals, and my eager eyes had seen him. And I had seen his eyes flash, his lips tighten, and haggard lines form for a moment on his dusty face. That was all. But I put two and two together, and knew that the two tired saddle-horses were just one more added touch of ominousness to the situation.

"I guess they're keeping an eye on us, Laban," was my father's sole comment.

It was at Fillmore that I saw a man that I was to see again. He was a tall, broad-shouldered man, well on in middle age, with all the evidence of good health and immense strength—strength not alone of body but of will. Unlike most men I was accustomed to about me, he was smooth-shaven. Several days' growth of beard showed that he was already well-grayed. His mouth was unusually wide, with thin lips tightly compressed as if he had lost many of his front teeth. His nose was large, square, and thick. So was his face square, wide between the cheekbones, underhung with massive jaws, and topped with a broad, intelligent forehead. And the eyes, rather small, a little more than the width of an eye apart, were the bluest blue I had ever seen.

It was at the flour-mill at Fillmore that I first saw this man. Father, with several of our company, had gone there to try to buy flour, and I, disobeying my mother in my curiosity to see more of our enemies, had tagged along unperceived. This man was one of four or five who stood in a group with the miller during the interview.

"You seen that smooth-faced old cuss?" Laban said to father, after we had got outside and were returning to camp.

Father nodded.

"Well, that's Lee," Laban continued. "I seen'm in Salt Lake. He's a regular son-of-a-gun. Got nineteen wives and fifty children, they all say. An' he's rank crazy on religion. Now, what's he followin' us up for through this God-forsaken country?"

Our weary, doomed drifting went on. The little settlements, wherever water and soil permitted, were from twenty to fifty miles apart. Between stretched the barrenness of sand and alkali and drought. And at every settlement our peaceful attempts to buy food were vain. They denied us harshly, and wanted to know who of us had sold them food when we drove them from Missouri. It was useless on our part to tell them we were from Arkansas. From Arkansas we truly were, but they insisted on our being Missourians.

At Beaver, five days' journey south from Fillmore, we saw Lee again. And again we saw hard-ridden horses tethered before the houses. But we did not see Lee at Parowan.

Cedar City was the last settlement. Laban, who had ridden on ahead, came back and reported to father. His first news was significant.

"I seen that Lee skedaddling out as I rid in, Captain. An' there's more men-folk an' horses in Cedar City than the size of the place 'd warrant."

But we had no trouble at the settlement. Beyond refusing to sell us food, they left us to ourselves. The women and children stayed in the houses, and though some of the men appeared in sight they did not, as on former occasions, enter our camp and taunt us.

It was at Cedar City that the Wainwright baby died. I remember Mrs. Wainwright weeping and pleading with Laban to try to get some cow's milk.

"It may save the baby's life," she said. "And they've got cow's milk. I saw fresh cows with my own eyes. Go on, please, Laban. It won't hurt you to try. They can only refuse. But they won't. Tell them it's for a baby, a wee little baby. Mormon women have mother's hearts. They couldn't refuse a cup of milk for a wee little baby."

And Laban tried. But, as he told father afterward, he did not get to see any Mormon women. He saw only the Mormon men, who turned him away.

This was the last Mormon outpost. Beyond lay the vast desert, with, on the other side of it, the dream land, ay, the myth land, of California. As our wagons rolled out of the place in the early morning I, sitting beside my father on the driver's seat, saw Laban give expression to his feelings. We had gone perhaps half a mile, and were topping a low rise that would sink Cedar City from view, when Laban turned his horse around, halted it, and stood up in the stirrups. Where he had halted was a new-made grave, and I knew it for the Wainwright baby's—not the first of our graves since we had crossed the Wasatch mountains.

He was a weird figure of a man. Aged and lean, long-faced, hollow-cheeked, with matted, sunburnt hair that fell below the shoulders of his buckskin shirt, his face was distorted with hatred and helpless rage. Holding his long rifle in his bridle-hand, he shook his free fist at Cedar City.

"God's curse on all of you!" he cried out. "On your children, and on your babes unborn. May drought destroy your crops. May you eat sand seasoned with the venom of rattlesnakes. May the sweet water of your springs turn to bitter alkali. May . . ."

Here his words became indistinct as our wagons rattled on; but his heaving shoulders and brandishing fist attested that he had only begun to lay the curse. That he expressed the general feeling in our train was evidenced by the many women who leaned from the wagons, thrusting out gaunt forearms and shaking bony, labour-malformed fists at the last of Mormondom. A man, who walked in the sand and goaded the oxen of the wagon behind ours, laughed and waved his goad. It was unusual, that laugh, for there had been no laughter in our train for many days.

"Give 'm hell, Laban," he encouraged. "Them's my sentiments."

And as our train rolled on I continued to look back at Laban, standing in his stirrups by the baby's grave. Truly he was a weird figure, with his long hair, his moccasins, and fringed leggings. So old and weather-beaten was his buckskin shirt that ragged filaments, here and there, showed where proud fringes once had been. He was a man of flying tatters. I remember, at his waist, dangled dirty tufts of hair that, far back in the journey, after a shower of rain, were wont to show glossy black. These I knew were Indian scalps, and the sight of them always thrilled me.

"It will do him good," father commended, more to himself than to me. "I've been looking for days for him to blow up."

"I wish he'd go back and take a couple of scalps," I volunteered.

My father regarded me quizzically.

"Don't like the Mormons, eh, son?"

I shook my head and felt myself swelling with the inarticulate hate that possessed me.

"When I grow up," I said, after a minute, "I'm goin' gunning for them."

"You, Jesse!" came my mother's voice from inside the wagon. "Shut your mouth instanter." And to my father: "You ought to be ashamed letting the boy talk on like that."

Two days' journey brought us to Mountain Meadows, and here, well beyond the last settlement, for the first time we did not form the wagon-circle. The wagons were roughly in a circle, but there were many gaps, and the wheels were not chained. Preparations were made to stop a week. The cattle must be rested for the real desert, though this was desert enough in all seeming. The same low hills of sand were about us, but sparsely covered with scrub brush. The flat was sandy, but there was some grass—more than we had encountered in many days. Not more than a hundred feet from camp was a weak spring that barely supplied human needs. But farther along the bottom various other weak springs emerged from the hillsides, and it was at these that the cattle watered.

We made camp early that day, and, because of the programme to stay a week, there was a general overhauling of soiled clothes by the women, who planned to start washing on the morrow. Everybody worked till nightfall. While some of the men mended harness others repaired the frames and ironwork of the wagons. There was much heating and hammering of iron and tightening of bolts and nuts. And I remember coming upon Laban, sitting cross-legged in the shade of a wagon and sewing away till nightfall on a new pair of moccasins. He was the only man in our train who wore moccasins and buckskin, and I have an impression that he had not belonged to our company when it left Arkansas. Also, he had neither wife, nor family, nor wagon of his own. All he possessed was his horse, his rifle, the clothes he stood up in, and a couple of blankets that were hauled in the Mason wagon.

Next morning it was that our doom fell. Two days' journey beyond the last Mormon outpost, knowing that no Indians were about and apprehending nothing from the Indians on any count, for the first time we had not chained our wagons in the solid circle, placed guards on the cattle, nor set a night-watch.

My awakening was like a nightmare. It came as a sudden blast of sound. I was only stupidly awake for the first moments and did nothing except to try to analyze and identify the various noises that went to compose the blast that continued without letup. I could hear near and distant explosions of rifles, shouts and curses of men, women screaming, and children bawling. Then I could make out the thuds and squeals of bullets that hit wood and iron in the wheels and under-construction of the wagon. Whoever it was that was shooting, the aim was too low.

When I started to rise, my mother, evidently just in the act of dressing, pressed me down with her hand. Father, already up and about, at this stage erupted into the wagon.

"Out of it!" he shouted. "Quick! To the ground!"

He wasted no time. With a hook-like clutch that was almost a blow, so swift was it, he flung me bodily out of the rear end of the wagon. I had barely time to crawl out from under when father, mother, and the baby came down pell-mell where I had been.

"Here, Jesse!" father shouted to me, and I joined him in scooping out sand behind the shelter of a wagon-wheel. We worked bare-handed and wildly. Mother joined in.

"Go ahead and make it deeper, Jesse," father ordered.

He stood up and rushed away in the gray light, shouting commands as he ran. (I had learned by now my surname. I was Jesse Fancher. My father was Captain Fancher.)

"Lie down!" I could hear him. "Get behind the wagon wheels and burrow in the sand! Family men, get the women and children out of the wagons! Hold your fire! No more shooting! Hold your fire and be ready for the rush when it comes! Single men, join Laban at the right, Cochrane at the left, and me in the centre! Don't stand up! Crawl for it!"

But no rush came. For a quarter of an hour the heavy and irregular firing continued. Our damage had come in the first moments of surprise when a number of the early-rising men were caught exposed in the light of the campfires they were building. The Indians—for Indians Laban declared them to be—had attacked us from the open, and were lying down and firing at us. In the growing light father made ready for them. His position was near to where I lay in the burrow with mother so that I heard him when he cried out:

"Now! all together!"

From left, right, and centre our rifles loosed in a volley. I had popped my head up to see, and I could make out more than one stricken Indian. Their fire immediately ceased, and I could see them scampering back on foot across the open, dragging their dead and wounded with them.

All was work with us on the instant. While the wagons were being dragged and chained into the circle with tongues inside—I saw women and little boys and girls flinging their strength on the wheel spokes to help—we took toll of our losses. First, and gravest of all, our last animal had been run off. Next, lying about the fires they had been building, were seven of our men. Four were dead, and three were dying. Other men, wounded, were being cared for by the women. Little Rish Hardacre had been struck in the arm by a heavy ball. He was no more than six, and I remember looking on with mouth agape while his mother held him on her lap and his father set about bandaging the wound. Little Rish had stopped crying. I could see the tears on his cheeks while he stared wonderingly at a sliver of broken bone sticking out of his forearm.

Granny White was found dead in the Foxwell wagon. She was a fat and helpless old woman who never did anything but sit down all the time and smoke a pipe. She was the mother of Abby Foxwell. And Mrs. Grant had been killed. Her husband sat beside her body. He was very quiet. There were no tears in his eyes. He just sat there, his rifle across his knees, and everybody left him alone.

Under father's directions the company was working like so many beavers. The men dug a big rifle pit in the centre of the corral, forming a breastwork out of the displaced sand. Into this pit the women dragged bedding, food, and all sorts of necessaries from the wagons. All the children helped. There was no whimpering, and little or no excitement. There was work to be done, and all of us were folks born to work.

The big rifle pit was for the women and children. Under the wagons, completely around the circle, a shallow trench was dug and an earthwork thrown up. This was for the fighting men.

Laban returned from a scout. He reported that the Indians had withdrawn the matter of half a mile and were holding a powwow. Also he had seen them carry six of their number off the field, three of which, he said, were deaders.

From time to time, during the morning of that first day, we observed clouds of dust that advertised the movements of considerable bodies of mounted men. These clouds of dust came toward us, hemming us in on all sides. But we saw no living creature. One cloud of dust only moved away from us. It was a large cloud, and everybody said it was our cattle being driven off. And our forty great wagons that had rolled over the Rockies and half across the continent stood in a helpless circle. Without cattle they could roll no farther.

At noon Laban came in from another scout. He had seen fresh Indians arriving from the south, showing that we were being closed in. It was at this time that we saw a dozen white men ride out on the crest of a low hill to the east and look down on us.

"That settles it," Laban said to father. "The Indians have been put up to it."

"They're white like us," I heard Abby Foxwell complain to mother. "Why don't they come in to us?"

"They ain't whites," I piped up, with a wary eye for the swoop of mother's hand. "They're Mormons."

That night, after dark, three of our young men stole out of camp. I saw them go. They were Will Aden, Abel Milliken, and Timothy Grant.

"They are heading for Cedar City to get help," father told mother while he was snatching a hasty bite of supper.

Mother shook her head.

"There's plenty of Mormons within calling distance of camp," she said. "If they won't help, and they haven't shown any signs, then the Cedar City ones won't either."

"But there are good Mormons and bad Mormons—" father began.

"We haven't found any good ones so far," she shut him off.

Not until morning did I hear of the return of Abel Milliken and Timothy Grant, but I was not long in learning. The whole camp was downcast by reason of their report. The three had gone only a few miles when they were challenged by white men. As soon as Will Aden spoke up, telling that they were from the Fancher Company, going to Cedar City for help, he was shot down. Milliken and Grant escaped back with the news, and the news settled the last hope in the hearts of our company. The whites were behind the Indians, and the doom so long apprehended was upon us.

This morning of the second day our men, going for water, were fired upon. The spring was only a hundred feet outside our circle, but the way to it was commanded by the Indians who now occupied the low hill to the east. It was close range, for the hill could not have been more than fifteen rods away. But the Indians were not good shots, evidently, for our men brought in the water without being hit.

Beyond an occasional shot into camp the morning passed quietly. We had settled down in the rifle pit, and, being used to rough living, were comfortable enough.

Of course it was bad for the families of those who had been killed, and there was the taking care of the wounded. I was forever stealing away from mother in my insatiable curiosity to see everything that was going on, and I managed to see pretty much of everything. Inside the corral, to the south of the big rifle pit, the men dug a hole and buried the seven men and two women all together. Only Mrs. Hastings, who had lost her husband and father, made much trouble. She cried and screamed out, and it took the other women a long time to quiet her.

On the low hill to the east the Indians kept up a tremendous powwowing and yelling. But beyond an occasional harmless shot they did nothing.

"What's the matter with the ornery cusses?" Laban impatiently wanted to know. "Can't they make up their minds what they're goin' to do, an' then do it?"

It was hot in the corral that afternoon. The sun blazed down out of a cloudless sky, and there was no wind. The men, lying with their rifles in the trench under the wagons, were partly shaded; but the big rifle pit, in which were over a hundred women and children, was exposed to the full power of the sun. Here, too, were the wounded men, over whom we erected awnings of blankets. It was crowded and stifling in the pit, and I was for ever stealing out of it to the firing-line, and making a great to-do at carrying messages for father.

Our grave mistake had been in not forming the wagon-circle so as to inclose the spring. This had been due to the excitement of the first attack, when we did not know how quickly it might be followed by a second one. And now it was too late. At fifteen rods' distance from the Indian position on the hill we did not dare unchain our wagons. Inside the corral, south of the graves, we constructed a latrine, and, north of the rifle pit in the centre, a couple of men were told off by father to dig a well for water.

In the mid-afternoon of that day, which was the second day, we saw Lee again. He was on foot, crossing diagonally over the meadow to the northwest just out of rifle-shot from us. Father hoisted one of mother's sheets on a couple of ox-goads lashed together. This was our white flag. But Lee took no notice of it, continuing on his way.

Laban was for trying a long shot at him, but father stopped him, saying that it was evident the whites had not made up their minds what they were going to do with us, and that a shot at Lee might hurry them into making up their minds the wrong way.

"Here, Jesse," father said to me, tearing a strip from the sheet and fastening it to an ox-goad. "Take this and go out and try to talk to that man. Don't tell him anything about what's happened to us. Just try to get him to come in and talk with us."

As I started to obey, my chest swelling with pride in my mission, Jed Dunham cried out that he wanted to go with me. Jed was about my own age.

"Dunham, can your boy go along with Jesse?" father asked Jed's father. "Two's better than one. They'll keep each other out of mischief."

So Jed and I, two youngsters of nine, went out under the white flag to talk with the leader of our enemies. But Lee would not talk. When he saw us coming he started to sneak away. We never got within calling distance of him, and after a while he must have hidden in the brush; for we never laid eyes on him again, and we knew he couldn't have got clear away.

Jed and I beat up the brush for hundreds of yards all around. They hadn't told us how long we were to be gone, and since the Indians did not fire on us we kept on going. We were away over two hours, though had either of us been alone he would have been back in a quarter of the time. But Jed was bound to outbrave me, and I was equally bound to outbrave him.

Our foolishness was not without profit. We walked boldly about under our white flag, and learned how thoroughly our camp was beleaguered. To the south of our train, not more than half a mile away, we made out a large Indian camp. Beyond, on the meadow, we could see Indian boys riding hard on their horses.

Then there was the Indian position on the hill to the east. We managed to climb a low hill so as to look into this position. Jed and I spent half an hour trying to count them, and concluded, with much guessing, that there must be at least a couple of hundred. Also, we saw white men with them and doing a great deal of talking.

North-east of our train, not more than four hundred yards from it, we discovered a large camp of whites behind a low rise of ground. And beyond we could see fifty or sixty saddle-horses grazing. And a mile or so away, to the north, we saw a tiny cloud of dust approaching. Jed and I waited until we saw a single man, riding fast, gallop into the camp of the whites.

When we got back into the corral the first thing that happened to me was a smack from mother for having stayed away so long; but father praised Jed and me when we gave our report.

"Watch for an attack now maybe, Captain," Aaron Cochrane said to father. "That man the boys seen has rid in for a purpose. The whites are holding the Indians till they get orders from higher up. Maybe that man brung the orders one way or the other. They ain't sparing horseflesh, that's one thing sure."

Half an hour after our return Laban attempted a scout under a white flag. But he had not gone twenty feet outside the circle when the Indians opened fire on him and sent him back on the run.

Just before sundown I was in the rifle pit holding the baby, while mother was spreading the blankets for a bed. There were so many of us that we were packed and jammed. So little room was there that many of the women the night before had sat up and slept with their heads bowed on their knees. Right alongside of me, so near that when he tossed his arms about he struck me on the shoulder, Silas Dunlap was dying. He had been shot in the head in the first attack, and all the second day was out of his head and raving and singing doggerel. One of his songs, that he sang over and over, until it made mother frantic nervous, was:

"Said the first little devil to the second little devil,
'Give me some tobaccy from your old tobaccy box.'
Said the second little devil to the first little devil,
'Stick close to your money and close to your rocks,
An' you'll always have tobaccy in your old tobaccy box.'"

I was sitting directly alongside of him, holding the baby, when the attack burst on us. It was sundown, and I was staring with all my eyes at Silas Dunlap, who was just in the final act of dying. His wife, Sarah, had one hand resting on his forehead. Both she and her Aunt Martha were crying softly. And then it came—explosions and bullets from hundreds of rifles. Clear around from east to west, by way of the north, they had strung out in half a circle and were pumping lead in our position. Everybody in the rifle pit flattened down. Lots of the younger children set up a-squalling, and it kept the women busy hushing them. Some of the women screamed at first, but not many.

Thousands of shots must have rained in on us in the next few minutes. How I wanted to crawl out to the trench under the wagons where our men were keeping up a steady but irregular fire! Each was shooting on his own whenever he saw a man to pull trigger on. But mother suspected me, for she made me crouch down and keep right on holding the baby.

I was just taking a look at Silas Dunlap—he was still quivering—when the little Castleton baby was killed. Dorothy Castleton, herself only about ten, was holding it, so that it was killed in her arms. She was not hurt at all. I heard them talking about it, and they conjectured that the bullet must have struck high on one of the wagons and been deflected down into the rifle pit. It was just an accident, they said, and that except for such accidents we were safe where we were.

When I looked again Silas Dunlap was dead, and I suffered distinct disappointment in being cheated out of witnessing that particular event. I had never been lucky enough to see a man actually die before my eyes.

Dorothy Castleton got hysterics over what had happened, and yelled and screamed for a long time and she set Mrs. Hastings going again. Altogether such a row was raised that father sent Watt Cummings crawling back to us to find out what was the matter.

Well along into twilight the heavy firing ceased, although there were scattering shots during the night. Two of our men were wounded in this second attack, and were brought into the rifle pit. Bill Tyler was killed instantly, and they buried him, Silas Dunlap, and the Castleton baby, in the dark alongside of the others.

All during the night men relieved one another at sinking the well deeper; but the only sign of water they got was damp sand. Some of the men fetched a few pails of water from the spring, but were fired upon, and they gave it up when Jeremy Hopkins had his left hand shot off at the wrist.

Next morning, the third day, it was hotter and dryer than ever. We awoke thirsty, and there was no cooking. So dry were our mouths that we could not eat. I tried a piece of stale bread mother gave me, but had to give it up. The firing rose and fell. Sometimes there were hundreds shooting into the camp. At other times came lulls in which not a shot was fired. Father was continually cautioning our men not to waste shots because we were running short of ammunition.

And all the time the men went on digging the well. It was so deep that they were hoisting the sand up in buckets. The men who hoisted were exposed, and one of them was wounded in the shoulder. He was Peter Bromley, who drove oxen for the Bloodgood wagon, and he was engaged to marry Jane Bloodgood. She jumped out of the rifle pit and ran right to him while the bullets were flying and led him back into shelter. About midday the well caved in, and there was lively work digging out the couple who were buried in the sand. Amos Wentworth did not come to for an hour. After that they timbered the well with bottom boards from the wagons and wagon tongues, and the digging went on. But all they could get, and they were twenty feet down, was damp sand. The water would not seep.

By this time the conditions in the rifle pit were terrible. The children were complaining for water, and the babies, hoarse from much crying, went on crying. Robert Carr, another wounded man, lay about ten feet from mother and me. He was out of his head, and kept thrashing his arms about and calling for water. And some of the women were almost as bad, and kept raving against the Mormons and

Indians. Some of the women prayed a great deal, and the three grown Demdike sisters, with their mother, sang gospel hymns. Other women got damp sand that was hoisted out of the bottom of the well, and packed it against the bare bodies of the babies to try to cool and soothe them.

The two Fairfax brothers couldn't stand it any longer, and, with pails in their hands, crawled out under a wagon and made a dash for the spring. Giles never got half way, when he went down. Roger made it there and back without being hit. He brought two pails part-full, for some splashed out when he ran. Giles crawled back, and when they helped him into the rifle pit he was bleeding at the mouth and coughing.

Two part-pails of water could not go far among over a hundred of us, not counting the men. Only the babies, and the very little children, and the wounded men, got any. I did not get a sip, although mother dipped a bit of cloth into the several spoonfuls she got for the baby and wiped my mouth out. She did not even do that for herself, for she left me the bit of damp rag to chew.

The situation grew unspeakably worse in the afternoon. The quiet sun blazed down through the clear windless air and made a furnace of our hole in the sand. And all about us were the explosions of rifles and yells of the Indians. Only once in a while did father permit a single shot from the trench, and at that only by our best marksmen, such as Laban and Timothy Grant. But a steady stream of lead poured into our position all the time. There were no more disastrous ricochets, however; and our men in the trench, no longer firing, lay low and escaped damage. Only four were wounded, and only one of them very badly.

Father came in from the trench during a lull in the firing. He sat for a few minutes alongside mother and me without speaking. He seemed to be listening to all the moaning and crying for water that was going up. Once he climbed out of the rifle pit and went over to investigate the well. He brought back only damp sand, which he plastered thick on the chest and shoulders of Robert Carr. Then he went to where Jed Dunham and his mother were, and sent for Jed's father to come in from the trench. So closely packed were we that when anybody moved about inside the rifle pit he had to crawl carefully over the bodies of those lying down.

After a time father came crawling back to us.

"Jesse," he asked, "are you afraid of the Indians?"

I shook my head emphatically, guessing that I was to be sent on another proud mission.

"Are you afraid of the damned Mormons?"

"Not of any damned Mormon," I answered, taking advantage of the opportunity to curse our enemies without fear of the avenging back of mother's hand.

I noted the little smile that curled his tired lips for the moment when he heard my reply.

"Well, then, Jesse," he said, "will you go with Jed to the spring for water?"

I was all eagerness.

"We're going to dress the two of you up as girls," he continued, "so that maybe they won't fire on you."

I insisted on going as I was, as a male human that wore pants; but I surrendered quickly enough when father suggested that he would find some other boy to dress up and go along with Jed.

A chest was fetched in from the Chattox wagon. The Chattox girls were twins and of about a size with Jed and me. Several of the women got around to help.

They were the Sunday dresses of the Chattox twins, and had come in the chest all the way from Arkansas.

In her anxiety mother left the baby with Sarah Dunlap, and came as far as the trench with me. There, under a wagon and behind the little breastwork of sand, Jed and I received our last instructions. Then we crawled out and stood up in the open. We were dressed precisely alike—white stockings, white dresses, with big blue sashes, and white sunbonnets. Jed's right and my left hand were clasped together. In each of our free hands we carried two small pails.

"Take it easy," father cautioned, as we began our advance. "Go slow. Walk like girls."

Not a shot was fired. We made the spring safely, filled our pails, and lay down and took a good drink ourselves. With a full pail in each hand we made the return trip. And still not a shot was fired.

I cannot remember how many journeys we made—fully fifteen or twenty. We walked slowly, always going out with hands clasped, always coming back slowly with four pails of water. It was astonishing how thirsty we were. We lay down several times and took long drinks.

But it was too much for our enemies. I cannot imagine that the Indians would have withheld their fire for so long, girls or no girls, had they not obeyed instructions from the whites who were with them. At any rate Jed and I were just starting on another trip when a rifle went off from the Indian hill, and then another.

"Come back!" mother cried out.

I looked at Jed, and found him looking at me. I knew he was stubborn and had made up his mind to be the last one in. So I started to advance, and at the same instant he started.

"You!—Jesse!" cried my mother. And there was more than a smacking in the way she said it.

Jed offered to clasp hands, but I shook my head.

"Run for it," I said.

And while we hotfooted it across the sand it seemed all the rifles on Indian hill were turned loose on us. I got to the spring a little ahead, so that Jed had to wait for me to fill my pails.

"Now run for it," he told me; and from the leisurely way he went about filling his own pails I knew he was determined to be in last.

So I crouched down, and, while I waited, watched the puffs of dust raised by the bullets. We began the return side by side and running.

"Not so fast," I cautioned him, "or you'll spill half the water."

That stung him, and he slacked back perceptibly. Midway I stumbled and fell headlong. A bullet, striking directly in front of me, filled my eyes with sand. For a moment I thought I was shot.

"Done it a-purpose," Jed sneered as I scrambled to my feet. He had stood and waited for me.

I caught his idea. He thought I had fallen deliberately in order to spill my water and go back for more. This rivalry between us was a serious matter—so serious, indeed, that I immediately took advantage of what he had imputed and raced back to the spring. And Jed Dunham, scornful of the bullets that were puffing dust all around him, stood there upright in the open and waited for me.

We came in side by side, with honours even in our boys' foolhardiness. But when we delivered the water Jed had only one pailful. A bullet had gone through the other pail close to the bottom.

Mother took it out on me with a lecture on disobedience. She must have known, after what I had done, that father wouldn't let her smack me; for, while she was lecturing, father winked at me across her shoulder. It was the first time he had ever winked at me.

Back in the rifle pit Jed and I were heroes. The women wept and blessed us, and kissed us and mauled us. And I confess I was proud of the demonstration, although, like Jed, I let on that I did not like all such making-over. But Jeremy Hopkins, a great bandage about the stump of his left wrist, said we were the stuff white men were made out of—men like Daniel Boone, like Kit Carson, and Davy Crockett. I was prouder of that than all the rest.

The remainder of the day I seem to have been bothered principally with the pain of my right eye caused by the sand that had been kicked into it by the bullet. The eye was bloodshot, mother said; and to me it seemed to hurt just as much whether I kept it open or closed. I tried both ways.

Things were quieter in the rifle pit, because all had had water, though strong upon us was the problem of how the next water was to be procured. Coupled with this was the known fact that our ammunition was almost exhausted. A thorough overhauling of the wagons by father had resulted in finding five pounds of powder. A very little more was in the flasks of the men.

I remembered the sundown attack of the night before, and anticipated it this time by crawling to the trench before sunset. I crept into a place alongside of Laban. He was busy chewing tobacco, and did not notice me. For some time I watched him, fearing that when he discovered me he would order me back. He would take a long squint out between the wagon wheels, chew steadily a while, and then spit carefully into a little depression he had made in the sand.

"How's tricks?" I asked finally. It was the way he always addressed me.

"Fine," he answered. "Most remarkable fine, Jesse, now that I can chew again. My mouth was that dry that I couldn't chew from sun-up to when you brung the water."

Here a man showed head and shoulders over the top of the little hill to the north-east occupied by the whites. Laban sighted his rifle on him for a long minute. Then he shook his head.

"Four hundred yards. Nope, I don't risk it. I might get him, and then again I mightn't, an' your dad is mighty anxious about the powder."

"What do you think our chances are?" I asked, man-fashion, for, after my water exploit, I was feeling very much the man.

Laban seemed to consider carefully for a space ere he replied.

"Jesse, I don't mind tellin' you we're in a damned bad hole. But we'll get out, oh, we'll get out, you can bet your bottom dollar."

"Some of us ain't going to get out," I objected.

"Who, for instance?" he queried.

"Why, Bill Tyler, and Mrs. Grant, and Silas Dunlap, and all the rest."

"Aw, shucks, Jesse—they're in the ground already. Don't you know everybody has to bury their dead as they traipse along? They've ben doin' it for thousands of years I reckon, and there's just as many alive as ever they was. You see, Jesse, birth and death go hand-in-hand. And they're born as fast as they die—faster, I reckon, because they've increased and multiplied. Now you, you might a-got killed this afternoon packin' water. But you're here, ain't you, a-gassin' with me an' likely to grow up an' be the father of a fine large family in Californy. They say everything grows large in Californy."

This cheerful way of looking at the matter encouraged me to dare sudden expression of a long covetousness.

"Say, Laban, supposin' you got killed here——"

"Who?—me?" he cried.

"I'm just sayin' supposin'," I explained.

"Oh, all right then. Go on. Supposin' I am killed?"

"Will you give me your scalps?"

"Your ma'll smack you if she catches you a-wearin' them," he temporized.

"I don't have to wear them when she's around. Now if you got killed, Laban, somebody'd have to get them scalps. Why not me?"

"Why not?" he repeated. "That's correct, and why not you? All right, Jesse. I like you, and your pa. The minute I'm killed the scalps is yourn, and the scalpin' knife, too. And there's Timothy Grant for witness. Did you hear, Timothy?"

Timothy said he had heard, and I lay there speechless in the stifling trench, too overcome by my greatness of good fortune to be able to utter a word of gratitude.

I was rewarded for my foresight in going to the trench. Another general attack was made at sundown, and thousands of shots were fired into us. Nobody on our side was scratched. On the other hand, although we fired barely thirty shots, I saw Laban and Timothy Grant each get an Indian. Laban told me that from the first only the Indians had done the shooting. He was certain that no white had fired a shot. All of which sorely puzzled him. The whites neither offered us aid nor attacked us, and all the while were on visiting terms with the Indians who were attacking us.

Next morning found the thirst harsh upon us. I was out at the first hint of light. There had been a heavy dew, and men, women, and children were lapping it up with their tongues from off the wagon-tongues, brake-blocks, and wheel-tyres.

There was talk that Laban had returned from a scout just before daylight; that he had crept close to the position of the whites; that they were already up; and that in the light of their camp-fires he had seen them praying in a large circle. Also he reported from what few words he caught that they were praying about us and what was to be done with us.

"May God send them the light then," I heard one of the Demdike sisters say to Abby Foxwell.

"And soon," said Abby Foxwell, "for I don't know what we'll do a whole day without water, and our powder is about gone."

Nothing happened all morning. Not a shot was fired. Only the sun blazed down through the quiet air. Our thirst grew, and soon the babies were crying and the younger children whimpering and complaining. At noon Will Hamilton took two large pails and started for the spring. But before he could crawl under the wagon Ann Demdike ran and got her arms around him and tried to hold him back. But he talked to her, and kissed her, and went on. Not a shot was fired, nor was any fired all the time he continued to go out and bring back water.

"Praise God!" cried old Mrs. Demdike. "It is a sign. They have relented."

This was the opinion of many of the women.

About two o'clock, after we had eaten and felt better, a white man appeared, carrying a white flag. Will Hamilton went out and talked to him, came back and talked with father and the rest of our men, and then went out to the stranger again. Farther back we could see a man standing and looking on, whom we recognized as Lee.

With us all was excitement. The women were so relieved that they were crying and kissing one another, and old Mrs. Demdike and others were hallelujahing and blessing God. The proposal, which our men had accepted, was that we would put ourselves under the flag of truce and be protected from the Indians.

"We had to do it," I heard father tell mother.

He was sitting, droop-shouldered and dejected, on a wagon-tongue.

"But what if they intend treachery?" mother asked.

He shrugged his shoulders.

"We've got to take the chance that they don't," he said. "Our ammunition is gone."

Some of our men were unchaining one of our wagons and rolling it out of the way. I ran across to see what was happening. In came Lee himself, followed by two empty wagons, each driven by one man. Everybody crowded around Lee. He said that they had had a hard time with the Indians keeping them off of us, and that Major Higbee, with fifty of the Mormon militia, were ready to take us under their charge.

But what made father and Laban and some of the men suspicious was when Lee said that we must put all our rifles into one of the wagons so as not to arouse the animosity of the Indians. By so doing we would appear to be the prisoners of the Mormon militia.

Father straightened up and was about to refuse when he glanced to Laban, who replied in an undertone:

"They ain't no more use in our hands than in the wagon, seein' as the powder's gone."

Two of our wounded men who could not walk were put into the wagons, and along with them were put all the little children. Lee seemed to be picking them out over eight and under eight. Jed and I were large for our age, and we were nine besides; so Lee put us with the older bunch and told us we were to march with the women on foot.

When he took our baby from mother and put it in a wagon she started to object. Then I saw her lips draw tightly together, and she gave in. She was a gray-eyed, strong-featured, middle-aged woman, large-boned and fairly stout. But the long journey and hardship had told on her, so that she was hollow-cheeked and gaunt, and like all the women in the company she wore an expression of brooding, never-ceasing anxiety.

It was when Lee described the order of march that Laban came to me. Lee said that the women and the children that walked should go first in the line, following behind the two wagons. Then the men, in single file, should follow the women. When Laban heard this he came to me, untied the scalps from his belt, and fastened them to my waist.

"But you ain't killed yet," I protested.

"You bet your life I ain't," he answered lightly. "I've just reformed, that's all.

This scalp-wearin' is a vain thing and heathen." He stopped a moment as if he had forgotten something, then, as he turned abruptly on his heel to regain the men of our company, he called over his shoulder, "Well, so long, Jesse."

I was wondering why he should say good-bye when a white man came riding into the corral. He said Major Higbee had sent him to tell us to hurry up, because the Indians might attack at any moment.

So the march began, the two wagons first. Lee kept along with the women and walking children. Behind us, after waiting until we were a couple of hundred feet in advance, came our men. As we emerged from the corral we could see the militia just a short distance away. They were leaning on their rifles and standing in a long line about six feet apart. As we passed them I could not help noticing how solemn-faced they were. They looked like men at a funeral. So did the women notice this, and some of them began to cry.

I walked right behind my mother. I had chosen this position so that she would not catch sight of my scalps. Behind me came the three Demdike sisters, two of them helping the old mother. I could hear Lee calling all the time to the men who drove the wagons not to go so fast. A man that one of the Demdike girls said must be Major Higbee sat on a horse watching us go by. Not an Indian was in sight.

By the time our men were just abreast of the militia—I had just looked back to try to see where Jed Dunham was—the thing happened. I heard Major Higbee cry out in a loud voice, "Do your duty!" All the rifles of the militia seemed to go off at once, and our men were falling over and sinking down. All the Demdike women went down at one time. I turned quickly to see how mother was, and she was down. Right alongside of us, out of the bushes, came hundreds of Indians, all shooting. I saw the two Dunlap sisters start on the run across the sand, and took after them, for whites and Indians were all killing us. And as I ran I saw the driver of one of the wagons shooting the two wounded men. The horses of the other wagon were plunging and rearing and their driver was trying to hold them.

It was when the little boy that was I was running after the Dunlap girls that blackness came upon him. All memory there ceases, for Jesse Fancher there ceased, and, as Jesse Fancher, ceased forever. The form that was Jesse Fancher, the body that was his, being matter and apparitional, like an apparition passed and was not. But the imperishable spirit did not cease. It continued to exist, and, in its next incarnation, became the residing spirit of that apparitional body known as Darrell Standing's and which soon is to be taken out and hanged and sent into the nothingness whither all apparitions go.

There is a lifer here in Folsom, Matthew Davies, of old pioneer stock, who is trusty of the scaffold and execution chamber. He is an old man, and his folks crossed the plains in the early days. I have talked with him, and he has verified the massacre in which Jesse Fancher was killed. When this old lifer was a child there was much talk in his family of the Mountain Meadows Massacre. The children in the wagons, he said, were saved, because they were too young to tell tales.

All of which I submit. Never, in my life of Darrell Standing, have I read a line or heard a word spoken of the Fancher Company that perished at Mountain Meadows. Yet, in the jacket in San Quentin prison, all this knowledge came to me. I could not create this knowledge out of nothing, any more than could I create dynamite out of nothing. This knowledge and these facts I have related have but one explanation. They are out of the spirit content of me—the spirit that, unlike matter, does not perish.

In closing this chapter I must state that Matthew Davies also told me that some years after the massacre Lee was taken by United States Government officials to the Mountain Meadows and there executed on the site of our old corral.

1915

The Short Story Writer

TO THE MAN ON TRAIL

"Dump it in."

"But I say, Kid, isn't that going it a little too strong? Whisky and alcohol's bad enough; but when it comes to brandy and pepper sauce and——"

"Dump it in. Who's making this punch, anyway?" And Malemute Kid smiled benignantly through the clouds of steam. "By the time you've been in this country as long as I have, my son, and lived on rabbit tracks and salmon belly, you'll learn that Christmas comes only once per annum. And a Christmas without punch is sinking a hole to bedrock with nary a pay streak."

"Stack up on that fer a high cyard," approved Big Jim Belden, who had come down from his claim on Mazy May to spend Christmas, and who, as everyone knew, had been living the two months past on straight moose meat. "Hain't fergot the hooch we-uns made on the Tanana, hev yeh?"

"Well, I guess yes. Boys, it would have done your hearts good to see that whole tribe fighting drunk—and all because of a glorious ferment of sugar and sour dough. That was before your time," Malemute Kid said as he turned to Stanley Prince, a young mining expert who had been in two years. "No white women in the country then, and Mason wanted to get married. Ruth's father was chief of the Tananas, and objected, like the rest of the tribe. Stiff? Why, I used my last pound of sugar; finest work in that line I ever did in my life. You should have seen the chase, down the river and across the portage."

"But the squaw?" asked Louis Savoy, the tall French Canadian, becoming interested; for he had heard of this wild deed when at Forty Mile the preceding winter.

Then Malemute Kid, who was a born raconteur, told the unvarnished tale of the Northland Lochinvar. More than one rough adventurer of the North felt his heartstrings draw closer and experienced vague yearnings for the sunnier pastures of the Southland, where life promised something more than a barren struggle with cold and death.

"We struck the Yukon just behind the first ice run," he concluded, "and the tribe only a quarter of an hour behind. But that saved us; for the second run broke the jam above and shut them out. When they finally got into Nuklukyeto, the whole post was ready for them. And as to the forgathering, ask Father Roubeau here: he performed the ceremony."

The Jesuit took the pipe from his lips but could only express his gratification with patriarchal smiles, while Protestant and Catholic vigorously applauded.

"By gar!" ejaculated Louis Savoy, who seemed overcome by the romance of it. "*La petite* squaw; *mon* Mason *brav*. By gar!"

Then, as the first tin cups of punch went round, Bettles the Unquenchable sprang to his feet and struck up his favorite drinking song:

"There's Henry Ward Beecher
And Sunday-school teachers,
All drink of the sassafras root;
But you bet all the same,
If it had its right name,
It's the juice of the forbidden fruit."

"Oh, the juice of the forbidden fruit,"

roared out the bacchanalian chorus,

"Oh, the juice of the forbidden fruit;
But you bet all the same,
If it had its right name,
It's the juice of the forbidden fruit."

Malemute Kid's frightful concoction did its work; the men of the camps and trails unbent in its genial glow, and jest and song and tales of past adventure went round the board. Aliens from a dozen lands, they toasted each and all. It was the Englishman, Prince, who pledged "Uncle Sam, the precocious infant of the New World"; the Yankee, Bettles, who drank to "The Queen, God bless her"; and together, Savoy and Meyers, the German trader, clanged their cups to Alsace and Lorraine.

Then Malemute Kid arose, cup in hand, and glanced at the greased-paper window, where the frost stood full three inches thick. "A health to the man on trail this night; may his grub hold out; may his dogs keep their legs; may his matches never miss fire."

Crack! Crack! They heard the familiar music of the dog whip, the whining howl of the Malemutes, and the crunch of a sled as it drew up to the cabin. Conversation languished while they waited the issue.

"An old-timer; cares for his dogs and then himself," whispered Malemute Kid to Prince as they listened to the snapping jaws and the wolfish snarls and yelps of pain which proclaimed to their practiced ears that the stranger was beating back their dogs while he fed his own.

Then came the expected knock, sharp and confident, and the stranger entered. Dazzled by the light, he hesitated a moment at the door, giving to all a chance for scrutiny. He was a striking personage, and a most picturesque one, in his Arctic dress of wool and fur. Standing six foot two or three, with proportionate breadth of shoulders and depth of chest, his smooth-shaven face nipped by the cold to a gleaming pink, his long lashes and eyebrows white with ice, and the ear and neck flaps of his great wolfskin cap loosely raised, he seemed, of a verity, the Frost King, just stepped in out of the night. Clasped outside his Mackinaw jacket, a beaded belt held two large Colt's revolvers and a hunting knife, while he carried, in addition to the inevitable dog whip, a smokeless rifle of the largest bore and latest pattern. As he came forward, for all his step was firm and elastic, they could see that fatigue bore heavily upon him.

An awkward silence had fallen, but his hearty "What cheer, my lads?" put them quickly at ease, and the next instant Malemute Kid and he had gripped hands. Though they had never met, each had heard of the other, and the recognition was mutual. A sweeping introduction and a mug of punch were forced upon him before he could explain his errand.

"How long since that basket sled, with three men and eight dogs, passed?" he asked.

"An even two days ahead. Are you after them?"

"Yes; my team. Run them off under my very nose, the cusses. I've gained two days on them already—pick them up on the next run."

"Reckon they'll show spunk?" asked Belden, in order to keep up the conversation, for Malemute Kid already had the coffeepot on and was busily frying bacon and moose meat.

The stranger significantly tapped his revolvers.

"When'd yeh leave Dawson?"

"Twelve o'clock."

"Last night?"—as a matter of course.

"Today."

A murmur of surprise passed round the circle. And well it might; for it was just midnight, and seventy-five miles of rough river trail was not to be sneered at for a twelve hours' run.

The talk soon became impersonal, however, harking back to the trails of childhood. As the young stranger ate of the rude fare Malemute Kid attentively studied his face. Nor was he long in deciding that it was fair, honest, and open, and that he liked it. Still youthful, the lines had been firmly traced by toil and hardship. Though genial in conversation, and mild when at rest, the blue eyes gave promise of the hard steel-glitter which comes when called into action, especially against odds. The heavy jaw and square-cut chin demonstrated rugged pertinacity and indomitability. Nor, though the attributes of the lion were there, was there wanting the certain softness, the hint of womanliness, which bespoke the emotional nature.

"So thet's how me an' the ol' woman got spliced," said Belden, concluding the exciting tale of his courtship. "'Here we be, Dad,' sez she. 'An' may yeh be damned,' sez he to her, an' then to me, 'Jim, yeh—yeh git outen them good duds o' yourn; I want a right peart slice o' thet forty acre plowed 'fore dinner.' An' then he turns on her an' sez, 'An' yeh, Sal; yeh sail inter them dishes.' An' then he sort o' sniffled an' kissed her. An' I was thet happy—but he seen me an' roars out, 'Yeh, Jim!' An' yeh bet I dusted fer the barn."

"Any kids waiting for you back in the States?" asked the stranger.

"Nope; Sal died 'fore any come. Thet's why I'm here." Belden abstractedly began to light his pipe, which had failed to go out, and then brightened up with, "How 'bout yerself, stranger—married man?"

For reply, he opened his watch, slipped it from the thong which served for a chain, and passed it over. Belden picked up the slush lamp, surveyed the inside of the case critically, and, swearing admiringly to himself, handed it over to Louis

Savoy. With numerous "By gars!" he finally surrendered it to Prince, and they noticed that his hands trembled and his eyes took on a peculiar softness. And so it passed from horny hand to horny hand—the pasted photograph of a woman, the clinging kind that such men fancy, with a babe at the breast. Those who had not yet seen the wonder were keen with curiosity; those who had became silent and retrospective. They could face the pinch of famine, the grip of scurvy, or the quick death by field or flood; but the pictured semblance of a stranger woman and child made women and children of them all.

"Never have seen the youngster yet—he's a boy, she says, and two years old," said the stranger as he received the treasure back. A lingering moment he gazed upon it, then snapped the case and turned away, but not quick enough to hide the restrained rush of tears.

Malemute Kid led him to a bunk and bade him turn in.

"Call me at four sharp. Don't fail me," were his last words, and a moment later he was breathing in the heaviness of exhausted sleep.

"By Jove! He's a plucky chap," commented Prince. "Three hours' sleep after seventy-five miles with the dogs, and then the trail again. Who is he, Kid?"

"Jack Westondale. Been in going on three years, with nothing but the name of working like a horse, and any amount of bad luck to his credit. I never knew him, but Sitka Charley told me about him."

"It seems hard that a man with a sweet young wife like his should be putting in his years in this Godforsaken hole, where every year counts two on the outside."

"The trouble with him is clean grit and stubbornness. He's cleaned up twice with a stake, but lost it both times."

Here the conversation was broken off by an uproar from Bettles, for the effect had begun to wear away. And soon the bleak years of monotonous grub and deadening toil were being forgotten in rough merriment. Malemute Kid alone seemed unable to lose himself, and cast many an anxious look at his watch. Once he put on his mittens and beaver-skin cap, and, leaving the cabin, fell to rummaging about in the cache.

Nor could he wait the hour designated; for he was fifteen minutes ahead of time in rousing his guest. The young giant had stiffened badly, and brisk rubbing was necessary to bring him to his feet. He tottered painfully out of the cabin, to find his dogs harnessed and everything ready for the start. The company wished him good luck and a short chase, while Father Roubeau, hurriedly blessing him, led the stampede for the cabin; and small wonder, for it is not good to face seventy-four degrees below zero with naked ears and hands.

Malemute Kid saw him to the main trail, and there, gripping his hand heartily, gave him advice.

"You'll find a hundred pounds of salmon eggs on the sled," he said. "The dogs will go as far on that as with one hundred and fifty of fish, and you can't get dog food at Pelly, as you probably expected." The stranger started, and his eyes flashed, but he did not interrupt. "You can't get an ounce of food for dog or man till you reach Five Fingers, and that's a stiff two hundred miles. Watch out for open water on the Thirty Mile River, and be sure you take the big cutoff above Le Barge."

"How did you know it? Surely the news can't be ahead of me already?"

"I don't know it; and what's more, I don't want to know it. But you never owned that team you're chasing. Sitka Charley sold it to them last spring. But he sized you up to me as square once, and I believe him. I've seen your face; I like it. And I've seen—why, damn you, hit the high places for salt water and that wife of yours, and——" Here the Kid unmittened and jerked out his sack.

"No; I don't need it," and the tears froze on his cheeks as he convulsively gripped Malemute Kid's hand.

"Then don't spare the dogs; cut them out of the traces as fast as they drop; buy them, and think they're cheap at ten dollars a pound. You can get them at Five Fingers, Little Salmon, and Hootalinqua. And watch out for wet feet," was his parting advice. "Keep a-traveling up to twenty-five, but if it gets below that, build a fire and change your socks."

Fifteen minutes had barely elapsed when the jingle of bells announced new arrivals. The door opened, and a mounted policeman of the Northwest Territory entered, followed by two half-breed dog drivers. Like Westondale, they were heavily armed and showed signs of fatigue. The half-breeds had been borne to the trail and bore it easily; but the young policeman was badly exhausted. Still, the dogged obstinacy of his race held him to the pace he had set, and would hold him till he dropped in his tracks.

"When did Westondale pull out?" he asked. "He stopped here, didn't he?" This was supererogatory, for the tracks told their own tale too well.

Malemute Kid had caught Belden's eye, and he, scenting the wind, replied evasively, "A right peart while back."

"Come, my man; speak up," the policeman admonished.

"Yeh seem to want him right smart. Hez he ben gittin' cantankerous down Dawson way?"

"Held up Harry McFarland's for forty thousand; exchanged it at the P. C. store for a check on Seattle; and who's to stop the cashing of it if we don't overtake him? When did he pull out?"

Every eye suppressed its excitement, for Malemute Kid had given the cue, and the young officer encountered wooden faces on every hand.

Striding over to Prince, he put the question to him. Though it hurt him, gazing into the frank, earnest face of his fellow countryman, he replied inconsequentially on the state of the trail.

Then he espied Father Roubeau, who could not lie. "A quarter of an hour ago," the priest answered; "but he had four hours' rest for himself and dogs."

"Fifteen minutes' start, and he's fresh! My God!" The poor fellow staggered back, half fainting from exhaustion and disappointment, murmuring something about the run from Dawson in ten hours and the dogs being played out.

Malemute Kid forced a mug of punch upon him; then he turned for the door, ordering the dog drivers to follow. But the warmth and promise of rest were too tempting, and they objected strenuously. The Kid was conversant with their French patois, and followed it anxiously.

They swore that the dogs were gone up; that Siwash and Babette would have to be shot before the first mile was covered; that the rest were almost as bad; and that it would be better for all hands to rest up.

"Lend me five dogs?" he asked, turning to Malemute Kid.

But the Kid shook his head.

"I'll sign a check on Captain Constantine for five thousand—here's my papers—I'm authorized to draw at my own discretion."

Again the silent refusal.

"Then I'll requisition them in the name of the Queen."

Smiling incredulously, the Kid glanced at his well-stocked arsenal, and the Englishman, realizing his impotency, turned for the door. But the dog drivers still objecting, he whirled upon them fiercely, calling them women and curs. The swart face of the older half-breed flushed angrily as he drew himself up and promised in good, round terms that he would travel his leader off his legs, and would then be delighted to plant him in the snow.

The young officer—and it required his whole will—walked steadily to the door, exhibiting a freshness he did not possess. But they all knew and appreciated his proud effort; nor could he veil the twinges of agony that shot across his face. Covered with frost, the dogs were curled up in the snow, and it was almost impossible to get them to their feet. The poor brutes whined under the stinging lash, for the dog drivers were angry and cruel; nor till Babette, the leader, was cut from the traces, could they break out the sled and get under way.

"A dirty scoundrel and a liar!" "By gar! Him no good!" "A thief!" "Worse than an Indian!" It was evident that they were angry—first at the way they had been deceived; and second at the outraged ethics of the Northland, where honesty, above all, was man's prime jewel. "An' we gave the cuss a hand, after knowin' what he'd did." All eyes turned accusingly upon Malemute Kid, who rose from the corner where he had been making Babette comfortable, and silently emptied the bowl for a final round of punch.

"It's a cold night, boys—a bitter cold night," was the irrelevant commencement of his defense. "You've all traveled trail, and know what that stands for. Don't jump a dog when he's down. You've only heard one side. A whiter man than Jack Westondale never ate from the same pot nor stretched blanket with you or me. Last fall he gave his whole clean-up, forty thousand, to Joe Castrell, to buy in on Dominion. Today he'd be a millionaire. But while he stayed behind at Circle City, taking care of his partner with the scurvy, what does Castrell do? Goes into McFarland's, jumps the limit, and drops the whole sack. Found him dead in the snow the next day. And poor Jack laying his plans to go out this winter to his wife and the boy he's never seen. You'll notice he took exactly what his partner lost—forty thousand. Well, he's gone out; and what are you going to do about it?"

The Kid glanced round the circle of his judges, noted the softening of their faces, then raised his mug aloft. "So a health to the man on trail this night; may his grub hold out; may his dogs keep their legs; may his matches never miss fire. God prosper him; good luck go with him; and——"

"Confusion to the Mounted Police!" cried Bettles, to the crash of the empty cups.

1899

THE WHITE SILENCE

"Carmen won't last more than a couple of days." Mason spat out a chunk of ice and surveyed the poor animal ruefully, then put her foot in his mouth and proceeded to bite out the ice which clustered cruelly between the toes.

"I never saw a dog with a highfalutin' name that ever was worth a rap," he said, as he concluded his task and shoved her aside. "They just fade away and die under the responsibility. Did ye ever see one go wrong with a sensible name like Cassiar, Siwash, or Husky? No, sir! Take a look at Shookum here, he's—"

Snap! The lean brute flashed up, the white teeth just missing Mason's throat.

"Ye will, will ye?" A shrewd clout behind the ear with the butt of the dog whip stretched the animal in the snow, quivering softly, a yellow slaver dripping from its fangs.

"As I was saying, just look at Shookum here—he's got the spirit. Bet ye he eats Carmen before the week's out."

"I'll bank another proposition against that," replied Malemute Kid, reversing the frozen bread placed before the fire to thaw. "We'll eat Shookum before the trip is over. What d'ye say, Ruth?"

The Indian woman settled the coffee with a piece of ice, glanced from Malemute Kid to her husband, then at the dogs, but vouchsafed no reply. It was such a palpable truism that none was necessary. Two hundred miles of unbroken trail in prospect, with a scant six days' grub for themselves and none for the dogs, could admit no other alternative. The two men and the woman grouped about the fire and began their meager meal. The dogs lay in their harnesses, for it was a midday halt, and watched each mouthful enviously.

"No more lunches after today," said Malemute Kid. "And we've got to keep a close eye on the dogs—they're getting vicious. They'd just as soon pull a fellow down as not, if they get a chance."

"And I was president of an Epworth once, and taught in the Sunday school." Having irrelevantly delivered himself of this, Mason fell into a dreamy contemplation of his steaming moccasins, but was aroused by Ruth filling his cup. "Thank God, we've got slathers of tea! I've seen it growing, down in Tennessee. What wouldn't I give for a hot corn pone just now! Never mind, Ruth; you won't starve much longer, nor wear moccasins either."

The woman threw off her gloom at this, and in her eyes welled up a great love for her white lord—the first white man she had ever seen—the first man whom she had known to treat a woman as something better than a mere animal or beast of burden.

"Yes, Ruth," continued her husband, having recourse to the macaronic jargon in which it was alone possible for them to understand each other; "wait till we clean up and pull for the Outside. We'll take the White Man's canoe and go to the Salt Water. Yes, bad water, rough water—great mountains dance up and down all the time. And so big, so far, so far away—you travel ten sleep, twenty sleep, forty sleep"—he graphically enumerated the days on his fingers—"all the time water, bad water. Then you come to great village, plenty people, just the same mosquitoes next summer. Wigwams oh, so high—ten, twenty pines. Hi-yu skookum!"

He paused impotently, cast an appealing glance at Malemute Kid, then laboriously placed the twenty pines, end on end, by sign language. Malemute Kid smiled with cheery cynicism; but Ruth's eyes were wide with wonder, and with pleasure; for she half believed he was joking, and such condescension pleased her poor woman's heart.

"And then you step into a—a box, and pouf! up you go." He tossed his empty cup in the air by way of illustration and, as he deftly caught it, cried: "And biff!

down you come. Oh, great medicine men! You go Fort Yukon, I go Arctic City—twenty-five sleep—big string, all the time—I catch him string—I say, 'Hello, Ruth! How are ye?'—and you say, 'Is that my good husband?'—and I say, 'Yes'—and you say, 'No can bake good bread, no more soda'—then I say, 'Look in cache, under flour; good-by.' You look and catch plenty soda. All the time you Fort Yukon, me Arctic City. Hi-yu medicine man!"

Ruth smiled so ingenuously at the fairy story that both men burst into laughter. A row among the dogs cut short the wonders of the Outside, and by the time the snarling combatants were separated, she had lashed the sleds and all was ready for the trail.

"Mush! Baldy! Hi! Mush on!" Mason worked his whip smartly and, as the dogs whined low in the traces, broke out the sled with the gee pole. Ruth followed with the second team, leaving Malemute Kid, who had helped her start, to bring up the rear. Strong man, brute that he was, capable of felling an ox at a blow, he could not bear to beat the poor animals, but humored them as a dog driver rarely does—nay, almost wept with them in their misery.

"Come, mush on there, you poor sore-footed brutes!" he murmured, after several ineffectual attempts to start the load. But his patience was at last rewarded, and though whimpering with pain, they hastened to join their fellows.

No more conversation; the toil of the trail will not permit such extravagance. And of all deadening labors, that of the Northland trail is the worst. Happy is the man who can weather a day's travel at the price of silence, and that on a beaten track.

And of all heartbreaking labors, that of breaking trail is the worst. At every step the great webbed shoe sinks till the snow is level with the knee. Then up, straight up, the deviation of a fraction of an inch being a certain precursor of disaster, the snowshoe must be lifted till the surface is cleared; then forward, down, and the other foot is raised perpendicularly for the matter of half a yard. He who tries this for the first time, if haply he avoids bringing his shoes in dangerous propinquity and measures not his length on the treacherous footing, will give up exhausted at the end of a hundred yards; he who can keep out of the way of the dogs for a whole day may well crawl into his sleeping bag with a clear conscience and a pride which passeth all understanding; and he who travels twenty sleeps on the Long Trail is a man whom the gods may envy.

The afternoon wore on, and with the awe, born of the White Silence, the voiceless travelers bent to their work. Nature has many tricks wherewith she convinces man of his finity—the ceaseless flow of the tides, the fury of the storm, the shock of the earthquake, the long roll of heaven's artillery—but the most tremendous, the most stupefying of all, is the passive phase of the White Silence. All movement ceases, the sky clears, the heavens are as brass; the slightest whisper seems sacrilege, and man becomes timid, affrighted at the sound of his own voice. Sole speck of life journeying across the ghostly wastes of a dead world, he trembles at his audacity, realizes that his is a maggot's life, nothing more. Strange thoughts arise unsummoned, and the mystery of all things strives for utterance. And the fear of death, of God, of the universe, comes over him—the hope of the Resurrection and the Life, the yearning for immortality, the vain striving of the imprisoned essence—it is then, if ever, man walks alone with God.

So wore the day away. The river took a great bend, and Mason headed his team for the cutoff across the narrow neck of land. But the dogs balked at the high bank. Again and again, though Ruth and Malemute Kid were shoving on the sled, they slipped back. Then came the concerted effort. The miserable creatures, weak from hunger, exerted their last strength. Up–up–the sled poised on the top of the bank; but the leader swung the string of dogs behind him to the right, fouling Mason's snowshoes. The result was grievous. Mason was whipped off his feet; one of the dogs fell in the traces; and the sled toppled back, dragging everything to the bottom again.

Slash! the whip fell among the dogs savagely, especially upon the one which had fallen.

"Don't, Mason," entreated Malemute Kid; "the poor devil's on its last legs. Wait and we'll put my team on."

Mason deliberately withheld the whip till the last word had fallen, then out flashed the long lash, completely curling about the offending creature's body. Carmen–for it was Carmen–cowered in the snow, cried piteously, then rolled over on her side.

It was a tragic moment, a pitiful incident of the trail–a dying dog, two comrades in anger. Ruth glanced solicitously from man to man. But Malemute Kid restrained himself, though there was a world of reproach in his eyes, and, bending over the dog, cut the traces. No word was spoken. The teams were double-spanned and the difficulty overcome; the sleds were under way again, the dying dog dragging herself along in the rear. As long as an animal can travel, it is not shot, and this last chance is accorded it–the crawling into camp, if it can, in the hope of a moose being killed.

Already penitent for his angry action, but too stubborn to make amends, Mason toiled on at the head of the cavalcade, little dreaming that danger hovered in the air. The timber clustered thick in the sheltered bottom, and through this they threaded their way. Fifty feet or more from the trail towered a lofty pine. For generations it had stood there, and for generations destiny had had this one end in view–perhaps the same had been decreed of Mason.

He stooped to fasten the loosened thong of his moccasin. The sleds came to a halt, and the dogs lay down in the snow without a whimper. The stillness was weird; not a breath rustled the frost-encrusted forest; the cold and silence of outer space had chilled the heart and smote the trembling lips of nature. A sigh pulsed through the air–they did not seem to actually hear it, but rather felt it, like the premonition of movement in a motionless void. Then the great tree, burdened with its weight of years and snow, played its last part in the tragedy of life. He heard the warning crash and attempted to spring up but, almost erect, caught the blow squarely on the shoulder.

The sudden danger, the quick death–how often had Malemute Kid faced it! The pine needles were still quivering as he gave his commands and sprang into action. Nor did the Indian girl faint or raise her voice in idle wailing, as might many of her white sisters. At his order, she threw her weight on the end of a quickly extemporized handspike, easing the pressure and listening to her husband's groans, while Malemute Kid attacked the tree with his ax. The steel rang merrily as it bit into the frozen trunk, each stroke being accompanied by a forced, audible respiration, the "Huh!" "Huh!" of the woodsman.

At last the Kid laid the pitiable thing that was once a man in the snow. But worse than his comrade's pain was the dumb anguish in the woman's face, the blended look of hopeful, hopeless query. Little was said; those of the Northland are early taught the futility of words and the inestimable value of deeds. With the temperature at sixty-five below zero, a man cannot lie many minutes in the snow and live. So the sled lashings were cut, and the sufferer, rolled in furs, laid on a couch of boughs. Before him roared a fire, built of the very wood which wrought the mishap. Behind and partially over him was stretched the primitive fly—a piece of canvas, which caught the radiating heat and threw it back and down upon him—a trick which men may know who study physics at the fount.

And men who have shared their bed with death know when the call is sounded. Mason was terribly crushed. The most cursory examination revealed it. His right arm, leg, and back were broken; his limbs were paralyzed from the hips; and the likelihood of internal injuries was large. An occasional moan was his only sign of life.

No hope; nothing to be done. The pitiless night crept slowly by—Ruth's portion, the despairing stoicism of her race, and Malemute Kid adding new lines to his face of bronze. In fact, Mason suffered least of all, for he spent his time in eastern Tennessee, in the Great Smoky Mountains, living over the scenes of his childhood. And most pathetic was the melody of his long-forgotten Southern vernacular, as he raved of swimming holes and coon hunts and watermelon raids. It was as Greek to Ruth, but the Kid understood and felt—felt as only one can feel who has been shut out for years from all that civilization means.

Morning brought consciousness to the stricken man, and Malemute Kid bent closer to catch his whispers.

"You remember when we foregathered on the Tanana, four years come next ice run? I didn't care so much for her then. It was more like she was pretty, and there was a smack of excitement about it, I think. But d'ye know, I've come to think a heap of her. She's been a good wife to me, always at my shoulder in the pinch. And when it comes to trading, you know there isn't her equal. D'ye recollect the time she shot the Moosehorn Rapids to pull you and me off that rock, the bullets whipping the water like hailstones?—and the time of the famine at Nuklukyeto?—or when she raced the ice run to bring the news? Yes, she's been a good wife to me, better'n that other one. Didn't know I'd been there? Never told you, eh? Well, I tried it once, down in the States. That's why I'm here. Been raised together, too. I came away to give her a chance for divorce. She got it.

"But that's got nothing to do with Ruth. I had thought of cleaning up and pulling for the Outside next year—her and I—but it's too late. Don't send her back to her people, Kid. It's beastly hard for a woman to go back. Think of it!—nearly four years on our bacon and beans and flour and dried fruit, and then to go back to her fish and caribou. It's not good for her to have tried our ways, to come to know they're better'n her people's, and then return to them. Take care of her, Kid—why don't you—but no, you always fought shy of them—and you never told me why you came to this country. Be kind to her, and send her back to the States as soon as you can. But fix it so she can come back—liable to get homesick, you know.

"And the youngster—it's drawn us closer, Kid. I only hope it is a boy. Think of it!—flesh of my flesh, Kid. He mustn't stop in this country. And if it's a girl, why, she can't. Sell my furs; they'll fetch at least five thousand, and I've got as much more with the company. And handle my interests with yours. I think that bench claim will show up. See that he gets a good schooling; and, Kid, above all, don't let him come back. This country was not made for white men.

"I'm a gone man, Kid. Three or four sleeps at the best. You've got to go on. You must go on! Remember, it's my wife, it's my boy—O God! I hope it's a boy! You can't stay by me—and I charge you, a dying man, to pull on."

"Give me three days," pleaded Malemute Kid. "You may change for the better; something may turn up."

"No."

"Just three days."

"You must pull on."

"Two days."

"It's my wife and my boy, Kid. You would not ask it."

"One day."

"No, no! I charge——"

"Only one day. We can shave it through on the grub, and I might knock over a moose."

"No—all right; one day, but not a minute more. And, Kid, don't—don't leave me to face it alone. Just a shot, one pull on the trigger. You understand. Think of it! Think of it! Flesh of my flesh, and I'll never live to see him!

"Send Ruth here. I want to say good-by and tell her that she must think of the boy and not wait till I'm dead. She might refuse to go with you if I didn't. Good-by, old man; good-by.

"Kid! I say—a—sink a hole above the pup, next to the slide. I panned out forty cents on my shovel there.

"And, Kid!" He stooped lower to catch the last faint words, the dying man's surrender of his pride. "I'm sorry—for—you know—Carmen."

Leaving the girl crying softly over her man, Malemute Kid slipped into his parka and snowshoes, tucked his rifle under his arm, and crept away into the forest. He was no tyro in the stern sorrows of the Northland, but never had he faced so stiff a problem as this. In the abstract, it was a plain, mathematical proposition—three possible lives as against one doomed one. But now he hesitated. For five years, shoulder to shoulder, on the rivers and trails, in the camps and mines, facing death by field and flood and famine, had they knitted the bonds of their comradeship. So close was the tie that he had often been conscious of a vague jealousy of Ruth, from the first time she had come between. And now it must be severed by his own hand.

Though he prayed for a moose, just one moose, all game seemed to have deserted the land, and nightfall found the exhausted man crawling into camp, light-handed, heavyhearted. An uproar from the dogs and shrill cries from Ruth hastened him.

Bursting into the camp, he saw the girl in the midst of the snarling pack, laying about her with an ax. The dogs had broken the iron rule of their masters and were rushing the grub. He joined the issue with his rifle reversed, and the hoary game of natural selection was played out with all the ruthlessness of its primeval environment. Rifle and ax went up and down, hit or missed with monotonous regularity; lithe bodies flashed, with wild eyes and dripping fangs; and man and beast fought for supremacy to the bitterest conclusion. Then the beaten brutes crept to the edge of the firelight, licking their wounds, voicing their misery to the stars.

The whole stock of dried salmon had been devoured, and perhaps five pounds of flour remained to tide them over two hundred miles of wilderness. Ruth returned to her husband, while Malemute Kid cut up the warm body of one of the dogs, the skull of which had been crushed by the ax. Every portion was carefully put away, save the hide and offal, which were cast to his fellows of the moment before.

Morning brought fresh trouble. The animals were turning on each other. Carmen, who still clung to her slender thread of life, was downed by the pack. The lash fell among them unheeded. They cringed and cried under the blows, but refused to scatter till the last wretched bit had disappeared—bones, hide, hair, everything.

Malemute Kid went about his work, listening to Mason, who was back in Tennessee, delivering tangled discourses and wild exhortations to his brethren of other days.

Taking advantage of neighboring pines, he worked rapidly, and Ruth watched him make a cache similar to those sometimes used by hunters to preserve their meat from the wolverines and dogs. One after the other, he bent the tops of two small pines toward each other and nearly to the ground, making them fast with thongs of moosehide. Then he beat the dogs into submission and harnessed them to two of the sleds, loading the same with everything but the furs which enveloped Mason. These he wrapped and lashed tightly about him, fastening either end of the robes to the bent pines. A single stroke of his hunting knife would release them and send the body high in the air.

Ruth had received her husband's last wishes and made no struggle. Poor girl, she had learned the lesson of obedience well. From a child, she had bowed, and seen all women bow, to the lords of creation, and it did not seem in the nature of things for woman to resist. The Kid permitted her one outburst of grief, as she kissed her husband—her own people had no such custom—then led her to the foremost sled and helped her into her snowshoes. Blindly, instinctively, she took the gee pole and whip, and "mushed" the dogs out on the trail. Then he returned to Mason, who had fallen into a coma, and long after she was out of sight crouched by the fire, waiting, hoping, praying for his comrade to die.

It is not pleasant to be alone with painful thoughts in the White Silence. The silence of gloom is merciful, shrouding one as with protection and breathing a thousand intangible sympathies; but the bright White Silence, clear and cold, under steely skies, is pitiless.

An hour passed—two hours—but the man would not die. At high noon the sun, without raising its rim above the southern horizon, threw a suggestion of fire athwart the heavens, then quickly drew it back. Malemute Kid roused and dragged himself to his comrade's side. He cast one glance about him. The White Silence seemed to sneer, and a great fear came upon him. There was a sharp report; Mason swung into his aerial sepulcher, and Malemute Kid lashed the dogs into a wild gallop as he fled across the snow.

1899

AN ODYSSEY OF THE NORTH

I

The sleds were singing their eternal lament to the creaking of the harnesses and the tinkling bells of the leaders; but the men and dogs were tired and made no sound. The trail was heavy with new-fallen snow, and they had come far, and the runners, burdened with flintlike quarters of frozen moose, clung tenaciously to the unpacked surface and held back with a stubbornness almost human. Darkness was coming on, but there was no camp to pitch that night. The snow fell gently through the pulseless air, not in flakes, but in tiny frost crystals of delicate design. It was very warm—barely ten below zero—and the men did not mind. Meyers and Bettles had raised their ear flaps, while Malemute Kid had even taken off his mittens.

The dogs had been fagged out early in the afternoon, but they now began to show new vigor. Among the more astute there was a certain restlessness—an impatience at the restraint of the traces, an indecisive quickness of movement, a sniffing of snouts and pricking of ears. These became incensed at their more phlegmatic brothers, urging them on with numerous sly nips on their hinder quarters. Those, thus chidden, also contracted and helped spread the contagion. At last the leader of the foremost sled uttered a sharp whine of satisfaction, crouching lower in the snow and throwing himself against the collar. The rest followed suit. There was an ingathering of back bands, a tightening of traces; the sleds leaped forward, and the men clung to the gee poles, violently accelerating the uplift of their feet that they might escape going under the runners. The weariness of the day fell from them, and they whooped encouragement to the dogs. The animals responded with joyous yelps. They were swinging through the gathering darkness at a rattling gallop.

"Gee! Gee!" the men cried, each in turn, as their sleds abruptly left the main trail, heeling over on single runners like luggers on the wind.

Then came a hundred yards' dash to the lighted parchment window, which told its own story of the home cabin, the roaring Yukon stove, and the steaming pots of tea. But the home cabin had been invaded. Threescore huskies chorused defiance, and as many furry forms precipitated themselves upon the dogs which drew the first sled. The door was flung open, and a man, clad in the scarlet tunic of the Northwest Police, waded knee-deep among the furious brutes, calmly and impartially dispensing soothing justice with the butt end of a dog whip. After that the men shook hands; and in this wise was Malemute Kid welcomed to his own cabin by a stranger.

Stanley Prince, who should have welcomed him, and who was responsible for the Yukon stove and hot tea aforementioned, was busy with his guests. There were a dozen or so of them, as nondescript a crowd as ever served the Queen in the enforcement of her laws or the delivery of her mails. They were of many breeds, but their common life had formed of them a certain type—a lean and wiry type, with trail-hardened muscles, and sun-browned faces, and untroubled souls which gazed frankly forth, clear-eyed and steady. They drove the dogs of the Queen, wrought fear in the hearts of her enemies, ate of her meager fare, and were happy. They had seen life, and done deeds, and lived romances; but they did not know it.

And they were very much at home. Two of them were sprawled upon Malemute Kid's bunk, singing chansons which their French forebears sang in the days when first they entered the Northwest land and mated with its Indian women. Bettles' bunk had suffered a similar invasion, and three or four lusty *voyageurs* worked their toes among its blankets as they listened to the tale of one who had served on the boat brigade with Wolseley when he fought his way to Khartoum. And when he tired, a cowboy told of courts and kings and lords and ladies he had seen when Buffalo Bill toured the capitals of Europe. In a corner two half-breeds, ancient comrades in a lost campaign, mended harnesses and talked of the days when the Northwest flamed with insurrection and Louis Riel was king.

Rough jests and rougher jokes went up and down, and great hazards by trail and river were spoken of in the light of commonplaces, only to be recalled by virtue of some grain of humor or ludicrous happening. Prince was led away by these uncrowned heroes who had seen history made, who regarded the great and the romantic as but the ordinary and the incidental in the routine of life. He passed his precious tobacco among them with lavish disregard, and rusty chains of reminiscence were loosened, and forgotten odysseys resurrected for his especial benefit.

When conversation dropped and the travelers filled the last pipes and unlashed their tight-rolled sleeping furs, Prince fell back upon his comrade for further information.

"Well, you know what the cowboy is," Malemute Kid answered, beginning to unlace his moccasins; "and it's not hard to guess the British blood in his bed partner. As for the rest, they're all children of the *coureurs du bois*, mingled with God knows how many other bloods. The two turning in by the door are the regulation 'breeds' or *Boisbrûles*. That lad with the worsted breech scarf—notice his eyebrows and the turn of his jaw—shows a Scotchman wept in his mother's smoky tepee. And that handsome-looking fellow putting the capote under his head is a French half-breed—you heard him talking; he doesn't like the two Indians turning in next to him. You see, when the 'breeds' rose under Riel the full-bloods kept the peace, and they've not lost much love for one another since."

"But I say, what's that glum-looking fellow by the stove? I'll swear he can't talk English. He hasn't opened his mouth all night."

"You're wrong. He knows English well enough. Did you follow his eyes when he listened? I did. But he's neither kith nor kin to the others. When they talked their own patois you could see he didn't understand. I've been wondering myself what he is. Let's find out."

"Fire a couple of sticks into the stove!" Malemute Kid commanded, raising his voice and looking squarely at the man in question.

He obeyed at once.

"Had discipline knocked into him somewhere," Prince commented in a low tone.

Malemute Kid nodded, took off his socks, and picked his way among recumbent men to the stove. There he hung his damp footgear among a score or so of mates.

"When do you expect to get to Dawson?" he asked tentatively.

The man studied him a moment before replying. "They say seventy-five mile. So? Maybe two days."

The very slightest accent was perceptible, while there was no awkward hesitancy or groping for words.

"Been in the country before?"

"No."

"Northwest Territory?"

"Yes."

"Born there?"

"No."

"Well, where the devil were you born? You're none of these." Malemute Kid swept his hand over the dog drivers, even including the two policemen who had turned into Prince's bunk. "Where did you come from? I've seen faces like yours before, though I can't remember just where."

"I know you," he irrelevantly replied, at once turning the drift of Malemute Kid's questions.

"Where? Ever see me?"

"No; your partner, him priest, Pastilik, long time ago. Him ask me if I see you, Malemute Kid. Him give me grub. I no stop long. You hear him speak 'bout me?"

"Oh! you're the fellow that traded the otter skins for the dogs?"

The man nodded, knocked out his pipe, and signified his disinclination for conversation by rolling up in his furs. Malemute Kid blew out the slush lamp and crawled under the blankets with Prince.

"Well, what is he?"

"Don't know—turned me off, somehow, and then shut up like a clam. But he's a fellow to whet your curiosity. I've heard of him. All the coast wondered about him eight years ago. Sort of mysterious, you know. He came down out of the North, in the dead of winter, many a thousand miles from here, skirting Bering Sea and traveling as though the devil were after him. No one ever learned where he came from, but he must have come far. He was badly travel-worn when he got food from the Swedish missionary on Golovin Bay and asked the way south. We heard of this afterward. Then he abandoned the shore line, heading right across Norton Sound. Terrible weather, snowstorms and high winds, but he pulled through where a thousand other men would have died, missing St. Michaels and making the land at Pastilik. He'd lost all but two dogs, and was nearly gone with starvation.

"He was so anxious to go on that Father Roubeau fitted him out with grub; but he couldn't let him have any dogs, for he was only waiting my arrival to go on a trip himself. Mr. Ulysses knew too much to start on without animals, and fretted around for several days. He had on his sled a bunch of beautifully cured otter skins, sea otters, you know, worth their weight in gold. There was also at Pastilik an old Shylock of a Russian trader, who had dogs to kill. Well, they didn't dicker very long, but when the Strange One headed south again, it was in the rear of a spanking dog team. Mr. Shylock, by the way, had the otter skins. I saw them, and they were magnificent. We figured it up and found the dogs brought him at least five hundred apiece. And it wasn't as if the Strange One didn't know the value of sea otter; he was an Indian of some sort, and what little he talked showed he'd been among white men.

"After the ice passed out of the sea, word came up from Nunivak Island that he'd gone in there for grub. Then he dropped from sight, and this is the first heard of him in eight years. Now where did he come from? and what was he doing there? and why did he come from there? He's Indian, he's been nobody knows where, and he's had discipline, which is unusual for an Indian. Another mystery of the North for you to solve, Prince."

"Thanks awfully, but I've got too many on hand as it is," he replied.

Malemute Kid was already breathing heavily; but the young mining engineer gazed straight up through the thick darkness, waiting for the strange orgasm which stirred his blood to die away. And when he did sleep, his brain worked on, and for the nonce he, too, wandered through the white unknown, struggled with the dogs on endless trails, and saw men live, and toil, and die like men.

The next morning, hours before daylight, the dog drivers and policemen pulled out for Dawson. But the powers that saw to Her Majesty's interests and ruled the destinies of her lesser creatures gave the mailmen little rest, for a week later they appeared at Stuart River, heavily burdened with letters for Salt Water. However, their dogs had been replaced by fresh ones; but, then, they were dogs.

The men had expected some sort of a layover in which to rest up; besides, this Klondike was a new section of the Northland, and they had wished to see a little something of the Golden City where dust flowed like water and dance halls rang with never-ending revelry. But they dried their socks and smoked their evening pipes with much the same gusto as on their former visit, though one or two bold spirits speculated on desertion and the possibility of crossing the unexplored Rockies to the east, and thence, by the Mackenzie Valley, of gaining their old stamping grounds in the Chippewyan country. Two or three even decided to return to their homes by that route when their terms of service had expired, and they began to lay plans forthwith, looking forward to the hazardous undertaking in much the same way a city-bred man would to a day's holiday in the woods.

He of the Otter Skins seemed very restless, though he took little interest in the discussion, and at last he drew Malemute Kid to one side and talked for some time in low tones. Prince cast curious eyes in their direction, and the mystery deepened when they put on caps and mittens and went outside. When they returned, Malemute Kid placed his gold scales on the table, weighed out the matter of sixty ounces, and transferred them to the Strange One's sack. Then the chief of the dog drivers joined the conclave, and certain business was transacted with him. The next day the gang went on upriver, but He of the Otter Skins took several pounds of grub and turned his steps back toward Dawson.

"Didn't know what to make of it," said Malemute Kid in response to Prince's queries; "but the poor beggar wanted to be quit of the service for some reason or other—at least it seemed a most important one to him, though he wouldn't let on what. You see, it's just like the army: he signed for two years, and the only way to get free was to buy himself out. He couldn't desert and then stay here, and he was just wild to remain in the country. Made up his mind when he got to Dawson, he said; but no one knew him, hadn't a cent, and I was the only one he'd spoken two words with. So he talked it over with the lieutenant-governor, and made arrangements in case he could get the money from me—loan, you know. Said he'd pay back in the year, and, if I wanted, would put me onto something rich. Never'd seen it, but knew it was rich.

"And talk! why, when he got me outside he was ready to weep. Begged and pleaded; got down in the snow to me till I hauled him out of it. Palavered around like a crazy man. Swore he's worked to this very end for years and years, and couldn't bear to be disappointed now. Asked him what end, but he wouldn't say.

Said they might keep him on the other half of the trail and he wouldn't get to Dawson in two years, and then it would be too late. Never saw a man take on so in my life. And when I said I'd let him have it, had to yank him out of the snow again. Told him to consider it in the light of a grubstake. Think he'd have it? No sir! Swore he'd give me all he found, make me rich beyond the dreams of avarice, and all such stuff. Now a man who puts his life and time against a grubstake ordinarily finds it hard enough to turn over half of what he finds. Something behind all this, Prince; just you make a note of it. We'll hear of him if he stays in the country——"

"And if he doesn't?"

"Then my good nature gets a shock, and I'm sixty some odd ounces out."

The cold weather had come on with the long nights, and the sun had begun to play his ancient game of peekaboo along the southern snow line ere aught was heard of Malemute Kid's grubstake. And then, one bleak morning in early January, a heavily laden dog train pulled into his cabin below Stuart River. He of the Otter Skins was there, and with him walked a man such as the gods have almost forgotten how to fashion. Men never talked of luck and pluck and five-hundred-dollar dirt without bringing in the name of Axel Gunderson; nor could tales of nerve or strength or daring pass up and down the campfire without the summoning of his presence. And when the conversation flagged, it blazed anew at mention of the woman who shared his fortunes.

As has been noted, in the making of Axel Gunderson the gods had remembered their old-time cunning and cast him after the manner of men who were born when the world was young. Full seven feet he towered in his picturesque costume which marked a king of Eldorado. His chest, neck, and limbs were those of a giant. To bear his three hundred pounds of bone and muscle, his snowshoes were greater by a generous yard than those of other men. Rough-hewn, with rugged brow and massive jaw and unflinching eyes of palest blue, his face told the tale of one who knew but the law of might. Of the yellow of ripe corn silk, his frost-incrusted hair swept like day across the night and fell far down his coat of bearskin. A vague tradition of the sea seemed to cling about him as he swung down the narrow trail in advance of the dogs; and he brought the butt of his dog whip against Malemute Kid's door as a Norse sea rover, on southern foray, might thunder for admittance at the castle gate.

Prince bared his womanly arms and kneaded sour-dough bread, casting, as he did so, many a glance at the three guests—three guests the like of which might never come under a man's roof in a lifetime. The Strange One, whom Malemute Kid had surnamed Ulysses, still fascinated him; but his interest chiefly gravitated between Axel Gunderson and Axel Gunderson's wife. She felt the day's journey, for she had softened in comfortable cabins during the many days since her husband mastered the wealth of frozen pay streaks, and she was tired. She rested against his great breast like a slender flower against a wall, replying lazily to Malemute Kid's good-natured banter, and stirring Prince's blood strangely with an occasional sweep of her deep, dark eyes. For Prince was a man, and healthy, and had seen few women in many months. And she was older than he, and an Indian besides. But she was different from all native wives he had met: she had traveled—had been in his country among others, he gathered from the conversation; and she knew most of the things the women of his own race knew, and much more that it was not in the nature of things for them to know. She could make a meal of sun-dried fish or a bed in the snow; yet she teased them with tantalizing details of many-course dinners, and caused strange internal dissensions to arise at the mention of various quondam dishes which they had well-nigh forgotten. She knew the ways of the moose, the bear, and the little blue fox, and of the wild amphibians of the Northern seas; she was skilled in the lore of the woods and the streams, and the tale writ by man and bird and beast upon the delicate snow crust was to her an open book; yet Prince caught the appreciative twinkle in her eye as she read the Rules of the Camp. These rules had been fathered by the Unquenchable Bettles at a time when his blood ran high, and were remarkable for the terse simplicity of their humor. Prince always turned them to the wall before the arrival of ladies; but who could suspect that this native wife—— Well, it was too late now.

This, then, was the wife of Axel Gunderson, a woman whose name and fame had traveled with her husband's, hand in hand, through all the Northland. At table, Malemute Kid baited her with the assurance of an old friend, and Prince shook off the shyness of first acquaintance and joined in. But she held her own in the unequal contest, while her husband, slower in wit, ventured naught but applause. And he was very proud of her; his every look and action revealed the magnitude of the place she occupied in his life. He of the Otter Skins ate in silence, forgotten in the merry battle; and long ere the others were done he pushed back from the table and went out among the dogs. Yet all too soon his fellow travelers drew on their mittens and parkas and followed him.

There had been no snow for many days, and the sleds slipped along the hard-packed Yukon trail as easily as if it had been glare ice. Ulysses led the first sled; with the second came Prince and Axel Gunderson's wife; while Malemute Kid and the yellow-haired giant brought up the third.

"It's only a hunch, Kid," he said, "but I think it's straight. He's never been there, but he tells a good story, and shows a map I heard of when I was in the Kootenay country years ago. I'd like to have you go along; but he's a strange one, and swore point-blank to throw it up if anyone was brought in. But when I come back you'll get first tip, and I'll stake you next to me, and give you a half share in the town site besides.

"No! no!" he cried, as the other strove to interrupt. "I'm running this, and before I'm done it'll need two heads. If it's all right, why, it'll be a second Cripple Creek, man; do you hear?—a second Cripple Creek! It's quartz, you know, not placer; and if we work it right we'll corral the whole thing—millions upon millions. I've heard of the place before, and so have you. We'll build a town—thousands of workmen—good waterways—steamship lines—big carrying trade—light-draught steamers for head reaches—survey a railroad, perhaps—sawmills—electric-light plant—do our own banking—commercial company—syndicate—— Say! just you hold your hush till I get back!"

The sleds came to a halt where the trail crossed the mouth of Stuart River. An unbroken sea of frost, its wide expanse stretched away into the unknown east. The snowshoes were withdrawn from the lashings of the sleds. Axel Gunderson shook hands and stepped to the fore, his great webbed shoes sinking a fair half yard into the feathery surface and packing the snow so the dogs should not wallow. His wife fell in behind the last sled, betraying long practice in the art of handling the awkward footgear. The stillness was broken with cheery farewells; the dogs whined; and He of the Otter Skins talked with his whip to a recalcitrant wheeler.

An hour later the train had taken on the likeness of a black pencil crawling in a long, straight line across a mighty sheet of foolscap.

II

One night, many weeks later, Malemute Kid and Prince fell to solving chess problems from the torn page of an ancient magazine. The Kid had just returned from his Bonanza properties and was resting up preparatory to a long moose hunt. Prince, too, had been on creek and trail nearly all winter, and had grown hungry for a blissful week of cabin life.

"Interpose the black knight, and force the king. No, that won't do. See, the next move——"

"Why advance the pawn two squares? Bound to take it in transit, and with the bishop out of the way——"

"But hold on! That leaves a hole, and——"

"No; it's protected. Go ahead! You'll see it works."

It was very interesting. Somebody knocked at the door a second time before Malemute Kid said, "Come in." The door swung open. Something staggered in. Prince caught one square look and sprang to his feet. The horror in his eyes caused Malemute Kid to whirl about; and he, too, was startled, though he had seen bad things before. The thing tottered blindly toward them. Prince edged away till he reached the nail from which hung his Smith & Wesson.

"My God! what is it?" he whispered to Malemute Kid.

"Don't know. Looks like a case of freezing and no grub," replied the Kid, sliding away in the opposite direction. "Watch out! It may be mad," he warned, coming back from closing the door.

The thing advanced to the table. The bright flame of the slush lamp caught its eye. It was amused, and gave voice to eldritch cackles which betokened mirth. Then, suddenly, he—for it was a man—swayed back, with a hitch to his skin trousers, and began to sing a chantey, such as men lift when they swing around the capstan circle and the sea snorts in their ears:

"Yan-kee ship come down de ri-ib-er,
Pull! my bully boys! Pull!
D'yeh want—to know de captain ru-uns her?
Pull! my bully boys! Pull!
Jon-a-than Jones ob South Caho-li-in-a,
Pull! my bully—"

He broke off abruptly, tottered with a wolfish snarl to the meat shelf, and before they could intercept was tearing with his teeth at a chunk of raw bacon. The struggle was fierce between him and Malemute Kid; but his mad strength left him as suddenly as it had come, and he weakly surrendered the spoil. Between them they got him upon a stool, where he sprawled with half his body across the table. A small dose of whiskey strengthened him, so that he could dip a spoon into the sugar caddy which Malemute Kid placed before him. After his appetite had been somewhat cloyed, Prince, shuddering as he did so, passed him a mug of weak beef tea.

The creature's eyes were alight with a somber frenzy, which blazed and waned with every mouthful. There was very little skin to the face. The face, for that matter, sunken and emaciated, bore little likeness to human countenance. Frost after frost had bitten deeply, each depositing its stratum of scab upon the half-healed scar that went before. This dry, hard surface was of a bloody-black color, serrated by grievous cracks wherein the raw red flesh peeped forth. His skin garments were dirty and in tatters, and the fur of one side was singed and burned away, showing where he had lain upon his fire.

Malemute Kid pointed to where the sun-tanned hide had been cut away, strip by strip—the grim signature of famine.

"Who—are—you?" slowly and distinctly enunciated the Kid.

The man paid no heed.

"Where do you come from?"

"Yan-kee ship come down de ri-ib-er," was the quavering response.

"Don't doubt the beggar came down the river," the Kid said, shaking him in an endeavor to start a more lucid flow of talk.

But the man shrieked at the contact, clapping a hand to his side in evident pain. He rose slowly to his feet, half leaning on the table.

"She laughed at me—so—with the hate in her eye; and she—would—not—come."

His voice died away, and he was sinking back when Malemute Kid gripped him by the wrist and shouted, "Who? Who would not come?"

"She, Unga. She laughed, and struck at me, so, and so. And then——"

"Yes?"

"And then——"

"And then what?"

"And then he lay very still in the snow a long time. He is—still in—the—snow."

The two men looked at each other helplessly.

"Who is in the snow?"

"She, Unga. She looked at me with the hate in her eye, and then——"

"Yes, yes."

"And then she took the knife, so; and once, twice—she was weak. I traveled very slow. And there is much gold in that place, very much gold."

"Where is Unga?" For all Malemute Kid knew, she might be dying a mile away. He shook the man savagely, repeating again and again, "Where is Unga? Who is Unga?"

"She—is—in—the—snow."

"Go on!" The Kid was pressing his wrist cruelly.

"So—I—would—be—in—the snow—but—I—had—a—debt—to—pay. It—was—heavy—I—had—a—debt—to—pay—a—debt—to—pay I—had——" The faltering monosyllables ceased as he fumbled in his pouch and drew forth a buckskin sack. "A—debt—to—pay—five—pounds—of—gold—grub—stake—Mal—e—mute—Kid—I——" The exhausted head dropped upon the table; nor could Malemute Kid rouse it again.

"It's Ulysses," he said quietly, tossing the bag of dust on the table. "Guess it's all day with Axel Gunderson and the woman. Come on, let's get him between the blankets. He's Indian; he'll pull through and tell a tale besides."

As they cut his garments from him, near his right breast could be seen two unhealed, hard-lipped knife thrusts.

III

"I will talk of the things which were in my own way; but you will understand.

I will begin at the beginning, and tell of myself and the woman, and, after that, of the man."

He of the Otter Skins drew over to the stove as do men who have been deprived of fire and are afraid the Promethean gift may vanish at any moment. Malemute Kid picked up the slush lamp and placed it so its light might fall upon the face of the narrator. Prince slid his body over the edge of the bunk and joined them.

"I am Naass, a chief, and the son of a chief, born between a sunset and a rising, on the dark seas, in my father's oomiak. All of a night the men toiled at the paddles, and the women cast out the waves which threw in upon us, and we fought with the storm. The salt spray froze upon my mother's breast till her breath passed with the passing of the tide. But I—I raised my voice with the wind and the storm, and lived.

"We dwelt in Akatan——"

"Where?" asked Malemute Kid.

"Akatan, which is in the Aleutians; Akatan, beyond Chignik, beyond Kardalak, beyond Unimak. As I say, we dwelt in Akatan, which lies in the midst of the sea on the edge of the world. We farmed the salt seas for the fish, the seal, and the otter; and our homes shouldered about one another on the rocky strip between the rim of the forest and the yellow beach where our kayaks lay. We were not many, and the world was very small. There were strange lands to the east—islands like Akatan; so we thought all the world was islands and did not mind.

"I was different from my people. In the sands of the beach were the crooked timbers and wave-warped planks of a boat such as my people never built; and I remember on the point of the island which overlooked the ocean three ways there stood a pine tree which never grew there, smooth and straight and tall. It is said the two men came to that spot, turn about, through many days, and watched with the passing of the light. These two men came from out of the sea in the boat which lay in pieces on the beach. And they were white like you, and weak as the little children when the seal have gone away and the hunters come home empty. I know of these things from the old men and the old women, who got them from their fathers and mothers before them. These strange white men did not take kindly to our ways at first, but they grew strong, what of the fish and the oil, and fierce. And they built them each his own house, and took the pick of our women, and in time children came. Thus he was born who was to become the father of my father's father.

"As I said, I was different from my people, for I carried the strong, strange blood of this white man who came out of the sea. It is said we had other laws in the days before these men; but they were fierce and quarrelsome, and fought with our men till there were no more left who dared to fight. Then they made themselves chiefs, and took away our old laws and gave us new ones, insomuch that the man was the son of his father, and not his mother, as our way had been. They also ruled that the son, first-born, should have all things which were his father's before him, and that the brothers and sisters should shift for themselves. And they gave us other laws. They showed us new ways in the catching of fish and the killing of bear which were thick in the woods; and they taught us to lay by bigger stores for the time of famine. And these things were good.

"But when they had become chiefs, and there were no more men to face their anger, they fought, these strange white men, each with the other. And the one whose blood I carry drove his seal spear the length of an arm through the other's body. Their children took up the fight, and their children's children; and there was great hatred between them, and black doings, even to my time, so that in each family but one lived to pass down the blood of them that went before. Of my blood I was alone; of the other man's there was but a girl. Unga, who lived with her mother. Her father and my father did not come back from the fishing one night; but afterward they washed up to the beach on the big tides, and they held very close to each other.

"The people wondered, because of the hatred between the houses, and the old men shook their heads and said the fight would go on when children were born to her and children to me. They told me this as a boy, till I came to believe, and to look upon Unga as a foe, who was to be the mother of children which were to fight with mine. I thought of these things day by day, and when I grew to a stripling I came to ask why this should be so. And they answered, 'We do not know, but that in such way your fathers did.' And I marveled that those which were to come should fight the battles of those that were gone, and in it I could see no right. But the people said it must be, and I was only a stripling.

"And they said I must hurry, that my blood might be the older and grow strong before hers. This was easy, for I was head man, and the people looked up to me because of the deeds and the laws of my fathers, and the wealth which was mine. Any maiden would come to me, but I found none to my liking. And the old men and the mothers of maidens told me to hurry, for even then were the hunters bidding high to the mother of Unga; and should her children grow strong before mine, mine would surely die.

"Nor did I find a maiden till one night coming back from the fishing. The sunlight was lying, so, low and full in the eyes, the wind free, and the kayaks racing with the white seas. Of a sudden the kayak of Unga came driving past me, and she looked upon me, so, with her black hair flying like a cloud of night and the spray wet on her cheek. As I say, the sunlight was full in the eyes, and I was a stripling; but somehow it was all clear, and I knew it to be the call of kind to kind. As she whipped ahead she looked back within the space of two strokes—looked as only the woman Unga could look—and again I knew it as the call of kind. The people shouted as we ripped past the lazy oomiaks and left them far behind. But she was quick at the paddle, and my heart was like the belly of a sail, and I did not gain. The wind freshened, the sea whitened, and, leaping like the seals on the windward breech, we roared down the golden pathway of the sun."

Naass was crouched half out of his stool, in the attitude of one driving a paddle, as he ran the race anew. Somewhere across the stove he beheld the tossing kayak and the flying hair of Unga. The voice of the wind was in his ears, and its salt beat fresh upon his nostrils.

"But she made the shore, and ran up the sand, laughing, to the house of her mother. And a great thought came to me that night—a thought worthy of him that was chief over all the people of Akatan. So, when the moon was up, I went down to the house of her mother, and looked upon the goods of Yash-Noosh, which were piled by the door—the goods of Yash-Noosh, a strong hunter who had it in mind to be the father of the children of Unga. Other young men had piled their goods there and taken them away again; and each young man had made a pile greater than the one before.

"And I laughed to the moon and the stars, and went to my own house where my wealth was stored. And many trips I made, till my pile was greater by the fingers of one hand than the pile of Yash-Noosh. There were fish, dried in the sun and smoked; and forty hides of the hair seal, and half as many of the fur, and each hide was tied at the mouth and big bellied with oil; and ten skins of bear which I killed in the woods when they came out in the spring. And there were beads and blankets and scarlet cloths, such as I got in trade from the people who lived to the east, and who got them in trade from the people who lived still beyond in the east. And I looked upon the pile of Yash-Noosh and laughed, for I was head man in Akatan, and my wealth was greater than the wealth of all my young men, and my fathers had done deeds, and given laws, and put their names for all time in the mouths of the people.

"So, when the morning came, I went down to the beach, casting out of the corner of my eye at the house of the mother of Unga. My offer yet stood untouched. And the women smiled, and said sly things one to the other. I wondered, for never had such a price been offered; and that night I added more to the pile, and put beside it a kayak of well-tanned skins which never yet had swam in the sea. But in the day it was yet there, open to the laughter of all men. The mother of Unga was crafty, and I grew angry at the shame in which I stood before my people. So that night I added till it became a great pile, and I hauled up my oomiak, which was of the value of twenty kayaks. And in the morning there was no pile.

"Then made I preparation for the wedding, and the people that lived even to the east came for the food of the feast and the potlatch token. Unga was older than I by the age of four suns in the way we reckoned the years. I was only a stripling; but then I was a chief, and the son of a chief, and it did not matter.

"But a ship shoved her sails above the floor of the ocean, and grew larger with the breath of the wind. From her scuppers she ran clear water, and the men were in haste and worked hard at the pumps. On the bow stood a mighty man, watching the depth of the water and giving commands with a voice of thunder. His eyes were of the pale blue of the deep waters, and his head was maned like that of a sea lion. And his hair was yellow, like the straw of a southern harvest or the manila rope yarns which sailormen plait.

"Of late years we had seen ships from afar, but this was the first to come to the beach of Akatan. The feast was broken, and the women and children fled to the houses, while we men strung our bows and waited with spears in hand. But when the ship's forefoot smelled the beach the strange men took no notice of us, being busy with their own work. With the falling of the tide they careened the schooner and patched a great hole in her bottom. So the women crept back, and the feast went on.

"When the tide rose, the sea wanderers kedged the schooner to deep water and then came among us. They bore presents and were friendly; so I made room for them, and out of the largeness of my heart gave them tokens such as I gave all the guests, for it was my wedding day, and I was head man in Akatan. And he with the mane of the sea lion was there, so tall and strong that one looked to see the earth shake with the fall of his feet. He looked much and straight at Unga, with his arms folded, so, and stayed till the sun went away and the stars came out. Then he went down to his ship. After that I took Unga by the hand and led her to my own house. And there was singing and great laughter, and the women said sly things, after the manner of women at such times. But we did not care. Then the people left us alone and went home.

"The last noise had not died away when the chief of the sea wanderers came in by the door. And he had with him black bottles, from which we drank and made merry. You see, I was only a stripling, and had lived all my days on the edge of the world. So my blood became as fire, and my heart as light as the froth that flies from the surf to the cliff. Unga sat silent among the skins in the corner, her eyes wide, for she seemed to fear. And he with the mane of the sea lion looked upon her straight and long. Then his men came in with bundles of goods, and he piled before me wealth such as was not in all Akatan. There were guns, both large and small, and powder and shot and shell, and bright axes and knives of steel, and cunning tools, and strange things the like of which I had never seen. When he showed me by sign that it was all mine, I thought him a great man to be so free; but he showed me also that Unga was to go away with him in his ship. Do you understand?—that Unga was to go away with him in his ship. The blood of my fathers flamed hot on the sudden, and I made to drive him through with my spear. But the spirit of the bottles had stolen the life from my arm, and he took me by the neck, so, and knocked my head against the wall of the house. And I was made weak like a newborn child, and my legs would no more stand under me. Unga screamed, and she laid hold of the things of the house with her hands, till they fell all about us as he dragged her to the door. Then he took her in his great arms, and when she tore at his yellow hair laughed with a sound like that of the big bull seal in the rut.

"I crawled to the beach and called upon my people, but they were afraid. Only Yash-Noosh was a man, and they struck him on the head with an oar, till he lay with his face in the sand and did not move. And they raised the sails to the sound of their songs, and the ship went away on the wind.

"The people said it was good, for there would be no more war of the bloods in Akatan; but I said never a word, waiting till the time of the full moon, when I put fish and oil in my kayak and went away to the east. I saw many islands and many people, and I, who had lived on the edge, saw that the world was very large. I talked by signs; but they had not seen a schooner nor a man with the mane of a sea lion, and they pointed always to the east. And I slept in queer places, and ate odd things, and met strange faces. Many laughed, for they thought me light of head; but sometimes old men turned my face to the light and blessed me, and the eyes of the young women grew soft as they asked me of the strange ship, and Unga, and the men of the sea.

"And in this manner, through rough seas and great storms, I came to Unalaska. There were two schooners there, but neither was the one I sought. So I passed on to the east, with the world growing ever larger, and in the island of Unamok there was no word of the ship, nor in Kadiak, nor in Atognak. And so I came one day to a rocky land, where men dug great holes in the mountain. And there was a schooner, but not my schooner, and men loaded upon it the rocks which they dug. This I thought childish, for all the world was made of rocks; but they gave me food and set me to work. When the schooner was deep in the water, the captain gave me money and told me to go; but I asked which way he went, and he pointed south. I made signs that I would go with him, and he laughed at first, but then, being short of men, took me to help work the ship. So I came to talk after their manner, and to heave on ropes, and to reef the stiff sails in sudden squalls, and to take my turn at the wheel. But it was not strange, for the blood of my fathers was the blood of the men of the sea.

"I had thought it an easy task to find him I sought, once I got among his own people; and when we raised the land one day, and passed between a gateway of the sea to a port, I looked for perhaps as many schooners as there were fingers to my hands. But the ships lay against the wharves for miles, packed like so many little fish; and when I went among them to ask for a man with the mane of a sea lion, they laughed, and answered me in the tongues of many peoples. And I found that they hailed from the uttermost parts of the earth.

"And I went into the city to look upon the face of every man. But they were like the cod when they run thick on the banks, and I could not count them. And the noise smote upon me till I could not hear, and my head was dizzy with much movement. So I went on and on, through the lands which sang in the warm sunshine; where the harvests lay rich on the plains; and where great cities were fat with men that lived like women, with false words in their mouths and their hearts black with the lust of gold. And all the while my people of Akatan hunted and fished, and were happy in the thought that the world was small.

"But the look in the eyes of Unga coming home from the fishing was with me always, and I knew I would find her when the time was met. She walked down quiet lanes in the dusk of the evening, or led me chases across the thick fields wet with the morning dew, and there was a promise in her eyes such as only the woman Unga could give.

"So I wandered through a thousand cities. Some were gentle and gave me food, and others laughed, and still others cursed; but I kept my tongue between my teeth, and went strange ways and saw strange sights. Sometimes I, who was a chief and the son of a chief, toiled for men—men rough of speech and hard as iron, who wrung gold from the sweat and sorrow of their fellow men. Yet no word did I get of my quest till I came back to the sea like a homing seal to the rookeries. But this was at another port, in another country which lay to the north. And there I heard dim tales of the yellow-haired sea wanderer, and I learned that he was a hunter of seals, and that even then he was abroad on the ocean.

"So I shipped on a seal schooner with the lazy Siwashes, and followed his trackless trail to the north where the hunt was then warm. And we were away weary months, and spoke many of the fleet, and heard much of the wild doings of him I sought; but never once did we raise him above the sea. We went north, even to the Pribilofs, and killed the seals in herds on the beach, and brought their warm bodies aboard till our scuppers ran grease and blood and no man could stand upon the deck. Then were we chased by a ship of slow steam, which fired upon us with great guns. But we put on sail till the sea was over our decks and washed them clean, and lost ourselves in a fog.

"It is said, at this time, while we fled with fear at our hearts, that the yellow-haired sea wanderer put in to the Pribilofs, right to the factory, and while the part of his men held the servants of the company, the rest loaded ten thousand green skins from the salt houses. I say it is said, but I believe; for in the voyages I made on the coast with never a meeting the northern seas rang with his wildness and daring, till the three nations which have lands there sought him with their ships. And I heard of Unga, for the captains sang loud in her praise, and she was always with him. She had learned the ways of his people, they said, and was happy. But I knew better—knew that her heart harked back to her own people by the yellow beach of Akatan.

"So, after a long time, I went back to the port which is by a gateway of the sea, and there I learned that he had gone across the girth of the great ocean to hunt for the seal to the east of the warm land which runs south from the Russian seas. And I, who was become a sailorman, shipped with men of his own race, and went after him in the hunt of the seal. And there were few ships off that new land; but we hung on the flank of the seal pack and harried it north through all the spring of the year. And when the cows were heavy with pup and crossed the Russian line, our men grumbled and were afraid. For there was much fog, and every day men were lost in the boats. They would not work, so the captain turned the ship back toward the way it came. But I knew the yellow-haired sea wanderer was unafraid, and would hang by the pack, even to the Russian Isles, where few men go. So I took a boat, in the black of night, when the lookout dozed on the fo'c'slehead, and went alone to the warm, long land. And I journeyed south to meet the men by Yeddo Bay, who are wild and unafraid. And the Yoshiwara girls were small, and bright like steel, and good to look upon; but I could not stop, for I knew that Unga rolled on the tossing floor by the rookeries of the north.

"The men by Yeddo Bay had met from the ends of the earth, and had neither gods nor homes, sailing under the flag of the Japanese. And with them I went to the rich beaches of Copper Island, where our salt piles became high with skins. And in that silent sea we saw no man till we were ready to come away. Then one day the fog lifted on the edge of a heavy wind, and there jammed down upon us a schooner, with close in her wake the cloudy funnels of a Russian man-of-war. We fled away on the beam of the wind, with the schooner jamming still closer and plunging ahead three feet to our two. And upon her poop was the man with the mane of the sea lion, pressing the rails under with the canvas and laughing in his strength of life. And Unga was there—I knew her on the moment—but he sent her below when the cannons began to talk across the sea. As I say, with three feet to our two, till we saw the rudder lift green at every jump—and I swinging on to the wheel and cursing, with my back to the Russian shot. For we knew he had it in mind to run before us, that he might get away while we were caught. And they knocked our masts out of us till we dragged into the wind like a wounded gull; but he went on over the edge of the sky line—he and Unga.

"What could we? The fresh hides spoke for themselves. So they took us to a Russian port, and after that to a lone country, where they set us to work in the mines to dig salt. And some died, and—and some did not die."

Naass swept the blanket from his shoulders, disclosing the gnarled and twisted flesh, marked with the unmistakable striations of the knout. Prince hastily covered him, for it was not nice to look upon.

"We were there a weary time and sometimes men got away to the south, but they always came back. So, when we who hailed from Yeddo Bay rose in the night and took the guns from the guards, we went to the north. And the land was very large, with plains, soggy with water, and great forests. And the cold came, with much snow on the ground, and no man knew the way. Weary months we journeyed through the endless forest—I do not remember, now, for there was little food and often we lay down to die. But at last we came to the cold sea, and but three were left to look upon it. One had shipped from Yeddo as captain, and he knew in his head the lay of the great lands, and of the place where men may cross from one to the other on the ice. And he led us—I do not know, it was so long—till there were but two. When we came to that place we found five of the strange people which live in that country, and they had dogs and skins, and we were very poor. We fought in the snow till they died, and the captain died, and the dogs and skins were mine. Then I crossed on the ice, which was broken, and once I drifted till a gale from the west put me upon the shore. And after that, Golovin Bay, Pastilik, and the priest. Then south, south, to the warm sunlands where first I wandered.

"But the sea was no longer fruitful, and those who went upon it after the seal went to little profit and great risk. The fleets scattered, and the captains and the men had no word of those I sought. So I turned away from the ocean which never rests, and went among the lands, where the trees, the houses, and the mountains sit always in one place and do not move. I journeyed far, and came to learn many things, even to the way of reading and writing from books. It was well I should do this, for it came upon me that Unga must know these things, and that someday, when the time was met—we—you understand, when the time was met.

"So I drifted, like those little fish which raise a sail to the wind but cannot steer. But my eyes and my ears were open always, and I went among men who traveled much, for I knew they had but to see those I sought to remember. At last there came a man, fresh from the mountains, with pieces of rock in which the free gold stood to the size of peas, and he had heard, he had met, he knew them. They were rich, he said, and lived in the place where they drew the gold from the ground.

"It was in a wild country, and very far away; but in time I came to the camp, hidden between the mountains, where men worked night and day, out of the sight of the sun. Yet the time was not come. I listened to the talk of the people. He had gone away—they had gone away—to England, it was said, in the matter of bringing men with much money together to form companies. I saw the house they had lived in; more like a palace, such as one sees in the old countries. In the nighttime I crept in through a window that I might see in what manner he treated her. I went from room to room, and in such way thought kings and queens must live, it was all so very good. And they all said he treated her like a queen, and many marveled as to what breed of woman she was for there was other blood in her veins, and she was different from the women of Akatan, and no one knew her for what she was. Aye, she was a queen; but I was a chief, and the son of a chief, and I had paid for her an untold price of skin and boat and bead.

"But why so many words? I was a sailorman, and knew the way of the ships on the seas. I followed to England, and then to other countries. Sometimes I heard of them by word of mouth, sometimes I read of them in the papers; yet never once could I come by them, for they had much money, and traveled fast, while I was a poor man. Then came trouble upon them, and their wealth slipped away one day like a curl of smoke. The papers were full of it at the time; but after that nothing was said, and I knew they had gone back where more gold could be got from the ground.

"They had dropped out of the world, being now poor, and so I wandered from camp to camp, even north to the Kootenay country, where I picked up the cold scent. They had come and gone, some said this way, and some that, and still others that they had gone to the country of the Yukon. And I went this way, and I went that, ever journeying from place to place, till it seemed I must grow weary of the world which was so large. But in the Kootenay I traveled a bad trail, and a long trail, with a breed of the Northwest, who saw fit to die when the famine pinched. He had been to the Yukon by an unknown way over the mountains, and when he knew his time was near gave me the map and the secret of a place where he swore by his gods there was much gold.

"After that all the world began to flock into the north. I was a poor man; I sold myself to be a driver of dogs. The rest you know. I met him and her in Dawson. She did not know me, for I was only a stripling, and her life had been large, so she had no time to remember the one who had paid for her an untold price.

"So? You bought me from my term of service. I went back to bring things about in my own way, for I had waited long, and now that I had my hand upon him was in no hurry. As I say, I had it in mind to do my own way, for I read back in my life, through all I had seen and suffered, and remembered the cold and hunger of the endless forest by the Russian seas. As you know, I led him into the east—him and Unga—into the east where many have gone and few returned. I led them to the spot where the bones and the curses of men lie with the gold which they may not have.

"The way was long and the trail unpacked. Our dogs were many and ate much; nor could our sleds carry till the break of spring. We must come back before the river ran free. So here and there we cached grub, that our sleds might be lightened and there be no chance of famine on the back trip. At the McQuestion there were three men, and near them we built a cache, as also did we at the Mayo, where was a hunting camp of a dozen Pellys which had crossed the divide from the south. After that, as we went on into the east, we saw no men; only the sleeping river, the moveless forest, and the White Silence of the North. As I say, the way was long and the trail unpacked. Sometimes, in a day's toil, we made no more than eight miles, or ten, and at night we slept like dead men. And never once did they dream that I was Naass, head man of Akatan, the righter of wrongs.

"We now made smaller caches, and in the nighttime it was a small matter to go back on the trail we had broken and change them in such way that one might deem the wolverines the thieves. Again there be places where there is a fall to the river, and the water is unruly, and the ice makes above and is eaten away beneath. In such a spot the sled I drove broke through, and the dogs; and to him and Unga it was ill luck, but no more. And there was much grub on that sled, and the dogs the strongest. But he laughed, for he was strong of life, and gave the dogs that were left little grub till we cut them from the harnesses one by one and fed them to their mates. We would go home light, he said, traveling and eating from cache to cache, with neither dogs nor sleds; which was true, for our grub was very short, and the last dog died in the traces the night we came to the gold and the bones and the curses of men.

"To reach that place—and the map spoke true—in the heart of the great mountains, we cut ice steps against the wall of a divide. One looked for a valley beyond, but there was no valley; the snow spread away, level as the great harvest plains, and here and there about us mighty mountains shoved their white heads among the stars. And midway on that strange plain which should have been a valley the earth and the snow fell away, straight down toward the heart of the world. Had we not been sailormen our heads would have swung round with the sight, but we stood on the dizzy edge that we might see a way to get down. And on one side, and one side only, the wall had fallen away till it was like the slope of the decks in a topsail breeze. I do not know why this thing should be so, but it was so. 'It is the mouth of hell,' he said; 'let us go down.' And we went down.

"And on the bottom there was a cabin, built by some man, of logs which he had cast down from above. It was a very old cabin, for men had died there alone at different times, and on pieces of birch bark which were there we read their last words and their curses. One had died of scurvy; another's partner had robbed him of his last grub and powder and stolen away; a third had been mauled by a bald-face grizzly; a fourth had hunted for game and starved—and so it went, and they had been loath to leave the gold, and had died by the side of it in one way or another. And the worthless gold they had gathered yellowed the floor of the cabin like in a dream.

"But his soul was steady, and his head clear, this man I had led thus far. 'We have nothing to eat,' he said, 'and we will only look upon this gold, and see whence it comes and how much there be. Then we will go away quick, before it gets into our eyes and steals away our judgment. And in this way we may return in the end, with more grub, and possess it all.' So we looked upon the great vein, which cut the wall of the pit as a true vein should, and we measured it, and traced it from above and below, and drove the stakes of the claims and blazed the trees in token of our rights. Then, our knees shaking with lack of food, and a sickness in our bellies, and our hearts chugging close to our mouths, we climbed the mighty wall for the last time and turned our faces to the back trip.

"The last stretch we dragged Unga between us, and we fell often, but in the end we made the cache. And lo, there was no grub. It was well done, for he thought it the wolverines, and damned them and his gods in the one breath. But Unga was brave, and smiled, and put her hand in his, till I turned away that I might hold myself. 'We will rest by the fire,' she said, 'till morning, and we will gather strength from our moccasins.' So we cut the tops of our moccasins in strips, and boiled them half of the night, that we might chew them and swallow them. And in the morning we talked of our chance. The next cache was five days' journey; we could not make it. We must find game.

" 'We will go forth and hunt,' he said.

" 'Yes,' said I, 'we will go forth and hunt.'

"And he ruled that Unga stay by the fire and save her strength. And we went forth, he in quest of the moose and I to the cache I had changed. But I ate little, so they might not see in me much strength. And in the night he fell many times as he drew into camp. And I, too, made to suffer great weakness, stumbling over my showshoes as though each step might be my last. And we gathered strength from our moccasins.

"He was a great man. His soul lifted his body to the last; nor did he cry aloud, save for the sake of Unga. On the second day I followed him, that I might not miss the end. And he lay down to rest often. That night he was near gone; but in the morning he swore weakly and went forth again. He was like a drunken man, and I looked many times for him to give up, but his was the strength of the strong, and his soul the soul of a giant, for he lifted his body through all the weary day. And he shot two ptarmigan, but would not eat them. He needed no fire; they meant life; but his thought was for Unga, and he turned toward camp. He no longer walked, but crawled on hand and knee through the snow. I came to him, and read death in his eyes. Even then it was not too late to eat of the ptarmigan. He cast away his rifle and carried the birds in his mouth like a dog. I walked by his side, upright. And he looked at me during the moments he rested, and wondered that I was so strong. I could see it, though he no longer spoke; and when his lips moved, they moved without sound. As I say, he was a great man, and my heart spoke for softness; but I read back in my life, and remembered the cold and hunger of the endless forest by the Russian seas. Besides, Unga was mine, and I had paid for her an untold price of skin and boat and bead.

"And in this manner we came through the white forest, with the silence heavy upon us like a damp sea mist. And the ghosts of the past were in the air and all about us; and I saw the yellow beach of Akatan, and the kayaks racing home from the fishing, and the houses on the rim of the forest. And the men who had made themselves chiefs were there, the lawgivers whose blood I bore and whose blood I had wedded in Unga. Aye, and Yash-Noosh walked with me, the wet sand in his hair, and his war spear, broken as he fell upon it, still in his hand. And I knew the time was met, and saw in the eyes of Unga the promise.

"As I say, we came thus through the forest, till the smell of the camp smoke was in our nostrils. And I bent above him, and tore the ptarmigan from his teeth. He turned on his side and rested, the wonder mounting in his eyes, and the hand which was under slipping slow toward the knife at his hip. But I took it from him, smiling close in his face. Even then he did not understand. So I made to drink from black bottles, and to build high upon the snow a pile of goods, and to live again the things which happened on the night of my marriage. I spoke no word, but he understood. Yet was he unafraid. There was a sneer to his lips, and cold anger, and he gathered new strength with the knowledge. It was not far, but the snow was deep, and he dragged himself very slow. Once he lay so long I turned him over and gazed into his eyes. And sometimes he looked forth, and sometimes death. And when I loosed him he struggled on again. In this way we came to the fire. Unga was at his side on the instant. His lips moved without sound; then he pointed at me, that Unga might understand. And after that he lay in the snow, very still, for a long while. Even now is he there in the snow.

"I said no word till I had cooked the ptarmigan. Then I spoke to her, in her own tongue, which she had not heard in many years. She straightened herself, so, and her eyes were wonder-wide, and she asked who I was, and where I had learned that speech.

"'I am Naass,' I said.

"'You?' she said. 'You?' And she crept close that she might look upon me.

"'Yes,' I answered; 'I am Naass, head man of Akatan, the last of the blood, as you are the last of the blood.'

"And she laughed. By all the things I have seen and the deeds I have done may I never hear such a laugh again. It put the chill to my soul, sitting there in the White Silence, alone with death and this woman who laughed.

"'Come!' I said, for I thought she wandered. 'Eat of the food and let us be gone. It is a far fetch from here to Akatan.'

"But she shoved her face in his yellow mane, and laughed till it seemed the heavens must fall about our ears. I had thought she would be overjoyed at the sight of me, and eager to go back to the memory of old times, but this seemed a strange form to take.

"'Come!' I cried, taking her strong by the hand. 'The way is long and dark. Let us hurry!'

"'Where?' she asked, sitting up, and ceasing from her strange mirth.

"'To Akatan,' I answered, intent on the light to grow on her face at the thought. But it became like his, with a sneer to the lips, and cold anger.

"'Yes,' she said; 'we will go, hand in hand, to Akatan, you and I. And we will live in the dirty huts, and eat of the fish and oil, and bring forth a spawn—a spawn to be proud of all the days of our life. We will forget the world and be happy, very happy. It is good, most good. Come! Let us hurry. Let us go back to Akatan.'

"And she ran her hand through his yellow hair, and smiled in a way which was not good. And there was no promise in her eyes.

"I sat silent, and marveled at the strangeness of woman. I went back to the night when he dragged her from me and she screamed and tore at his hair—at his hair which now she played with and would not leave. Then I remembered the price and the long years of waiting; and I gripped her close, and dragged her away as he had done. And she held back, even as on that night, and fought like a she-cat for its whelp. And when the fire was between us and the man, I loosed her, and she sat and listened. And I told her of all that lay between, of all that had happened to me on strange seas, of all that I had done in strange lands; of my weary quest, and the hungry years, and the promise which had been mine from the first. Aye, I told all, even to what had passed that day between the man and me, and in the days yet young. And as I spoke I saw the promise grow in her eyes, full and large like the break of dawn. And I read pity there, the tenderness of woman, the love, the heart and the soul of Unga. And I was a stripling again, for the look was the look of Unga as she ran up the beach, laughing, to the home of her mother. The stern unrest was gone, and the hunger, and the weary waiting. The time was met. I felt the call of her breast, and it seemed there I must pillow my head and forget. She opened her arms to me, and I came against her. Then, sudden, the hate flamed in her eye, her hand was at my hip. And once, twice, she passed the knife.

"'Dog!' she sneered, as she flung me into the snow. 'Swine!' And then she laughed till the silence cracked, and went back to her dead.

"As I say, once she passed the knife, and twice; but she was weak with hunger, and it was not meant that I should die. Yet was I minded to stay in that place, and to close my eyes in the last long sleep with those whose lives had crossed with mine and led my feet on unknown trails. But there lay a debt upon me which would not let me rest.

"And the way was long, the cold bitter, and there was little grub. The Pellys had found no moose, and had robbed my cache. And so had the three white men, but they lay thin and dead in their cabin as I passed. After that I do not remember, till I came here, and found food and fire—much fire."

As he finished, he crouched closely, even jealously, over the stove. For a long while the slush-lamp shadows played tragedies upon the wall.

"But Unga!" cried Prince, the vision still strong upon him.

"Unga? She would not eat of the ptarmigan. She lay with her arms about his neck, her face deep in his yellow hair. I drew the fire close, that she might not feel the frost, but she crept to the other side. And I built a fire there; yet it was little good, for she would not eat. And in this manner they still lie up there in the snow."

"And you?" asked Malemute Kid.

"I do not know; but Akatan is small, and I have little wish to go back and live on the edge of the world. Yet is there small use in life. I can go to Constantine, and he will put irons upon me, and one day they will tie a piece of rope, so, and I will sleep good. Yet—no; I do not know."

"But, Kid," protested Prince, "this is murder!"

"Hush!" commanded Malemute Kid. "There be things greater than our wisdom, beyond our justice. The right and the wrong of this we cannot say, and it is not for us to judge."

Naass drew yet closer to the fire. There was a great silence, and in each man's eyes many pictures came and went.

1900

JAN, THE UNREPENTANT

For there's never a law of God or man
Runs north of Fifty-three.

Jan rolled over, clawing and kicking. He was fighting hand and foot now, and he fought grimly, silently. Two of the three men who hung upon him shouted directions to each other, and strove to curb the short, hairy devil who would not curb. The third man howled. His finger was between Jan's teeth.

"Quit yer tantrums, Jan, an' ease up!" panted Red Bill, getting a strangle-hold on Jan's neck. "Why on earth can't yeh hang decent and peaceable?"

But Jan kept his grip on the third man's finger, and squirmed over the floor of the tent, into the pots and pans.

"Youah no gentleman, suh," reproved Mr. Taylor, his body following his finger, and endeavoring to accommodate itself to every jerk of Jan's head. "You hev killed Mistah Gordon, as brave and honorable a gentleman as ever hit the trail aftah the dogs. Youah a murderah, suh, and without honah."

"An' yer no comrade," broke in Red Bill. "If you was, you'd hang 'thout rampin' around an' roarin'. Come on, Jan, there's a good fellow. Don't give us no more trouble. Jes' quit, an' we'll hang yeh neat and handy, an' be done with it."

"Steady, all!" Lawson, the sailorman, bawled. "Jam his head into the bean pot and batten down."

"But my fingah, suh," Mr. Taylor protested.

"Leggo with y'r finger, then! Always in the way!"

"But I can't, Mistah Lawson. It's in the critter's gullet, and nigh chewed off as 't is."

"Stand by for stays!" As Lawson gave the warning, Jan half lifted himself, and the struggling quartet floundered across the tent into a muddle of furs and blankets. In its passage it cleared the body of a man, who lay motionless, bleeding from a bullet-wound in the neck.

All this was because of the madness which had come upon Jan—the madness which comes upon a man who has stripped off the raw skin of earth and grovelled long in primal nakedness, and before whose eyes rise the fat vales of the homeland, and into whose nostrils steals the whiff of hay, and grass, and flower, and new-turned soil. Through five frigid years Jan had sown the seed. Stuart River, Forty Mile, Circle City, Koyokuk, Kotzebue, had marked his bleak and strenuous agriculture, and now it was Nome that bore the harvest,—not the Nome of golden

From *The God of His Fathers*, copyright 1901 by McClure, Phillips & Co.

beaches and ruby sands, but the Nome of '97, before Anvil City was located, or Eldorado District organized.

John Gordon was a Yankee, and should have known better. But he passed the sharp word at a time when Jan's blood-shot eyes blazed and his teeth gritted in torment. And because of this, there was a smell of saltpetre in the tent, and one lay quietly, while the other fought like a cornered rat, and refused to hang in the decent and peaceable manner suggested by his comrades.

"If you will allow me, Mistah Lawson, befoah we go further in this rumpus, I would say it wah a good idea to pry this hyer varmint's teeth apart. Neither will he bite off, nor will he let go. He has the wisdom of the sarpint, suh, the wisdom of the sarpint."

"Lemme get the hatchet to him!" vociferated the sailor. "Lemme get the hatchet!" He shoved the steel edge close to Mr. Taylor's finger and used the man's teeth as a fulcrum. Jan held on and breathed through his nose, snorting like a grampus. "Steady, all! Now she takes it!"

"Thank you, suh; it is a powerful relief." And Mr. Taylor proceeded to gather into his arms the victim's wildly waving legs.

But Jan upreared in his Berserker rage; bleeding, frothing, cursing; five frozen years thawing into sudden hell. They swayed backward and forward, panted, sweated, like some cyclopean, many-legged monster rising from the lower deeps. The slush-lamp went over, drowned in its own fat, while the midday twilight scarce percolated through the dirty canvas of the tent.

"For the love of Gawd, Jan, get yer senses back!" pleaded Red Bill. "We ain't goin' to hurt yeh, 'r kill yeh, 'r anythin' of that sort. Jes' want to hang yeh, that's all, an' you a-messin' round an' rampagin' somethin' terrible. To think of travellin' trail together an' then bein' treated this-a way. Wouldn't 'bleeved it of yeh, Jan!"

"He's got too much steerage-way. Grab holt his legs, Taylor, and heave 'm over!"

"Yes, suh, Mistah Lawson. Do you press youah weight above, after I give the word." The Kentuckian groped about him in the murky darkness. "Now, suh, now is the accepted time!"

There was a great surge, and a quarter of a ton of human flesh tottered and crashed to its fall against the side-wall. Pegs drew and guy-ropes parted, and the tent, collapsing, wrapped the battle in its greasy folds.

"Yer only makin' it harder fer yerself," Red Bill continued, at the same time driving both his thumbs into a hairy throat, the possessor of which he had pinned down. "You've made nuisance enough a' ready, an' it'll take half the day to get things straightened when we've strung yeh up."

"I'll thank you to leave go, suh," spluttered Mr. Taylor.

Red Bill grunted and loosed his grip, and the twain crawled out into the open. At the same instant Jan kicked clear of the sailor, and took to his heels across the snow.

"Hi! you lazy devils! Buck! Bright! Sic 'm! Pull 'm down!" sang out Lawson, lunging through the snow after the fleeing man. Buck and Bright, followed by the rest of the dogs, outstripped him and rapidly overhauled the murderer.

There was no reason that these men should do this; no reason for Jan to run away; no reason for them to attempt to prevent him. On the one hand stretched the barren snow-land; on the other, the frozen sea. With neither food nor shelter, he could not run far. All they had to do was to wait till he wandered back to the tent, as he inevitably must, when the frost and hunger laid hold of him. But these men did not stop to think. There was a certain taint of madness running in the veins of all of them. Besides, blood had been spilled, and upon them was the blood-lust, thick and hot. "Vengeance is mine," saith the Lord, and He saith it in temperate climes where the warm sun steals away the energies of men. But in the Northland they have discovered that prayer is only efficacious when backed by muscle, and they are accustomed to doing things for themselves. God is everywhere, they have heard, but he flings a shadow over the land for half the year that they may not find him; so they grope in darkness, and it is not to be wondered that they often doubt, and deem the Decalogue out of gear.

Jan ran blindly, reckoning not of the way of his feet, for he was mastered by the verb "to live." To live! To exist! Buck flashed gray through the air, but missed. The man struck madly at him, and stumbled. Then the white teeth of Bright closed on his mackinaw jacket, and he pitched into the snow. *To live! To exist!* He fought wildly as ever, the centre of a tossing heap of men and dogs. His left hand gripped a wolf-dog by the scruff of the back, while the arm was passed around the neck of Lawson. Every struggle of the dog helped to throttle the hapless sailor. Jan's right hand was buried deep in the curling tendrils of Red Bill's shaggy head, and beneath all, Mr. Taylor lay pinned and helpless. It was a deadlock, for the strength of his madness was prodigious; but suddenly, without apparent reason, Jan loosed his various grips and rolled over quietly on his back. His adversaries drew away a little, dubious and disconcerted. Jan grinned viciously.

"Mine friends," he said, still grinning, "you haf asked me to be politeful, und now I am politeful. Vot piziness vood you do mit me?"

"That's right, Jan. Be ca'm," soothed Red Bill. "I knowed you'd come to yer senses afore long. Jes' be ca'm now, an' we'll do the trick with neatness and despatch."

"Vot piziness? Vot trick?"

"The hangin'. An' yeh oughter thank yer lucky stars for havin' a man what knows his business. I've did it afore now, more'n once, down in the States, an' I can do it to a T."

"Hang who? Me?"

"Yep."

"Ha! ha! Shust hear der man speak foolishness! Gif me a hand, Bill, und I vill get up und be hung."

He crawled stiffly to his feet and looked about him.

"Herr Gott! listen to der man! He vood hang me! Ho! ho! ho! I tank not! Yes, I tank not!"

"And I tank yes, you swab," Lawson spoke up mockingly, at the same time cutting a sled-lashing and coiling it up with ominous care. "Judge Lynch holds court this day."

"Von liddle while." Jan stepped back from the proffered noose. "I haf somedings to ask und to make der great proposition. Kentucky, you know about der Shudge Lynch?"

"Yes, suh. It is an institution of free men and of gentlemen, and it is an ole one and time-honored. Corruption may wear the robe of magistracy, suh, but Judge Lynch can always be relied upon to give justice without court fees. I repeat, suh, without court fees. Law may be bought and sold, but in this enlightened land justice is free as the air we breathe, strong as the licker we drink, prompt as—"

"Cut it short! Find out what the beggar wants," interrupted Lawson, spoiling the peroration.

"Vell, Kentucky, tell me dis: von man kill von odder man, Shudge Lynch hang dot man?"

"If the evidence is strong enough—yes, suh."

"An' the evidence in this here case is strong enough to hang a dozen men, Jan," broke in Red Bill.

"Nefer you mind, Bill. I talk mit you next. Now von anodder ding I ask Kentucky. If Shudge Lynch hang not der man, vot den?"

"If Judge Lynch does not hang the man, then the man goes free, and his hands are washed clean of blood. And further, suh, our great and glorious constitution has said, to wit: that no man may twice be placed in jeopardy of his life for one and the same crime, or words to that effect."

"Und dey can't shoot him, or hit him mit a club over der head alongside, or do nodings more mit him?"

"No, suh."

"Goot! You hear vot Kentucky speaks, all you noddleheads? Now I talk mit Bill. You know der piziness, Bill, und you hang me up brown, eh? Vot you say?"

"'Betcher life, an', Jan, if yeh don't give no more trouble ye'll be almighty proud of the job. I'm a connesoor."

"You haf der great head, Bill, und know somedings or two. Und you know two und one makes tree—ain't it?"

Bill nodded.

"Und when you haf two dings, you haf not tree dings—ain't it? Now you follow mit me close und I show you. It takes tree dings to hang. First ding, you haf to haf der man. Goot! I am der man. Second ding, you haf to haf der rope. Lawson haf der rope. Goot! Und tird ding, you haf to haf someding to tie der rope to. Sling your eyes over der landscape und find der tird ding to tie der rope to? Eh? Vot you say?"

Mechanically they swept the ice and snow with their eyes. It was a homogeneous scene, devoid of contrasts or bold contours, dreary, desolate, and monotonous,—the ice-packed sea, the slow slope of the beach, the background of low-lying hills, and over all thrown the endless mantle of snow.

"No trees, no bluffs, no cabins, no telegraph poles, nothin'," moaned Red Bill; "nothin' respectable enough nor big enough to swing the toes of a five-foot man clear o' the ground. I give it up." He looked yearningly at that portion of Jan's anatomy which joins the head and shoulders. "Give it up," he repeated sadly to Lawson. "Throw the rope down. Gawd never intended this here country for livin' purposes, an' that's a cold frozen fact."

Jan grinned triumphantly. "I tank I go mit der tent und haf a smoke."

"Ostensiblee y'r correct, Bill, me son," spoke up Lawson; "but y'r a dummy, and you can lay to that for another cold frozen fact. Takes a sea farmer to learn you landsmen things. Ever hear of a pair of shears? Then clap y'r eyes to this."

The sailor worked rapidly. From the pile of dunnage where they had pulled up the boat the preceding fall, he unearthed a pair of long oars. These he lashed together, at nearly right angles, close to the ends of the blades. Where the handles rested he kicked holes through the snow to the sand. At the point of intersection he attached two guy-ropes, making the end of one fast to a cake of beach-ice. The other guy he passed over to Red Bill.

"Here, me son, lay holt o' that and run it out."

And to his horror, Jan saw his gallows rise in the air. "No! no!" he cried, recoiling and putting up his fists. "It is not goot! I vill not hang! Come, you noddleheads! I vill lick you, all together, von after der odder! I vill blay hell! I vill do eferydings! Und I vill die pefore I hang!"

The sailor permitted the two other men to clinch with the mad creature. They rolled and tossed about furiously, tearing up snow and tundra, their fierce struggle writing a tragedy of human passion on the white sheet spread by nature. And ever and anon a hand or foot of Jan emerged from the tangle, to be gripped by Lawson and lashed fast with rope-yarns. Pawing, clawing, blaspheming, he was conquered and bound, inch by inch, and drawn to where the inexorable shears lay like a pair of gigantic dividers on the snow. Red Bill adjusted the noose, placing the hangman's knot properly under the left ear. Mr. Taylor and Lawson tailed onto the running-guy, ready at the word to elevate the gallows. Bill lingered, contemplating his work with artistic appreciation.

"Herr Gott! Vood you look at it!"

The horror in Jan's voice caused the rest to desist. The fallen tent had uprisen, and in the gathering twilight it flapped ghostly arms about and titubated toward them drunkenly. But the next instant John Gordon found the opening and crawled forth.

"What the flaming–!" For the moment his voice died away in his throat as his eyes took in the tableau. "Hold on! I'm not dead!" he cried out, coming up to the group with stormy countenance.

"Allow me, Mistah Gordon, to congratulate you upon youah escape," Mr. Taylor ventured. "A close shave, suh, a powahful close shave."

"Congratulate hell! I might have been dead and rotten and no thanks to you, you–!" And thereat John Gordon delivered himself of a vigorous flood of English, terse, intensive, denunciative, and composed solely of expletives and adjectives.

"Simply creased me," he went on when he had eased himself sufficiently. "Ever crease cattle, Taylor?"

"Yes, suh, many a time down in God's country."

"Just so. That's what happened to me. Bullet just grazed the base of my skull at the top of the neck. Stunned me but no harm done." He turned to the bound man. "Get up, Jan. I'm going to lick you to a standstill or you're going to apologize. The rest of you lads stand clear."

"I tank not. Shust tie me loose und you see," replied Jan, the Unrepentant, the devil within him still unconquered. "Und after as I lick you, I take der rest of der noddleheads, von after der odder, altogedder!"

1900

THE MAN WITH THE GASH

Jacob Kent had suffered from cupidity all the days of his life. This, in turn, had engendered a chronic distrustfulness, and his mind and character had become so warped that he was a very disagreeable man to deal with. He was also a victim to somnambulic propensities, and very set in his ideas. He had been a weaver of cloth from the cradle, until the fever of Klondike had entered his blood and torn him away from his loom. His cabin stood midway between Sixty Mile Post and the Stuart River; and men who made it a custom to travel the trail to Dawson likened him to a robber baron, perched in his fortress and exacting toll from the caravans that used his ill-kept roads. Since a certain amount of history was required in the construction of this figure, the less cultured wayfarers from Stuart River were prone to describe him after a still more primordial fashion, in which a command of strong adjectives was to be chiefly noted.

This cabin was not his, by the way, having been built several years previously by a couple of miners who had got out a raft of logs at that point for a grub-stake. They had been most hospitable lads, and, after they abandoned it, travelers who knew the route made it an object to arrive there at nightfall. It was very handy, saving them all the time and toil of pitching camp; and it was an unwritten rule that the last man left a neat pile of firewood for the next comer. Rarely a night passed but from half a dozen to a score of men crowded into its shelter. Jacob Kent noted these things, exercised squatter sovereignty, and moved in. Thenceforth, the weary travelers were mulcted a dollar per head for the privilege of sleeping on the floor, Jacob Kent weighing the dust and never failing to steal the down-weight. Besides, he so contrived that his transient guests chopped his wood for him and carried his water. This was rank piracy, but his victims were an easy-going breed, and while they detested him, they yet permitted him to flourish in his sins.

One afternoon in April he sat by his door,—for all the world like a predatory spider,—marvelling at the heat of the returning sun, and keeping an eye on the trail for prospective flies. The Yukon lay at his feet, a sea of ice, disappearing around two great bends to the north and south, and stretching an honest two miles from bank to bank. Over its rough breast ran the sled-trail, a slender sunken line, eighteen inches wide and two thousand miles in length, with more curses distributed to the linear foot than any other road in or out of all Christendom.

Jacob Kent was feeling particularly good that afternoon. The record had been broken the previous night, and he had sold his hospitality to no less than twenty-eight visitors. True, it had been quite uncomfortable, and four had snored beneath his bunk all night; but then it had added appreciable weight to the sack in which he kept his gold dust. That sack, with its glittering yellow treasure, was at once the chief delight and the chief bane of his existence. Heaven and hell lay within its slender mouth. In the nature of things, there being no privacy to his one-roomed dwelling, he was tortured by a constant fear of theft. It would be very easy for these bearded, desperate-looking strangers to make away with it. Often he dreamed that such was the case, and awoke in the grip of nightmare. A select number of these robbers haunted him through his dreams, and he came to know them quite well, especially the bronzed leader with the gash on his right cheek. This fellow was the most persistent of the lot, and, because of him, he had, in his waking moments, constructed several score of hiding-places in and about the cabin. After a concealment he would breathe freely again, perhaps for several nights, only to collar the Man with the Gash in the very act of unearthing the sack. Then, on awakening in the midst of the usual struggle, he would at once get up and transfer the bag to a new and more ingenious crypt. It was not that he was the direct victim of these phantasms; but he believed in omens and thought-transference, and he deemed these dream-robbers to be the astral projection of real personages who happened at those particular moments, no matter where they were in the flesh, to be harboring designs, in the spirit, upon his wealth. So he continued to bleed the unfortunates who crossed his threshold, and at the same time to add to his trouble with every ounce that went into the sack.

As he sat sunning himself, a thought came to Jacob Kent that brought him to his feet with a jerk. The pleasures of life had culminated in the continual weighing and reweighing of his dust; but a shadow had been thrown upon this pleasant avocation, which he had hitherto failed to brush aside. His gold-scales were quite small; in fact, their maximum was a pound and a half,–eighteen ounces,–while his hoard mounted up to something like three and a third times that. He had never been able to weigh it all at one operation, and hence considered himself to have been shut out from a new and most edifying coign of contemplation. Being denied this, half the pleasure of possession had been lost; nay, he felt that this miserable obstacle actually minimized the fact, as it did the strength, of possession. It was the solution of this problem flashing across his mind that had just brought him to his feet. He searched the trail carefully in either direction. There was nothing in sight, so he went inside.

In a few seconds he had the table cleared away and the scales set up. On one side he placed the stamped disks to the equivalent of fifteen ounces, and balanced it with dust on the other. Replacing the weights with dust, he then had thirty ounces precisely balanced. These, in turn, he placed together on one side and again balanced with more dust. By this time the gold was exhausted, and he was sweating liberally. He trembled with ecstasy, ravished beyond measure. Nevertheless he dusted the sack thoroughly, to the last least grain, till the balance was overcome and one side of the scales sank to the table. Equilibrium, however, was restored by the addition of a pennyweight and five grains to the opposite side. He stood, head thrown back, transfixed. The sack was empty, but the potentiality of the scales had become immeasurable. Upon them he could weigh any amount, from the tiniest grain to pounds upon pounds. Mammon laid hot fingers on his heart. The sun swung on its westering way till it flashed through the open doorway, full upon the yellow-burdened scales. The precious heaps, like the golden breasts of a bronze Cleopatra, flung back the light in a mellow glow. Time and space were not.

"Gawd blime me! but you 'ave the makin' of several quid there, 'aven't you?"

Jacob Kent wheeled about, at the same time reaching for his double-barrelled shotgun, which stood handy. But when his eyes lit on the intruder's face, he staggered back dizzily. *It was the face of the Man with the Gash!*

The man looked at him curiously.

"Oh, that's all right," he said, waving his hand deprecatingly. "You needn't think as I'll 'arm you or your blasted dust.

"You're a rum 'un, you are," he added reflectively, as he watched the sweat pouring from off Kent's face and the quavering of his knees.

"W'y don't you pipe up an' say somethin'?" he went on, as the other struggled for breath. "Wot's gone wrong o' your gaff? Anythink the matter?"

"W–w–where'd you get it?" Kent at last managed to articulate, raising a shaking forefinger to the ghastly scar which seamed the other's cheek.

"Shipmate stove me down with a marlin-spike from the main-royal. An' now as you 'ave your figger'ead in trim, wot I want to know is, wot's it to you? That's wot I want to know—wot's it to you? Gawd blime me! do it 'urt you? Ain't it smug enough for the likes o' you? That's wot I want to know!"

"No, no," Kent answered, sinking upon a stool with a sickly grin. "I was just wondering."

"Did you ever see the like?" the other went on truculently.

"No."

"Ain't it a beute?"

"Yes." Kent nodded his head approvingly, intent on humoring this strange visitor, but wholly unprepared for the outburst which was to follow his effort to be agreeable.

"You blasted, bloomin', burgoo-eatin' son-of-a-sea-swab! Wot do you mean, a sayin' the most onsightly thing Gawd Almighty ever put on the face o' man is a beute? Wot do you mean, you—"

And thereat this fiery son of the sea broke off into a string of Oriental profanity, mingling gods and devils, lineages and men, metaphors and monsters, with so savage a virility that Jacob Kent was paralyzed. He shrank back, his arms lifted as though to ward off physical violence. So utterly unnerved was he that the other paused in the mid-swing of a gorgeous peroration and burst into thunderous laughter.

"The sun's knocked the bottom out o' the trail," said the Man with the Gash, between departing paroxysms of mirth. "An' I only 'ope as you'll appreciate the hoppertunity of consortin' with a man o' my mug. Get steam up in that fire-box o' your'n. I'm goin' to unrig the dogs an' grub 'em. An' don't be shy o' the wood, my lad; there's plenty more where that come from, and it's you've got the time to sling an axe. An' tote up a bucket o' water while you're about it. Lively! or I'll run you down, so 'elp me!"

Such a thing was unheard of. Jacob Kent was making the fire, chopping wood, packing water—doing menial tasks for a guest! When Jim Cardegee left Dawson, it was with his head filled with the iniquities of this roadside Shylock; and all along the trail his numerous victims had added to the sum of his crimes. Now, Jim Cardegee, with the sailor's love for a sailor's joke, had determined, when he pulled into the cabin, to bring its inmate down a peg or so. That he had succeeded beyond expectation he could not help but remark, though he was in the dark as to the part the gash on his cheek had played in it. But while he could not understand, he saw the terror it created, and resolved to exploit it as remorselessly as would any modern trader a choice bit of merchandise.

"Strike me blind, but you're a 'ustler," he said admiringly, his head cocked to one side, as his host bustled about. "You never 'ort to 'ave gone Klondiking. It's the keeper of a pub' you was laid out for. An' it's often as I 'ave 'eard the lads up an' down the river speak o' you, but I 'adn't no idea you was so jolly nice."

Jacob Kent experienced a tremendous yearning to try his shotgun on him, but the fascination of the gash was too potent. This was the real Man with the Gash, the man who had so often robbed him in the spirit. This, then, was the embodied entity of the being whose astral form had been projected into his dreams, the man who had so frequently harbored designs against his hoard; hence—there could be no other conclusion—this Man with the Gash had now come in the flesh to dispossess him. And that gash! He could no more keep his eyes from it than stop the beating of his heart. Try as he would, they wandered back to that one point as inevitably as the needle to the pole.

"Do it 'urt you?" Jim Cardegee thundered suddenly, looking up from the spreading of his blankets and encountering the rapt gaze of the other. "It strikes me as 'ow it 'ud be the proper thing for you to draw your jib, douse the glim, an' turn in, seein' as 'ow it worrits you. Jes' lay to that, you swab, or so 'elp me I'll take a pull on your peak-purchases!"

Kent was so nervous that it took three puffs to blow out the slush-lamp, and he crawled into his blankets without even removing his moccasins. The sailor was soon snoring lustily from his hard bed on the floor, but Kent lay staring up into the blackness, one hand on the shotgun, resolved not to close his eyes the whole night. He had not had an opportunity to secrete his five pounds of gold, and it lay in the ammunition box at the head of his bunk. But, try as he would, he at last dozed off with the weight of his dust heavy on his soul. Had he not inadvertently fallen asleep with his mind in such condition, the somnambulic demon would not have been invoked, nor would Jim Cardegee have gone mining next day with a dish-pan.

The fire fought a losing battle, and at last died away, while the frost penetrated the mossy chinks between the logs and chilled the inner atmosphere. The dogs outside ceased their howling, and, curled up in the snow, dreamed of salmon-stocked heavens where dog-drivers and kindred task-masters were not. Within, the sailor lay like a log, while his host tossed restlessly about, the victim of strange fantasies. As midnight drew near he suddenly threw off the blankets and got up. It was remarkable that he could do what he then did without ever striking a light. Perhaps it was because of the darkness that he kept his eyes shut, and perhaps it was for fear he would see the terrible gash on the cheek of his visitor; but, be this as it may, it is a fact that, unseeing, he opened his ammunition box, put a heavy charge into the muzzle of the shotgun without spilling a particle, rammed it down with double wads, and then put everything away and got back into bed.

Just as daylight laid its steel-gray fingers on the parchment window, Jacob Kent awoke. Turning on his elbow, he raised the lid and peered into the ammunition box. Whatever he saw, or whatever he did not see, exercised a very peculiar effect upon him, considering his neurotic temperament. He glanced at the sleeping man on the floor, let the lid down gently, and rolled over on his back. It was an unwonted calm that rested on his face. Not a muscle quivered. There was not the least sign of excitement or perturbation. He lay there a long while, thinking, and when he got up and began to move about, it was in a cool, collected manner, without noise and without hurry.

It happened that a heavy wooden peg had been driven into the ridge-pole just above Jim Cardegee's head. Jacob Kent, working softly, ran a piece of half-inch manila over it, bringing both ends to the ground. One end he tied about his waist, and in the other he rove a running noose. Then he cocked his shotgun and laid it within reach, by the side of numerous moose-hide thongs. By an effort of will he bore the sight of the scar, slipped the noose over the sleeper's head, and drew it taut by throwing back on his weight, at the same time seizing the gun and bringing it to bear.

Jim Cardegee awoke, choking, bewildered, staring down the twin wells of steel.

"Where is it?" Kent asked, at the same time slacking on the rope.

"You blasted—ugh—"

Kent merely threw back his weight, shutting off the other's wind.

"Bloomin'–Bur–ugh–"

"Where is it?" Kent repeated.

"Wot?" Cardegee asked, as soon as he had caught his breath.

"The gold-dust."

"Wot gold-dust?" the perplexed sailor demanded.

"You know well enough,–mine."

"Ain't seen nothink of it. Wot do ye take me for? A safe-deposit? Wot 'ave I got to do with it, any'ow?"

"Mebbe you know, and mebbe you don't know, but anyway, I'm going to stop your breath till you do know. And if you lift a hand, I'll blow your head off!"

"Vast heavin'!" Cardegee roared, as the rope tightened.

Kent eased away a moment, and the sailor, wriggling his neck as though from the pressure, managed to loosen the noose a bit and work it up so the point of contact was just under the chin.

"Well?" Kent questioned, expecting the disclosure.

But Cardegee grinned. "Go ahead with your 'angin', you bloomin' old pot-wolloper!"

Then, as the sailor had anticipated, the tragedy became a farce. Cardegee being the heavier of the two, Kent, throwing his body backward and down, could not lift him clear of the ground. Strain and strive to the uttermost, the sailor's feet still stuck to the floor and sustained a part of his weight. The remaining portion was supported by the point of contact just under his chin. Failing to swing him clear, Kent clung on, resolved to slowly throttle him or force him to tell what he had done with the hoard. But the Man with the Gash would not throttle. Five, ten, fifteen minutes passed, and at the end of that time, in despair, Kent let his prisoner down.

"Well," he remarked, wiping away the sweat, "if you won't hang you'll shoot. Some men wasn't born to be hanged, anyway."

"An' it's a pretty mess as you'll make o' this 'ere cabin floor." Cardegee was fighting for time. "Now, look 'ere, I'll tell you wot we do; we'll lay our 'eads 'longside an' reason together. You've lost some dust. You say as 'ow I know, an' I say as 'ow I don't. Let's get a hobservation an' shape a course–"

"Vast heavin'!" Kent dashed in, maliciously imitating the other's enunciation. "I'm going to shape all the courses of this shebang, and you observe; and if you do anything more, I'll bore you as sure as Moses!"

"For the sake of my mother–"

"Whom God have mercy upon if she loves you. Ah! Would you?" He frustrated a hostile move on the part of the other by pressing the cold muzzle against his forehead. "Lay quiet, now! If you lift as much as a hair, you'll get it."

It was rather an awkward task, with the trigger of the gun always within pulling distance of the finger; but Kent was a weaver, and in a few minutes had the sailor tied hand and foot. Then he dragged him without and laid him by the side of the cabin, where he could overlook the river and watch the sun climb to the meridian.

"Now I'll give you till noon, and then–"

"Wot?"

"You'll be hitting the brimstone trail. But if you speak up, I'll keep you till the next bunch of mounted police come by."

"Well, Gawd blime me, if this ain't a go! 'Ere I be, innercent as a lamb, an' 'ere you be, lost all o' your top 'amper an' out o' your reckonin', run me foul an' goin' to rake me into 'ell-fire. You bloomin' old pirut! You—"

Jim Cardegee loosed the strings of his profanity and fairly outdid himself. Jacob Kent brought out a stool that he might enjoy it in comfort. Having exhausted all the possible combinations of his vocabulary, the sailor quieted down to hard thinking, his eyes constantly gauging the progress of the sun, which tore up the eastern slope of the heavens with unseemly haste. His dogs, surprised that they had not long since been put to harness, crowded around him. His helplessness appealed to the brutes. They felt that something was wrong, though they knew not what, and they crowded about, howling their mournful sympathy.

"Chook! Mush-on! you Siwashes!" he cried, attempting, in a vermicular way, to kick at them, and discovering himself to be tottering on the edge of a declivity. As soon as the animals had scattered, he devoted himself to the significance of that declivity which he felt to be there but could not see. Nor was he long in arriving at a correct conclusion. In the nature of things, he figured, man is lazy. He does no more than he has to. When he builds a cabin he must put dirt on the roof. From these premises it was logical that he should carry that dirt no further than was absolutely necessary. Therefore, he lay upon the edge of the hole from which the dirt had been taken to roof Jacob Kent's cabin. This knowledge, properly utilized, might prolong things, he thought; and he then turned his attention to the moose-hide thongs which bound him. His hands were tied behind him, and pressing against the snow, they were wet with the contact. This moistening of the raw-hide he knew would tend to make it stretch, and, without apparent effort, he endeavored to stretch it more and more.

He watched the trail hungrily, and when in the direction of Sixty Mile a dark speck appeared for a moment against the white background of an ice-jam, he cast an anxious eye at the sun. It had climbed nearly to the zenith. Now and again he caught the black speck clearing the hills of ice and sinking into the intervening hollows; but he dared not permit himself more than the most cursory glances for fear of rousing his enemy's suspicion. Once, when Jacob Kent rose to his feet and searched the trail with care, Cardegee was frightened, but the dog-sled had struck a piece of trail running parallel with a jam, and remained out of sight till the danger was past.

"I'll see you 'ung for this," Cardegee threatened, attempting to draw the other's attention. "An' you'll rot in 'ell, jes' you see if you don't.

"I say," he cried, after another pause; "d'ye b'lieve in ghosts?" Kent's sudden start made him sure of his ground, and he went on: "Now a ghost 'as the right to 'aunt a man wot don't do wot he says; and you can't shuffle me off till eight bells —wot I mean is twelve o'clock—can you? 'Cos if you do, it'll 'appen as 'ow I'll 'aunt you. D'ye 'ear? A minute, a second too quick, an' I'll 'aunt you, so 'elp me, I will!"

Jacob Kent looked dubious, but declined to talk.

"'Ow's your chronometer? Wot's your longitude? 'Ow do you know as your time's correct?" Cardegee persisted, vainly hoping to beat his executioner out of a few minutes. "Is it Barrack's time you 'ave, or is it the Company time? 'Cos if you do it before the stroke o' the bell, I'll not rest. I give you fair warnin'. I'll come back. An' if you 'aven't the time, 'ow will you know? That's wot I want—'ow will you tell?"

"I'll send you off all right," Kent replied.

"Got a sun-dial here."

"No good. Thirty-two degrees variation o' the needle."

"Stakes are all set."

" 'Ow did you set 'em? Compass?"

"No; lined them up with the North Star."

"Sure?"

"Sure."

Cardegee groaned, then stole a glance at the trail. The sled was just clearing a rise, barely a mile away, and the dogs were in full lope, running lightly.

" 'Ow close is the shadows to the line?"

Kent walked to the primitive timepiece and studied it. "Three inches," he announced, after a careful survey.

"Say, jes' sing out 'eight bells' afore you pull the gun, will you?"

Kent agreed, and they lapsed into silence. The thongs about Cardegee's wrists were slowly stretching, and he had begun to work them over his hands.

"Say, 'ow close is the shadows?"

"One inch."

The sailor wriggled slightly to assure himself that he would topple over at the right moment, and slipped the first turn over his hands.

" 'Ow close?"

"Half an inch." Just then Kent heard the jarring churn of the runners and turned his eyes to the trail. The driver was lying flat on the sled and the dogs swinging down the straight stretch to the cabin. Kent whirled back, bringing his rifle to shoulder.

"It ain't eight bells yet!" Cardegee expostulated. "I'll 'aunt you, sure!"

Jacob Kent faltered. He was standing by the sun-dial, perhaps ten paces from his victim. The man on the sled must have seen that something unusual was taking place, for he had risen to his knees, his whip singing viciously among the dogs. The shadows swept into line. Kent looked along the sights.

"Make ready!" he commanded solemnly. "Eight b–"

But just a fraction of a second too soon, Cardegee rolled backward into the hole. Kent held his fire and ran to the edge. Bang! The gun exploded full in the sailor's face as he rose to his feet. But no smoke came from the muzzle; instead, a sheet of flame burst from the side of the barrel near its butt, and Jacob Kent went down. The dogs dashed up the bank, dragging the sled over his body, and the driver sprang off as Jim Cardegee freed his hands and drew himself from the hole.

"Jim!" The new-comer recognized him. "What's the matter?"

"Wot's the matter? Oh, nothink at all. It jest 'appens as I do little things like this for my 'ealth. Wot's the matter, you bloomin' idjit? Wot's the matter, eh? Cast me loose or I'll show you wot! 'Urry up, or I'll 'olystone the decks with you!"

"Huh!" he added, as the other went to work with his sheath-knife. "Wot's the matter? I want to know. Jes' tell me that, will you, wot's the matter? Hey?"

Kent was quite dead when they rolled him over. The gun, an old-fashioned, heavy-weighted muzzle-loader, lay near him. Steel and wood had parted company. Near the butt of the right-hand barrel, with lips pressed outward, gaped a fissure several inches in length. The sailor picked it up, curiously. A glittering stream of yellow dust ran out through the crack. The facts of the case dawned upon Jim Cardegee.

"Strike me standin'!" he roared; " 'ere's a go! 'Ere's 'is bloomin' dust! Gawd blime me, an' you, too, Charley, if you don't run an' get the dish-pan!"

1900

THE LAW OF LIFE

Old Koskoosh listened greedily. Though his sight had long since faded, his hearing was still acute, and the slightest sound penetrated to the glimmering intelligence which yet abode behind the withered forehead, but which no longer gazed forth upon the things of the world. Ah! That was Sit-cum-to-ha, shrilly anathematizing the dogs as she cuffed and beat them into the harnesses. Sit-cum-to-ha was his daughter's daughter, but she was too busy to waste a thought upon her broken grandfather, sitting alone there in the snow, forlorn and helpless. Camp must be broken. The long trail waited while the short day refused to linger. Life called her, and the duties of life, not death. And he was very close to death now.

The thought made the old man panicky for the moment, and he stretched forth a palsied hand which wandered tremblingly over the small heap of dry wood beside him. Reassured that it was indeed there, his hand returned to the shelter of his mangy furs, and he again fell to listening. The sulky crackling of half-frozen hides told him that the chief's moose-skin lodge had been struck, and even then was being rammed and jammed into portable compass. The chief was his son, stalwart and strong, headman of the tribesmen, and a mighty hunter. As the women toiled with the camp luggage, his voice rose, chiding them for their slowness. Old Koskoosh strained his ears. It was the last time he would hear that voice. There went Geehow's lodge! And Tusken's! Seven, eight, nine; only the shaman's could be still standing. There! They were at work upon it now. He could hear the shaman grunt as he piled it on the sled. A child whimpered, and a woman soothed it with soft, crooning gutturals. Little Koo-tee, the old man thought, a fretful child, and not overstrong. It would die soon, perhaps, and they would burn a hole through the frozen tundra and pile rocks above to keep the wolverines away. Well, what did it matter? A few years at best, and as many an empty belly as a full one. And in the end, Death waited, ever-hungry and hungriest of them all.

What was that? Oh, the men lashing the sleds and drawing tight the thongs. He listened, who would listen no more. The whiplashes snarled and bit among the dogs. Hear them whine! How they hated the work and the trail! They were off! Sled after sled churned slowly away into the silence. They were gone. They had passed out of his life, and he faced the last bitter hour alone. No. The snow crunched beneath a moccasin; a man stood beside him; upon his head a hand rested gently. His son was good to do this thing. He remembered other old men whose sons had not waited after the tribe. But his son had. He wandered away into the past, till the young man's voice brought him back.

"It is well with you?" he asked.

And the old man answered, "It is well."

"There be wood beside you," the younger man continued, "and the fire burns bright. The morning is gray, and the cold has broken. It will snow presently. Even now it is snowing."

"Aye, even now is it snowing."

"The tribesmen hurry. Their bales are heavy and their bellies flat with lack of feasting. The trail is long and they travel fast. I go now. It is well?"

"It is well. I am as a last year's leaf, clinging lightly to the stem. The first breath that blows, and I fall. My voice is become like an old woman's. My eyes no longer show me the way of my feet, and my feet are heavy, and I am tired. It is well."

He bowed his head in content till the last noise of the complaining snow had died away, and he knew his son was beyond recall. Then his hand crept out in haste to the wood. It alone stood between him and the eternity that yawned in upon him. At last the measure of his life was a handful of faggots. One by one they would go to feed the fire, and just so, step by step, death would creep upon him. When the last stick had surrendered up its heat, the frost would begin to gather strength. First his feet would yield, then his hands; and the numbness would travel, slowly, from the extremities to the body. His head would fall forward upon his knees, and he would rest. It was easy. All men must die.

He did not complain. It was the way of life, and it was just. He had been born close to the earth, close to the earth had he lived, and the law thereof was not new to him. It was the law of all flesh. Nature was not kindly to the flesh. She had no concern for that concrete thing called the individual. Her interest lay in the species, the race. This was the deepest abstraction old Koskoosh's barbaric mind was capable of, but he grasped it firmly. He saw it exemplified in all life. The rise of the sap, the bursting greenness of the willow bud, the fall of the yellow leaf—in this alone was told the whole history. But one task did Nature set the individual. Did he not perform it, he died. Did he perform it, it was all the same, he died. Nature did not care; there were plenty who were obedient, and it was only the obedience in this matter, not the obedient, which lived and lived always. The tribe of Koskoosh was very old. The old men he had known when a boy had known old men before them. Therefore it was true that the tribe lived, that it stood for the obedience of all its members, way down into the forgotten past, whose very resting places were unremembered. They did not count; they were episodes. They had passed away like clouds from a summer sky. He also was an episode and would pass away. Nature did not care. To life she set one task, gave one law. To perpetuate was the task of life, its law was death. A maiden was a good creature to look upon, full-breasted and strong, with spring to her step and light in her eyes. But her task was yet before her. The light in her eyes brightened, her step quickened, she was now bold with the young men, now timid, and she gave them of her own unrest. And ever she grew fairer and yet fairer to look upon, till some hunter, able no longer to withhold himself, took her to his lodge to cook and toil for him and to become the mother of his children. And with the coming of her offspring her looks left her. Her limbs dragged and shuffled, her eyes dimmed and bleared, and only the little children found joy against the withered cheek of the old squaw by the fire. Her task was done. But a little while, on the first pinch of famine or the first long trail, and she would be left, even as he had been left, in the snow, with a little pile of wood. Such was the law.

He placed a stick carefully upon the fire and resumed his meditations. It was the same everywhere, with all things. The mosquitoes vanished with the first frost.

The little tree squirrel crawled away to die. When age settled upon the rabbit it became slow and heavy and could no longer outfoot its enemies. Even the big bald-face grew clumsy and blind and quarrelsome, in the end to be dragged down by a handful of yelping huskies. He remembered how he had abandoned his own father on an upper reach of the Klondike one winter, the winter before the missionary came with his talk books and his box of medicines. Many a time had Koskoosh smacked his lips over the recollection of that box, though now his mouth refused to moisten. The "painkiller" had been especially good. But the missionary was a bother after all, for he brought no meat into the camp, and he ate heartily, and the hunters grumbled. But he chilled his lungs on the divide by the Mayo, and the dogs afterward nosed the stones away and fought over his bones.

Koskoosh placed another stick on the fire and harked back deeper into the past. There was the time of the great famine, when the old men crouched empty-bellied to the fire, and let fall from their lips dim traditions of the ancient day when the Yukon ran wide open for three winters, and then lay frozen for three summers. He had lost his mother in that famine. In the summer the salmon run had failed, and the tribe looked forward to the winter and the coming of the caribou. Then the winter came, but with it there were no caribou. Never had the like been known, not even in the lives of the old men. But the caribou did not come, and it was the seventh year, and the rabbits had not replenished, and the dogs were naught but bundles of bones. And through the long darkness the children wailed and died, and the women, and the old men; and not one in ten of the tribe lived to meet the sun when it came back in the spring. That *was* a famine!

But he had seen times of plenty, too, when the meat spoiled on their hands, and the dogs were fat and worthless with overeating—times when they let the game go unkilled, and the women were fertile, and the lodges were cluttered with sprawling men-children and women-children. Then it was the men became high-stomached, and revived ancient quarrels, and crossed the divides to the south to kill the Pellys, and to the west that they might sit by the dead fires of the Tananas. He remembered, when a boy, during a time of plenty, when he saw a moose pulled down by the wolves. Zing-ha lay with him in the snow and watched—Zing-ha, who later became the craftiest of hunters, and who, in the end, fell through an air hole on the Yukon. They found him, a month afterward, just as he had crawled halfway out and frozen stiff to the ice.

But the moose. Zing-ha and he had gone out that day to play at hunting after the manner of their fathers. On the bed of the creak they struck the fresh track of a moose, and with it the tracks of many wolves. "An old one," Zing-ha, who was quicker at reading the sign, said, "an old one who cannot keep up with the herd. The wolves have cut him out from his brothers, and they will never leave him." And it was so. It was their way. By day and by night, never resting, snarling on his heels, snapping at his nose, they would stay by him to the end. How Zing-ha and he felt the blood lust quicken! The finish would be a sight to see!

Eager-footed, they took the trail, and even he, Koskoosh, slow of sight and an unversed tracker, could have followed it blind, it was so wide. Hot were they on the heels of the chase, reading the grim tragedy, fresh-written, at every step. Now they came to where the moose had made a stand. Thrice the length of a grown man's body, in every direction, had the snow been stamped about and uptossed In the midst were the deep impressions of the splay-hoofed game, and all about, everywhere, were the lighter footmarks of the wolves. Some, while their brothers harried the kill, had lain to one side and rested. The full-stretched impress of their bodies in the snow was as perfect as though made the moment before. One wolf had been caught in a wild lunge of the maddened victim and trampled to death. A few bones, well picked, bore witness.

Again, they ceased the uplift of their snowshoes at a second stand. Here the great animal had fought desperately. Twice had he been dragged down, as the snow attested, and twice had he shaken his assailants clear and gained footing once more. He had done his task long since, but none the less was life dear to him. Zing-ha said it was a strange thing, a moose once down to get free again; but this one certainly had. The shaman would see signs and wonders in this when they told him.

And yet again, they came to where the moose had made to mount the bank and gain the timber. But his foes had laid on from behind, till he reared and fell back upon them, crushing two deep into the snow. It was plain the kill was at hand, for their brothers had left them untouched. Two more stands were hurried past, brief in time length and very close together. The trail was red now, and the clean stride of the great beast had grown short and slovenly. Then they heard the first sounds of the battle—not the full-throated chorus of the chase, but the short, snappy bark which spoke of close quarters and teeth to flesh. Crawling up the wind, Zing-ha bellied it through the snow, and with him crept he, Koskoosh, who was to be chief of the tribesmen in the years to come. Together they shoved aside the underbranches of a young spruce and peered forth. It was the end they saw.

The picture, like all of youth's impressions, was still strong with him, and his dim eyes watched the end played out as vividly as in that far-off time. Koskoosh marveled at this, for in the days which followed, when he was a leader of men and a head of councilors, he had done great deeds and made his name a curse in the mouths of the Pellys, to say naught of the strange white man he had killed, knife to knife, in open fight.

For long he pondered on the days of his youth, till the fire died down and the frost bit deeper. He replenished it with two sticks this time, and gauged his grip on life by what remained. If Sit-cum-to-ha had only remembered her grandfather, and gathered a larger armful, his hours would have been longer. It would have been easy. But she was ever a careless child, and honored not her ancestors from the time the Beaver, son of the son of Zing-ha, first cast eyes upon her. Well, what mattered it? Had he not done likewise in his own quick youth? For a while he listened to the silence. Perhaps the heart of his son might soften, and he would come back with the dogs to take his old father on with the tribe to where the caribou ran thick and the fat hung heavy upon them.

He strained his ears, his restless brain for the moment stilled. Not a stir, nothing. He alone took breath in the midst of the great silence. It was very lonely. Hark! What was that? A chill passed over his body. The familiar, long-drawn howl broke the void, and it was close at hand. Then on his darkened eyes was projected the vision of the moose—the old bull moose—the torn flanks and bloody sides, the riddled mane, and the great branching horns, down low and tossing to the last. He saw the flashing forms of gray, the gleaming eyes, the lolling tongues, the slavered fangs. And he saw the inexorable circle close in till it became a dark point in the midst of the stamped snow.

A cold muzzle thrust against his cheek, and at its touch his soul leaped back to the present. His hand shot into the fire and dragged out a burning faggot. Overcome for the nonce by his hereditary fear of man, the brute retreated, raising a prolonged call to his brothers; and greedily they answered, till a ring of crouching, jaw-slobbered gray was stretched round about. The old man listened to the drawing in of this circle. He waved his brand wildly, and sniffs turned to snarls; but the panting brutes refused to scatter. Now one wormed his chest forward, dragging his haunches after, now a second, now a third; but never a one drew back. Why should he cling to life? he asked, and dropped the blazing stick into the snow. It sizzled and went out. The circle grunted uneasily but held its own. Again he saw the last stand of the old bull moose, and Koskoosh dropped his head wearily upon his knees. What did it matter after all? Was it not the law of life?

1901

THE ONE THOUSAND DOZEN

David Rasmunsen was a hustler, and, like many a greater man, a man of the one idea. Wherefore, when the clarion call of the North rang on his ear, he conceived an adventure in eggs and bent all his energy to its achievement. He figured briefly and to the point, and the adventure became iridescent-hued, splendid. That eggs would sell at Dawson for five dollars a dozen was a safe working premise. Whence it was incontrovertible that one thousand dozen would bring, in the Golden Metropolis, five thousand dollars.

On the other hand, expense was to be considered, and he considered it well, for he was a careful man, keenly practical, with a hard head and a heart that imagination never warmed. At fifteen cents a dozen, the initial cost of his thousand dozen would be one hundred and fifty dollars, a mere bagatelle in face of the enormous profit. And suppose, just suppose, to be wildly extravagant for once, that transportation for himself and eggs should run up eight hundred and fifty more; he would still have four thousand clear cash and clean when the last egg was disposed of and the last dust had rippled into his sack.

"You see, Alma,"—he figured it over with his wife, the cosy dining room submerged in a sea of maps, government surveys, guidebooks, and Alaskan itineraries, —"you see, expenses don't really begin till you make Dyea—fifty dollars'll cover it with a first-class passage thrown in. Now from Dyea to Lake Linderman, Indian packers take your goods over for twelve cents a pound, twelve dollars a hundred, or one hundred and twenty dollars a thousand. Say I have fifteen hundred pounds, it'll cost one hundred and eighty dollars—call it two hundred and be safe. I am creditably informed by a Klondiker just come out that I can buy a boat for three hundred. But the same man says I'm sure to get a couple of passengers for one hundred and fifty each, which will give me the boat for nothing, and, further, they can help me manage it. And . . . that's all; I put my eggs ashore from the boat at Dawson. Now let me see how much is that?"

"Fifty dollars from San Francisco to Dyea, two hundred from Dyea to Linderman, passengers pay for the boat—two hundred and fifty all told," she summed up swiftly.

"And a hundred for my clothes and personal outfit," he went on happily; "that leaves a margin of five hundred for emergencies. And what possible emergencies can arise?"

Alma shrugged her shoulders and elevated her brows. If that vast Northland was capable of swallowing up a man and a thousand dozen eggs, surely there was room and to spare for whatever else he might happen to possess. So she thought, but she said nothing. She knew David Rasmunsen too well to say anything.

"Doubling the time because of chance delays, I should make the trip in two months. Think of it, Alma! Four thousand in two months! Beats the paltry hundred a month I'm getting now. Why, we'll build further out where we'll have more space, gas in every room, and a view, and the rent of the cottage'll pay taxes, insurance, and water, and leave something over. And then there's always the chance of my striking it and coming out a millionnaire. Now tell me, Alma, don't you think I'm very moderate?"

And Alma could hardly think otherwise. Besides, had not her own cousin,—though a remote and distant one to be sure, the black sheep, the harum-scarum, the ne'er-do-well,—had not he come down out of that weird North country with a hundred thousand in yellow dust, to say nothing of a half-ownership in the hole from which it came?

David Rasmunsen's grocer was surprised when he found him weighing eggs in the scales at the end of the counter, and Rasmunsen himself was more surprised when he found that a dozen eggs weighed a pound and a half—fifteen hundred pounds for his thousand dozen! There would be no weight left for his clothes, blankets, and cooking utensils, to say nothing of the grub he must necessarily consume by the way. His calculations were all thrown out, and he was just proceeding to recast them when he hit upon the idea of weighing small eggs. "For whether they be large or small, a dozen eggs is a dozen eggs," he observed sagely to himself; and a dozen small ones he found to weigh but a pound and a quarter. Thereat the city of San Francisco was overrun by anxious-eyed emissaries, and commission houses and dairy associations were startled by a sudden demand for eggs running not more than twenty ounces to the dozen.

Rasmunsen mortgaged the little cottage for a thousand dollars, arranged for his wife to make a prolonged stay among her own people, threw up his job, and started North. To keep within his schedule he compromised on a second-class passage, which, because of the rush, was worse than steerage; and in the late summer, a pale and wabbly man, he disembarked with his eggs on the Dyea beach. But it did not take him long to recover his land legs and appetite. His first interview with the Chilkoot packers straightened him up and stiffened his backbone. Forty cents a pound they demanded for the twenty-eight-mile portage, and while he caught his breath and swallowed, the price went up to forty-three. Fifteen husky Indians put the straps on his packs at forty-five, but took them off at an offer of forty-seven from a Skaguay Crœsus in dirty shirt and ragged overalls who had lost his horses on the White Pass Trail and was now making a last desperate drive at the country by way of Chilkoot.

But Rasmunsen was clean grit, and at fifty cents found takers, who, two days later, set his eggs down intact at Linderman. But fifty cents a pound is a thousand dollars a ton, and his fifteen hundred pounds had exhausted his emergency fund and left him stranded at the Tantalus point where each day he saw the fresh-whip-sawed boats departing for Dawson. Further, a great anxiety brooded over the camp where the boats were built. Men worked frantically, early and late, at the height of their endurance, calking, nailing, and pitching in a frenzy of haste for which adequate explanation was not far to seek. Each day the snow-line crept farther down the bleak, rock-shouldered peaks, and gale followed gale, with sleet and slush and snow, and in the eddies and quiet places young ice formed and thickened through the fleeting hours. And each morn, toil-stiffened men turned wan faces across the lake to see if the freeze-up had come. For the freeze-up heralded the death of their hope—the hope that they would be floating down the swift river ere navigation closed on the chain of lakes.

To harrow Rasmunsen's soul further, he discovered three competitors in the egg business. It was true that one, a little German, had gone broke and was himself forlornly back-tripping the last pack of the portage; but the other two had boats nearly completed and were daily supplicating the god of merchants and traders to stay the iron hand of winter for just another day. But the iron hand closed down over the land. Men were being frozen in the blizzard, which swept Chilkoot, and Rasmunsen frosted his toes ere he was aware. He found a chance to go passenger with his freight in a boat just shoving off through the rubble, but two hundred, hard cash, was required, and he had no money.

"Ay tank you yust wait one leedle w'ile," said the Swedish boat-builder, who had struck his Klondike right there and was wise enough to know it—"one leedle w'ile und I make you a tam fine skiff boat, sure Pete."

With this unpledged word to go on, Rasmunsen hit the back trail to Crater Lake, where he fell in with two press correspondents whose tangled baggage was strewn from Stone House, over across the Pass, and as far as Happy Camp.

"Yes," he said with consequence. "I've a thousand dozen eggs at Linderman, and my boat's just about got the last seam calked. Consider myself in luck to get it. Boats are at a premium, you know, and none to be had."

Whereupon and almost with bodily violence the correspondents clamored to go with him, fluttered greenbacks before his eyes, and spilled yellow twenties from hand to hand. He could not hear of it, but they overpersuaded him, and he reluctantly consented to take them at three hundred apiece. Also they pressed upon him the passage money in advance. And while they wrote to their respective journals concerning the good Samaritan with the thousand dozen eggs, the good Samaritan was hurrying back to the Swede at Linderman.

"Here, you! Gimme that boat!" was his salutation, his hand jingling the correspondents' gold pieces and his eyes hungrily bent upon the finished craft.

The Swede regarded him stolidly and shook his head.

"How much is the other fellow paying? Three hundred? Well, here's four. Take it."

He tried to press it upon him, but the man backed away.

"Ay tank not. Ay say him get der skiff boat. You yust wait—"

"Here's six hundred. Last call. Take it or leave it. Tell'm it's a mistake."

The Swede wavered. "Ay tank yes," he finally said, and the last Rasmunsen saw of him his vocabulary was going to wreck in a vain effort to explain the mistake to the other fellows.

The German slipped and broke his ankle on the steep hogback above Deep Lake, sold out his stock for a dollar a dozen, and with the proceeds hired Indian packers to carry him back to Dyea. But on the morning Rasmunsen shoved off with his correspondents, his two rivals followed suit.

"How many you got?" one of them, a lean little New Englander, called out.

"One thousand dozen," Rasmunsen answered proudly.

"Huh! I'll go you even stakes I beat you in with my eight hundred."

The correspondents offered to lend him the money; but Rasmunsen declined, and the Yankee closed with the remaining rival, a brawny son of the sea and sailor of ships and things, who promised to show them all a wrinkle or two when it came to cracking on. And crack on he did, with a large tarpaulin squaresail which pressed the bow half under at every jump. He was the first to run out of Linderman, but, disdaining the portage, piled his loaded boat on the rocks in the boiling rapids. Rasmunsen and the Yankee, who likewise had two passengers, portaged across on their backs and then lined their empty boats down through the bad water to Bennett.

Bennett was a twenty-five-mile lake, narrow and deep, a funnel between the mountains through which storms ever romped. Rasmunsen camped on the sand-pit at its head, where were many men and boats bound north in the teeth of the Arctic winter. He awoke in the morning to find a piping gale from the south, which caught the chill from the whited peaks and glacial valleys and blew as cold as north wind ever blew. But it was fair, and he also found the Yankee staggering past the first bold headland with all sail set. Boat after boat was getting under way, and the correspondents fell to with enthusiasm.

"We'll catch him before Cariboo Crossing," they assured Rasmunsen, as they ran up the sail and the *Alma* took the first icy spray over her bow.

Now Rasmunsen all his life had been prone to cowardice on water, but he clung to the kicking steering-oar with set face and determined jaw. His thousand dozen were there in the boat before his eyes, safely secured beneath the correspondents' baggage, and somehow, before his eyes, were the little cottage and the mortgage for a thousand dollars.

It was bitter cold. Now and again he hauled in the steering-sweep and put out a fresh one while his passengers chopped the ice from the blade. Wherever the spray struck, it turned instantly to frost, and the dipping boom of the spritsail was quickly fringed with icicles. The *Alma* strained and hammered through the big seas till the seams and butts began to spread, but in lieu of bailing the correspondents chopped ice and flung it overboard. There was no let-up. The mad race with winter was on, and the boats tore along in a desperate string.

"W-w-we can't stop to save our souls!" one of the correspondents chattered, from cold, not fright.

"That's right! Keep her down the middle, old man!" the other encouraged.

Rasmunsen replied with an idiotic grin. The iron-bound shores were in a lather of foam, and even down the middle the only hope was to keep running away from the big seas. To lower sail was to be overtaken and swamped. Time and again they passed boats pounding among the rocks, and once they saw one on the edge of the breakers about to strike. A little craft behind them, with two men, jibed over and turned bottom up.

"W-w-watch out, old man!" cried he of the chattering teeth.

Rasmunsen grinned and tightened his aching grip on the sweep. Scores of times had the send of the sea caught the big square stern of the *Alma* and thrown her off from dead before it till the after leach of the spritsail fluttered hollowly, and each time, and only with all his strength, had he forced her back. His grin by then had become fixed, and it disturbed the correspondents to look at him.

They roared down past an isolated rock a hundred yards from shore. From its wave-drenched top a man shrieked wildly, for the instant cutting the storm with his voice. But the next instant the *Alma* was by, and the rock growing a black speck in the troubled froth.

"That settles the Yankee! Where's the sailor?" shouted one of his passengers.

Rasmunsen shot a glance over his shoulder at a black squaresail. He had seen it leap up out of the gray to windward, and for an hour, off and on, had been watching it grow. The sailor had evidently repaired damages and was making up for lost time.

"Look at him come!"

Both passengers stopped chopping ice to watch. Twenty miles of Bennett were behind them—room and to spare for the sea to toss up its mountains toward the sky. Sinking and soaring like a storm god, the sailor drove by them. The huge sail seemed to grip the boat from the crests of the waves, to tear it bodily out of the water, and fling it crashing and smothering down into the yawning troughs.

"The sea'll never catch him!"

"But he'll r-r-run her nose under!"

Even as they spoke, the black tarpaulin swooped from sight behind a big comber. The next wave rolled over the spot, and the next, but the boat did not reappear. The *Alma* rushed by the place. A little riffraff of oars and boxes was seen. An arm thrust up and a shaggy head broke surface a score of yards away.

For a time there was silence. As the end of the lake came in sight, the waves began to leap aboard with such steady recurrence that the correspondents no longer chopped ice but flung the water out with buckets. Even this would not do, and, after a shouted conference with Rasmunsen, they attacked the baggage. Flour, bacon, beans, blankets, cooking stove, ropes, odds and ends, everything they could get hands on, flew overboard. The boat acknowledged it at once, taking less water and rising more buoyantly.

"That'll do!" Rasmunsen called sternly, as they applied themselves to the top layer of eggs.

"The h-hell it will!" answered the shivering one, savagely. With the exception of their notes, films, and cameras, they had sacrificed their outfit. He bent over, laid hold of an egg-box, and began to worry it out from under the lashing.

"Drop it! Drop it, I say!"

Rasmunsen had managed to draw his revolver, and with the crook of his arm over the sweep head was taking aim. The correspondent stood up on the thwart, balancing back and forth, his face twisted with menace and speechless anger.

"My God!"

So cried his brother correspondent, hurling himself, face downward, into the bottom of the boat. The *Alma*, under the divided attention of Rasmunsen, had been caught by a great mass of water and whirled around. The after leach hollowed, the sail emptied and jibed, and the boom, sweeping with terrific force across the boat, carried the angry correspondent overboard with a broken back. Mast and sail had gone over the side as well. A drenching sea followed, as the boat lost headway, and Rasmunsen sprang to the bailing bucket.

Several boats hurtled past them in the next half-hour,—small boats, boats of their own size, boats afraid, unable to do aught but run madly on. Then a ten-ton barge, at imminent risk of destruction, lowered sail to windward and lumbered down upon them.

"Keep off! Keep off!" Rasmunsen screamed.

But his low gunwale ground against the heavy craft, and the remaining correspondent clambered aboard. Rasmunsen was over the eggs like a cat and in the bow of the *Alma*, striving with numb fingers to bend the hauling-lines together.

"Come on!" a red-whiskered man yelled at him.

"I've a thousand dozen eggs here," he shouted back. "Gimme a tow! I'll pay you!"

"Come on!" they howled in chorus.

A big whitecap broke just beyond, washing over the barge and leaving the *Alma* half swamped. The men cast off, cursing him as they ran up their sail. Rasmunsen cursed back and fell to bailing. The mast and sail, like a sea anchor, still fast by the halyards, held the boat head on to wind and sea and gave him a chance to fight the water out.

Three hours later, numbed, exhausted, blathering like a lunatic, but still bailing, he went ashore on an ice-strewn beach near Cariboo Crossing. Two men, a government courier and a half-breed voyageur, dragged him out of the surf, saved his cargo, and beached the *Alma*. They were paddling out of the country in a Peterborough, and gave him shelter for the night in their storm-bound camp. Next morning they departed, but he elected to stay by his eggs. And thereafter the name and fame of the man with the thousand dozen eggs began to spread through the land. Gold-seekers who made in before the freeze-up carried the news of his coming. Grizzled old-timers of Forty Mile and Circle City, sour doughs with leathern jaws and bean-calloused stomachs, called up dream memories of chickens and green things at mention of his name. Dyea and Skaguay took an interest in his being, and questioned his progress from every man who came over the passes, while Dawson—golden, omeletless Dawson—fretted and worried, and waylaid every chance arrival for word of him.

But of this, Rasmunsen knew nothing. The day after the wreck he patched up the *Alma* and pulled out. A cruel east wind blew in his teeth from Tagish, but he got the oars over the side and bucked manfully into it, though half the time he was drifting backward and chopping ice from the blades. According to the custom of the country, he was driven ashore at Windy Arm; three times on Tagish saw him swamped and beached; and Lake Marsh held him at the freeze-up. The *Alma* was crushed in the jamming of the floes, but the eggs were intact. These he back-tripped two miles across the ice to the shore, where he built a cache, which stood for years after and was pointed out by men who knew.

Half a thousand frozen miles stretched between him and Dawson, and the waterway was closed. But Rasmunsen, with a peculiar tense look in his face, struck back up the lakes on foot. What he suffered on that lone trip, with naught but a single blanket, an axe, and a handful of beans, is not given to ordinary mortals to know. Only the Arctic adventurer may understand. Suffice that he was caught in a blizzard on Chilkoot and left two of his toes with the surgeon at Sheep Camp. Yet he stood on his feet and washed dishes in the scullery of the *Pawona* to the Puget Sound, and from there passed coal on a P. S. boat to San Francisco.

It was a haggard, unkempt man who limped across the shining office floor to raise a second mortgage from the bank people. His hollow cheeks betrayed themselves through the scraggly beard, and his eyes seemed to have retired into deep caverns where they burned with cold fires. His hands were grained from exposure and hard work, and the nails were rimmed with tight-packed dirt and coal dust. He spoke vaguely of eggs and ice-packs, winds and tides; but when they declined to let him have more than a second thousand, his talk became incoherent, concerning itself chiefly with the price of dogs and dog-food, and such things as snowshoes and moccasins and winter trails. They let him have fifteen hundred, which was more than the cottage warranted, and breathed easier when he scrawled his signature and passed out the door.

Two weeks later he went over Chilkoot with three dog sleds of five dogs each. One team he drove, the two Indians with him driving the other. At Lake Marsh they broke out the cache and loaded up. But there was no trail. He was the first in over the ice, and to him fell the task of packing the snow and hammering away through the rough river jams. Behind him he often observed a camp-fire smoke trickling thinly up through the quiet air, and he wondered why the people did not overtake him. For he was a stranger to the land and did not understand. Nor could he understand his Indians when they tried to explain. This they conceived to be a hardship, but when they balked and refused to break camp of mornings, he drove them to their work at pistol point.

When he slipped through an ice bridge near the White Horse and froze his foot, tender yet and oversensitive from the previous freezing, the Indians looked for him to lie up. But he sacrificed a blanket, and, with his foot incased in an enormous moccasin, big as a water-bucket, continued to take his regular turn with the front sled. Here was the cruelest work, and they respected him, though on the side they rapped their foreheads with their knuckles and significantly shook their heads. One night they tried to run away, but the zip-zip of his bullets in the snow brought them back, snarling but convinced. Whereupon, being only savage Chilkat men, they put their heads together to kill him; but he slept like a cat, and, waking or sleeping, the chance never came. Often they tried to tell him the import of the smoke wreath in the rear, but he could not comprehend and grew suspicious of them. And when they sulked or shirked, he was quick to let drive at them between the eyes, and quick to cool their heated souls with sight of his ready revolver.

And so it went—with mutinous men, wild dogs, and a trail that broke the heart. He fought the men to stay with him, fought the dogs to keep them away from the eggs, fought the ice, the cold, and the pain of his foot, which would not heal. As fast as the young tissue renewed, it was bitten and seared by the frost, so that a running sore developed, into which he could almost shove his fist. In the mornings, when he first put his weight upon it, his head went dizzy, and he was near to fainting from the pain; but later on in the day it usually grew numb, to recommence when he crawled into his blankets and tried to sleep. Yet he, who had been a clerk and sat at a desk all his days, toiled till the Indians were exhausted, and even outworked the dogs. How hard he worked, how much he suffered, he did not know. Being a man of the one idea, now that the idea had come, it mastered him. In the foreground of his consciousness was Dawson, in the background his thousand dozen eggs, and midway between the two his ego fluttered, striving alway to draw them together to a glittering golden point. This golden point was the five thousand dollars, the consummation of the idea and the point of departure for whatever new idea might present itself. For the rest, he was a mere automaton. He was unaware of other things, seeing them as through a glass darkly, and giving them no thought. The work of his hands he did with machine-like wisdom; likewise the work of his head. So the look on his face grew very tense, till even the Indians were afraid of it, and marvelled at the strange white man who had made them slaves and forced them to toil with such foolishness.

Then came a snap on Lake Le Barge, when the cold of outer space smote the tip of the planet, and the frost ranged sixty and odd degrees below zero. Here, laboring with open mouth that he might breathe more freely, he chilled his lungs, and for the rest of the trip he was troubled with a dry, hacking cough, especially irritable in smoke of camp or under stress of undue exertion. On the Thirty Mile River he found much open water, spanned by precarious ice bridges and fringed with narrow rim ice, tricky and uncertain. The rim ice was impossible to reckon on, and he dared it without reckoning, falling back on his revolver when his drivers demurred. But on the ice bridges, covered with snow though they were, precautions could be taken. These they crossed on their snowshoes, with long poles, held crosswise in their hands, to which to cling in case of accident. Once over, the dogs were called to follow. And on such a bridge, where the absence of the centre ice was masked by the snow, one of the Indians met his end. He went through as quickly and neatly as a knife through thin cream, and the current swept him from view down under the stream ice.

That night his mate fled away through the pale moonlight, Rasmunsen futilely puncturing the silence with his revolver—a thing that he handled with more celerity than cleverness. Thirty-six hours later the Indian made a police camp on the Big Salmon.

"Um—um—um funny mans—what you call?—top um head all loose," the interpreter explained to the puzzled captain. "Eh? Yep, clazy, much clazy mans. Eggs, eggs, all a time eggs—savvy? Come bime-by."

It was several days before Rasmunsen arrived, the three sleds lashed together, and all the dogs in a single team. It was awkward, and where the going was bad he was compelled to back-trip it sled by sled, though he managed most of the time, through herculean efforts, to bring all along on the one haul. He did not seem moved when the captain of police told him his man was hitting the high places for Dawson, and was by that time, probably, halfway between Selkirk and Stewart. Nor did he appear interested when informed that the police had broken the trail as far as Pelly; for he had attained to a fatalistic acceptance of all natural dispensations, good or ill. But when they told him that Dawson was in the bitter clutch of famine, he smiled, threw the harness on his dogs, and pulled out.

But it was at his next halt that the mystery of the smoke was explained. With the word at Big Salmon that the trail was broken to Pelly, there was no longer any need for the smoke wreath to linger in his wake; and Rasmunsen, crouching over his lonely fire, saw a motley string of sleds go by. First came the courier and the half-breed who had hauled him out from Bennett; then mail-carriers for Circle City, two sleds of them, and a mixed following of ingoing Klondikers. Dogs and men were fresh and fat, while Rasmunsen and his brutes were jaded and worn down to the skin and bone. They of the smoke wreath had travelled one day in three, resting and reserving their strength for the dash to come when broken trail was met with; while each day he had plunged and floundered forward, breaking the spirit of his dogs and robbing them of their mettle.

As for himself, he was unbreakable. They thanked him kindly for his efforts in their behalf, those fat, fresh men,—thanked him kindly, with broad grins and ribald laughter; and now, when he understood, he made no answer. Nor did he cherish silent bitterness. It was immaterial. The idea—the fact behind the idea—was not changed. Here he was and his thousand dozen; there was Dawson; the problem was unaltered.

At the Little Salmon, being short of dog food, the dogs got into his grub, and from there to Selkirk he lived on beans—coarse, brown beans, big beans, grossly nutritive, which griped his stomach and doubled him up at two-hour intervals. But the Factor at Selkirk had a notice on the door of the Post to the effect that no steamer had been up the Yukon for two years, and in consequence grub was beyond price. He offered to swap flour, however, at the rate of a cupful for each egg, but Rasmunsen shook his head and hit the trail. Below the Post he managed to buy frozen horse hide for the dogs, the horses having been slain by the Chilkat cattle men, and the scraps and offal preserved by the Indians. He tackled the hide himself, but the hair worked into the bean sores of his mouth, and was beyond endurance.

Here at Selkirk, he met the forerunners of the hungry exodus of Dawson, and from there on they crept over the trail, a dismal throng. "No grub!" was the song they sang. "No grub, and had to go." "Everybody holding candles for a rise in the spring." "Flour dollar'n a half a pound, and no sellers."

"Eggs?" one of them answered. "Dollar apiece, but they ain't none."

Rasmunsen made a rapid calculation. "Twelve thousand dollars," he said aloud.

"Hey?" the man asked.

"Nothing," he answered, and *mushed* the dogs along.

When he arrived at Stewart River, seventy miles from Dawson, five of his dogs were gone, and the remainder were falling in the traces. He, also, was in the traces, hauling with what little strength was left in him. Even then he was barely crawling along ten miles a day. His cheek-bones and nose, frost-bitten again and again, were turned bloody-black and hideous. The thumb, which was separated from the fingers by the gee-pole, had likewise been nipped and gave him great pain. The monstrous moccasin still incased his foot, and strange pains were beginning to rack the leg. At Sixty Mile, the last beans, which he had been rationing for some time, were finished; yet he steadfastly refused to touch the eggs. He could not reconcile his mind to the legitimacy of it, and staggered and fell along the way to Indian River. Here a fresh-killed moose and an open-handed old-timer gave him and his dogs new strength, and at Ainslie's he felt repaid for it all when a stampede, ripe from Dawson in five hours, was sure he could get a dollar and a quarter for every egg he possessed.

He came up the steep bank by the Dawson barracks with fluttering heart and shaking knees. The dogs were so weak that he was forced to rest them, and, waiting, he leaned limply against the gee-pole. A man, an eminently decorous-looking man, came sauntering by in a great bearskin coat. He glanced at Rasmunsen curiously, then stopped and ran a speculative eye over the dogs and the three lashed sleds.

"What you got?" he asked.

"Eggs," Rasmunsen answered huskily, hardly able to pitch his voice above a whisper.

"Eggs! Whoopee! Whoopee!" He sprang up into the air, gyrated madly, and finished with half a dozen war steps. "You don't say—all of 'em?"

"All of 'em?"

"Say, you must be the Egg Man." He walked around and viewed Rasmunsen from the other side. "Come, now, ain't you the Egg Man?"

Rasmunsen didn't know, but supposed he was, and the man sobered down a bit.

"What d'ye expect to get for 'em?" he asked cautiously.

Rasmunsen became audacious. "Dollar'n a half," he said.

"Done!" the man came back promptly. "Gimme a dozen."

"I—I mean a dollar'n a half apiece," Rasmunsen hesitatingly explained.

"Sure. I heard you. Make it two dozen. Here's the dust."

The man pulled out a healthy gold sack the size of a small sausage and knocked it negligently against the gee-pole. Rasmunsen felt a strange trembling in the pit of his stomach, a tickling of the nostrils, and an almost overwhelming desire to sit down and cry. But a curious, wide-eyed crowd was beginning to collect, and man after man was calling out for eggs. He was without scales, but the man with the bearskin coat fetched a pair and obligingly weighed in the dust while Rasmunsen passed out the goods. Soon there was a pushing and shoving and shouldering, and a great clamor. Everybody wanted to buy and to be served first. And as the excitement grew, Rasmunsen cooled down. This would never do. There must be something behind the fact of their buying so eagerly. It would be wiser if he rested first and sized up the market. Perhaps eggs were worth two dollars apiece. Anyway, whenever he wished to sell, he was sure of a dollar and a half. "Stop!" he cried, when a couple of hundred had been sold. "No more now. I'm played out. I've got to get a cabin, and then you can come and see me."

A groan went up at this, but the man with the bearskin coat approved. Twenty-four of the frozen eggs went rattling in his capacious pockets and he didn't care whether the rest of the town ate or not. Besides, he could see Rasmunsen was on his last legs.

"There's a cabin right around the second corner from the Monte Carlo," he told him—"the one with the sody-bottle window. It ain't mine, but I've got charge of it. Rents for ten a day and cheap for the money. You move right in, and I'll see you later. Don't forget the sody-bottle window."

"Tra-la-loo!" he called back a moment later. "I'm goin' up the hill to eat eggs and dream of home."

On his way to the cabin, Rasmunsen recollected he was hungry and bought a small supply of provisions at the N. A. T. & T. store—also a beefsteak at the butcher shop and dried salmon for the dogs. He found the cabin without difficulty and left the dogs in the harness while he started the fire and got the coffee under way.

"A dollar'n a half apiece—one thousand dozen—eighteen thousand dollars!" He kept muttering it to himself, over and over, as he went about his work.

As he flopped the steak into the frying-pan the door opened. He turned. It was the man with the bearskin coat. He seemed to come in with determination, as though bound on some explicit errand, but as he looked at Rasmunsen an expression of perplexity came into his face.

"I say—now I say—" he began, then halted.

Rasmunsen wondered if he wanted the rent.

"I say, damn it, you know, them eggs is bad."

Rasmunsen staggered. He felt as though some one had struck him an astounding blow between the eyes. The walls of the cabin reeled and tilted up. He put out his hand to steady himself and rested it on the stove. The sharp pain and the smell of the burning flesh brought him back to himself.

"I see," he said slowly, fumbling in his pocket for the sack. "You want your money back."

"It ain't the money," the man said, "but hain't you got any eggs—good?"

Rasmunsen shook his head. "You'd better take the money."

But the man refused and backed away. "I'll come back," he said, "when you've taken stock, and get what's comin'."

Rasmunsen rolled the chopping-block into the cabin and carried in the eggs. He went about it quite calmly. He took up the hand-axe, and, one by one, chopped the eggs in half. These halves he examined carefully and let fall to the floor. At first he sampled from the different cases, then deliberately emptied one case at a time. The heap on the floor grew larger. The coffee boiled over and the smoke of the burning beefsteak filled the cabin. He chopped steadfastly and monotonously till the last case was finished.

Somebody knocked at the door, knocked again, and let himself in.

"What a mess!" he remarked, as he paused and surveyed the scene.

The severed eggs were beginning to thaw in the heat of the stove, and a miserable odor was growing stronger.

"Must a-happened on the steamer," he suggested.

Rasmunsen looked at him long and blankly.

"I'm Murray, Big Jim Murray, everybody knows me," the man volunteered. "I'm just hearin' your eggs is rotten, and I'm offerin' you two hundred for the batch. They ain't good as salmon, but still they're fair scoffin's for dogs."

Rasmunsen seemed turned to stone. He did not move. "You go to hell," he said passionlessly.

"Now just consider. I pride myself it's a decent price for a mess like that, and it's better'n nothin'. Two hundred. What you say?"

"You go to hell," Rasmunsen repeated softly, "and get out of here."

Murray gaped with a great awe, then went out carefully, backward, with his eyes fixed on the other's face.

Rasmunsen followed him out and turned the dogs loose. He threw them all the salmon he had bought, and coiled a sled-lashing up in his hand. Then he reëntered the cabin and drew the latch in after him. The smoke from the cindered steak made his eyes smart. He stood on the bunk, passed the lashing over the ridge-pole, and measured the swing-off with his eye. It did not seem to satisfy, for he put the stool on the bunk and climbed upon the stool. He drove a noose in the end of the lashing and slipped his head through. The other end he made fast. Then he kicked the stool out from under.

1903

BÂTARD

Bâtard was a devil. This was recognized throughout the Northland. "Hell's Spawn" he was called by many men, but his master, Black Leclère, chose for him the shameful name "Bâtard." Now Black Leclère was also a devil, and the twain were well matched. There is a saying that when two devils come together, hell is to pay. This is to be expected, and this certainly was to be expected when Bâtard and

Black Leclère came together. The first time they met, Bâtard was a part-grown puppy, lean and hungry, with bitter eyes; and they met with snap and snarl, and wicked looks, for Leclère's upper lip had a wolfish way of lifting and showing the white, cruel teeth. And it lifted then, and his eyes glinted viciously, as he reached for Bâtard and dragged him out from the squirming litter. It was certain that they divined each other, for on the instant Bâtard had buried his puppy fangs in Leclère's hand, and Leclère, thumb and finger, was coolly choking his young life out of him.

"*Sacredam,*" the Frenchman said softly, flirting the quick blood from his bitten hand and gazing down on the little puppy choking and gasping in the snow.

Leclère turned to John Hamlin, storekeeper of the Sixty Mile Post. "Dat fo' w'at Ah lak heem. 'Ow moch, eh, you, M'sieu'? 'Ow moch? Ah buy heem, now; Ah buy heem queek."

And because he hated him with an exceeding bitter hate, Leclère bought Bâtard and gave him his shameful name. And for five years the twain adventured across the Northland, from St. Michael's and the Yukon delta to the head-reaches of the Pelly and even so far as the Peace River, Athabasca, and the Great Slave. And they acquired a reputation for uncompromising wickedness, the like of which never before attached itself to man and dog.

Bâtard did not know his father,—hence his name,—but, as John Hamlin knew, his father was a great gray timber wolf. But the mother of Bâtard, as he dimly remembered her, was snarling, bickering, obscene, husky, full-fronted and heavy-chested, with a malign eye, a cat-like grip on life, and a genius for trickery and evil. There was neither faith nor trust in her. Her treachery alone could be relied upon, and her wild-wood amours attested her general depravity. Much of evil and much of strength were there in these, Bâtard's progenitors, and, bone and flesh of their bone and flesh, he had inherited it all. And then came Black Leclère, to lay his heavy hand on the bit of pulsating puppy life, to press and prod and mould till it became a big bristling beast, acute in knavery, overspilling with hate, sinister, malignant, diabolical. With a proper master Bâtard might have made an ordinary, fairly efficient sled-dog. He never got the chance: Leclère but confirmed him in his congenital iniquity.

The history of Bâtard and Leclère is a history of war—of five cruel, relentless years, of which their first meeting is fit summary. To begin with, it was Leclère's fault, for he hated with understanding and intelligence, while the long-legged, ungainly puppy hated only blindly, instinctively, without reason or method. At first there were no refinements of cruelty (these were to come later), but simple beatings and crude brutalities. In one of these Bâtard had an ear injured. He never regained control of the riven muscles, and ever after the ear drooped limply down to keep keen the memory of his tormentor. And he never forgot.

His puppyhood was a period of foolish rebellion. He was always worsted, but he fought back because it was his nature to fight back. And he was unconquerable. Yelping shrilly from the pain of lash and club, he none the less contrived always to throw in the defiant snarl, the bitter vindictive menace of his soul which fetched without fail more blows and beatings. But his was his mother's tenacious grip on life. Nothing could kill him. He flourished under misfortune, grew fat with famine, and out of his terrible struggle for life developed a preternatural intelligence. His were the stealth and cunning of the husky, his mother, and the fierceness and valor of the wolf, his father.

Possibly it was because of his father that he never wailed. His puppy yelps passed with his lanky legs, so that he became grim and taciturn, quick to strike, slow to warn. He answered curse with snarl, and blow with snap, grinning the while his implacable hatred; but never again, under the extremest agony, did Leclère bring from him the cry of fear nor of pain. This unconquerableness but fanned Leclère's wrath and stirred him to greater deviltries.

Did Leclère give Bâtard half a fish and to his mates whole ones, Bâtard went forth to rob other dogs of their fish. Also he robbed caches and expressed himself in a thousand rogueries, till he became a terror to all dogs and masters of dogs. Did Leclère beat Bâtard and fondle Babette,—Babette who was not half the worker he was,—why, Bâtard threw her down in the snow and broke her hind leg in his heavy jaws, so that Leclère was forced to shoot her. Likewise, in bloody battles, Bâtard mastered all his team-mates, set them the law of trail and forage, and made them live to the law he set.

In five years he heard but one kind word, received but one soft stroke of a hand, and then he did not know what manner of things they were. He leaped like the untamed thing he was, and his jaws were together in a flash. It was the missionary at Sunrise, a newcomer in the country, who spoke the kind word and gave the soft stroke of the hand. And for six months after, he wrote no letters home to the States, and the surgeon at McQuestion travelled two hundred miles on the ice to save him from blood-poisoning.

Men and dogs looked askance at Bâtard when he drifted into their camps and posts. The men greeted him with feet threateningly lifted for the kick, the dogs with bristling manes and bared fangs. Once a man did kick Bâtard, and Bâtard, with quick wolf snap, closed his jaws like a steel trap on the man's calf and crunched down to the bone. Whereat the man was determined to have his life, only Black Leclère, with ominous eyes and naked hunting-knife, stepped in between. The killing of Bâtard—ah, *sacredam, that* was a pleasure Leclère reserved for himself. Some day it would happen, or else—bah! who was to know? Anyway, the problem would be solved.

For they had become problems to each other. The very breath each drew was a challenge and a menace to the other. Their hate bound them together as love could never bind. Leclère was bent on the coming of the day when Bâtard should wilt in spirit and cringe and whimper at his feet. And Bâtard—Leclère knew what was in Bâtard's mind, and more than once had read it in Bâtard's eyes. And so clearly had he read, that when Bâtard was at his back, he made it a point to glance often over his shoulder.

Men marvelled when Leclère refused large money for the dog. "Some day you'll kill him and be out his price," said John Hamlin once, when Bâtard lay panting in the snow where Leclère had kicked him, and no one knew whether his ribs were broken, and no one dared look to see.

"Dat," said Leclère, dryly, "dat is my biz'ness, M'sieu'."

And the men marvelled that Bâtard did not run away. They did not understand. But Leclère understood. He was a man who lived much in the open, beyond the sound of human tongue, and he had learned the voices of wind and storm, the sigh of night, the whisper of dawn, the clash of day. In a dim way he could hear the green things growing, the running of the sap, the bursting of the bud. And he knew the subtle speech of the things that moved, of the rabbit in the snare, the moody raven beating the air with hollow wing, the baldface shuffling under the moon, the wolf like a gray shadow gliding betwixt the twilight and the dark. And to him Bâtard spoke clear and direct. Full well he understood why Bâtard did not run away, and he looked more often over his shoulder.

When in anger, Bâtard was not nice to look upon, and more than once had he leapt for Leclère's throat, to be stretched quivering and senseless in the snow, by the butt of the ever ready dogwhip. And so Bâtard learned to bide his time. When he reached his full strength and prime of youth, he thought the time had come. He was broad-chested, powerfully muscled, of far more than ordinary size, and his neck from head to shoulders was a mass of bristling hair—to all appearances a full-blooded wolf. Leclère was lying asleep in his furs when Bâtard deemed the time to be ripe. He crept upon him stealthily, head low to earth and lone ear laid back, with a feline softness of tread. Bâtard breathed gently, very gently, and not till he was close at hand did he raise his head. He paused for a moment, and looked at the bronzed bull throat, naked and knotty, and swelling to a deep and steady pulse. The slaver dripped down his fangs and slid off his tongue at the sight, and in that moment he remembered his drooping ear, his uncounted blows and prodigious wrongs, and without a sound sprang on the sleeping man.

Leclère awoke to the pang of the fangs in his throat, and, perfect animal that he was, he awoke clear-headed and with full comprehension. He closed on Bâtard's windpipe with both his hands, and rolled out of his furs to get his weight uppermost. But the thousands of Bâtard's ancestors had clung at the throats of unnumbered moose and caribou and dragged them down, and the wisdom of those ancestors was his. When Leclère's weight came on top of him, he drove his hind legs upward and in, and clawed down chest and abdomen, ripping and tearing through skin and muscle. And when he felt the man's body wince above him and lift, he worried and shook at the man's throat. His team-mates closed around in a snarling circle, and Bâtard, with failing breath and fading sense, knew that their jaws were hungry for him. But that did not matter—it was the man, the man above him, and he ripped and clawed, and shook and worried, to the last ounce of his strength. But Leclère choked him with both his hands, till Bâtard's chest heaved and writhed for the air denied, and his eyes glazed and set, and his jaws slowly loosened, and his tongue protruded black and swollen.

"Eh? *Bon*, you devil!" Leclère gurgled, mouth and throat clogged with his own blood, as he shoved the dizzy dog from him.

And then Leclère cursed the other dogs off as they fell upon Bâtard. They drew back into a wider circle, squatting alertly on their haunches and licking their chops, the hair on every neck bristling and erect.

Bâtard recovered quickly, and at sound of Leclère's voice, tottered to his feet and swayed weakly back and forth.

"A-h-ah! You beeg devil!" Leclère spluttered. "Ah fix you; Ah fix you plentee, by *Gar!*"

Bâtard, the air biting into his exhausted lungs like wine, flashed full into the man's face, his jaws missing and coming together with a metallic clip. They rolled over and over on the snow, Leclère striking madly with his fists. Then they separated, face to face, and circled back and forth before each other. Leclère could have drawn his knife. His rifle was at his feet. But the beast in him was up and raging. He would do the thing with his hands—and his teeth. Bâtard sprang in, but Leclère knocked him over with a blow of the fist, fell upon him, and buried his teeth to the bone in the dog's shoulder.

It was a primordial setting and a primordial scene, such as might have been in the savage youth of the world. An open space in a dark forest, a ring of grinning wolf-dogs, and in the centre two beasts, locked in combat, snapping and snarling, raging madly about, panting, sobbing, cursing, straining, wild with passion, in a fury of murder, ripping and tearing and clawing in elemental brutishness.

But Leclère caught Bâtard behind the ear, with a blow from his fist, knocking him over, and, for the instant, stunning him. Then Leclère leaped upon him with his feet, and sprang up and down, striving to grind him into the earth. Both Bâtard's hind legs were broken ere Leclère ceased that he might catch breath.

"A-a-ah! A-a-ah!" he screamed, incapable of speech, shaking his fist, through sheer impotence of throat and larynx.

But Bâtard was indomitable. He lay there in a helpless welter, his lip feebly lifting and writhing to the snarl he had not the strength to utter. Leclère kicked him, and the tired jaws closed on the ankle, but could not break the skin.

Then Leclère picked up the whip and proceeded almost to cut him to pieces, at each stroke of the lash crying: "Dis taim Ah break you! Eh? By *Gar!* Ah break you!"

In the end, exhausted, fainting from loss of blood, he crumpled up and fell by his victim, and when the wolf-dogs closed in to take their vengeance, with his last consciousness dragged his body on top Bâtard to shield him from their fangs.

This occurred not far from Sunrise, and the missionary, opening the door to Leclère a few hours later, was surprised to note the absence of Bâtard from the team. Nor did his surprise lessen when Leclère threw back the robes from the sled, gathered Bâtard into his arms, and staggered across the threshold. It happened that the surgeon of McQuestion, who was something of a gadabout, was up on a gossip, and between them they proceeded to repair Leclère.

"*Merci, non,*" said he. "Do you fix firs' de dog. To die? *Non.* Eet is not good. Becos' heem Ah mus' yet break. Dat fo' w'at he mus' not die."

The surgeon called it a marvel, the missionary a miracle, that Leclère pulled through at all; and so weakened was he, that in the spring the fever got him, and he went on his back again. Bâtard had been in even worse plight, but his grip on life prevailed, and the bones of his hind legs knit, and his organs righted themselves, during the several weeks he lay strapped to the floor. And by the time Leclère, finally convalescent, sallow and shaky, took the sun by the cabin door, Bâtard had reasserted his supremacy among his kind, and brought not only his own team-mates but the missionary's dogs into subjection.

He moved never a muscle, nor twitched a hair, when, for the first time, Leclère tottered out on the missionary's arm, and sank down slowly and with infinite caution on the three-legged stool.

"*Bon!*" he said. "*Bon!* De good sun!" And he stretched out his wasted hands and washed them in the warmth.

Then his gaze fell on the dog, and the old light blazed back in his eyes. He touched the missionary lightly on the arm. "*Mon père,* dat is one beeg devil, dat Bâtard. You will bring me one pistol, so, dat Ah drink de sun in peace."

And thenceforth for many days he sat in the sun before the cabin door. He never dozed, and the pistol lay always across his knees. Bâtard had a way, the first thing each day, of looking for the weapon in its wonted place. At sight of it he would lift his lip faintly in token that he understood, and Leclère would lift his own lip in an answering grin. One day the missionary took note of the trick.

"Bless me!" he said. "I really believe the brute comprehends."

Leclère laughed softly. "Look you, *mon père*. Dat w'at Ah now spik, to dat does he lissen."

As if in confirmation, Bâtard just perceptibly wriggled his lone ear up to catch the sound.

"Ah say 'keel.' "

Bâtard growled deep down in his throat, the hair bristled along his neck, and every muscle went tense and expectant.

"Ah lift de gun, so, like dat." And suiting action to word, he sighted the pistol at Bâtard.

Bâtard, with a single leap, sideways, landed around the corner of the cabin out of sight.

"Bless me!" he repeated at intervals.

Leclère grinned proudly.

"But why does he not run away?"

The Frenchman's shoulders went up in the racial shrug that means all things from total ignorance to infinite understanding.

"Then why do you not kill him?"

Again the shoulders went up.

"*Mon père*," he said after a pause, "de taim is not yet. He is one beeg devil. Some taim Ah break heem, so, an' so, all to leetle bits. Hey? Some taim. *Bon!*"

A day came when Leclère gathered his dogs together and floated down in a bateau to Forty Mile, and on to the Porcupine, where he took a commission from the P. C. Company, and went exploring for the better part of a year. After that he poled up the Koyokuk to deserted Arctic City, and later came drifting back, from camp to camp, along the Yukon. And during the long months Bâtard was well lessoned. He learned many tortures, and, notably, the torture of hunger, the torture of thirst, the torture of fire, and, worst of all, the torture of music.

Like the rest of his kind, he did not enjoy music. It gave him exquisite anguish, racking him nerve by nerve, and ripping apart every fibre of his being. It made him howl, long and wolf-like, as when the wolves bay the stars on frosty nights. He could not help howling. It was his one weakness in the contest with Leclère, and it was his shame. Leclère, on the other hand, passionately loved music—as passionately as he loved strong drink. And when his soul clamored for expression, it usually uttered itself in one or the other of the two ways, and more usually in both ways. And when he had drunk, his brain a-lilt with unsung song and the devil in him aroused and rampant, his soul found its supreme utterance in torturing Bâtard.

"Now we will haf a leetle museek," he would say. "Eh? W'at you t'ink, Bâtard?"

It was only an old and battered harmonica, tenderly treasured and patiently repaired; but it was the best that money could buy, and out of its silver reeds he drew weird vagrant airs that men had never heard before. Then Bâtard, dumb of throat, with teeth tight clenched, would back away, inch by inch, to the farthest cabin corner. And Leclère, playing, playing, a stout club tucked under his arm, followed the animal up, inch by inch, step by step, till there was no further retreat.

At first Bâtard would crowd himself into the smallest possible space, grovelling close to the floor; but as the music came nearer and nearer, he was forced to uprear, his back jammed into the logs, his fore legs fanning the air as though to beat off the rippling waves of sound. He still kept his teeth together, but severe muscular contractions attacked his body, strange twitchings and jerkings, till he was all a-quiver and writhing in silent torment. As he lost control, his jaws spasmodically wrenched apart, and deep throaty vibrations issued forth, too low in the register of sound for human ear to catch. And then, nostrils distended, eyes dilated, hair bristling in helpless rage, arose the long wolf howl. It came with a slurring rush upward, swelling to a great heart-breaking burst of sound, and dying away in sadly cadenced woe—then the next rush upward, octave upon octave; the bursting heart; and the infinite sorrow and misery, fainting, fading, falling, and dying slowly away.

It was fit for hell. And Leclère, with fiendish ken, seemed to divine each particular nerve and heartstring, and with long wails and tremblings and sobbing minors to make it yield up its last shred of grief. It was frightful, and for twenty-four hours after, Bâtard was nervous and unstrung, starting at common sounds, tripping over his own shadow, but, withal, vicious and masterful with his team-mates. Nor did he show signs of a breaking spirit. Rather did he grow more grim and taciturn, biding his time with an inscrutable patience that began to puzzle and weigh upon Leclère. The dog would lie in the firelight, motionless, for hours, gazing straight before him at Leclère, and hating him with his bitter eyes.

Often the man felt that he had bucked against the very essence of life—the unconquerable essence that swept the hawk down out of the sky like a feathered thunderbolt, that drove the great gray goose across the zones, that hurled the spawning salmon through two thousand miles of boiling Yukon flood. At such times he felt impelled to express his own unconquerable essence; and with strong drink, wild music, and Bâtard, he indulged in vast orgies, wherein he pitted his puny strength in the face of things, and challenged all that was, and had been, and was yet to be.

"Dere is somet'ing dere," he affirmed, when the rhythmed vagaries of his mind touched the secret chords of Bâtard's being and brought forth the long lugubrious howl. "Ah pool eet out wid bot' my han's, so, an' so. Ha! Ha! Eet is fonee! Eet is ver' fonee! De priest chant, de womans pray, de mans swear, de leetle bird go *peep-peep*, Bâtard, heem go *yow-yow*—an' eet is all de ver' same t'ing. Ha! Ha!"

Father Gautier, a worthy priest, once reproved him with instances of concrete perdition. He never reproved him again.

"Eet may be so, *mon père*," he made answer. "An' Ah t'ink Ah go troo hell a-snappin', lak de hemlock troo de fire. Eh, *mon père?*"

But all bad things come to an end as well as good, and so with Black Leclère. On the summer low water, in a poling boat, he left McDougall for Sunrise. He left McDougall in company with Timothy Brown, and arrived at Sunrise by himself. Further, it was known that they had quarrelled just previous to pulling out; for the *Lizzie*, a wheezy ten-ton sternwheeler, twenty-four hours behind, beat Leclère in by three days. And when he did get in, it was with a clean-drilled bullet-hole through his shoulder muscle, and a tale of ambush and murder.

A strike had been made at Sunrise, and things had changed considerably. With the infusion of several hundred gold-seekers, a deal of whiskey, and half a dozen equipped gamblers, the missionary had seen the page of his years of labor with the Indians wiped clean. When the squaws became preoccupied with cooking beans and keeping the fire going for the wifeless miners, and the bucks with swapping their warm furs for black bottles and broken timepieces, he took to his bed, said "bless me" several times, and departed to his final accounting in a rough-hewn, oblong box. Whereupon the gamblers moved their roulette and faro tables into the mission house, and the click of chips and clink of glasses went up from dawn till dark and to dawn again.

Now Timothy Brown was well beloved among these adventurers of the north. The one thing against him was his quick temper and ready fist,—a little thing, for which his kind heart and forgiving hand more than atoned. On the other hand, there was nothing to atone for Black Leclère. He was "black," as more than one remembered deed bore witness, while he was as well hated as the other was beloved. So the men of Sunrise put an antiseptic dressing on his shoulder and haled him before Judge Lynch.

It was a simple affair. He had quarrelled with Timothy Brown at McDougall. With Timothy Brown he had left McDougall. Without Timothy Brown he had arrived at Sunrise. Considered in the light of his evilness, the unanimous conclusion was that he had killed Timothy Brown. On the other hand, Leclère acknowledged their facts, but challenged their conclusion, and gave his own explanation. Twenty miles out of Sunrise he and Timothy Brown were poling the boat along the rocky shore. From that shore two rifle-shots rang out. Timothy Brown pitched out of the boat and went down bubbling red, and that was the last of Timothy Brown. He, Leclère, pitched into the bottom of the boat with a stinging shoulder. He lay very quiet, peeping at the shore. After a time two Indians stuck up their heads and came out to the water's edge, carrying between them a birch-bark canoe. As they launched it, Leclère let fly. He potted one, who went over the side after the manner of Timothy Brown. The other dropped into the bottom of the canoe, and then canoe and poling boat went down the stream in a drifting battle. After that they hung up on a split current, and the canoe passed on one side of an island, the poling boat on the other. That was the last of the canoe, and he came on into Sunrise. Yes, from the way the Indian in the canoe jumped, he was sure he had potted him. That was all.

This explanation was not deemed adequate. They gave him ten hours' grace while the *Lizzie* steamed down to investigate. Ten hours later she came wheezing back to Sunrise. There had been nothing to investigate. No evidence had been found to back up his statements. They told him to make his will, for he possessed a fifty-thousand-dollar Sunrise claim, and they were a law-abiding as well as a law-giving breed.

Leclère shrugged his shoulders. "Bot one t'ing," he said; "a leetle, w'at you call, favor—a leetle favor, dat is eet. I gif my feefty t'ousan' dollair to de church. I gif my husky dog, Bâtard, to de devil. De leetle favor? Firs' you hang heem, an' den you hang me. Eet is good, eh?"

Good it was, they agreed, that Hell's Spawn should break trail for his master across the last divide, and the court was adjourned down to the river bank, where a big spruce tree stood by itself. Slackwater Charley put a hangman's knot in the end of a hauling-line, and the noose was slipped over Leclère's head and pulled tight around his neck. His hands were tied behind his back, and he was assisted to the top of a cracker box. Then the running end of the line was passed over an overhanging branch, drawn taut, and made fast. To kick the box out from under would leave him dancing on the air.

"Now for the dog," said Webster Shaw, sometime mining engineer. "You'll have to rope him, Slackwater."

Leclère grinned. Slackwater took a chew of tobacco, rove a running noose, and proceeded leisurely to coil a few turns in his hand. He paused once or twice to brush particularly offensive mosquitoes from off his face. Everybody was brushing mosquitoes, except Leclère, about whose head a small cloud was visible. Even Bâtard, lying full-stretched on the ground, with his forepaws rubbed the pests away from eyes and mouth.

But while Slackwater waited for Bâtard to lift his head, a faint call came down the quiet air, and a man was seen waving his arms and running across the flat from Sunrise. It was the storekeeper.

"C-call 'er off, boys," he panted, as he came in among them.

"Little Sandy and Bernadotte's jes' got in," he explained with returning breath. "Landed down below an' come up by the short cut. Got the Beaver with 'm. Picked 'm up in his canoe, stuck in a back channel, with a couple of bullet holes in 'm. Other buck was Klok-Kutz, the one that knocked spots out of his squaw and dusted."

"Eh? W'at Ah say? Eh?" Leclère cried exultantly. "Dat de one fo' sure! Ah know. Ah spik true."

"The thing to do is teach these damned Siwashes a little manners," spoke Webster Shaw. "They're getting fat and sassy, and we'll have to bring them down a peg. Round in all the bucks and string up the Beaver for an object lesson. That's the programme. Come on and let's see what he's got to say for himself."

"Heh, M'sieu'!" Leclère called, as the crowd began to melt away through the twilight in the direction of Sunrise. "Ah lak ver' moch to see de fon."

"Oh, we'll turn you loose when we come back," Webster Shaw shouted over his shoulder. "In the meantime meditate on your sins and the ways of providence. It will do you good, so be grateful."

As is the way with men who are accustomed to great hazards, whose nerves are healthy and trained to patience, so it was with Leclère, who settled himself to the long wait—which is to say that he reconciled his mind to it. There was no settling of the body, for the taut rope forced him to stand rigidly erect. The least relaxation of the leg muscles pressed the rough-fibred noose into his neck, while the upright position caused him much pain in his wounded shoulder. He projected his under lip and expelled his breath upward along his face, to blow the mosquitoes away from his eyes. But the situation had its compensation. To be snatched from the maw of death was well worth a little bodily suffering, only it was unfortunate that he should miss the hanging of the Beaver.

And so he mused, till his eyes chanced to fall upon Bâtard, head between forepaws and stretched on the ground asleep. And then Leclère ceased to muse. He studied the animal closely, striving to sense if the sleep were real or feigned. Bâtard's sides were heaving regularly, but Leclère felt that the breath came and went a shade too quickly; also he felt that there was a vigilance or alertness to every hair that belied unshackling sleep. He would have given his Sunrise claim to be assured that the dog was not awake, and once, when one of his joints cracked, he looked quickly and guiltily at Bâtard to see if he roused. He did not rouse then, but a few minutes later he got up slowly and lazily, stretched, and looked carefully about him.

"*Sacredam*," said Leclère, under his breath. Assured that no one was in sight or hearing, Bâtard sat down, curled his upper lip almost into a smile, looked up at Leclère, and licked his chops.

"Ah see my feenish," the man said, and laughed sardonically aloud.

Bâtard came nearer, the useless ear wabbling, the good ear cocked forward with devilish comprehension. He thrust his head on one side quizzically, and advanced with mincing, playful steps. He rubbed his body gently against the box till it shook and shook again. Leclère teetered carefully to maintain his equilibrium.

"Bâtard," he said calmly, "look out. Ah keel you."

Bâtard snarled at the word, and shook the box with greater force. Then he upreared, and with his forepaws threw his weight against it higher up. Leclère kicked out with one foot, but the rope bit into his neck and checked so abruptly as nearly to overbalance him.

"Hi, ya! *Chook! Mush-on!*" he screamed.

Bâtard retreated, for twenty feet or so, with a fiendish levity in his bearing that Leclère could not mistake. He remembered the dog often breaking the scum of ice on the water hole, by lifting up and throwing his weight upon it; and, remembering, he understood what he now had in mind. Bâtard faced about and paused. He showed his white teeth in a grin, which Leclère answered; and then hurled his body through the air, in full charge, straight for the box.

Fifteen minutes later, Slackwater Charley and Webster Shaw, returning, caught a glimpse of a ghostly pendulum swinging back and forth in the dim light. As they hurriedly drew in closer, they made out the man's inert body, and a live thing that clung to it, and shook and worried, and gave to it the swaying motion.

"Hi, ya! *Chook!* you Spawn of Hell," yelled Webster Shaw.

But Bâtard glared at him, and snarled threateningly, without loosing his jaws.

Slackwater Charley got out his revolver, but his hand was shaking, as with a chill, and he fumbled.

"Here, you take it," he said, passing the weapon over.

Webster Shaw laughed shortly, drew a sight between the gleaming eyes, and pressed the trigger. Bâtard's body twitched with the shock, threshed the ground spasmodically for a moment, and went suddenly limp. But his teeth still held fast locked.

1903

ALL GOLD CANYON

It was the green heart of the canyon, where the walls swerved back from the rigid plan and relieved their harshness of line by making a little sheltered nook and filling it to the brim with sweetness and roundness and softness. Here all things rested. Even the narrow stream ceased its turbulent downrush long enough to form a quiet pool. Knee-deep in the water, with drooping head and half-shut eyes, drowsed a red-coated, many-antlered buck.

On one side, beginning at the very lip of the pool, was a tiny meadow, a cool, resilient surface of green that extended to the base of the frowning wall. Beyond the pool a gentle slope of earth ran up and up to meet the opposing wall. Fine grass covered the slope—grass that was spangled with flowers, with here and there patches of color, orange and purple and golden. Below, the canyon was shut in. There was no view. The walls leaned together abruptly and the canyon ended in a chaos of rocks, moss-covered and hidden by a green screen of vines and creepers and boughs of trees. Up the canyon rose far hills and peaks, the big foothills, pine-covered and remote. And far beyond, like clouds upon the border of the sky, towered minarets of white, where the Sierra's eternal snows flashed austerely the blazes of the sun.

There was no dust in the canyon. The leaves and flowers were clean and virginal. The grass was young velvet. Over the pool three cottonwoods sent their snowy fluffs fluttering down the quiet air. On the slope the blossoms of the wine-wooded manzanita filled the air with springtime odors, while the leaves, wise with experience, were already beginning their vertical twist against the coming aridity of summer. In the open spaces on the slope, beyond the farthest shadow-reach of the manzanita, poised the mariposa lilies, like so many flights of jeweled moths suddenly arrested and on the verge of trembling into flight again. Here and there that woods harlequin, the madroña, permitting itself to be caught in the act of changing its pea-green trunk to madder red, breathed its fragrance into the air from great clusters of waxen bells. Creamy white were these bells, shaped like lilies of the valley, with the sweetness of perfume that is of the springtime.

There was not a sigh of wind. The air was drowsy with its weight of perfume. It was a sweetness that would have been cloying had the air been heavy and humid. But the air was sharp and thin. It was as starlight transmuted into atmosphere, shot through and warmed by sunshine, and flower-drenched with sweetness.

An occasional butterfly drifted in and out through the patches of light and shade. And from all about rose the low and sleepy hum of mountain bees—feasting sybarites that jostled one another good-naturedly at the board, nor found time for rough discourtesy. So quietly did the little stream drip and ripple its way through the canyon that it spoke only in faint and occasional gurgles. The voice of the stream was as a drowsy whisper, ever interrupted by dozings and silences, ever lifted again in the awakenings.

The motion of all things was a drifting in the heart of the canyon. Sunshine and butterflies drifted in and out among the trees. The hum of the bees and the whisper of the stream were a drifting of sound. And the drifting sound and drifting color seemed to weave together in the making of a delicate and intangible fabric which was the spirit of the place. It was a spirit of peace that was not of death, but of smooth-pulsing life, of quietude that was not silence, of movement that was not action, of repose that was quick with existence without being violent with struggle and travail. The spirit of the place was the spirit of the peace of the living, somnolent with the easement and content of prosperity, and undisturbed by rumors of far wars.

The red-coated, many-antlered buck acknowledged the lordship of the spirit of the place and dozed knee-deep in the cool, shaded pool. There seemed no flies to vex him and he was languid with rest. Sometimes his ears moved when the stream awoke and whispered; but they moved lazily, with foreknowledge that it was merely the stream grown garrulous at discovery that it had slept.

But there came a time when the buck's ears lifted and tensed with swift eagerness for sound. His head was turned down the canyon. His sensitive, quivering nostrils scented the air. His eyes could not pierce the green screen through which the stream rippled away, but to his ears came the voice of a man. It was a steady, monotonous, singsong voice. Once the buck heard the harsh clash of metal upon rock. At the sound he snorted with a sudden start that jerked him through the air from water to meadow, and his feet sank into the young velvet, while he pricked his ears and again scented the air. Then he stole across the tiny meadow, pausing once and again to listen, and faded away out of the canyon like a wraith, soft-footed and without sound.

The clash of steel-shod soles against the rocks began to be heard, and the man's voice grew louder. It was raised in a sort of chant and became distinct with nearness, so that the words could be heard:

"Tu'n around an' tu'n yo' face
Untoe them sweet hills of grace.
(D' pow'rs of sin yo' am scornin'!)
Look about an' look aroun',
Fling yo' sin pack on d' groun'.
(Yo' will meet wid d' Lord in d' mornin'!)"

A sound of scrambling accompanied the song, and the spirit of the place fled away on the heels of the red-coated buck. The green screen was burst asunder, and a man peered out at the meadow and the pool and the sloping sidehill. He was a deliberate sort of man. He took in the scene with one embracing glance, then ran his eyes over the details to verify the general impression. Then, and not until then, did he open his mouth in vivid and solemn approval:

"Smoke of life an' snakes of purgatory! Will you just look at that! Wood an' water an' grass an' a sidehill! A pocket hunter's delight an' a cayuse's paradise! Cool green for tired eyes! Pink pills for pale people ain't in it. A secret pasture for prospectors and a resting place for tired burros, by damn!"

He was a sandy-complexioned man in whose face geniality and humor seemed the salient characteristics. It was a mobile face, quick-changing to inward mood and thought. Thinking was in him a visible process. Ideas chased across his face like windflaws across the surface of a lake. His hair, sparse and unkempt of growth, was as indeterminate and colorless as his complexion. It would seem that all the color of his frame had gone into his eyes, for they were startlingly blue. Also they were laughing and merry eyes, within them much of the naïveté and wonder of the child; and yet, in an unassertive way, they contained much of calm self-reliance and strength of purpose founded upon self-experience and experience of the world.

From out the screen of vines and creepers he flung ahead of him a miner's pick and shovel and gold pan. Then he crawled out himself into the open. He was clad in faded overalls and black cotton shirt, with hobnailed brogans on his feet, and on his head a hat whose shapelessness and stains advertised the rough usage of wind and rain and sun and camp smoke. He stood erect, seeing wide-eyed the secrecy of the scene and sensuously inhaling the warm, sweet breath of the canyon garden through nostrils that dilated and quivered with delight. His eyes narrowed to laughing slits of blue, his face wreathed itself in joy, and his mouth curled in a smile as he cried aloud:

"Jumping dandelions and happy hollyhocks, but that smells good to me! Talk about your attar o' roses an' cologne factories! They ain't in it!"

He had the habit of soliloquy. His quick-changing facial expressions might tell every thought and mood, but the tongue, perforce, ran hard after, repeating, like a second Boswell.

The man lay down on the lip of the pool and drank long and deep of its water. "Tastes good to me," he murmured, lifting his head and gazing across the pool at the sidehill, while he wiped his mouth with the back of his hand. The sidehill attracted his attention. Still lying on his stomach, he studied the hill formation long and carefully. It was a practiced eye that traveled up the slope to the crumbling canyon wall and back and down again to the edge of the pool. He scrambled to his feet and favored the sidehill with a second survey.

"Looks good to me," he concluded, picking up his pick and shovel and gold pan.

He crossed the stream below the pool, stepping agilely from stone to stone. Where the sidehill touched the water he dug up a shovelful of dirt and put it into the gold pan. He squatted down, holding the pan in his two hands, and partly immersing it in the stream. Then he imparted to the pan a deft circular motion that sent the water sluicing in and out through the dirt and gravel. The larger and the lighter particles worked to the surface, and these, by a skillful dipping movement of the pan, he spilled out and over the edge. Occasionally, to expedite matters, he rested the pan and with his fingers raked out the large pebbles and pieces of rock.

The contents of the pan diminished rapidly until only fine dirt and the smallest bits of gravel remained. At this stage he began to work very deliberately and carefully. It was fine washing, and he washed fine and finer, with a keen scrutiny and delicate and fastidious touch. At last the pan seemed empty of everything but water; but with a quick semicircular flirt that sent the water flying over the shallow rim into the stream he disclosed a layer of black sand on the bottom of the pan. So thin was this layer that it was like a streak of paint. He examined it closely. In the midst of it was a tiny golden speck. He dribbled a little water in over the depressed edge of the pan. With a quick flirt he sent the water sluicing across the bottom, turning the grains of black sand over and over. A second tiny golden speck rewarded his effort.

The washing had now become very fine—fine beyond all need of ordinary placer mining. He worked the black sand, a small portion at a time, up the shallow rim of the pan. Each small portion he examined sharply, so that his eyes saw every grain of it before he allowed it to slide over the edge and away. Jealously, bit by bit, he let the black sand slip away. A golden speck, no larger than a pin point, appeared on the rim, and by his manipulation of the water it returned to the bottom of the pan. And in such fashion another speck was disclosed, and another. Great was his care of them. Like a shepherd he herded his flock of golden specks so that not one should be lost. At last, of the pan of dirt nothing remained but his golden herd. He counted it, and then, after all his labor, sent it flying out of the pan with one final swirl of water.

But his blue eyes were shining with desire as he rose to his feet. "Seven," he muttered aloud, asserting the sum of the specks for which he had toiled so hard and which he had so wantonly thrown away. "Seven," he repeated, with the emphasis of one trying to impress a number on his memory.

He stood still a long while, surveying the hillside. In his eyes was a curiosity, new-aroused and burning. There was an exultance about his bearing and a keenness like that of a hunting animal catching the fresh scent of game.

He moved down the stream a few steps and took a second panful of dirt.

Again came the careful washing, the jealous herding of the golden specks, and the wantonness with which he sent them flying into the stream when he had counted their number.

"Five," he muttered, and repeated, "five."

He could not forbear another survey of the hill before filling the pan farther down the stream. His golden herds diminished. "Four, three, two, two, one," were his memory tabulations as he moved down the stream. When but one speck of gold rewarded his washing he stopped and built a fire of dry twigs. Into this he thrust the gold pan and burned it till it was blue-black. He held up the pan and examined it critically. Then he nodded approbation. Against such a color background he could defy the tiniest yellow speck to elude him.

Still moving down the stream, he panned again. A single speck was his reward. A third pan contained no gold at all. Not satisfied with this, he panned three times again, taking his shovels of dirt within a foot of one another. Each pan proved empty of gold, and the fact, instead of discouraging him, seemed to give him satisfaction. His elation increased with each barren washing, until he arose, exclaiming jubilantly:

"If it ain't the real thing, may God knock off my head with sour apples!"

Returning to where he had started operations, he began to pan up the stream. At first his golden herds increased—increased prodigiously. "Fourteen, eighteen, twenty-one, twenty-six," ran his memory tabulations. Just above the pool he struck his richest pan—thirty-five colors.

"Almost enough to save," he remarked regretfully as he allowed the water to sweep them away.

The sun climbed to the top of the sky. The man worked on. Pan by pan he went up the stream, the tally of results steadily decreasing.

"It's just booful, the way it peters out," he exulted when a shovelful of dirt contained no more than a single speck of gold.

And when no specks at all were found in several pans he straightened up and favored the hillside with a confident glance.

"Aha! Mr. Pocket!" he cried out as though to an auditor hidden somewhere above him beneath the surface of the slope. "Aha! Mr. Pocket! I'm a-comin', I'm a-comin', an' I'm shorely gwine to get yer! You heah me, Mr. Pocket? I'm gwine to get yer as shore as punkins ain't cauliflowers!"

He turned and flung a measuring glance at the sun poised above him in the azure of the cloudless sky. Then he went down the canyon, following the line of shovel holes he had made in filling the pans. He crossed the stream below the pool and disappeared through the green screen. There was little opportunity for the spirit of the place to return with its quietude and repose, for the man's voice, raised in ragtime song, still dominated the canyon with possession.

After a time, with a greater clashing of steel-shod feet on rock, he returned. The green screen was tremendously agitated. It surged back and forth in the throes of a struggle. There was a loud grating and clanging of metal. The man's voice leaped to a higher pitch and was sharp with imperativeness. A large body plunged and panted. There was a snapping and ripping and rending, and amid a shower of falling leaves a horse burst through the screen. On its back was a pack, and from this trailed broken vines and torn creepers. The animal gazed with astonished eyes at the scene into which it had been precipitated, then dropped its head to the grass and began contentedly to graze. A second horse scrambled into view, slipping once on the mossy rocks and regaining equilibrium when its hoofs sank into the yielding surface of the meadow. It was riderless, though on its back was a high-horned Mexican saddle, scarred and discolored by long usage.

The man brought up the rear. He threw off pack and saddle, with an eye to camp location, and gave the animals their freedom to graze. He unpacked his food and got out frying pan and coffeepot. He gathered an armful of dry wood, and with a few stones made a place for his fire.

"My," he said, "but I've got an appetite! I could scoff iron filings an' horseshoe nails an' thank you kindly, ma'am, for a second helpin'."

He straightened up, and while he reached for matches in the pocket of his overalls his eyes traveled across the pool to the sidehill. His fingers had clutched the matchbox, but they relaxed their hold and the hand came out empty. The man wavered perceptibly. He looked at his preparations for cooking and he looked at the hill.

"Guess I'll take another whack at her," he concluded, starting to cross the stream.

"They ain't no sense in it, I know," he mumbled apologetically. "But keepin' grub back an hour ain't goin' to hurt none, I reckon."

A few feet back from his first line of test pans he started a second line. The sun dropped down the western sky, the shadows lengthened, but the man worked on. He began a third line of test pans. He was crosscutting the hillside, line by line, as he ascended. The center of each line produced the richest pans, while the ends came where no colors showed in the pan. And as he ascended the hillside the lines grew perceptibly shorter. The regularity with which their length diminished served to indicate that somewhere up the slope the last line would be so short as to have scarcely length at all, and that beyond could come only a point. The design was growing into an inverted V. The converging sides of this V marked the boundaries of the gold-bearing dirt.

The apex of the V was evidently the man's goal. Often he ran his eye along the converging sides and on up the hill, trying to divine the apex, the point where the gold-bearing dirt must cease. Here resided "Mr. Pocket"—for so the man familiarly addressed the imaginary point above him on the slope, crying out:

"Come down out o' that, Mr. Pocket! Be right smart an' agreeable, an' come down!"

"All right," he would add later, in a voice resigned to determination. "All right, Mr. Pocket. It's plain to me I got to come right up an' snatch you out bald-headed. An' I'll do it! I'll do it!" he would threaten still later.

Each pan he carried down to the water to wash, and as he went higher up the hill the pans grew richer, until he began to save the gold in an empty baking-powder can which he carried carelessly in his lap pocket. So engrossed was he in his toil that he did not notice the long twilight of oncoming night. It was not until he tried vainly to see the gold colors in the bottom of the pan that he realized the passage of time. He straightened up abruptly. An expression of whimsical wonderment and awe overspread his face as he drawled:

"Gosh darn my buttons, if I didn't plumb forget dinner!"

He stumbled across the stream in the darkness and lighted his long-delayed fire. Flapjacks and bacon and warmed-over beans constituted his supper. Then he smoked a pipe by the smoldering coals, listening to the night noises and watching the moonlight stream through the canyon. After that he unrolled his bed, took off his heavy shoes, and pulled the blankets up to his chin. His face showed white in the moonlight, like the face of a corpse. But it was a corpse that knew its resurrection, for the man rose suddenly on one elbow and gazed across at his hillside.

"Good night, Mr. Pocket," he called sleepily. "Good night."

He slept through the early gray of morning until the direct rays of the sun smote his closed eyelids, when he awoke with a start and looked about him until he had established the continuity of his existence and identified his present self with the days previously lived.

To dress, he had merely to buckle on his shoes. He glanced at his fireplace and at his hillside, wavered, but fought down the temptation and started the fire.

"Keep yer shirt on, Bill; keep yer shirt on," he admonished himself. "What's the good of rushin'? No use in gettin' all het up an' sweaty. Mr. Pocket'll wait for you. He ain't a-runnin' away before you can get yer breakfast. Now what you want, Bill, is something fresh in yer bill o' fare. So it's up to you to go an' get it."

He cut a short pole at the water's edge and drew from one of his pockets a bit of line and a draggled fly that had once been a royal coachman.

"Mebbe they'll bite in the early morning," he muttered as he made his first cast into the pool. And a moment later he was gleefully crying: "What'd I tell you, eh? What'd I tell you?"

He had no reel nor any inclination to waste time, and by main strength, and swiftly, he drew out of the water a flashing ten-inch trout. Three more, caught in rapid succession, furnished his breakfast. When he came to the steppingstones on his way to his hillside, he was struck by a sudden thought, and paused.

"I'd just better take a hike downstream a ways," he said. "There's no tellin' what cuss may be snoopin' around."

But he crossed over on the stones, and with a "I really oughter take that hike" the need of the precaution passed out of his mind and he fell to work.

At nightfall he straightened up. The small of his back was stiff from stooping toil, and as he put his hand behind him to soothe the protesting muscles he said:

"Now what d'ye think of that, by damn? I clean forgot my dinner again! If I don't watch out I'll sure be degeneratin' into a two-meal-a-day crank."

"Pockets is the damnedest things I ever see for makin' a man absent-minded," he communed that night as he crawled into his blankets. Nor did he forget to call up the hillside, "Good night, Mr. Pocket! Good night!"

Rising with the sun, and snatching a hasty breakfast, he was early at work. A fever seemed to be growing in him, nor did the increasing richness of the test pans allay this fever. There was a flush in his cheek other than that made by the heat of the sun, and he was oblivious to fatigue and the passage of time. When he filled a pan with dirt he ran down the hill to wash it; nor could he forbear running up the hill again, panting and stumbling profanely, to refill the pan.

He was now a hundred yards from the water, and the inverted V was assuming definite proportions. The width of the pay dirt steadily decreased, and the man extended in his mind's eye the sides of the V to their meeting place far up the hill. This was his goal, the apex of the V, and he panned many times to locate it.

"Just about two yards above that manzanita bush an' a yard to the right," he finally concluded.

Then the temptation seized him. "As plain as the nose on your face," he said as he abandoned his laborious crosscutting and climbed to the indicated apex. He filled a pan and carried it down the hill to wash. It contained no trace of gold. He dug deep, and he dug shallow, filling and washing a dozen pans, and was unrewarded even by the tiniest golden specks. He was enraged at having yielded to the temptation, and cursed himself blasphemously and pridelessly. Then he went down the hill and took up the crosscutting.

"Slow an' certain, Bill; slow an' certain," he crooned. "Short cuts to fortune ain't in your line, an' it's about time you know it. Get wise, Bill; get wise. Slow an' certain's the only hand you can play; so go to it, an' keep to it, too."

As the crosscuts decreased, showing that the sides of the V were converging, the depth of the V increased. The gold trace was dipping into the hill. It was only at thirty inches beneath the surface that he could get colors in his pan. The dirt he found at twenty-five inches from the surface, and at thirty-five inches, yielded barren pans. At the base of the V, by the water's edge, he had found the gold colors at the grass roots. The higher he went up the hill, the deeper the gold dipped. To dig a hole three feet deep in order to get one test pan was a task of no mean magnitude; while between the man and the apex intervened an untold number of such holes to be dug. "An' there's no tellin' how much deeper it'll pitch," he sighed in a moment's pause, while his fingers soothed his aching back.

Feverish with desire, with aching back and stiffening muscles, with pick and shovel gouging and mauling the soft brown earth, the man toiled up the hill. Before him was the smooth slope, spangled with flowers and made sweet with their breath. Behind him was devastation. It looked like some terrible eruption breaking out on the smooth skin of the hill. His slow progress was like that of a slug, befouling beauty with a monstrous trail.

Though the dipping gold trace increased the man's work, he found consolation in the increasing richness of the pans. Twenty cents, thirty cents, fifty cents, sixty cents, were the values of the gold found in the pans, and at nightfall he washed his banner pan, which gave him a dollar's worth of gold dust from a shovelful of dirt.

"I'll just bet it's my luck to have some inquisitive cuss come buttin' in here on my pasture," he mumbled sleepily that night as he pulled the blankets up to his chin.

Suddenly he sat upright. "Bill!" he called sharply. "Now listen to me, Bill; d'ye hear! It's up to you, tomorrow mornin', to mosey round an' see what you can see. Understand? Tomorrow morning, an' don't you forget it!"

He yawned and glanced across at his sidehill. "Good night, Mr. Pocket," he called.

In the morning he stole a march on the sun, for he had finished breakfast when its first rays caught him, and he was climbing the wall of the canyon where it crumbled away and gave footing. From the outlook at the top he found himself in the midst of loneliness. As far as he could see, chain after chain of mountains heaved themselves into his vision. To the east his eyes, leaping the miles between range and range and between many ranges, brought up at last against the white-peaked Sierras—the main crest, where the backbone of the Western world reared itself against the sky. To the north and south he could see more distinctly the cross systems that broke through the main trend of the sea of mountains. To the west the ranges fell away, one behind the other, diminishing and fading into the gentle foothills that, in turn, descended into the great valley which he could not see.

And in all that mighty sweep of earth he saw no sign of man nor of the handiwork of man—save only the torn bosom of the hillside at his feet. The man looked long and carefully. Once, far down his own canyon, he thought he saw in the air a faint hint of smoke. He looked again and decided that it was the purple haze of the hills made dark by a convolution of the canyon wall at its back.

"Hey, you, Mr. Pocket!" he called down into the canyon. "Stand out from under! I'm a-comin', Mr. Pocket! I'm a-comin'!"

The heavy brogans on the man's feet made him appear clumsy-footed, but he swung down from the giddy height as lightly and airily as a mountain goat. A rock, turning under his foot on the edge of the precipice, did not disconcert him. He seemed to know the precise time required for the turn to culminate in disaster, and in the meantime he utilized the false footing itself for the momentary earth contact necessary to carry him on into safety. Where the earth sloped so steeply that it was impossible to stand for a second upright, the man did not hesitate. His foot pressed the impossible surface for but a fraction of the fatal second and gave him the bound that carried him onward. Again, where even the fraction of a second's footing was out of the question, he would swing his body past by a moment's handgrip on a jutting knob of rock, a crevice, or a precariously rooted shrub. At last, with a wild leap and yell, he exchanged the face of the wall for an earth slide and finished the descent in the midst of several tons of sliding earth and gravel.

His first pan of the morning washed out over two dollars in coarse gold. It was from the center of the V. To either side the diminution in the values of the pans was swift. His lines of crosscutting holes were growing very short. The converging sides of the inverted V were only a few yards apart. Their meeting point was only a few yards above him. But the pay streak was dipping deeper and deeper into the earth. By early afternoon he was sinking the test holes five feet before the pans could show the gold trace.

For that matter the gold trace had become something more than a trace; it was a placer mine in itself, and the man resolved to come back after he had found the pocket and work over the ground. But the increasing richness of the pans began to worry him. By late afternoon the worth of the pans had grown to three and four dollars. The man scratched his head perplexedly and looked a few feet up the hill at the manzanita bush that marked approximately the apex of the V. He nodded his head and said oracularly:

"It's one o' two things, Bill; one o' two things. Either Mr. Pocket's spilled himself all out an' down the hill, or else Mr. Pocket's that damned rich you maybe won't be able to carry him all away with you. And that'd be hell, wouldn't it, now?" He chuckled at contemplation of so pleasant a dilemma.

Nightfall found him by the edge of the stream, his eyes wrestling with the gathering darkness over the washing of a five-dollar pan.

"Wisht I had an electric light to go on working," he said.

He found sleep difficult that night. Many times he composed himself and closed his eyes for slumber to overtake him; but his blood pounded with too strong desire, and as many times his eyes opened and he murmured wearily, "Wisht it was sunup."

Sleep came to him in the end, but his eyes were open with the first paling of the stars, and the gray of dawn caught him with breakfast finished and climbing the hillside in the direction of the secret abiding place of Mr. Pocket.

The first crosscut the man made, there was space for only three holes, so narrow had become the pay streak and so close was he to the fountainhead of the golden stream he had been following for four days.

"Be ca'm, Bill; be ca'm," he admonished himself as he broke ground for the final hole where the sides of the V had at last come together in a point.

"I've got the almighty cinch on you, Mr. Pocket, an' you can't lose me," he said many times as he sank the hole deeper and deeper.

Four feet, five feet, six feet, he dug his way down into the earth. The digging grew harder. His pick grated on broken rock. He examined the rock. "Rotten quartz," was his conclusion as, with the shovel, he cleared the bottom of the hole of loose dirt. He attacked the crumbling quartz with the pick, bursting the disintegrating rock asunder with every stroke.

He thrust his shovel into the loose mass. His eye caught a gleam of yellow. He dropped the shovel and squatted suddenly on his heels. As a farmer rubs the clinging earth from fresh-dug potatoes, so the man, a piece of rotten quartz held in both hands, rubbed the dirt away.

"Sufferin' Sardanopolis!" he cried. "Lumps an' chunks of it! Lumps an' chunks of it!"

It was only half rock he held in his hand. The other half was virgin gold. He dropped it into his pan and examined another piece. Little yellow was to be seen, but with his strong fingers he crumbled the rotten quartz away till both hands were filled with glowing yellow. He rubbed the dirt away from fragment after fragment, tossing them into the gold pan. It was a treasure hole. So much had the quartz rotted away that there was less of it than there was of gold. Now and again he found a piece to which no rock clung—a piece that was all gold. A chunk, where the pick had laid open the heart of the gold, glittered like a handful of yellow jewels, and he cocked his head at it and slowly turned it around and over to observe the rich play of the light upon it.

"Talk about yer Too Much Gold diggin's!" the man snorted contemptuously. "Why, this diggin'd make it look like thirty cents. This diggin' is all gold. An' right here an' now I name this yere canyon 'All Gold Canyon,' b' gosh!"

Still squatting on his heels, he continued examining the fragments and tossing them into the pan. Suddenly there came to him a premonition of danger. It seemed a shadow had fallen upon him. But there was no shadow. His heart had given a great jump up into his throat and was choking him. Then his blood slowly chilled and he felt the sweat of his shirt cold against his flesh.

He did not spring up nor look around. He did not move. He was considering the nature of the premonition he had received, trying to locate the source of the mysterious force that had warned him, striving to sense the imperative presence of the unseen thing that threatened him. There is an aura of things hostile, made manifest by messengers too refined for the senses to know; and this aura he felt, but knew not how he felt it. His was the feeling as when a cloud passes over the sun. It seemed that between him and life had passed something dark and smothering and menacing; a gloom, as it were, that swallowed up life and made for death—his death.

Every force of his being impelled him to spring up and confront the unseen danger, but his soul dominated the panic, and he remained squatting on his heels, in his hands a chunk of gold. He did not dare to look around, but he knew by now that there was something behind him and above him. He made believe to be interested in the gold in his hand. He examined it critically, turned it over and over, and rubbed the dirt from it. And all the time he knew that something behind him was looking at the gold over his shoulder.

Still feigning interest in the chunk of gold in his hand, he listened intently and he heard the breathing of the thing behind him. His eyes searched the ground in front of him for a weapon, but they saw only the uprooted gold, worthless to him now in his extremity. There was his pick, a handy weapon on occasion; but this was not such an occasion. The man realized his predicament. He was in a narrow hole that was seven feet deep. His head did not come to the surface of the ground. He was in a trap.

He remained squatting on his heels. He was quite cool and collected; but his mind, considering every factor, showed him only his helplessness. He continued rubbing the dirt from the quartz fragments and throwing the gold into the pan. There was nothing else for him to do. Yet he knew that he would have to rise up, sooner or later, and face the danger that breathed at his back. The minutes passed, and with the passage of each minute he knew that by so much he was nearer the time when he must stand up or else—and his wet shirt went cold against his flesh again at the thought—or else he might receive death as he stooped there over his treasure.

Still he squatted on his heels, rubbing dirt from gold and debating in just what manner he should rise up. He might rise up with a rush and claw his way out of the hole to meet whatever threatened on the even footing aboveground. Or he might rise up slowly and carelessly, and feign casually to discover the thing that breathed at his back. His instinct and every fighting fiber of his body favored the mad, clawing rush to the surface. His intellect, and the craft thereof, favored the slow and cautious meeting with the thing that menaced and which he could not see. And while he debated, a loud, crashing noise burst on his ear. At the same instant he received a stunning blow on the left side of the back, and from the point of impact felt a rush of flame through his flesh. He sprang up in the air, but halfway to his feet collapsed. His body crumpled in like a leaf withered in sudden heat, and he came down, his chest across his pan of gold, his face in the dirt and rock, his legs tangled and twisted because of the restricted space at the bottom of the hole. His legs twitched convulsively several times. His body was shaken as with a mighty ague. There was a slow expansion of the lungs, accompanied by a deep sigh. Then the air was slowly, very slowly, exhaled, and his body as slowly flattened itself down into inertness.

Above, revolver in hand, a man was peering down over the edge of the hole. He peered for a long time at the prone and motionless body beneath him. After a while the stranger sat down on the edge of the hole so that he could see into it, and rested the revolver on his knee. Reaching his hand into a pocket, he drew out a wisp of brown paper. Into this he dropped a few crumbs of tobacco. The combination became a cigarette, brown and squat, with the ends turned in. Not once did he take his eyes from the body at the bottom of the hole. He lighted the cigarette and drew its smoke into his lungs with a caressing intake of the breath. He smoked slowly. Once the cigarette went out and he relighted it. And all the while he studied the body beneath him.

In the end he tossed the cigarette stub away and rose to his feet. He moved to the edge of the hole. Spanning it, a hand resting on each edge, and with the revolver still in the right hand, he muscled his body down into the hole. While his feet were yet a yard from the bottom he released his hands and dropped down.

At the instant his feet struck bottom he saw the pocket miner's arm leap out, and his own legs knew a swift, jerking grip that overthrew him. In the nature of the jump his revolver hand was above his head. Swiftly as the grip had flashed about his legs, just as swiftly he brought the revolver down. He was still in the air, his fall in process of completion, when he pulled the trigger. The explosion was deafening in the confined space. The smoke filled the hole so that he could see nothing. He struck the bottom on his back, and like a cat's the pocket miner's body was on top of him. Even as the miner's body passed on top, the stranger crooked in his right arm to fire; and even in that instant the miner, with a quick thrust of elbow, struck his wrist. The muzzle was thrown up and the bullet thudded into the dirt of the side of the hole.

The next instant the stranger felt the miner's hand grip his wrist. The struggle was now for the revolver. Each man strove to turn it against the other's body. The smoke in the hole was clearing. The stranger, lying on his back, was beginning to see dimly. But suddenly he was blinded by a handful of dirt deliberately flung into his eyes by his antagonist. In that moment of shock his grip on the revolver was broken. In the next moment he felt a smashing darkness descend upon his brain, and in the midst of the darkness even the darkness ceased.

But the pocket miner fired again and again, until the revolver was empty. Then he tossed it from him and, breathing heavily, sat down on the dead man's legs.

The miner was sobbing and struggling for breath. "Measly skunk!" he panted; "a-campin' on my trail an' lettin' me do the work, an' then shootin' me in the back!"

He was half crying from anger and exhaustion. He peered at the face of the dead man. It was sprinkled with loose dirt and gravel, and it was difficult to distinguish the features.

"Never laid eyes on him before," the miner concluded his scrutiny. "Just a common an' ordinary thief, damn him! An' he shot me in the back! He shot me in the back!"

He opened his shirt and felt himself, front and back, on his left side.

"Went clean through, and no harm done!" he cried jubilantly. "I'll bet he aimed all right, all right; but he drew the gun over when he pulled the trigger—the cuss! But I fixed 'm! Oh, I fixed 'm!"

His fingers were investigating the bullet hole in his side, and a shade of regret passed over his face. "It's goin' to be stiffer'n hell," he said. "An' it's up to me to get mended an' get out o' here."

He crawled out of the hole and went down the hill to his camp. Half an hour later he returned, leading his pack horse. His open shirt disclosed the rude bandages with which he had dressed his wound. He was slow and awkward with his left-hand movements, but that did not prevent his using the arm.

The bight of the pack rope under the dead man's shoulders enabled him to heave the body out of the hole. Then he set to work gathering up his gold. He worked steadily for several hours, pausing often to rest his stiffening shoulder and to exclaim:

"He shot me in the back, the measly skunk! He shot me in the back!"

When his treasure was quite cleaned up and wrapped securely into a number of blanket-covered parcels, he made an estimate of its value.

"Four hundred pounds, or I'm a Hottentot," he concluded. "Say two hundred in quartz an' dirt—that leaves two hundred pounds of gold. Bill! Wake up! Two hundred pounds of gold! Forty thousand dollars! An' it's yourn—all yourn!"

He scratched his head delightedly and his fingers blundered into an unfamiliar groove. They quested along it for several inches. It was a crease through his scalp where the second bullet had plowed.

He walked angrily over to the dead man.

"You would, would you?" he bullied. "You would, eh? Well, I fixed you good an' plenty, an' I'll give you decent burial, too. That's more'n you'd have done for me."

He dragged the body to the edge of the hole and toppled it in. It struck the bottom with a dull crash, on its side, the face twisted up to the light. The miner peered down at it.

"An' you shot me in the back!" he said accusingly.

With pick and shovel he filled the hole. Then he loaded the gold on his horse. It was too great a load for the animal, and when he had gained his camp he transferred part of it to his saddle horse. Even so, he was compelled to abandon a portion of his outfit—pick and shovel and gold pan, extra food and cooking utensils, and divers odds and ends.

The sun was at the zenith when the man forced the horses at the screen of vines and creepers. To climb the huge boulders the animals were compelled to uprear and struggle blindly through the tangled mass of vegetation. Once the saddle horse fell heavily and the man removed the pack to get the animal on its feet. After it started on its way again the man thrust his head out from among the leaves and peered up at the hillside.

"The measly skunk!" he said, and disappeared.

There was a ripping and tearing of vines and boughs. The trees surged back and forth, marking the passage of the animals through the midst of them. There was a clashing of steel-shod hoofs on stone, and now and again an oath or a sharp cry of command. Then the voice of the man was raised in song:

"Tu'n around an' tu'n yo' face
Untoe them sweet hills of grace.
(D' pow'rs of sin yo' am scornin'!)
Look about an' look aroun',
Fling yo' sin pack on d' groun'.
(Yo' will meet wid d' Lord in d' mornin'!)"

The song grew faint and fainter, and through the silence crept back the spirit of the place. The stream once more drowsed and whispered; the hum of the mountain bees rose sleepily. Down through the perfume-weighted air fluttered the snowy fluffs of the cottonwoods. The butterflies drifted in and out among the trees, and over all blazed the quiet sunshine. Only remained the hoofmarks in the meadow and the torn hillside to mark the boisterous trail of the life that had broken the peace of the place and passed on.

1905

THE APOSTATE

Now I wake me up to work;
I pray the Lord I may not shirk.
If I should die before the night,
I pray the Lord my work's all right.

Amen.

"If you don't git up, Johnny, I won't give you a bite to eat!"

The threat had no effect on the boy. He clung stubbornly to sleep, fighting for its oblivion as the dreamer fights for his dream. The boy's hands loosely clenched themselves, and he made feeble, spasmodic blows at the air. These blows were intended for his mother, but she betrayed practised familiarity in avoiding them as she shook him roughly by the shoulder.

"Lemme 'lone!"

It was a cry that began, muffled, in the deeps of sleep, that swiftly rushed upward, like a wail, into passionate belligerence, and that died away and sank down into an inarticulate whine. It was a bestial cry, as of a soul in torment, filled with infinite protest and pain.

But she did not mind. She was a sad-eyed, tired-faced woman, and she had grown used to this task, which she repeated every day of her life. She got a grip on the bedclothes and tried to strip them down; but the boy, ceasing his punching, clung to them desperately. In a huddle, at the foot of the bed, he still remained covered. Then she tried dragging the bedding to the floor. The boy opposed her. She braced herself. Hers was the superior weight, and the boy and bedding gave, the former instinctively following the latter in order to shelter against the chill of the room that bit into his body.

As he toppled on the edge of the bed it seemed that he must fall head-first to the floor. But consciousness fluttered up in him. He righted himself and for a moment perilously balanced. Then he struck the floor on his feet. On the instant his mother seized him by the shoulders and shook him. Again his fists struck out, this time with more force and directness. At the same time his eyes opened. She released him. He was awake.

"All right," he mumbled.

She caught up the lamp and hurried out, leaving him in darkness.

"You'll be docked," she warned back to him.

He did not mind the darkness. When he had got into his clothes, he went out into the kitchen. His tread was very heavy for so thin and light a boy. His legs dragged with their own weight, which seemed unreasonable because they were such skinny legs. He drew a broken-bottomed chair to the table.

"Johnny!" his mother called sharply.

He arose as sharply from the chair, and, without a word, went to the sink. It was a greasy, filthy sink. A smell came up from the outlet. He took no notice of it.

That a sink should smell was to him part of the natural order, just as it was a part of the natural order that the soap should be grimy with dish-water and hard to lather. Nor did he try very hard to make it lather. Several splashes of the cold water from the running faucet completed the function. He did not wash his teeth. For that matter he had never seen a toothbrush, nor did he know that there existed beings in the world who were guilty of so great a foolishness as tooth washing.

"You might wash yourself wunst a day without bein' told," his mother complained.

She was holding a broken lid on the pot as she poured two cups of coffee. He made no remark, for this was a standing quarrel between them, and the one thing upon which his mother was hard as adamant. "Wunst" a day it was compulsory that he should wash his face. He dried himself on a greasy towel, damp and dirty and ragged, that left his face covered with shreds of lint.

"I wish we didn't live so far away," she said, as he sat down. "I try to do the best I can. You know that. But a dollar on the rent is such a savin', an' we've more room here. You know that."

He scarcely followed her. He had heard it all before, many times. The range of her thought was limited, and she was ever harkening back to the hardship worked upon them by living so far from the mills.

"A dollar means more grub," he remarked sententiously. "I'd sooner do the walkin' an' git the grub."

He ate hurriedly, half chewing the bread and washing the unmasticated chunks down with coffee. The hot and muddy liquid went by the name of coffee. Johnny thought it was coffee—and excellent coffee. That was one of the few of life's illusions that remained to him. He had never drunk real coffee in his life.

In addition to the bread, there was a small piece of cold pork. His mother refilled his cup with coffee. As he was finishing the bread, he began to watch if more was forthcoming. She intercepted his questioning glance.

"Now, don't be hoggish, Johnny," was her comment. "You've had your share. Your brothers an' sisters are smaller'n you."

He did not answer the rebuke. He was not much of a talker. Also, he ceased his hungry glancing for more. He was uncomplaining, with a patience that was as terrible as the school in which it had been learned. He finished his coffee, wiped his mouth on the back of his hand, and started to rise.

"Wait a second," she said hastily. "I guess the loaf kin stand you another slice—a thin un."

There was legerdemain in her actions. With all the seeming of cutting a slice from the loaf for him, she put loaf and slice back in the bread box and conveyed to him one of her own two slices. She believed she had deceived him, but he had noted her sleight-of-hand. Nevertheless, he took the bread shamelessly. He had a philosophy that his mother, what of her chronic sickliness, was not much of an eater anyway.

She saw that he was chewing the bread dry, and reached over and emptied her coffee cup into his.

"Don't set good somehow on my stomach this morning," she explained.

A distant whistle, prolonged and shrieking, brought both of them to their feet. She glanced at the tin alarm-clock on the shelf. The hands stood at half-past five. The rest of the factory world was just arousing from sleep. She drew a shawl about her shoulders, and on her head put a dingy hat, shapeless and ancient.

"We've got to run," she said, turning the wick of the lamp and blowing down the chimney.

They groped their way out and down the stairs. It was clear and cold, and Johnny shivered at the first contact with the outside air. The stars had not yet begun to pale in the sky, and the city lay in blackness. Both Johnny and his mother shuffled their feet as they walked. There was no ambition in the leg muscles to swing the feet clear of the ground.

After fifteen silent minutes, his mother turned off to the right.

"Don't be late," was her final warning from out of the dark that was swallowing her up.

He made no response, steadily keeping on his way. In the factory quarter, doors were opening everywhere, and he was soon one of a multitude that pressed onward through the dark. As he entered the factory gate the whistle blew again. He glanced at the east. Across a ragged sky-line of housetops a pale light was beginning to creep. This much he saw of the day as he turned his back upon it and joined his work gang.

He took his place in one of many long rows of machines. Before him, above a bin filled with small bobbins, were large bobbins revolving rapidly. Upon these he wound the jute twine of the small bobbins. The work was simple. All that was required was celerity. The small bobbins were emptied so rapidly, and there were so many large bobbins that did the emptying, that there were no idle moments.

He worked mechanically. When a small bobbin ran out, he used his left hand for a brake, stopping the large bobbin and at the same time, with thumb and forefinger, catching a flying end of twine. Also, at the same time, with his right hand, he caught up the loose twine-end of a small bobbin. These various acts with both hands were performed simultaneously and swiftly. Then there would come a flash of his hands as he looped the weaver's knot and released the bobbin. There was nothing difficult about weaver's knots. He once boasted he could tie them in his sleep. And for that matter, he sometimes did, toiling centuries long in a single night at tying an endless succession of weaver's knots.

Some of the boys shirked, wasting time and machinery by not replacing the small bobbins when they ran out. And there was an overseer to prevent this. He caught Johnny's neighbor at the trick, and boxed his ears.

"Look at Johnny there—why ain't you like him?" the overseer wrathfully demanded.

Johnny's bobbins were running full blast, but he did not thrill at the indirect praise. There had been a time . . . but that was long ago, very long ago. His apathetic face was expressionless as he listened to himself being held up as a shining example. He was the perfect worker. He knew that. He had been told so, often. It was a commonplace, and besides it didn't seem to mean anything to him any more. From the perfect worker he had evolved into the perfect machine. When his work went wrong, it was with him as with the machine, due to faulty material. It would have been as possible for a perfect nail-die to cut imperfect nails as for him to make a mistake.

And small wonder. There had never been a time when he had not been in intimate relationship with machines. Machinery had almost been bred into him, and at any rate he had been brought up on it. Twelve years before, there had been a small flutter of excitement in the loom room of this very mill. Johnny's mother had fainted. They stretched her out on the floor in the midst of the shrieking machines. A couple of elderly women were called from their looms. The foreman assisted. And in a few minutes there was one more soul in the loom room than had entered by the doors. It was Johnny, born with the pounding, crashing roar of the looms in his ears, drawing with his first breath the warm, moist air that was thick with flying lint. He had coughed that first day in order to rid his lungs of the lint; and for the same reason he had coughed ever since.

The boy alongside of Johnny whimpered and sniffed. The boy's face was convulsed with hatred for the overseer who kept a threatening eye on him from a distance; but every bobbin was running full. The boy yelled terrible oaths into the whirling bobbins before him; but the sound did not carry half a dozen feet, the roaring of the room holding it in and containing it like a wall.

Of all this Johnny took no notice. He had a way of accepting things. Besides, things grow monotonous by repetition, and this particular happening he had witnessed many times. It seemed to him as useless to oppose the overseer as to defy the will of a machine. Machines were made to go in certain ways and to perform certain tasks. It was the same with the overseer.

But at eleven o'clock there was excitement in the room. In an apparently occult way the excitement instantly permeated everywhere. The one-legged boy who worked on the other side of Johnny bobbed swiftly across the floor to a bin truck that stood empty. Into this he dived out of sight, crutch and all. The superintendent of the mill was coming along, accompanied by a young man. He was well dressed and wore a starched shirt—a gentleman, in Johnny's classification of men, and also, "the Inspector."

He looked sharply at the boys as he passed along. Sometimes he stopped and asked questions. When he did so, he was compelled to shout at the top of his lungs, at which moments his face was ludicrously contorted with the strain of making himself heard. His quick eye noted the empty machine alongside of Johnny's, but he said nothing. Johnny also caught his eye, and he stopped abruptly. He caught Johnny by the arm to draw him back a step from the machine; but with an exclamation of surprise he released the arm.

"Pretty skinny," the superintendent laughed anxiously.

"Pipe stems," was the answer. "Look at those legs. The boy's got the rickets—incipient, but he's got them. If epilepsy doesn't get him in the end, it will be because tuberculosis gets him first."

Johnny listened, but did not understand. Furthermore he was not interested in future ills. There was an immediate and more serious ill that threatened him in the form of the inspector.

"Now, my boy, I want you to tell me the truth," the inspector said, or shouted, bending close to the boy's ear to make him hear. "How old are you?"

"Fourteen," Johnny lied, and he lied with the full force of his lungs. So loudly did he lie that it started him off in a dry, hacking cough that lifted the lint which had been settling in his lungs all morning.

"Looks sixteen at least," said the superintendent.

"Or sixty," snapped the inspector.

"He's always looked that way."

"How long?" asked the inspector, quickly.

"For years. Never gets a bit older."

"Or younger, I dare say. I suppose he's worked here all those years?"

"Off and on—but that was before the new law was passed," the superintendent hastened to add.

"Machine idle?" the inspector asked, pointing at the unoccupied machine beside Johnny's, in which the part-filled bobbins were flying like mad.

"Looks that way." The superintendent motioned the overseer to him and shouted in his ear and pointed at the machine. "Machine's idle," he reported back to the inspector.

They passed on, and Johnny returned to his work, relieved in that the ill had been averted. But the one-legged boy was not so fortunate. The sharp-eyed inspector haled him out at arm's length from the bin truck. His lips were quivering, and his face had all the expression of one upon whom was fallen profound and irremediable disaster. The overseer looked astounded, as though for the first time he had laid eyes on the boy, while the superintendent's face expressed shock and displeasure.

"I know him," the inspector said. "He's twelve years old. I've had him discharged from three factories inside the year. This makes the fourth."

He turned to the one-legged boy. "You promised me, word and honor, that you'd go to school."

The one-legged boy burst into tears. "Please, Mr. Inspector, two babies died on us, and we're awful poor."

"What makes you cough that way?" the inspector demanded, as though charging him with crime.

And as in denial of guilt, the one-legged boy replied: "It ain't nothin'. I jes' caught a cold last week, Mr. Inspector, that's all."

In the end the one-legged boy went out of the room with the inspector, the latter accompanied by the anxious and protesting superintendent. After that monotony settled down again. The long morning and the longer afternoon wore away and the whistle blew for quitting time. Darkness had already fallen when Johnny passed out through the factory gate. In the interval the sun had made a golden ladder of the sky, flooded the world with its gracious warmth, and dropped down and disappeared in the west behind a ragged sky-line of housetops.

Supper was the family meal of the day—the one meal at which Johnny encountered his younger brothers and sisters. It partook of the nature of an encounter, to him, for he was very old, while they were distressingly young. He had no patience with their excessive and amazing juvenility. He did not understand it. His own childhood was too far behind him. He was like an old and irritable man, annoyed by the turbulence of their young spirits that was to him arrant silliness. He glowered silently over his food, finding compensation in the thought that they would soon have to go to work. That would take the edge off them and make them sedate and dignified—like him. Thus it was, after the fashion of the human, that Johnny made of himself a yardstick with which to measure the universe.

During the meal, his mother explained in various ways and with infinite repetition that she was trying to do the best she could; so that it was with relief, the scant meal ended, that Johnny shoved back his chair and arose. He debated for a moment between bed and the front door, and finally went out the latter. He did not go far. He sat down on the stoop, his knees drawn up and his narrow shoulders drooping forward, his elbows on his knees and the palms of his hands supporting his chin.

As he sat there, he did no thinking. He was just resting. So far as his mind was concerned, it was asleep. His brothers and sisters came out, and with other children played noisily about him. An electric globe on the corner lighted their frolics. He was peevish and irritable, that they knew; but the spirit of adventure lured them into teasing him. They joined hands before him, and, keeping time with their bodies, chanted in his face weird and uncomplimentary doggerel. At first he snarled curses at them—curses he had learned from the lips of various foremen. Finding this futile, and remembering his dignity, he relapsed into dogged silence.

His brother Will, next to him in age, having just passed his tenth birthday, was the ringleader. Johnny did not possess particularly kindly feelings toward him. His life had early been embittered by continual giving over and giving way to Will. He had a definite feeling that Will was greatly in his debt and was ungrateful about it. In his own playtime, far back in the dim past, he had been robbed of a large part of that playtime by being compelled to take care of Will. Will was a baby then, and then, as now, their mother had spent her days in the mills. To Johnny had fallen the part of little father and little mother as well.

Will seemed to show the benefit of the giving over and the giving way. He was well-built, fairly rugged, as tall as his elder brother and even heavier. It was as though the life-blood of the one had been diverted into the other's veins. And in spirits it was the same. Johnny was jaded, worn out, without resilience, while his younger brother seemed bursting and spilling over with exuberance.

The mocking chant rose louder and louder. Will leaned closer as he danced, thrusting out his tongue. Johnny's left arm shot out and caught the other around the neck. At the same time he rapped his bony fist to the other's nose. It was a pathetically bony fist, but that it was sharp to hurt was evidenced by the squeal of pain it produced. The other children were uttering frightened cries, while Johnny's sister, Jennie, had dashed into the house.

He thrust Will from him, kicked him savagely on the shins, then reached for him and slammed him face downward in the dirt. Nor did he release him till the face had been rubbed into the dirt several times. Then the mother arrived, an anæmic whirlwind of solicitude and maternal wrath.

"Why can't he leave me alone?" was Johnny's reply to her upbraiding. "Can't he see I'm tired?"

"I'm as big as you," Will raged in her arms, his face a mess of tears, dirt, and blood. "I'm as big as you now, an' I'm goin' to git bigger. Then I'll lick you—see if I don't."

"You ought to be to work, seein' how big you are," Johnny snarled. "That's what's the matter with you. You ought to be to work. An' it's up to your ma to put you to work."

"But he's too young," she protested. "He's only a little boy."

"I was younger'n him when I started to work."

Johnny's mouth was open, further to express the sense of unfairness that he felt, but the mouth closed with a snap. He turned gloomily on his heel and stalked into the house and to bed. The door of his room was open to let in warmth from the kitchen. As he undressed in the semi-darkness he could hear his mother talking with a neighbor woman who had dropped in. His mother was crying, and her speech was punctuated with spiritless sniffles.

"I can't make out what's gittin' into Johnny," he could hear her say. "He didn't used to be this way. He was a patient little angel.

"An' he *is* a good boy," she hastened to defend. "He's worked faithful, an' he did go to work too young. But it wasn't my fault. I do the best I can, I'm sure."

Prolonged sniffling from the kitchen, and Johnny murmured to himself as his eyelids closed down, "You betcher life I've worked faithful."

The next morning he was torn bodily by his mother from the grip of sleep. Then came the meagre breakfast, the tramp through the dark, and the pale glimpse of day across the housetops as he turned his back on it and went in through the factory gate. It was another day, of all the days, and all the days were alike.

And yet there had been variety in his life—at the times he changed from one job to another, or was taken sick. When he was six, he was little mother and father to Will and the other children still younger. At seven he went into the mills—winding bobbins. When he was eight, he got work in another mill. His new job was marvellously easy. All he had to do was to sit down with a little stick in his hand and guide a stream of cloth that flowed past him. This stream of cloth came out of the maw of a machine, passed over a hot roller, and went on its way elsewhere. But he sat always in the one place, beyond the reach of daylight, a gas-jet flaring over him, himself part of the mechanism.

He was very happy at that job, in spite of the moist heat, for he was still young and in possession of dreams and illusions. And wonderful dreams he dreamed as he watched the steaming cloth streaming endlessly by. But there was no exercise about the work, no call upon his mind, and he dreamed less and less, while his mind grew torpid and drowsy. Nevertheless, he earned two dollars a week, and two dollars represented the difference between acute starvation and chronic underfeeding.

But when he was nine, he lost his job. Measles was the cause of it. After he recovered, he got work in a glass factory. The pay was better, and the work demanded skill. It was piece-work, and the more skilful he was, the bigger wages he earned. Here was incentive. And under this incentive he developed into a remarkable worker.

It was simple work, the tying of glass stoppers into small bottles. At his waist he carried a bundle of twine. He held the bottles between his knees so that he might work with both hands. Thus, in a sitting position and bending over his own knees, his narrow shoulders grew humped and his chest was contracted for ten hours each day. This was not good for the lungs, but he tied three hundred dozen bottles a day.

The superintendent was very proud of him, and brought visitors to look at him. In ten hours three hundred dozen bottles passed through his hands. This meant that he had attained machine-like perfection. All waste movements were eliminated. Every motion of his thin arms, every movement of a muscle in the thin fingers, was swift and accurate. He worked at high tension, and the result was that he grew nervous. At night his muscles twitched in his sleep, and in the daytime he could not relax and rest. He remained keyed up and his muscles continued to twitch. Also he grew sallow and his lint-cough grew worse. Then pneumonia laid hold of the feeble lungs within the contracted chest, and he lost his job in the glass-works.

Now he had returned to the jute mills where he had first begun with winding bobbins. But promotion was waiting for him. He was a good worker. He would next go on the starcher, and later he would go into the loom room. There was nothing after that except increased efficiency

The machinery ran faster than when he had first gone to work, and his mind ran slower. He no longer dreamed at all, though his earlier years had been full of dreaming. Once he had been in love. It was when he first began guiding the cloth over the hot roller, and it was with the daughter of the superintendent. She was much older than he, a young woman, and he had seen her at a distance only a paltry half-dozen times. But that made no difference. On the surface of the cloth stream that poured past him, he pictured radiant futures wherein he performed prodigies of toil, invented miraculous machines, won to the mastership of the mills, and in the end took her in his arms and kissed her soberly on the brow.

But that was all in the long ago, before he had grown too old and tired to love. Also, she had married and gone away, and his mind had gone to sleep. Yet it had been a wonderful experience, and he often used to look back upon it as other men and women look back upon the time they believed in fairies. He had never believed in fairies nor Santa Claus; but he had believed implicitly in the smiling future his imagination had wrought into the steaming cloth stream.

He had become a man very early in life. At seven, when he drew his first wages, began his adolescence. A certain feeling of independence crept up in him, and the relationship between him and his mother changed. Somehow, as an earner and breadwinner, doing his own work in the world, he was more like an equal with her. Manhood, full-blown manhood, had come when he was eleven, at which time he had gone to work on the night shift for six months. No child works on the night shift and remains a child.

There had been several great events in his life. One of these had been when his mother bought some California prunes. Two others had been the two times when she cooked custard. Those had been events. He remembered them kindly. And at that time his mother had told him of a blissful dish she would sometime make—"floating island," she had called it, "better than custard." For years he had looked forward to the day when he would sit down to the table with floating island before him, until at last he had relegated the idea of it to the limbo of unattainable ideals.

Once he found a silver quarter lying on the sidewalk. That, also, was a great event in his life, withal a tragic one. He knew his duty on the instant the silver flashed on his eyes, before even he had picked it up. At home, as usual, there was not enough to eat, and home he should have taken it as he did his wages every Saturday night. Right conduct in this case was obvious; but he never had any spending of his money, and he was suffering from candy hunger. He was ravenous for the sweets that only on red-letter days he had ever tasted in his life.

He did not attempt to deceive himself. He knew it was sin, and deliberately he sinned when he went on a fifteen-cent candy debauch. Ten cents he saved for a future orgy; but not being accustomed to the carrying of money, he lost the ten cents. This occurred at the time when he was suffering all the torments of conscience, and it was to him an act of divine retribution. He had a frightened sense of the closeness of an awful and wrathful God. God had seen, and God had been swift to punish, denying him even the full wages of sin.

In memory he always looked back upon that event as the one great criminal deed of his life, and at the recollection his conscience always awoke and gave him another twinge. It was the one skeleton in his closet. Also, being so made and circumstanced, he looked back upon the deed with regret. He was dissatisfied with the manner in which he had spent the quarter. He could have invested it better, and, out of his later knowledge of the quickness of God, he would have beaten God out by spending the whole quarter at one fell swoop. In retrospect he spent the quarter a thousand times, and each time to better advantage.

There was one other memory of the past, dim and faded, but stamped into his soul everlasting by the savage feet of his father. It was more like a nightmare than a remembered vision of a concrete thing—more like the race-memory of man that makes him fall in his sleep and that goes back to his arboreal ancestry.

This particular memory never came to Johnny in broad daylight when he was wide awake. It came at night, in bed, at the moment that his consciousness was sinking down and losing itself in sleep. It always aroused him to frightened wakefulness, and for the moment, in the first sickening start, it seemed to him that he lay crosswise on the foot of the bed. In the bed were the vague forms of his father and mother. He never saw what his father looked like. He had but one impression of his father, and that was that he had savage and pitiless feet.

His earlier memories lingered with him, but he had no late memories. All days were alike. Yesterday or last year were the same as a thousand years—or a minute. Nothing ever happened. There were no events to mark the march of time. Time did not march. It stood always still. It was only the whirling machines that moved, and they moved nowhere—in spite of the fact that they moved faster.

When he was fourteen, he went to work on the starcher. It was a colossal event. Something had at last happened that could be remembered beyond a night's sleep or a week's pay-day. It marked an era. It was a machine Olympiad, a thing to date from. "When I went to work on the starcher," or "after," or "before I went to work on the starcher," were sentences often on his lips.

He celebrated his sixteenth birthday by going into the loom room and taking a loom. Here was an incentive again, for it was piece-work. And he excelled, because the clay of him had been moulded by the mills into the perfect machine. At the end of three months he was running two looms, and, later, three and four.

At the end of his second year at the looms he was turning out more yards than any other weaver, and more than twice as much as some of the less skilful ones. And at home things began to prosper as he approached the full stature of his earning power. Not, however, that his increased earnings were in excess of need. The children were growing up. They ate more. And they were going to school, and school-books cost money. And somehow, the faster he worked, the faster climbed the prices of things. Even the rent went up, though the house had fallen from bad to worse disrepair.

He had grown taller; but with his increased height he seemed leaner than ever. Also, he was more nervous. With the nervousness increased his peevishness and irritability. The children had learned by many bitter lessons to fight shy of him. His mother respected him for his earning power, but somehow her respect was tinctured with fear.

There was no joyousness in life for him. The procession of the days he never saw. The nights he slept away in twitching unconsciousness. The rest of the time he worked, and his consciousness was machine consciousness. Outside this his mind was a blank. He had no ideals, and but one illusion; namely, that he drank excellent coffee. He was a work-beast. He had no mental life whatever; yet deep down in the crypts of his mind, unknown to him, were being weighed and sifted every hour of his toil, every movement of his hands, every twitch of his muscles, and preparations were making for a future course of action that would amaze him and all his little world.

It was in the late spring that he came home from work one night aware of unusual tiredness. There was a keen expectancy in the air as he sat down to the table, but he did not notice. He went through the meal in moody silence, mechanically eating what was before him. The children um'd and ah'd and made smacking noises with their mouths. But he was deaf to them.

"D'ye know what you're eatin'?" his mother demanded at last, desperately.

He looked vacantly at the dish before him, and vacantly at her.

"Floatin' island," she announced triumphantly.

"Oh," he said.

"Floating island!" the children chorused loudly.

"Oh," he said. And after two or three mouthfuls, he added, "I guess I ain't hungry to-night."

He dropped the spoon, shoved back his chair, and arose wearily from the table.

"An' I guess I'll go to bed."

His feet dragged more heavily than usual as he crossed the kitchen floor. Undressing was a Titan's task, a monstrous futility, and he wept weakly as he crawled into bed, one shoe still on. He was aware of a rising, swelling something inside his head that made his brain thick and fuzzy. His lean fingers felt as big as his wrist, while in the ends of them was a remoteness of sensation vague and fuzzy like his brain. The small of his back ached intolerably. All his bones ached. He ached everywhere. And in his head began the shrieking, pounding, crashing, roaring of a million looms. All space was filled with flying shuttles. They darted in and out, intricately, amongst the stars. He worked a thousand looms himself, and ever they speeded up, faster and faster, and his brain unwound, faster and faster, and became the thread that fed the thousand flying shuttles.

He did not go to work next morning. He was too busy weaving colossally on the thousand looms that ran inside his head. His mother went to work, but first she sent for the doctor. It was a severe attack of la grippe, he said. Jennie served as nurse and carried out his instructions.

It was a very severe attack, and it was a week before Johnny dressed and tottered feebly across the floor. Another week, the doctor said, and he would be fit to return to work. The foreman of the loom room visited him on Sunday afternoon, the first day of his convalescence. The best weaver in the room, the foreman told his mother. His job would be held for him. He could come back to work a week from Monday.

"Why don't you thank 'im, Johnny?" his mother asked anxiously.

"He's ben that sick he ain't himself yet," she explained apologetically to the visitor.

Johnny sat hunched up and gazing steadfastly at the floor. He sat in the same position long after the foreman had gone. It was warm outdoors, and he sat on the stoop in the afternoon. Sometimes his lips moved. He seemed lost in endless calculations.

Next morning, after the day grew warm, he took his seat on the stoop. He had pencil and paper this time with which to continue his calculations, and he calculated painfully and amazingly.

"What comes after millions?" he asked at noon, when Will came home from school. "An' how d'ye work 'em?"

That afternoon finished his task. Each day, but without paper and pencil, he returned to the stoop. He was greatly absorbed in the one tree that grew across the street. He studied it for hours at a time, and was unusually interested when the wind swayed its branches and fluttered its leaves. Throughout the week he seemed lost in a great communion with himself. On Sunday, sitting on the stoop, he laughed aloud, several times, to the perturbation of his mother, who had not heard him laugh in years.

Next morning, in the early darkness, she came to his bed to rouse him. He had had his fill of sleep all week, and awoke easily. He made no struggle, nor did he attempt to hold on to the bedding when she stripped it from him. He lay quietly, and spoke quietly.

"It ain't no use, ma."

"You'll be late," she said, under the impression that he was still stupid with sleep.

"I'm awake, ma, an' I tell you it ain't no use. You might as well lemme alone. I ain't goin' to git up."

"But you'll lose your job!" she cried.

"I ain't goin' to git up," he repeated in a strange, passionless voice.

She did not go to work herself that morning. This was sickness beyond any sickness she had ever known. Fever and delirium she could understand; but this was insanity. She pulled the bedding up over him and sent Jennie for the doctor.

When that person arrived, Johnny was sleeping gently, and gently he awoke and allowed his pulse to be taken.

"Nothing the matter with him," the doctor reported. "Badly debilitated, that's all. Not much meat on his bones."

"He's always been that way," his mother volunteered.

"Now go 'way, ma, an' let me finish my snooze."

Johnny spoke sweetly and placidly, and sweetly and placidly he rolled over on his side and went to sleep.

At ten o'clock he awoke and dressed himself. He walked out into the kitchen, where he found his mother with a frightened expression on her face.

"I'm goin' away, ma," he announced, "an' I jes' want to say good-by."

She threw her apron over her head and sat down suddenly and wept. He waited patiently.

"I might a-known it," she was sobbing.

"Where?" she finally asked, removing the apron from her head and gazing up at him with a stricken face in which there was little curiosity.

"I don't know—anywhere."

As he spoke, the tree across the street appeared with dazzling brightness on his inner vision. It seemed to lurk just under his eyelids, and he could see it whenever he wished.

"An' your job?" she quavered.

"I ain't never goin' to work again."

"My God, Johnny!" she wailed, "don't say that!"

What he had said was blasphemy to her. As a mother who hears her child deny God, was Johnny's mother shocked by his words.

"What's got into you, anyway?" she demanded, with a lame attempt at imperativeness.

"Figures," he answered. "Jes' figures. I've ben doin' a lot of figurin' this week, an' it's most surprisin'."

"I don't see what that's got to do with it," she sniffled.

Johnny smiled patiently, and his mother was aware of a distinct shock at the persistent absence of his peevishness and irritability.

"I'll show you," he said. "I'm plum' tired out. What makes me tired? Moves. I've ben movin' ever since I was born. I'm tired of movin', an' I ain't goin' to move any more. Remember when I worked in the glass-house? I used to do three hundred dozen a day. Now I reckon I made about ten different moves to each bottle. That's thirty-six thousan' moves a day. Ten days, three hundred an' sixty thousan' moves a day. One month, one million an' eighty thousan' moves. Chuck out the eighty thousan'—" he spoke with the complacent beneficence of a philanthropist—"chuck out the eighty thousan', that leaves a million moves a month —twelve million moves a year.

"At the looms I'm movin' twic'st as much. That makes twenty-five million moves a year, an' it seems to me I've ben a movin' that way 'most a million years.

"Now this week I ain't moved at all. I ain't made one move in hours an' hours. I tell you it was swell, jes' settin' there, hours an' hours, an' doin' nothin'. I ain't never ben happy before. I never had any time. I've ben movin' all the time. That ain't no way to be happy. An' I ain't goin' to do it any more. I'm jes' goin' to set, an' set, an' rest, an' rest, and then rest some more."

"But what's goin' to come of Will an' the children?" she asked despairingly.

"That's it, 'Will an' the children,'" he repeated.

But there was no bitterness in his voice. He had long known his mother's ambition for the younger boy, but the thought of it no longer rankled. Nothing mattered any more. Not even that.

"I know, ma, what you've ben plannin' for Will—keepin' him in school to make a bookkeeper out of him. But it ain't no use, I've quit. He's got to go to work."

"An' after I have brung you up the way I have," she wept, starting to cover her head with the apron and changing her mind.

"You never brung me up," he answered with sad kindliness. "I brung myself up, ma, an' I brung up Will. He's bigger'n me, an' heavier, an' taller. When I was a kid, I reckon I didn't git enough to eat. When he come along an' was a kid, I was workin' an' earnin' grub for him too. But that's done with. Will can go to work, same as me, or he can go to hell, I don't care which. I'm tired. I'm goin' now. Ain't you goin' to say good-by?"

She made no reply. The apron had gone over her head again, and she was crying. He paused a moment in the doorway.

"I'm sure I done the best I knew how," she was sobbing.

He passed out of the house and down the street. A wan delight came into his face at the sight of the lone tree. "Jes' ain't goin' to do nothin'," he said to himself, half aloud, in a crooning tone. He glanced wistfully up at the sky, but the bright sun dazzled and blinded him.

It was a long walk he took, and he did not walk fast. It took him past the jute-mill. The muffled roar of the loom room came to his ears, and he smiled. It was a gentle, placid smile. He hated no one, not even the pounding, shrieking machines. There was no bitterness in him, nothing but an inordinate hunger for rest.

The houses and factories thinned out and the open spaces increased as he approached the country. At last the city was behind him, and he was walking down a leafy lane beside the railroad track. He did not walk like a man. He did not look like a man. He was a travesty of the human. It was a twisted and stunted and nameless piece of life that shambled like a sickly ape, arms loose-hanging, stoop-shouldered, narrow-chested, grotesque and terrible.

He passed by a small railroad station and lay down in the grass under a tree. All afternoon he lay there. Sometimes he dozed, with muscles that twitched in his sleep. When awake, he lay without movement, watching the birds or looking up at the sky through the branches of the tree above him. Once or twice he laughed aloud, but without relevance to anything he had seen or felt.

After twilight had gone, in the first darkness of the night, a freight train rumbled into the station. When the engine was switching cars on to the side-track, Johnny crept along the side of the train. He pulled open the side-door of an empty box-car and awkwardly and laboriously climbed in. He closed the door. The engine whistled. Johnny was lying down, and in the darkness he smiled.

1911

LOVE OF LIFE

This out of all will remain—
They have lived and have tossed:
So much of the game will be gain,
Though the gold of the dice has been lost.

They limped painfully down the bank, and once the foremost of the two men staggered among the rough-strewn rocks. They were tired and weak, and their faces had the drawn expression of patience which comes of hardship long endured. They were heavily burdened with blanket packs which were strapped to their shoulders. Head straps, passing across the forehead, helped support these packs. Each man carried a rifle. They walked in a stooped posture, the shoulders well forward, the head still farther forward, the eyes bent upon the ground.

"I wish we had just about two of them cartridges that's layin' in that cache of ourn," said the second man.

His voice was utterly and drearily expressionless. He spoke without enthusiasm; and the first man, limping into the milky stream that foamed over the rocks, vouchsafed no reply.

The other man followed at his heels. They did not remove their footgear, though the water was icy cold—so cold that their ankles ached and their feet went numb. In places the water dashed against their knees, and both men staggered for footing.

The man who followed slipped on a smooth boulder, nearly fell, but recovered himself with a violent effort, at the same time uttering a sharp exclamation of pain. He seemed faint and dizzy and put out his free hand while he reeled, as though seeking support against the air. When he had steadied himself he stepped forward, but reeled again and nearly fell. Then he stood still and looked at the other man, who had never turned his head.

The man stood still for fully a minute, as though debating with himself. Then he called out:

"I say, Bill, I've sprained my ankle."

Bill staggered on through the milky water. He did not look around. The man watched him go, and though his face was expressionless as ever, his eyes were like the eyes of a wounded deer.

The other man limped up the farther bank and continued straight on without looking back. The man in the stream watched him. His lips trembled a little, so that the rough thatch of brown hair which covered them was visibly agitated. His tongue even strayed out to moisten them.

"Bill!" he cried out.

It was the pleading cry of a strong man in distress, but Bill's head did not turn. The man watched him go, limping grotesquely and lurching forward with stammering gait up the slow slope toward the soft sky line of the low-lying hill. He watched him go till he passed over the crest and disappeared. Then he turned his gaze and slowly took in the circle of the world that remained to him now that Bill was gone.

Near the horizon the sun was smoldering dimly, almost obscured by formless mists and vapors, which gave an impression of mass and density without outline or tangibility. The man pulled out his watch, the while resting his weight on one leg. It was four o'clock, and as the season was near the last of July or first of August—he did not know the precise date within a week or two—he knew that the sun roughly marked the northwest. He looked to the south and knew that somewhere beyond those bleak hills lay the Great Bear Lake; also he knew that in that direction the Arctic Circle cut its forbidding way across the Canadian Barrens. This stream in which he stood was a feeder to the Coppermine River, which in turn flowed north and emptied into Coronation Gulf and the Arctic Ocean. He had never been there, but he had seen it, once, on a Hudson's Bay Company chart.

Again his gaze completed the circle of the world about him. It was not a heartening spectacle. Everywhere was soft sky line. The hills were all low-lying. There were no trees, no shrubs, no grasses—naught but a tremendous and terrible desolation that sent fear swiftly dawning into his eyes.

"Bill!" he whispered, once and twice; "Bill!"

He cowered in the midst of the milky water, as though the vastness were pressing in upon him with overwhelming force, brutally crushing him with its complacent awfulness. He began to shake as with an ague fit, till the gun fell from his hand with a splash. This served to rouse him. He fought with his fear and pulled himself together, groping in the water and recovering the weapon. He hitched his pack farther over on his left shoulder, so as to take a portion of its weight from off the injured ankle. Then he proceeded, slowly and carefully, wincing with pain, to the bank.

He did not stop. With a desperation that was madness, unmindful of the pain, he hurried up the slope to the crest of the hill over which his comrade had disappeared—more grotesque and comical by far than that limping, jerking comrade. But at the crest he saw a shallow valley, empty of life. He fought with his fear again, overcame it, hitched the pack still farther over on his left shoulder, and lurched on down the slope.

The bottom of the valley was soggy with water, which the thick moss held, spongelike, close to the surface. This water squirted out from under his feet at every step, and each time he lifted a foot the action culminated in a sucking sound as the wet moss reluctantly released its grip. He picked his way from muskeg to muskeg, and followed the other man's footsteps along and across the rocky ledges which thrust like islets through the sea of moss.

Though alone, he was not lost. Farther on, he knew, he would come to where dead spruce and fir, very small and wizened, bordered the shore of a little lake, the *titchin-nichilie*, in the tongue of the country, the "land of little sticks." And into that lake flowed a small stream, the water of which was not milky. There was rush grass on that stream—this he remembered well—but no timber, and he would follow it till its first trickle ceased at a divide. He would cross this divide to the first trickle of another stream, flowing to the west, which he would follow until it emptied into the river Dease, and here he would find a cache under an upturned canoe and piled over with many rocks. And in this cache would be ammunition for his empty gun, fishhooks and lines, a small net—all the utilities for the killing and snaring of food. Also he would find flour—not much—a piece of bacon, and some beans.

Bill would be waiting for him there, and they would paddle away south down the Dease to the Great Bear Lake. And south across the lake they would go, ever south, till they gained the Mackenzie. And south, still south, they would go, while the winter raced vainly after them, and the ice formed in the eddies, and the days grew chill and crisp, south to some warm Hudson's Bay Company post, where timber grew tall and generous and there was grub without end.

These were the thoughts of the man as he strove onward. But hard as he strove with his body, he strove equally hard with his mind, trying to think that Bill had not deserted him, that Bill would surely wait for him at the cache. He was compelled to think this thought, or else there would not be any use to strive, and he would have lain down and died. And as the dim ball of the sun sank slowly into the northwest he covered every inch—and many times—of his and Bill's flight south before the downcoming winter. And he conned the grub of the cache and the grub of the Hudson's Bay Company post over and over again. He had not eaten for two days; for a far longer time he had not had all he wanted to eat. Often he stooped and picked pale muskeg berries, put them into his mouth, and chewed and swallowed them. A muskeg berry is a bit of seed enclosed in a bit of water. In the mouth the water melts away and the seed chews sharp and bitter. The man knew there was no nourishment in the berries, but he chewed them patiently with a hope greater than knowledge and defying experience.

At nine o'clock he stubbed his toe on a rocky ledge, and from sheer weariness and weakness staggered and fell. He lay for some time, without movement, on his side. Then he slipped out of the pack straps and clumsily dragged himself into a sitting posture. It was not yet dark, and in the lingering twilight he groped about among the rocks for shreds of dry moss. When he had gathered a heap he built a fire—a smoldering, smudgy fire—and put a tin pot of water on to boil.

He unwrapped his pack and the first thing he did was to count his matches. There were sixty-seven. He counted them three times to make sure. He divided them into several portions, wrapping them in oil paper, disposing of one bunch in his empty tobacco pouch, of another bunch in the inside band of his battered hat, of a third bunch under his shirt on the chest. This accomplished, a panic came upon him, and he unwrapped them all and counted them again. There were still sixty-seven.

He dried his wet footgear by the fire. The moccasins were in soggy shreds. The blanket socks were worn through in places, and his feet were raw and bleeding. His ankle was throbbing, and he gave it an examination. It had swollen to the size of his knee. He tore a long strip from one of his two blankets and bound the ankle tightly. He tore other strips and bound them about his feet to serve for both moccasins and socks. Then he drank the pot of water, steaming hot, wound his watch, and crawled between his blankets.

He slept like a dead man. The brief darkness around midnight came and went. The sun arose in the northeast—at least the day dawned in that quarter, for the sun was hidden by gray clouds.

At six o'clock he awoke, quietly lying on his back. He gazed straight up into the gray sky and knew that he was hungry. As he rolled over on his elbow he was startled by a loud snort, and saw a bull caribou regarding him with alert curiosity. The animal was not more than fifty feet away, and instantly into the man's mind leaped the vision and the savor of a caribou steak sizzling and frying over a fire. Mechanically he reached for the empty gun, drew a bead, and pulled the trigger. The bull snorted and leaped away, his hoofs rattling and clattering as he fled across the ledges.

The man cursed and flung the empty gun from him. He groaned aloud as he started to drag himself to his feet. It was a slow and arduous task. His joints were like rusty hinges. They worked harshly in their sockets, with much friction, and each bending or unbending was accomplished only through a sheer exertion of will. When he finally gained his feet, another minute or so was consumed in straightening up, so that he could stand erect as a man should stand.

He crawled up a small knoll and surveyed the prospect. There were no trees, no bushes, nothing but a gray sea of moss scarcely diversified by gray rocks, gray lakelets, and gray streamlets. The sky was gray. There was no sun nor hint of sun. He had no idea of north, and he had forgotten the way he had come to this spot the night before. But he was not lost. He knew that. Soon he would come to the land of the little sticks. He felt that it lay off to the left somewhere, not far—possibly just over the next low hill.

He went back to put his pack into shape for traveling. He assured himself of the existence of his three separate parcels of matches, though he did not stop to count them. But he did linger, debating, over a squat moose-hide sack. It was not large. He could hide it under his two hands. He knew that it weighed fifteen pounds—as much as all the rest of the pack—and it worried him. He finally set it to one side and proceeded to roll the pack. He paused to gaze at the squat moose-hide sack. He picked it up hastily with a defiant glance about him, as though the desolation were trying to rob him of it; and when he rose to his feet to stagger on into the day, it was included in the pack on his back.

He bore away to the left, stopping now and again to eat muskeg berries. His ankle had stiffened, his limp was more pronounced, but the pain of it was as nothing compared with the pain of his stomach. The hunger pangs were sharp. They gnawed and gnawed until he could not keep his mind steady on the course he must pursue to gain the land of little sticks. The muskeg berries did not allay this gnawing, while they made his tongue and roof of his mouth sore with their irritating bite.

He came upon a valley where rock ptarmigan rose on whirring wings from the ledges and muskegs. "Ker—ker—ker" was the cry they made. He threw stones at them but could not hit them. He placed his pack on the ground and stalked them as a cat stalks a sparrow. The sharp rocks cut through his pants legs till his knees left a trail of blood; but the hurt was lost in the hurt of his hunger. He squirmed over the wet moss, saturating his clothes and chilling his body; but he was not aware of it, so great was his fever for food. And always the ptarmigan rose, whirring, before him, till their "Ker–ker–ker" became a mock to him, and he cursed them and cried aloud at them with their own cry.

Once he crawled upon one that must have been asleep. He did not see it till it shot up in his face from its rocky nook. He made a clutch as startled as was the rise of the ptarmigan, and there remained in his hand three tail feathers. As he watched its flight he hated it, as though it had done him some terrible wrong. Then he returned and shouldered his pack.

As the day wore along he came into valleys or swales where game was more plentiful. A band of caribou passed by, twenty and odd animals, tantalizingly within rifle range. He felt a wild desire to run after them, a certitude that he could run them down. A black fox came toward him, carrying a ptarmigan in his mouth. The man shouted. It was a fearful cry, but the fox, leaping away in fright, did not drop the ptarmigan.

Late in the afternoon he followed a stream, milky with lime, which ran through sparse patches of rush grass. Grasping these rushes firmly near the root, he pulled up what resembled a young onion sprout no larger than a shingle nail. It was tender, and his teeth sank into it with a crunch that promised deliciously of food. But its fibers were tough. It was composed of stringy filaments saturated with water, like the berries, and devoid of nourishment. He threw off his pack and went into the rush grass on hands and knees, crunching and munching, like some bovine creature.

He was very weary and often wished to rest—to lie down and sleep; but he was continually driven on, not so much by his desire to gain the land of little sticks as by his hunger. He searched little ponds for frogs and dug up the earth with his nails for worms, though he knew in spite that neither frogs nor worms existed so far north.

He looked into every pool of water vainly, until, as the long twilight came on, he discovered a solitary fish, the size of a minnow, in such a pool. He plunged his arm in up to the shoulder, but it eluded him. He reached for it with both hands and stirred up the milky mud at the bottom. In his excitement he fell in, wetting himself to the waist. Then the water was too muddy to admit of his seeing the fish, and he was compelled to wait until the sediment had settled.

The pursuit was renewed, till the the water was again muddied. But he could not wait. He unstrapped the tin bucket and began to bail the pool. He bailed wildly at first, splashing himself and flinging the water so short a distance that it ran back into the pool. He worked more carefully, striving to be cool, though his heart was pounding against his chest and his hands were trembling. At the end of half an hour the pool was nearly dry. Not a cupful of water remained. And there was no fish. He found a hidden crevice among the stones through which it had escaped to the adjoining and larger pool—a pool which he could not empty in a night and a day. Had he known of the crevice, he could have closed it with a rock at the beginning and the fish would have been his.

Thus he thought, and crumpled up and sank down upon the wet earth. At first he cried softly to himself, then he cried loudly to the pitiless desolation that ringed him around; and for a long time after he was shaken by great dry sobs.

He built a fire and warmed himself by drinking quarts of hot water, and made camp on a rocky ledge in the same fashion he had the night before. The last thing he did was to see that his matches were dry and to wind his watch. The blankets were wet and clammy. His ankle pulsed with pain. But he knew only that he was hungry, and through his restless sleep he dreamed of feasts and banquets and of food served and spread in all imaginable ways.

He awoke chilled and sick. There was no sun. The gray of earth and sky had become deeper, more profound. A raw wind was blowing, and the first flurries of snow were whitening the hilltops. The air about him thickened and grew white while he made a fire and boiled more water. It was wet snow, half rain, and the flakes were large and soggy. At first they melted as soon as they came in contact with the earth, but ever more fell, covering the ground, putting out the fire, spoiling his supply of moss fuel.

This was a signal for him to strap on his pack and stumble onward, he knew not where. He was not concerned with the land of little sticks, nor with Bill and the cache under the upturned canoe by the river Dease. He was mastered by the verb "to eat." He was hunger-mad. He took no heed of the course he pursued, so long as that course led him through the swale bottoms. He felt his way through the wet snow to the watery muskeg berries, and went by feel as he pulled up the rush grass by the roots. But it was tasteless stuff and did not satisfy. He found a weed that tasted sour and he ate all he could find of it, which was not much, for it was a creeping growth, easily hidden under the several inches of snow.

He had no fire that night, nor hot water, and crawled under his blanket to sleep the broken hunger sleep. The snow turned into a cold rain. He awakened many times to feel it falling on his upturned face. Day came—a gray day and no sun. It had ceased raining. The keenness of his hunger had departed. Sensibility, as far as concerned the yearning for food, had been exhausted. There was a dull, heavy ache in his stomach, but it did not bother him so much. He was more rational, and once more he was chiefly interested in the land of little sticks and the cache by the river Dease.

He ripped the remnant of one of his blankets into strips and bound his bleeding feet. Also he recinched the injured ankle and prepared himself for a day of travel. When he came to his pack he paused long over the squat moose-hide sack, but in the end it went with him.

The snow had melted under the rain, and only the hilltops showed white. The sun came out, and he succeeded in locating the points of the compass, though he knew now that he was lost. Perhaps, in his previous days' wanderings, he had edged away too far to the left. He now bore off to the right to counteract the possible deviation from his true course.

Though the hunger pangs were no longer so exquisite, he realized that he was weak. He was compelled to pause for frequent rests, when he attacked the muskeg berries and rush-grass patches. His tongue felt dry and large, as though covered with a fine hairy growth, and it tasted bitter in his mouth. His heart gave him a great deal of trouble. When he had traveled a few minutes it would begin a remorseless thump, thump, thump, and then leap up and away in a painful flutter of beats that choked him and made him go faint and dizzy.

In the middle of the day he found two minnows in a large pool. It was impossible to bail it, but he was calmer now and managed to catch them in his tin bucket. They were no longer than his little finger, but he was not particularly hungry. The dull ache in his stomach had been growing duller and fainter. It seemed almost that his stomach was dozing. He ate the fish raw, masticating with painstaking care, for the eating was an act of pure reason. While he had no desire to eat, he knew that he must eat to live.

In the evening he caught three more minnows, eating two and saving the third for breakfast. The sun had dried stray shreds of moss, and he was able to warm himself with hot water. He had not covered more than ten miles that day; and the next day, traveling whenever his heart permitted him, he covered no more than five miles. But his stomach did not give him the slightest uneasiness. It had gone to sleep. He was in a strange country, too, and the caribou were growing more plentiful, also the wolves. Often their yelps drifted across the desolation, and once he saw three of them slinking away before his path.

Another night; and in the morning, being more rational, he untied the leather string that fastened the squat moose-hide sack. From its open mouth poured a yellow stream of coarse gold dust and nuggets. He roughly divided the gold in halves, caching one half on a prominent ledge, wrapped in a piece of blanket, and returning the other half to the sack. He also began to use strips of the one remaining blanket for his feet. He still clung to his gun, for there were cartridges in that cache by the river Dease.

This was a day of fog, and this day hunger awoke in him again. He was very weak and was afflicted with a giddiness which at times blinded him. It was no uncommon thing now for him to stumble and fall; and stumbling once, he fell squarely into a ptarmigan nest. There were four newly hatched chicks, a day old—little specks of pulsating life no more than a mouthful; and he ate them ravenously, thrusting them alive into his mouth and crunching them like eggshells between his teeth. The mother ptarmigan beat about him with great outcry. He used his gun as a club with which to knock her over, but she dodged out of reach. He threw stones at her and with one chance shot broke a wing. Then she fluttered away, running, trailing the broken wing, with him in pursuit.

The little chicks had no more than whetted his appetite. He hopped and bobbed clumsily along on his injured ankle, throwing stones and screaming hoarsely at times; at other times hopping and bobbing silently along, picking himself up grimly and patiently when he fell, or rubbing his eyes with his hand when the giddiness threatened to overpower him.

The chase led him across swampy ground in the bottom of the valley, and he came upon footprints in the soggy moss. They were not his own—he could see that. They must be Bill's. But he could not stop, for the mother ptarmigan was running on. He would catch her first, then he would return and investigate.

He exhausted the mother ptarmigan; but he exhausted himself. She lay panting on her side. He lay panting on his side, a dozen feet away, unable to crawl to her. And as he recovered she recovered, fluttering out of reach as his hungry hand went out to her. The chase was resumed. Night settled down and she escaped. He stumbled from weakness and pitched head foremost on his face, cutting his cheek, his pack upon his back. He did not move for a long while; then he rolled over on his side, wound his watch, and lay there until morning.

Another day of fog. Half of his last blanket had gone into foot-wrappings. He failed to pick up Bill's trail. It did not matter. His hunger was driving him too compellingly—only—only he wondered if Bill, too, were lost. By midday the irk of his pack became too oppressive. Again he divided the gold, this time merely spilling half of it on the ground. In the afternoon he threw the rest of it away, there remaining to him only the half blanket, the tin bucket, and the rifle.

A hallucination began to trouble him. He felt confident that one cartridge remained to him. It was in the chamber of the rifle and he had overlooked it. On the other hand, he knew all the time that the chamber was empty. But the hallucination persisted. He fought it off for hours, then threw his rifle open and was confronted with emptiness. The disappointment was as bitter as though he had really expected to find the cartridge.

He plodded on for half an hour, when the hallucination arose again. Again he fought it, and still it persisted, till for very relief he opened his rifle to unconvince himself. At times his mind wandered farther afield, and he plodded on, a mere automaton, strange conceits and whimsicalities gnawing at his brain like worms. But these excursions out of the real were of brief duration, for ever the pangs of the hunger bite called him back. He was jerked back abruptly once from such an excursion by a sight that caused him nearly to faint. He reeled and swayed, doddering like a drunken man to keep from falling. Before him stood a horse. A horse! He could not believe his eyes. A thick mist was in them, intershot with sparkling points of light. He rubbed his eyes savagely to clear his vision, and beheld not a horse but a great brown bear. The animal was studying him with bellicose curiosity.

The man had brought his gun halfway to his shoulder before he realized. He lowered it and drew his hunting knife from its beaded sheath at his hip. Before him was meat and life. He ran his thumb along the edge of his knife. It was sharp. The point was sharp. He would fling himself upon the bear and kill it. But his heart began its warning thump, thump, thump. Then followed the wild upward leap and tattoo of flutters, the pressing as of an iron band about his forehead, the creeping of the dizziness into his brain.

His desperate courage was evicted by a great surge of fear. In his weakness, what if the animal attacked him? He drew himself up to his most imposing stature, gripping the knife and staring hard at the bear. The bear advanced clumsily a couple of steps, reared up, and gave vent to a tentative growl. If the man ran, he would run after him; but the man did not run. He was animated now with the courage of fear. He, too, growled, savagely, terribly, voicing the fear that is to life germane and that lies twisted about life's deepest roots.

The bear edged away to one side, growling menacingly, himself appalled by this mysterious creature that appeared upright and unafraid. But the man did not move. He stood like a statue till the danger was past, when he yielded to a fit of trembling and sank down into the wet moss.

He pulled himself together and went on, afraid now in a new way. It was not the fear that he should die passively from lack of food, but that he should be destroyed violently before starvation had exhausted the last particle of the endeavor in him that made toward surviving. There were the wolves. Back and forth across the desolation drifted their howls, weaving the very air into a fabric of menace that was so tangible that he found himself, arms in the air, pressing it back from him as it might be the walls of a wind-blown tent.

Now and again the wolves, in packs of two and three, crossed his path. But they sheered clear of him. They were not in sufficient numbers, and besides, they were hunting the caribou, which did not battle, while this strange creature that walked erect might scratch and bite.

In the late afternoon he came upon scattered bones where the wolves had made a kill. The debris had been a caribou calf an hour before, squawking and running and very much alive. He contemplated the bones, clean-picked and polished, pink with the cell life in them which had not yet died. Could it possibly be that he might be that ere the day was done! Such was life, eh? A vain and fleeting thing. It was only life that pained. There was no hurt in death. To die was to sleep. It meant cessation, rest. Then why was he not content to die?

But he did not moralize long. He was squatting in the moss, a bone in his mouth, sucking at the shreds of life that still dyed it faintly pink. The sweet meaty taste, thin and elusive almost as a memory, maddened him. He closed his jaws on the bones and crunched. Sometimes it was the bone that broke, sometimes his teeth. Then he crushed the bones between rocks, pounded them to a pulp, and swallowed them. He pounded his fingers, too, in his haste, and yet found a moment in which to feel surprise at the fact that his fingers did not hurt much when caught under the descending rock.

Came frightful days of snow and rain. He did not know when he made camp, when he broke camp. He traveled in the night as much as in the day. He rested wherever he fell, crawled on whenever the dying life in him flickered up and burned less dimly. He, as a man, no longer strove. It was the life in him, unwilling to die, that drove him on. He did not suffer. His nerves had become blunted, numb, while his mind was filled with weird visions and delicious dreams.

But ever he sucked and chewed on the crushed bones of the caribou calf, the least remnants of which he had gathered up and carried with him. He crossed no more hills or divides, but automatically followed a large stream which flowed through a wide and shallow valley. He did not see this stream nor this valley. He saw nothing save visions. Soul and body walked or crawled side by side, yet apart, so slender was the thread that bound them.

He awoke in his right mind, lying on his back on a rocky ledge. The sun was shining bright and warm. Afar off he heard the squawking of caribou calves. He was aware of vague memories of rain and wind and snow, but whether he had been beaten by the storm for two days or two weeks he did not know.

For some time he lay without movement, the genial sunshine pouring upon him and saturating his miserable body with its warmth. A fine day, he thought. Perhaps he could manage to locate himself. By a painful effort he rolled over on his side. Below him flowed a wide and sluggish river. Its unfamiliarity puzzled him. Slowly he followed it with his eyes, winding in wide sweeps among the bleak, bare hills, bleaker and barer and lower-lying than any hills he had yet encountered. Slowly, deliberately, without excitement or more than the most casual interest, he followed the course of the strange stream toward the sky line and saw it emptying into a bright and shining sea. He was still unexcited. Most unusual, he thought, a vision or a mirage—more likely a vision, a trick of his disordered mind. He was confirmed in this by sight of a ship lying at anchor in the midst of the shining sea. He closed his eyes for a while, then opened them. Strange how the vision persisted! Yet not strange. He knew there were no seas or ships in the heart of the barren lands, just as he had known there was no cartridge in the empty rifle.

He heard a snuffle behind him—a half-choking gasp or cough. Very slowly, because of his exceeding weakness and stiffness, he rolled over on his other side. He could see nothing near at hand, but he waited patiently. Again came the snuffle and cough, and outlined between two jagged rocks not a score of feet away he made out the gray head of a wolf. The sharp ears were not pricked so sharply as he had seen them on other wolves; the eyes were bleared and bloodshot, the head seemed to droop limply and forlornly. The animal blinked continually in the sunshine. It seemed sick. As he looked it snuffled and coughed again.

This, at least, was real, he thought, and turned on the other side so that he might see the reality of the world which had been veiled from him before by the vision. But the sea still shone in the distance and the ship was plainly discernible. Was it reality after all? He closed his eyes for a long while and thought, and then it came to him. He had been making north by east, away from the Dease Divide and into the Coppermine Valley. This wide and sluggish river was the Coppermine. That shining sea was the Arctic Ocean. That ship was a whaler, strayed east, far east, from the mouth of the Mackenzie, and it was lying at anchor in Coronation Gulf. He remembered the Hudson's Bay Company chart he had seen long ago, and it was all clear and reasonable to him.

He sat up and turned his attention to immediate affairs. He had worn through the blanket wrappings, and his feet were shapeless lumps of raw meat. His last blanket was gone. Rifle and knife were both missing. He had lost his hat somewhere, with the bunch of matches in the band, but the matches against his chest were safe and dry inside the tobacco pouch and oil paper. He looked at his watch. It marked eleven o'clock and was still running. Evidently he had kept it wound.

He was calm and collected. Though extremely weak, he had no sensation of pain. He was not hungry. The thought of food was not even pleasant to him, and whatever he did was done by his reason alone. He ripped off his pants legs to the knees and bound them about his feet. Somehow he had succeeded in retaining the tin bucket. He would have some hot water before he began what he foresaw was to be a terrible journey to the ship.

His movements were slow. He shook as with a palsy. When he started to collect dry moss he found he could not rise to his feet. He tried again and again, then contented himself with crawling about on hands and knees. Once he crawled near to the sick wolf. The animal dragged itself reluctantly out of his way, licking its chops with a tongue which seemed hardly to have the strength to curl. The man noticed that the tongue was not the customary healthy red. It was a yellowish brown and seemed coated with a rough and half-dry mucus.

After he had drunk a quart of hot water the man found he was able to stand, and even to walk as well as a dying man might be supposed to walk. Every minute or so he was compelled to rest. His steps were feeble and uncertain, just as the wolf's that trailed him were feeble and uncertain; and that night, when the shining sea was blotted out by blackness, he knew he was nearer to it by no more than four miles.

Throughout the night he heard the cough of the sick wolf, and now and then the squawking of the caribou calves. There was life all around him, but it was strong life, very much alive and well, and he knew the sick wolf clung to the sick man's trail in the hope that the man would die first. In the morning, on opening his eyes, he beheld it regarding him with a wistful and hungry stare. It stood crouched, with tail between its legs, like a miserable and woebegone dog. It shivered in the chill morning wind and grinned dispiritedly when the man spoke to it in a voice that achieved no more than a hoarse whisper.

The sun rose brightly, and all morning the man tottered and fell toward the ship on the shining sea. The weather was perfect. It was the brief Indian summer of the high latitudes. It might last a week. Tomorrow or next day it might be gone.

In the afternoon the man came upon a trail. It was of another man, who did not walk, but who dragged himself on all fours. The man thought it might be Bill, but he thought in a dull, uninterested way. He had no curiosity. In fact sensation and emotion had left him. He was no longer susceptible to pain. Stomach and nerves had gone to sleep. Yet the life that was in him drove him on. He was very weary, but it refused to die. It was because it refused to die that he still ate muskeg berries and minnows, drank his hot water, and kept a wary eye on the sick wolf.

He followed the trail of the other man who dragged himself along, and soon came to the end of it—a few fresh-picked bones where the soggy moss was marked by the foot pads of many wolves. He saw a squat moose-hide sack, mate to his own, which had been torn by sharp teeth. He picked it up, though its weight was almost too much for his feeble fingers. Bill had carried it to the last. Ha-ha! He would have the laugh on Bill. He would survive and carry it to the ship in the shining sea. His mirth was hoarse and ghastly, like a raven's croak, and the sick wolf joined him, howling lugubriously. The man ceased suddenly. How could he have the laugh on Bill if that were Bill; if those bones, so pinky-white and clean, were Bill?

He turned away. Well, Bill had deserted him; but he would not take the gold, nor would he suck Bill's bones. Bill would have, though, had it been the other way around, he mused as he staggered on.

He came to a pool of water. Stooping over in quest of minnows, he jerked his head back as though he had been stung. He had caught sight of his reflected face. So horrible was it that sensibility awoke long enough to be shocked. There were three minnows in the pool, which was too large to drain; and after several ineffectual attempts to catch them in the tin bucket he forbore. He was afraid, because of his great weakness, that he might fall in and drown. It was for this reason that he did not trust himself to the river astride one of the many drift logs which lined its sandspits.

That day he decreased the distance between him and the ship by three miles; the next day by two—for he was crawling now as Bill had crawled; and the end of the fifth day found the ship still seven miles away and him unable to make even a mile a day. Still the Indian summer held on, and he continued to crawl and faint, turn and turn about; and ever the sick wolf coughed and wheezed at his heels. His knees had become raw meat like his feet, and though he padded them with the shirt from his back it was a red track he left behind him on the moss and stones. Once, glancing back, he saw the wolf licking hungrily his bleeding trail, and he saw sharply what his own end might be—unless—unless he could get the wolf. Then began as grim a tragedy of existence as was ever played—a sick man that crawled, a sick wolf that limped, two creatures dragging their dying carcasses across the desolation and hunting each other's lives.

Had it been a well wolf, it would not have mattered so much to the man; but the thought of going to feed the maw of that loathsome and all but dead thing was repugnant to him. He was finicky. His mind had begun to wander again and to be perplexed by hallucinations, while his lucid intervals grew rarer and shorter.

He was awakened once from a faint by a wheeze close in his ear. The wolf leaped lamely back, losing its footing and falling in its weakness. It was ludicrous, but he was not amused. Nor was he even afraid. He was too far gone for that. But his mind was for the moment clear, and he lay and considered. The ship was no more than four miles away. He could see it quite distinctly when he rubbed the mists out of his eyes, and he could see the white sail of a small boat cutting the water of the shining sea. But he could never crawl those four miles. He knew that, and was very calm in the knowledge. He knew that he could not crawl half a mile. And yet he wanted to live. It was unreasonable that he should die after all he had undergone. Fate asked too much of him. And, dying, he declined to die. It was stark madness, perhaps, but in the very grip of death he defied death and refused to die.

He closed his eyes and composed himself with infinite precaution. He steeled himself to keep above the suffocating languor that lapped like a rising tide through all the wells of his being. It was very like a sea, this deadly languor that rose and rose and drowned his consciousness bit by bit. Sometimes he was all but submerged, swimming through oblivion with a faltering stroke; and again, by some strange alchemy of soul, he would find another shred of will and strike out more strongly.

Without movement he lay on his back, and he could hear, slowly drawing near and nearer, the wheezing intake and output of the sick wolf's breath. It drew closer, ever closer, through an infinitude of time, and he did not move. It was at his ear. The harsh dry tongue grated like sandpaper against his cheek. His hands shot out —or at least he willed them to shoot out. The fingers were curved like talons, but they closed on empty air. Swiftness and certitude require strength, and the man had not this strength.

The patience of the wolf was terrible. The man's patience was no less terrible. For half a day he lay motionless, fighting off unconsciousness and waiting for the thing that was to feed upon him and upon which he wished to feed. Sometimes the languid sea rose over him and he dreamed long dreams; but ever through it all, waking and dreaming, he waited for the wheezing breath and the harsh caress of the tongue.

He did not hear the breath, and he slipped slowly from some dream to the feel of the tongue along his hand. He waited. The fangs pressed softly; the pressure increased; the wolf was exerting its last strength in an effort to sink teeth in the food for which it had waited so long. But the man had waited long, and the lacerated hand closed on the jaw. Slowly, while the wolf struggled feebly and the hand clutched feebly, the other hand crept across to a grip. Five minutes later the whole weight of the man's body was on top of the wolf. The hands had not sufficient strength to choke the wolf, but the face of the man was pressed close to the throat of the wolf and the mouth of the man was full of hair. At the end of half an hour the man was aware of a warm trickle in his throat. It was not pleasant. It was like molten lead being forced into his stomach, and it was forced by his will alone. Later the man rolled over on his back and slept.

There were some members of a scientific expedition on the whaleship *Bedford*. From the deck they remarked a strange object on the shore. It was moving down the beach toward the water. They were unable to classify it, and, being scientific men, they climbed into the whaleboat alongside and went ashore to see. And they saw something that was alive but which could hardly be called a man. It was blind, unconscious. It squirmed along the ground like some monstrous worm. Most of its efforts were ineffectual, but it was persistent, and it writhed and twisted and went ahead perhaps a score of feet an hour.

Three weeks afterward the man lay in a bunk on the whaleship *Bedford*, and with tears streaming down his wasted cheeks told who he was and what he had undergone. He also babbled incoherently of his mother, of sunny southern California, and a home among the orange groves and flowers.

The days were not many after that when he sat at table with the scientific men and ship's officers. He gloated over the spectacle of so much food, watching it anxiously as it went into the mouths of others. With the disappearance of each mouthful an expression of deep regret came into his eyes. He was quite sane, yet he hated those men at mealtime. He was haunted by a fear that the food would not last. He inquired of the cook, the cabin boy, the captain, concerning the food stores. They reassured him countless times; but he could not believe them, and pried cunningly about the lazaret to see with his own eyes.

It was noticed that the man was getting fat. He grew stouter with each day. The scientific men shook their heads and theorized. They limited the man at his meals, but still his girth increased and he swelled prodigiously under his shirt.

The sailors grinned. They knew. And when the scientific men set a watch on the man they knew. They saw him slouch for'ard after breakfast, and, like a mendicant, with outstretched palm, accost a sailor. The sailor grinned and passed him a fragment of sea biscuit. He clutched it avariciously, looked at it as a miser looks at gold, and thrust it into his shirt bosom. Similar were the donations from other grinning sailors.

The scientific men were discreet. They let him alone. But they privily examined his bunk. It was lined with hardtack; the mattress was stuffed with hardtack; every nook and cranny was filled with hardtack. Yet he was sane. He was taking precautions against another possible famine—that was all. He would recover from it, the scientific men said; and he did, ere the *Bedford's* anchor rumbled down in San Francisco Bay.

1906

THE PASSING OF MARCUS O'BRIEN

"It is the judgment of this court that you vamose the camp . . . in the customary way, sir, in the customary way."

Judge Marcus O'Brien was absent-minded, and Mucluc Charley nudged him in the ribs. Marcus O'Brien cleared his throat and went on:—

"Weighing the gravity of the offence, sir, and the extenuating circumstances, it is the opinion of this court, and its verdict, that you be outfitted with three days' grub. That will do, I think."

Arizona Jack cast a bleak glance out over the Yukon. It was a swollen, chocolate flood, running a mile wide and nobody knew how deep. The earth-bank on which he stood was ordinarily a dozen feet above the water, but the river was now growling at the top of the bank, devouring, instant by instant, tiny portions of the top-standing soil. These portions went into the gaping mouths of the endless army of brown swirls and vanished away. Several inches more, and Red Cow would be flooded.

"It won't do," Arizona Jack said bitterly. "Three days' grub ain't enough."

"There was Manchester," Marcus O'Brien replied gravely. "He didn't get any grub."

"And they found his remains grounded on the Lower River an' half eaten by huskies," was Arizona Jack's retort. "And his killin' was without provocation. Joe Deeves never did nothin', never warbled once, an' jes' because his stomach was out of order, Manchester ups an' plugs him. You ain't givin' me a square deal, O'Brien, I tell you that straight. Give me a week's grub, and I play even to win out. Three days' grub, an' I cash in."

"What for did you kill Ferguson?" O'Brien demanded. "I haven't any patience for these unprovoked killings. And they've got to stop. Red Cow's none so populous. It's a good camp, and there never used to be any killings. Now they're epidemic. I'm sorry for you, Jack, but you've got to be made an example of. Ferguson didn't provoke enough for a killing."

"Provoke!" Arizona Jack snorted. "I tell you, O'Brien, you don't savve. You ain't got no artistic sensibilities. What for did I kill Ferguson? What for did Ferguson sing 'Then I wisht I was a little bird'? That's what I want to know. Answer me that. What for did he sing 'little bird, little bird'? One little bird was enough. I could a-stood one little bird. But no, he must sing two little birds. I gave 'm a chanst. I went to him almighty polite and requested him kindly to discard one little bird. I pleaded with him. There was witnesses that testified to that."

"An' Ferguson was no jay-throated songster," some one spoke up from the crowd.

O'Brien betrayed indecision.

"Ain't a man got a right to his artistic feelin's?" Arizona Jack demanded. "I gave Ferguson warnin'. It was violatin' my own nature to go on listenin' to his little birds. Why, there's music sharps that fine-strung an' keyed-up they'd kill for heaps less'n I did. I'm willin' to pay for havin' artistic feelin's. I can take my medicine an' lick the spoon, but three days' grub is drawin' it a shade fine, that's all, an' I hereby register my kick. Go on with the funeral."

O'Brien was still wavering. He glanced inquiringly at Mucluc Charley.

"I should say, Judge, that three days' grub was a mite severe," the latter suggested; "but you're runnin' the show. When we elected you judge of this here trial court, we agreed to abide by your decisions, an' we've done it, too, b'gosh, an' we're goin' to keep on doin' it."

"Mebbe I've been a trifle harsh, Jack," O'Brien said apologetically—"I'm that worked up over those killings; an' I'm willing to make it a week's grub." He cleared his throat magisterially and looked briskly about him. "And now we might as well get along and finish up the business. The boat's ready. You go and get the grub, Leclaire. We'll settle for it afterward."

Arizona Jack looked grateful, and, muttering something about "damned little birds," stepped aboard the open boat that rubbed restlessly against the bank. It was a large skiff, built of rough pine planks that had been sawed by hand from the standing timber of Lake Lindeman, a few hundred miles above, at the foot of Chilcoot. In the boat were a pair of oars and Arizona Jack's blankets. Leclaire brought the grub, tied up in a flour-sack, and put it on board. As he did so, he whispered:—

"I gave you good measure, Jack. You done it with provocation."

"Cast her off!" Arizona Jack cried.

Somebody untied the painter and threw it in. The current gripped the boat and whirled it away. The murderer did not bother with the oars, contenting himself with sitting in the stern-sheets and rolling a cigarette. Completing it, he struck a match and lighted up. Those that watched on the bank could see the tiny puffs of smoke. They remained on the bank till the boat swung out of sight around the bend half a mile below. Justice had been done.

The denizens of Red Cow imposed the law and executed sentences without the delays that mark the softness of civilization. There was no law on the Yukon save what they made for themselves. They were compelled to make it for themselves. It was in an early day that Red Cow flourished on the Yukon—1887—and the Klondike and its populous stampedes lay in the unguessed future. The men of Red Cow did not even know whether their camp was situated in Alaska or in the Northwest Territory, whether they drew breath under the stars and stripes or under the British flag. No surveyor had ever happened along to give them their latitude and longitude. Red Cow was situated somewhere along the Yukon, and that was sufficient for them. So far as flags were concerned, they were beyond all jurisdiction. So far as the law was concerned, they were in No-Man's land.

They made their own law, and it was very simple. The Yukon executed their decrees. Some two thousand miles below Red Cow the Yukon flowed into Bering Sea through a delta a hundred miles wide. Every mile of those two thousand miles was savage wilderness. It was true, where the Porcupine flowed into the Yukon inside the Arctic Circle there was a Hudson Bay Company trading post. But that was many hundreds of miles away. Also, it was rumored that many hundreds of miles farther on there were missions. This last, however, was merely rumor; the men of Red Cow had never been there. They had entered the lone land by way of Chilcoot and the head-waters of the Yukon.

The men of Red Cow ignored all minor offences. To be drunk and disorderly and to use vulgar language were looked upon as natural and inalienable rights. The men of Red Cow were individualists, and recognized as sacred but two things, property and life. There were no women present to complicate their simple morality. There were only three log-cabins in Red Cow—the majority of the population of forty men living in tents or brush shacks; and there was no jail in which to confine malefactors, while the inhabitants were too busy digging gold or seeking gold to take a day off and build a jail. Besides, the paramount question of grub negatived such a procedure. Wherefore, when a man violated the rights of property or life, he was thrown into an open boat and started down the Yukon. The quantity of grub he received was proportioned to the gravity of the offence. Thus, a common thief might get as much as two weeks' grub; an uncommon thief might get no more than half of that. A murderer got no grub at all. A man found guilty of manslaughter would receive grub for from three days to a week. And Marcus O'Brien had been elected judge, and it was he who apportioned the grub. A man who broke the law took his chances. The Yukon swept him away, and he might or might not win to Bering Sea. A few days' grub gave him a fighting chance. No grub meant practically capital punishment, though there was a slim chance, all depending on the season of the year.

Having disposed of Arizona Jack and watched him out of sight, the population turned from the bank and went to work on its claims—all except Curly Jim, who ran the one faro layout in all the Northland and who speculated in prospect-holes on the side. Two things happened that day that were momentous. In the late morning Marcus O'Brien struck it. He washed out a dollar, a dollar and a half, and two dollars, from three successive pans. He had found the streak. Curly Jim looked into the hole, washed a few pans himself, and offered O'Brien ten thousand dollars for all rights—five thousand in dust, and, in lieu of the other five thousand, a half interest in his faro layout. O'Brien refused the offer. He was there to make money out of the earth, he declared with heat, and not out of his fellow-men. And anyway, he didn't like faro. Besides, he appraised his strike at a whole lot more than ten thousand.

The second event of moment occurred in the afternoon, when Siskiyou Pearly ran his boat into the bank and tied up. He was fresh from the Outside, and had in his possession a four-months-old newspaper. Furthermore, he had half a dozen barrels of whiskey, all consigned to Curly Jim. The men of Red Cow quit work. They sampled the whiskey—at a dollar a drink, weighed out on Curly's scales; and they discussed the news. And all would have been well, had not Curly Jim conceived a nefarious scheme, which was, namely, first to get Marcus O'Brien drunk, and next, to buy his mine from him.

The first half of the scheme worked beautifully. It began in the early evening, and by nine o'clock O'Brien had reached the singing stage. He clung with one arm around Curly Jim's neck, and even essayed the late lamented Ferguson's song about the little birds. He considered he was quite safe in this, what of the fact that the only man in camp with artistic feelings was even then speeding down the Yukon on the breast of a five-mile current.

But the second half of the scheme failed to connect. No matter how much whiskey was poured down his neck, O'Brien could not be brought to realize that it was his bounden and friendly duty to sell his claim. He hesitated, it is true, and trembled now and again on the verge of giving in. Inside his muddled head, however, he was chuckling to himself. He was up to Curly Jim's game, and liked the hands that were being dealt him. The whiskey was good. It came out of one special barrel, and was about a dozen times better than that in the other five barrels.

Siskiyou Pearly was dispensing drinks in the bar-room to the remainder of the population of Red Cow, while O'Brien and Curly had out their business orgy in the kitchen. But there was nothing small about O'Brien. He went into the bar-room and returned with Mucluc Charley and Percy Leclaire.

"Business 'sociates of mine, business 'sociates," he announced, with a broad wink to them and a guileless grin to Curly. "Always trust their judgment, always trust 'em. They're all right. Give 'em some fire-water, Curly, an' le's talk it over."

This was ringing in; but Curly Jim, making a swift revaluation of the claim, and remembering that the last pan he washed had turned out seven dollars, decided that it was worth the extra whiskey, even if it was selling in the other room at a dollar a drink.

"I'm not likely to consider," O'Brien was hiccoughing to his two friends in the course of explaining to them the question at issue. "Who? Me?—sell for ten thousand dollars! No, indeed. I'll dig the gold myself, an' then I'm goin' down to God's country,—Southern California,—that's the place for me to end my declinin' days —an' then I'll start . . . as I said before, then I'll start . . . what did I say I was goin' to start?"

"Ostrich farm," Mucluc Charley volunteered.

"Sure, just what I'm goin' to start." O'Brien abruptly steadied himself and looked with awe at Mucluc Charley. "How did you know? Never said so. Jes' thought I said so. You're a min' reader, Charley. Le's have another."

Curly Jim filled the glasses and had the pleasure of seeing four dollars' worth of whiskey disappear, one dollar's worth of which he punished himself—O'Brien insisted that he drink as frequently as his guests.

"Better take the money now," Leclaire argued. "Take you two years to dig it out the hole, an' all that time you might be hatchin' teeny little baby ostriches an' pulling feathers out the big ones."

O'Brien considered the proposition and nodded approval. Curly Jim looked gratefully at Leclaire and refilled the glasses.

"Hold on there!" spluttered Mucluc Charley, whose tongue was beginning to wag loosely and trip over itself. "As your father confessor—there I go—as your brother—Oh hell!" He paused and collected himself for another start. "As your frien'—business frien', I should say, I would suggest, rather—I would take the liberty, as it was, to mention—I mean, suggest, that there may be more ostriches . . . O hell!" He downed another glass, and went on more carefully. "What I'm drivin' at is . . . what am I drivin' at?" He smote the side of his head sharply half a dozen times with the heel of his palm to shake up his ideas. "I got it!" he cried jubilantly. "Supposen there's slathers more'n ten thousand dollars in that hole!"

O'Brien, who apparently was all ready to close the bargain, switched about.

"Great!" he cried. "Splen'd idea. Never thought of it all by myself." He took Mucluc Charley warmly by the hand. "Good frien'! Good 's'ciate!" He turned belligerently on Curly Jim. "Maybe hundred thousand dollars in that hole. You wouldn't rob your old frien', would you, Curly? Course you wouldn't. I know you . . . better'n yourself, better'n yourself. Le's have another. We're good frien's, all of us, I say, all of us."

And so it went, and so went the whiskey, and so went Curly Jim's hopes up and down. Now Leclaire argued in favor of immediate sale, and almost won the reluctant O'Brien over, only to lose him to the more brilliant counter-argument of Mucluc Charley. And again, it was Mucluc Charley who presented convincing reasons for the sale and Percy Leclaire who held stubbornly back. A little later it was O'Brien himself who insisted on selling, while both friends, with tears and curses, strove to dissuade him. The more whiskey they downed, the more fertile of imagination they became. For one sober pro or con they found a score of drunken ones; and they convinced one another so readily that they were perpetually changing sides in the argument.

The time came when both Mucluc Charley and Leclaire were firmly set upon the sale, and they gleefully obliterated O'Brien's objections as fast as he entered them. O'Brien grew desperate. He exhausted his last argument and sat speechless. He looked pleadingly at the friends who had deserted him. He kicked Mucluc Charley's shins under the table, but that graceless hero immediately unfolded a new and most logical reason for the sale. Curly Jim got pen and ink and paper and wrote out the bill of sale. O'Brien sat with pen poised in hand.

"Le's have one more," he pleaded. "One more before I sign away a hundred thousan' dollars."

Curly Jim filled the glasses triumphantly. O'Brien downed his drink and bent forward with wobbling pen to affix his signature. Before he had made more than a blot, he suddenly started up, impelled by the impact of an idea colliding with his consciousness. He stood upon his feet and swayed back and forth before them, reflecting in his startled eyes the thought process that was taking place behind.

Then he reached his conclusion. A benevolent radiance suffused his countenance. He turned to the faro dealer, took his hand, and spoke solemnly.

"Curly, you're my frien'. There's my han'. Shake. Ol' man, I won't do it. Won't sell. Won't rob a frien'. No son-of-a-gun will ever have chance to say Marcus O'Brien robbed frien' 'cause frien' was drunk. You're drunk, Curly, an' won't rob you. Jes' had thought—never thought it before—don't know what the matter 'ith me, but never thought it before. Suppose, jes' suppose, Curly, my ol' frien', jes' suppose there ain't ten thousan' in whole damn claim. You'd be robbed. No, sir; won't do it. Marcus O'Brien makes money out of the groun', not out of his frien's."

Percy Leclaire and Mucluc Charley drowned the faro dealer's objections in applause for so noble a sentiment. They fell upon O'Brien from either side, their arms lovingly about his neck, their mouths so full of words they could not hear Curly's offer to insert a clause in the document to the effect that if there weren't ten thousand in the claim he would be given back the difference between yield and purchase price. The longer they talked the more maudlin and the more noble the discussion became. All sordid motives were banished. They were a trio of philanthropists striving to save Curly Jim from himself and his own philanthropy. They insisted that he was a philanthropist. They refused to accept for a moment that there could be found one ignoble thought in all the world. They crawled and climbed and scrambled over high ethical plateaus and ranges, or drowned themselves in metaphysical seas of sentimentality.

Curly Jim sweated and fumed and poured out the whiskey. He found himself with a score of arguments on his hands, not one of which had anything to do with the gold-mine he wanted to buy. The longer they talked the farther away they got from that gold-mine, and at two in the morning Curly Jim acknowledged himself beaten. One by one he led his helpless guests across the kitchen floor and thrust them outside. O'Brien came last, and the three, with arms locked for mutual aid, titubated gravely on the stoop.

"Good business man, Curly," O'Brien was saying. "Must say like your style—fine an' generous, free-handed hospital . . . hospital . . . hospitality. Credit to you. Nothin' base 'n graspin' in your make-up. As I was sayin'—"

But just then the faro dealer slammed the door. The three laughed happily on the stoop. They laughed for a long time. Then Mucluc Charley essayed speech.

"Funny—laughed so hard—ain't what I want to say. My idea is . . . . what wash it? Oh, got it! Funny how ideas slip. Elusive idea—chasin' elusive idea—great sport. Ever chase rabbits, Percy, my frien'? I had dog—great rabbit dog. Whash 'is name? Don't know name—never had no name—forget name—elusive name—chasin' elusive name—no, idea—elusive idea, but got it—what I want to say was—O hell!"

Thereafter there was silence for a long time. O'Brien slipped from their arms to a sitting posture on the stoop, where he slept gently. Mucluc Charley chased the elusive idea through all the nooks and crannies of his drowning consciousness. Leclaire hung fascinated upon the delayed utterance. Suddenly the other's hand smote him on the back.

"Got it!" Mucluc Charley cried in stentorian tones.

The shock of the jolt broke the continuity of Leclaire's mental process.

"How much to the pan?" he demanded.

"Pan nothin'!" Mucluc Charley was angry. "Idea—got it—got leg-hold—ran it down."

Leclaire's face took on a rapt, admiring expression, and again he hung upon the other's lips.

". . . O hell!" said Mucluc Charley.

At this moment the kitchen door opened for an instant, and Curly Jim shouted, "Go home!"

"Funny," said Mucluc Charley. "Shame idea—very shame as mine. Le's go home."

They gathered O'Brien up between them and started. Mucluc Charley began aloud the pursuit of another idea. Leclaire followed the pursuit with enthusiasm. But O'Brien did not follow it. He neither heard, nor saw, nor knew anything. He was a mere wobbling automaton, supported affectionately and precariously by his two business associates.

They took the path down by the bank of the Yukon. Home did not lie that way, but the elusive idea did. Mucluc Charley giggled over the idea that he could not catch for the edification of Leclaire. They came to where Siskiyou Pearly's boat lay moored to the bank. The rope with which it was tied ran across the path to a pine stump. They tripped over it and went down, O'Brien underneath. A faint flash of consciousness lighted his brain. He felt the impact of bodies upon his and struck out madly for a moment with his fists. Then he went to sleep again. His gentle snore arose on the air, and Mucluc Charley began to giggle.

"New idea," he volunteered, "brand new idea. Jes' caught it—no trouble at all. Came right up an' I patted it on the head. It's mine. 'Brien's drunk—beashly drunk. Shame—damn shame—learn'm lesshon. Thash Pearly's boat. Put 'Brien in Pearly's boat. Casht off—let her go down Yukon. 'Brien wake up in mornin'. Current too strong—can't row boat 'gainst current—mush walk back. Come back madder 'n hatter. You an' me headin' for tall timber. Learn 'm lesshon jes' shame, learn 'm lesshon."

Siskiyou Pearly's boat was empty, save for a pair of oars. Its gunwale rubbed against the bank alongside of O'Brien. They rolled him over into it. Mucluc Charley cast off the painter, and Leclaire shoved the boat out into the current. Then, exhausted by their labors, they lay down on the bank and slept.

Next morning all Red Cow knew of the joke that had been played on Marcus O'Brien. There were some tall bets as to what would happen to the two perpetrators when the victim arrived back. In the afternoon a lookout was set, so that they would know when he was sighted. Everybody wanted to see him come in. But he didn't come, though they sat up till midnight. Nor did he come next day, nor the next. Red Cow never saw Marcus O'Brien again, and though many conjectures were entertained, no certain clew was ever gained to dispel the mystery of his passing.

* * *

Only Marcus O'Brien knew, and he never came back to tell. He awoke next morning in torment. His stomach had been calcined by the inordinate quantity of whiskey he had drunk, and was a dry and raging furnace. His head ached all over, inside and out; and, worse than that, was the pain in his face. For six hours countless thousands of mosquitoes had fed upon him, and their ungrateful poison had swollen his face tremendously. It was only by a severe exertion of will that he was able to open narrow slits in his face through which he could peer. He happened to move his hands, and they hurt. He squinted at them, but failed to recognize them, so puffed were they by the mosquito virus. He was lost, or rather, his identity was lost to him. There was nothing familiar about him, which, by association of ideas, would cause to rise in his consciousness the continuity of his existence. He was divorced utterly from his past, for there was nothing about him to resurrect in his consciousness a memory of that past. Besides, he was so sick and miserable that he lacked energy and inclination to seek after who and what he was.

It was not until he discovered a crook in a little finger, caused by an unset breakage of years before, that he knew himself to be Marcus O'Brien. On the instant his past rushed into his consciousness. When he discovered a blood-blister under a thumb-nail, which he had received the previous week, his self-identification became doubly sure, and he knew that those unfamiliar hands belonged to Marcus O'Brien, or, just as much to the point, that Marcus O'Brien belonged to the hands. His first thought was that he was ill—that he had had river fever. It hurt him so much to open his eyes that he kept them closed. A small floating branch struck the boat a sharp rap. He thought it was some one knocking on the cabin door, and said, "Come in." He waited for a while, and then said testily, "Stay out, then, damn you." But just the same he wished they would come in and tell him about his illness.

But as he lay there, the past night began to reconstruct itself in his brain. He hadn't been sick at all, was his thought; he had merely been drunk, and it was time for him to get up and go to work. Work suggested his mine, and he remembered that he had refused ten thousand dollars for it. He sat up abruptly and squeezed open his eyes. He saw himself in a boat, floating on the swollen brown flood of the Yukon. The spruce-covered shores and islands were unfamiliar. He was stunned for a time. He couldn't make it out. He could remember the last night's orgy, but there was no connection between that and his present situation.

He closed his eyes and held his aching head in his hands. What had happened? Slowly the dreadful thought arose in his mind. He fought against it, strove to drive it away, but it persisted: he had killed somebody. That alone could explain why he was in an open boat drifting down the Yukon. The law of Red Cow that he had so long administered had now been administered to him. He had killed some one and been set adrift. But whom? He racked his aching brain for the answer, but all that came was a vague memory of bodies falling upon him and of striking out at them. Who were they? Maybe he had killed more than one. He reached to his belt. The knife was missing from its sheath. He had done it with that undoubtedly. But there must have been some reason for the killing. He opened his eyes and in a panic began to search about the boat. There was no grub, not an ounce of grub. He sat down with a groan. He had killed without provocation. The extreme rigor of the law had been visited upon him.

For half an hour he remained motionless, holding his aching head and trying to think. Then he cooled his stomach with a drink of water from overside and felt better. He stood up, and alone on the wide-stretching Yukon, with naught but the primeval wilderness to hear, he cursed strong drink. After that he tied up to a huge floating pine that was deeper sunk in the current than the boat and that consequently drifted faster. He washed his face and hands, sat down in the stern-sheets, and did some more thinking. It was late in June. It was two thousand miles to Bering Sea. The boat was averaging five miles an hour. There was no darkness in such high latitudes at that time of the year, and he could run the river every hour of the twenty-four. This would mean, daily, a hundred and twenty miles. Strike out the twenty for accidents, and there remained a hundred miles a day. In twenty days he would reach Bering Sea. And this would involve no expenditure of energy; the river did the work. He could lie down in the bottom of the boat and husband his strength.

For two days he ate nothing. Then, drifting into the Yukon Flats, he went ashore on the low-lying islands and gathered the eggs of wild geese and ducks. He had no matches, and ate the eggs raw. They were strong, but they kept him going. When he crossed the Arctic Circle, he found the Hudson Bay Company's post. The brigade had not yet arrived from the Mackenzie, and the post was completely out of grub. He was offered wild-duck eggs, but he informed them that he had a bushel of the same on the boat. He was also offered a drink of whiskey, which he refused with an exhibition of violent repugnance. He got matches, however, and after that he cooked his eggs. Toward the mouth of the river head-winds delayed him, and he was twenty-four days on the egg diet. Unfortunately, while asleep, he had drifted by both the missions of St. Paul and Holy Cross. And he could sincerely say, as he afterward did, that talk about missions on the Yukon was all humbug. There weren't any missions, and he was the man to know.

Once on Bering Sea he exchanged the egg diet for seal diet, and he never could make up his mind which he liked least. In the fall of the year he was rescued by a United States revenue cutter, and the following winter he made quite a hit in San Francisco as a temperance lecturer. In this field he found his vocation. "Avoid the bottle" is his slogan and battle-cry. He manages subtly to convey the impression that in his own life a great disaster was wrought by the bottle. He has even mentioned the loss of a fortune that was caused by that hell-bait of the devil, but behind that incident his listeners feel the loom of some terrible and unguessed evil for which the bottle is responsible. He has made a success in his vocation, and has grown gray and respected in the crusade against strong drink. But on the Yukon the passing of Marcus O'Brien remains tradition. It is a mystery that ranks at par with the disappearance of Sir John Franklin.

1908

TO BUILD A FIRE

Day had broken cold and gray, exceedingly cold and gray, when the man turned aside from the main Yukon trail and climbed the high earth-bank, where a dim and little-travelled trail led eastward through the fat spruce timberland. It was a steep bank, and he paused for breath at the top, excusing the act to himself by looking at his watch. It was nine o'clock. There was no sun nor hint of sun, though there was not a cloud in the sky. It was a clear day, and yet there seemed an intangible pall over the face of things, a subtle gloom that made the day dark, and that was due to the absence of sun. This fact did not worry the man. He was used to the lack of sun. It had been days since he had seen the sun, and he knew that a few more days must pass before that cheerful orb, due south, would just peep above the sky line and dip immediately from view.

The man flung a look back along the way he had come. The Yukon lay a mile wide and hidden under three feet of ice. On top of this ice were as many feet of snow. It was all pure white, rolling in gentle undulations where the ice jams of the freeze-up had formed. North and south, as far as his eye could see, it was unbroken white, save for a dark hairline that curved and twisted from around the spruce-covered island to the south, and that curved and twisted away into the north, where it disappeared behind another spruce-covered island. This dark hairline was the trail—the main trail—that led south five hundred miles to the Chilcoot Pass, Dyea, and salt water; and that led north seventy miles to Dawson, and still on to the north a thousand miles to Nulato, and finally to St. Michael, on Bering Sea, a thousand miles and half a thousand more.

But all this—the mysterious, far-reaching hairline trail, the absence of sun from the sky, the tremendous cold, and the strangeness and weirdness of it all—made no impression on the man. It was not because he was long used to it. He was a newcomer in the land, a *chechaquo*, and this was his first winter. The trouble with him was that he was without imagination. He was quick and alert in the things of life, but only in the things, and not in the significances. Fifty degrees below zero meant eighty-odd degrees of frost. Such fact impressed him as being cold and uncomfortable, and that was all. It did not lead him to meditate upon his frailty as a creature of temperature, and upon man's frailty in general, able only to live within certain narrow limits of heat and cold; and from there on it did not lead him to the conjectural field of immortality and man's place in the universe. Fifty degrees below zero stood for a bite of frost that hurt and that must be guarded against by the use of mittens, ear flaps, warm moccasins, and thick socks. Fifty degrees below zero was to him just precisely fifty degrees below zero. That there should be anything more to it than that was a thought that never entered his head.

As he turned to go on, he spat speculatively. There was a sharp, explosive crackle that startled him. He spat again. And again, in the air, before it could fall to the snow, the spittle crackled. He knew that at fifty below spittle crackled on the snow, but this spittle had crackled in the air. Undoubtedly it was colder than fifty below—how much colder he did not know. But the temperature did not matter. He was bound for the old claim on the left fork of Henderson Creek, where the boys were already. They had come over across the divide from the Indian Creek country, while he had come the roundabout way to take a look at the possibilities of getting out logs in the spring from the islands in the Yukon. He would be in to camp by six o'clock; a bit after dark, it was true, but the boys would be there, a fire would be going, and a hot supper would be ready. As for lunch, he pressed his hand against the protruding bundle under his jacket. It was also under his shirt, wrapped up in a handkerchief and lying against the naked skin. It was the only way to keep the biscuits from freezing. He smiled agreeably to himself as he thought of those biscuits, each cut open and sopped in bacon grease, and each enclosing a generous slice of fried bacon.

He plunged in among the big spruce trees. The trail was faint. A foot of snow had fallen since the last sled had passed over, and he was glad he was without a sled, travelling light. In fact, he carried nothing but the lunch wrapped in the handkerchief. He was surprised, however, at the cold. It certainly was cold, he concluded, as he rubbed his numb nose and cheekbones with his mittened hand. He was a warm-whiskered man, but the hair on his face did not protect the high cheekbones and the eager nose that thrust itself aggressively into the frosty air.

At the man's heels trotted a dog, a big native husky, the proper wolf dog, gray-coated and without any visible or temperamental difference from its brother, the wild wolf. The animal was depressed by the tremendous cold. It knew that it was no time for travelling. Its instinct told it a truer tale than was told to the man by the man's judgment. In reality, it was not merely colder than fifty below zero; it was colder than sixty below, than seventy below. It was seventy-five below zero. Since the freezing point is thirty-two above zero, it meant that one hundred and seven degrees of frost obtained. The dog did not know anything about thermometers. Possibly in its brain there was no sharp consciousness of a condition of very cold such as was in the man's brain. But the brute had its instinct. It experienced a vague but menacing apprehension that subdued it and made it slink along at the man's heels, and that made it question eagerly every unwonted movement of the man as if expecting him to go into camp or to seek shelter somewhere and build a fire. The dog had learned fire, and it wanted fire, or else to burrow under the snow and cuddle its warmth away from the air.

The frozen moisture of its breathing had settled on its fur in a fine powder of frost, and especially were its jowls, muzzle, and eyelashes whitened by its crystalled breath. The man's red beard and mustache were likewise frosted, but more solidly, the deposit taking the form of ice and increasing with every warm, moist breath he exhaled. Also, the man was chewing tobacco, and the muzzle of ice held his lips so rigidly that he was unable to clear his chin when he expelled the juice. The result was that a crystal beard of the color and solidity of amber was increasing its length on his chin. If he fell down it would shatter itself, like glass, into brittle fragments. But he did not mind the appendage. It was the penalty all tobacco chewers paid in that country, and he had been out before in two cold snaps. They had not been so cold as this, he knew, but by the spirit thermometer at Sixty Mile he knew they had been registered at fifty below and at fifty-five.

He held on through the level stretch of woods for several miles, crossed a wide flat of nigger heads, and dropped down a bank to the frozen bed of a small stream. This was Henderson Creek, and he knew he was ten miles from the forks. He looked at his watch. It was ten o'clock. He was making four miles an hour, and he calculated that he would arrive at the forks at half-past twelve. He decided to celebrate that event by eating his lunch there.

The dog dropped in again at his heels, with a tail drooping discouragement, as the man swung along the creek bed. The furrow of the old sled trail was plainly visible, but a dozen inches of snow covered the marks of the last runners. In a month no man had come up or down that silent creek. The man held steadily on. He was not much given to thinking, and just then particularly he had nothing to think about save that he would eat lunch at the forks and that at six o'clock he would be in camp with the boys. There was nobody to talk to; and, had there been, speech would have been impossible because of the ice muzzle on his mouth. So he continued monotonously to chew tobacco and to increase the length of his amber beard.

Once in a while the thought reiterated itself that it was very cold and that he had never experienced such cold. As he walked along he rubbed his cheekbones and nose with the back of his mittened hand. He did this automatically, now and again changing hands. But, rub as he would, the instant he stopped his cheekbones went numb, and the following instant the end of his nose went numb. He was sure to frost his cheeks; he knew that, and experienced a pang of regret that he had not devised a nose strap of the sort Bud wore in cold snaps. Such a strap passed across the cheeks, as well, and saved them. But it didn't matter much, after all. What were frosted cheeks? A bit painful, that was all; they were never serious.

Empty as the man's mind was of thoughts, he was keenly observant, and he noticed the changes in the creek, the curves and bends and timber jams, and always he sharply noted where he placed his feet. Once, coming around a bend, he shied abruptly, like a startled horse, curved away from the place where he had been walking, and retreated several paces back along the trail. The creek he knew was frozen clear to the bottom—no creek could contain water in that arctic winter—but he knew also that there were springs that bubbled out from the hillsides and ran along under the snow and on top the ice of the creek. He knew that the coldest snaps never froze these springs, and he knew likewise their danger. They were traps. They hid pools of water under the snow that might be three inches deep, or three feet. Sometimes a skin of ice half an inch thick covered them, and in turn was covered by the snow. Sometimes there were alternate layers of water and ice skin, so that when one broke through he kept on breaking through for a while, sometimes wetting himself to the waist.

That was why he had shied in such panic. He had felt the give under his feet and heard the crackle of a snow-hidden ice skin. And to get his feet wet in such a temperature meant trouble and danger. At the very least it meant delay, for he would be forced to stop and build a fire, and under its protection to bare his feet while he dried his socks and moccasins. He stood and studied the creek bed and its banks, and decided that the flow of water came from the right. He reflected awhile, rubbing his nose and cheeks, then skirted to the left, stepping gingerly and testing the footing for each step. Once clear of the danger, he took a fresh chew of tobacco and swung along at his four-mile gait.

In the course of the next two hours he came upon several similar traps. Usually the snow above the hidden pools had a sunken, candied appearance that advertised the danger. Once again, however, he had a close call; and once, suspecting danger, he compelled the dog to go on in front. The dog did not want to go. It hung back until the man shoved it forward, and then it went quickly across the white, unbroken surface. Suddenly it broke through, floundered to one side, and got away to firmer footing. It had wet its forefeet and legs, and almost immediately the water that clung to it turned to ice. It made quick efforts to lick the ice off its legs, then dropped down in the snow and began to bite out the ice that had formed between the toes. This was a matter of instinct. To permit the ice to remain would mean sore feet. It did not know this. It merely obeyed the mysterious prompting that arose from the deep crypts of its being. But the man knew, having achieved a judgment on the subject, and he removed the mitten from his right hand and helped tear out the ice particles. He did not expose his fingers more than a minute, and was astonished at the swift numbness that smote them. It certainly was cold. He pulled on the mitten hastily, and beat the hand savagely across his chest.

At twelve o'clock the day was at its brightest. Yet the sun was too far south on its winter journey to clear the horizon. The bulge of the earth intervened between it and Henderson Creek, where the man walked under a clear sky at noon and cast no shadow. At half-past twelve, to the minute, he arrived at the forks of the creek. He was pleased at the speed he had made. If he kept it up, he would certainly be with the boys by six. He unbuttoned his jacket and shirt and drew forth his lunch. The action consumed no more than a quarter of a minute, yet in that brief moment the numbness laid hold of the exposed fingers. He did not put the mitten on, but, instead, struck the fingers a dozen sharp smashes against his leg. Then he sat down on a snow-covered log to eat. The sting that followed upon the striking of his fingers against his leg ceased so quickly that he was startled. He had had no chance to take a bite of biscuit. He struck the fingers repeatedly and returned them to the mitten, baring the other hand for the purpose of eating. He tried to take a mouthful, but the ice muzzle prevented. He had forgotten to build a fire and thaw out. He chuckled at his foolishness, and as he chuckled he noted the numbness creeping into the exposed fingers. Also, he noted that the stinging which had first come to his toes when he sat down was already passing away. He wondered whether the toes were warm or numb. He moved them inside the moccasins and decided that they were numb.

He pulled the mitten on hurriedly and stood up. He was a bit frightened. He stamped up and down until the stinging returned into the feet. It certainly was cold, was his thought. That man from Sulphur Creek had spoken the truth when telling how cold it sometimes got in the country. And he had laughed at him at the time! That showed one must not be too sure of things. There was no mistake about it, it *was* cold. He strode up and down, stamping his feet and threshing his arms, until reassured by the returning warmth. Then he got out matches and proceeded to make a fire. From the undergrowth, where high water of the previous spring had lodged a supply of seasoned twigs, he got his firewood. Working carefully from a small beginning, he soon had a roaring fire, over which he thawed the ice from his face and in the protection of which he ate his biscuits. For the moment the cold of space was outwitted. The dog took satisfaction in the fire, stretching out close enough for warmth and far enough away to escape being singed.

When the man had finished, he filled his pipe and took his comfortable time over a smoke. Then he pulled on his mittens, settled the ear flaps of his cap firmly about his ears, and took the creek trail up the left fork. The dog was disappointed and yearned back toward the fire. This man did not know cold. Possibly all the generations of his ancestry had been ignorant of cold, of real cold, of cold one hundred and seven degrees below freezing point. But the dog knew; all its ancestry knew, and it had inherited the knowledge. And it knew that it was not good to walk abroad in such fearful cold. It was the time to lie snug in a hole in the snow and wait for a curtain of cloud to be drawn across the face of outer space whence this cold came. On the other hand, there was no keen intimacy between the dog and the man. The one was the toil slave of the other, and the only caresses it had ever received were the caresses of the whip lash and of harsh and menacing throat sounds that threatened the whip lash. So the dog made no effort to communicate its apprehension to the man. It was not concerned in the welfare of the man; it was for its own sake that it yearned back toward the fire. But the man whistled, and spoke to it with the sound of whip lashes, and the dog swung in at the man's heels and followed after.

The man took a chew of tobacco and proceeded to start a new amber beard. Also, his moist breath quickly powdered with white his mustache, eyebrows, and lashes. There did not seem to be so many springs on the left fork of the Henderson, and for half an hour the man saw no signs of any. And then it happened. At a place where there were no signs, where the soft, unbroken snow seemed to advertise solidity beneath, the man broke through. It was not deep. He wet himself halfway to the knees before he floundered out to the firm crust.

He was angry, and cursed his luck aloud. He had hoped to get into camp with the boys at six o'clock, and this would delay him an hour, for he would have to build a fire and dry out his footgear. This was imperative at that low temperature—he knew that much; and he turned aside to the bank, which he climbed. On top, tangled in the underbrush about the trunks of several small spruce trees, was a high-water deposit of dry firewood—sticks and twigs, principally, but also larger portions of seasoned branches and fine, dry, last year's grasses. He threw down several large pieces on top of the snow. This served for a foundation and prevented the young flame from drowning itself in the snow it otherwise would melt. The flame he got by touching a match to a small shred of birch bark that he took from his pocket. This burned even more readily than paper. Placing it on the foundation, he fed the young flame with wisps of dry grass and with the tiniest dry twigs.

He worked slowly and carefully, keenly aware of his danger. Gradually, as the flame grew stronger, he increased the size of the twigs with which he fed it. He squatted in the snow, pulling the twigs out from their entanglement in the brush and feeding directly to the flame. He knew there must be no failure. When it is seventy-five below zero, a man must not fail in his first attempt to build a fire—that is, if his feet are wet. If his feet are dry, and he fails, he can run along the trail for half a mile and restore his circulation. But the circulation of wet and freezing feet cannot be restored by running when it is seventy-five below. No matter how fast he runs, the wet feet will freeze the harder.

All this the man knew. The old-timer on Sulphur Creek had told him about it the previous fall, and now he was appreciating the advice. Already all sensation had gone out of his feet. To build the fire he had been forced to remove his mittens, and the fingers had quickly gone numb. His pace of four miles an hour had kept his heart pumping blood to the surface of his body and to all the extremities. But the instant he stopped, the action of the pump eased down. The cold of space smote the unprotected tip of the planet, and he, being on that unprotected tip, received the full force of the blow. The blood of his body recoiled before it. The blood was alive, like the dog, and like the dog it wanted to hide away and cover itself up from the fearful cold. So long as he walked four miles an hour, he pumped that blood, willy-nilly, to the surface; but now it ebbed away and sank down into the recesses of his body. The extremities were the first to feel its absence. His wet feet froze the faster, and his exposed fingers numbed the faster, though they had not yet begun to freeze. Nose and cheeks were already freezing, while the skin of all his body chilled as it lost its blood.

But he was safe. Toes and nose and cheeks would be only touched by the frost, for the fire was beginning to burn with strength. He was feeding it with twigs the size of his finger. In another minute he would be able to feed it with branches the size of his wrist, and then he could remove his wet footgear, and, while it dried, he could keep his naked feet warm by the fire, rubbing them at first, of course, with snow. The fire was a success. He was safe. He remembered the advice of the old-timer on Sulphur Creek, and smiled. The old-timer had been very serious in laying down the law that no man must travel alone in the Klondike after fifty below. Well, here he was; he had had the accident; he was alone; and he had saved himself. Those old-timers were rather womanish, some of them, he thought. All a man had to do was to keep his head, and he was all right. Any man who was a man could travel alone. But it was surprising, the rapidity with which his cheeks and nose were freezing. And he had not thought his fingers could go lifeless in so short a time. Lifeless they were, for he could scarcely make them move together to grip a twig, and they seemed remote from his body and from him. When he touched a twig, he had to look and see whether or not he had hold of it. The wires were pretty well down between him and his finger ends.

All of which counted for little. There was the fire, snapping and crackling and promising life with every dancing flame. He started to untie his moccasins. They were coated with ice; the thick German socks were like sheaths of iron halfway to the knees; and the moccasin strings were like rods of steel all twisted and knotted as by some conflagration. For a moment he tugged with his numb fingers, then, realizing the folly of it, he drew his sheath knife.

But before he could cut the strings, it happened. It was his own fault or, rather, his mistake. He should not have built the fire under the spruce tree. He should have build it in the open. But it had been easier to pull the twigs from the brush and drop them directly on the fire. Now the tree under which he had done this carried a weight of snow on its boughs. No wind had blown for weeks, and each bough was fully freighted. Each time he had pulled a twig he had communicated a slight agitation to the tree—an imperceptible agitation, so far as he was concerned, but an agitation sufficient to bring about the disaster. High up in the tree one bough capsized its load of snow. This fell on the boughs beneath, capsizing them. This process continued, spreading out and involving the whole tree. It grew like an avalanche, and it descended without warning upon the man and the fire, and the fire was blotted out! Where it had burned was a mantle of fresh and disordered snow.

The man was shocked. It was as though he had just heard his own sentence of death. For a moment he sat and stared at the spot where the fire had been. Then he grew very calm. Perhaps the old-timer on Sulphur Creek was right. If he had only had a trail mate he would have been in no danger now. The trail mate could have built the fire. Well, it was up to him to build the fire over again, and this second time there must be no failure. Even if he succeeded, he would most likely lose some toes. His feet must be badly frozen by now, and there would be some time before the second fire was ready.

Such were his thoughts, but he did not sit and think them. He was busy all the time they were passing through his mind. He made a new foundation for a fire, this time in the open, where no treacherous tree could blot it out. Next he gathered dry grasses and tiny twigs from the high-water flotsam. He could not bring his fingers together to pull them out, but he was able to gather them by the handful. In this way he got many rotten twigs and bits of green moss that were undesirable, but it was the best he could do. He worked methodically, even collecting an armful of the larger branches to be used later when the fire gathered strength. And all the while the dog sat and watched him, a certain yearning wistfulness in its eyes, for it looked upon him as the fire provider, and the fire was slow in coming.

When all was ready, the man reached in his pocket for a second piece of birch bark. He knew the bark was there, and, though he could not feel it with his fingers, he could hear its crisp rustling as he fumbled for it. Try as he would, he could not clutch hold of it. And all the time, in his consciousness, was the knowledge that each instant his feet were freezing. This thought tended to put him in a panic, but he fought against it and kept calm. He pulled on his mittens with his teeth, and threshed his arms back and forth, beating his hands with all his might against his sides. He did this sitting down, and he stood up to do it; and all the while the dog sat in the snow, its wolf brush of a tail curled around warmly over its forefeet, its sharp wolf ears pricked forward intently as it watched the man. And the man, as he beat and threshed with his arms and hands, felt a great surge of envy as he regarded the creature that was warm and secure in its natural covering.

After a time he was aware of the first faraway signals of sensation in his beaten fingers. The faint tingling grew stronger till it evolved into a stinging ache that was excruciating, but which the man hailed with satisfaction. He stripped the mitten from his right hand and fetched forth the birch bark. The exposed fingers were quickly going numb again. Next he brought out his bunch of sulphur matches. But the tremendous cold had already driven the life out of his fingers. In his effort to separate one match from the others, the whole bunch fell in the snow. He tried to pick it out of the snow, but failed. The dead fingers could neither touch nor clutch. He was very careful. He drove the thought of his freezing feet, and nose, and cheeks, out of his mind, devoting his whole soul to the matches. He watched, using the sense of vision in place of that of touch, and when he saw his fingers on each side the bunch, he closed them—that is, he willed to close them, for the wires were down, and the fingers did not obey. He pulled the mitten on the right hand, and beat it fiercely against his knee. Then, with both mittened hands, he scooped the bunch of matches, along with much snow, into his lap. Yet he was no better off.

After some manipulation he managed to get the bunch between the heels of his mittened hands. In this fashion he carried it to his mouth. The ice crackled and snapped when by a violent effort he opened his mouth. He drew the lower jaw in, curled the upper lip out of the way, and scraped the bunch with his upper teeth in order to separate a match. He succeeded in getting one, which he dropped on his lap. He was no better off. He could not pick it up. Then he devised a way. He picked it up in his teeth and scratched it on his leg. Twenty times he scratched before he succeeded in lighting it. As it flamed he held it with his teeth to the birch bark. But the burning brimstone went up his nostrils and into his lungs, causing him to cough spasmodically. The match fell into the snow and went out.

The old-timer on Sulphur Creek was right, he thought in the moment of controlled despair that ensued: after fifty below, a man should travel with a partner. He beat his hands, but failed in exciting any sensation. Suddenly he bared both hands, removing the mittens with his teeth. He caught the whole bunch between the heels of his hands. His arm muscles not being frozen enabled him to press the hand heels tightly against the matches. Then he scratched the bunch along his leg. It flared into flame, seventy sulphur matches at once! There was no wind to blow them out. He kept his head to one side to escape the strangling fumes, and held the blazing bunch to the birch bark. As he so held it, he became aware of sensation in his hand. His flesh was burning. He could smell it. Deep down below the surface he could feel it. The sensation developed into pain that grew acute. And still he endured it, holding the flame of the matches clumsily to the bark that would not light readily because his own burning hands were in the way, absorbing most of the flame.

At last, when he could endure no more, he jerked his hands apart. The blazing matches fell sizzling into the snow, but the birch bark was alight. He began laying dry grasses and the tiniest twigs on the flame. He could not pick and choose, for he had to lift the fuel between the heels of his hands. Small pieces of rotten wood and green moss clung to the twigs, and he bit them off as well as he could with his teeth. He cherished the flame carefully and awkwardly. It meant life, and it must not perish. The withdrawal of blood from the surface of his body now made him begin to shiver, and he grew more awkward. A large piece of green moss fell squarely on the little fire. He tried to poke it out with his fingers, but his shivering frame made him poke too far, and he disrupted the nucleus of the little fire, the burning grasses and tiny twigs separating and scattering. He tried to poke them together again, but in spite of the tenseness of the effort, his shivering got away with him, and the twigs were hopelessly scattered. Each twig gushed a puff of smoke and went out. The fire provider had failed. As he looked apathetically about him, his eyes chanced on the dog, sitting across the ruins of the fire from him, in the snow, making restless, hunching movements, slightly lifting one forefoot and then the other, shifting its weight back and forth on them with wistful eagerness.

The sight of the dog put a wild idea into his head. He remembered the tale of the man, caught in a blizzard, who killed a steer and crawled inside the carcass, and so was saved. He would kill the dog and bury his hands in the warm body until the numbness went out of them. Then he could build another fire. He spoke to the dog, calling it to him; but in his voice was a strange note of fear that frightened the animal, who had never known the man to speak in such way before. Something was the matter, and its suspicious nature sensed danger—it knew not what danger, but somewhere, somehow, in its brain arose an apprehension of the man. It flattened its ears down at the sound of the man's voice, and its restless, hunching movements and the liftings and shiftings of its forefeet became more pronounced; but it would not come to the man. He got on his hands and knees and crawled toward the dog. This unusual posture again excited suspicion, and the animal sidled mincingly away.

The man sat up in the snow for a moment and struggled for calmness. Then he pulled on his mittens, by means of his teeth, and got upon his feet. He glanced down at first in order to assure himself that he was really standing up, for the absence of sensation in his feet left him unrelated to the earth. His erect position in itself started to drive the webs of suspicion from the dog's mind; and when he spoke peremptorily, with the sound of whip lashes in his voice, the dog rendered its customary allegiance and came to him. As it came within reaching distance, the man lost his control. His arms flashed out to the dog, and he experienced genuine surprise when he discovered that his hands could not clutch, that there was neither bend nor feeling in the fingers. He had forgotten for the moment that they were frozen and that they were freezing more and more. All this happened quickly, and before the animal could get away, he encircled its body with his arms. He sat down in the snow, and in this fashion held the dog, while it snarled and whined and struggled.

But it was all he could do, hold its body encircled in his arms and sit there. He realized that he could not kill the dog. There was no way to do it. With his helpless hands he could neither draw nor hold his sheath knife nor throttle the animal. He released it, and it plunged wildly away, with tail between its legs, and still snarling. It halted forty feet away and surveyed him curiously, with ears sharply pricked forward.

The man looked down at his hands in order to locate them, and found them hanging on the ends of his arms. It struck him as curious that one should have to use his eyes in order to find out where his hands were. He began threshing his arms back and forth, beating the mittened hands against his sides. He did this for five minutes, violently, and his heart pumped enough blood up to the surface to put a stop to his shivering. But no sensation was aroused in the hands. He had an impression that they hung like weights on the ends of his arms, but when he tried to run the impression down, he could not find it.

A certain fear of death, dull and oppressive, came to him. This fear quickly became poignant as he realized that it was no longer a mere matter of freezing his fingers and toes, or of losing his hands and feet, but that it was a matter of life and death with the chances against him. This threw him into a panic, and he turned and ran up the creek bed along the old, dim trail. The dog joined in behind and kept up with him. He ran blindly, without intention, in fear such as he had never known in his life. Slowly, as he plowed and floundered through the snow, he began to see things again—the banks of the creek, the old timber jams, the leafless aspens, and the sky. The running made him feel better. He did not shiver. Maybe, if he ran on, his feet would thaw out; and, anyway, if he ran far enough, he would reach camp and the boys. Without doubt he would lose some fingers and toes and some of his face; but the boys would take care of him, and save the rest of him when he got there. And at the same time there was another thought in his mind that said he would never get to the camp and the boys; that it was too many miles away, that the freezing had too great a start on him, and that he would soon be stiff and dead. This thought he kept in the background and refused to consider. Sometimes it pushed itself forward and demanded to be heard, but he thrust it back and strove to think of other things.

It struck him as curious that he could run at all on feet so frozen that he could not feel them when they struck the earth and took the weight of his body. He seemed to himself to skim along above the surface, and to have no connection with the earth. Somewhere he had once seen a winged Mercury, and he wondered if Mercury felt as he felt when skimming over the earth.

His theory of running until he reached camp and the boys had one flaw in it: he lacked the endurance. Several times he stumbled, and finally he tottered, crumpled up, and fell. When he tried to rise, he failed. He must sit and rest, he decided, and next time he would merely walk and keep on going. As he sat and regained his breath, he noted that he was feeling quite warm and comfortable. He was not shivering, and it even seemed that a warm glow had come to his chest and trunk. And yet, when he touched his nose or cheeks, there was no sensation. Running would not thaw them out. Nor would it thaw out his hands and feet. Then the thought came to him that the frozen portions of his body must be extending. He tried to keep this thought down, to forget it, to think of something else; he was aware of the panicky feeling that it caused, and he was afraid of the panic. But the thought asserted itself, and persisted, until it produced a vision of his body totally frozen. This was too much, and he made another wild run along the trail. Once he slowed down to a walk, but the thought of the freezing extending itself made him run again.

And all the time the dog ran with him, at his heels. When he fell down a second time, it curled its tail over its forefeet and sat in front of him, facing him, curiously eager and intent. The warmth and security of the animal angered him, and he cursed it till it flattened down its ears appeasingly. This time the shivering came more quickly upon the man. He was losing in his battle with the frost. It was creeping into his body from all sides. The thought of it drove him on, but he ran no more than a hundred feet, when he staggered and pitched headlong. It was his last panic. When he had recovered his breath and control, he sat up and entertained in his mind the conception of meeting death with dignity. However, the conception did not come to him in such terms. His idea of it was that he had been making a fool of himself, running around like a chicken with its head cut off—such was the simile that occurred to him. Well, he was bound to freeze anyway, and he might as well take it decently. With this new-found peace of mind came the first glimmerings of drowsiness. A good idea, he thought, to sleep off to death. It was like taking an anesthetic. Freezing was not so bad as people thought. There were lots worse ways to die.

He pictured the boys finding his body next day. Suddenly he found himself with them, coming along the trail and looking for himself. And, still with them, he came around a turn in the trail and found himself lying in the snow. He did not belong with himself any more, for even then he was out of himself, standing with the boys and looking at himself in the snow. It certainly was cold, was his thought. When he got back to the States he could tell the folks what real cold was. He drifted on from this to a vision of the old-timer on Sulphur Creek. He could see him quite clearly, warm and comfortable, and smoking a pipe.

"You were right, old hoss; you were right," the man mumbled to the old-timer of Sulphur Creek.

Then the man drowsed off into what seemed to him the most comfortable and satisfying sleep he had ever known. The dog sat facing him and waiting. The brief day drew to a close in a long, slow twilight. There were no signs of a fire to be made, and, besides, never in the dog's experience had it known a man to sit like that in the snow and make no fire. As the twilight drew on, its eager yearning for the fire mastered it, and with a great lifting and shifting of forefeet, it whined softly, then flattened its ears down in anticipation of being chidden by the man. But the man remained silent. Later the dog whined loudly. And still later it crept close to the man and caught the scent of death. This made the animal bristle and back away. A little longer it delayed, howling under the stars that leaped and danced and shone brightly in the cold sky. Then it turned and trotted up the trail in the direction of the camp it knew, where were the other food providers and fire providers.

1908

FLUSH OF GOLD

Lon McFane was a bit grumpy, what of losing his tobacco pouch, or else he might have told me, before we got to it, something about the cabin at Surprise Lake. All day, turn and turn about, we had spelled each other at going to the fore and breaking trail for the dogs. It was heavy snow-shoe work, and did not tend to make a man voluble, yet Lon McFane might have found breath enough at noon, when we stopped to boil coffee, with which to tell me. But he didn't. Surprise Lake?—it was Surprise Cabin to me. I had never heard of it before. I confess I was a bit tired. I had been looking for Lon to stop and make camp any time for an hour; but I had too much pride to suggest making camp or to ask him his intentions; and yet he was my man, hired at a handsome wage to mush my dogs for me and to obey my

From *Lost Face*, copyright 1910 by The Macmillan Company.

commands. I guess I was a bit grumpy myself. He said nothing, and I was resolved to ask nothing, even if we tramped on all night.

We came upon the cabin abruptly. For a week of trail we had met no one, and, in my mind, there had been little likelihood of meeting any one for a week to come. And yet there it was, right before my eyes, a cabin, with a dim light in the window and smoke curling up from the chimney.

"Why didn't you tell me—" I began, but was interrupted by Lon, who muttered:—

"Surprise Lake—it lies up a small feeder half a mile on. It's only a pond."

"Yes, but the cabin—who lives in it?"

"A woman," was the answer, and the next moment Lon had rapped on the door, and a woman's voice bade him enter.

"Have you seen Dave recently?" she asked.

"Nope," Lon answered carelessly. "I've been in the other direction, down Circle City way. Dave's up Dawson way, ain't he?"

The woman nodded, and Lon fell to unharnessing the dogs, while I unlashed the sled and carried the camp outfit into the cabin. The cabin was a large, one-room affair, and the woman was evidently alone in it. She pointed to the stove, where water was already boiling, and Lon set about the preparation of supper, while I opened the fish-bag and fed the dogs. I looked for Lon to introduce us, and was vexed that he did not, for they were evidently old friends.

"You are Lon McFane, aren't you?" I heard her ask him. "Why, I remember you now. The last time I saw you it was on a steamboat, wasn't it? I remember. . . ."

Her speech seemed suddenly to be frozen by the spectacle of dread which, I knew, from the terror I saw mounting in her eyes, must be on her inner vision. To my astonishment, Lon was affected by her words and manner. His face showed desperate, for all his voice sounded hearty and genial, as he said:—

"The last time we met was at Dawson, Queen's Jubilee, or Birthday, or something—don't you remember?—the canoe races in the river, and the obstacle races down the main street?"

The terror faded out of her eyes and her whole body relaxed. "Oh, yes, I do remember," she said. "And you won one of the canoe races."

"How's Dave been makin' it lately? Strikin' it as rich as ever, I suppose?" Lon asked, with apparent irrelevance.

She smiled and nodded, and then, noticing that I had unlashed the bed roll, she indicated the end of the cabin where I might spread it. Her own bunk, I noticed, was made up at the opposite end.

"I thought it was Dave coming when I heard your dogs," she said.

After that she said nothing, contenting herself with watching Lon's cooking operations, and listening the while as for the sound of dogs along the trail. I lay back on the blankets and smoked and watched. Here was mystery; I could make that much out, but no more could I make out. Why in the deuce hadn't Lon given me the tip before we arrived? I looked at her face, unnoticed by her, and the longer I looked the harder it was to take my eyes away. It was a wonderfully beautiful face, unearthly, I may say, with a light in it or an expression or something that was never on land or sea. Fear and terror had completely vanished, and it was a placidly beautiful face—if by "placid" one can characterize that intangible and occult something that I cannot say was a radiance or a light any more than I can say it was an expression.

Abruptly, as if for the first time, she became aware of my presence.

"Have you seen Dave recently?" she asked me. It was on the tip of my tongue to say "Dave who?" when Lon coughed in the smoke that arose from the sizzling bacon. The bacon might have caused that cough, but I took it as a hint and left my question unasked. "No, I haven't," I answered. "I'm new in this part of the country—"

"But you don't mean to say," she interrupted, "that you've never heard of Dave—of Big Dave Walsh?"

"You see," I apologized, "I'm new in the country. I've put in most of my time in the Lower Country, down Nome way."

"Tell him about Dave," she said to Lon.

Lon seemed put out, but he began in that hearty, genial manner that I had noticed before. It seemed a shade too hearty and genial, and it irritated me.

"Oh, Dave is a fine man," he said. "He's a man, every inch of him, and he stands six feet four in his socks. His word is as good as his bond. The man lies who ever says Dave told a lie, and that man will have to fight with me, too, as well—if there's anything left of him when Dave gets done with him. For Dave is a fighter. Oh, yes, he's a scrapper from way back. He got a grizzly with a '38 popgun. He got clawed some, but he knew what he was doin'. He went into the cave on purpose to get that grizzly. 'Fraid of nothing. Free an' easy with his money, or his last shirt an' match when out of money. Why, he drained Surprise Lake here in three weeks an' took out ninety thousand, didn't he?" She flushed and nodded her head proudly. Through his recital she had followed every word with keenest interest. "An' I must say," Lon went on, "that I was disappointed sore on not meeting Dave here to-night."

Lon served supper at one end of the table of whip-sawed spruce, and we fell to eating. A howling of the dogs took the woman to the door. She opened it an inch and listened.

"Where is Dave Walsh?" I asked, in an undertone. "Dead," Lon answered. "In hell, maybe. I don't know. Shut up."

"But you just said that you expected to meet him here to-night," I challenged.

"Oh, shut up, can't you," was Lon's reply, in the same cautious undertone.

The woman had closed the door and was returning, and I sat and meditated upon the fact that this man who told me to shut up received from me a salary of two hundred and fifty dollars a month and his board.

Lon washed the dishes, while I smoked and watched the woman. She seemed more beautiful than ever—strangely and weirdly beautiful, it is true. After looking at her steadfastly for five minutes, I was compelled to come back to the real world and to glance at Lon McFane. This enabled me to know, without discussion, that the woman, too, was real. At first I had taken her for the wife of Dave Walsh; but if Dave Walsh were dead, as Lon had said, then she could be only his widow.

It was early to bed, for we faced a long day on the morrow; and as Lon crawled in beside me under the blankets, I ventured a question.

"That woman's crazy, isn't she?"

"Crazy as a loon," he answered.

And before I could formulate my next question, Lon McFane, I swear, was off to sleep. He always went to sleep that way—just crawled into the blankets, closed his eyes, and was off, a demure little heavy breathing rising on the air. Lon never snored.

And in the morning it was quick breakfast, feed the dogs, load the sled, and hit the trail. We said good-by as we pulled out, and the woman stood in the doorway and watched us off. I carried the vision of her unearthly beauty away with me, just under my eyelids, and all I had to do, any time, was to close them and see her again. The way was unbroken, Surprise Lake being far off the travelled trails, and Lon and I took turn about at beating down the feathery snow with our big, webbed shoes so that the dogs could travel. "But you said you expected to meet Dave Walsh at the cabin," trembled on the tip of my tongue a score of times. I did not utter it. I would wait until we knocked off in the middle of the day. And when the middle of the day came, we went right on, for, as Lon explained, there was a camp of moose hunters at the forks of the Teelee, and we could make there by dark. But we didn't make there by dark, for Bright, the lead-dog, broke his shoulder-blade, and we lost an hour over him before we shot him. Then, crossing a timber jam on the frozen bed of the Teelee, the sled suffered a wrenching capsize, and it was a case of make camp and repair the runner. I cooked supper and fed the dogs while Lon made the repairs, and together we got in the night's supply of ice and firewood. Then we sat on our blankets, our moccasins steaming on upended sticks before the fire, and had our evening smoke.

"You didn't know her?" Lon queried suddenly. I shook my head.

"You noticed the color of her hair and eyes and her complexion, well, that's where she got her name—she was like the first warm glow of a golden sunrise. She was called Flush of Gold. Ever heard of her?"

Somewhere I had a confused and misty remembrance of having heard the name, yet it meant nothing to me. "Flush of Gold," I repeated; "sounds like the name of a dance-house girl." Lon shook his head. "No, she was a good woman, at least in that sense, though she sinned greatly just the same."

"But why do you speak always of her in the past tense, as though she were dead?"

"Because of the darkness on her soul that is the same as the darkness of death. The Flush of Gold that I knew, that Dawson knew, and that Forty Mile knew before that, is dead. That dumb, lunatic creature we saw last night was not Flush of Gold."

"And Dave?" I queried.

"He built that cabin," Lon answered. "He built it for her . . . and for himself. He is dead. She is waiting for him there. She half believes he is not dead. But who can know the whim of a crazed mind? Maybe she wholly believes he is not dead. At any rate, she waits for him there in the cabin he built. Who would rouse the dead? Then who would rouse the living that are dead? Not I, and that is why I let on to expect to meet Dave Walsh there last night. I'll bet a stack that I'd a been more surprised than she if I *had* met him there last night."

"I do not understand," I said. "Begin at the beginning, as a white man should, and tell me the whole tale."

And Lon began. "Victor Chauvet was an old Frenchman—born in the south of France. He came to California in the days of gold. He was a pioneer. He found no gold, but, instead, became a maker of bottled sunshine—in short, a grape-grower and wine-maker. Also, he followed gold excitements. That is what brought him to Alaska in the early days, and over the Chilcoot and down the Yukon long before the Carmack strike. The old town site of Ten Mile was Chauvet's. He carried the first mail into Arctic City. He staked those coal-mines on the Porcupine a dozen years ago. He grubstaked Loftus into the Nippennuck Country. Now it happened that

Victor Chauvet was a good Catholic, loving two things in this world, wine and woman. Wine of all kinds he loved, but of woman, only one, and she was the mother of Marie Chauvet."

Here I groaned aloud, having meditated beyond self-control over the fact that I paid this man two hundred and fifty dollars a month.

"What's the matter now?" he demanded.

"Matter?" I complained. "I thought you were telling the story of Flush of Gold. I don' want a biography of your old French winebibber."

Lon calmly lighted his pipe, took one good puff, then put the pipe aside. "And you asked me to begin at the beginning," he said.

"Yes," said I; "the beginning."

"And the beginning of Flush of Gold is the old French winebibber, for he was the father of Marie Chauvet, and Marie Chauvet was the Flush of Gold. What more do you want? Victor Chauvet never had much luck to speak of. He managed to live, and to get along, and to take good care of Marie, who resembled the one woman he had loved. He took very good care of her. Flush of Gold was the pet name he gave her. Flush of Gold Creek was named after her—Flush of Gold town site, too. The old man was great on town sites, only he never landed them.

"Now, honestly," Lon said, with one of his lightning changes, "you've seen her, what do you think of her—of her looks, I mean? How does she strike your beauty sense?"

"She is remarkably beautiful," I said. "I never saw anything like her in my life. In spite of the fact, last night, that I guessed she was mad, I could not keep my eyes off of her. It wasn't curiosity. It was wonder, sheer wonder, she was so strangely beautiful."

"She was more strangely beautiful before the darkness fell upon her," Lon said softly. "She was truly the Flush of Gold. She turned all men's hearts . . . and heads. She recalls, with an effort, that I once won a canoe race at Dawson—I, who once loved her, and was told by her of her love for me. It was her beauty that made all men love her. She'd a got the apple from Paris, on application, and there wouldn't have been any Trojan War, and to top it off she'd have thrown Paris down. And now she lives in darkness, and she who was always fickle, for the first time is constant—and constant to a shade, to a dead man she does not realize is dead.

"And this is the way it was. You remember what I said last night of Dave Walsh—Big Dave Walsh? He was all that I said, and more, many times more. He came into this country in the late eighties—that's a pioneer for you. He was twenty years old then. He was a young bull. When he was twenty-five he could lift clear of the ground thirteen fifty-pound sacks of flour. At first, each fall of the year, famine drove him out. It was a lone land in those days. No river steamboats, no grub, nothing but salmon bellies and rabbit tracks. But after famine chased him out three years, he said he'd had enough of being chased; and the next year he stayed. He lived on straight meat when he was lucky enough to get it; he ate eleven dogs that winter; but he stayed. And the next winter he stayed, and the next. He never did leave the country again. He was a bull, a great bull. He could kill the strongest man in the country with hard work. He could outpack a Chilcat Indian, he could outpaddle a Stick, and he could travel all day with wet feet when the thermometer registered fifty below zero, and that's going some, I tell you, for vitality. You'd freeze your feet at twenty-five below if you wet them and tried to keep on.

"Dave Walsh was a bull for strength. And yet he was soft and easy-natured. Anybody could do him, the latest short-horn in camp could lie his last dollar out of him. 'But it doesn't worry me,' he had a way of laughing off his softness; 'it doesn't keep me awake nights.' Now don't get the idea that he had no backbone. You remember about the bear he went after with the popgun. When it came to fighting, Dave was the blamedest ever. He was the limit, if by that I may describe his unlimitedness when he got into action. He was easy and kind with the weak, but the strong had to give trail when he went by. And he was a man that men liked, which is the finest word of all, a man's man.

"Dave never took part in the big stampede to Dawson when Carmack made the Bonanza strike. You see, Dave was just then over on Mammon Creek strikin' it himself. He discovered Mammon Creek. Cleaned eighty-four thousand up that winter, and opened up the claim so that it promised a couple of hundred thousand for the next winter. Then, summer bein' on and the ground sloshy, he took a trip up the Yukon to Dawson to see what Carmack's strike looked like. And there he saw Flush of Gold. I remember the night. I shall always remember. It was something sudden, and it makes one shiver to think of a strong man with all the strength withered out of him by one glance from the soft eyes of a weak, blond, female creature like Flush of Gold. It was at her dad's cabin, old Victor Chauvet's. Some friend had brought Dave along to talk over town sites on Mammon Creek. But little talking did he do, and what he did was mostly gibberish. I tell you the sight of Flush of Gold had sent Dave clean daffy. Old Victor Chauvet insisted after Dave left that he had been drunk. And so he had. He was drunk, but Flush of Gold was the strong drink that made him so.

"That settled it, that first glimpse he caught of her. He did not start back down the Yukon in a week, as he had intended. He lingered on a month, two months, all summer. And we who had suffered understood, and wondered what the outcome would be. Undoubtedly, in our minds, it seemed that Flush of Gold had met her master. And why not? There was romance sprinkled all over Dave Walsh. He was a Mammon King, he had made the Mammon Creek strike; he was an old sour dough, one of the oldest pioneers in the land—men turned to look at him when he went by, and said to one another in awed undertones, 'There goes Dave Walsh.' And why not? He stood six feet four; he had yellow hair himself that curled on his neck; and he was a bull—a yellow-maned bull just turned thirty-one.

"And Flush of Gold loved him, and, having danced him through a whole summer's courtship, at the end their engagement was made known. The fall of the year was at hand, Dave had to be back for the winter's work on Mammon Creek, and Flush of Gold refused to be married right away. Dave put Dusky Burns in charge of the Mammon Creek claim, and himself lingered on in Dawson. Little use. She wanted her freedom a while longer; she must have it, and she would not marry until next year. And so, on the first ice, Dave Walsh went alone down the Yukon behind his dogs, with the understanding that the marriage would take place when he arrived on the first steamboat of the next year.

"Now Dave was as true as the Pole Star, and she was as false as a magnetic needle in a cargo of loadstone. Dave was as steady and solid as she was fickle and fly-away, and in some way Dave, who never doubted anybody, doubted her. It was the jealousy of his love, perhaps, and maybe it was the message ticked off from her soul to his; but at any rate Dave was worried by fear of her inconstancy. He was afraid to trust her till the next year, he had so to trust her, and he was pretty well beside himself. Some of it I got from old Victor Chauvet afterwards, and from all that I have pieced together I conclude that there was something of a scene before Dave pulled north with his dogs. He stood up before the old Frenchman, with Flush of Gold beside him, and announced that they were plighted to each other. He was very dramatic, with fire in his eyes, old Victor said. He talked something about 'until death do us part'; and old Victor especially remembered that at one place Dave took her by the shoulder with his great paw and almost shook her as he said: 'Even unto death are you mine, and I would rise from the grave to claim you.' Old Victor distinctly remembered those words: 'Even unto death are you mine, and I would rise from the grave to claim you.' And he told me afterwards that Flush of Gold was pretty badly frightened, and that he afterwards took Dave to one side privately and told him that that wasn't the way to hold Flush of Gold—that he must humor her and gentle her if he wanted to keep her.

"There is no discussion in my mind but that Flush of Gold was frightened. She was a savage herself in her treatment of men, while men had always treated her as a soft and tender and too utterly-utter something that must not be hurt. She didn't know what harshness was . . . until Dave Walsh, standing his six feet four, a big bull, gripped her and pawed her and assured her that she was his until death, and then some. And besides, in Dawson, that winter, was a music-player,—one of those macaroni-eating, greasy-tenor-Eyetalian-dago propositions,—and Flush of Gold lost her heart to him. Maybe it was only fascination—I don't know. Sometimes it seems to me that she really did love Dave Walsh. Perhaps it was because he had frightened her with that even-unto-death, rise-from-the-grave stunt of his that she in the end inclined to the dago music-player. But it is all guesswork, and the facts are sufficient. He wasn't a dago; he was a Russian count—this was straight; and he wasn't a professional piano-player or anything of the sort. He played the violin and the piano, and he sang,—sang well,—but it was for his own pleasure and for the pleasure of those he sang for. He had money, too—and right here let me say that Flush of Gold never cared a rap for money. She was fickle, but she was never sordid.

"But to be getting along. She was plighted to Dave, and Dave was coming up on the first steamboat to get her—that was the summer of '98, and the first steamboat was to be expected the middle of June. And Flush of Gold was afraid to throw Dave down and face him afterwards. It was all planned suddenly. The Russian music-player, the Count, was her obedient slave. She planned it, I know. I learned as much from old Victor afterwards. The Count took his orders from her, and caught that first steamboat down. It was the *Golden Rocket*. And so did Flush of Gold catch it. And so did I. I was going to Circle City, and I was flabbergasted when I found Flush of Gold on board. I didn't see her name down on the passenger list. She was with the Count fellow all the time, happy and smiling, and I noticed that the Count fellow was down on the list as having his wife along. There it was, stateroom, number, and all. The first I knew that he was married, only I didn't see anything of the wife . . . unless Flush of Gold was so counted. I wondered if they'd got married ashore before starting. There'd been talk about them in Dawson, you see, and bets had been laid that the Count fellow had cut Dave out.

"I talked with the purser. He didn't know anything more about it than I did; he didn't know Flush of Gold, anyway, and besides, he was almost rushed to death. You know what a Yukon steamboat is, but you can't guess what the *Golden Rocket* was when it left Dawson that June of 1898. She was a hummer. Being the first steamer out, she carried all the scurvy patients and hospital wrecks. Then she must have carried a couple of millions of Klondike dust and nuggets, to say nothing of a packed and jammed passenger list, deck passengers galore, and bucks and squaws and dogs without end. And she was loaded down to the guards with freight and baggage. There was a mountain of the same on the fore-lower-deck, and each little stop along the way added to it. I saw the box come aboard at Teelee Portage, and I knew it for what it was, though I little guessed the joker that was in it. And they piled it on top of everything else on the fore-lower-deck, and they didn't pile it any too securely either. The mate expected to come back to it again, and then forgot about it. I thought at the time that there was something familiar about the big husky dog that climbed over the baggage and freight and lay down next to the box. And then we passed the *Glendale*, bound up for Dawson. As she saluted us, I thought of Dave on board of her and hurrying to Dawson for Flush of Gold. I turned and looked at her where she stood by the rail. Her eyes were bright, but she looked a bit frightened by the sight of the other steamer, and she was leaning closely to the Count fellow as for protection. She needn't have leaned so safely against him, and I needn't have been so sure of a disappointed Dave Walsh arriving at Dawson. For Dave Walsh wasn't on the *Glendale*. There were a lot of things I didn't know, but was soon to know—for instance, that the pair was not yet married. Inside half an hour preparations for the marriage took place. What of the sick men in the main cabin, and of the crowded condition of the *Golden Rocket*, the likeliest place for the ceremony was found forward, on the lower deck, in an open space next to the rail and gang-plank and shaded by the mountain of freight with the big box on top and the sleeping dog beside it. There was a missionary on board, getting off at Eagle City, which was the next stop, so they had to use him quick. That's what they'd planned to do, get married on the boat.

"But I've run ahead of the facts. The reason Dave Walsh wasn't on the *Glendale* was because he was on the *Golden Rocket*. It was this way. After loiterin' in Dawson on account of Flush of Gold, he went down to Mammon Creek on the ice. And there he found Dusky Burns doing so well with the claim, there was no need for him to be around. So he put some grub on the sled, harnessed the dogs, took an Indian along, and pulled out for Surprise Lake. He always had a liking for that section. Maybe you don't know how the creek turned out to be a four-flusher; but the prospects were good at the time, and Dave proceeded to build his cabin and hers. That's the cabin we slept in. After he finished it, he went off on a moose hunt to the forks of the Teelee, takin' the Indian along.

"And this is what happened. Came on a cold snap. The juice went down forty, fifty, sixty below zero. I remember that snap—I was at Forty Mile; and I remember the very day. At eleven o'clock in the morning the spirit thermometer at the N. A. T. & T. Company's store went down to seventy-five below zero. And that morning, near the forks of the Teelee, Dave Walsh was out after moose with that blessed Indian of his. I got it all from the Indian afterwards—we made a trip over the ice together to Dyea. That morning Mr. Indian broke through the ice and wet himself to the waist. Of course he began to freeze right away. The proper thing was to build a fire. But Dave Walsh was a bull. It was only half a mile to camp, where a fire was already burning. What was the good of building another? He threw Mr. Indian over his shoulder—and ran with him—half a mile—with the thermometer at seventy-five below. You know what that means. Suicide. There's no other name for it. Why, that buck Indian weighed over two hundred himself, and

Dave ran half a mile with him. Of course he froze his lungs. Must have frozen them near solid. It was a tomfool trick for any man to do. And anyway, after lingering horribly for several weeks, Dave Walsh died.

"The Indian didn't know what to do with the corpse. Ordinarily he'd have buried him and let it go at that. But he knew that Dave Walsh was a big man, worth lots of money, a *hi-yu skookum* chief. Likewise he'd seen the bodies of other *hi-yu skookums* carted around the country like they were worth something. So he decided to take Dave's body to Forty Mile, which was Dave's headquarters. You know how the ice is on the grass roots in this country—well, the Indian planted Dave under a foot of soil—in short, he put Dave on ice. Dave could have stayed there a thousand years and still been the same old Dave. You understand—just the same as a refrigerator. Then the Indian brings over a whipsaw from the cabin at Surprise Lake and makes lumber enough for the box. Also, waiting for the thaw, he goes out and shoots about ten thousand pounds of moose. This he keeps on ice, too. Came the thaw. The Teelee broke. He built a raft and loaded it with the meat, the big box with Dave inside, and Dave's team of dogs, and away they went down the Teelee.

"The raft got caught on a timber jam and hung up two days. It was scorching hot weather, and Mr. Indian nearly lost his moose meat. So when he got to Teelee Portage he figured a steamboat would get to Forty Mile quicker than his raft. He transferred his cargo, and there you are, fore-lower deck of the *Golden Rocket*, Flush of Gold being married, and Dave Walsh in his big box casting the shade for her. And there's one thing I clean forgot. No wonder I thought the husky dog that came aboard at Teelee Portage was familiar. It was Pee-lat, Dave Walsh's lead-dog and favorite—a terrible fighter, too. He was lying down beside the box.

"Flush of Gold caught sight of me, called me over, shook hands with me, and introduced me to the Count. She was beautiful. I was as mad for her then as ever. She smiled into my eyes and said I must sign as one of the witnesses. And there was no refusing her. She was ever a child, cruel as children are cruel. Also, she told me she was in possession of the only two bottles of champagne in Dawson—or that had been in Dawson the night before; and before I knew it I was scheduled to drink her and the Count's health. Everybody crowded 'round, the captain of the steamboat, very prominent, trying to ring in on the wine, I guess. It was a funny wedding. On the upper deck the hospital wrecks, with various feet in the grave, gathered and looked down to see. There were Indians all jammed in the circle, too, big bucks, and their squaws and kids, to say nothing of about twenty-five snarling wolf-dogs. The missionary lined the two of them up and started in with the service. And just then a dog-fight started, high up on the pile of freight—Pee-lat lying beside the big box, and a white-haired brute belonging to one of the Indians. The fight wasn't explosive at all. The brutes just snarled at each other from a distance—tapping at each other long-distance, you know, saying dast and dassent, dast and dassent. The noise was rather disturbing, but you could hear the missionary's voice above it.

"There was no particularly easy way of getting at the two dogs, except from the other side of the pile. But nobody was on that side—everybody watching the ceremony, you see. Even then everything might have been all right if the captain hadn't thrown a club at the dogs. That was what precipitated everything. As I say, if the captain hadn't thrown that club, nothing might have happened.

"The missionary had just reached the point where he was saying 'In sickness and in health,' and 'Until death do us part.' And just then the captain threw the club. I saw the whole thing. It landed on Pee-lat, and at that instant the white brute jumped him. The club caused it. Their two bodies struck the box, and it began to slide, its lower end tilting down. It was a long oblong box, and it slid down slowly until it reached the perpendicular, when it came down on the run. The onlookers on that side the circle had time to get out from under. Flush of Gold and the Count, on the opposite side of the circle, were facing the box; the missionary had his back to it. The box must have fallen ten feet straight up and down, and it hit end on.

"Now mind you, not one of us knew that Dave Walsh was dead. We thought he was on the *Glendale*, bound for Dawson. The missionary had edged off to one side, and so Flush of Gold faced the box when it struck. It was like in a play. It couldn't have been better planned. It struck on end, and on the right end; the whole front of the box came off; and out swept Dave Walsh on his feet, partly wrapped in a blanket, his yellow hair flying and showing bright in the sun. Right out of the box, on his feet, he swept upon Flush of Gold. She didn't know he was dead, but it was unmistakable, after hanging up two days on a timber jam, that he was rising all right from the dead to claim her. Possibly that is what she thought. At any rate, the sight froze her. She couldn't move. She just sort of wilted and watched Dave Walsh coming for her. And he got her. It looked almost as though he threw his arms around her, but whether or not this happened, down to the deck they went together. We had to drag Dave Walsh's body clear before we could get hold of her. She was in a faint, but it would have been just as well if she had never come out of that faint; for when she did, she fell to screaming the way insane people do. She kept it up for hours, till she was exhausted. Oh, yes, she recovered. You saw her last night, and know how much recovered she is. She is not violent, it is true, but she lives in darkness. She believes that she is waiting for Dave Walsh, and so she waits in the cabin he built for her. She is no longer fickle. It is nine years now that she had been faithful to Dave Walsh, and the outlook is that she'll be faithful to him to the end."

Lon McFane pulled down the top of the blankets and prepared to crawl in.

"We have her grub hauled to her each year," he added, "and in general keep an eye on her. Last night was the first time she ever recognized me, though."

"Who are the *we?*" I asked.

"Oh," was the answer, "the Count and old Victor Chauvet and me. Do you know, I think the Count is the one to be really sorry for. Dave Walsh never did know that she was false to him. And she does not suffer. Her darkness is merciful to her."

I lay silently under the blankets for the space of a minute.

"Is the Count still in the country?" I asked.

But there was a gentle sound of heavy breathing, and I knew Lon McFane was asleep.

1908

LOST FACE

It was the end. Subienkow had traveled a long trail of bitterness and horror, homing like a dove for the capitals of Europe, and here, farther away than ever, in Russian America, the trail ceased. He sat in the snow, arms tied behind him, waiting the torture. He stared curiously before him at a huge Cossack, prone in the snow, moaning in his pain. The men had finished handling the giant and turned him over to the women. That they exceeded the fiendishness of the men the man's cries attested.

Subienkow looked on and shuddered. He was not afraid to die. He had carried his life too long in his hands, on that weary trail from Warsaw to Nulato, to shudder at mere dying. But he objected to the torture. It offended his soul. And this offense, in turn, was not due to the mere pain he must endure, but to the sorry spectacle the pain would make of him. He knew that he would pray, and beg, and entreat, even as Big Ivan and the others that had gone before. This would not be nice. To pass out bravely and cleanly, with a smile and a jest—ah, that would have been the way. But to lose control, to have his soul upset by the pangs of the flesh, to screech and gibber like an ape, to become the veriest beast—ah, that was what was so terrible.

There had been no chance to escape. From the beginning, when he dreamed the fiery dream of Poland's independence, he had become a puppet in the hands of fate. From the beginning, at Warsaw, at St. Petersburg, in the Siberian mines, in Kamchatka, on the crazy boats of the fur thieves, fate had been driving him to this end. Without doubt, in the foundations of the world was graved this end for him—for him, who was so fine and sensitive, whose nerves scarcely sheltered under his skin, who was a dreamer and a poet and an artist. Before he was dreamed of, it had been determined that the quivering bundle of sensitiveness that constituted him should be doomed to live in raw and howling savagery, and to die in this far land of night, in this dark place beyond the last boundaries of the world.

He sighed. So that thing before him was Big Ivan—Big Ivan the giant, the man without nerves, the man of iron, the Cossack turned freebooter of the seas, who was as phlegmatic as an ox, with a nervous system so low that what was pain to ordinary men was scarcely a tickle to him. Well, well, trust these Nulato Indians to find Big Ivan's nerves and trace them to the roots of his quivering soul. They were certainly doing it. It was inconceivable that a man could suffer so much and yet live. Big Ivan was paying for his low order of nerves. Already he had lasted twice as long as any of the others.

Subienkow felt that he could not stand the Cossack's sufferings much longer. Why didn't Ivan die? He would go mad if that screaming did not cease. But when it did cease, his turn would come. And there was Yakaga awaiting him, too, grinning at him even now in anticipation—Yakaga, whom only last week he had kicked out of the fort, and upon whose face he had laid the lash of his dog whip. Yakaga would attend to him. Doubtlessly Yakaga was saving for him more refined tortures, more exquisite nerve-racking. Ah! That must have been a good one, from the way Ivan screamed. The squaws bending over him stepped back with laughter and clapping of hands. Subienkow saw the monstrous thing that had been perpetrated, and began to laugh hysterically. The Indians looked at him in wonderment that he should laugh. But Subienkow could not stop.

This would never do. He controlled himself, the spasmodic twitchings slowly dying away. He strove to think of other things, and began reading back in his own life. He remembered his mother and his father, and the little spotted pony, and the French tutor who had taught him dancing and sneaked him an old worn copy of Voltaire. Once more he saw Paris, and dreary London, and gay Vienna, and Rome. And once more he saw that wild group of youths who had dreamed, even as he, the dream of an independent Poland with a king of Poland on the throne at Warsaw. Ah, there it was that the long trail began. Well, he had lasted longest. One by one, beginning with the two executed at St. Petersburg, he took up the count of the passing of those brave spirits. Here one had been beaten to death by a jailer, and there, on that bloodstained highway of the exiles, where they had marched for endless months, beaten and maltreated by their Cossack guards, another had dropped by the way. Always it had been savagery—brutal, bestial savagery. They had died—of fever, in the mines, under the knout. The last two had died after the escape, in the battle with the Cossacks, and he alone had won to Kamchatka with the stolen papers and the money of a traveler he had left lying in the snow.

It had been nothing but savagery. All the years, with his heart in studios and theaters and courts, he had been hemmed in by savagery. He had purchased his life with blood. Everybody had killed. He had killed that traveler for his passports. He had proved that he was a man of parts by dueling with two Russian officers on a single day. He had had to prove himself in order to win to a place among the fur thieves. He had had to win to that place. Behind him lay the thousand-years-long road across all Siberia and Russia. He could not escape that way. The only way was ahead, across the dark and icy sea of Bering to Alaska. The way had led from savagery to deeper savagery. On the scurvy-rotten ships of the fur thieves, out of food and out of water, buffeted by the interminable storms of that stormy sea, men had become animals. Thrice he had sailed east from Kamchatka. And thrice, after all manner of hardship and suffering, the survivors had come back to Kamchatka. There had been no outlet for escape, and he could not go back the way he had come, for the mines and the knout awaited him.

Again, the fourth and last time, he had sailed east. He had been with those who first found the fabled Seal Islands; but he had not returned with them to share the wealth of furs in the mad orgies of Kamchatka. He had sworn never to go back. He knew that to win to those dear capitals of Europe he must go on. So he had changed ships and remained in the dark new land. His comrades were Slavonian hunters and Russian adventurers, Mongols and Tatars and Siberian aborigines; and through the savages of the New World they had cut a path of blood. They had massacred whole villages that refused to furnish the fur tribute; and they in turn had been massacred by ships' companies. He, with one Finn, had been the sole survivors of such a company. They had spent a winter of solitude and starvation on a lonely Aleutian isle, and their rescue in the spring by another fur ship had been one chance in a thousand.

But always the terrible savagery had hemmed him in. Passing from ship to ship, and ever refusing to return, he had come to the ship that explored south. All down the Alaskan coast they had encountered nothing but hosts of savages. Every anchorage among the beetling islands or under the frowning cliffs of the mainland had meant a battle or a storm. Either the gales blew, threatening destruction, or the war canoes came off, manned by howling natives with the war paint on their faces, who came to learn the bloody virtues of the sea rovers' gunpowder. South, south they had coasted, clear to the myth land of California. Here, it was said, were Spanish adventurers who had fought their way up from Mexico. He had had hopes of those Spanish adventurers. Escaping to them, the rest would have been easy—a year or two, what did it matter more or less?—and he would win to Mexico, then a ship, and Europe would be his. But they had met no Spaniards. Only had they encountered the same impregnable wall of savagery. The denizens of the confines of the world, painted for war, had driven them back from the shores. At last, when one boat was cut off and every man killed, the commander had abandoned the quest and sailed back to the North.

The years had passed. He had served under Tebenkoff when Michaelovski Redoubt was built. He had spent two years in the Kuskokwim country. Two summers, in the month of June, he had managed to be at the head of Kotzebue Sound. Here, at this time, the tribes assembled for barter; here were to be found spotted deerskins from Siberia, ivory from the Diomedes, walrus skins from the shores of the Arctic, strange stone lamps, passing in trade from tribe to tribe, no one knew whence, and, once, a hunting knife of English make; and here, Subienkow knew, was the school in which to learn geography. For he met Eskimos from Norton Sound, from King Island and St. Lawrence Island, from Cape Prince of Wales, and Point Barrow. Such places had other names, and their distances were measured in days.

It was a vast region these trading savages came from, and a vaster region from which, by repeated trade, their stone lamps and that steel knife had come. Subienkow bullied and cajoled and bribed. Every far journeyer or strange tribesman was brought before him. Perils unaccountable and unthinkable were mentioned, as well as wild beasts, hostile tribes, impenetrable forests, and mighty mountain ranges; but always from beyond came the rumor and the tale of white-skinned men, blue of eye and fair of hair, who fought like devils and who sought always for furs. They were to the east—far, far to the east. No one had seen them. It was the word that had been passed along.

It was a hard school. One could not learn geography very well through the medium of strange dialects, from dark minds that mingled fact and fable and that measured distances by "sleeps" that varied according to the difficulty of the going. But at last came the whisper that gave Subienkow courage. In the east lay a great river where were these blue-eyed men. The river was called the Yukon. South of Michaelovski Redoubt emptied another great river which the Russians knew as the Kwikpak. These two rivers were one, ran the whisper.

Subienkow returned to Michaelovski. For a year he urged an expedition up the Kwikpak. Then arose Malakoff, the Russian half-breed, to lead the wildest and most ferocious of the hell's broth of mongrel adventurers who had crossed from Kamchatka. Subienkow was his lieutenant. They threaded the mazes of the great delta of the Kwikpak, picked up the first low hills on the northern bank, and for half a thousand miles, in skin canoes loaded to the gunwales with trade goods and ammunition, fought their way against the five-knot current of a river that ran from two to ten miles wide in a channel many fathoms deep. Malakoff decided to build the fort at Nulato. Subienkow urged to go farther. But he quickly reconciled himself to

Nulato. The long winter was coming on. It would be better to wait. Early the following summer, when the ice was gone, he would disappear up the Kwikpak and work his way to the Hudson's Bay Company's posts. Malakoff had never heard the whisper that the Kwikpak was the Yukon, and Subienkow did not tell him.

Came the building of the fort. It was enforced labor. The tiered walls of logs arose to the sighs and groans of the Nulato Indians. The lash was laid upon their backs, and it was the iron hand of the freebooters of the sea that laid on the lash. There were Indians that ran away, and when they were caught they were brought back and spread-eagled before the fort, where they and their tribe learned the efficacy of the knout. Two died under it; others were injured for life; and the rest took the lesson to heart and ran away no more. The snow was flying ere the fort was finished, and then it was the time for furs. A heavy tribute was laid upon the tribe. Blows and lashings continued, and that the tribute should be paid, the women and children were held as hostages and treated with the barbarity that only the fur thieves knew.

Well, it had been a sowing of blood, and now was come the harvest. The fort was gone. In the light of its burning, half the fur thieves had been cut down. The other half had passed under the torture. Only Subienkow remained, or Subienkow and Big Ivan, if that whimpering, moaning thing in the snow could be called Big Ivan. Subienkow caught Yakaga grinning at him. There was no gainsaying Yakaga. The mark of the lash was still on his face. After all, Subienkow could not blame him, but he disliked the thought of what Yakaga would do to him. He thought of appealing to Makamuk, the head chief; but his judgment told him that such appeal was useless. Then, too, he thought of bursting his bonds and dying fighting. Such an end would be quick. But he could not break his bonds. Caribou thongs were stronger than he. Still devising, another thought came to him. He signed for Makamuk, and that an interpreter who knew the coast dialect should be brought.

"Oh, Makamuk," he said, "I am not minded to die. I am a great man, and it were foolishness for me to die. In truth, I shall not die. I am not like these other carrion."

He looked at the moaning thing that had once been Big Ivan, and stirred it contemptuously with his toe.

"I am too wise to die. Behold, I have a great medicine. I alone know this medicine. Since I am not going to die, I shall exchange this medicine with you."

"What is this medicine?" Makamuk demanded.

"It is a strange medicine."

Subienkow debated with himself for a moment, as if loath to part with the secret.

"I will tell you. A little bit of this medicine rubbed on the skin makes the skin hard like a rock, hard like iron, so that no cutting weapon can cut it. The strongest blow of a cutting weapon is a vain thing against it. A bone knife becomes like a piece of mud; and it will turn the edge of the iron knives we have brought among you. What will you give me for the secret of the medicine?"

"I will give you your life," Makamuk made answer through the interpreter.

Subienkow laughed scornfully.

"And you shall be a slave in my house until you die."

The Pole laughed more scornfully.

"Untie my hands and feet and let us talk," he said.

The chief made the sign; and when he was loosed Subienkow rolled a cigarette and lighted it.

"This is foolish talk," said Makamuk. "There is no such medicine. It cannot be. A cutting edge is stronger than any medicine."

The chief was incredulous, and yet he wavered. He had seen too many deviltries of fur thieves that worked. He could not wholly doubt.

"I will give you your life; but you shall not be a slave," he announced.

"More than that."

Subienkow played his game as coolly as if he were bartering for a fox skin.

"It is a very great medicine. It has saved my life many times. I want a sled and dogs, and six of your hunters to travel with me down the river and give me safety to one day's sleep from Michaelovski Redoubt."

"You must live here, and teach us all of your deviltries," was the reply.

Subienkow shrugged his shoulders and remained silent. He blew cigarette smoke out on the icy air, and curiously regarded what remained of the big Cossack.

"That scar!" Makamuk said suddenly, pointing to the Pole's neck, where a livid mark advertised the slash of a knife in a Kamchatkan brawl. "The medicine is not good. The cutting edge was stronger than the medicine."

"It was a strong man that drove the stroke." (Subienkow considered.) "Stronger than you, stronger than your strongest hunter, stronger than he."

Again, with the toe of his moccasin, he touched the Cossack—a grisly spectacle, no longer conscious—yet in whose dismembered body the pain-racked life clung and was loath to go.

"Also the medicine was weak. For at that place there were no berries of a certain kind, of which I see you have plenty in this country. The medicine here will be strong."

"I will let you go downriver," said Makamuk; "and the sled and the dogs and the six hunters to give you safety shall be yours."

"You are slow," was the cool rejoinder. "You have committed an offense against my medicine in that you did not at once accept my terms. Behold, I now demand more. I want one hundred beaver skins." (Makamuk sneered.) "I want one hundred pounds of dried fish." (Makamuk nodded, for fish were plentiful and cheap.) "I want two sleds—one for me and one for my furs and fish. And my rifle must be returned to me. If you do not like the price, in a little while the price will grow."

Yakaga whispered to the chief.

"But how can I know your medicine is true medicine?" Makamuk asked.

"It is very easy. First, I shall go into the woods——"

Again Yakaga whispered to Makamuk, who made a suspicious dissent.

"You can send twenty hunters with me," Subienkow went on. "You see, I must get the berries and the roots with which to make the medicine. Then, when you have brought the two sleds and loaded on them the fish and the beaver skins and the rifle, and when you have told off the six hunters who will go with me—then, when all is ready, I will rub the medicine on my neck, so, and lay my neck there on that log. Then can your strongest hunter take the ax and strike three times on my neck. You yourself can strike the three times."

Makamuk stood with gaping mouth, drinking in this latest and most wonderful magic of the fur thieves.

"But first," the Pole added hastily, "between each blow I must put on fresh medicine. The ax is heavy and sharp, and I want no mistakes."

"All that you have asked shall be yours," Makamuk cried in a rush of acceptance. "Proceed to make your medicine."

Subienkow concealed his elation. He was playing a desperate game, and there must be no slips. He spoke arrogantly.

"You have been slow. My medicine is offended. To make the offense clean you must give me your daughter."

He pointed to the girl, an unwholesome creature, with a cast in one eye and a bristling wolf tooth. Makamuk was angry, but the Pole remained imperturbable, rolling and lighting another cigarette.

"Make haste," he threatened. "If you are not quick, I shall demand yet more."

In the silence that followed, the dreary Northland scene faded from before him, and he saw once more his native land, and France, and once, as he glanced at the wolf-toothed girl, he remembered another girl, a singer and a dancer, whom he had known when first as a youth he came to Paris.

"What do you want with the girl?" Makamuk asked.

"To go down the river with me." Subienkow glanced her over critically. "She will make a good wife, and it is an honor worthy of my medicine to be married to your blood."

Again he remembered the singer and dancer and hummed aloud a song she had taught him. He lived the old life over, but in a detached, impersonal sort of way, looking at the memory pictures of his own life as if they were pictures in a book of anybody's life. The chief's voice, abruptly breaking the silence, startled him.

"It shall be done," said Makamuk. "The girl shall go down the river with you. But be it understood that I myself strike the three blows with the ax on your neck."

"But each time I shall put on the medicine," Subienkow answered, with a show of ill-concealed anxiety.

"You shall put the medicine on between each blow. Here are the hunters who shall see you do not escape. Go into the forest and gather your medicine."

Makamuk had been convinced of the worth of the medicine by the Pole's rapacity. Surely nothing less than the greatest of medicines could enable a man in the shadow of death to stand up and drive an old woman's bargain.

"Besides," whispered Yakaga, when the Pole, with his guard, had disappeared among the spruce trees, "when you have learned the medicine you can easily destroy him."

"But how can I destroy him?" Makamuk argued. "His medicine will not let me destroy him."

"There will be some part where he has not rubbed the medicine," was Yakaga's reply. "We will destroy him through that part. It may be his ears. Very well; we will thrust a spear in one ear and out the other. Or it may be his eyes. Surely the medicine will be much too strong to rub on his eyes."

The chief nodded. "You are wise, Yakaga. If he possesses no other devil things, we will then destroy him."

Subienkow did not waste time in gathering the ingredients for his medicine. He selected whatsoever came to hand such as spruce needles, the inner bark of the willow, a strip of birch bark, and a quantity of mossberries, which he made the hunters dig up for him from beneath the snow. A few frozen roots completed his supply, and he led the way back to camp.

Makamuk and Yakaga crouched beside him, noting the quantities and kinds of the ingredients he dropped into the pot of boiling water.

"You must be careful that the mossberries go in first," he explained.

"And—oh yes, one other thing—the finger of a man. Here, Yakaga, let me cut off your finger."

But Yakaga put his hands behind him and scowled.

"Just a small finger," Subienkow pleaded.

"Yakaga, give him your finger," Makamuk commanded.

"There be plenty of fingers lying around," Yakaga grunted, indicating the human wreckage in the snow of the score of persons who had been tortured to death.

"It must be the finger of a live man," the Pole objected.

"Then shall you have the finger of a live man." Yakaga strode over to the Cossack and sliced off a finger.

"He is not yet dead," he announced, flinging the bloody trophy in the snow at the Pole's feet. "Also, it is a good finger, because it is large."

Subienkow dropped it into the fire under the pot and began to sing. It was a French love song that with great solemnity he sang into the brew.

"Without these words I utter into it the medicine is worthless," he explained. "The words are the chiefest strength of it. Behold, it is ready."

"Name the words slowly, that I may know them," Makamuk commanded.

"Not until after the test. When the ax flies back three times from my neck, then will I give you the secret of the words."

"But if the medicine is not good medicine?" Makamuk queried anxiously.

Subienkow turned upon him wrathfully.

"My medicine is always good. However, if it is not good, then do by me as you have done to the others. Cut me up a bit at a time, even as you have cut him up." He pointed to the Cossack. "The medicine is now cool. Thus I rub it on my neck, saying this further medicine."

With great gravity he slowly intoned a line of the "Marseillaise," at the same time rubbing the villainous brew thoroughly into his neck.

An outcry interrupted his play acting. The giant Cossack, with a last resurgence of his tremendous vitality, had arisen to his knees. Laughter and cries of surprise and applause arose from the Nulatos, as Big Ivan began flinging himself about in the snow with mighty spasms.

Subienkow was made sick by the sight, but he mastered his qualms and made believe to be angry.

"This will not do," he said. "Finish him, and then we will make the test. Here, you, Yakaga, see that his noise ceases."

While this was being done, Subienkow turned to Makamuk.

"And remember, you are to strike hard. This is not baby work. Here, take the ax and strike the log, so that I can see you strike like a man."

Makamuk obeyed, striking twice, precisely and with vigor, cutting out a large chip.

"It is well." Subienkow looked about him at the circle of savage faces that somehow seemed to symbolize the wall of savagery that had hemmed him about ever since the Czar's police had first arrested him in Warsaw. "Take your ax, Makamuk, and stand so. I shall lie down. When I raise my hand, strike, and strike with all your might. And be careful that no one stands behind you. The medicine is good, and the ax may bounce from off my neck and right out of your hands."

He looked at the two sleds, with the dogs in harness, loaded with furs and fish.

His rifle lay on top of the beaver skins. The six hunters who were to act as his guard stood by the sleds.

"Where is the girl?" the Pole demanded. "Bring her up to the sleds before the test goes on."

When this had been carried out, Subienkow lay down in the snow, resting his head on the log like a tired child about to sleep. He had lived so many dreary years that he was indeed tired.

"I laugh at you and your strength, O Makamuk," he said. "Strike, and strike hard."

He lifted his hand. Makamuk swung the ax, a broadax for the squaring of logs. The bright steel flashed through the frosty air, poised for a perceptible instant above Makamuk's head, then descended upon Subienkow's bare neck. Clear through flesh and bone it cut its way, biting deeply into the log beneath. The amazed savages saw the head bounce a yard away from the blood-spouting trunk.

There was a great bewilderment and silence, while slowly it began to dawn in their minds that there had been no medicine. The fur thief had outwitted them. Alone, of all their prisoners, he had escaped the torture. That had been the stake for which he played. A great roar of laughter went up. Makamuk bowed his head in shame. The fur thief had fooled him. He had lost face before all his people. Still they continued to roar out their laughter. Makamuk turned, and with bowed head stalked away. He knew that thenceforth he would be no longer known as Makamuk. He would be Lost Face; the record of his shame would be with him until he died; and whenever the tribes gathered in the spring for the salmon, or in the summer for the trading, the story would pass back and forth across the campfires of how the fur thief died peaceably, at a single stroke, by the hand of Lost Face.

"Who was Lost Face?" he could hear, in anticipation, some insolent young buck demand. "Oh, Lost Face," would be the answer, "he who once was Makamuk in the days before he cut off the fur thief's head."

1908

A PIECE OF STEAK

With the last morsel of bread Tom King wiped his plate clean of the last particle of flour gravy and chewed the resulting mouthful in a slow and meditative way. When he arose from the table, he was oppressed by the feeling that he was distinctly hungry. Yet he alone had eaten. The two children in the other room had been sent early to bed in order that in sleep they might forget they had gone supperless. His wife had touched nothing, and had sat silently and watched him with solicitous eyes. She was a thin, worn woman of the working class, though signs of an earlier prettiness were not wanting in her face. The flour for the gravy she had borrowed from the neighbor across the hall. The last two ha'pennies had gone to buy the bread.

He sat down by the window on a rickety chair that protested under his weight, and quite mechanically he put his pipe in his mouth and dipped into the side pocket of his coat. The absence of any tobacco made him aware of his action, and with a scowl for his forgetfulness he put the pipe away. His movements were slow, almost hulking, as though he were burdened by the heavy weight of his muscles. He was a solid-bodied, stolid-looking man, and his appearance did not suffer from being overprepossessing. His rough clothes were old and slouchy. The uppers of his shoes were too weak to carry the heavy resoling that was itself of no recent date. And his cotton shirt, a cheap, two-shilling affair, showed a frayed collar and ineradicable paint stains.

But it was Tom King's face that advertised him unmistakably for what he was. It was the face of a typical prize fighter; of one who had put in long years of service in the squared ring and, by that means, developed and emphasized all the marks of the fighting beast. It was distinctly a lowering countenance, and, that no feature of it might escape notice, it was clean-shaven. The lips were shapeless and constituted a mouth harsh to excess, that was like a gash in his face. The jaw was aggressive, brutal, heavy. The eyes, slow of movement and heavy-lidded, were almost expressionless under the shaggy, indrawn brows. Sheer animal that he was, the eyes were the most animal-like feature about him. They were sleepy, lionlike—the eyes of a fighting animal. The forehead slanted quickly back to the hair, which, clipped close, showed every bump of a villainous-looking head. A nose, twice broken and molded variously by countless blows, and a cauliflower ear, permanently swollen and distorted to twice its size, completed his adornment, while the beard, fresh-shaven as it was, sprouted in the skin and gave the face a blue-black stain.

Altogether, it was the face of a man to be afraid of in a dark alley or lonely place. And yet Tom King was not a criminal, nor had he ever done anything criminal. Outside of brawls, common to his walk in life, he had harmed no one. Nor had he ever been known to pick a quarrel. He was a professional, and all the fighting brutishness of him was reserved for his professional appearances. Outside the ring he was slow-going, easy-natured, and, in his younger days, when money was flush, too openhanded for his own good. He bore no grudges and had few enemies. Fighting was a business with him. In the ring he struck to hurt, struck to maim, struck to destroy; but there was no animus in it. It was a plain business proposition. Audiences assembled and paid for the spectacle of men knocking each other out. The winner took the big end of the purse. When Tom King faced the Woolloomooloo Gouger, twenty years before, he knew that the Gouger's jaw was only four months healed after having been broken in a Newcastle bout. And he had played for that jaw and broken it again in the ninth round, not because he bore the Gouger any ill will, but because that was the surest way to put the Gouger out and win the big end of the purse. Nor had the Gouger borne him any ill will for it. It was the game, and both knew the game and played it.

Tom King had never been a talker, and he sat by the window, morosely silent, staring at his hands. The veins stood out on the backs of the hands, large and swollen; and the knuckles, smashed and battered and malformed, testified to the use to which they had been put. He had never heard that a man's life was the life of his arteries, but well he knew the meaning of those big, upstanding veins. His heart had pumped too much blood through them at top pressure. They no longer did the work. He had stretched the elasticity out of them, and with their distention had passed his endurance. He tired easily now. No longer could he do a fast twenty rounds, hammer and tongs, fight, fight, fight, from gong to gong, with fierce rally on top of fierce rally, beaten to the ropes and in turn beating his opponent to the ropes, and rallying fiercest and fastest of all in that last, twentieth round, with the house on its feet and yelling, himself rushing, striking, ducking, raining showers of blows upon showers of blows and receiving showers of blows in return, and all the time the heart faithfully pumping the surging blood through the adequate veins. The veins, swollen at the time, had always shrunk down again, though not quite—each time, imperceptibly at first, remaining just a trifle larger than before. He stared at them and at his battered knuckles, and, for the moment, caught a vision of the youthful excellence of those hands before the first knuckle had been smashed on the head of Benny Jones, otherwise known as the Welsh Terror.

The impression of his hunger came back on him.

"Blimey, but couldn't I go a piece of steak!" he muttered aloud, clenching his huge fists and spitting out a smothered oath.

"I tried both Burke's an' Sawley's," his wife said half apologetically.

"An' they wouldn't?" he demanded.

"Not a ha'penny. Burke said——" She faltered.

"G'wan! Wot'd he say?"

"As how 'e was thinkin' Sandel 'ud do ye tonight, an' as how yer score was comfortable big as it was."

Tom King grunted but did not reply. He was busy thinking of the bull terrier he had kept in his younger days to which he had fed steaks without end. Burke would have given him credit for a thousand steaks—then. But times had changed. Tom King was getting old; and old men, fighting before second-rate clubs, couldn't expect to run bills of any size with the tradesmen.

He had got up in the morning with a longing for a piece of steak, and the longing had not abated. He had not had a fair training for this fight. It was a drought year in Australia, times were hard, and even the most irregular work was difficult to find. He had had no sparring partner, and his food had not been of the best nor always sufficient. He had done a few days' navvy work when he could get it, and he had run around the Domain in the early mornings to get his legs in shape. But it was hard, training without a partner and with a wife and two kiddies that must be fed. Credit with the tradesmen had undergone very slight expansion when he was matched with Sandel. The secretary of the Gayety Club had advanced him three pounds—the loser's end of the purse—and beyond that had refused to go. Now and again he had managed to borrow a few shillings from old pals, who would have lent more only that it was a drought year and they were hard put themselves. No—and there was no use in disguising the fact—his training had not been satisfactory. He should have had better food and no worries. Besides, when a man is forty, it is harder to get into condition than when he is twenty.

"What time is it, Lizzie?" he asked.

His wife went across the hall to inquire, and came back.

"Quarter before eight."

"They'll be startin' the first bout in a few minutes," he said. "Only a tryout. Then there's a four-round spar 'tween Dealer Wells an' Gridley, an' a ten-round go 'tween Starlight an' some sailor bloke. I don't come on for over an hour."

At the end of another silent ten minutes he rose to his feet.

"Truth is, Lizzie, I ain't had proper trainin'."

He reached for his hat and started for the door. He did not offer to kiss her—he never did on going out—but on this night she dared to kiss him, throwing her arms around him and compelling him to bend down to her face. She looked quite small against the massive bulk of the man.

"Good luck, Tom," she said. "You gotter do 'im."

"Ay, I gotter do 'im," he repeated. "That's all there is to it. I jus' gotter do 'im."

He laughed with an attempt at heartiness, while she pressed more closely against him. Across her shoulders he looked around the bare room. It was all he had in the world, with the rent overdue, and her and the kiddies. And he was leaving it to go out into the night to get meat for his mate and cubs—not like a modern workingman going to his machine grind, but in the old, primitive, royal, animal way, by fighting for it.

"I gotter do 'im," he repeated, this time a hint of desperation in his voice. "If it's a win, it's thirty quid—an' I can pay all that's owin', with a lump o' money left over. If it's a lose, I get naught—not even a penny for me to ride home on the tram. The secretary's give all that's comin' from a loser's end. Good-by, old woman. I'll come straight home if it's a win."

"An' I'll be waitin' up," she called to him along the hall.

It was full two miles to the Gayety, and as he walked along he remembered how in his palmy days—he had once been the heavyweight champion of New South Wales—he would have ridden in a cab to the fight, and how, most likely, some heavy backer would have paid for the cab and ridden with him. There were Tommy Burns and that Yankee, Jack Johnson—they rode about in motorcars. And he walked! And, as any man knew, a hard two miles was not the best preliminary to a fight. He was an old un, and the world did not wag well with old uns. He was good for nothing now except navvy work, and his broken nose and swollen ear were against him even in that. He found himself wishing that he had learned a trade. It would have been better in the long run. But no one had told him, and he knew, deep down in his heart, that he would not have listened if they had. It had been so easy. Big money—sharp, glorious fights—periods of rest and loafing in between—a following of eager flatterers, the slaps on the back, the shakes of the hand, the toffs glad to buy him a drink for the privilege of five minutes' talk—and the glory of it, the yelling houses, the whirlwind finish, the referee's "King wins!" and his name in the sporting columns next day.

Those had been times! But he realized now, in his slow, ruminating way, that it was the old uns he had been putting away. He was Youth, rising; and they were Age, sinking. No wonder it had been easy—they with their swollen veins and battered knuckles and weary in the bones of them from the long battles they had already fought. He remembered the time he put out old Stowsher Bill, at Rush-Cutters Bay, in the eighteenth round, and how old Bill had cried afterward in the dressing room like a baby. Perhaps old Bill's rent had been overdue. Perhaps he'd had at home a missus an' a couple of kiddies. And perhaps Bill, that very day of the fight, had had a hungering for a piece of steak. Bill had fought game and taken incredible punishment. He could see now, after he had gone through the mill himself, that Stowsher Bill had fought for a bigger stake, that night twenty years ago, than had young Tom King, who had fought for glory and easy money. No wonder Stowsher Bill had cried afterward in the dressing room.

Well, a man had only so many fights in him, to begin with. It was the iron law of the game. One man might have a hundred hard fights in him, another man only twenty; each, according to the make of him and the quality of his fiber, had a definite number, and when he had fought them he was done. Yes, he had had more fights in him than most of them, and he had had far more than his share of the hard, grueling fights—the kind that worked the heart and lungs to bursting, that took the elastic out of the arteries and made hard knots of muscle out of youth's sleek suppleness, that wore out nerve and stamina and made brain and bones weary from excess of effort and endurance overwrought. Yes, he had done better than all of them. There was none of his old fighting partners left. He was the last of the old guard. He had seen them all finished, and he had had a hand in finishing some of them.

They had tried him out against the old uns, and one after another he had put them away—laughing when, like old Stowsher Bill, they cried in the dressing room. And now he was an old un, and they tried out the youngsters on him. There was that bloke Sandel. He had come over from New Zealand with a record behind him. But nobody in Australia knew anything about him, so they put him up against old Tom King. If Sandel made a showing, he would be given better men to fight, with bigger purses to win; so it was to be depended upon that he would put up a fierce battle. He had everything to win by it—money and glory and career; and Tom King was the grizzled old chopping block that guarded the highway to fame and fortune. And he had nothing to win except thirty quid, to pay to the landlord and the tradesmen. And as Tom King thus ruminated, there came to his stolid vision the form of youth, glorious youth, rising exultant and invincible, supple of muscle and silken of skin, with heart and lungs that had never been tired and torn and that laughed at limitation of effort. Yes, youth was the nemesis. It destroyed the old uns and recked not that, in so doing, it destroyed itself. It enlarged its arteries and smashed its knuckles, and was in turn destroyed by youth. For youth was ever youthful. It was only age that grew old.

At Castlereagh Street he turned to the left, and three blocks along came to the Gayety. A crowd of young larrikins hanging outside the door made respectful way for him, and he heard one say to another: "That's 'im! That's Tom King!"

Inside, on the way to his dressing room, he encountered the secretary, a keen-eyed, shrewd-faced young man, who shook his hand.

"How are you feelin', Tom?" he asked.

"Fit as a fiddle," King answered, though he knew that he lied, and that if he had a quid he would give it right there for a good piece of steak.

When he emerged from the dressing room, his seconds behind him, and came down the aisle to the squared ring in the center of the hall, a burst of greeting and applause went up from the waiting crowd. He acknowledged salutations right and left, though few of the faces did he know. Most of them were the faces of kiddies unborn when he was winning his first laurels in the squared ring. He leaped lightly to the raised platform and ducked through the ropes to his corner, where he sat down on a folding stool. Jack Ball, the referee, came over and shook his hand. Ball was a broken-down pugilist who for over ten years had not entered the ring as a principal. King was glad that he had him for referee. They were both old uns. If he should rough it with Sandel a bit beyond the rules, he knew Ball could be depended upon to pass it by.

Aspiring young heavyweights, one after another, were climbing into the ring and being presented to the audience by the referee. Also he issued their challenges for them.

"Young Pronto," Bill announced, "from North Sydney, challenges the winner for fifty pounds side bet."

The audience applauded, and applauded again as Sandel himself sprang through the ropes and sat down in his corner. Tom King looked across the ring at him curiously, for in a few minutes they would be locked together in merciless combat, each trying with all the force of him to knock the other into unconsciousness. But little could he see, for Sandel, like himself, had trousers and sweater on over his ring costume. His face was strongly handsome, crowned with a curly mop of yellow hair, while his thick, muscular neck hinted at bodily magnificence.

Young Pronto went to one corner and then the other, shaking hands with the principals and dropping down out of the ring. The challenges went on. Ever youth climbed through the ropes—youth unknown but insatiable, crying out to mankind that with strength and skill it would match issues with the winner. A few years before, in his own heyday of invincibleness, Tom King would have been amused and bored by these preliminaries. But now he sat fascinated, unable to shake the vision of youth from his eyes. Always were these youngsters rising up in the boxing game, springing through the ropes and shouting their defiance; and always were the old uns going down before them. They climbed to success over the bodies of the old uns. And ever they came, more and more youngsters—youth unquenchable and irresistible—and ever they put the old uns away, themselves becoming old uns and traveling the same downward path, while behind them, ever pressing on them, was youth eternal—the new babies, grown lusty and dragging their elders down, with behind them more babies to the end of time—youth that must have its will and that will never die.

King glanced over to the press box and nodded to Morgan, of the *Sportsman*, and Corbett, of the *Referee*. Then he held out his hands, while Sid Sullivan and Charley Bates, his seconds, slipped on his gloves and laced them tight, closely watched by one of Sandel's seconds, who first examined critically the tapes on King's knuckles. A second of his own was in Sandel's corner, performing a like office. Sandel's trousers were pulled off, and as he stood up his sweater was skinned off over his head. And Tom King, looking, saw youth incarnate, deep-chested, heavy-thewed, with muscles that slipped and slid like live things under the white satin skin. The whole body was acrawl with life, and Tom King knew that it was a life that had never oozed its freshness out through the aching pores during the long fights wherein youth paid its toll and departed not quite so young as when it entered.

The two men advanced to meet each other, and as the gong sounded and the seconds clattered out of the ring with the folding stools, they shook hands and instantly took their fighting attitudes. And instantly, like a mechanism of steel and springs balanced on a hair trigger, Sandel was in and out and in again, landing a left to the eyes, a right to the ribs, ducking a counter, dancing lightly away and dancing menacingly back again. He was swift and clever. It was a dazzling exhibition. The house yelled its approbation. But King was not dazzled. He had fought too many fights and too many youngsters. He knew the blows for what they were—too quick and too deft to be dangerous. Evidently Sandel was going to rush things from the start. It was to be expected. It was the way of youth, expending its splendor and excellence in wild insurgence and furious onslaught, overwhelming opposition with its own unlimited glory of strength and desire.

Sandel was in and out, here, there, and everywhere, light-footed and eager-hearted, a living wonder of white flesh and stinging muscle that wove itself into a dazzling fabric of attack, slipping and leaping like a flying shuttle from action to action through a thousand actions, all of them centered upon the destruction of Tom King, who stood between him and fortune. And Tom King patiently endured. He knew his business, and he knew youth now that youth was no longer his. There was nothing to do till the other lost some of his steam, was his thought, and he grinned to himself as he deliberately ducked so as to receive a heavy blow on the top of his head. It was a wicked thing to do, yet eminently fair according to the rules of the boxing game. A man was supposed to take care of his own knuckles, and if he insisted on hitting an opponent on the top of the head he did so at his own peril. King could have ducked lower and let the blow whiz harmlessly past, but he remembered his own early fights and how he smashed his first knuckle on the head of the Welsh Terror. He was but playing the game. That duck had accounted for one of Sandel's knuckles. Not that Sandel would mind it now. He would go on, superbly regardless, hitting as hard as ever throughout the fight. But later on, when the long ring battles had begun to tell, he would regret that knuckle and look back and remember how he smashed it on Tom King's head.

The first round was all Sandel's, and he had the house yelling with the rapidity of his whirlwind rushes. He overwhelmed King with avalanches of punches, and King did nothing. He never struck once, contenting himself with covering up, blocking and ducking and clinching to avoid punishment. He occasionally feinted, shook his head when the weight of a punch landed, and moved stolidly about, never leaping or springing or wasting an ounce of strength. Sandel must foam the froth of youth away before discreet age could dare to retaliate. All King's movements were slow and methodical, and his heavy-lidded, slow-moving eyes gave him the appearance of being half asleep or dazed. Yet they were eyes that saw everything, that had been trained to see everything through all his twenty years and odd in the ring. They were eyes that did not blink or waver before an impending blow, but that coolly saw and measured distance.

Seated in his corner for the minute's rest at the end of the round, he lay back with outstretched legs, his arms resting on the right angle of the ropes, his chest and abdomen heaving frankly and deeply as he gulped down the air driven by the towels of his seconds. He listened with closed eyes to the voices of the house, "Why don't yeh fight, Tom?" many were crying. "Yeh ain't afraid of 'im, are yeh?"

"Muscle-bound," he heard a man on a front seat comment. "He can't move quicker. Two to one on Sandel, in quids."

The gong struck and the two men advanced from their corners. Sandel came forward fully three quarters of the distance, eager to begin again; but King was content to advance the shorter distance. It was in line with his policy of economy. He had not been well trained, and he had not had enough to eat, and every step counted. Besides, he had already walked two miles to the ringside. It was a repetition of the first round, with Sandel attacking like a whirlwind and with the audience indignantly demanding why King did not fight. Beyond feinting and several slowly delivered and ineffectual blows he did nothing save block and stall and clinch. Sandel wanted to make the pace fast, while King, out of his wisdom, refused to accommodate him. He grinned with a certain wistful pathos in his ring-battered countenance, and went on cherishing his strength with the jealousy of which only age is capable. Sandel was youth, and he threw his strength away with the munificent abandon of youth. To King belonged the ring generalship, the wisdom bred of long, aching fights. He watched with cool eyes and head, moving slowly and waiting for Sandel's froth to foam away. To the majority of the onlookers it seemed as though King was hopelessly outclassed, and they voiced their opinion in offers of three to one on Sandel. But there were wise ones, a few, who knew King of old time, and who covered what they considered easy money.

The third round began as usual, one-sided, with Sandel doing all the leading and delivering all the punishment. A half minute had passed when Sandel, overconfident, left an opening. King's eyes and right arm flashed in the same instant. It was his first real blow—a hook, with the twisted arch of the arm to make it rigid, and with all the weight of the half-pivoted body behind it. It was like a sleepy-seeming lion suddenly thrusting out a lightning paw. Sandel, caught on the side of the jaw, was felled like a bullock. The audience gasped and murmured awe-stricken applause. The man was not muscle-bound, after all, and he could drive a blow like a trip hammer.

Sandel was shaken. He rolled over and attempted to rise, but the sharp yells from his seconds to take the count restrained him. He knelt on one knee, ready to rise, and waited, while the referee stood over him, counting the seconds loudly in his ear. At the ninth he rose in fighting attitude, and Tom King, facing him, knew regret that the blow had not been an inch nearer the point of the jaw. That would have been a knockout, and he could have carried the thirty quid home to the missus and the kiddies.

The round continued to the end of its three minutes, Sandel for the first time respectful of his opponent and King slow of movement and sleepy-eyed as ever. As the round neared its close, King, warned of the fact by sight of the seconds crouching outside ready for the spring in through the ropes, worked the fight around to his own corner. And when the gong struck, he sat down immediately on the waiting stool, while Sandel had to walk all the way across the diagonal of the square to his own corner. It was a little thing, but it was the sum of little things that counted. Sandel was compelled to walk that many more steps, to give up that much energy, and to lose a part of the precious minute of rest. At the beginning of every round King loafed slowly out from his corner, forcing his opponent to advance the greater distance. The end of every round found the fight maneuvered by King into his own corner so that he could immediately sit down.

Two more rounds went by, in which King was parsimonious of effort and Sandel prodigal. The latter's attempt to force a fast pace made King uncomfortable, for a fair percentage of the multitudinous blows showered upon him went home. Yet King persisted in his dogged slowness, despite the crying of the young hotheads for him to go in and fight. Again, in the sixth round, Sandel was careless, again Tom King's fearful right flashed out to the jaw, and again Sandel took the nine seconds' count.

By the seventh round Sandel's pink of condition was gone, and he settled down to what he knew was to be the hardest fight in his experience. Tom King was an old un, but a better old un than he had ever encountered—an old un who never lost his head, who was remarkably able at defense, whose blows had the impact of a knotted club, and who had a knockout in either hand. Nevertheless, Tom King dared not hit often. He never forgot his battered knuckles, and knew that every hit must count if the knuckles were to last out the fight. As he sat in his corner, glancing across at his opponent, the thought came to him that the sum of his wisdom and Sandel's youth would constitute a world's champion heavyweight. But that was the trouble. Sandel would never become a world champion. He lacked the wisdom, and the only way for him to get it was to buy it with youth; and when wisdom was his, youth would have been spent in buying it.

King took every advantage he knew. He never missed an opportunity to clinch, and in effecting most of the clinches his shoulder drove stiffly into the other's ribs. In the philosophy of the ring a shoulder was as good as a punch so far as damage was concerned, and a great deal better so far as concerned expenditure of effort. Also in the clinches King rested his weight on his opponent, and was loath to let go. This compelled the interference of the referee, who tore them apart, always assisted by Sandel, who had not yet learned to rest. He could not refrain from using those glorious flying arms and writhing muscles of his, and when the other rushed into a clinch, striking shoulder against ribs, and with head resting under Sandel's left arm, Sandel almost invariably swung his right behind his own back and into the projecting face. It was a clever stroke, much admired by the audience, but it was not dangerous, and was, therefore, just that much wasted strength. But Sandel was tireless and unaware of limitations, and King grinned and doggedly endured.

Sandel developed a fierce right to the body, which made it appear that King was taking an enormous amount of punishment, and it was only the old ringsters who appreciated the deft touch of King's left glove to the other's biceps just before the impact of the blow. It was true, the blow landed each time; but each time it was robbed of its power by that touch on the biceps. In the ninth round, three times inside a minute, King's right hooked its twisted arch to the jaw; and three times Sandel's body, heavy as it was, was leveled to the mat. Each time he took the nine seconds allowed him and rose to his feet, shaken and jarred, but still strong. He had lost much of his speed, and he wasted less effort. He was fighting grimly; but he continued to draw upon his chief asset, which was youth. King's chief asset was experience. As his vitality had dimmed and his vigor abated, he had replaced them with cunning, with wisdom born of the long fights and with a careful shepherding of strength. Not alone had he learned never to make a superfluous movement, but he had learned how to seduce an opponent into throwing his strength away. Again and again, by feint of foot and hand and body, he continued to inveigle Sandel into leaping back, ducking, or countering. King rested, but he never permitted Sandel to rest. It was the strategy of age.

Early in the tenth round King began stopping the other's rushes with straight lefts to the face, and Sandel, grown wary, responded by drawing the left, then by ducking it and delivering his right in a swinging hook to the side of the head. It was too high up to be vitally effective; but when first it landed King knew the old, familiar descent of the black veil of unconsciousness across his mind. For the instant, or for the slightest fraction of an instant, rather, he ceased. In the one moment he saw his opponent ducking out of his field of vision and the background of white, watching faces; in the next moment he again saw his opponent and the background of faces. It was as if he had slept for a time and just opened his eyes again, and yet the interval of unconsciousness was so microscopically short that there had been no time for him to fall. The audience saw him totter and his knees give, and then saw him recover and tuck his chin deeper into the shelter of his left shoulder.

Several times Sandel repeated the blow, keeping King partially dazed, and then the latter worked out his defense, which was also a counter. Feinting with his left, he took a half step backward, at the same time uppercutting with the whole strength of his right. So accurately was it timed that it landed squarely on Sandel's face in the full, downward sweep of the duck, and Sandel lifted in the air and curled backward, striking the mat on his head and shoulders. Twice King achieved this, then turned loose and hammered his opponent to the ropes. He gave Sandel no chance to rest or to set himself, but smashed blow in upon blow till the house rose to its feet and the air was filled with an unbroken roar of applause. But Sandel's strength and endurance were superb, and he continued to stay on his feet. A knockout seemed certain, and a captain of police, appalled at the dreadful punishment, arose by the ringside to stop the fight. The gong struck for the end of the round and Sandel staggered to his corner, protesting to the captain that he was sound and strong. To prove it, he threw two back air-springs, and the police captain gave in.

Tom King, leaning back in his corner and breathing hard, was disappointed. If the fight had been stopped, the referee, perforce, would have rendered him the decision and the purse would have been his. Unlike Sandel, he was not fighting for glory or career, but for thirty quid. And now Sandel would recuperate in the minute of rest.

Youth will be served—this saying flashed into King's mind, and he remembered the first time he had heard it, the night when he had put away Stowsher Bill. The toff who had bought him a drink after the fight and patted him on the shoulder had used those words. Youth will be served! The toff was right. And on that night in the long ago he had been youth. Tonight youth sat in the opposite corner. As for himself, he had been fighting for half an hour now, and he was an old man. Had he fought like Sandel, he would not have lasted fifteen minutes. But the point was that he did not recuperate. Those upstanding arteries and that sorely tried heart would not enable him to gather strength in the intervals between the rounds. And he had not had sufficient strength in him to begin with. His legs were heavy under him and beginning to cramp. He should not have walked those two miles to the fight. And there was the steak which he had got up longing for that morning. A great and terrible hatred rose up in him for the butchers who had refused him credit. It was hard for an old man to go into a fight without enough to eat. And a piece of steak was such a little thing, a few pennies at best; yet it meant thirty quid to him.

With the gong that opened the eleventh round Sandel rushed, making a show of freshness which he did not really possess. King knew it for what it was—a bluff as old as the game itself. He clinched to save himself, then, going free, allowed Sandel to get set. This was what King desired. He feinted with his left, drew the answering duck and swinging upward hook, then made the half step backward, delivered the uppercut full to the face and crumpled Sandel over to the mat. After that he never let him rest, receiving punishment himself, but inflicting far more, smashing Sandel to the ropes, hooking and driving all manner of blows into him, tearing away from his clinches or punching him out of attempted clinches, and ever when Sandel would have fallen, catching him with one uplifting hand and with the other immediately smashing him into the ropes where he could not fall.

The house by this time had gone mad, and it was his house, nearly every voice yelling: "Go it, Tom!" "Get 'im! Get 'im!" "You've got 'im, Tom! You've got 'im!" It was to be a whirlwind finish, and that was what a ringside audience paid to see.

And Tom King, who for half an hour had conserved his strength, now expended it prodigally in the one great effort he knew he had in him. It was his one chance—

now or not at all. His strength was waning fast, and his hope was that before the last of it ebbed out of him he would have beaten his opponent down for the count. And as he continued to strike and force, coolly estimating the weight of his blows and the quality of the damage wrought, he realized how hard a man Sandel was to knock out. Stamina and endurance were his to an extreme degree, and they were the virgin stamina and endurance of youth. Sandel was certainly a coming man. He had it in him. Only out of such rugged fiber were successful fighters fashioned.

Sandel was reeling and staggering, but Tom King's legs were cramping and his knuckles going back on him. Yet he steeled himself to strike the fierce blows, every one of which brought anguish to his tortured hands. Though now he was receiving practically no punishment, he was weakening as rapidly as the other. His blows went home, but there was no longer the weight behind them, and each blow was the result of a severe effort of will. His legs were like lead, and they dragged visibly under him; while Sandel's backers, cheered by this symptom, began calling encouragement to their man.

King was spurred to a burst of effort. He delivered two blows in succession—a left, a trifle too high, to the solar plexus, and a right cross to the jaw. They were not heavy blows, yet so weak and dazed was Sandel that he went down and lay quivering. The referee stood over him, shouting the count of the fatal seconds in his ear. If before the tenth second was called he did not rise, the fight was lost. The house stood in hushed silence. King rested on trembling legs. A mortal dizziness was upon him, and before his eyes the sea of faces sagged and swayed, while to his ears, as from a remote distance, came the count of the referee. Yet he looked upon the fight as his. It was impossible that a man so punished could rise.

Only youth could rise, and Sandel rose. At the fourth second he rolled over on his face and groped blindly for the ropes. By the seventh second he had dragged himself to his knee, where he rested, his head rolling groggily on his shoulders. As the referee cried "Nine!" Sandel stood upright, in proper stalling position, his left arm wrapped about his face, his right wrapped about his stomach. Thus were his vital points guarded, while he lurched forward toward King in the hope of effecting a clinch and gaining more time.

At the instant Sandel arose, King was at him, but the two blows he delivered were muffled on the stalled arms. The next moment Sandel was in the clinch and holding on desperately while the referee strove to drag the two men apart. King helped to force himself free. He knew the rapidity with which youth recovered, and he knew that Sandel was his if he could prevent that recovery. One stiff punch would do it. Sandel was his, indubitably his. He had outgeneraled him, outfought him, outpointed him. Sandel reeled out of the clinch, balanced on the hairline between defeat or survival. One good blow would topple him over and down and out. And Tom King, in a flash of bitterness, remembered the piece of steak and wished that he had it then behind that necessary punch he must deliver. He nerved himself for the blow, but it was not heavy enough nor swift enough. Sandel swayed but did not fall, staggering back to the ropes and holding on. King staggered after him, and, with a pang like that of dissolution, delivered another blow. But his body had deserted him. All that was left of him was a fighting intelligence that was dimmed and clouded from exhaustion. The blow that was aimed for the jaw struck no higher than the shoulder. He had willed the blow higher, but the tired muscles had not been able to obey. And, from the impact of the blow, Tom King himself reeled back and nearly fell. Once again he strove. This time his punch missed altogether, and from absolute weakness he fell against Sandel and clinched, holding on to him to save himself from sinking to the floor.

King did not attempt to free himself. He had shot his bolt. He was gone. And youth had been served. Even in the clinch he could feel Sandel growing stronger against him. When the referee thrust them apart, there, before his eyes, he saw youth recuperate. From instant to instant Sandel grew stronger. His punches, weak and futile at first, became stiff and accurate. Tom King's bleared eyes saw the gloved fist driving at his jaw, and he willed to guard it by interposing his arm. He saw the danger, willed the act; but the arm was too heavy. It seemed burdened with a hundredweight of lead. It would not lift itself, and he strove to lift it with his soul. Then the gloved fist landed home. He experienced a sharp snap that was like an electric spark, and simultaneously the veil of blackness enveloped him.

When he opened his eyes again he was in his corner, and he heard the yelling of the audience like the roar of the surf at Bondi Beach. A wet sponge was being pressed against the base of his brain, and Sid Sullivan was blowing cold water in a refreshing spray over his face and chest. His gloves had already been removed, and Sandel, bending over him, was shaking his hand. He bore no ill will toward the man who had put him out, and he returned the grip with a heartiness that made his battered knuckles protest. Then Sandel stepped to the center of the ring and the audience hushed its pandemonium to hear him accept young Pronto's challenge and offer to increase the side bet to one hundred pounds. King looked on apathetically while his seconds mopped the streaming water from him, dried his face, and prepared him to leave the ring. He felt hungry. It was not the ordinary, gnawing kind, but a great faintness, a palpitation at the pit of the stomach that communicated itself to all his body. He remembered back into the fight to the moment when he had Sandel swaying and tottering on the hairline balance of defeat. Ah, that piece of steak would have done it! He had lacked just that for the decisive blow, and he had lost. It was all because of the piece of steak.

His seconds were half supporting him as they helped him through the ropes. He tore free from them, ducked through the ropes unaided, and leaped heavily to the floor, following on their heels as they forced a passage for him down the crowded center aisle. Leaving the dressing room for the street, in the entrance to the hall, some young fellow spoke to him.

"W'y didn't yuh go in an' get 'im when yuh 'ad 'im?" the young fellow asked.

"Aw, go to hell!" said Tom King, and passed down the steps to the sidewalk.

The doors of the public house at the corner were swinging wide, and he saw the lights and the smiling barmaids, heard the many voices discussing the fight and the prosperous chink of money on the bar. Somebody called to him to have a drink. He hesitated perceptibly, then refused and went on his way.

He had not a copper in his pocket, and the two-mile walk home seemed very long. He was certainly getting old. Crossing the Domain he sat down suddenly on a bench, unnerved by the thought of the missus sitting up for him, waiting to learn the outcome of the fight. That was harder than any knockout, and it seemed almost impossible to face.

He felt weak and sore, and the pain of his smashed knuckles warned him that, even if he could find a job at navvy work, it would be a week before he could grip a pick handle or a shovel. The hunger palpitation at the pit of the stomach was sickening. His wretchedness overwhelmed him, and into his eyes came an unwonted moisture. He covered his face with his hands, and, as he cried, he remembered

Stowsher Bill and how he had served him that night in the long ago. Poor old Stowsher Bill! He could understand now why Bill had cried in the dressing room.

1909

THE SEED OF McCOY

The *Pyrenees*, her iron sides pressed low in the water by her cargo of wheat, rolled sluggishly, and made it easy for the man who was climbing aboard from out a tiny outrigger canoe. As his eyes came level with the rail, so that he could see inboard, it seemed to him that he saw a dim, almost indiscernible haze. It was more like an illusion, like a blurring film that had spread abruptly over his eyes. He felt an inclination to brush it away, and the same instant he thought that he was growing old and that it was time to send to San Francisco for a pair of spectacles.

As he came over the rail he cast a glance aloft at the tall masts, and, next, at the pumps. They were not working. There seemed nothing the matter with the big ship, and he wondered why she had hoisted the signal of distress. He thought of his happy islanders, and hoped it was not disease. Perhaps the ship was short of water or provisions. He shook hands with the captain whose gaunt face and care-worn eyes made no secret of the trouble, whatever it was. At the same moment the new-comer was aware of a faint, indefinable smell. It seemed like that of burnt bread, but different.

He glanced curiously about him. Twenty feet away a weary-faced sailor was calking the deck. As his eye lingered on the man, he saw suddenly arise from under his hands a faint spiral of haze that curled and twisted and was gone. By now he had reached the deck. His bare feet were pervaded by a dull warmth that quickly penetrated the thick calluses. He knew now the nature of the ship's distress. His eyes roved swiftly forward, where the full crew of weary-faced sailors regarded him eagerly. The glance from his liquid brown eyes swept over them like a benediction, soothing them, wrapping them about as in the mantle of a great peace. "How long has she been afire, Captain?" he asked in a voice so gentle and unperturbed that it was as the cooing of a dove.

At first the captain felt the peace and content of it stealing in upon him; then the consciousness of all that he had gone through and was going through smote him, and he was resentful. By what right did this ragged beach-comber, in dungaree trousers and a cotton shirt, suggest such a thing as peace and content to him and his overwrought, exhausted soul? The captain did not reason this; it was the unconscious process of emotion that caused his resentment.

"Fifteen days," he answered shortly. "Who are you?"

"My name is McCoy," came the answer in tones that breathed tenderness and compassion.

"I mean, are you the pilot?"

McCoy passed the benediction of his gaze over the tall, heavy-shouldered man with the haggard, unshaven face who had joined the captain.

"I am as much a pilot as anybody," was McCoy's answer. "We are all pilots here, Captain, and I know every inch of these waters."

But the captain was impatient.

"What I want is some of the authorities. I want to talk with them, and blame quick."

"Then I'll do just as well."

Again that insidious suggestion of peace, and his ship a raging furnace beneath his feet! The captain's eyebrows lifted impatiently and nervously, and his fist clenched as if he were about to strike a blow with it.

"Who in hell are you?" he demanded.

"I am the chief magistrate," was the reply in a voice that was still the softest and gentlest imaginable.

The tall, heavy-shouldered man broke out in a harsh laugh that was partly amusement, but mostly hysterical. Both he and the captain regarded McCoy with incredulity and amazement. That this barefooted beach-comber should possess such high-sounding dignity was inconceivable. His cotton shirt, unbuttoned, exposed a grizzled chest and the fact that there was no undershirt beneath. A worn straw hat failed to hide the ragged gray hair. Halfway down his chest descended an untrimmed patriarchal beard. In any slop-shop, two shillings would have outfitted him complete as he stood before them.

"Any relation to the McCoy of the *Bounty*?" the captain asked.

"He was my great-grandfather."

"Oh," the captain said, then bethought himself. "My name is Davenport, and this is my first mate, Mr. Konig."

They shook hands.

"And now to business." The captain spoke quickly, the urgency of a great haste pressing his speech. "We've been on fire for over two weeks. She's ready to break all hell loose any moment. That's why I held for Pitcairn. I want to beach her, or scuttle her, and save the hull."

"Then you made a mistake, Captain," said McCoy. "You should have slacked away for Mangareva. There's a beautiful beach there, in a lagoon where the water is like a mill-pond."

"But we're here, ain't we?" the first mate demanded. "That's the point. We're here, and we've got to do something."

McCoy shook his head kindly.

"You can do nothing here. There is no beach. There isn't even anchorage."

"Gammon!" said the mate. "Gammon!" he repeated loudly, as the captain signalled him to be more soft-spoken. "You can't tell me that sort of stuff. Where d'ye keep your own boats, hey—your schooner, or cutter, or whatever you have? Hey? Answer me that."

McCoy smiled as gently as he spoke. His smile was a caress, an embrace that surrounded the tired mate and sought to draw him into the quietude and rest of McCoy's tranquil soul.

"We have no schooner or cutter," he replied. "And we carry our canoes to the top of the cliff."

"You've got to show me," snorted the mate. "How d'ye get around to the other islands, heh? Tell me that."

"We don't get around. As governor of Pitcairn, I sometimes go. When I was younger, I was away a great deal—sometimes on the trading schooners, but mostly on the missionary brig. But she's gone now, and we depend on passing vessels. Sometimes we have had as high as six calls in one year. At other times, a year, and even longer, has gone by without one passing ship. Yours is the first in seven months."

"And you mean to tell me—" the mate began.

But Captain Davenport interfered.

"Enough of this. We're losing time. What is to be done, Mr. McCoy?"

The old man turned his brown eyes, sweet as a woman's, shoreward, and both captain and mate followed his gaze around from the lonely rock of Pitcairn to the crew clustering forward and waiting anxiously for the announcement of a decision. McCoy did not hurry. He thought smoothly and slowly, step by step, with the certitude of a mind that was never vexed or outraged by life.

"The wind is light now," he said finally. "There is a heavy current setting to the westward."

"That's what made us fetch to leeward," the captain interrupted, desiring to vindicate his seamanship.

"Yes, that is what fetched you to leeward," McCoy went on. "Well, you can't work up against this current to-day. And if you did, there is no beach. Your ship will be a total loss."

He paused, and captain and mate looked despair at each other.

"But I will tell you what you can do. The breeze will freshen to-night around midnight—see those tails of clouds and that thickness to windward, beyond the point there? That's where she'll come from, out of the southeast, hard. It is three hundred miles to Mangareva. Square away for it. There is a beautiful bed for your ship there."

The mate shook his head.

"Come in to the cabin, and we'll look at the chart," said the captain.

McCoy found a stifling, poisonous atmosphere in the pent cabin. Stray waftures of invisible gases bit his eyes and made them sting. The deck was hotter, almost unbearably hot to his bare feet. The sweat poured out of his body. He looked almost with apprehension about him. This malignant, internal heat was astounding. It was a marvel that the cabin did not burst into flames. He had a feeling of being in a huge bake-oven where the heat might at any moment increase tremendously and shrivel him up like a blade of grass.

As he lifted one foot and rubbed the hot sole against the leg of his trousers, the mate laughed in a savage, snarling fashion.

"The anteroom of hell," he said. "Hell herself is right down there under your feet."

"It's hot!" McCoy cried involuntarily, mopping his face with a bandana handkerchief.

"Here's Mangareva," the captain said, bending over the table and pointing to a black speck in the midst of the white blankness of the chart. "And here, in between, is another island. Why not run for that?"

McCoy did not look at the chart.

"That's Crescent Island," he answered. "It is uninhabited, and it is only two or three feet above water. Lagoon, but no entrance. No, Mangareva is the nearest place for your purpose."

"Mangareva it is, then," said Captain Davenport, interrupting the mate's growling objection. "Call the crew aft, Mr. Konig."

The sailors obeyed, shuffling wearily along the deck and painfully endeavoring to make haste. Exhaustion was evident in every movement. The cook came out of his galley to hear, and the cabin-boy hung about near him.

When Captain Davenport had explained the situation and announced his intention of running for Mangareva, an uproar broke out. Against a background of throaty rumbling arose inarticulate cries of rage, with here and there a distinct curse, or word, or phrase. A shrill Cockney voice soared and dominated for a moment, crying: "Gawd! After bein' in 'ell for fifteen days—an' now 'e wants us to sail this floatin' 'ell to sea again!"

The captain could not control them, but McCoy's gentle presence seemed to rebuke and calm them, and the muttering and cursing died away, until the full crew, save here and there an anxious face directed at the captain, yearned dumbly toward the green-clad peaks and beetling coast of Pitcairn.

Soft as a spring zephyr was the voice of McCoy:

"Captain, I thought I heard some of them say they were starving."

"Ay," was the answer, "and so we are. I've had a sea-biscuit and a spoonful of salmon in the last two days. We're on whack. You see, when we discovered the fire, we battened down immediately to suffocate the fire. And then we found how little food there was in the pantry. But it was too late. We didn't dare break out the lazarette. Hungry? I'm just as hungry as they are."

He spoke to the men again, and again the throat-rumbling and cursing arose, their faces convulsed and animal-like with rage. The second and third mates had joined the captain, standing behind him at the break of the poop. Their faces were set and expressionless; they seemed bored, more than anything else, by this mutiny of the crew. Captain Davenport glanced questioningly at his first mate, and that person merely shrugged his shoulders in token of his helplessness.

"You see," the captain said to McCoy, "you can't compel sailors to leave the safe land and go to sea on a burning vessel. She has been their floating coffin for over two weeks now. They are worked out, and starved out, and they've got enough of her. We'll beat up for Pitcairn."

But the wind was light, the *Pyrenees'* bottom was foul, and she could not beat up against the strong westerly current. At the end of two hours she had lost three miles. The sailors worked eagerly, as if by main strength they could compel the *Pyrenees* against the adverse elements. But steadily, port tack and starboard tack, she sagged off to the westward. The captain paced restlessly up and down, pausing occasionally to survey the vagrant smoke-wisps and to trace them back to the portions of the deck from which they sprang. The carpenter was engaged constantly in attempting to locate such places, and, when he succeeded, in calking them tighter and tighter.

"Well, what do you think?" the captain finally asked McCoy, who was watching the carpenter with all a child's interest and curiosity in his eyes.

McCoy looked shoreward, where the land was disappearing in the thickening haze.

"I think it would be better to square away for Mangareva. With that breeze that is coming, you'll be there to-morrow evening."

"But what if the fire breaks out? It is liable to do it any moment."

"Have your boats ready in the falls. The same breeze will carry your boats to Mangareva if the ship burns out from under."

Captain Davenport debated for a moment, and then McCoy heard the question he had not wanted to hear, but which he knew was surely coming.

"I have no chart of Mangareva. On the general chart it is only a fly-speck. I would not know where to look for the entrance into the lagoon. Will you come along and pilot her in for me?"

McCoy's serenity was unbroken.

"Yes, Captain," he said, with the same quiet unconcern with which he would have accepted an invitation to dinner; "I'll go with you to Mangareva."

Again the crew was called aft, and the captain spoke to them from the break of the poop.

"We've tried to work her up, but you see how we've lost ground. She's setting off in a two-knot current. This gentleman is the Honorable McCoy, Chief Magistrate and Governor of Pitcairn Island. He will come along with us to Mangareva. So you see the situation is not so dangerous. He would not make such an offer if he thought he was going to lose his life. Besides, whatever risk there is, if he of his own free will comes on board and takes it, we can do no less. What do you say for Mangareva?"

This time there was no uproar. McCoy's presence, the surety and calm that seemed to radiate from him, had had its effect. They conferred with one another in low voices. There was little urging. They were virtually unanimous, and they shoved the Cockney out as their spokesman. That worthy was overwhelmed with consciousness of the heroism of himself and his mates, and with flashing eyes he cried:

"By Gawd! if 'e will, we will!"

The crew mumbled its assent and started forward.

"One moment, Captain," McCoy said, as the other was turning to give orders to the mate. "I must go ashore first."

Mr. Konig was thunderstruck, staring at McCoy as if he were a madman.

"Go ashore!" the captain cried. "What for? It will take you three hours to get there in your canoe."

McCoy measured the distance of the land away, and nodded.

"Yes, it is six now. I won't get ashore till nine. The people cannot be assembled earlier than ten. As the breeze freshens up to-night, you can begin to work up against it, and pick me up at daylight to-morrow morning."

"In the name of reason and common-sense," the captain burst forth, "what do you want to assemble the people for? Don't you realize that my ship is burning beneath me?"

McCoy was as placid as a summer sea, and the other's anger produced not the slightest ripple upon it.

"Yes, Captain," he cooed in his dovelike voice, "I do realize that your ship is burning. That is why I am going with you to Mangareva. But I must get permission to go with you. It is our custom. It is an important matter when the governor leaves the island. The people's interests are at stake, and so they have the right to vote their permission or refusal. But they will give it, I know that."

"Are you sure?"

"Quite sure."

"Then if you know they will give it, why bother with getting it? Think of the delay—a whole night."

"It is our custom," was the imperturbable reply. "Also, I am the governor, and I must make arrangements for the conduct of the island during my absence."

"But it is only a twenty-four-hour run to Mangareva," the captain objected. "Suppose it took you six times that long to return to windward; that would bring you back by the end of a week."

McCoy smiled his large, benevolent smile.

"Very few vessels come to Pitcairn, and when they do, they are usually from San Francisco or from around the Horn. I shall be fortunate if I get back in six months. I may be away a year, and I may have to go to San Francisco in order to find a vessel that will bring me back. My father once left Pitcairn to be gone three months, and two years passed before he could get back. Then, too, you are short of food. If you have to take to the boats, and the weather comes up bad, you may be days in reaching land. I can bring off two canoe loads of food in the morning. Dried bananas will be best. As the breeze freshens, you beat up against it. The nearer you are, the bigger loads I can bring off. Good-by."

He held out his hand. The captain shook it, and was reluctant to let go. He seemed to cling to it as a drowning sailor clings to a life-buoy.

"How do I know you will come back in the morning?" he asked.

"Yes, that's it!" cried the mate. "How do we know but what he's skinning out to save his own hide?"

McCoy did not speak. He looked at them sweetly and benignantly, and it seemed to them that they received a message from his tremendous certitude of soul.

The captain released his hand, and, with a last sweeping glance that embraced the crew in its benediction, McCoy went over the rail and descended into his canoe.

The wind freshened, and the *Pyrenees*, despite the foulness of her bottom, won half a dozen miles away from the westerly current. At daylight, with Pitcairn three miles to windward, Captain Davenport made out two canoes coming off to him. Again McCoy clambered up the side and dropped over the rail to the hot deck. He was followed by many packages of dried bananas, each package wrapped in dry leaves.

"Now, Captain," he said, "swing the yards and drive for dear life. You see, I am no navigator," he explained a few minutes later, as he stood by the captain aft, the latter with gaze wandering from aloft to overside as he estimated the *Pyrenees'* speed. "You must fetch her to Mangareva. When you have picked up the land, then I will pilot her in. What do you think she is making?"

"Eleven," Captain Davenport answered, with a final glance at the water rushing past.

"Eleven. Let me see, if she keeps up that gait, we'll sight Mangareva between eight and nine o'clock to-morrow morning. I'll have her on the beach by ten, or by eleven at latest. And then your troubles will be all over."

It almost seemed to the captain that the blissful moment had already arrived, such was the persuasive convincingness of McCoy. Captain Davenport had been under the fearful strain of navigating his burning ship for over two weeks, and he was beginning to feel that he had had enough.

A heavier flaw of wind struck the back of his neck and whistled by his ears. He measured the weight of it, and looked quickly overside.

"The wind is making all the time," he announced. "The old girl's doing nearer twelve than eleven right now. If this keeps up, we'll be shortening down to-night."

All day the *Pyrenees*, carrying her load of living fire, tore across the foaming sea.

By nightfall, royals and topgallantsails were in, and she flew on into the darkness, with great, crested seas roaring after her. The auspicious wind had had its effect, and fore and aft a visible brightening was apparent. In the second dog-watch some careless soul started a song, and by eight bells the whole crew was singing.

Captain Davenport had his blankets brought up and spread on top the house.

"I've forgotten what sleep is," he explained to McCoy. "I'm all in. But give me a call at any time you think necessary."

At three in the morning he was aroused by a gentle tugging at his arm. He sat up quickly, bracing himself against the skylight, stupid yet from his heavy sleep. The wind was thrumming its war-song in the rigging, and a wild sea was buffeting the *Pyrenees*. Amidships she was wallowing first one rail under and then the other, flooding the waist more often than not. McCoy was shouting something he could not hear. He reached out, clutched the other by the shoulder, and drew him close so that his own ear was close to the other's lips.

"It's three o'clock," came McCoy's voice, still retaining its dovelike quality, but curiously muffled, as if from a long way off. "We've run two hundred and fifty. Crescent Island is only thirty miles away, somewhere there dead ahead. There's no lights on it. If we keep running, we'll pile up, and lose ourselves as well as the ship."

"What d' ye think—heave to?"

"Yes; heave to till daylight. It will only put us back four hours."

So the *Pyrenees*, with her cargo of fire, was hove to, bitting the teeth of the gale and fighting and smashing the pounding seas. She was a shell, filled with a conflagration, and on the outside of the shell, clinging precariously, the little motes of men, by pull and haul, helped her in the battle.

"It is most unusual, this gale," McCoy told the captain, in the lee of the cabin. "By rights there should be no gale at this time of the year. But everything about the weather has been unusual. There has been a stoppage of the trades, and now it's howling right out of the trade quarter." He waved his hand into the darkness, as if his vision could dimly penetrate for hundreds of miles. "It is off to the westward. There is something big making off there somewhere—a hurricane or something. We're lucky to be so far to the eastward. But this is only a little blow," he added. "It can't last. I can tell you that much."

By daylight the gale had eased down to normal. But daylight revealed a new danger. It had come on thick. The sea was covered by a fog, or, rather, by a pearly mist that was fog-like in density, in so far as it obstructed vision, but that was no more than a film on the sea, for the sun shot it through and filled it with a glowing radiance.

The deck of the *Pyrenees* was making more smoke than on the preceding day, and the cheerfulness of officers and crew had vanished. In the lee of the galley the cabin-boy could be heard whimpering. It was his first voyage, and the fear of death was at his heart. The captain wandered about like a lost soul, nervously chewing his mustache, scowling, unable to make up his mind what to do.

"What do you think?" he asked, pausing by the side of McCoy, who was making a breakfast off fried bananas and a mug of water.

McCoy finished the last banana, drained the mug, and looked slowly around. In his eyes was a smile of tenderness as he said:

"Well, Captain, we might as well drive as burn. Your decks are not going to hold out forever. They are hotter this morning. You haven't a pair of shoes I can wear? It is getting uncomfortable for my bare feet."

The *Pyrenees* shipped two heavy seas as she was swung off and put once more before it, and the first mate expressed a desire to have all that water down in the hold, if only it could be introduced without taking off the hatches. McCoy ducked his head into the binnacle and watched the course set.

"I'd hold her up some more, Captain," he said. "She's been making drift when hove to."

"I've set it to a point higher already," was the answer. "Isn't that enough?"

"I'd make it two points, Captain. This bit of a blow kicked that westerly current ahead faster than you imagine."

Captain Davenport compromised on a point and a half, and then went aloft, accompanied by McCoy and the first mate, to keep a lookout for land. Sail had been made, so that the *Pyrenees* was doing ten knots. The following sea was dying down rapidly. There was no break in the pearly fog, and by ten o'clock Captain Davenport was growing nervous. All hands were at their stations, ready, at the first warning of land ahead, to spring like fiends to the task of bringing the *Pyrenees* up on the wind. That land ahead, a surf-washed outer reef, would be perilously close when it revealed itself in such a fog.

Another hour passed. The three watchers aloft stared intently into the pearly radiance.

"What if we miss Mangareva?" Captain Davenport asked abruptly.

McCoy, without shifting his gaze, answered softly:

"Why, let her drive, Captain. That is all we can do. All the Paumotus are before us. We can drive for a thousand miles through reefs and atolls. We are bound to fetch up somewhere."

"Then drive it is." Captain Davenport evidenced his intention of descending to the deck. "We've missed Mangareva. God knows where the next land is. I wish I'd held her up that other half-point," he confessed a moment later. "This cursed current plays the devil with a navigator."

"The old navigators called the Paumotus the Dangerous Archipelago," McCoy said, when they had regained the poop. "This very current was partly responsible for that name."

"I was talking with a sailor chap in Sydney, once," said Mr. Konig. "He'd been trading in the Paumotus. He told me insurance was eighteen per cent. Is that right?"

McCoy smiled and nodded.

"Except that they don't insure," he explained. "The owners write off twenty per cent of the cost of their schooners each year."

"My God!" Captain Davenport groaned. "That makes the life of a schooner only five years!" He shook his head sadly, murmuring, "Bad waters! bad waters!"

Again they went into the cabin to consult the big general chart; but the poisonous vapors drove them coughing and gasping on deck.

"Here is Moerenhout Island." Captain Davenport pointed it out on the chart, which he had spread on the house. "It can't be more than a hundred miles to leeward."

"A hundred and ten." McCoy shook his head doubtfully. "It might be done, but it is very difficult. I might beach her, and then again I might put her on the reef. A bad place, a very bad place."

"We'll take the chance," was Captain Davenport's decision, as he set about working out the course.

Sail was shortened early in the afternoon, to avoid running past in the night; and in the second dog-watch the crew manifested its regained cheerfulness. Land was so very near, and their troubles would be over in the morning.

But morning broke clear, with a blazing tropic sun. The southeast trade had swung around to the eastward, and was driving the *Pyrenees* through the water at an eight-knot clip. Captain Davenport worked up his dead reckoning, allowing generously for drift, and announced Moerenhout Island to be not more than ten miles off. The *Pyrenees* sailed the ten miles; she sailed ten miles more; and the lookouts at the three mastheads saw naught but the naked, sun-washed sea.

"But the land is there, I tell you," Captain Davenport shouted to them from the poop.

McCoy smiled soothingly, but the captain glared about him like a madman, fetched his sextant, and took a chronometer sight.

"I knew I was right," he almost shouted, when he had worked up the observation. "Twenty-one, fifty-five, south; one-thirty-six, two, west. There you are. We're eight miles to windward yet. What did you make it out, Mr. Konig?"

The first mate glanced at his own figures, and said in a low voice:

"Twenty-one, fifty-five all right; but my longitude's one-thirty-six, forty-eight. That puts us considerably to leeward—"

But Captain Davenport ignored his figures with so contemptuous a silence as to make Mr. Konig grit his teeth and curse savagely under his breath.

"Keep her off," the captain ordered the man at the wheel. "Three points—steady there, as she goes!"

Then he returned to his figures and worked them over. The sweat poured from his face. He chewed his mustache, his lips, and his pencil, staring at the figures as a man might at a ghost. Suddenly, with a fierce, muscular outburst, he crumpled the scribbled paper in his fist and crushed it under foot. Mr. Konig grinned vindictively and turned away, while Captain Davenport leaned against the cabin and for half an hour spoke no word, contenting himself with gazing to leeward with an expression of musing hopelessness on his face.

"Mr. McCoy," he broke silence abruptly. "The chart indicates a group of islands, but not how many, off there to the north'ard, or nor'-nor'westward, about forty miles—the Acteon Islands. What about them?"

"There are four, all low," McCoy answered. "First to the southeast is Matuerui—no people, no entrance to the lagoon. Then comes Tenarunga. There used to be about a dozen people there, but they may be all gone now. Anyway, there is no entrance for a ship—only a boat entrance, with a fathom of water. Vehauga and Teua-raro are the other two. No entrances, no people, very low. There is no bed for the *Pyrenees* in that group. She would be a total wreck."

"Listen to that!" Captain Davenport was frantic. "No people! No entrances! What in the devil are islands good for?

"Well, then," he barked suddenly, like an excited terrier, "the chart gives a whole mess of islands off to the nor'west. What about them? What one has an entrance where I can lay my ship?"

McCoy calmly considered. He did not refer to the chart. All these islands, reefs, shoals, lagoons, entrances, and distances were marked on the chart of his memory. He knew them as the city dweller knows his buildings, streets, and alleys.

"Papakena and Vanavana are off there to the westward, or west-nor'westward a hundred miles and a bit more," he said. "One is uninhabited, and I heard that the people on the other had gone off to Cadmus Island. Anyway, neither lagoon has an entrance. Ahunui is another hundred miles on to the nor'west. No entrance, no people."

"Well, forty miles beyond them are two islands?" Captain Davenport queried, raising his head from the chart.

McCoy shook his head.

"Paros and Manuhungi—no entrances, no people. Nengo-Nengo is forty miles beyond them, in turn, and it has no people and no entrance. But there is Hao Island. It is just the place. The lagoon is thirty miles long and five miles wide. There are plenty of people. You can usually find water. And any ship in the world can go through the entrance."

He ceased and gazed solicitously at Captain Davenport, who, bending over the chart with a pair of dividers in hand, had just emitted a low groan.

"Is there any lagoon with an entrance anywhere nearer than Hao Island?" he asked.

"No, Captain; that is the nearest."

"Well, it's three hundred and forty miles." Captain Davenport was speaking very slowly, with decision. "I won't risk the responsibility of all these lives. I'll wreck her on the Acteons. And she's a good ship, too," he added regretfully, after altering the course, this time making more allowance than ever for the westerly current.

An hour later the sky was overcast. The southeast trade still held, but the ocean was a checker-board of squalls.

"We'll be there by one o'clock," Captain Davenport announced confidently. "By two o'clock at the outside. McCoy, you put her ashore on the one where the people are."

The sun did not appear again, nor, at one o'clock, was any land to be seen. Captain Davenport looked astern at the *Pyrenees'* canting wake.

"Good Lord!" he cried. "An easterly current! Look at that!"

Mr. Konig was incredulous. McCoy was noncommittal, though he said that in the Paumotus there was no reason why it should not be an easterly current. A few minutes later a squall robbed the *Pyrenees* temporarily of all her wind, and she was left rolling heavily in the trough.

"Where's that deep lead? Over with it, you there!" Captain Davenport held the lead-line and watched it sag off to the northeast. "There, look at that! Take hold of it for yourself."

McCoy and the mate tried it, and felt the line thrumming and vibrating savagely to the grip of the tidal stream.

"A four-knot current," said Mr. Konig.

"An easterly current instead of a westerly," said Captain Davenport, glaring accusingly at McCoy, as if to cast the blame for it upon him.

"That is one of the reasons, Captain, for insurance being eighteen per cent in these waters," McCoy answered cheerfully. "You never can tell. The currents are always changing. There was a man who wrote books, I forget his name, in the yacht *Casco*. He missed Takaroa by thirty miles and fetched Tikei, all because of the shifting currents. You are up to windward now, and you'd better keep off a few points."

"But how much has this current set me?" the captain demanded irately. "How am I to know how much to keep off?"

"I don't know, Captain," McCoy said with great gentleness.

The wind returned, and the *Pyrenees*, her deck smoking and shimmering in the bright gray light, ran off dead to leeward. Then she worked back, port tack and starboard tack, crisscrossing her track, combing the sea for the Acteon Islands, which the masthead lookouts failed to sight.

Captain Davenport was beside himself. His rage took the form of sullen silence, and he spent the afternoon in pacing the poop or leaning against the weather-shrouds. At nightfall, without even consulting McCoy, he squared away and headed into the northwest. Mr. Konig, surreptitiously consulting chart and binnacle, and McCoy, openly and innocently consulting the binnacle, knew that they were running for Hao Island. By midnight the squalls ceased, and the stars came out. Captain Davenport was cheered by the promise of a clear day.

"I'll get an observation in the morning," he told McCoy, "though what my latitude is, is a puzzler. But I'll use the Sumner method, and settle that. Do you know the Sumner line?"

And thereupon he explained it in detail to McCoy.

The day proved clear, the trade blew steadily out of the east, and the *Pyrenees* just as steadily logged her nine knots. Both the captain and the mate worked out the position on a Sumner line, and agreed, and at noon agreed again, and verified the morning sights by the noon sights.

"Another twenty-four hours and we'll be there," Captain Davenport assured McCoy. "It's a miracle the way the old girl's decks hold out. But they can't last. They can't last. Look at them smoke, more and more every day. Yet it was a tight deck to begin with, fresh-calked in 'Frisco. I was surprised when the fire first broke out and we battened down. Look at that!"

He broke off to gaze with dropped jaw at a spiral of smoke that coiled and twisted in the lee of the mizzenmast twenty feet above the deck.

"Now, how did that get there?" he demanded indignantly.

Beneath it there was no smoke. Crawling up from the deck, sheltered from the wind by the mast, by some freak it took form and visibility at that height. It writhed away from the mast, and for a moment overhung the captain like some threatening portent. The next moment the wind whisked it away, and the captain's jaw returned to place.

"As I was saying, when we first battened down, I was surprised. It was a tight deck, yet it leaked smoke like a sieve. And we've calked and calked ever since. There must be tremendous pressure underneath to drive so much smoke through."

That afternoon the sky became overcast again, and squally, drizzly weather set in. The wind shifted back and forth between southeast and northeast, and at midnight the *Pyrenees* was caught aback by a sharp squall from the southwest, from which point the wind continued to blow intermittently.

"We won't make Hao until ten or eleven," Captain Davenport complained at seven in the morning, when the fleeting promise of the sun had been erased by hazy cloud masses in the eastern sky. And the next moment he was plaintively demanding, "And what are the currents doing?"

Lookouts at the mastheads could report no land, and the day passed in drizzling calms and violent squalls. By nightfall a heavy sea began to make from the west. The barometer had fallen to 29.50. There was no wind, and still the ominous sea continued to increase. Soon the *Pyrenees* was rolling madly in the huge waves that marched in an unending procession from out of the darkness of the west. Sail was shortened as fast as both watches could work, and, when the tired crew had finished, its grumbling and complaining voices, peculiarly animal-like and menacing, could be heard in the darkness. Once the starboard watch was called aft to lash down and make secure, and the men openly advertised their sullenness and unwillingness. Every slow movement was a protest and a threat. The atmosphere was moist and sticky like mucilage, and in the absence of wind all hands seemed to pant and gasp for air. The sweat stood out on faces and bare arms, and Captain Davenport for one, his face more gaunt and care-worn than ever, and his eyes troubled and staring, was oppressed by a feeling of impending calamity.

"It's off to the westward," McCoy said encouragingly. "At worst, we'll be only on the edge of it."

But Captain Davenport refused to be comforted, and by the light of a lantern read up the chapter in his *Epitome* that related to the strategy of shipmasters in cyclonic storms. From somewhere amidships the silence was broken by a low whimpering from the cabin-boy.

"Oh, shut up!" Captain Davenport yelled suddenly and with such force as to startle every man on board and to frighten the offender into a wild wail of terror.

"Mr. Konig," the captain said in a voice that trembled with rage and nerves, "will you kindly step for'ard and stop that brat's mouth with a deck mop?"

But it was McCoy who went forward, and in a few minutes had the boy comforted and asleep.

Shortly before daybreak the first breath of air began to move from out the southeast, increasing swiftly to a stiff and stiffer breeze. All hands were on deck waiting for what might be behind it.

"We're all right now, Captain," said McCoy, standing close to his shoulder. "The hurricane is to the west'ard, and we are south of it. This breeze is the in-suck. It won't blow any harder. You can begin to put sail on her."

"But what's the good? Where shall I sail? This is the second day without observations, and we should have sighted Hao Island yesterday morning. Which way does it bear, north, south, east, or what? Tell me that, and I'll make sail in a jiffy."

"I am no navigator, Captain," McCoy said in his mild way.

"I used to think I was one," was the retort, "before I got into these Paumotus."

At mid-day the cry of "Breakers ahead!" was heard from the lookout. The *Pyrenees* was kept off, and sail after sail was loosed and sheeted home. The *Pyrenees* was sliding through the water and fighting a current that threatened to set her down upon the breakers. Officers and men were working like mad, cook and cabin-boy, Captain Davenport himself, and McCoy all lending a hand. It was a close shave. It was a low shoal, a bleak and perilous place over which the seas broke unceasingly, where no man could live, and on which not even sea-birds could rest. The *Pyrenees* was swept within a hundred yards of it before the wind carried her clear, and at this moment the panting crew, its work done, burst out in a torrent of curses upon the head of McCoy—of McCoy who had come on board, and proposed the run to Mangareva, and lured them all away from the safety of Pitcairn Island to certain destruction in this baffling and terrible stretch of sea. But McCoy's tranquil soul was undisturbed. He smiled at them with simple and gracious benevolence, and, somehow, the exalted goodness of him seemed to penetrate to their dark and somber souls, shaming them, and from very shame stilling the curses vibrating in their throats.

"Bad waters! bad waters!" Captain Davenport was murmuring as his ship forged clear; but he broke off abruptly to gaze at the shoal which should have been dead astern, but which was already on the *Pyrenees'* weather-quarter and working up rapidly to windward.

He sat down and buried his face in his hands. And the first mate saw, and McCoy saw, and the crew saw, what he had seen. South of the shoal an easterly current had set them down upon it; north of the shoal an equally swift westerly current had clutched the ship and was sweeping her away.

"I've heard of these Paumotus before," the captain groaned, lifting his blanched face from his hands. "Captain Moyendale told me about them after losing his ship on them. And I laughed at him behind his back. God forgive me, I laughed at him. What shoal is that?" he broke off, to ask McCoy.

"I don't know, Captain."

"Why don't you know?"

"Because I never saw it before, and because I have never heard of it. I do know that it is not charted. These waters have never been thoroughly surveyed."

"Then you don't know where we are?"

"No more than you do," McCoy said gently.

At four in the afternoon cocoanut-trees were sighted, apparently growing out of the water. A little later the low land of an atoll was raised above the sea.

"I know where we are now, Captain." McCoy lowered the glasses from his eyes. "That's Resolution Island. We are forty miles beyond Hao Island, and the wind is in our teeth."

"Get ready to beach her then. Where's the entrance?"

"There's only a canoe passage. But now that we know where we are, we can run for Barclay de Tolley. It is only one hundred and twenty miles from here, due nor'-nor'west. With this breeze we can be there by nine o'clock to-morrow morning."

Captain Davenport consulted the chart and debated with himself.

"If we wreck her here," McCoy added, "we'd have to make the run to Barclay de Tolley in the boats just the same."

The captain gave his orders, and once more the *Pyrenees* swung off for another run across the inhospitable sea.

And the middle of the next afternoon saw despair and mutiny on her smoking deck. The current had accelerated, the wind had slackened, and the *Pyrenees* had sagged off to the west. The lookout sighted Barclay de Tolley to the eastward, barely visible from the masthead, and vainly and for hours the *Pyrenees* tried to beat up to it. Ever, like a mirage, the cocoanut-trees hovered on the horizon, visible only from the masthead. From the deck they were hidden by the bulge of the world.

Again Captain Davenport consulted McCoy and the chart. Makemo lay seventy-five miles to the southwest. Its lagoon was thirty miles long, and its entrance was excellent. When Captain Davenport gave his orders, the crew refused duty. They announced that they had had enough of hell-fire under their feet. There was the land. What if the ship could not make it? They could make it in the boats. Let her burn, then. Their lives amounted to something to them. They had served faithfully the ship, now they were going to serve themselves.

They sprang to the boats, brushing the second and third mates out of the way, and proceeded to swing the boats out and to prepare to lower away. Captain Davenport and the first mate, revolvers in hand, were advancing to the break of the poop, when McCoy, who had climbed on top of the cabin, began to speak.

He spoke to the sailors, and at the first sound of his dovelike, cooing voice they paused to hear. He extended to them his own ineffable serenity and peace. His soft voice and simple thoughts flowed out to them in a magic stream, soothing them against their wills. Long forgotten things came back to them, and some remembered lullaby songs of childhood and the content and rest of the mother's arm at the end of the day. There was no more trouble, no more danger, no more irk, in all the world. Everything was as it should be, and it was only a matter of course that they should turn their backs upon the land and put to sea once more with hell-fire hot beneath their feet.

McCoy spoke simply; but it was not what he spoke. It was his personality that spoke more eloquently than any word he could utter. It was an alchemy of soul occultly subtile and profoundly deep—a mysterious emanation of the spirit, seductive, sweetly humble, and terribly imperious. It was illumination in the dark crypts of their souls, a compulsion of purity and gentleness vastly greater than that which resided in the shining, death-spitting revolvers of the officers.

The men wavered reluctantly where they stood, and those who had loosed the turns made them fast again. Then one, and then another, and then all of them, began to sidle awkwardly away.

McCoy's face was beaming with childlike pleasure as he descended from the top of the cabin. There was no trouble. For that matter there had been no trouble averted. There never had been any trouble, for there was no place for such in the blissful world in which he lived.

"You hypnotized 'em," Mr. Konig grinned at him, speaking in a low voice.

"Those boys are good," was the answer. "Their hearts are good. They have had a hard time, and they have worked hard, and they will work hard to the end."

Mr. Konig had no time to reply. His voice was ringing out orders, the sailors were springing to obey, and the *Pyrenees* was paying slowly off from the wind until her bow should point in the direction of Makemo.

The wind was very light, and after sundown almost ceased. It was insufferably warm, and fore and aft men sought vainly to sleep. The deck was too hot to lie upon, and poisonous vapors, oozing through the seams, crept like evil spirits over the ship, stealing into the nostrils and windpipes of the unwary and causing fits of sneezing and coughing. The stars blinked lazily in the dim vault overhead; and the full moon, rising in the east, touched with its light the myriads of wisps and threads and spidery films of smoke that intertwined and writhed and twisted along the deck, over the rails, and up the masts and shrouds.

"Tell me," Captain Davenport said, rubbing his smarting eyes, "what happened with that *Bounty* crowd after they reached Pitcairn? The account I read said they burnt the *Bounty*, and that they were not discovered until many years later. But what happened in the meantime? I've always been curious to know. They were men with their necks in the rope. There were some native men, too. And then there were women. That made it look like trouble right from the jump."

"There was trouble," McCoy answered. "They were bad men. They quarrelled about the women right away. One of the mutineers, Williams, lost his wife. All the women were Tahitian women. His wife fell from the cliffs when hunting sea-birds. Then he took the wife of one of the native men away from him. All the native men were made very angry by this, and they killed off nearly all the mutineers. Then the mutineers that escaped killed off all the native men. The women helped. And the natives killed each other. Everybody killed everybody. They were terrible men.

"Timiti was killed by two other natives while they were combing his hair in friendship. The white men had sent them to do it. Then the white men killed them. The wife of Tullaloo killed him in a cave because she wanted a white man for husband. They were very wicked. God had hidden His face from them. At the end of two years all the native men were murdered, and all the white men except four. They were Young, John Adams, McCoy, who was my great-grandfather, and Quintal. He was a very bad man, too. Once, just because his wife did not catch enough fish for him, he bit off her ear."

"They were a bad lot!" Mr. Konig exclaimed.

"Yes, they were very bad," McCoy agreed and went on serenely cooing of the blood and lust of his iniquitous ancestry. "My great-grandfather escaped murder in order to die by his own hand. He made a still and manufactured alcohol from the roots of the ti-plant. Quintal was his chum, and they got drunk together all the time. At last McCoy got delirium tremens, tied a rock to his neck, and jumped into the sea.

"Quintal's wife, the one whose ear he bit off, also got killed by falling from the cliffs. Then Quintal went to Young and demanded his wife, and went to Adams and demanded his wife. Adams and Young were afraid of Quintal. They knew he would kill them. So they killed him, the two of them together, with a hatchet. Then Young died. And that was about all the trouble they had."

"I should say so," Captain Davenport snorted. "There was nobody left to kill."

"You see, God had hidden His face," McCoy said.

By morning no more than a faint air was blowing from the eastward, and, unable to make appreciable southing by it, Captain Davenport hauled up full-and-by on the port track. He was afraid of that terrible westerly current which had cheated him out of so many ports of refuge. All day the calm continued, and all night, while the sailors, on a short ration of dried banana, were grumbling. Also, they were growing weak and complaining of stomach pains caused by the straight banana diet. All day the current swept the *Pyrenees* to the westward, while there was no wind to bear her south. In the middle of the first dog-watch, cocoanut-trees were sighted due south, their tufted heads rising above the water and marking the low-lying atoll beneath.

"That is Taenga Island," McCoy said. "We need a breeze to-night, or else we'll miss Makemo."

"What's become of the southeast trade?" the captain demanded. "Why don't it blow? What's the matter?"

"It is the evaporation from the big lagoons—there are so many of them," McCoy explained. "The evaporation upsets the whole system of trades. It even causes the wind to back up and blow gales from the southwest. This is the Dangerous Archipelago, Captain."

Captain Davenport faced the old man, opened his mouth, and was about to curse, but paused and refrained. McCoy's presence was a rebuke to the blasphemies that stirred in his brain and trembled in his larynx. McCoy's influence had been growing during the many days they had been together. Captain Davenport was an autocrat of the sea, fearing no man, never bridling his tongue, and now he found himself unable to curse in the presence of this old man with the feminine brown eyes and the voice of a dove. When he realized this, Captain Davenport experienced a distinct shock. This old man was merely the seed of McCoy, of McCoy of the *Bounty*, the mutineer fleeing from the hemp that waited him in England, the McCoy who was a power for evil in the early days of blood and lust and violent death on Pitcairn Island.

Captain Davenport was not religious, yet in that moment he felt a mad impulse to cast himself at the other's feet—and to say he knew not what. It was an emotion that so deeply stirred him, rather than a coherent thought, and he was aware in some vague way of his own unworthiness and smallness in the presence of this other man who possessed the simplicity of a child and the gentleness of a woman.

Of course he could not so humble himself before the eyes of his officers and men. And yet the anger that had prompted the blasphemy still raged in him. He suddenly smote the cabin with his clenched hand and cried:

"Look here, old man, I won't be beaten. These Paumotus have cheated and tricked me and made a fool of me. I refuse to be beaten. I am going to drive this ship, and drive and drive and drive clear through the Paumotus to China but what I find a bed for her. If every man deserts, I'll stay by her. I'll show the Paumotus. They can't fool me. She's a good girl, and I'll stick by her as long as there's a plank to stand on. You hear me?"

"And I'll stay with you, Captain," McCoy said.

During the night, light, baffling airs blew out of the south, and the frantic captain, with his cargo of fire, watched and measured his westward drift and went off by himself at times to curse softly so that McCoy should not hear.

Daylight showed more palms growing out of the water to the south.

"That's the leeward point of Makemo," McCoy said. "Katiu is only a few miles to the west. We may make that."

But the current, sucking between the two islands, swept them to the northwest, and at one in the afternoon they saw the palms of Katiu rise above the sea and sink back into the sea again.

A few minutes later, just as the captain had discovered that a new current from the northeast had gripped the *Pyrenees*, the masthead lookouts raised cocoanut palms in the northwest.

"It is Raraka," said McCoy. "We won't make it without wind. The current is drawing us down to the southwest. But we must watch out. A few miles farther on a current flows north and turns in a circle to the northwest. This will sweep us away from Fakarava, and Fakarava is the place for the *Pyrenees* to find her bed."

"They can sweep all they da—all they well please," Captain Davenport remarked with heat. "We'll find a bed for her somewhere just the same."

But the situation on the *Pyrenees* was reaching a culmination. The deck was so hot that it seemed an increase of a few degrees would cause it to burst into flames. In many places even the heavy-soled shoes of the men were no protection, and they were compelled to step lively to avoid scorching their feet. The smoke had increased and grown more acrid. Every man on board was suffering from inflamed eyes, and they coughed and strangled like a crew of tuberculosis patients. In the afternoon the boats were swung out and equipped. The last several packages of dried bananas were stored in them, as well as the instruments of the officers. Captain Davenport even put the chronometer into the longboat, fearing the blowing up of the deck at any moment.

All night this apprehension weighed heavily on all, and in the first morning light, with hollow eyes and ghastly faces, they stared at one another as if in surprise that the *Pyrenees* still held together and that they still were alive.

Walking rapidly at times, and even occasionally breaking into an undignified hop-skip-and-run, Captain Davenport inspected his ship's deck.

"It is a matter of hours now, if not of minutes," he announced on his return to the poop.

The cry of land came down from the masthead. From the deck the land was invisible, and McCoy went aloft, while the captain took advantage of the opportunity to curse some of the bitterness out of his heart. But the cursing was suddenly stopped by a dark line on the water which he sighted to the northeast. It was not a squall, but a regular breeze—the disrupted trade-wind, eight points out of its direction but resuming business once more.

"Hold her up, Captain," McCoy said as soon as he reached the poop. "That's the easterly point of Fakarava, and we'll go in through the passage full-tilt, the wind abeam, and every sail drawing."

At the end of an hour, the cocoanut-trees and the low-lying land were visible from the deck. The feeling that the end of the *Pyrenees'* resistance was imminent weighed heavily on everybody. Captain Davenport had the three boats lowered and dropped short astern, a man in each to keep them apart. The *Pyrenees* closely skirted the shore, the surf-whitened atoll a bare two cable-lengths away.

"Get ready to wear her, Captain," McCoy warned.

And a minute later the land parted, exposing a narrow passage and the lagoon beyond, a great mirror, thirty miles in length and a third as broad.

"Now, Captain."

For the last time the yards of the *Pyrenees* swung around as she obeyed the wheel and headed into the passage. The turns had scarcely been made, and nothing had been coiled down, when the men and mates swept back to the poop in panic terror. Nothing had happened, yet they averred that something was going to happen. They could not tell why. They merely knew that it was about to happen. McCoy started forward to take up his position on the bow in order to con the vessel in; but the captain gripped his arm and whirled him around.

"Do it from here," he said. "That deck's not safe. What's the matter?" he demanded the next instant. "We're standing still."

McCoy smiled.

"You are bucking a seven-knot current, Captain," he said. "That is the way the full ebb runs out of this passage."

At the end of another hour the *Pyrenees* had scarcely gained her length, but the wind freshened and she began to forge ahead.

"Better get into the boats, some of you," Captain Davenport commanded.

His voice was still ringing, and the men were just beginning to move in obedience, when the amidship deck of the *Pyrenees*, in a mass of flame and smoke, was flung upward into the sails and rigging, part of it remaining there and the rest falling into the sea. The wind being abeam, was what had saved the men crowded aft. They made a blind rush to gain the boats, but McCoy's voice, carrying its convincing message of vast calm and endless time, stopped them.

"Take it easy," he was saying. "Everything is all right. Pass that boy down somebody, please."

The man at the wheel had forsaken it in a funk, and Captain Davenport had leaped and caught the spokes in time to prevent the ship from yawing in the current and going ashore.

"Better take charge of the boats," he said to Mr. Konig. "Tow one of them short, right under the quarter. . . . When I go over, it'll be on the jump."

Mr. Konig hesitated, then went over the rail and lowered himself into the boat.

"Keep her off half a point, Captain."

Captain Davenport gave a start. He had thought he had the ship to himself.

"Ay, ay; half a point it is," he answered.

Amidships the *Pyrenees* was an open, flaming furnace, out of which poured an immense volume of smoke which rose high above the masts and completely hid the forward part of the ship. McCoy, in the shelter of the mizzen-shrouds, continued his difficult task of conning the ship through the intricate channel. The fire was working aft along the deck from the seat of explosion, while the soaring tower of canvas on the mainmast went up and vanished in a sheet of flame. Forward, though they could not see them, they knew that the head-sails were still drawing.

"If only she don't burn all her canvas off before she makes inside," the captain groaned.

"She'll make it," McCoy assured him with supreme confidence. "There is plenty of time. She is bound to make it. And once inside, we'll put her before it; that will keep the smoke away from us and hold back the fire from working aft."

A tongue of flame sprang up the mizzen, reached hungrily for the lowest tier of canvas, missed it, and vanished. From aloft a burning shred of rope-stuff fell square on the back of Captain Davenport's neck. He acted with the celerity of one stung by a bee as he reached up and brushed the offending fire from his skin.

"How is she heading, Captain?"

"Nor'west by west."

"Keep her west-nor'west."

Captain Davenport put the wheel up and steadied her.

"West by north, Captain."

"West by north she is."

"And now west."

Slowly, point by point, as she entered the lagoon, the *Pyrenees* described the circle that put her before the wind; and point by point, with all the calm certitude of a thousand years of time to spare, McCoy chanted the changing course.

"Another point, Captain."

"A point it is."

Captain Davenport whirled several spokes over, suddenly reversing and coming back one to check her.

"Steady."

"Steady she is—right on it."

Despite the fact that the wind was now astern, the heat was so intense that Captain Davenport was compelled to steal sidelong glances into the binnacle, letting go the wheel, now with one hand, now with the other, to rub or shield his blistering cheeks. McCoy's beard was crinkling and shrivelling and the smell of it, strong in the other's nostrils, compelled him to look toward McCoy with sudden solicitude. Captain Davenport was letting go the spokes alternately with his hands in order to rub their blistering backs against his trousers. Every sail on the mizzenmast vanished in a rush of flame, compelling the two men to crouch and shield their faces.

"Now," said McCoy, stealing a glance ahead at the low shore, "four points up, Captain, and let her drive."

Shreds and patches of burning rope and canvas were falling about them and upon them. The tarry smoke from a smouldering piece of rope at the captain's feet set him off into a violent coughing fit, during which he still clung to the spokes.

The *Pyrenees* struck, her bow lifted, and she ground ahead gently to a stop. A shower of burning fragments, dislodged by the shock, fell about them. The ship moved ahead again and struck a second time. She crushed the fragile coral under her keel, drove on, and struck a third time.

"Hard over," said McCoy. "Hard over?" he questioned gently, a minute later.

"She won't answer," was the reply.

"All right. She is swinging around." McCoy peered over the side. "Soft, white sand. Couldn't ask better. A beautiful bed."

As the *Pyrenees* swung around her stern away from the wind, a fearful blast of smoke and flame poured aft. Captain Davenport deserted the wheel in blistering agony. He reached the painter of the boat that lay under the quarter, then looked for McCoy, who was standing aside to let him go down.

"You first," the captain cried, gripping him by the shoulder and almost throwing him over the rail. But the flame and smoke were too terrible, and he followed hard after McCoy, both men wriggling on the rope and sliding down into the boat together. A sailor in the bow, without waiting for orders, slashed the painter through with his sheath-knife. The oars, poised in readiness, bit into the water, and the boat shot away.

"A beautiful bed, Captain," McCoy murmured, looking back.

"Ay, a beautiful bed, and all thanks to you," was the answer.

The three boats pulled away for the white beach of pounded coral, beyond which, on the edge of a cocoanut grove, could be seen a half-dozen grass-houses, and a score or more of excited natives, gazing wide-eyed at the conflagration that had come to land.

The boats grounded and they stepped out on the white beach.

"And now," said McCoy, "I must see about getting back to Pitcairn."

1909

THE MEXICAN

Nobody knew his history—they of the Junta least of all. He was their "little mystery," their "big patriot," and in his way he worked as hard for the coming Mexican Revolution as did they. They were tardy in recognizing this, for not one of the Junta liked him. The day he first drifted into their crowded, busy rooms they all suspected him of being a spy—one of the bought tools of the Diaz secret service.

Too many of the comrades were in civil and military prisons scattered over the United States, and others of them, in irons, were even then being taken across the border to be lined up against adobe walls and shot.

At the first sight the boy did not impress them favorably. Boy he was, not more than eighteen and not overlarge for his years. He announced that he was Felipe Rivera, and that it was his wish to work for the revolution. That was all—not a wasted word, no further explanation. He stood waiting. There was no smile on his lips, no geniality in his eyes. Big, dashing Paulino Vera felt an inward shudder. Here was something forbidding, terrible, inscrutable. There was something venomous and snakelike in the boy's black eyes. They burned like cold fire, as with a vast, concentrated bitterness. He flashed them from the faces of the conspirators to the typewriter which little Mrs. Sethby was industriously operating. His eyes rested on hers but an instant—she had chanced to look up—and she, too, sensed the nameless something that made her pause. She was compelled to read back in order to regain the swing of the letter she was writing.

Paulino Vera looked questioningly at Arrellano and Ramos, and questioningly they looked back and to each other. The indecision of doubt brooded in their eyes. This slender boy was the Unknown, vested with all the menace of the Unknown. He was unrecognizable, something quite beyond the ken of honest, ordinary revolutionists whose fiercest hatred for Diaz and his tyranny after all was only that of honest and ordinary patriots. Here was something else, they knew not what. But Vera, always the most impulsive, the quickest to act, stepped into the breach.

"Very well," he said coldly. "You say you want to work for the revolution. Take off your coat. Hang it over there. I will show you—come—where are the buckets and cloths. The floor is dirty. You will begin by scrubbing it, and by scrubbing the floors of the other rooms. The spittoons need to be cleaned. Then there are the windows."

"Is it for the revolution?" the boy asked.

"It is for the revolution," Vera answered.

Rivera looked cold suspicion at all of them, then proceeded to take off his coat.

"It is well," he said.

And nothing more. Day after day he came to his work—sweeping, scrubbing, cleaning. He emptied the ashes from the stoves, brought up the coal and kindling, and lighted the fires before the most energetic one of them was at his desk.

"Can I sleep here?" he asked once.

Aha! So that was it—the hand of Diaz showing through! To sleep in the rooms of the Junta meant access to their secrets, to the lists of names, to the addresses of comrades down on Mexican soil. The request was denied, and Rivera never spoke of it again. He slept they knew not where, and ate they knew not where nor how. Once Arrellano offered him a couple of dollars. Rivera declined the money with a shake of the head. When Vera joined in and tried to press it upon him, he said:

"I am working for the revolution."

It takes money to raise a modern revolution, and always the Junta was pressed. The members starved and toiled, and the longest day was none too long, and yet there were times when it appeared as if the revolution stood or fell on no more than the matter of a few dollars. Once, the first time, when the rent of the house was two months behind and the landlord was threatening dispossession, it was Felipe Rivera, the scrub boy in the poor, cheap clothes, worn and threadbare, who laid sixty dollars in gold on May Sethby's desk. There were other times. Three hundred letters, clicked out on the busy typewriters (appeals for assistance, for sanctions from the organized labor groups, requests for square news deals to the editors of newspapers, protests against the highhanded treatment of revolutionists by the United States courts), lay unmailed, awaiting postage. Vera's watch had disappeared—the old-fashioned gold repeater that had been his father's. Likewise had gone the plain gold band from May Sethby's third finger. Things were desperate. Ramos and Arrellano pulled their long mustaches in despair. The letters must go off, and the post office allowed no credit to purchasers of stamps. Then it was that Rivera put on his hat and went out. When he came back he laid a thousand two-cent stamps on May Sethby's desk.

"I wonder if it is the cursed gold of Diaz?" said Vera to the comrades.

They elevated their brows and could not decide. And Felipe Rivera, the scrubber for the revolution, continued, as occasion arose, to lay down gold and silver for the Junta's use.

And still they could not bring themselves to like him. They did not know him. His ways were not theirs. He gave no confidences. He repelled all probing. Youth that he was, they could never nerve themselves to dare to question him.

"A great and lonely spirit, perhaps, I do not know, I do not know," Arrellano said helplessly.

"He is not human," said Ramos.

"His soul has been seared," said May Sethby. "Light and laughter have been burned out of him. He is like one dead, and yet he is fearfully alive."

"He has been through hell," said Vera. "No man could look like that who has not been through hell—and he is only a boy."

Yet they could not like him. He never talked, never inquired, never suggested. He would stand listening, expressionless, a thing dead, save for his eyes, coldly burning, while their talk of the revolution ran high and warm. From face to face and speaker to speaker his eyes would turn, boring like gimlets of incandescent ice, disconcerting and perturbing.

"He is no spy," Vera confided to May Sethby. "He is a patriot—mark me, the greatest patriot of us all. I know it, I feel it, here in my heart and head I feel it. But him I know not at all."

"He has a bad temper," said May Sethby.

"I know," said Vera with a shudder. "He has looked at me with those eyes of his. They do not love; they threaten; they are savage as a wild tiger's. I know, if I should prove unfaithful to the cause, that he would kill me. He has no heart. He is pitiless as steel, keen and cold as frost. He is like moonshine in a winter night when a man freezes to death on some lonely mountaintop. I am not afraid of Diaz and all his killers; but this boy, of him am I afraid. I tell you true. I am afraid. He is the breath of death."

Yet Vera it was who persuaded the others to give the first trust to Rivera. The line of communication between Los Angeles and Lower California had broken down. Three of the comrades had dug their own graves and been shot into them. Two more were United States prisoners in Los Angeles. Juan Alvarado, the federal commander, was a monster. All their plans did he checkmate. They could no longer gain access to the active revolutionists, and the incipient ones, in Lower California.

Young Rivera was given his instructions and dispatched south. When he returned, the line of communication was re-established, and Juan Alvarado was dead.

He had been found in bed, a knife hilt-deep in his breast. This had exceeded Rivera's instructions, but they of the Junta knew the times of his movements. They did not ask him. He said nothing. But they looked at one another and conjectured.

"I have told you," said Vera. "Diaz has more to fear from this youth than from any man. He is implacable. He is the hand of God."

The bad temper, mentioned by May Sethby, and sensed by them all, was evidenced by physical proofs. Now he appeared with a cut lip, a blackened cheek, or a swollen ear. It was patent that he brawled, somewhere in that outside world where he ate and slept, gained money, and moved in ways unknown to them. As the time passed he had come to set type for the little revolutionary sheet they published weekly. There were occasions when he was unable to set type, when his knuckles were bruised and battered, when his thumbs were injured and helpless, when one arm or the other hung wearily at his side while his face was drawn with unspoken pain.

"A wastrel," said Arrellano.

"A frequenter of low places," said Ramos.

"But where does he get the money?" Vera demanded. "Only today, just now, have I learned that he paid the bill for white paper—one hundred and forty dollars."

"There are his absences," said May Sethby. "He never explains them."

"We should set a spy upon him," Ramos propounded.

"I should not care to be that spy," said Vera. "I fear you would never see me again, save to bury me. He has a terrible passion. Not even God would he permit to stand between him and the way of his passion."

"I feel like a child before him," Ramos confessed.

"To me he is power—he is the primitive, the wild wolf, the striking rattlesnake, the stinging centipede," said Arrellano.

"He is the revolution incarnate," said Vera. "He is the flame and the spirit of it, the insatiable cry for vengeance that makes no cry but that slays noiselessly. He is a destroying angel moving through the still watches of the night."

"I could weep over him," said May Sethby. "He knows nobody. He hates all people. Us he tolerates, for we are the way of his desire. He is alone . . . lonely." Her voice broke in a half sob and there was dimness in her eyes.

Rivera's ways and times were truly mysterious. There were periods when they did not see him for a week at a time. Once he was away a month. These occasions were always capped by his return, when, without advertisement or speech, he laid gold coins on May Sethby's desk. Again, for days and weeks, he spent all his time with the Junta. And yet again, for irregular periods, he would disappear through the heart of each day, from early morning until late afternoon. At such times he came early and remained late. Arrellano had found him at midnight, setting type with fresh-swollen knuckles, or mayhap it was his lip, new-split, that still bled.

II

The time of the crisis approached. Whether or not the revolution would be depended upon the Junta, and the Junta was hard-pressed. The need for money was greater than ever before, while money was harder to get. Patriots had given their last cent and now could give no more. Section-gang laborers—fugitive peons from

Mexico—were contributing half their scanty wages. But more than that was needed. The heartbreaking, conspiring, undermining toil of years approached fruition. The time was ripe. The revolution hung on the balance. One shove more, one last heroic effort, and it would tremble across the scales to victory. They knew their Mexico. Once started, the revolution would take care of itself. The whole Diaz machine would go down like a house of cards. The border was ready to rise. One Yankee, with a hundred I.W.W. men, waited the word to cross over the border and begin the conquest of Lower California. But he needed guns. And clear across to the Atlantic, the Junta in touch with them all and all of them needing guns, mere adventurers, soldiers of fortune, bandits, disgruntled American union men, socialists, anarchists, roughnecks, Mexican exiles, peons escaped from bondage, whipped miners from the bullpens of Cœur d'Alene and Colorado who desired only the more vindictively to fight—all the flotsam and jetsam of wild spirits from the madly complicated modern world. And it was guns and ammunition, ammunition and guns—the unceasing and eternal cry.

Fling this heterogeneous, bankrupt, vindictive mass across the border, and the revolution was on. The customhouse, the northern ports of entry, would be captured. Diaz could not resist. He dared not throw the weight of his armies against them, for he must hold the south. And through the south the flame would spread despite. The people would rise. The defenses of city after city would crumple up. State after state would totter down. And at last, from every side, the victorious armies of the revolution would close in on the city of Mexico itself, Diaz's last stronghold.

But the money. They had the men, impatient and urgent, who would use the guns. They knew the traders who would sell and deliver the guns. But to culture the revolution thus far had exhausted the Junta. The last dollar had been spent, the last resource and the last starving patriot milked dry, and the great adventure still trembled on the scales. Guns and ammunition! The ragged battalions must be armed. But how? Ramos lamented his confiscated estates. Arrellano wailed the spendthriftness of his youth. May Sethby wondered if it would have been different had they of the Junta been more economical in the past.

"To think that the freedom of Mexico should stand or fall on a few paltry thousands of dollars," said Paulino Vera.

Despair was in all their faces. José Amarillo, their last hope, a recent convert who had promised money, had been apprehended at his hacienda in Chihuahua and shot against his own stable wall. The news had just come through.

Rivera, on his knees, scrubbing, looked up, with suspended brush, his bare arms flecked with soapy, dirty water.

"Will five thousand do it?" he asked.

They looked their amazement. Vera nodded and swallowed. He could not speak, but he was on the instant invested with a vast faith.

"Order the guns," Rivera said, and thereupon was guilty of the longest flow of words they had ever heard him utter. "The time is short. In three weeks I shall bring you the five thousand. It is well. The weather will be warmer for those who fight. Also, it is the best I can do."

Vera fought his faith. It was incredible. Too many fond hopes had been shattered since he had begun to play the revolution game. He believed this threadbare scrubber of the revolution, and yet he dared not believe.

"You are crazy," he said.

"In three weeks," said Rivera. "Order the guns."

He got up, rolled down his sleeves, and put on his coat.

"Order the guns," he said. "I am going now."

III

After hurrying and scurrying, much telephoning and bad language, a night session was held in Kelly's office. Kelly was rushed with business; also, he was unlucky. He had brought Danny Ward out from New York, arranged the fight for him with Billy Carthey, the date was three weeks away, and for two days now, carefully concealed from the sporting writers, Carthey had been lying up, badly injured. There was no one to take his place. Kelly had been burning the wires east to every eligible lightweight, but they were tied up with dates and contracts. And now hope had revived, though faintly.

"You've got a hell of a nerve," Kelly addressed Rivera, after one look, as soon as they got together.

Hate that was malignant was in Rivera's eyes, but his face remained impassive.

"I can lick Ward," was all he said.

"How do you know? Ever see him fight?"

Rivera shook his head.

"He can beat you up with one hand and both eyes closed."

Rivera shrugged his shoulders.

"Haven't you got anything to say?" the fight promoter snarled.

"I can lick him."

"Who'd you ever fight, anyway?" Michael Kelly demanded. Michael was the promoter's brother, and ran the Yellowstone Poolrooms, where he made goodly sums on the fight game.

Rivera favored him with a bitter, unanswering stare.

The promoter's secretary, a distinctively sporty young man, sneered audibly.

"Well, you know Roberts." Kelly broke the hostile silence. "He ought to be here. I've sent for him. Sit down and wait, though from the looks of you, you haven't got a chance. I can't throw the public down with a bum fight. Ringside seats are selling at fifteen dollars, you know that."

When Roberts arrived it was patent that he was mildly drunk. He was a tall, lean, slack-jointed individual, and his walk, like his talk, was a smooth and languid drawl.

Kelly went straight to the point.

"Look here, Roberts, you've been braggin' you discovered this little Mexican. You know Carthey's broke his arm. Well, this little yellow streak has the gall to blow in today and say he'll take Carthey's place. What about it?"

"It's all right, Kelly," came the slow response. "He can put up a fight."

"I suppose you'll be sayin' next that he can lick Ward," Kelly snapped.

Roberts considered judicially.

"No, I won't say that. Ward's a topnotcher and a ring general. But he can't hash-house Rivera in short order. I know Rivera. Nobody can get his goat. He ain't got a goat that I could ever discover. And he's a two-handed fighter. He can throw in the sleep-makers from any position."

"Never mind that. What kind of a show can he put up? You've been conditioning and training fighters all your life. I take off my hat to your judgment. Can he give the public a run for its money?"

"He sure can, and he'll worry Ward a mighty heap on top of it. You don't know that boy. I do. I discovered him. He ain't got a goat. He's a devil. He's a wizzy-wooz if anybody should ask you. He'll make Ward sit up with a show of local talent that'll make the rest of you sit up. I won't say he'll lick Ward, but he'll put up such a show that you'll all know he's a comer."

"All right." Kelly turned to his secretary. "Ring up Ward. I warned him to show up if I thought it worth while. He's right across at the Yellowstone, throwin' chests and doing the popular." Kelly turned back to the conditioner. "Have a drink?"

Roberts sipped his highball and unburdened himself.

"Never told you how I discovered the little cuss. It was a couple of years ago he showed up out at the quarters. I was getting Prayne ready for his fight with Delaney. Prayne's wicked. He ain't got a tickle of mercy in his make-up. He'd chopped up his pardners something cruel, and I couldn't find a willing boy that'd work with him. I'd noticed this little starved Mexican kid hanging around, and I was desperate. So I grabbed him, slammed on the gloves, and put him in. He was tougher'n rawhide, but weak. And he didn't know the first letter in the alphabet of boxing. Prayne chopped him to ribbons. But he hung on for two sickening rounds, when he fainted. Starvation, that was all. Battered? You couldn't have recognized him. I gave him half a dollar and a square meal. You oughta seen him wolf it down. He hadn't had a bite for a couple of days. That's the end of him, thinks I. But next day he showed up, stiff an' sore, ready for another half and a square meal. And he done better as time went by. Just a born fighter, and tough beyond belief. He hasn't a heart. He's a piece of ice. And he never talked eleven words in a string since I know him. He saws wood and does his work."

"I've seen 'm," the secretary said. "He's worked a lot for you."

"All the big little fellows has tried out on him," Roberts answered. "And he's learned from 'em. I've seen some of them he could lick. But his heart wasn't in it. I reckoned he never liked the game. He seemed to act that way."

"He's been fighting some before the little clubs the last few months," Kelly said.

"Sure. But I don't know what struck 'm. All of a sudden his heart got into it. He just went out like a streak and cleaned up all the little local fellows. Seemed to want the money, and he's won a bit, though his clothes don't look it. He's peculiar. Nobody knows his business. Nobody knows how he spends his time. Even when he's on the job, he plumb up and disappears most of each day soon as his work is done. Sometimes he just blows away for weeks at a time. But he don't take advice. There's a fortune in it for the fellow that gets the job of managin' him, only he won't consider it. And you watch him hold out for the cash money when you get down to terms."

It was at this stage that Danny Ward arrived. Quite a party it was. His manager and trainer were with him, and he breezed in like a gusty draft of geniality, good nature, and all-conqueringness. Greetings flew about, a joke here, a retort there, a smile or a laugh for everybody. Yet it was his way, and only partly sincere. He was a good actor, and he had found geniality a most valuable asset in the game of getting on in the world. But down underneath he was the deliberate, cold-blooded fighter and businessman. The rest was a mask. Those who knew him or trafficked with him said that when it came to brass tacks he was Danny on the Spot. He was invariably present at all business discussions, and it was urged by some that his manager was a blind whose only function was to serve as Danny's mouthpiece.

Rivera's way was different. Indian blood, as well as Spanish, was in his veins, and he sat back in a corner, silent, immobile, only his black eyes passing from face to face and noting everything.

"So that's the guy," Danny said, running an appraising eye over his proposed antagonist. "How de do, old chap."

Rivera's eyes burned venomously, but he made no sign of acknowledgment. He disliked all gringos, but this gringo he hated with an immediacy that was unusual even in him.

"Gawd!" Danny protested facetiously to the promoter. "You ain't expectin' me to fight a deef mute." When the laughter subsided he made another hit. "Los Angeles must be on the dink when this is the best you can scare up. What kindergarten did you get 'm from?"

"He's a good little boy, Danny, take it from me," Roberts defended. "Not as easy as he looks."

"And half the house is sold already," Kelly pleaded. "You'll have to take 'm on, Danny. It's the best we can do."

Danny ran another careless and unflattering glance over Rivera and sighed.

"I gotta be easy with 'm, I guess. If only he don't blow up."

Roberts snorted.

"You gotta be careful," Danny's manager warned. "No taking chances with a dub that's likely to sneak a lucky one across."

"Oh, I'll be careful all right, all right," Danny smiled. "I'll get 'm at the start an' nurse 'm along for the dear public's sake. What d'ye say to fifteen rounds, Kelly—an' then the hay for him?"

"That'll do," was the answer. "As long as you make it realistic."

"Then let's get down to biz." Danny paused and calculated. "Of course, sixty-five per cent of gate receipts, same as with Carthey. But the split'll be different. Eighty will just about suit me." And to his manager, "That right?"

The manager nodded.

"Here, you, did you get that?" Kelly asked Rivera.

Rivera shook his head.

"Well, it's this way," Kelly exposited. "The purse'll be sixty-five per cent of the gate receipts. You're a dub, and an unknown. You and Danny split, twenty per cent goin' to you, an' eighty to Danny. That's fair, isn't it, Roberts?"

"Very fair, Rivera," Roberts agreed. "You see, you ain't got a reputation yet."

"What will sixty-five per cent of the gate receipts be?" Rivera demanded.

"Oh, maybe five thousand, maybe as high as eight thousand," Danny broke in to explain. "Something like that. Your share'll come to something like a thousand or sixteen hundred. Pretty good for takin' a licking from a guy with my reputation. What d'ye say?"

Then Rivera took their breaths away.

"Winner takes all," he said with finality.

A dead silence prevailed.

"It's like candy from a baby," Danny's manager proclaimed.

Danny shook his head.

"I've been in the game too long," he explained. "I'm not casting reflections on the referee or the present company. I'm not sayin' nothing about bookmakers an' frame-ups that sometimes happen. But what I do say is that it's poor business for a fighter like me. I play safe. There's no tellin'. Mebbe I break my arm, eh? Or some guy slips me a bunch of dope." He shook his head solemnly. "Win or lose, eighty is my split. What d'ye say, Mexican?"

Rivera shook his head.

Danny exploded. He was getting down to brass tacks now.

"Why, you dirty little greaser! I've a mind to knock your block off right now."

Roberts drawled his body to interposition between hostilities.

"Winner takes all," Rivera repeated sullenly.

"Why do you stand out that way?" Danny asked.

"I can lick you," was the straight answer.

Danny half started to take off his coat. But, as his manager knew, it was a grandstand play. The coat did not come off, and Danny allowed himself to be placated by the group. Everybody sympathized with him. Rivera stood alone.

"Look here, you little fool," Kelly took up the argument. "You're nobody. We know what you've been doing the last few months—putting away little local fighters. But Danny is class. His next fight after this will be for the championship. And you're unknown. Nobody ever heard of you out of Los Angeles."

"They will," Rivera answered with a shrug, "after this fight."

"You think for a second you can lick me?" Danny blurted in.

Rivera nodded.

"Oh, come; listen to reason," Kelly pleaded. "Think of the advertising."

"I want the money," was Rivera's answer.

"You couldn't win from me in a thousand years," Danny assured him.

"Then what are you holding out for?" Rivera countered. "If the money's that easy, why don't you go after it?"

"I will, so help me!" Danny cried with abrupt conviction. "I'll beat you to death in the ring, my boy—you monkeyin' with me this way. Make out the articles, Kelly. Winner take all. Play it up in the sportin' columns. Tell 'em it's a grudge fight. I'll show this fresh kid a few."

Kelly's secretary had begun to write, when Danny interrupted.

"Hold on!" He turned to Rivera. "Weights?"

"Ringside," came the answer.

"Not on your life, fresh kid. If winner takes all, we weigh in at 10 A.M."

"And winner takes all?" Rivera queried.

Danny nodded. That settled it. He would enter the ring in his full ripeness of strength.

"Weigh in at ten," Rivera said.

The secretary's pen went on scratching.

"It means five pounds," Roberts complained to Rivera. "You've given too much away. You've thrown the fight right there. Danny'll be as strong as a bull. You're a fool. He'll lick you sure. You ain't got the chance of a dewdrop in hell."

Rivera's answer was a calculated look of hatred. Even this gringo he despised, and him had he found the whitest gringo of them all.

IV

Barely noticed was Rivera as he entered the ring. Only a very slight and very scattering ripple of halfhearted handclapping greeted him. The house did not believe in him. He was the lamb led to slaughter at the hands of the great Danny.

Besides, the house was disappointed. It had expected a rushing battle between Danny Ward and Billy Carthey, and here it must put up with this poor little tyro. Still further, it had manifested its disapproval of the change by betting two, and even three, to one on Danny. And where a betting audience's money is, there is its heart.

The Mexican boy sat down in his corner and waited. The slow minutes lagged by. Danny was making him wait. It was an old trick, but ever it worked on the young, new fighters. They grew frightened, sitting thus and facing their own apprehensions and a callous, tobacco-smoking audience. But for once the trick failed. Roberts was right. Rivera had no goat. He, who was more delicately co-ordinated, more finely nerved and strung than any of them, had no nerves of this sort. The atmosphere of foredoomed defeat in his own corner had no effect on him. His handlers were gringos and strangers. Also they were scrubs—the dirty driftage of the fight game, without honor, without efficiency. And they were chilled, as well, with certitude that theirs was the losing corner.

"Now you gotta be careful," Spider Hagerty warned him. Spider was his chief second. "Make it last as long as you can—them's my instructions from Kelly. If you don't, the papers'll call it another bum fight and give the game a bigger black eye in Los Angeles."

All of which was not encouraging. But Rivera took no notice. He despised prize fighting. It was the hated game of the hated gringo. He had taken up with it, as a chopping block for others in the training quarters, solely because he was starving. The fact that he was marvelously made for it had meant nothing. He hated it. Not until he had come in to the Junta had he fought for money, and he had found the money easy. Not first among the sons of men had he been to find himself successful at a despised vocation.

He did not analyze. He merely knew that he must win this fight. There could be no other outcome. For behind him, nerving him to this belief, were profounder forces than any the crowded house dreamed. Danny Ward fought for money and for the easy ways of life that money would bring. But the things Rivera fought for burned in his brain—blazing and terrible visions, that, with eyes wide open, sitting lonely in the corner of the ring and waiting for his tricky antagonist, he saw as clearly as he had lived them.

He saw the white-walled, water-power factories of Rio Blanco. He saw the six thousand workers, starved and wan, and the little children, seven and eight years of age, who toiled long shifts for ten cents a day. He saw the perambulating corpses, the ghastly death's heads of men who labored in the dye rooms. He remembered that he had heard his father call the dye rooms the "suicide holes," where a year was death. He saw the little patio, and his mother cooking and moiling at crude housekeeping and finding time to caress and love him. And his father he saw, large, big-mustached, and deep-chested, kindly above all men, who loved all men and whose heart was so large that there was love to overflowing still left for the mother and the little muchacho playing in the corner of the patio. In those days his name had not been Felipe Rivera. It had been Fernandez, his father's and mother's name. Him had they called Juan. Later he had changed it himself, for he had found the name of Fernandez hated by prefects of police, *jefes políticos*, and *rurales*.

Big, hearty Joaquin Fernandez! A large place he occupied in Rivera's visions. He had not understood at the time, but, looking back, he could understand. He could see him setting type in the little printery, or scribbling endless hasty, nervous lines on the much-cluttered desk. And he could see the strange evenings, when workmen, coming secretly in the dark like men who did ill deeds, met with his father and talked long hours where he, the muchacho, lay not always asleep in the corner.

As from a remote distance he could hear Spider Hagerty saying to him: "No layin' down at the start. Them's instructions. Take a beatin' an' earn your dough."

Ten minutes had passed, and he still sat in his corner. There were no signs of Danny, who was evidently playing the trick to the limit.

But more visions burned before the eye of Rivera's memory. The strike, or, rather, the lockout, because the workers of Rio Blanco had helped their striking brothers of Puebla. The hunger, the expeditions in the hills for berries, the roots and herbs that all ate and that twisted and pained the stomachs of all of them. And then the nightmare; the waste of ground before the company's store; the thousands of starving workers; General Rosalio Martinez and the soldiers of Porfirio Diaz; and the death-spitting rifles that seemed never to cease spitting, while the workers' wrongs were washed and washed again in their own blood. And that night! He saw the flatcars, piled high with the bodies of the slain, consigned to Vera Cruz, food for the sharks of the bay. Again he crawled over the grisly heaps, seeking and finding, stripped and mangled, his father and his mother. His mother he especially remembered—only her face projecting, her body burdened by the weight of dozens of bodies. Again the rifles of the soldiers of Porfirio Diaz cracked, and again he dropped to the ground and slunk away like some hunted coyote of the hills.

To his ears came a great roar, as of the sea, and he saw Danny Ward, leading his retinue of trainers and seconds, coming down the center aisle. The house was in wild uproar for the popular hero who was bound to win. Everybody proclaimed him. Everybody was for him. Even Rivera's own seconds warmed to something akin to cheerfulness when Danny ducked jauntily through the ropes and entered the ring. His face continually spread to an unending succession of smiles, and when Danny smiled he smiled in every feature, even to the laughter wrinkles of the corners of the eyes and into the depths of the eyes themselves. Never was there so genial a fighter. His face was a running advertisement of good feeling, of good-fellowship. He knew everybody. He joked, and laughed, and greeted his friends through the ropes. Those farther away, unable to suppress their admiration, cried loudly: "Oh, you Danny!" It was a joyous ovation of affection that lasted a full five minutes.

Rivera was disregarded. For all that the audience noticed, he did not exist. Spider Hagerty's bloated face bent down close to his.

"No gettin' scared," the Spider warned. "An' remember instructions. You gotta last. No layin' down. If you lay down, we got instructions to beat you up in the dressing rooms. Savvy? You just gotta fight."

The house began to applaud. Danny was crossing the ring to him. Danny bent over, caught Rivera's right hand in both his own and shook it with impulsive heartiness. Danny's smile-wreathed face was close to his. The audience yelled its appreciation of Danny's display of sporting spirit. He was greeting his opponent with the fondness of a brother. Danny's lips moved, and the audience, interpreting the unheard words to be those of a kindly-natured sport, yelled again. Only Rivera heard the low words.

"You little Mexican rat," hissed from between Danny's gaily smiling lips, "I'll fetch the yellow outa you."

Rivera made no move. He did not rise. He merely hated with his eyes.

"Get up, you dog!" some man yelled through the ropes from behind.

The crowd began to hiss and boo him for his unsportsmanlike conduct, but he sat unmoved. Another great outburst of applause was Danny's as he walked back across the ring.

When Danny stripped, there were ohs! and ahs! of delight. His body was perfect, alive with easy suppleness and health and strength. The skin was white as a woman's, and as smooth. All grace, and resilience, and power resided therein. He had proved it in scores of battles. His photographs were in all the physical-culture magazines.

A groan went up as Spider Hagerty peeled Rivera's sweater over his head. His body seemed leaner because of the swarthiness of the skin. He had muscles, but they made no display like his opponent's. What the audience neglected to see was the deep chest. Nor could it guess the toughness of the fiber of the flesh, the instantaneousness of the cell explosions of the muscles, the fineness of the nerves that wired every part of him into a splendid fighting mechanism. All the audience saw was a brown-skinned boy of eighteen with what seemed the body of a boy. With Danny it was different. Danny was a man of twenty-four, and his body was a man's body. The contrast was still more striking as they stood together in the center of the ring receiving the referee's last instructions.

Rivera noticed Roberts sitting directly behind the newspapermen. He was drunker than usual, and his speech was correspondingly slower.

"Take it easy, Rivera," Roberts drawled. "He can't kill you, remember that. He'll rush you at the go-off, but don't get rattled. You just cover up, and stall, and clinch. He can't hurt you much. Just make believe to yourself that he's choppin' out on you at the trainin' quarters."

Rivera made no sign that he had heard.

"Sullen little devil," Roberts muttered to the man next to him. "He always was that way."

But Rivera forgot to look his usual hatred. A vision of countless rifles blinded his eyes. Every face in the audience, far as he could see, to the high dollar seats, was transformed into a rifle. And he saw the long Mexican border arid and sun-washed and aching, and along it he saw the ragged bands that delayed only for the guns.

Back in his corner he waited, standing up. His seconds had crawled out through the ropes, taking the canvas stool with them. Diagonally across the squared ring, Danny faced him. The gong struck, and the battle was on. The audience howled its delight. Never had it seen a battle open more convincingly. The papers were right. It was a grudge fight. Three quarters of the distance Danny covered in the rush to get together, his intention to eat up the Mexican lad plainly advertised. He assailed with not one blow, nor two, nor a dozen. He was a gyroscope of blows, a whirlwind of destruction. Rivera was nowhere. He was overwhelmed, buried beneath avalanches of punches delivered from every angle and position by a past master in the art. He was overborne, swept back against the ropes, separated by the referee, and swept back against the ropes again.

It was not a fight. It was a slaughter, a massacre. Any audience, save a prize-fighting one, would have exhausted its emotions in that first minute. Danny was certainly showing what he could do—a splendid exhibition. Such was the certainty of the audience, as well as its excitement and favoritism, that it failed to take notice that the Mexican still stayed on his feet. It forgot Rivera. It rarely saw him, so closely was he enveloped in Danny's man-eating attack. A minute of this went by, and two minutes. Then, in a separation, it caught a clear glimpse of the Mexican. His lip was cut, his nose was bleeding. As he turned and staggered into a clinch the welts of oozing blood, from his contacts with the ropes, showed in red bars across his back. But what the audience did not notice was that his chest was not heaving and that his eyes were coldly burning as ever. Too many aspiring champions, in the cruel welter of the training camps, had practiced this man-eating attack on him. He had learned to live through for a compensation of from half a dollar a go up to fifteen dollars a week—a hard school, and he was schooled hard.

Then happened the amazing thing. The whirling, blurring mix-up ceased suddenly. Rivera stood alone. Danny, the redoubtable Danny, lay on his back. His body quivered as consciousness strove to return to it. He had not staggered and sunk down, nor had he gone over in a long slumping fall. The right hook of Rivera had dropped him in mid-air with the abruptness of death. The referee shoved Rivera back with one hand and stood over the fallen gladiator counting the seconds. It is the custom of prize-fighting audiences to cheer a clean knockdown blow. But this audience did not cheer. The thing had been too unexpected. It watched the toll of the seconds in tense silence, and through this silence the voice of Roberts rose exultantly:

"I told you he was a two-handed fighter!"

By the fifth second Danny was rolling over on his face, and when seven was counted he rested on one knee, ready to rise after the count of nine and before the count of ten. If his knee still touched the floor at "ten" he was considered "down" and also "out." The instant his knee left the floor he was considered "up," and in that instant it was Rivera's right to try and put him down again. Rivera took no chances. The moment that knee left the floor he would strike again. He circled around, but the referee circled in between, and Rivera knew that the seconds he counted were very slow. All gringos were against him, even the referee.

At "nine" the referee gave Rivera a sharp thrust back. It was unfair, but it enabled Danny to rise, the smile back on his lips. Doubled partly over, with arms wrapped about face and abdomen, he cleverly stumbled into a clinch. By all the rules of the game the referee should have broken it, but he did not, and Danny clung on like a surf-battered barnacle and moment by moment recuperated. The last minute of the round was going fast. If he could live to the end he would have a full minute in his corner to revive. And live to the end he did, smiling through all desperateness and extremity.

"The smile that won't come off!" somebody yelled, and the audience laughed loudly in its relief.

"The kick that greaser's got is something God-awful," Danny gasped in his corner to his adviser while his handlers worked frantically over him.

The second and third rounds were tame. Danny, a tricky and consummate ring general, stalled and blocked and held on, devoting himself to recovering from that dazing first-round blow. In the fourth round he was himself again. Jarred and shaken, nevertheless his good condition had enabled him to regain his vigor. But he tried no man-eating tactics. The Mexican had proved a tartar. Instead he brought to bear his best fighting powers. In tricks and skill and experience he was the master, and though he could land nothing vital, he proceeded scientifically to chop and wear down his opponent. He landed three blows to Rivera's one, but they were punishing blows only, and not deadly. It was the sum of many of them that constituted deadliness. He was respectful of this two-handed dub with the amazing short-arm kicks in both his fists.

In defense Rivera developed a disconcerting straight left. Again and again, attack after attack he straight-lefted away from him with accumulated damage to Danny's mouth and nose. But Danny was protean. That was why he was the coming champion. He could change from style to style of fighting at will. He now devoted himself to infighting. In this he was particularly wicked, and it enabled him to avoid the other's straight left. Here he set the house wild repeatedly, capping it with a marvelous lock-break and lift of an inside uppercut that raised the Mexican in the air and dropped him to the mat. Rivera rested on one knee, making the most of the count, and in the soul of him he knew the referee was counting short seconds on him.

Again, in the seventh, Danny achieved the diabolical inside uppercut. He succeeded only in staggering Rivera, but in the ensuing moment of defenseless helplessness he smashed him with another blow through the ropes. Rivera's body bounced on the heads of the newspapermen below, and they boosted him back to the edge of the platform outside the ropes. Here he rested on one knee, while the referee raced off the seconds. Inside the ropes, through which he must duck to enter the ring, Danny waited for him. Nor did the referee intervene or thrust Danny back.

The house was beside itself with delight.

"Kill 'm, Danny, kill 'm!" was the cry.

Scores of voices took it up until it was like a war chant of wolves.

Danny did his best, but Rivera, at the count of eight, instead of nine, came unexpectedly through the ropes and safely into a clinch. Now the referee worked, tearing him away so that he could be hit, giving Danny every advantage that an unfair referee can give.

But Rivera lived, and the daze cleared from his brain. It was all of a piece. They were the hated gringos and they were all unfair. And in the worst of it visions continued to flash and sparkle in his brain—long lines of railroad track that simmered across the desert; *rurales* and American constables; prisons and calabooses; tramps at water tanks—all the squalid and painful panorama of his odyssey after Rio Blanco and the strike. And, resplendent and glorious, he saw the great red revolution sweeping across his land. The guns were there before him. Every hated face was a gun. It was for the guns he fought. He was the guns. He was the revolution. He fought for all Mexico.

The audience began to grow incensed with Rivera. Why didn't he take the licking that was appointed him? Of course he was going to be licked, but why should he be so obstinate about it? Very few were interested in him, and they were the certain, definite percentage of a gambling crowd that plays long shots. Believing Danny to be the winner, nevertheless they had put their money on the Mexican at four to ten and one to three. More than a trifle was up on the point of how many rounds Rivera could last. Wild money had appeared at the ringside proclaiming that he could not last seven rounds, or even six. The winners of this, now that their cash risk was happily settled, had joined in cheering on the favorite.

Rivera refused to be licked. Through the eighth round his opponent strove vainly to repeat the uppercut. In the ninth Rivera stunned the house again. In the midst of a clinch he broke the lock with a quick, lithe movement, and in the narrow space between their bodies his right lifted from the waist. Danny went to the floor and took the safety of the count. The crowd was appalled. He was being bested at his own game. His famous right uppercut had been worked back on him. Rivera made no attempt to catch him as he arose at "nine." The referee was openly blocking that play, though he stood clear when the situation was reversed and it was Rivera who required to rise.

Twice in the tenth Rivera put through the right uppercut, lifted from waist to opponent's chin. Danny grew desperate. The smile never left his face, but he went back to his man-eating rushes. Whirlwind as he would, he could not damage Rivera, while Rivera, through the blur and whirl, dropped him to the mat three times in succession. Danny did not recuperate so quickly now, and by the eleventh round he was in a serious way. But from then till the fourteenth he put up the gamest exhibition of his career. He stalled and blocked, fought parsimoniously, and strove to gather strength. Also he fought as foully as a successful fighter knows how. Every trick and device he employed, butting in the clinches with the seeming of accident, pinioning Rivera's glove between arm and body, heeling his glove on Rivera's mouth to clog his breathing. Often, in the clinches, through his cut and smiling lips he snarled insults unspeakable and vile in Rivera's ear. Everybody, from the referee to the house, was with Danny and was helping Danny. And they knew what he had in mind. Bested by this surprise box of an unknown, he was pinning all on a single punch. He offered himself for punishment, fished, and feinted, and drew, for that one opening that would enable him to whip a blow through with all his strength and turn the tide. As another and greater fighter had done before him, he might do—a right and left, to solar plexus and across the jaw. He could do it, for he was noted for the strength of punch that remained in his arms as long as he could keep his feet.

Rivera's seconds were not half caring for him in the intervals between rounds. Their towels made a showing but drove little air into his panting lungs. Spider Hagerty talked advice to him, but Rivera knew it was wrong advice. Everybody was against him. He was surrounded by treachery. In the fourteenth round he put Danny down again, and himself stood resting, hands dropped at side, while the referee counted. In the other corner Rivera had been noting suspicious whisperings. He saw Michael Kelly make his way to Roberts and bend and whisper. Rivera's ears were a cat's, desert-trained, and he caught snatches of what was said. He wanted to hear more, and when his opponent arose he maneuvered the fight into a clinch over against the ropes.

"Got to," he could hear Michael, while Roberts nodded. "Danny's got to win—I stand to lose a mint. I've got a ton of money covered—my own. It he lasts the fifteenth I'm bust. The boy'll mind you. Put something across."

And thereafter Rivera saw no more visions. They were trying to job him. Once again he dropped Danny and stood resting, his hands at his side. Roberts stood up.

"That settled him," he said. "Go to your corner."

He spoke with authority, as he had often spoken to Rivera at the training quarters. But Rivera looked hatred at him and waited for Danny to rise. Back in his corner in the minute interval, Kelly, the promoter, came and talked to Rivera.

"Throw it, damn you," he rasped in a harsh low voice. "You gotta lay down, Rivera. Stick with me and I'll make your future. I'll let you lick Danny next time. But here's where you lay down."

Rivera showed with his eyes that he heard, but he made neither sign of assent nor dissent.

"Why don't you speak?" Kelly demanded angrily.

"You lose anyway," Spider Hagerty supplemented. "The referee'll take it away from you. Listen to Kelly and lay down."

"Lay down, kid," Kelly pleaded, "and I'll help you to the championship."

Rivera did not answer.

"I will, so help me, kid."

At the strike of the gong Rivera sensed something impending. The house did not. Whatever it was, it was there inside the ring with him and very close. Danny's earlier surety seemed returned to him. The confidence of his advance frightened Rivera. Some trick was about to be worked. Danny rushed, but Rivera refused the encounter. He side-stepped away into safety. What the other wanted was a clinch. It was in some way necessary to the trick. Rivera backed and circled away, yet he knew, sooner or later, the clinch and the trick would come. Desperately he resolved to draw it. He made as if to effect the clinch with Danny's next rush. Instead, at the last instant, just as their bodies should have come together, Rivera darted nimbly back. And in the same instant Danny's corner raised a cry of foul. Rivera had fooled them. The referee paused irresolutely. The decision that trembled on his lips was never uttered, for a shrill, boy's voice from the gallery piped, "Raw work!"

Danny cursed Rivera openly, and forced him, while Rivera danced away. Also Rivera made up his mind to strike no more blows at the body. In this he threw away half his chance of winning, but he knew if he was to win at all it was with the outfighting that remained to him. Given the least opportunity, they would lie a foul on him. Danny threw all caution to the winds. For two rounds he tore after and into the boy who dared not meet him at close quarters. Rivera was struck again and again; he took blows by the dozens to avoid the perilous clinch. During this supreme final rally of Danny's the audience rose to its feet and went mad. It did not understand. All it could see was that its favorite was winning after all.

"Why don't you fight?" it demanded wrathfully of Rivera. "You're yellow! You're yellow!" "Open up, you cur! Open up!" "Kill 'm, Danny! Kill 'm!" "You sure got 'm! Kill 'm!"

In all the house, bar none, Rivera was the only cold man. By temperament and blood he was the hottest-passioned there; but he had gone through such vastly greater heats that this collective passion of ten thousand throats, rising surge on surge, was to his brain no more than the velvet cool of a summer twilight.

Into the seventeenth round Danny carried his rally. Rivera, under a heavy blow, drooped and sagged. His hands dropped helplessly as he reeled backward. Danny thought it was his chance. The boy was at his mercy. Thus Rivera, feigning, caught him off his guard, lashing out a clean drive to the mouth. Danny went down. When he arose Rivera felled him with a down-chop of the right on neck and jaw. Three times he repeated this. It was impossible for any referee to call these blows foul.

"Oh, Bill! Bill!" Kelly pleaded to the referee.

"I can't," that official lamented back. "He won't give me a chance."

Danny, battered and heroic, still kept coming up. Kelly and others near to the ring began to cry out to the police to stop it, though Danny's corner refused to throw in the towel. Rivera saw the fat police captain starting awkwardly to climb through the ropes, and was not sure what it meant. There were so many ways of cheating in this game of the gringos. Danny, on his feet, tottered groggily and helplessly before him. The referee and the captain were both reaching for Rivera when he struck the last blow. There was no need to stop the fight, for Danny did not rise.

"Count!" Rivera cried hoarsely to the referee.

And when the count was finished Danny's seconds gathered him up and carried him to his corner.

"Who wins?" Rivera demanded.

Reluctantly the referee caught his gloved hand and held it aloft. There were no congratulations for Rivera. He walked to his corner unattended, where his seconds had not yet placed his stool. He leaned backward on the ropes and looked his hatred at them, swept it on and about him till the whole ten thousand gringos were included. His knees trembled under him, and he was sobbing from exhaustion. Before his eyes the hated faces swayed back and forth in the giddiness of nausea. Then he remembered they were the guns. The guns were his. The revolution could go on.

1910

THE STRENGTH OF THE STRONG

Parables don't lie, but liars will parable.
—Lip-King.

Old Long Beard paused in his narrative, licked his greasy fingers, and wiped them on his naked sides where his one piece of ragged bearskin failed to cover him. Crouched around him, on their hams, were three young men, his grandsons, Deer-Runner, Yellow-Head, and Afraid-of-the-Dark. In appearance they were much the same. Skins of wild animals partly covered them. They were lean and meager of build, narrow-hipped and crooked-legged, and at the same time deep-chested, with heavy arms and enormous hands. There was much hair on their chests and shoulders, and on the outsides of their arms and legs. Their heads were matted with uncut hair, long locks of which often strayed before their eyes, beady and black and glittering like the eyes of birds. They were narrow between the eyes and broad between the cheeks, while their lower jaws were projecting and massive.

It was a night of clear starlight, and below them, stretching away remotely, lay range on range of forest-covered hills. In the distance the heavens were red from the glow of a volcano. At their backs yawned the black mouth of a cave, out of which, from time to time, blew draughty gusts of wind. Immediately in front of them blazed a fire. At one side, partly devoured, lay the carcass of a bear, with about it, at a respectable distance, several large dogs, shaggy and wolf-like. Beside each man lay his bow and arrows and a huge club. In the cave mouth a number of rude spears leaned against the rock.

"So that was how we moved from the cave to the tree," old Long Beard spoke up.

They laughed boisterously, like big children, at recollection of a previous story his words called up. Long Beard laughed, too, the five-inch bodkin of bone, thrust midway through the cartilage of his nose, leaping and dancing and adding to his ferocious appearance. He did not exactly say the words recorded, but he made animal-like sounds with his mouth that meant the same thing.

"And that is the first I remember of the Sea Valley," Long Beard went on. "We were a very foolish crowd. We did not know the secret of strength. For, behold, each family lived by itself, and took care of itself. There were thirty families, but we got no strength from one another. We were in fear of each other all the time. No one ever paid visits. In the top of our tree we built a grass house, and on the platform outside was a pile of rocks, which were for the heads of any that might chance to try to visit us. Also, we had our spears and arrows. We never walked under the trees of the other families, either. My brother did, once, under old Boo-oogh's tree, and he got his head broken and that was the end of him.

"Old Boo-oogh was very strong. It was said he could pull a grown man's head right off. I never heard of him doing it, because no man would give him a chance. Father wouldn't. One day, when father was down on the beach, Boo-oogh took after mother. She couldn't run fast, for the day before she had got her leg clawed by a bear when she was up on the mountain gathering berries. So Boo-oogh caught her and carried her up into his tree. Father never got her back. He was afraid. Old Boo-oogh made faces at him.

"But father did not mind. Strong-Arm was another strong man. He was one of the best fishermen. But one day, climbing after sea gull eggs, he had a fall from the cliff. He was never strong after that. He coughed a great deal, and his shoulders drew near to each other. So father took Strong-Arm's wife. When he came around and coughed under our tree, father laughed at him and threw rocks at him. It was our way in those days. We did not know how to add strength together and become strong."

"Would a brother take a brother's wife?" Deer-Runner demanded.

"Yes, if he had gone to live in another tree by himself."

"But we do not do such things now," Afraid-of-the-Dark objected.

"It is because I have taught your fathers better." Long Beard thrust his hairy paw into the bear meat and drew out a handful of suet, which he sucked with a meditative air. Again he wiped his hands on his naked sides and went on. "What I am telling you happened in the long ago, before we knew any better."

"You must have been fools not to know better," was Deer-Runner's comment, Yellow-Head grunting approval.

"So we were, but we became bigger fools, as you shall see. Still, we did learn better, and this was the way of it. We Fish-Eaters had not learned to add our strength until our strength was the strength of all of us. But the Meat-Eaters, who lived across the divide in the Big Valley, stood together, hunted together, fished together, and fought together. One day they came into our valley. Each family of us got into its own cave and tree. There were only ten Meat-Eaters, but they fought together, and we fought each family by itself."

Long Beard counted long and perplexedly on his fingers.

"There were sixty men of us," was what he managed to say with fingers and lips combined. "And we were very strong, only we did not know it. So we watched the ten men attack Boo-oogh's tree. He made a good fight, but he had no chance.

We looked on. When some of the Meat-Eaters tried to climb the tree, Boo-oogh had to show himself in order to drop stones on their heads, whereupon the other Meat-Eaters, who were waiting for that very thing, shot him full of arrows. And that was the end of Boo-oogh.

"Next, the Meat-Eaters got One-Eye and his family in his cave. They built a fire in the mouth and smoked him out, like we smoked out the bear there to-day. Then they went after Six-Fingers, up his tree, and, while they were killing him and his grown son, the rest of us ran away. They caught some of our women, and killed two old men who could not run fast and several children. The women they carried away with them to the Big Valley.

"After that the rest of us crept back, and, somehow, perhaps because we were in fear and felt the need for one another, we talked the thing over. It was our first council—our first real council. And in that council we formed our first tribe. For we had learned the lesson. Of the ten Meat-Eaters, each man had had the strength of ten, for the ten had fought as one man. They had added their strength together. But of the thirty families and the sixty men of us, we had had the strength of but one man, for each had fought alone.

"It was a great talk we had, and it was hard talk, for we did not have the words then as now with which to talk. The Bug made some of the words long afterward, and so did others of us make words from time to time. But in the end we agreed to add our strength together and to be as one man when the Meat-Eaters came over the divide to steal our women. And that was the tribe.

"We set two men on the divide, one for the day and one for the night, to watch if the Meat-Eaters came. These were the eyes of the tribe. Then, also, day and night, there were to be ten men awake with their clubs and spears and arrows in their hands, ready to fight. Before, when a man went after fish, or clams, or gull-eggs, he carried his weapons with him, and half the time he was getting food and half the time watching for fear some other man would get him. Now that was all changed. The men went out without their weapons and spent all their time getting food. Likewise, when the women went into the mountains after roots and berries, five of the ten men went with them to guard them. While all the time, day and night, the eyes of the tribe watched from the top of the divide.

"But troubles came. As usual, it was about the women. Men without wives wanted other men's wives, and there was much fighting between men, and now and again one got his head smashed or a spear through his body. While one of the watchers was on top the divide, another man stole his wife, and he came down to fight. Then the other watcher was in fear that someone would take his wife, and he came down likewise. Also, there was trouble among the ten men who carried always their weapons, and they fought five against five, till some ran away down the coast and the others ran after them.

"So it was that the tribe was left without eyes or guards. We had not the strength of sixty. We had no strength at all. So we held a council and made our first laws. I was but a cub at the time, but I remember. We said that, in order to be strong, we must not fight one another, and we made a law that when a man killed another, him would the tribe kill. We made another law that whoso stole another man's wife, him would the tribe kill. We said that whatever man had too great strength, and by that strength hurt his brothers in the tribe, him would we kill that his strength might hurt no more. For, if we let his strength hurt, the brothers would become afraid and the tribe would fall apart, and we would be as weak as when the Meat-Eaters first came upon us and killed Boo-oogh.

"Knuckle-Bone was a strong man, a very strong man, and he knew not law. He knew only his own strength, and in the fullness thereof he went forth and took the wife of Three-Clams. Three-Clams tried to fight, but Knuckle-Bone clubbed out his brains. Yet had Knuckle-Bone forgotten that all the men of us had added our strength to keep the law among us, and him we killed, at the foot of his tree, and hung his body on a branch as a warning that the law was stronger than any man. For we were the law, all of us, and no man was greater than the law.

"Then there were other troubles, for know, O Deer-Runner, and Yellow-Head, and Afraid-of-the-Dark, that it is not easy to make a tribe. There were many things, little things, that it was a great trouble to call all the men together to have a council about. We were having councils morning, noon, and night, and in the middle of the night. We could find little time to go out and get food, what of the councils, for there was always some little thing to be settled, such as naming two new watchers to take the place of the old ones on the hill, or naming how much food should fall to the share of the men who kept their weapons always in their hands and got no food for themselves.

"We stood in need of a chief man to do these things, who would be the voice of the council, and who would account to the council for the things he did. So we named Fith-Fith the chief man. He was a strong man, too, and very cunning, and when he was angry he made noises just like that, *fith-fith*, like a wildcat.

"The ten men who guarded the tribe were set to work making a wall of stones across the narrow part of the valley. The women and large children helped, as did other men, until the wall was strong. After that, all the families came down out of their caves and trees and built grasshouses behind the shelter of the wall. These houses were large and much better than the caves and trees, and everybody had a better time of it because the men had added their strength together and become a tribe. Because of the wall and the guards and the watchers, there was more time to hunt and fish and pick roots and berries; there was more food, and better food, and no one went hungry. And Three-Legs, so named because his legs had been smashed when a boy and who walked with a stick—Three-Legs got the seed of the wild corn and planted it in the ground in the valley near his house. Also, he tried planting fat roots and other things he found in the mountain valleys.

"Because of the safety in the Sea Valley, which was because of the wall and the watchers and the guards, and because there was food in plenty for all without having to fight for it, many families came in from the coast valleys on both sides and from the high back mountains where they had lived more like wild animals than men. And it was not long before the Sea Valley filled up, and in it were countless families. But, before this happened, the land, which had been free to all and belonged to all, was divided up. Three-Legs began it when he planted corn. But most of us did not care about the land. We thought the marking of the boundaries with fences of stone was a foolishness. We had plenty to eat, and what more did we want? I remember that my father and I built stone fences for Three-Legs and were given corn in return.

"So only a few got all the land, and Three-Legs got most of it. Also, others that had taken land gave it to the few that held on, being paid in return with corn and fat roots, and bearskins, and fishes which the farmers got from the fishermen in exchange for corn. And, the first thing we knew, all the land was gone.

"It was about this time that Fith-Fith died and Dog-Tooth, his son, was made chief. He demanded to be made chief anyway, because his father had been chief before him. Also, he looked upon himself as a greater chief than his father. He was a good chief at first, and worked hard, so that the council had less and less to do. Then arose a new voice in the Sea Valley. It was Twisted-Lip. We had never thought much of him, until he began to talk with the spirits of the dead. Later we called him Big-Fat, because he ate over-much, and did no work, and grew round and large. One day Big-Fat told us that the secrets of the dead were his, and that he was the voice of God. He became great friends with Dog-Tooth, who commanded that we build Big-Fat a grasshouse. And Big-Fat put taboos all around this house and kept God inside.

"More and more Dog-Tooth became greater than the council, and when the council grumbled and said it would name a new chief, Big-Fat spoke with the voice of God and said no. Also, Three-Legs and the others who held the land stood behind Dog-Tooth. Moreover, the strongest man in the council was Sea-Lion, and him the land-owners gave land to secretly, along with many bearskins and baskets of corn. So Sea-Lion said that Big-Fat's voice was truly the voice of God and must be obeyed. And soon afterward Sea-Lion was named the voice of Dog-Tooth and did most of his talking for him.

"Then there was Little-Belly, a little man, so thin in the middle that he looked as if he had never had enough to eat. Inside the mouth of the river, after the sandbar had combed the strength of the breakers, he built a big fish-trap. No man had ever seen or dreamed a fish-trap before. He worked weeks on it, with his son and his wife, while the rest of us laughed at their labors. But, when it was done, the first day he caught more fish in it than could the whole tribe in a week, whereat there was great rejoicing. There was only one other place in the river for a fish-trap, but, when my father and I and a dozen other men started to make a very large trap, the guards came from the big grasshouse we had built for Dog-Tooth. And the guards poked us with their spears and told us begone, because Little-Belly was going to build a trap there himself on the word of Sea-Lion, who was the voice of Dog-Tooth.

"There was much grumbling, and my father called a council. But, when he rose to speak, him the Sea-Lion thrust through the throat with a spear and he died. And Dog-Tooth and Little-Belly, and Three-Legs and all that held land said it was good. And Big-Fat said it was the will of God. And after that all men were afraid to stand up in the council, and there was no more council.

"Another man, Pig-Jaw, began to keep goats. He had heard about it as among the Meat-Eaters, and it was not long before he had many flocks. Other men, who had no land and no fish-traps, and who else would have gone hungry, were glad to work for Pig-Jaw, caring for his goats, guarding them from wild dogs and tigers, and driving them to the feeding pastures in the mountains. In return, Pig-Jaw gave them goat meat to eat and goat-skins to wear, and sometimes they traded the goat meat for fish and corn and fat roots.

It was this time that money came to be. Sea-Lion was the man who first thought of it, and he talked it over with Dog-Tooth and Big-Fat. You see, these three were the ones that got a share of everything in the Sea Valley. One basket out of every three of corn was theirs, one fish out of every three, one goat out of every three.

In return, they fed the guards and the watchers, and kept the rest for themselves. Sometimes, when a big haul of fish was made, they did not know what to do with all their share. So Sea-Lion set the women to making money out of shell—little round pieces, with a hole in each one, and all made smooth and fine. These were strung on strings, and the strings were called money.

"Each string was of the value of thirty fish, or forty fish, but the women, who made a string a day, were given two fish each. The fish came out of the shares of Dog-Tooth, Big-Fat, and Sea-Lion, which they three did not eat. So all the money belonged to them. Then they told Three-Legs and the other land owners that they would take their share of corn and roots in money, Little-Belly that they would take their share of fish in money, the Pig-Jaw that they would take their share of goats and cheese in money. Thus, a man who had nothing, worked for one who had, and was paid in money. With this money he bought corn, and fish, and meat, and cheese. And Three-Legs and all owners of things paid Dog-Tooth and Sea-Lion and Big-Fat their share in money. And they paid the guards and watchers in money, and the guards and watchers bought their food with the money. And, because money was cheap, Dog-Tooth made many more men into guards. And, because money was cheap to make, a number of men began to make money out of shell themselves. But the guards stuck spears in them and shot them full of arrows, because they were trying to break up the tribe. It was bad to break up the tribe, for then the Meat-Eaters would come over the divide and kill them all.

"Big-Fat was the voice of God, but he took Broken-Rib and made him into a priest, so that he became the voice of Big-Fat and did most of his talking for him. And both had other men to be servants to them. So, also, did Little-Belly and Three-Legs and Pig-Jaw have other men to lie in the sun about their grasshouses and carry messages for them and give commands. And more and more were men taken away from work, so that those that were left worked harder than ever before. It seemed that men desired to do no work and strove to seek out other ways whereby men should work for them. Crooked-Eyes found such a way. He made the first fire-brew out of corn. And thereafter he worked no more, for he talked secretly with Dog-Tooth and Big-Fat and the other masters, and it was agreed that he should be the only one to make fire-brew. But Crooked-Eyes did no work himself. Men made the brew for him, and he paid them in money. Then he sold the fire-brew for money, and all men bought. And many strings of money did he give Dog-Tooth and Sea-Lion and all of them.

"Big-Fat and Broken-Rib stood by Dog-Tooth when he took his second wife, and his third wife. They said Dog-Tooth was different from other men and second only to God that Big-Fat kept in his taboo house, and Dog-Tooth said so, too, and wanted to know who were they to grumble about how many wives he took. Dog-Tooth had a big canoe made, and many more men he took from work, who did nothing and lay in the sun, save only when Dog-Tooth went in the canoe, when they paddled for him. And he made Tiger-Face head man over all the guards, so that Tiger-Face became his right arm, and when he did not like a man Tiger-Face killed that man for him. And Tiger-Face, also, made another man to be his right arm, and to give commands, and to kill for him.

"But this was the strange thing: as the days went by we who were left worked harder and harder, and yet did we get less and less to eat."

"But what of the goats and the corn and the fat roots and the fish-trap," spoke up

Afraid-of-the-Dark, "what of all this? Was there not more food to be gained by man's work?"

"It is so," Long-Beard agreed. "Three men on the fish-trap got more fish than the whole tribe before there was a fish-trap. But have I not said we were fools? The more food we were able to get, the less food did we have to eat."

"But was it not plain that the many men who did not work ate it all up?" Yellow-Head demanded.

Long-Beard nodded his head sadly. "Dog-Tooth's dogs were stuffed with meat, and the men who lay in the sun and did no work were rolling in fat, and, at the same time, there were little children crying themselves to sleep with hunger biting them with every wail."

Deer-Runner was spurred by the recital of famine to tear out a chunk of bear-meat and broil it on a stick over the coals. This he devoured with smacking lips, while Long-Beard went on:

"When we grumbled Big-Fat arose, and with the voice of God said that God had chosen the wise men to own the land and the goats and the fish-trap and the fire-brew, and that without these wise men we would all be animals, as in the days when we lived in trees.

"And there arose one who became a singer of songs for the king. Him they called the Bug, because he was small and ungainly of face and limb and excelled not in work or deed. He loved the fattest marrow bones, the choicest fish, the milk warm from the goats, the first corn that was ripe, and the snug place by the fire. And thus, becoming singer of songs to the king, he found a way to do nothing and be fat. And when the people grumbled more and more, and some threw stones at the king's grass house, the Bug sang a song of how good it was to be a Fish-Eater. In his song he told that the Fish-Eaters were the chosen of God and the finest men God had made. He sang of the Meat-Eaters as pigs and crows, and sang how fine and good it was for the Fish-Eaters to fight and die doing God's work, which was the killing of Meat-Eaters. The words of his song were like fire in us, and we clamored to be led against the Meat-Eaters. And we forgot that we were hungry, and why we had grumbled, and were glad to be led by Tiger-Face over the divide, where we killed many Meat-Eaters and were content.

"But things were no better in the Sea Valley. The only way to get food was to work for Three-Legs or Little-Belly or Pig-Jaw; for there was no land that a man might plant with corn for himself. And often there were more men than Three-Legs and the others had work for. So these men went hungry, and so did their wives and children and their old mothers. Tiger-Face said they could become guards if they wanted to, and many of them did, and thereafter they did no work except to poke spears in the men who did work and who grumbled at feeding so many idlers.

"And when we grumbled, ever the Bug sang new songs. He said that Three-Legs and Pig-Jaw and the rest were strong men, and that was why they had so much. He said that we should be glad to have strong men with us, else would we perish of our own worthlessness and the Meat-Eaters. Therefore, we should be glad to let such strong men have all they could lay hands on. And Big-Fat and Pig-Jaw and Tiger-Face and all the rest said it was true.

"'All right,' said Long-Fang, 'then will I, too, be a strong man.' And he got himself corn and began to make fire-brew and sell it for strings of money. And, when Crooked-Eyes complained, Long-Fang said that he was himself a strong man, and that if Crooked-Eyes made any more noise he would bash his brains out for him. Whereat Crooked-Eyes was afraid and went and talked with Three-Legs and Pig-Jaw. And all three went and talked to Dog-Tooth. And Dog-Tooth spoke to Sea-Lion, and Sea-Lion sent a runner with a message to Tiger-Face. And Tiger-Face sent his guards, who burned Long-Fang's house along with the fire-brew he had made. Also, they killed him and all his family. And Big-Fat said it was good, and the Bug sang another song about how good it was to observe the law, and what a fine land the Sea Valley was, and how every man who loved the Sea Valley should go forth and kill the bad Meat-Eaters. And again his song was as fire to us, and we forgot to grumble.

"It was very strange. When Little-Belly caught too many fish, so that it took a great many to sell for a little money, he threw many of the fish back into the sea, so that more money would be paid for what was left. And Three-Legs often let many large fields lie idle so as to get more money for his corn. And the women, making so much money out of shell that much money was needed to buy with, Dog-Tooth stopped the making of money. And the women had no work, so they took the places of the men. I worked on the fish-trap, getting a string of money every five days. But my sister now did my work, getting a string of money for every ten days. The women worked cheaper, and there was less food, and Tiger-Face said for us to become guards. Only I could not become a guard because I was lame of one leg and Tiger-Face would not have me. And there were many like me. We were broken men and only fit to beg for work or to take care of the babies while the women worked."

Yellow-Head, too, was made hungry by the recital and broiled a piece of bear-meat on the coals.

"But why didn't you rise up, all of you, and kill Three-Legs and Pig-Jaw and Big-Fat and the rest and get enough to eat?" Afraid-in-the-Dark demanded.

"Because we could not understand," Long-Beard answered. "There was too much to think about, and, also, there were the guards sticking spears into us, and Big-Fat talking about God, and the Bug singing new songs. And when any man did think right, and said so, Tiger-Face and the guards got him, and he was tied out to the rocks at low tide so that the rising waters drowned him.

"It was a strange thing—the money. It was like the Bug's songs. It seemed all right, but it wasn't, and we were slow to understand. Dog-Tooth began to gather the money in. He put it in a big pile, in a grasshouse, with guards to watch it day and night. And the more money he piled in the house the dearer money became, so that a man worked a longer time for a string of money than before. Then, too, there was always talk of war with the Meat-Eaters, and Dog-Tooth and Tiger-Face filled many houses with corn, and dried fish, and smoked goat meat, and cheese. And with the food piled there in mountains the people had not enough to eat. But what did it matter? Whenever the people grumbled too loudly the Bug sang a new song, and Big-Fat said it was God's word that we should kill Meat-Eaters, and Tiger-Face led us over the divide to kill and be killed. I was not good enough to be a guard and lie fat in the sun, but, when we made war, Tiger-Face was glad to take me along. And when we had eaten all the food stored in the houses we stopped fighting and went back to work to pile up more food."

"Then were you all crazy," commented Deer-Runner.

"Then were we indeed all crazy," Long-Beard agreed. "It was strange, all of it. There was Split-Nose. He said everything was wrong. He said it was true that we grew strong by adding our strength together. And he said that, when we first formed the tribe, it was right that the men whose strength hurt the tribe should be shorn of their strength—men who bashed their brothers' heads and stole their brothers' wives. And now, he said, the tribe was not getting stronger, but was getting weaker, because there were men with another kind of strength that were hurting the tribe—men who had the strength of the land, like Three-Legs; who had the strength of the fish-trap, like Little-Belly; who had the strength of all the goat meat, like Pig-Jaw. The thing to do, Split-Nose said, was to shear these men of their evil strength; to make them go to work, all of them, and to let no man eat who did not work.

"And the Bug sang another song about men like Split-Nose, who wanted to go back and live in trees.

"Yet Split-Nose said no; that he did not want to go back, but ahead; that they grew strong only as they added their strength together; and that, if the Fish-Eaters would add their strength to the Meat-Eaters, there would be no more fighting and no more watchers and no more guards, and that, with all men working, there would be so much food that each man would have to work not more than two hours a day.

"Then the Bug sang again, and he sang that Split-Nose was lazy, and he sang also the 'Song of the Bees.' It was a strange song, and those who listened were made mad, as from the drinking of strong fire-brew. The song was of a swarm of bees, and of a robber wasp who had come in to live with the bees and who was stealing all their honey. The wasp was lazy and told them there was no need to work; also, he told them to make friends with the bears, who were not honey-stealers but only very good friends. And the Bug sang in crooked words, so that those who listened knew that the swarm was the Sea Valley tribe, that the bears were the Meat-Eaters, and that the lazy wasp was Split-Nose. And, when the Bug sang that the bees listened to the wasp till the swarm was near to perishing, the people growled and snarled, and when the Bug sang that at last the good bees arose and stung the wasp to death, the people picked up stones from the ground and stoned Split-Nose to death till there was naught to be seen of him but the heap of stones they had flung on top of him. And there were many poor people who worked long and hard and had not enough to eat that helped throw the stones on Split-Nose.

"And, after the death of Split-Nose, there was but one other man that dared rise up and speak his mind, and that man was Hair-Face. 'Where is the strength of the strong?' he asked. 'We are the strong, all of us, and we are stronger than Dog-Tooth and Tiger-Face and Three-Legs and Pig-Jaw and all the rest who do nothing and eat much and weaken us by the hurt of their strength which is bad strength. Men who are slaves are not strong. If the man who first found the virtue and use of fire had used his strength we would have been his slaves, as we are the slaves to-day of Little-Belly, who found the virtue and use of the fish-trap; and of the men who found the virtue and use of the land, and the goats, and the fire-brew. Before, we lived in trees, my brothers, and no man was safe. But we fight no more with one another. We have added our strength together. Then let us fight no more with the Meat-Eaters. Let us add our strength and their strength together. Then will we be indeed strong. And then we will go out together, the Fish-Eaters and the Meat-Eaters, and we will kill the tigers and the lions and the wolves and the wild dogs, and we will pasture our goats on all the hillsides and plant our corn and fat roots in all the high mountain valleys. In that day we will be so strong that all the wild animals will flee before us and perish. And nothing will withstand us, for the strength of each man will be the strength of all men in the world.'

"So said Hair-Face, and they killed him, because, they said, he was a wild man and wanted to go back and live in a tree. It was very strange. Whenever a man arose and wanted to go forward all those that stood still said he went backward and should be killed. And the poor people helped stone him, and were fools. We were all fools, except those who were fat and did no work. The fools were called wise, and the wise were stoned. Men who worked did not get enough to eat, and the men who did not work ate too much.

"And the tribe went on losing strength. The children were weak and sickly. And, because we ate not enough, strange sicknesses came among us and we died like flies. And then the Meat-Eaters came upon us. We had followed Tiger-Face too often over the divide and killed them. And now they came to repay in blood. We were too weak and sick to man the big wall. And they killed us, all of us, except some of the women, which they took away with them. The Bug and I escaped, and I hid in the wildest places, and became a hunter of meat and went hungry no more. I stole a wife from the Meat-Eaters, and went to live in the caves of the high mountains where they could not find me. And we had three sons, and each son stole a wife from the Meat-Eaters. And the rest you know, for are you not the sons of my sons?"

"But the Bug?" queried Deer-Runner. "What became of him?"

"He went to live with the Meat-Eaters and to be a singer of songs to the king. He is an old man now, but he sings the same old songs; and, when a man rises up to go forward, he sings that that man is walking backward to live in a tree."

Long-Beard dipped into the bear-carcass and sucked with toothless gums at a fist of suet.

"Some day," he said, wiping his hands on his sides, "all the fools will be dead and then all live men will go forward. The strength of the strong will be theirs, and they will add their strength together, so that, of all the men in the world, not one will fight with another. There will be no guards nor watchers on the walls. And all the hunting animals will be killed, and, as Hair-Face said, all the hillsides will be pastured with goats and all the high mountain valleys will be planted with corn and fat roots. And all men will be brothers, and no man will lie idle in the sun and be fed by his fellows. And all that will come to pass in the time when the fools are dead, and when there will be no more singers to stand still and sing the 'Song of the Bees.' Bees are not men."

1911

WAR

He was a young man, not more than twenty-four or five, and he might have sat his horse with the careless grace of his youth had he not been so catlike and tense. His black eyes roved everywhere, catching the movements of twigs and branches where small birds hopped, questing ever onward through the changing vistas of

From *The Night Born*, copyright 1913 by The Century Company.

trees and brush, and returning always to the clumps of undergrowth on either side. And as he watched, so did he listen, though he rode on in silence, save for the boom of heavy guns from far to the west. This had been sounding monotonously in his ears for hours, and only its cessation would have aroused his notice. For he had business closer to hand. Across his saddle-bow was balanced a carbine.

So tensely was he strung, that a bunch of quail, exploding into flight from under his horse's nose, startled him to such an extent that automatically, instantly, he had reined in and fetched the carbine halfway to his shoulder. He grinned sheepishly, recovered himself, and rode on. So tense was he, so bent upon the work he had to do, that the sweat stung his eyes unwiped, and unheeded rolled down his nose and spattered his saddle pommel. The band of his cavalryman's hat was fresh-stained with sweat. The roan horse under him was likewise wet. It was high noon of a breathless day of heat. Even the birds and squirrels did not dare the sun, but sheltered in shady hiding places among the trees.

Man and horse were littered with leaves and dusted with yellow pollen, for the open was ventured no more than was compulsory. They kept to the brush and trees, and invariably the man halted and peered out before crossing a dry glade or naked stretch of upland pasturage. He worked always to the north, though his way was devious, and it was from the north that he seemed most to apprehend that for which he was looking. He was no coward, but his courage was only that of the average civilized man, and he was looking to live, not die.

Up a small hillside he followed a cowpath through such dense scrub that he was forced to dismount and lead his horse. But when the path swung around to the west, he abandoned it and headed to the north again along the oak-covered top of the ridge.

The ridge ended in a steep descent—so steep that he zigzagged back and forth across the face of the slope, sliding and stumbling among the dead leaves and matted vines and keeping a watchful eye on the horse above that threatened to fall down upon him. The sweat ran from him, and the pollen-dust, settling pungently in mouth and nostrils, increased his thirst. Try as he would, nevertheless the descent was noisy, and frequently he stopped, panting in the dry heat and listening for any warning from beneath.

At the bottom he came out on a flat, so densely forested that he could not make out its extent. Here the character of the woods changed, and he was able to remount. Instead of the twisted hillside oaks, tall straight trees, big-trunked and prosperous, rose from the damp fat soil. Only here and there were thickets, easily avoided, while he encountered winding, park-like glades where the cattle had pastured in the days before war had run them off.

His progress was more rapid now, as he came down into the valley, and at the end of half an hour he halted at an ancient rail fence on the edge of a clearing. He did not like the openness of it, yet his path lay across to the fringe of trees that marked the banks of the stream. It was a mere quarter of a mile across that open, but the thought of venturing out in it was repugnant. A rifle, a score of them, a thousand, might lurk in that fringe by the stream.

Twice he essayed to start, and twice he paused. He was appalled by his own loneliness. The pulse of war that beat from the West suggested the companionship of battling thousands; here was naught but silence, and himself, and possible death-dealing bullets from a myriad ambushes. And yet his task was to find what he feared to find. He must go on, and on, till somewhere, some time, he encountered another man, or other men, from the other side, scouting, as he was scouting, to make report, as he must make report, of having come in touch.

Changing his mind, he skirted inside the woods for a distance, and again peeped forth. This time, in the middle of the clearing, he saw a small farmhouse. There were no signs of life. No smoke curled from the chimney, not a barnyard fowl clucked and strutted. The kitchen door stood open, and he gazed so long and hard into the black aperture that it seemed almost that a farmer's wife must emerge at any moment.

He licked the pollen and dust from his dry lips, stiffened himself, mind and body, and rode out into the blazing sunshine. Nothing stirred. He went on past the house, and approached the wall of trees and bushes by the river's bank. One thought persisted maddeningly. It was of the crash into his body of a high-velocity bullet. It made him feel very fragile and defenseless, and he crouched lower in the saddle.

Tethering his horse in the edge of the wood, he continued a hundred yards on foot till he came to the stream. Twenty feet wide it was, without perceptible current, cool and inviting, and he was very thirsty. But he waited inside his screen of leafage, his eyes fixed on the screen on the opposite side. To make the wait endurable, he sat down, his carbine resting on his knees. The minutes passed, and slowly his tenseness relaxed. At last he decided there was no danger; but just as he prepared to part the bushes and bend down to the water, a movement among the opposite bushes caught his eye.

It might be a bird. But he waited. Again there was an agitation of the bushes, and then, so suddenly that it almost startled a cry from him, the bushes parted and a face peered out. It was a face covered with several weeks' growth of ginger-colored beard. The eyes were blue and wide apart, with laughter-wrinkles in the corners that showed despite the tired and anxious expression of the whole face.

All this he could see with microscopic clearness, for the distance was no more than twenty feet. And all this he saw in such brief time, that he saw it as he lifted his carbine to his shoulder. He glanced along the sights, and knew that he was gazing upon a man who was as good as dead. It was impossible to miss at such point blank range.

But he did not shoot. Slowly he lowered the carbine and watched. A hand, clutching a water-bottle, became visible and the ginger beard bent downward to fill the bottle. He could hear the gurgle of the water. Then arm and bottle and ginger beard disappeared behind the closing bushes. A long time he waited, when, with thirst unslaked, he crept back to his horse, rode slowly across the sun-washed clearing, and passed into the shelter of the woods beyond.

II

Another day, hot and breathless. A deserted farmhouse, large, with many outbuildings and an orchard, standing in a clearing. From the woods, on a roan horse, carbine across pommel, rode the young man with the quick black eyes. He breathed with relief as he gained the house. That a fight had taken place here earlier in the season was evident. Clips and empty cartridges, tarnished with verdigris, lay on the ground, which, while wet, had been torn up by the hoofs of horses. Hard by the kitchen garden were graves, tagged and numbered. From the oak tree by the kitchen door, in tattered, weather-beaten garments, hung the bodies of two men.

The faces, shriveled and defaced, bore no likeness to the faces of men. The roan horse snorted beneath them, and the rider caressed and soothed it and tied it farther away.

Entering the house, he found the interior a wreck. He trod on empty cartridges as he walked from room to room to reconnoiter from the windows. Men had camped and slept everywhere, and on the floor of one room he came upon stains unmistakable where the wounded had been laid down.

Again outside, he led the horse around behind the barn and invaded the orchard. A dozen trees were burdened with ripe apples. He filled his pockets, eating while he picked. Then a thought came to him, and he glanced at the sun, calculating the time of his return to camp. He pulled off his shirt, tying the sleeves and making a bag. This he proceeded to fill with apples.

As he was about to mount his horse, the animal suddenly pricked up its ears. The man, too, listened, and heard, faintly, the thud of hoofs on soft earth. He crept to the corner of the barn and peered out. A dozen mounted men, strung out loosely, approaching from the opposite side of the clearing, were only a matter of a hundred yards or so away. They rode on to the house. Some dismounted, while others remained in the saddle as an earnest that their stay would be short. They seemed to be holding a council, for he could hear them talking excitedly in the detested tongue of the alien invader. The time passed, but they seemed unable to reach a decision. He put the carbine away in its boot, mounted, and waited impatiently, balancing the shirt of apples on the pommel.

He heard footsteps approaching, and drove his spurs so fiercely into the roan as to force a surprised groan from the animal as it leaped forward. At the corner of the barn he saw the intruder, a mere boy of nineteen or twenty for all of his uniform, jump back to escape being run down. At the same moment the roan swerved, and its rider caught a glimpse of the aroused men by the house. Some were springing from their horses, and he could see the rifles going to their shoulders. He passed the kitchen door and the dried corpses swinging in the shade, compelling his foes to run around the front of the house. A rifle cracked, and a second, but he was going fast, leaning forward, low in the saddle, one hand clutching the shirt of apples, the other guiding the horse.

The top bar of the fence was four feet high, but he knew his roan and leaped it at full career to the accompaniment of several scattered shots. Eight hundred yards straight away were the woods, and the roan was covering the distance with mighty strides. Every man was now firing. They were pumping their guns so rapidly that he no longer heard individual shots. A bullet went through his hat, but he was unaware, though he did know when another tore through the apples on the pommel. And he winced and ducked even lower when a third bullet, fired low, struck a stone between his horse's legs and ricochetted off through the air, buzzing and humming like some incredible insect.

The shots died down as the magazines were emptied, until, quickly, there was no more shooting. The young man was elated. Through that astonishing fusillade he had come unscathed. He glanced back. Yes, they had emptied their magazines. He could see several reloading. Others were running back behind the house for their horses. As he looked, two already mounted, came back into view around the corner, riding hard. And at the same moment, he saw the man with the unmistakable ginger beard kneel down on the ground, level his gun, and coolly take his time for the long shot.

The young man threw his spurs into the horse, crouched very low, and swerved in his flight in order to distract the other's aim. And still the shot did not come. With each jump of the horse, the woods sprang nearer. They were only two hundred yards away, and still the shot was delayed.

And then he heard it, the last thing he was to hear, for he was dead ere he hit the ground in the long crashing fall from the saddle. And they, watching at the house, saw him fall, saw his body bounce when it struck the earth, and saw the burst of red-cheeked apples that rolled about him. They laughed at the unexpected eruption of apples, and clapped their hands in applause of the long shot by the man with the ginger beard.

1911

THE PEARLS OF PARLAY

The Kanaka helmsman put the wheel down and the *Malahini* slipped into the eye of the wind and righted to an even keel. Her headsails emptied; there was a rat-tat of reef points and quick shifting of boom tackles, and she heeled over and filled away on the other tack. Though it was early morning and the wind brisk the five white men who lounged on the poop deck were scantily clad. David Grief and his guest, Gregory Mulhall, an Englishman, were still in pajamas, their naked feet thrust into Chinese slippers. The captain and mate were in thin undershirts and unstarched duck trousers, while the supercargo still held in his hands the undershirt he was reluctant to put on. The sweat stood out on his forehead and he seemed to thrust his bare chest thirstily into the wind that did not cool.

"Pretty muggy for a breeze like this," he complained.

"And what's it doing around in the west? That's what I want to know," was Grief's contribution to the general plaint.

"It won't last and it ain't been there long," said Hermann, the Holland mate. "She is been chop round all night—five minutes here, ten minutes there, one hour somewhere other quarter."

"Something makin', something makin'," Captain Warfield croaked, spreading his bushy beard with the fingers of both hands and shoving the thatch of his chin into the breeze in a vain search for coolness. "Weather's been crazy for a fortnight. Haven't had the proper trades in three weeks. Everything's mixed up. Barometer was pumping at sunset last night and it's pumping now, though the weather sharps say it don't mean anything. All the same, I've got a prejudice against seeing it pump. Gets on my nerves, sort of, you know. She was pumping that way the time we lost the *Lancaster*. I was only an apprentice, but I can remember that well enough. Brand-new four-masted steel ship; first voyage—broke the old man's heart. He'd been forty years in the company. Just faded away and died the next year."

Despite the wind and the early hour, the heat was suffocating. The wind whispered coolness but did not deliver coolness. It might have blown off the Sahara, save for the extreme humidity with which it was laden. There was no fog or mist, nor hint of fog or mist; yet the dimness of distance produced the impression.

There were no defined clouds; yet so thickly were the heavens covered by a messy cloud pall that the sun failed to shine through.

"Ready about!" Captain Warfield ordered with slow sharpness.

The brown, breechclouted Kanaka sailors moved languidly but quickly to head sheets and boom tackles.

"Hard alee!"

The helmsman ran the spokes over with no hint of gentling and the *Malahini* darted prettily into the wind and about.

"Jove! She's a witch!" was Mulhall's appreciation. "I didn't know you South Sea traders sailed yachts."

"She was a Gloucester fisherman originally," Grief explained, "and the Gloucester boats are all yachts when it comes to build, rig, and sailing."

"But you're heading right in—why don't you make it?" came the Englishman's criticism.

"Try it, Captain Warfield," Grief suggested. "Show him what a lagoon entrance is on a strong ebb."

"Close and by!" the captain ordered.

"Close and by!" the Kanaka repeated, easing half a spoke.

The *Malahini* laid squarely into the narrow passage, which was the lagoon entrance of a large, long, and narrow oval of an atoll. The atoll was shaped as if three atolls, in the course of building, had collided and coalesced and failed to rear the partition walls. Coconut palms grew in spots on the circle of sand and there were many gaps where the sand was too low to the sea for coconuts, through which could be seen the protected lagoon where the water lay flat like the ruffled surface of a mirror. Many square miles of water were in the irregular lagoon, all of which surged out on the ebb through the one narrow channel. So narrow was the channel, so large the outflow of water, that the passage was more like the rapids of a river than the mere tidal entrance to an atoll. The water boiled and whirled and swirled and drove outward in a white foam of stiff, serrated waves. Each heave and blow on her bows of the upstanding waves of the current swung the *Malahini* off the straight lead and wedged her as with wedges of steel toward the side of the passage. Part way in she was when her closeness to the coral edge compelled her to go about. On the opposite tack, broadside to the current, she swept seaward with the current's speed.

"Now's the time for that new and expensive engine of yours," Grief jeered good-naturedly.

That the engine was a sore point with Captain Warfield was patent. He had begged and badgered for it until, in the end, Grief had given his consent.

"It will pay for itself yet," the captain retorted. "You wait and see. It beats insurance; and you know the underwriters won't stand for insurance in the Paumotus."

Grief pointed to a small cutter beating up astern of them on the same course. "I'll wager five francs the little *Nuhiva* beats us in."

"Sure!" Captain Warfield agreed. "She's overpowered. We're like a liner alongside of her and we've only got forty horsepower. She's got ten horse, and she's a little skimming dish. She could skate across the froth of hell; but just the same she can't buck this current. It's running ten knots right now."

And at the rate of ten knots, buffeted and jerkily rolled, the *Malahini* went out to sea with the tide.

"She'll slacken in half an hour—then we'll make headway," Captain Warfield said with an irritation explained by his next words. "He has no right to call it Parlay. It's down on the Admiralty charts, and the French charts too, as Hikihoho. Bougainville discovered it and named it from the natives."

"What's the name matter?" the supercargo demanded, taking advantage of speech to pause with arms shoved into the sleeves of the undershirt. "There it is, right under our nose; and old Parlay is there with the pearls."

"Who see them pearls?" Hermann queried, looking from one to another.

"It's well known," was the supercargo's reply. He turned to the steersman. "Tell them, Tai-Hotauri."

The Kanaka, pleased and self-conscious, took and gave a spoke. "My brother dive for Parlay three-four month and he make much talk about pearl. Hikihoho very good place for pearl."

"And the pearl buyers have never got him to part with a pearl," the captain broke in.

"And they say the old man had a hatful for Armande when he sailed for Tahiti," the supercargo carried on the tale.

"That's fifteen years ago and he's been adding to it ever since—stored the shell as well. Everybody's seen that—hundreds of tons of it. They say the lagoon's fished clean now. Maybe that's why he's announced the auction."

"If he really sells what he has, this will be the biggest year's output of pearls in the Paumotus," Grief said.

"I say, now, look here!" Mulhall burst forth, harried by the humid heat as much as the rest of them. "What's it all about? Who's the old beachcomber anyway? What are all these pearls? Why so secretive about it?"

"Hikihoho belongs to old Parlay," the supercargo answered. "He's got a fortune in pearls, saved up for years and years; and he sent the word out weeks ago that he'd auction them off to the buyers tomorrow. See those schooners' masts sticking up inside the lagoon?"

"Eight—so I see," said Hermann.

"What are they doing in a dinky atoll like this?" the supercargo went on. "There isn't a schoonerload of copra a year in the place. They've come for the auction. That's why we're here. That's why the little *Nuhiva's* bumping along astern there—though what she can buy is beyond me. Narii Herring—he's an English Jew half-caste—owns and runs her, and his only assets are his nerve, his debts, and his whisky bills. He's a genius in such things. He owes so much there isn't a merchant in Papeete who isn't interested in his welfare. They go out of their way to throw work in his way. They've got to—and a dandy stunt it is for Narii. Now I owe nobody. What's the result? If I fell down in a fit on the beach they'd let me lie there and die. They wouldn't lose anything. But Narii Herring! What wouldn't they do if he fell in a fit? Their best wouldn't be too good for him. They've got too much money tied up in him to let him lie. They'd take him into their homes and hand-nurse him like a brother. Let me tell you, honesty in paying bills ain't what it's cracked up to be."

"What's this Narii chap got to do with it?" was the Englishman's short-tempered demand. And, turning to Grief, he said: "What's all this pearl nonsense? Begin at the beginning."

"You'll have to help me out," Grief warned the others as he began. "Old Parlay is a character. From what I've seen of him, I believe he's partly and mildly insane. Anyway, here's the story. Parlay's a full-blooded Frenchman. He told me once that he came from Paris. His accent is the true Parisian. He arrived down here in the old days. Went to trading and all the rest. That's how he got in on Hikihoho. Came in trading when trading was the real thing. About a hundred miserable Paumotans lived on the island. He married the Queen—native fashion. When she died everything was his. Measles came through and there weren't more than a dozen survivors. He fed them and worked them, and was King. Now before the Queen died she gave birth to a girl. That's Armande. When she was three he sent her to the convent at Papeete. When she was seven or eight he sent her to France. You begin to glimpse the situation. The best and most aristocratic convent in France was none too good for the only daughter of a Paumotan island king and capitalist—and you know the old-country French draw no color line. She was educated like a princess and she accepted herself in much the same way. Also she thought she was all white and never dreamed of a bar sinister.

"Now comes the tragedy. The old man had always been cranky and erratic, and he'd played the despot on Hikihoho so long that he'd got the idea in his head that there was nothing wrong with the King—or the princess either. When Armande was eighteen he sent for her. He had slews and slathers of money, as Yankee Bill would say. He'd built the big house on Hikihoho and a whacking fine bungalow in Papeete. She was to arrive on the mail boat from New Zealand and he sailed in his schooner to meet her at Papeete. And he might have carried the situation off, despite the hens and bull beasts of Papeete, if it hadn't been for the hurricane. That was the year, wasn't it, when Manu-Huni was swept and eleven hundred drowned?"

The others nodded and Captain Warfield said: "I was in the *Magpie* that blow and we went ashore, all hands and the cook—*Magpie* and all—a quarter of a mile into the coconuts at the head of Taiohae Bay—and it a supposedly hurricane-proof harbor."

"Well," Grief continued, "old Parlay got caught in the same blow and arrived in Papeete with his hatful of pearls three weeks too late. He'd had to jack up his schooner and build half a mile of ways before he could get her back into the sea.

"Meantime there was Armande at Papeete. Nobody called on her. She did, French fashion, make the initial calls on the governor and the port doctor. They saw her, but neither of their hen wives was at home to her or returned the call. She was out of caste—without caste—though she had never dreamed it; and that was the gentle way they broke the information to her. There was a gay young lieutenant on the French cruiser. He lost his heart to her, but not his head. You can imagine the shock to this young woman, refined, beautiful, raised like an aristocrat, pampered with the best of old France that money could buy! And you can guess the end." He shrugged his shoulders. "There was a Japanese servant in the bungalow. He saw it—said she did it with the proper spirit of the samurai. Took a stiletto—no thrust, no drive, no wild rush for annihilation—took the stiletto, placed the point carefully against her heart, and with both hands slowly and steadily pressed home.

"Old Parlay arrived after that with his pearls. There was one single one of them, they say, worth sixty thousand francs. Peter Gee saw it and has told me he offered that much for it. The old man went clean off for a while. They had him strait-jacketed in the Colonial Club for two days——"

"His wife's uncle, an old Paumotan, cut him out of the jacket and turned him loose," the supercargo corroborated.

"And then old Parlay proceeded to eat things up," Grief went on. "Pumped three bullets into the scalawag of a lieutenant——"

"Who lay in sick bay for three months," Captain Warfield contributed.

"Flung a glass of wine in the governor's face; fought a duel with the port doctor; beat up his native servants; wrecked the hospital; broke two ribs and the collarbone of a man nurse—and escaped; went down to his schooner, a gun in each hand, daring the chief of police and all the gendarmes to arrest him, and sailed for Hikihoho. And they say he's never left the island since."

The supercargo nodded. "That was fifteen years ago, and he's never budged."

"And added to his pearls," said the captain. "He's a blithering old lunatic. Makes my flesh creep. He's a regular Finn."

"What's that?" Mulhall asked.

"Bosses the weather—that's what the natives believe, at any rate. Ask Tai-Hotauri there. Hey, Tai-Hotauri, what you think old Parlay do along weather?"

"Just the same one big weather devil!" came the Kanaka's answer. "I know. He want big blow, he make big blow. He want no wind, no wind come."

"A regular old warlock," said Mulhall.

"No good luck, them pearl," Tai-Hotauri blurted out, rolling his head ominously. "He say he sell. Plenty schooner come. Then he make big hurricane; everybody finish, you see. All native men say so."

"It's hurricane season now," Captain Warfield laughed morosely. "They're not far wrong. It's making for something right now; and I'd feel better if the *Malahini* was a thousand miles away from here."

"He is a bit mad," Grief concluded. "I've tried to get his point of view. It's—well, it's mixed. For eighteen years he'd centered everything on Armande. Half the time he believes she's still alive—not yet come back from France. That's one of the reasons he held on to the pearls. And all the time he hates white men. He never forgets they killed her, though a great deal of the time he forgets she's dead."

"Hello! Where's your wind?"

The sails bellied emptily overhead and Captain Warfield grunted his disgust. Intolerable as the heat had been, in the absence of wind it was almost overpowering. The sweat oozed out on all their faces; and now one and then another drew deep breaths, involuntarily questing for more air.

"Here she comes again—an eight-point haul! Boom tackles across! Jump!"

The Kanakas sprang to the captain's orders and for five minutes the schooner laid directly into the passage—and even gained on the current. Again the breeze fell flat, then puffed from the old quarter, compelling a shift back of sheets and tackles.

"Here comes the *Nuhiva*," Grief said. "She's got her engine on. Look at her skim!"

"All ready?" the captain asked the engineer, a Portuguese half-caste, whose head and shoulders protruded from the small hatch just for'ard of the cabin, and who wiped the dripping sweat from his face with a bunch of greasy waste.

"Sure!" he replied.

"Then let her go!"

The engineer disappeared into his den and a moment later the exhaust muffler coughed and spluttered overside; but the schooner could not hold her lead. The little cutter traveled three feet to her two and was quickly alongside and forging ahead.

Only natives were on her deck and the man who was steering waved his hand in derisive greeting and farewell.

"That's Narii Herring," Grief told Mulhall, "the big fellow at the wheel—the nerviest and most conscienceless scoundrel in the Paumotus."

Five minutes later a cry of joy from their own Kanakas centered all eyes on the *Nuhiva.* Her engine had broken down and they were overtaking her. The *Malahini's* sailors sprang into the rigging and jeered as they went by; the little cutter, heeled over by the wind, was going backward on the tide.

"Some engine, that of ours!" Grief approved as the lagoon opened before them and the course was changed across it to the anchorage.

Captain Warfield was visibly cheered, though he merely grunted: "It'll pay for itself; never fear."

The *Malahini* ran well into the center of the little fleet ere she found swinging room to anchor.

"There's Isaacs on the *Dolly,*" Grief observed with a hand wave of greeting. "And Peter Gee's on the *Roberta.* Couldn't keep him away from a pearl sale like this. And there's Francini on the *Cactus.* They're all here—all the buyers. Old Parlay will surely get a price."

"They haven't repaired the engine yet," Captain Warfield grumbled gleefully. He was looking across the lagoon to where the *Nuhiva's* sails showed through the sparse coconuts.

II

The house of Parlay was a big two-story frame affair, built of California lumber, with a galvanized iron roof. So disproportionate was it to the slender ring of the atoll that it showed out upon the sand strip and above it like some monstrous excrescence. They of the *Malahini* paid the courtesy visit ashore immediately after anchoring. Other captains and buyers were in the big room examining the pearls that were to be auctioned next day. Paumotan servants, natives of Hikihoho and relatives of the owner, moved about, dispensing whisky and absinthe. And through the curious company moved Parlay himself, cackling and sneering, the withered wreck of what had once been a tall and powerful man. His eyes were deep-sunken and feverish, his cheeks fallen in and cavernous. The hair of his head seemed to have come out in patches and his mustache and imperial had been shed in the same lopsided way.

"Jove!" Mulhall muttered under his breath. "A long-legged Napoleon III—but burnt out, baked, and fire-crackled. And mangy! No wonder he crooks his head to one side. He's got to keep the balance."

"Goin' to have a blow," was the old man's greeting to Grief. "You must think a lot of pearls to come a day like this."

"They're worth going to inferno for," Grief laughed genially back, running his eyes over the surface of the table covered by the display.

"Other men have already made that journey for them," old Parlay cackled. "See this one!" He pointed to a large, perfect pearl, the size of a small walnut, that lay apart on a piece of chamois. "They offered me sixty thousand francs for it in Tahiti. They'll bid as much and more for it tomorrow if they aren't blown away. Well, that pearl was found by my cousin—my cousin by marriage. He was a native, you see. Also he was a thief. He hid it. It was mine. His cousin, who was also my cousin—we're all related here—killed him for it and fled away in a cutter to Noo-Nau. I pursued; but the chief of Noo-Nau had killed him for it before I got there. Oh yes, there are many dead men represented on the table there. Have a drink, Captain? Your face is not familiar. You are new in the islands?"

"It's Captain Robinson, of the *Roberta*," Grief said, introducing them.

Meantime Mulhall had shaken hands with Peter Gee.

"I never fancied there were so many pearls in the world," Mulhall said.

"Nor have I ever seen so many together at one time," Peter Gee admitted.

"What ought they to be worth?" asked Mulhall.

"Fifty or sixty thousand pounds—and that's to us buyers. In Paris . . ." He shrugged his shoulders.

Mulhall wiped the sweat from his eyes. All were sweating profusely and breathing hard. There was no ice, and the whisky and absinthe went down lukewarm.

"Yes, yes!" Parlay was cackling. "Many dead men lie on the table there. I know those pearls, all of them. You see those three—perfectly matched, aren't they? A diver from Easter Island got them for me inside a week. Next week a shark got him—took his arm off and blood poison did the business. And that big baroque there—nothing much; if I'm offered twenty francs for it tomorrow I'll be in luck—it came out of twenty-two fathoms of water. The man was from Rarotonga. He broke all diving records. He got it out of twenty-two fathoms. I saw him. And he burst his lungs at the same time, or got the bends; for he died in two hours. He died screaming. They could hear him for miles. He was the most powerful native I ever saw. Half a dozen of my divers have died of the bends. And more men will die—more men will die!"

"Oh, hush your croaking, Parlay!" chided one of the captains. "It ain't going to blow."

"If I was a strong young man I couldn't get up hook and get out fast enough," the old man retorted in the falsetto of age. "Not if I was a strong young man with the taste for wine yet in my mouth. But not you. You'll all stay. I wouldn't advise you if I thought you'd go. You can't drive buzzards away from the carrion. Have another drink, my brave sailormen. Well, well! What men will dare for a few little oyster drops! There they are, the beauties! Auction tomorrow at ten sharp. Old Parlay's selling out and the buzzards are gathering—old Parlay, who was a stronger man in his day than any of them and who will see most of them dead yet!"

"If he isn't a vile old beast!" the supercargo of the *Malahini* whispered to Peter Gee.

"What if she does blow?" said the captain of the *Dolly*. "Hikihoho's never been swept."

"The more reason she will be, then," Captain Warfield answered back. "I wouldn't trust her."

"Who's croaking now?" Grief reproved.

"I'd hate to lose that new engine before it paid for itself," Captain Warfield replied gloomily.

Parlay skipped with astonishing nimbleness across the crowded room to where a ship's barometer hung on the wall.

"Take a look, my brave sailormen!" he cried exultantly.

The man nearest read the glass. The sobering effect showed plainly on his face.

"It's dropped ten," was all he said, yet every face went anxious and there was a restlessness as if every man desired immediately to start for the door.

"Listen!" Parlay commanded.

In the silence the outer surf seemed to have become unusually loud. There was a great, rumbling roar.

"A big sea is beginning to set," someone said; and there was a movement to the windows, where all gathered.

Through the sparse coconuts they gazed seaward. An orderly succession of huge, smooth seas was rolling down upon the coral shore. For some minutes they gazed on the strange sight and talked in low voices, and in those few minutes it was manifest to all that the waves were increasing in size. It was uncanny, this rising sea in a dead calm, and their voices unconsciously sank lower. Old Parlay shocked them with his abrupt cackle.

"There is yet time to get away to sea, brave gentlemen. You can tow across the lagoon with your whaleboats."

"It's all right, old man," said Darling, the mate of the *Cactus*, a stalwart youngster of twenty-five. "The blow's to the south'ard and passing on. We'll not get a whiff of it."

An air of relief went through the room. Conversations were started, and the voices became louder. Several of the buyers even went back to the table to continue the examination of the pearls. Parlay's cackle rose higher.

"That's right," he encouraged. "If the world was coming to an end you'd go on buying."

"We'll buy these tomorrow," Isaacs assured him.

"Then you'll be doing your buying in hell!"

The chorus of incredulous laughter incensed the old man. He turned fiercely on Darling.

"Since when have children like you come to the knowledge of storms? And who is the man who has plotted the hurricane courses of the Paumotus? What books will you find it in? I sailed the Paumotus before the oldest of you drew breath. I know! To the eastward the paths of the hurricanes are on so wide a circle they make a straight line. To the westward here they make a sharp curve. Remember your chart. How did it happen the hurricane of '91 swept Auri and Hiolau? The curve, my brave boy, the curve! In an hour, or two or three at most, will come the wind. Listen to that!"

A vast, rumbling crash shook the coral foundations of the atoll. The house quivered to it. The native servants, with bottles of whisky and absinthe in their hands, shrank together as if for protection and stared with fear through the windows at the mighty wash of the wave lapping far up the beach to the corner of a copra shed.

Parlay looked at the barometer, giggled, and leered around at his guests. Captain Warfield strode across to see.

"Twenty-nine seventy-five!" he read. "She's gone down five more. The old devil's right. She's a-coming—and it's me, for one, for aboard!"

"It's growing dark," Isaacs half whimpered.

"Jove! It's like a stage," Mulhall said to Grief, looking at his watch. "Ten o'clock in the morning and it's like twilight. Down go the lights for the tragedy. Where's the slow music?"

In answer another rumbling crash shook the atoll and the house. Almost in a panic the company started for the door. In the dim light their sweaty faces appeared ghastly. Isaacs panted asthmatically in the suffocating heat.

"What's your haste?" Parlay chuckled and girded at his departing guests. "A last drink, brave gentlemen!" No one noticed him. As they took the shell-bordered path to the beach he stuck his head out at the door and called: "Don't forget, gentlemen—at ten tomorrow old Parlay sells his pearls!"

III

On the beach a curious scene took place. Whaleboat after whaleboat was being hurriedly manned and shoved off. It had grown still darker. The stagnant calm continued and the sand shook under their feet with each buffet of the sea on the outer shore. Narii Herring walked leisurely along the sand. He grinned at the very evident haste of the captains and buyers. With him were three of his Kanakas and also Tai-Hotauri.

"Get into the boat and take an oar," Captain Warfield ordered the latter.

Tai-Hotauri came over jauntily, while Narii Herring and his Kanakas paused and looked on from forty feet away.

"I work no more for you, skipper," Tai-Hotauri said insolently and loudly; but his face belied his words, for he was guilty of a prodigious wink. "Fire me, skipper," he huskily whispered with a second significant wink.

Captain Warfield took the cue and proceeded to do some acting himself. He raised his fist and his voice.

"Get into that boat, you swine," he thundered, "or I'll knock seven bells out of you!"

The Kanaka drew back truculently and Grief stepped between to placate his captain.

"I go to work on the *Nuhiva*," Tai-Hotauri said, rejoining the other group.

"Come back here!" the captain threatened.

"He's a free man, skipper," Narii Herring spoke up. "He's sailed with me in the past and he's sailing with me again—that's all."

"Come on; we must get on board," Grief urged. "Look how dark it's getting!"

Captain Warfield gave in, but as the boat shoved off he stood up in the stern sheets and shook his fist ashore.

"I'll settle with you yet, Narii!" he cried. "You're the only skipper in the group who steals other men's sailors." He sat down and in a lowered voice queried: "Now what's Tai-Hotauri up to? He's on to something; but what is it?"

IV

As the boat came alongside the *Malahini*, Hermann's anxious face greeted them over the rail.

"Bottom fall out from barometer," he announced. "She goin' to blow. I got starboard anchor overhaul."

"Overhaul the big one too," Captain Warfield ordered, taking charge. "And here, some of you, hoist in this boat. Lower her down to the deck and lash her, bottom up."

Men were busy at work on the decks of all the schooners. There was a great clanking of chains being overhauled; and now one craft and now another hove in, veered, and dropped a second anchor.

Like the *Malahini*, those that had third anchors were preparing to drop them when the wind showed what quarter it was to blow from.

The roar of the big surf continually grew, though the lagoon lay in mirrorlike calm. There was no sign of life where Parlay's big house perched on the sand. Boat and copra sheds and the sheds where the shell was stored were deserted.

"For two cents I'd up anchors and get out," Grief said. "I'd do it anyway if it were open sea; but those chains of atolls to the north and east have us pocketed. We've a better chance right there. What do you think, Captain Warfield?"

"I agree with you, though a lagoon is no millpond for riding it out. I wonder where she's going to start from? Hello! There goes one of Parlay's copra sheds!"

They could see the grass-thatched shed lift and collapse, while a froth of foam cleared the crest of the sand and ran down to the lagoon.

"Breached across!" Mulhall exclaimed. "That's something for a starter. There she comes again!"

The wreck of the shed was now flung up and left on the sand crest. A third wave buffeted it into fragments, which washed down the slope toward the lagoon.

"If she blow I would as be cooler yet," Hermann grunted. "No longer can I breathe. It is damn hot. I am dry like a stove."

He chopped open a drinking coconut with his heavy sheath knife and drained the contents. The rest of them followed his example, pausing once to watch one of Parlay's shell sheds go down in ruin. The barometer now registered 29.50.

"Must be pretty close to the center of the area of low pressure," Grief remarked cheerfully. "I was never through the eye of a hurricane before. It will be an experience for you too, Mulhall. From the speed the barometer's dropped it's going to be a big one."

Captain Warfield groaned, and all eyes were drawn to him. He was looking through the glasses down the length of the lagoon to the southeast.

"There she comes," he said quietly.

They did not need glasses to see. A flying film, strangely marked, seemed drawing over the surface of the lagoon. Abreast of it, along the atoll, traveling with equal speed, was a stiff bending of the coconut palms and a blur of flying leaves. The front of the wind on the water was a solid, sharply defined strip of dark-colored, wind-vexed water. In advance of this strip, like skirmishers, were flashes of wind-flaws. Behind this strip, a quarter of a mile in width, was a strip of what seemed glassy calm. Next came another dark strip of wind—and behind that the lagoon was all crisping, boiling whiteness.

"What is that calm streak?" Mulhall asked.

"Calm," Warfield answered.

"But it travels as fast as the wind," was the other's objection.

"It has to, or it would be overtaken and there wouldn't be any calm. It's a double-header. I saw a big squall like that off Savaii once. A regular double-header. Smash! It hit us; then it lulled to nothing and smashed us a second time. Stand by and hold on. Here she is on top of us. Look at the *Roberta!*"

The *Roberta*, lying nearest to the wind at slack chains, was swept off broadside like a straw. Then her chains brought her up, bow on to the wind, with an astonishing jerk. Schooner after schooner—the *Malahini* with them—was now sweeping away with the first gust and fetching up on taut chains.

Mulhall and several of the Kanakas were taken off their feet when the *Malahini* jerked to her anchor.

And then there was no wind. The flying calm streak had reached them. Grief lighted a match and the unshielded flame burned without flickering in the still air. A very dim twilight prevailed. The cloud-sky, lowering as it had been for hours, seemed now to have descended quite down upon the sea.

The *Roberta* tightened to her chains when the second head of the hurricane hit, as did schooner after schooner in swift succession. The sea, white with fury, boiled in tiny, spitting wavelets. The deck of the *Malahini* vibrated under their feet. The taut-stretched halyards beat a tattoo against the masts, and all the rigging, as if smitten by some mighty hand, set up a wild thrumming. It was impossible to face the wind and breathe. Mulhall, crouching with the others behind the shelter of the cabin, discovered this; and his lungs were filled in an instant with so great a volume of driven air which he could not expel that he nearly strangled ere he could turn his head away.

"It's incredible!" he gasped; but no one heard him.

Hermann and several Kanakas were crawling for'ard on hands and knees to let go the third anchor. Grief touched Captain Warfield and pointed to the *Roberta*. She was dragging down upon them. Warfield put his mouth to Grief's ear and shouted:

"We're dragging too!"

Grief sprang to the wheel and put it hard over, veering the *Malahini* to port. The third anchor took hold and the *Roberta* went by, stern first, a dozen yards away. They waved their hands to Peter Gee and Captain Robinson, who, with a number of sailors, were at work on the bow.

"He's knocking out the shackles!" Grief shouted. "Going to chance the passage! Got to! Anchors skating!"

"We're holding now!" came the answering shout. "There goes the *Cactus* down on the *Misi*. That settles them!"

The *Misi* had been holding, but the added windage of the *Cactus* was too much and the entangled schooners slid away across the boiling white. Their men could be seen chopping and fighting to get them apart. The *Roberta*, cleared of her anchors, with a patch of tarpaulin set for'ard, was heading for the passage at the northwestern end of the lagoon. They saw her make it and drive out to sea. The *Misi* and the *Cactus*, however, unable to get clear of each other, went ashore on the atoll half a mile from the passage.

The wind merely increased on itself and continued to increase. To face the full blast of it required all one's strength, and several minutes of crawling on deck against it tired a man to exhaustion. Hermann, with his Kanakas, plodded steadily, lashing and making secure, putting ever more gaskets on the sails. The wind ripped and tore their thin undershirts from their backs. They moved slowly, as if their bodies weighed tons, never releasing a handhold until another had been secured. Loose ends of rope stood out stiffly horizontal, and after whipping the loose ends frazzled and blew away.

Mulhall touched one and then another and pointed to the shore. The grass sheds had disappeared and Parlay's house rocked drunkenly. Because the wind blew lengthwise along the atoll the house had been sheltered by the miles of coconut trees; but the big seas, breaking across from outside, were undermining it and hammering it to pieces. Already tilted down the slope of sand, its end was imminent. Here and there in the coconut trees people had lashed themselves. The trees did not sway or thresh about. Bent over rigidly by the wind, they remained in that position and vibrated monstrously. Underneath, across the sand, surged the white spume of the breakers.

A big sea was likewise making down the length of the lagoon. It had plenty of room to kick up in the ten-mile stretch from the windward rim of the atoll, and all the schooners were bucking and plunging into it. The *Malahini* had begun shoving her bow and fo'c'sle head under the bigger ones, and at times her waist was filled rail-high with water.

"Now's the time for your engine!" Grief bellowed; and Captain Warfield, crawling over to where the engineer lay, shouted emphatic commands.

Under the engine, going full speed ahead, the *Malahini* behaved better. Though she continued to ship seas over her bow, she was not jerked down so fiercely by her anchors. On the other hand, she was unable to get any slack in the chains. The best her forty horsepower could do was to ease the strain.

Still the wind increased. The little *Nuhiva,* lying abreast of the *Malahini* and closer in to the beach, her engine still unrepaired and her captain ashore, was having a bad time of it. She buried herself so frequently and so deeply that they wondered each time if she could clear herself of the water.

At three in the afternoon, buried by a second sea before she could free herself of the preceding one, she did not come up.

Mulhall looked at Grief.

"Burst in her hatches!" was the bellowed answer.

Captain Warfield pointed to the *Winifred,* a little schooner plunging and burying outside of them, and shouted in Grief's ear. His voice came in patches of dim words, with intervals of silence when whisked away by the roaring wind.

"Rotten little tub! . . . Anchors hold. . . . But how she holds together! . . . Old as the ark."

An hour later Hermann pointed to her. Her for'ard bitts, foremast, and most of her bow were gone, having been jerked out of her by her anchors. She swung broadside, rolling in the trough and settling by the head; and in this plight she was swept away to leeward.

Five vessels now remained, and of them the *Malahini* was the only one with an engine. Fearing either the *Nuhiva's* or the *Mildred's* fate, two of them followed the *Roberta's* example, knocking out the chain shackles and running for the passage. The *Dolly* was the first, but her tarpaulin was carried away and she went to destruction on the lee rim of the atoll, near the *Misi* and the *Cactus.* Undeterred by this, the *Moana* let go and followed with the same result.

"Pretty good engine that, eh?" Captain Warfield yelled to his owner.

Grief put out his hand and shook. "She's paying for herself!" he yelled back. "The wind's shifting round to the south'ard and we ought to lie easier!"

Slowly and steadily, but with ever-increasing velocity, the wind veered round to the south and the southwest, till the three schooners that were left pointed directly in toward the beach. The wreck of Parlay's house was picked up, hurled into the lagoon, and blown out upon them. Passing the *Malahini,* it crashed into the *Papara,* lying a quarter of a mile astern. There was wild work for'ard on her and in a quarter of an hour the house went clear, but it had taken the *Papara's* foremast and bowsprit with it.

Inshore, on their port bow, lay the *Tahaa,* slim and yachtlike, but excessively oversparred. Her anchors still held, but her captain, finding no abatement in the wind, proceeded to reduce windage by chopping down his masts.

"Pretty good engine that!" Grief congratulated his skipper. "It will save our sticks for us yet."

Captain Warfield shook his head dubiously.

The sea on the lagoon went swiftly down with the change of wind, but they were beginning to feel the heave and lift of the outer sea breaking across the atoll. There were not so many trees remaining. Some had been broken short off, others uprooted. One tree they saw snapped off halfway up, three persons clinging to it, and whirled away by the wind into the lagoon. Two detached themselves from it and swam to the *Tahaa.* Not long after, just before darkness, they saw a man jump overboard from that schooner's stern and strike out strongly for the *Malahini* through the white, spitting wavelets.

"It's Tai-Hotauri," was Grief's judgment. "Now we'll have the news."

The Kanaka caught the bobstay, climbed over the bow, and crawled aft. Time was given him to breathe and then, behind the part shelter of the cabin, in broken snatches and largely by signs he told his story:

"Narii . . . damn robber! . . . He want steal . . . pearls. . . . Kill Parlay. . . . One man kill Parlay. . . . No man know what man. . . . Three Kanakas, Narii, me . . . five beans . . . hat. . . . Narii say one bean black. . . . Nobody know. . . . Kill Parlay. . . . Narii damn liar. . . . All beans black. . . . Five black. . . . Copra shed dark. . . . Every man get black bean. . . . Big wind come . . . no chance. . . . Everybody get up tree. . . . No good luck, them pearls, I tell you before . . . no good luck."

"Where's Parlay?" Grief shouted.

"Up tree. . . . Three of his Kanakas same tree; Narii and one Kanaka 'nother tree. . . . My tree blow to hell; then I come on board."

"Where are the pearls?"

"Up tree along Parlay. Mebbe Narii get them pearl yet."

In the ear of one after another Grief shouted Tai-Hotauri's story. Captain Warfield was particularly incensed and they could see him grinding his teeth.

Hermann went below and returned with a riding light, but the moment it was lifted above the level of the cabin wall the wind blew it out. He had better success with the binnacle lamp, which was lighted only after many collective attempts.

"A fine night of wind," Grief yelled in Mulhall's ear, "and blowing harder all the time!"

"How hard?"

"A hundred miles an hour—two hundred! I don't know. Harder than I've ever seen it."

The lagoon grew more and more troubled by the sea that swept across the atoll. Hundreds of leagues of ocean were being backed up by the hurricane, which more than overcame the lowering effect of the ebb tide. Immediately the tide began to rise, the increase in the size of the seas was noticeable. Moon and wind were heaping the South Pacific on Hikihoho atoll.

Captain Warfield returned from one of his periodical trips to the engine room with the word that the engineer lay in a faint.

"Can't let that engine stop!" he concluded helplessly.

"All right!" Grief shouted. "Bring him on deck. I'll spell him."

The hatch to the engine room was battened down, access being gained through a narrow passage from the cabin. The heat and gas fumes were stifling. Grief made one hasty, comprehensive examination of the engine and the fittings of the tiny room, then blew out the oil lamp. After that he worked in darkness, save for the glow from endless cigars that he went into the cabin to light. Even-tempered as he was, he soon began to give evidences of the strain of being pent in with a mechanical monster that toiled and sobbed and slubbered in the shouting dark. Naked to the waist, covered with grease and oil, bruised and skinned from being knocked about by the plunging, jumping vessel, his head swimming from the mixture of gas and air he was compelled to breathe, he labored on hour after hour, by turns petting, blessing, nursing, and cursing the engine and all its parts. The ignition began to go bad. The feed grew worse and, worst of all, the cylinders began to heat. In a consultation held in the cabin the half-caste engineer begged and pleaded to stop the engine for half an hour in order to cool it and to attend to the water circulation.

Captain Warfield was against any stopping. The half-caste swore that the engine would ruin itself and stop anyway, and for good. Grief, with glaring eyes, greasy and battered, yelled and cursed them both down and issued commands. Mulhall, the supercargo, and Hermann were set to work in the cabin at double-straining and triple-straining the gasoline.

A hole was chopped through the engine-room floor and a Kanaka heaved bilge water over the cylinders, while Grief continued to souse the running parts in oil.

"Didn't know you were a gasoline expert," Captain Warfield admired when Grief came into the cabin to catch a breath of little less impure air.

"I bathe in gasoline," he grated savagely through his teeth. "I eat it."

What other uses he might have found for it were never given, for at that moment all the men in the cabin, as well as the gasoline that was being strained, were smashed for'ard against the bulkhead as the *Malahini* took an abrupt, deep dive. For the space of several minutes, unable to gain their feet, they rolled back and forth and pounded and hammered from wall to wall. The schooner, swept by three big seas, creaked and groaned and quivered and, from the weight of water on her decks, behaved loggily. Grief crept to the engine, while Captain Warfield awaited his chance to get through the companionway and out on deck.

It was half an hour before he came back.

"Whaleboat's gone!" he reported. "Galley's gone! Everything gone except the deck and hatches! And if that engine hadn't been going we'd be gone! Keep up the good work!"

By midnight the engineer's lungs and head had been sufficiently cleared of gas fumes to let him relieve Grief, who went on deck to get his own head and lungs clear. He joined the others, who crouched behind the cabin, holding on with their hands and made doubly secure by rope lashings. It was a complicated huddle, for it was the only place of refuge for the Kanakas. Some of them had accepted the skipper's invitation into the cabin, but had been driven out by the fumes. The *Malahini* was being plunged down and swept frequently, and what they breathed was air and spray and water commingled.

"Making heavy weather of it, Mulhall!" Grief yelled to his guest between immersions.

Mulhall, strangling and choking, could only nod. The scuppers could not carry off the burden of water on the schooner's deck. She rolled it out and took it in over one rail and the other; and at times, nose thrown skyward, sitting down on her heel, she avalanched it aft. It surged along the poop gangways, poured over the top of the cabin, submerging and bruising those who clung on, and went out over the stern rail.

Mulhall saw him first and drew Grief's attention. It was Narii Herring, crouching and holding on where the dim binnacle light shone upon him. He was quite naked, save for a belt and a bare-bladed knife thrust between it and the skin.

Captain Warfield untied his lashings and made his way over the bodies of the others. When his face became visible in the light from the binnacle it was working with anger. They could see him shout, but the wind tore the sound away. He would not put his lips to Narii's ear. Instead he pointed over the side. Narii Herring understood. His white teeth showed in an amused and sneering smile, and he stood up—a magnificent figure of a man.

"It's murder!" Mulhall yelled to Grief.

"He'd have murdered old Parley!" Grief yelled back.

For the moment the poop was clear of water and the *Malahini* on an even keel. Narii made a bravado attempt to walk to the rail, but was flung down by the wind. Thereafter he crawled, disappearing in the darkness, though there was certitude in all of them that he had gone over the side. The *Malahini* dived deep; and when they emerged from the flood that swept aft Grief got Mulhall's ear.

"Can't lose him! He's the Fish Man of Tahiti! He'll cross the lagoon and land on the other rim of the atoll—if there's any atoll left."

Five minutes afterward, in another submergence, a mess of bodies poured down on them over the top of the cabin. These they seized and held till the water cleared, when they carried them below and learned their identity. Old Parlay lay on his back on the floor with closed eyes and without movement. The other two were his Kanaka cousins. All three were naked and bloody. The arm of one Kanaka hung helpless and broken at his side. The other Kanaka bled freely from a hideous scalp wound.

"Narii did that?" Mulhall demanded. Grief shook his head. "No; it's from being smashed along the deck and over the house!"

Something suddenly ceased, leaving them all in dizzying uncertainty. For a moment it was hard to realize there was no wind. With the absolute abruptness of a sword slash the wind had been chopped off. The schooner rolled and plunged, fetching up on her anchors with a crash that for the first time they could hear. Also, for the first time, they could hear the water washing about on deck. The engineer threw off the propeller and eased the engine down.

"We're in the dead center," Grief said. "Now for the shift. It will come as hard as ever." He looked at the barometer.

"Twenty-nine thirty-two," he read.

Not in a moment could he tone down the voice which for hours had shouted against the wind, and so loudly did he speak that, in the quiet, it hurt the others' ears.

"All his ribs are smashed," the supercargo said, feeling along Parlay's side. "He's still breathing; but he's a goner."

Old Parlay groaned, moved one arm impotently, and opened his eyes. In them was the light of recognition.

"My brave gentlemen," he whispered haltingly, "don't forget . . . the auction . . . at ten o'clock . . . in hell!"

His eyes drooped shut and the lower jaw threatened to drop, but he mastered the qualms of dissolution long enough to emit one final, loud, derisive cackle.

Above and below pandemonium broke out. The old familiar roar of the wind was with them. The *Malahini,* caught broadside, was pressed down almost on her beam-ends as she swung the arc compelled by her anchors. They rounded her into the wind, where she jerked to an even keel. The propeller was thrown on and the engine took up its work again.

"Northwest!" Captain Warfield shouted to Grief when he came on deck. "Hauled eight points like a shot!"

"Narii'll never get across the lagoon now!" Grief observed.

"Then he'll blow back to our side—worse luck!"

V

After the passing of the center the barometer began to rise. Equally rapid was the fall of the wind. When it was no more than a howling gale the engine lifted up in the air, parted its bedplates with a last convulsive effort of its forty horse-power, and lay down on its side. A wash of water from the bilge sizzled over it and the steam rose in clouds.

The engineer wailed his dismay, but Grief glanced over the wreck affectionately and went into the cabin to swab the grease off his chest and arms with bunches of cotton waste.

The sun was up and the gentlest of summer breezes blowing when he came on deck, after sewing up the scalp of one Kanaka and setting the other's arm. The *Malahini* lay close in to the beach. For'ard, Hermann and the crew were heaving in and straightening out the tangle of anchors.

The *Papara* and the *Tahaa* were gone; and Captain Warfield, through the glasses, was searching the opposite rim of the atoll.

"Not a stick left of them," he said. "That's what comes of not having engines. They must have dragged across before the big shift came."

Ashore, where Parlay's house had been, was no vestige of any house. For the space of three hundred yards, where the sea had breached, no tree or even stump was left. Here and there, farther along, stood an occasional palm, and there were numbers which had been snapped off above the ground.

In the crown of one surviving palm Tai-Hotauri asserted he saw something move. There were no boats left to the *Malahini,* and they watched him swim ashore and climb the tree.

When he came back they helped over the rail a young native girl of Parlay's household. But first she passed up to them a battered basket. In it was a litter of blind kittens—all dead save one that feebly mewed and staggered on awkward legs.

"Hello!" said Mulhall. "Who's that?"

Along the beach they saw a man walking. He moved casually, as if out for a morning stroll. Captain Warfield gritted his teeth. It was Narii Herring.

"Hello, Skipper," Narii called when he was abreast of them. "Can I come aboard and get some breakfast?"

Captain Warfield's face and neck began to swell and turn purple. He tried to speak, but choked.

"For two cents . . . ! For two cents . . . !" was all he could manage to articulate.

1911

THE RACE FOR NUMBER THREE

"Huh! Get onto the glad rags!"

Shorty surveyed his partner with simulated disapproval, and Smoke, vainly attempting to rub the wrinkles out of the pair of trousers he had just put on, was irritated.

"They sure fit you close for a second-hand buy," Shorty went on. "What was the tax?"

"One hundred and fifty for the suit," Smoke answered. "The man was nearly my own size. I thought it was remarkably reasonable. What are you kicking about?"

"Who? Me? Oh, nothin'. I was just thinkin' it was goin' some for a meat-eater that hit Dawson in an ice-jam, with no grub, one suit of underclothes, a pair of mangy moccasins, an' overalls that looked like they'd been through the wreck of the *Hesperus*. Pretty gay front, pardner. Say?"

"What do you want now?" Smoke demanded testily.

"What's her name?"

"There isn't any her, my friend. I'm to have dinner at Colonel Bowie's, if you want to know. The trouble with you, Shorty, is you're envious because I'm going into high society and you're not invited."

"Ain't you some late?" Shorty queried.

"What do you mean?"

"For dinner. They'll be eatin' supper when you get there."

Smoke was about to explain with crudely elaborate sarcasm when he caught the twinkle in the other's eye. He went on dressing, with fingers that had lost their deftness, tying a Windsor tie in a bow-knot at the throat of his soft cotton shirt.

"Wisht I hadn't sent all my starched shirts to the laundry," Shorty murmured sympathetically. "I might 'a' fitted you out."

By this time Smoke was straining at a pair of shoes. The woolen socks were too thick to go into them. He looked appealingly at Shorty, who shook his head.

"Nope. If I had thin ones I wouldn't lend 'em to you. Back to the moccasins, pardner. You'd sure freeze your toes in skimpy-fangled gear like that."

"I paid fifteen dollars for them, second hand," Smoke lamented.

"I reckon they won't be a man not in moccasins."

"But there are to be women, Shorty. I'm going to sit down and eat with real live women—Mrs. Bowie, and several others, so the colonel told me."

"Well, moccasins won't spoil their appetite none," was Shorty's comment. "Wonder what the colonel wants with you?"

"I don't know, unless he's heard about my finding Surprise Lake. It will take a fortune to drain it, and the Guggenheims are out for investment."

"Reckon that's it. That's right, stick to the moccasins. Gee! That coat is sure wrinkled, an' it fits you a mite too swift. Just peck around at your vittles. If you eat hearty you'll bust through. An' if them women folks gets to droppin' handkerchiefs, just let 'em lay. Don't do any pickin' up. Whatever you do, don't."

As became a high-salaried expert and the representative of the great house of Guggenheim, Colonel Bowie lived in one of the most magnificent cabins in Dawson. And there Smoke met the social elect of Dawson—not the mere pick-handle millionaires, but the ultra-cream of a mining city whose population had been recruited from all the world—men like Warburton Jones, the explorer and writer; Captain Consadine, of the Mounted Police; Haskell, gold commissioner of the Northwest Territory; and Baron Von Schroeder, an emperor's favorite with an international dueling reputation. And here, dazzling in evening gown, he met Joy Gastell, whom hitherto he had encountered only on trail, befurred and moccasined. At dinner he found himself beside her.

"I feel like a fish out of water," he confessed. "All you folks are so real grand, you know. Besides, I never dreamed such Oriental luxury existed in the Klondike. Look at Von Schroeder there. He's actually got a dinner-jacket, and Consadine's got a starched shirt. I noticed he wore moccasins just the same. How do you like *my* outfit?" He moved his shoulders about as if preening himself for Joy's approval.

"It looks as if you'd grown stout since you came over the pass," she laughed.

"Wrong. Guess again."

"It's somebody else's."

"You win. I bought it for a price from one of the clerks at the A. C. Company."

"It's a shame clerks are so narrow-shouldered," she sympathized. "And you haven't told me what you think of *my* outfit."

"I can't," he said. "I'm out of breath. I've been living on trail too long. This sort of thing comes to me with a shock, you know. I'd quite forgotten that women have arms and shoulders. To-morrow morning, like my friend Shorty, I'll wake up and know it's all a dream. Now the last time I saw you on Squaw Creek—"

"I was just a squaw," she broke in.

"I hadn't intended to say that. I was remembering that it was on Squaw Creek that I discovered you had feet."

"And I can never forget that you saved them for me," she said. "I've been wanting to see you ever since, to thank you." He shrugged his shoulders deprecatingly. "And that's why you are here to-night."

"You asked the colonel to invite me?"

"No; Mrs. Bowie. And I asked her to let me have you at table. And here's my chance. Everybody's talking. Listen. You know Mono Creek?"

"Yes."

"It has turned out rich, dreadfully rich. They estimated the claims as worth a million and more apiece. It was only located the other day."

"I remember the stampede."

"Well, the whole creek was staked to the sky-line, and all the feeders, too. And yet, right now, on the main creek, Number Three below Discovery is unrecorded. The creek was so far away from Dawson that the commissioner allowed sixty days for recording after location. Every claim was recorded except Number Three below. It was staked by Cyrus Johnson. And that was all. Cyrus Johnson has disappeared, and in six days the time for recording will be up. Then the man who stakes it, and reaches Dawson first and records it, gets it."

"A million dollars," Smoke murmured.

"Gilchrist, who has the next claim below, has got six hundred dollars in a single pan of bedrock. He's burned one hole down. And the claim on the other side is even richer. I know."

"But why doesn't everybody know?" Smoke queried skeptically.

"They're beginning to know. They kept it secret for a long time, and it is only now that it's coming out. Good dog-teams will be at a premium in another twenty-four hours. Now you've got to get away as decently as you can as soon as dinner is over. I've arranged it. An Indian will come with a message for you. You read it, let on that you're very much put out, make your excuses, and get away."

"I—er—I fail to follow."

"Ninny!" she exclaimed in a half-whisper. "What you must do is to get out to-night and hustle dog-teams. I know of two. There's Hanson's team, seven big Hudson Bay dogs—he's holding them at four hundred each. That's top price to-night, but it won't be to-morrow. And Sitka Charley has eight Malemutes he's asking thirty-five hundred for. To-morrow he'll laugh at an offer of five thousand. Then you've got your own team of dogs. And you'll have to buy several more teams. That's your work to-night. Get the best. It's dogs as well as men that will win this race. It's a hundred and ten miles, and you'll have to relay as frequently as you can."

"Oh, I see, you want me to go in for it," Smoke drawled.

"If you haven't the money for the dogs, I'll—" She faltered, but before she could continue, Smoke was speaking.

"I can buy the dogs. But aren't you afraid this is gambling?"

"After your exploits at roulette in the Elkhorn," she retorted, "I'm not afraid that you're afraid. It's a sporting proposition, if that's what you mean. A race for a million and with some of the stiffest dog-mushers and travelers in the country entered against you. They haven't entered yet, but by this time to-morrow they will, and dogs will be worth what the richest man can afford to pay. Big Olaf is in town. He came up from Circle City last month. He is one of the most terrible dog-mushers in the country, and if he enters he will be your most dangerous man. Arizona Bill is another. He's been a professional freighter and mail-carrier for years. If he goes in, interest will be centered on him and Big Olaf."

"And you intend me to come along as a sort of dark horse?"

"Exactly. And it will have its advantages. You will not be supposed to stand a show. After all, you know, you are still classed as a chekako. You haven't seen the four seasons go around. Nobody will take notice of you until you come into the home stretch in the lead."

"It's on the home stretch the dark horse is to show up its classy form, eh?"

She nodded, and continued earnestly: "Remember, I shall never forgive myself for the trick I played on the Squaw Creek stampede unless you win this Mono claim. And if any man can win this race against the old-timers, it's you."

It was the way she said it. He felt warm all over, and in his heart and head. He gave her a quick, searching look, involuntary and serious, and for the moment that her eyes met his steadily ere they fell, it seemed to him that he read something of vaster import than the claim Cyrus Johnson had failed to record.

"I'll do it," he said, "I'll win it."

The glad light in her eyes seemed to promise a greater meed than all the gold in the Mono claim. He was aware of a movement of her hand in her lap. Under the screen of the table-cloth he thrust his own hand across and met a firm grip of woman's fingers that sent another wave of warmth through him.

"What will Shorty say?" was the thought that flashed whimsically through his mind as he withdrew his hand. He glanced almost jealously at the faces of Von Schroeder and Jones, and wondered if they had not divined the remarkableness and deliciousness of this woman who sat beside him.

He was aroused by her voice, and realized that she had been speaking for some moments.

"So, you see, Arizona Bill is a white Indian," she was saying. "And Big Olaf is a bear-wrestler, a king of the snows, a mighty savage. He can out-travel and out-endure an Indian, and he's never known any other life than that of the wild and the frost."

"Who's that?" Captain Consadine broke in from across the table.

"Big Olaf," she answered. "I was just telling Mr. Bellew what a traveler he is."

"You're right," the captain's voice boomed. "Big Olaf is the greatest traveler in the Yukon. I'd back him against Old Nick himself for snow-bucking and ice-travel. He brought in the government despatches in 1895, and he did it after two couriers were frozen on Chilkoot and the third drowned in the open water of Thirty Mile."

Smoke had traveled in a leisurely fashion up to Mono Creek, fearing to tire his dogs before the big race. Also, he had familiarized himself with every mile of the trail and located his relay camps. So many men had entered the race that the hundred and ten miles of its course were almost a continuous village. Relay camps were everywhere along the trail. Von Schroeder, who had gone in purely for the sport, had no less than eleven dog-teams—a fresh one for every ten miles. Arizona Bill had been forced to content himself with eight teams. Big Olaf had seven, which was the complement of Smoke. In addition, over two score of other men were in the running. Not every day, even in the golden north, was a million dollars the prize for a dog-race. The country had been swept of dogs, and their prices had doubled and quadrupled in the course of the frantic speculation.

Number Three below Discovery was ten miles up Mono Creek from its mouth. The remaining hundred miles was to be run on the frozen breast of the Yukon. On Number Three itself were fifty tents and over three hundred dogs. The old stakes, blazed and scrawled sixty days before by Cyrus Johnson, still stood, and every man had gone over the boundaries of the claim again and again, for the race with the dogs was to be preceded by a foot and obstacle race. Each man had to relocate the claim for himself, and this meant that he must place two center-stakes and four corner-stakes and cross the creek twice, before he could start for Dawson with his dogs.

Furthermore, there were to be no "sooners." Not until the stroke of midnight of Friday night was the claim open for relocation, and not until the stroke of midnight could a man plant a stake. This was the ruling of the gold commissioner at Dawson, and Captain Consadine had sent up a squad of mounted police to enforce it. Discussion had arisen about the difference between sun-time and police-time, but Consadine had sent forth his fiat that police-time went, and, further, that it was the watch of Lieutenant Pollock that went.

The Mono trail ran along the level creek-bed, and, less than two feet in width, was like a groove, walled on either side by the snowfall of months. The problem of how forty-odd sleds and three hundred dogs were to start in so narrow a course was in everybody's mind.

"Huh!" said Shorty. "It's goin' to be the gosh-dangdest mix-up that ever was. I can't see no way out, Smoke, except main strength an' sweat an' to plow through. If the whole creek was glare-ice they ain't room for a dozen teams abreast. I got a hunch right now they's goin' to be a heap of scrappin' before they get strung out. An' if any of it comes our way, you got to let me do the punchin'."

Smoke squared his shoulders and laughed non-committally.

"No, you don't!" his partner cried in alarm. "No matter what happens, you don't dast hit. You can't handle dogs a hundred miles with a busted knuckle, an' that's what'll happen if you land on somebody's jaw."

Smoke nodded his head. "You're right, Shorty. I couldn't risk the chance."

"An' just remember," Shorty went on, "that I got to do all the shovin' for them first ten miles, an' you got to take it easy as you can. I'll sure jerk you through to the Yukon. After that it's up to you an' the dogs. Say, what d'ye think Schroeder's scheme is? He's got his first team a quarter of a mile down the creek, an' he'll know it by a green lantern. But we got him skinned. Me for the red flare every time."

The day had been clear and cold, but a blanket of cloud formed across the face of the sky, and the night came on warm and dark, with the hint of snow impending. The thermometer registered fifteen below zero, and in the Klondike winter fifteen below is esteemed very warm.

At a few minutes before midnight, leaving Shorty with the dogs five hundred yards down the creek, Smoke joined the racers on Number Three. There were forty-five of them waiting the start for the thousand thousand dollars Cyrus Johnson had left lying in the frozen gravel. Each man carried six stakes and a heavy wooden mallet, and was clad in a smock-like parka of heavy cotton drill.

Lieutenant Pollock, in a big bearskin coat, looked at his watch by the light of a fire. It lacked a minute of midnight. "Make ready," he said, as he raised a revolver in his right hand and watched the second-hand tick around.

Forty-five hoods were thrown back from the parkas, forty-five pairs of hands were unmittened, and forty-five pairs of moccasins pressed tensely into the packed snow. Also, forty-five stakes were thrust into the snow, and the same number of mallets lifted in the air.

The shot rang out, and the mallets fell. Cyrus Johnson's right to the million had expired.

Smoke drove in his stake and was away with the leading dozen. Fires had been lighted at the corners, and by each fire stood a policeman, list in hand, checking off the names of the runners. A man was supposed to call out his name and show his face. There was to be no staking by proxy while the real racer was off and away down the creek.

At the first corner, beside Smoke's stake, Von Schroeder placed his. The mallets struck at the same instant. As they hammered, more arrived from behind and with such impetuosity as to get in one another's way and cause jostling and shoving. Squirming through the press and calling his name to the policeman, Smoke saw the baron, struck in collision by one of the rushers, hurled clean off his feet into the snow. But Smoke did not wait. Others were still ahead of him. By the light of the vanishing fire, he was certain that he saw the back, hugely looming, of Big Olaf, and at the southwestern corner Big Olaf and he drove their stakes side by side.

It was no light work, this preliminary obstacle race. The boundaries of the claim totaled nearly a mile, and most of it was over the uneven surface of a snow-covered, niggerhead flat. All about Smoke men tripped and fell, and several times he pitched forward himself, jarringly, on hands and knees. Once, Big Olaf fell so immediately in front of him as to bring him down on top.

The upper center-stake was driven by the edge of the bank, and down the bank the racers plunged, across the frozen creek-bed, and up the other side. Here, as Smoke clambered, a hand gripped his ankle and jerked him back. In the flickering light of a distant fire, it was impossible to see who had played the trick. But Arizona Bill, who had been treated similarly, rose to his feet and drove his fist with a crunch into the offender's face. Smoke saw and heard as he was scrambling to his feet, but before he could make another lunge for the bank a fist dropped him half stunned into the snow. He staggered up, located the man, half swung a hook for his jaw, then remembered Shorty's warning and refrained. The next moment, struck below the knees by a hurtling body, he went down again.

It was a foretaste of what would happen when the men reached their sleds. Men were pouring over the other bank and piling into the jam. They swarmed up the bank in bunches, and in bunches were dragged back by their impatient fellows. More blows were struck, curses rose from the panting chests of those who still had wind to spare, and Smoke, curiously visioning the face of Joy Gastell, hoped that the mallets would not be brought into play. Overthrown, trod upon, groping in the snow for his lost stakes he at last crawled out of the crush and attacked the bank farther along. Others were doing this, and it was his luck to have many men in advance of him in the race for the northwestern corner.

Reaching the fourth corner, he tripped headlong, and in the sprawling fall lost his remaining stake. For five minutes he groped in the darkness before he found it, and all the time the panting runners were passing him. From the last corner to the creek he began overtaking men for whom the mile run had been too much. In the creek itself bedlam had broken loose. A dozen sleds were piled up and overturned, and nearly a hundred dogs were locked in combat. Among them men struggled, tearing the tangled animals apart, or beating them apart with clubs.

Leaping down the bank beyond the glutted passage, he gained the hard-footing of the sled-trail and made better time. Here, in packed harbors beside the narrow trail, sleds and men waited for runners that were still behind. From the rear came the whine and rush of dogs, and Smoke had barely time to leap aside into the deep snow. A sled tore past, and he made out the man kneeling and shouting madly. Scarcely was it by when it stopped with a crash of battle. The excited dogs of a harbored sled, resenting the passing animals, had got out of hand and sprung upon them.

Smoke plunged around and by. He could see the green lantern of Von Schroeder and, just below it, the red flare that marked his own team. Two men were guarding Von Schroeder's dogs, with short clubs interposed between them and the trail.

"Come on, you Smoke! Come on, you Smoke!" he could hear Shorty calling anxiously.

"Coming!" he gasped.

By the red flare, he could see the snow torn up and trampled, and from the way his partner breathed he knew a battle had been fought. He staggered to the sled, and, in the moment he was falling on it, Shorty's whip snapped as he yelled:

"Mush! you devils! Mush!"

The dogs sprang into the breast-bands, and the sled jerked abruptly ahead. They were big animals—Hanson's prize team of Hudson Bays—and Smoke had selected them for the first stage, which included the ten miles of Mono, the heavy going of the cut-off across the flat at the mouth, and the first ten miles of the Yukon stretch.

"How many are ahead?" he asked.

"You shut up an' save your wind," Shorty answered. "Hi! you brutes! Hit her up! Hit her up!"

He was running behind the sled, towing on a short rope. Smoke could not see him; nor could he see the sled on which he lay full length. The fires had been left in the rear, and they were tearing through a wall of blackness as fast as the dogs could spring into it. This blackness was almost sticky, so nearly did it take on the seeming of substance.

Smoke felt the sled heel up on one runner as it rounded an invisible curve, and from ahead came the snarls of beasts and the oaths of men. This was known afterward as the Barnes-Slocum jam. It was the teams of those two men which first collided, and into it, at full career, piled Smoke's seven big fighters. Scarcely more than semi-domesticated wolves, the excitement of that night on Mono Creek had sent every dog fighting mad. The Klondike dogs, driven without reins, cannot be stopped except by voice, so that there was no stopping this glut of struggle that heaped itself between the narrow rims of the creek. From behind, sled after sled hurled into the turmoil. Men who had their teams nearly extricated were overwhelmed by fresh avalanches of dogs—each animal well fed, well rested, and ripe for battle.

"It's knock down an' drag out an' plow through!" Shorty yelled in his partner's ear. "An' watch out for your knuckles! You drag dogs out an' let me do the punchin'!"

What happened in the next half-hour Smoke never distinctly remembered. At the end he emerged exhausted, sobbing for breath, his jaw sore from a fist-blow, his shoulder aching from the bruise of a club, the blood running warmly down one leg from the rip of a dog's fangs, and both sleeves of his parka torn to shreds. As in a dream, while the battle still raged behind, he helped Shorty reharness the dogs. One, dying, they cut from the traces, and in the darkness they felt their way to the repair of the disrupted harness.

"Now you lie down an' get your wind back," Shorty commanded.

And through the darkness the dogs sped, with unabated strength, down Mono Creek, across the long cut-off, and to the Yukon. Here, at the junction with the main river-trail, somebody had lighted a fire, and here Shorty said good-by. By the light of the fire, as the sled leaped behind the flying dogs, Smoke caught another of the unforgettable pictures of the Northland. It was of Shorty, swaying and sinking down limply in the snow, yelling his parting encouragement, one eye blackened and closed, knuckles bruised and broken, and one arm, ripped and fang-torn, gushing forth a steady stream of blood.

"How many ahead?" Smoke asked, as he dropped his tired Hudson Bays and sprang upon the waiting sled at the first relay-station.

"I counted eleven," the man called after him, for he was already away, behind the leaping dogs.

Fifteen miles they were to carry him on the next stage, which would fetch him to the mouth of White River. There were nine of them, but they composed his weakest team. The twenty-five miles between White River and Sixty Mile he had broken into two stages because of ice-jams, and here two of his heaviest, toughest teams were stationed.

He lay on the sled at full length, face down, holding on with both hands. Whenever the dogs slacked from topmost speed he rose to his knees, and, yelling and urging, clinging precariously with one hand, threw his whip into them. Poor team that it was, he passed two sleds before White River was reached. Here, at the freeze-up, a jam had piled a barrier, allowing the open water that formed for half a mile below to freeze smoothly. This smooth stretch enabled the racers to make flying exchanges of sleds, and down all the course they had placed their relays below the jams.

Over the jam and out onto the smooth, Smoke tore along, calling loudly, "Billy! Billy!"

Billy heard and answered, and by the light of the many fires on the ice, Smoke saw a sled swing in from the side and come abreast. Its dogs were fresh and overhauled his. As the sleds swerved toward each other he leaped across, and Billy promptly rolled off.

"Where's Big Olaf?" Smoke cried.

"Leading!" Billy's voice answered; and the fires were left behind, and Smoke was again flying through the wall of blackness.

In the jams of that relay, where the way led across a chaos of up-ended ice-cakes, and where Smoke slipped off the forward end of the sled and with a haul-rope toiled behind the wheel-dog, he passed three sleds. Accidents had happened, and he could hear the men cutting out dogs and mending harnesses.

Among the jams of the next short relay into Sixty Mile, he passed two more teams. And that he might know adequately what had happened to them, one of his own dogs wrenched a shoulder, was unable to keep up, and was dragged in the harness. Its teammates, angered, fell upon it with their fangs, and Smoke was forced to club them off with the heavy butt of his whip. As he cut the injured animal out, he heard the whining cries of dogs behind him and the voice of a man that was familiar. It was Von Schroeder. Smoke called a warning to prevent a rear-end collision, and the baron, hawing his animals and swinging on the gee-pole, went by a dozen feet to the side. Yet so impenetrable was the blackness that Smoke heard him pass but did not see him.

On the smooth stretch of ice beside the trading-post at Sixty Mile, Smoke overtook two more sleds. All had just changed teams, and for five minutes they ran abreast, each man on his knees and pouring whip and voice into the maddened dogs. But Smoke had studied out that portion of the trail, and now marked the tall pine on the bank that showed faintly in the light of the many fires. Below that pine was not merely darkness, but an abrupt cessation of the smooth stretch. There the trail, he knew, narrowed to a single sled-width. Leaning out ahead, he caught the haul-rope and drew his leaping sled up to the wheel-dog. He caught the animal by the hind legs and threw it. With a snarl of rage it tried to slash him with its fangs, but was dragged on by the rest of the team. Its body proved an efficient brake, and the two other teams, still abreast, dashed ahead into the darkness for the narrow way.

Smoke heard the crash and uproar of their collision, released his wheeler, sprang to the gee-pole, and urged his team to the right into the soft snow where the straining animals wallowed to their necks. It was exhausting work, but he won by the tangled teams and gained the hard-packed trail beyond.

On the relay out of Sixty Mile, Smoke had next to his poorest team, and though the going was good, he had set it a short fifteen miles. Two more teams would bring him into Dawson and to the gold-recorder's office, and Smoke had selected his best animals for the last two stretches. Sitka Charley himself waited with the eight Malemutes that would jerk Smoke along for twenty miles, and for the finish, with a fifteen-mile run, was his own team—the team he had had all winter and which had been with him in the search for Surprise Lake.

The two men he had left entangled at Sixty Mile failed to overtake him, and, on the other hand, his team failed to overtake any of the three that still led. His animals were willing, though they lacked stamina and speed, and little urging was needed to keep them jumping into it at their best. There was nothing for Smoke to do but to lie face downward and hold on. Now and again he would plunge out of the darkness into the circle of light about a blazing fire, catch a glimpse of furred men standing by harnessed and waiting dogs, and plunge into the darkness again. Mile after mile, with only the grind and jar of the runners in his ears, he sped on. Almost automatically he kept his place as the sled bumped ahead or half lifted and heeled on the swings and swerves of the bends.

The gray twilight of the morning was breaking as he exchanged his weary dogs for eight fresh Malemutes. Lighter animals than the Hudson Bays, they were capable of greater speed, and they ran with the supple tirelessness of true wolves. Sitka Charley called out the order of the teams ahead. Big Olaf led, Arizona Bill was second, and Von Schroeder third. These were the three best men in the country. In fact, ere Smoke had left Dawson, the popular betting had placed them in that order. While they were racing for a million, at least half a million had been staked by others on the outcome of the race. No one had bet on Smoke, who, despite his several known exploits, was still accounted a chekako with much to learn.

As daylight strengthened, Smoke caught sight of a sled ahead, and, in half an hour, his own lead-dog was leaping at its tail. Not until the man turned his head to exchange greetings, did Smoke recognize him as Arizona Bill. Von Schroeder had evidently passed him. The trail, hard-packed, ran too narrowly through the soft snow, and for another half-hour Smoke was forced to stay in the rear. Then they topped an ice-jam and struck a smooth stretch below, where were a number of relay-camps and where the snow was packed widely. On his knees, swinging his whip and yelling, Smoke drew abreast of Arizona Bill, then pulled ahead.

Bill dropped behind very slowly, though when the last relay-station was in sight he was fully half a mile in the rear. Ahead, bunched together, Smoke could see Big Olaf and Von Schroeder. Again Smoke arose to his knees, and he lifted his jaded dogs into a burst of speed such as a man only can who has the proper instinct for dog-driving. He drew up close to the tail of Von Schroeder's sled, and in this order the three sleds dashed out on the smooth going below a jam, where many men and many dogs waited. Dawson was fifteen miles away.

Von Schroeder, with his ten-mile relays, had changed five miles back and would change five miles ahead. So he held on, keeping his dogs at full leap. Big Olaf and Smoke made flying changes, and their fresh teams immediately regained what had been lost to the baron. Big Olaf led past, and Smoke followed into the narrow trail beyond.

"Still good, but not so good," Smoke paraphrased Spencer to himself.

Of Von Schroeder, now behind, he had no fear; but ahead was the greatest dog-driver in the country. To pass him seemed impossible. Again and again, many times, Smoke forced his leader to the other's sled-tail, and each time Big Olaf let out another link and drew away. Smoke contented himself with taking the pace, and hung on grimly. The race was not lost until one or the other won, and in fifteen miles many things could happen.

Three miles from Dawson something did happen. To Smoke's surprise, Big Olaf rose up and with oaths and leather proceeded to fetch out the last ounce of effort in his animals. It was a spurt that should have been reserved for the last hundred yards instead of being begun three miles from the finish. Sheer dog-killing that it was, Smoke followed. His own team was superb. No dogs on the Yukon had had harder work or were in better condition. Besides, Smoke had toiled with them, and eaten and bedded with them, and he knew each dog as an individual and how best to win in to the animal's intelligence and extract its last least shred of willingness.

They topped a small jam and struck the smooth going below. Big Olaf was barely fifty feet ahead. A sled shot out from the side and drew in toward him, and Smoke understood Big Olaf's terrific spurt. He had tried to gain a lead for the change. This fresh team that waited to jerk him down the homestretch had been a private surprise of his. Even the men who had backed him to win had no knowledge of it.

Smoke strove desperately to pass during the exchange of sleds. Lifting his dogs to the effort, he ate up the intervening fifty feet. With urging and pouring of leather, he went to the side and on until his head-dog was jumping abreast of Big Olaf's wheeler. On the other side, abreast, was the relay sled. At the speed they were going, Big Olaf did not dare try the flying leap. If he missed and fell off, Smoke would be in the lead, and the race would be lost.

Big Olaf tried to spurt ahead, and he lifted his dogs magnificently, but Smoke's leader still continued to jump beside Big Olaf's wheeler. For half a mile the three sleds tore and bounced along side by side. The smooth stretch was nearing its end when Big Olaf took the chance. As the flying sleds swerved toward each other, he leaped, and the instant he struck he was on his knees, with whip and voice spurting the fresh team. The smooth stretch pinched out into the narrow trail, and he jumped his dogs ahead and into it with a lead of barely a yard.

A man was not beaten until he was beaten, was Smoke's conclusion, and drive no matter how, Big Olaf failed to shake him off. No team Smoke had driven that night could have stood such a killing pace and kept up with fresh dogs—no team save this one. Nevertheless, the pace *was* killing it, and as they began to round the bluff at Klondike City, he could feel the pitch of strength going out of his animals. Almost imperceptibly they lagged behind, and foot by foot Big Olaf drew away until he led by a score of yards.

A great cheer went up from the population of Klondike City assembled on the ice. Here the Klondike entered the Yukon, and half a mile away, across the Klondike, on the north bank, stood Dawson. An outburst of madder cheering arose, and Smoke caught a glimpse of a sled shooting out to him. He recognized the splendid animals that drew it. They were Joy Gastell's. And Joy Gastell drove them. The hood of her squirrel-skin parka was tossed back, revealing the cameo-like oval of her face outlined against her heavily-massed hair. Mittens had been discarded, and with bare hands she clung to whip and sled.

"Jump!" she cried, as her leader snarled at Smoke's.

Smoke struck the sled behind her. It rocked violently from the impact of his body, but she was full up on her knees and swinging the whip.

"Hi! You! Mush on! Chook! Chook!" she was crying, and the dogs whined and yelped in eagerness of desire and effort to overtake Big Olaf.

And then, as the lead-dog caught the tail of Big Olaf's sled, and yard by yard drew up abreast, the great crowd on the Dawson bank went mad. It *was* a great crowd, for the men had dropped their tools on all the creeks and come down to see the outcome of the race, and a dead heat at the end of a hundred and ten miles justified any madness.

"When you're in the lead I'm going to drop off!" Joy cried out over her shoulder.

Smoke tried to protest.

"And watch out for the dip curve halfway up the bank," she warned.

Dog by dog, separated by half a dozen feet, the two teams were running abreast. Big Olaf, with whip and voice, held his own for a minute. Then, slowly, an inch at a time, Joy's leader began to forge past.

"Get ready!" she cried to Smoke. "I'm going to leave you in a minute. Get the whip."

And as he shifted his hand to clutch the whip, they heard Big Olaf roar a warning, but too late. His lead dog, incensed at being passed, swerved in to the attack. His fangs struck Joy's leader on the flank. The rival teams flew at one another's throats. The sleds overran the fighting brutes and capsized. Smoke struggled to his feet and tried to lift Joy up. But she thrust him from her, crying,

"Go!"

On foot, already fifty feet in advance, was Big Olaf, still intent on finishing the race. Smoke obeyed, and when the two men reached the foot of the Dawson bank, he was at the other's heels. But up the bank Big Olaf lifted his body hugely, regaining a dozen feet.

Five blocks down the main street was the gold-recorder's office. The street was packed as for the witnessing of a parade. Not so easily this time did Smoke gain to his giant rival, and when he did he was unable to pass. Side by side they ran along the narrow aisle between the solid walls of cheering men. Now one, now the other, with great convulsive jerks, gained an inch or so, only to lose it immediately after.

If the pace had been a killing one for their dogs, the one they now set themselves was no less so. But they were racing for a million dollars and greatest honor in the Yukon country. The only outside impression that came to Smoke on that last mad stretch was one of astonishment that there should be so many people in the Klondike. He had never seen them all at once before.

He felt himself involuntarily lag, and Big Olaf sprang a full stride in the lead. To Smoke it seemed that his heart would burst, while he had lost all consciousness of his legs. He knew they were flying under him, but he did not know how he continued to make them fly, nor how he put even greater pressure of will upon them and compelled them again to carry him to his giant competitor's side.

The open door of the recorder's office appeared ahead of them. Both men had made a final, futile spurt. Neither could draw away from the other, and side by side they hit the doorway, collided violently, and fell headlong on the office floor.

They sat up, but were too exhausted to rise. Big Olaf, the sweat pouring from him, breathing with tremendous, painful gasps, pawed the air and vainly tried to speak. Then he reached out his hand with unmistakable meaning; Smoke extended his, and they shook.

"It's a dead heat," Smoke could hear the recorder saying, but it was as if in a dream, and the voice was very thin and very far away. "And all I can say is that you both win. You'll have to divide the claim between you. You're partners."

Their two arms pumped up and down as they ratified the decision. Big Olaf nodded his head with great emphasis, and spluttered. At last he got it out.

"You damn chekako," was what he said, but in the saying of it was admiration. "I don't know how you done it, but you did."

Outside, the great crowd was noisily massed, while the office was packing and jamming. Smoke and Big Olaf essayed to rise, and each helped the other to his feet. Smoke found his legs weak under him, and staggered drunkenly. Big Olaf tottered toward him.

"I'm sorry my dogs jumped yours."

"It couldn't be helped," Smoke panted back. "I heard you yell."

"Say," Big Olaf went on with shining eyes. "That girl—one damn fine girl, eh?"

"One damn fine girl," Smoke agreed.

1912

SAMUEL

Margaret Henan would have been a striking figure under any circumstances, but never more so than when I first chanced upon her, a sack of grain of fully a hundredweight on her shoulder, as she walked with sure though tottering stride from the cart tail to the stable, pausing for an instant to gather strength at the foot of the steep steps that led to the grain bin. There were four of these steps, and she went up them, a step at a time, slowly, unwaveringly, and with so dogged a certitude that it never entered my mind that her strength could fail her and let that hundredweight sack fall from the lean and withered frame that well-nigh doubled under it. For she was patently an old woman, and it was her age that made me linger by the cart and watch.

Six times she went between the cart and the stable, each time with a full sack on her back, and beyond passing the time of day with me she took no notice of my presence. Then, the cart empty, she fumbled for matches and lighted a short clay pipe, pressing down the burning surface of the tobacco with a callused and apparently nerveless thumb. The hands were noteworthy. They were large-knuckled, sinewy, and malformed by labor, rimmed with calluses, the nails blunt and broken, and with here and there cuts and bruises, healed and healing, such as are common to the hands of hard-working men. On the back were huge, upstanding veins, eloquent of age and toil. Looking at them, it was hard to believe that they were the hands of the woman who had once been the belle of Island McGill. This last, of course, I learned later. At the time I knew neither her history nor her identity.

She wore heavy man's brogans. Her legs were stockingless, and I had noticed when she walked that her bare feet were thrust into the crinkly, ironlike shoes that sloshed about her lean ankles at every step. Her figure, shapeless and waistless, was garbed in a rough man's shirt and in a ragged flannel petticoat that had once been red. But it was her face, wrinkled, withered, and weather-beaten, surrounded by an aureole of unkempt and straggling wisps of grayish hair, that caught and held me. Neither drifted hair nor serried wrinkles could hide the splendid dome of a forehead, high and broad without verging in the slightest on the abnormal.

The sunken cheeks and pinched nose told little of the quality of the life that flickered behind those clear blue eyes of hers. Despite the minutiae of wrinkle work that somehow failed to wizen them, her eyes were clear as a girl's—clear, outlooking, and farseeing, and with an open and unblinking steadfastness of gaze that was disconcerting. The remarkable thing was the distance between them. It is a lucky man or woman who has the width of an eye between, but with Margaret Henan the width between her eyes was fully that of an eye and a half. Yet so symmetrically molded was her face that this remarkable feature produced no uncanny effect, and for that matter would have escaped the casual observer's notice. The mouth, shapeless and toothless, with down-turned corners and lips dry and parchmentlike, nevertheless lacked the muscular slackness so usual with age. The lips might have been those of a mummy save for that impression of rigid firmness they gave. Not that they were atrophied. On the contrary, they seemed tense and set with a muscular and spiritual determination. There, and in the eyes, was the secret of the certitude with which she carried the heavy sacks up the steep steps, with never a false step or overbalance, and emptied them in the grain bin.

"You are an old woman to be working like this," I ventured.

She looked at me with that strange, unblinking gaze, and she thought and spoke with the slow deliberateness that characterized everything about her, as if well aware of an eternity that was hers and in which there was no need for haste. Again I was impressed by the enormous certitude of her. In this eternity that seemed so indubitably hers there was time and to spare for safe footing and stable equilibrium—for certitude, in short. No more in her spiritual life than in carrying the hundredweights of grain was there a possibility of a misstep or an overbalancing. The feeling produced in me was uncanny. Here was a human soul that, save for the most glimmering of contacts, was beyond the humanness of me. And the more I learned of Margaret Henan in the weeks that followed the more mysteriously remote she became. She was as alien as a far journeyer from some other star, and no hint could she nor all the countryside give me of what norms of living, what heats of feeling or rules of philosophic contemplation actuated her in all that she had been and was.

"I wull be suvunty-two come Guid Friday a fortnight," she said in reply to my question.

"But you are an old woman to be doing this man's work, and a strong man's work at that," I insisted.

Again she seemed to immerse herself in that atmosphere of contemplative eternity, and so strangely did it affect me that I should not have been surprised to have awaked a century or so later and found her just beginning to enunciate her reply:

"The work hoz tull be done, an' I am beholden tull no one."

"But have you no children, no family relations?"

"Oh, aye, aplenty o' them, but they no see fut tull be helpun' me."

She drew out her pipe for a moment, then added, with a nod of her head toward the house, "I luv' wuth meself."

I glanced at the house, straw-thatched and commodious, at the large stable, and at the large array of fields I knew must belong with the place.

"It is a big bit of land for you to farm by yourself."

"Oh, aye, a bug but, suvunty acres. Ut kept me old mon buzzy, along wuth a son an' a hired mon, tull say naught o' extra honds un the harvest an' a maidservant un the house."

She clambered into the cart, gathered the reins in her hands, and quizzed me with her keen, shrewd eyes.

"Belike ye hail from over the watter–Ameruky, I'm meanun'?"

"Yes, I'm a Yankee," I answered.

"Ye wull no be findun' mony Island McGill folk stoppun' un Ameruky?"

"No; I don't remember ever meeting one in the States."

She nodded her head.

"They are home-lovun' bodies, though I wull no be sayun' they are no fair-traveled. Yet they come home ot the last, them oz are no lost ot sea or kult by fevers an' suchlike un foreign parts."

"Then your sons will have gone to sea and come home again?" I queried.

"Oh, aye, all savun' Samuel oz was drownded."

At the mention of Samuel I could have sworn to a strange light in her eyes, and it seemed to me, as by some telepathic flash, that I divined in her a tremendous wistfulness, an immense yearning. It seemed to me that here was the key to her inscrutableness, the clue that if followed properly would make all her strangeness plain. It came to me that here was a contact and that for the moment I was glimpsing into the soul of her. The question was tickling on my tongue, but she forestalled me.

She *tckh'd* to the horse, and with a "Guid day tull you, sir," drove off.

A simple, homely people are the folk of Island McGill, and I doubt if a more sober, thrifty, and industrious folk is to be found in all the world. Meeting them abroad–and to meet them abroad one must meet them on the sea, for a hybrid seafaring and farmer breed are they–one would never take them to be Irish. Irish they claim to be, speaking of the North of Ireland with pride and sneering at their Scottish brothers; yet Scotch they undoubtedly are, transplanted Scotch of long ago, it is true, but nonetheless Scotch, with a thousand traits, to say nothing of their tricks of speech and woolly utterance, which nothing less than their Scotch clannishness could have preserved to this late day.

A narrow loch, scarcely half a mile wide, separates Island McGill from the mainland of Ireland; and, once across this loch, one finds himself in an entirely different country. The Scotch impression is strong, and the people, to commence with, are Presbyterians. When it is considered that there is no public house in all the island and that seven thousand souls dwell therein, some idea may be gained of the temperateness of the community. Wedded to old ways, public opinion and the ministers are powerful influences, while fathers and mothers are revered and obeyed as in few other places in this modern world. Courting lasts never later than ten at night, and no girl walks out with her young man without her parents' knowledge and consent.

The young men go down to the sea and sow their wild oats in the wicked ports, returning periodically, between voyages, to live the old intensive morality, to court till ten o'clock, to sit under the minister each Sunday, and to listen at home to the same stern precepts that the elders preached to them from the time they were laddies. Much they learned of women in the ends of the earth, these seafaring sons, yet a canny wisdom was theirs and they never brought wives home with them. The one solitary exception to this had been the schoolmaster, who had been guilty of bringing a wife from half a mile the other side of the loch. For this he had never been forgiven, and he rested under a cloud for the remainder of his days. At his death the wife went back across the loch to her own people, and the blot on the escutcheon of Island McGill was erased. In the end the sailormen married girls of their own homeland and settled down to become exemplars of all the virtues for which the island was noted.

Island McGill was without a history. She boasted none of the events that go to make history. There had never been any wearing of the green, any Fenian conspiracies, any land disturbances. There had been but one eviction, and that purely technical—a test case, and on advice of the tenant's lawyer. So Island McGill was without annals. History had passed her by. She paid her taxes, acknowledged her crowned rulers, and left the world alone; all she asked in return was that the world leave her alone. The world was composed of two parts—Island McGill and the rest of it. And whatever was not Island McGill was outlandish and barbarian; and well she knew, for did not her seafaring sons bring home report of that world and its ungodly ways?

It was from the skipper of a Glasgow tramp, as passenger from Colombo to Rangoon, that I had first learned of the existence of Island McGill; and it was from him that I had carried the letter that gave me entrance to the house of Mrs. Ross, widow of a master mariner, with a daughter living with her and with two sons, master mariners themselves and out upon the sea. Mrs. Ross did not take in boarders, and it was Captain Ross's letter alone that had enabled me to get from her bed and board. In the evening, after my encounter with Margaret Henan, I questioned Mrs. Ross, and I knew on the instant that I had in truth stumbled upon mystery.

Like all Island McGill folk, as I was soon to discover, Mrs. Ross was at first averse to discussing Margaret Henan at all. Yet it was from her I learned that evening that Margaret Henan had once been one of the island belles. Herself the daughter of a well-to-do farmer, she had married Thomas Henan, equally well to do. Beyond the usual housewife's tasks she had never been accustomed to work. Unlike many of the island women, she had never lent a hand in the fields.

"But what of her children?" I asked.

"Two o' the sons, Jamie an' Timothy, uz married an' be goun' tull sea. Thot bug house close tull the post office uz Jamie's. The daughters thot ha' no married be luvun' wuth them as dud marry. An' the rest be dead."

"The Samuels," Clara interpolated, with what I suspected was a giggle.

She was Mrs. Ross's daughter, a strapping young woman with handsome features and remarkably handsome black eyes.

" 'Tuz naught tull be smuckerun' ot," her mother reproved her.

"The Samuels?" I intervened. "I don't understand."

"Her four sons thot died."

"And were they all named Samuel?"

"Aye."

"Strange," I commented in the lagging silence.

"Very strange," Mrs. Ross affirmed, proceeding stolidly with the knitting of the woolen singlet on her knees—one of the countless undergarments that she interminably knitted for her skipper sons.

"And it was only the Samuels that died?" I queried in further attempt.

"The others luv'd," was the answer. "A fine fomuly—no finer on the island. No better lods ever sailed out of Island McGill. The munuster held them up oz models tull pottern after. Nor was ever a whusper breathed again' the girls."

"But why is she left alone now in her old age?" I persisted. "Why don't her own flesh and blood look after her? Why does she live alone? Don't they ever go to see her or care for her?"

"Never a one un twenty years an' more now. She fetch't ut on tull herself. She drove them from the house just oz she drove old Tom Henan, thot was her husband, tull hus death."

"Drink?" I ventured.

Mrs. Ross shook her head scornfully, as if drink was a weakness beneath the weakest of Island McGill.

A long pause followed, during which Mrs. Ross knitted stolidly on, only nodding permission when Clara's young man, mate on one of the Shire Line sailing ships, came to walk out with her. I studied the half-dozen ostrich eggs, hanging in the corner against the wall like a cluster of some monstrous fruit. On each shell was painted precipitous and impossible seas through which full-rigged ships foamed with a lack of perspective only equaled by their sharp technical perfection. On the mantelpiece stood two large pearl shells, obviously a pair, intricately carved by the patient hands of New Caledonian convicts. In the center of the mantel was a stuffed bird of paradise, while about the room were scattered gorgeous shells from the southern seas, delicate sprays of coral sprouting from barnacled pipi shells and cased in glass, assagais from South Africa, stone axes from New Guinea, huge Alaskan tobacco pouches beaded with heraldic totem designs, a boomerang from Australia, divers ships in glass bottles, a cannibal *kai-kai* bowl from the Marquesas, and fragile cabinets from China and the Indies and inlaid with mother-of-pearl and precious woods.

I gazed at this varied trove brought home by sailor sons, and pondered the mystery of Margaret Henan, who had driven her husband to his death and been forsaken by all her kin. It was not the drink. Then what was it? Some shocking cruelty? Some amazing infidelity? Or some fearful, Old World peasant crime?

I broached my theories, but to all Mrs. Ross shook her head.

"Ut was no thot," she said. "Margaret was a guid wife an' a guid mother, an' I doubt she would harm a fly. She brought up her fomuly God-fearin' an' decent-minded. Her trouble was thot she took lunatuc—turned eediot."

Mrs. Ross tapped significantly on her forehead to indicate a state of addlement.

"But I talked with her this afternoon," I objected, "and I found her a sensible woman—remarkably bright for one of her years."

"Aye, an' I'm grantun' all thot you say," she went on calmly. "But I am no referrun' tull thot. I am referrun' tull her wucked-headed an' vucious stubbornness. No more stubborn woman ever luv'd than Margaret Henan. Ut was all on account o' Samuel, which was the name o' her eldest an' they do say her favorut brother—hum oz died by hus own hond all through the munuster's mustake un no registerun' the new church ot Dublin. Ut was a lesson thot the name was musfortunate, but she would no take ut, an' there was talk when she called her first child Samuel—hum thot died o' the croup. An' wuth thot what does she do but call the next one

Samuel, an' hum only three when he fell untull the tub o' hot watter an' was plain cooked tull death. Ut all come, I tell you, o' her wucked-headed an' foolush stubbornness. For a Samuel she must hov; an' ut was the death of the four of her sons. After the first, dudna her own mother go down un the dirt tull her feet, a-beggun' an' pleadun' wuth her no tull name her next one Samuel? But she was no tull be turned from her purpose. Margaret Henan was always set un her ways, an' never more so thon on thot name Samuel.

"She was fair lunatuc on Samuel. Dudna her neighbors, an' all kuth an' kun savun' them thot luv'd un the house wuth her, get up an' walk out ot the christenun' of the second—hum thot was cooked? Thot they dud, an' ot the very moment the munuster asked what would the bairn's name be. 'Samuel,' says she; an' wuth thot they got up an' walked out an' left the house. An' ot the door dudna her aunt Fannie, her mother's suster, turn an' say loud for all tull hear: 'What for wull she be wantun' tull murder the wee thung?' The munuster heard fine, an' dudna like ut, but, oz he told my Larry afterward, what could he do? Ut was the woman's wush, an' there was no law again' a mother callun' her child accordun' tull her wush.

"An' then was there no the third Samuel? An' when he was lost ot sea off the Cape, dudna she break all laws o' nature tull hov a fourth? She was forty-seven, I'm tellun' ye, an' she hod a chold ot forty-seven. Thunk on ut! Ot forty-seven! Ut was fair scand'lous."

From Clara, next morning, I got the tale of Margaret Henan's favorite brother; and from here and there, in the week that followed, I pieced together the tragedy of Margaret Henan. Samuel Dundee had been the youngest of Margaret's four brothers, and, as Clara told me, she had well-nigh worshiped him. He was going to sea at the time, skipper of one of the sailing ships of the Bank Line, when he married Agnes Hewitt. She was described as a slender wisp of a girl, delicately featured and with a nervous organization of the supersensitive order. Theirs had been the first marriage in the "new" church, and after a two weeks' honeymoon Samuel had kissed his bride good-by and sailed in command of the *Loughbank*, a big four-masted bark.

And it was because of the "new" church that the minister's blunder occurred. Nor was it the blunder of the minister alone, as one of the elders later explained; for it was equally the blunder of the whole presbytery of Coughleen, which included fifteen churches on Island McGill and the mainland. The old church, beyond repair, had been torn down and the new one built on the original foundation. Looking upon the foundation stones as similar to a ship's keel, it never entered the minister's nor the presbytery's head that the new church was legally any other than the old church.

"An' three couples was married the first week un the new church," Clara said. "First of all, Samuel Dundee an' Agnes Hewitt; the next day Albert Mahan an' Minnie Duncan; an' by the week end Eddie Troy and Flo Mackintosh—all sailormen, an' un sux weeks' time the last of them back tull their ships an' awa', an' no one o' them dreamin' of the wuckedness they'd been ot."

The Imp of the Perverse must have chuckled at the situation. All things favored. The marriages had taken place in the first week of May, and it was not till three months later that the minister, as required by law, made his quarterly report to the civil authorities in Dublin. Promptly came back the announcement that his church had no legal existence, not being registered according to the law's demands. This was overcome by prompt registration; but the marriages were not to be so easily remedied. The three sailor husbands were away, and their wives, in short, were not their wives.

"But the munuster was no for alarmin' the bodies," said Clara. He kept hus council an' bided hus time, waitin' for the lods tull be back from sea. Oz luck would have ut, he was away across the island tull a christenun' when Albert Mahan arrives home onexpected, hus shup just docked ot Dublin. Ut's nine o'clock ot night when the munuster, un hus sluppers an' dressun' gown, gets the news. Up he jumps an' calls for horse an' saddle, an' awa' he goes like the wund for Albert Mahan's. Albert uz just goun' tull bed an' hoz one shoe off when the munuster arrives.

" 'Come wuth me, the pair o' ye,' says he, breathless-like. 'What for, an' me dead weary an' goun' tull bed?' says Albert. 'Tull be lawful married,' says the munuster. Albert looks black an' says, 'Now, Munuster, ye wull be jokin',' but tull humself, oz I've heard hum tell mony a time, he uz wonderun' thot the munuster should a-took tull whusky ot hus time o' life."

" 'We be no married?' says Minnie. He shook his head. 'An' I om no Mussus Mahan?' 'No,' says he, 'ye are no Mussus Mahan. Ye are plain Muss Duncan.' 'But ye married us yoursel',' says she. 'I dud an' I dudna,' says he. An' wuth thot he tells them the whole upshot, an' Albert puts on hus shoe, an' they go with the munuster an' are married proper an' lawful, an' oz Albert Mahan says afterward mony's the time, ' 'Tus no every mon thot hoz two weddun' nights on Island McGill.' "

Six months later Eddie Troy came home and was promptly remarried. But Samuel Dundee was away on a three years' voyage and his ship fell overdue. Further to complicate the situation, a baby boy, past two years old, was waiting for him in the arms of his wife. The months passed, and the wife grew thin with worrying. "Ut's no meself I'm thunkun' on," she is reported to have said many times, "but ut's the puir fatherless bairn. Uf aught happened tull Samuel where wull the bairn stond?"

Lloyds posted the *Loughbank* as missing, and the owners ceased the monthly remittance of Samuel's half pay to his wife. It was the question of the child's legitimacy that preyed on her mind, and when all hope of Samuel's return was abandoned she drowned herself and the child in the loch. And here enters the greater tragedy. The *Loughbank* was not lost. By a series of sea disasters and delays too interminable to relate, she had made one of those long, unsighted passages such as occur once or twice in half a century. How the Imp must have held both his sides! Back from the sea came Samuel, and when they broke the news to him something else broke somewhere in his heart or head. Next morning they found him where he had tried to kill himself across the grave of his wife and child. Never in the history of Island McGill was there so fearful a deathbed. He spat in the minister's face and reviled him, and died blaspheming so terribly that those that tended on him did so with averted gaze and trembling hands.

And in the face of all this Margaret Henan named her first child Samuel.

How account for the woman's stubbornness? Or was it a morbid obsession that demanded a child of hers should be named Samuel? Her third child was a girl, named after herself, and the fourth was a boy again. Despite the strokes of fate that had already bereft her, and despite the loss of friends and relatives, she persisted in her resolve to name the child after her brother. She was shunned at church by those who had grown up with her. Her mother, after a final appeal, left her house with the warning that if the child were so named she would never speak to her again. And though the old lady lived thirty-odd years longer she kept her word. The minister agreed to christen the child any name but Samuel, and every other minister on Island McGill refused to christen it by the name she had chosen. There was talk on the part of Margaret Henan of going to law at the time, but in the end she carried the child to Belfast and there had it christened Samuel.

And then nothing happened. The whole island was confuted. The boy grew and prospered. The schoolmaster never ceased averring that it was the brightest lad he had ever seen. Samuel had a splendid constitution, a tremendous grip on life. To everybody's amazement he escaped the usual run of childish afflictions. Measles, whooping cough, and mumps knew him not. He was armor-clad against germs, immune to all disease. Headaches and earaches were things unknown. "Never so much oz a boil or a pumple," as one of the old bodies told me, ever marred his healthy skin. He broke school records in scholarship and athletics, and whipped every boy of his size or years on Island McGill.

It was a triumph for Margaret Henan. This paragon was hers, and it bore the cherished name. With the one exception of her mother, friends and relatives drifted back and acknowledged that they had been mistaken; though there were old crones who still abided by their opinion and who shook their heads ominously over their cups of tea. The boy was too wonderful to last. There was no escaping the curse of the name his mother had wickedly laid upon him. The young generation joined Margaret Henan in laughing at them, but the old crones continued to shake their heads.

Other children followed. Margaret Henan's fifth was a boy, whom she called Jamie, and in rapid succession followed three girls, Alice, Sara, and Nora, the boy Timothy, and two more girls, Florence and Katie. Katie was the last and eleventh, and Margaret Henan, at thirty-five, ceased from her exertions. She had done well by Island McGill and the Queen. Nine healthy children were hers. All prospered. It seemed her ill luck had shot its bolt with the deaths of her first two. Nine lived, and one of them was named Samuel.

Jamie elected to follow the sea, though it was not so much a matter of election as compulsion, for the eldest sons on Island McGill remained on the land while all other sons went to the salt plowing. Timothy followed Jamie, and by the time the latter had got his first command, a steamer in the bay trade out of Cardiff, Timothy was mate of a big sailing ship. Samuel, however, did not take kindly to the soil. The farmer's life had no attraction for him. His brothers went to sea, not out of desire, but because it was the only way for them to gain their bread; and he, who had no need to go, envied them when, returned from far voyages, they sat by the kitchen fire and told their bold tales of the wonderlands beyond the sea rim.

Samuel became a teacher, much to his father's disgust, and even took extra certificates, going to Belfast for his examinations. When the old master retired, Samuel took over his school. Secretly, however, he studied navigation, and it was Margaret's delight when he sat by the kitchen fire and, despite their masters' tickets, tangled up his brothers in the theoretics of their profession. Tom Henan alone was outraged when Samuel, schoolteacher, a gentleman, and heir to the Henan farm, shipped to sea before the mast. Margaret had an abiding faith in her son's star, and whatever he did she was sure was for the best. Like everything else connected with his glorious personality, there had never been known so swift a rise as in the case of Samuel. With barely two years' sea experience before the mast, he was taken from the fo'c'sle and made a provisional second mate. This occurred in a fever port on the west coast, and the committee of skippers that examined him agreed that he knew more of the science of navigation than they had remembered or forgotten. Two years later he sailed from Liverpool, mate of the *Starry Grace,* with both master's and extra master's tickets in his possession. And then it happened—the thing the old crones had been shaking their heads over for years.

It was told me by Gavin McNab, bosun of the *Starry Grace* at the time, himself an Island McGill man.

"Wull do I remember ut," he said. "We was runnin' our eastun' down, an' makun' heavy weather of ut. Oz fine a sailormon oz ever walked was Samuel Henan. I remember the look of hum wull thot last marnun', a-watchun' them bug seas curlun' up astern, an' a-watchun' the old girl an' seeun' how she took them—the skupper down below an' drunkun' for days. Ut was ot seven thot Henan brought her up on tull the wund, not darun' tull run longer un thot fearful sea. Ot eight, after havun' breakfast, he turns un, an' a half hour after up comes the skupper, bleary-eyed an' shaky an' holdun' on tull the componion. Ut was fair smokun', I om tellun' ye, an' there he stood, blunkun' an' noddun' an' talkun' tull humsel'. 'Keep off,' says he ot last tull the mon ot the wheel. 'My God!' says the second mate, standun' beside hum. The skupper never looks tull hum ot all, but keeps on mutterun' an' jabberun' tull humsel'. All of a suddent-like he straightuns up an' throws hus head back, an' says: 'Put your wheel over, me mon—now, domn ye! Are ye deef thot ye'll no be hearun' me?'

"Ut was a drunken mon's luck, for the *Starry Grace* wore off afore thot God-almighty gale wuthout shuppun' a bucket o' watter, the second mate shoutun' orders an' the crew jumpun' like mod. An' wuth thot the skupper nods contented-like tull humsel' an' goes below after more whusky. Ut was plain murder o' the lives o' all of us, for ut was no the time for the buggest shup afloat tull be runnun'. Run? Never hov I seen the like! Ut was beyond all thunkun', an' me goun' tull sea, boy an' mon, for forty year. I tell you ut was fair awesome.

"The face o' the second mate was white oz death, an' he stood ut alone for half an hour, when ut was too much for hum an' he went below an' called Samuel an' the third. Aye, a fine sailormon, thot Samuel, but ut was too much for hum. He looked an' studied, and looked an' studied, but he could no see hus way. He durst na heave tull. She would ha' been sweeput o' all honds an' stucks an' everythung afore she could-a fetch't up. There was naught tull do but keep on runnun'. An' uf ut worsened we were lost onyway, for soon or late thot overtakun' sea was sure tull sweep us clear over poop an' all.

"Dud I say ut was a God-almighty gale? Ut was worse nor thot. The devil humsel' must ha' hod a hond un the brewun' o' ut, ut was thot fearsome. I ha' looked on some sights, but I om no carun' tull look on the like o' thot again. No mon dared tull be un hus bunk. No, nor no mon on the decks. All honds of us stood on top the house an' held on an' watched. The three mates was on the poop, with two men ot the wheel, an' the only mon below was thot whusky-blighted captain snorun' drunk.

"An' then I see ut comun', a mile away, risun' above all the waves like an island un the sea—the buggest wave ever I looked upon. The three mates stood tulgether an' watched ut comun', a-prayun' like we thot she would no break un passun' us. But ut was no tull be. Ot the last, when she rose up like a mountain, curlun' above the stern an' blottun' out the sky, the mates scottered, the second an' third runnun' for the mizzen shrouds an' climbun' up, but the first runnun' tull the wheel tull lend a hond. He was a brave mon, thot Samuel Henan. He run straight un tull the face o' thot father o' all waves, no thunkun' on humself but thunkun' only o' the shup. The two men was lashed tull the wheel, but he would be ready tull hond un the case they was kult. An' then she took ut. We on the house could no see the poop for the thousand tons o' watter thot hod hut ut. Thot wave cleaned them out, took everythung along wuth ut—the two mates, climbun' up the mizzen ruggun', Samuel Henan runnun' tull the wheel, the two men ot the wheel, aye, an' the wheel utself. We never saw aught o' them, for she broached tull what o' the wheel goun', an' two men o' us was drownded off the house, no tull mention the carpenter thot we pucked up ot the break o' the poop wuth every bone o' hus body broke tull he was like so much jelly."

And here enters the marvel of it, the miraculous wonder of that woman's heroic spirit. Margaret Henan was forty-seven when the news came home of the loss of Samuel; and it was not long after that the unbelievable rumor went around Island McGill. I say unbelievable. Island McGill would not believe. Dr. Hall pooh-poohed it. Everybody laughed at it as a good joke. They traced back the gossip to Sara Dack, servant to the Henans, and who alone lived with Margaret and her husband. But Sara Dack persisted in her assertion and was called a low-mouthed liar. One or two dared question Tom Henan himself, but beyond black looks and curses for their presumption they elicited nothing from him.

The rumor died down, and the island fell to discussing in all its ramifications the loss of the *Grenoble* in the China Seas, with all her officers and half her crew born and married on Island McGill. But the rumor would not stay down. Sara Dack was louder in her assertions, the looks Tom Henan cast about him were blacker than ever, and Dr. Hall, after a visit to the Henan house, no longer pooh-poohed. Then Island McGill sat up, and there was a tremendous wagging of tongues. It was unnatural and ungodly. The like had never been heard. And when, as time passed, the truth of Sara Dack's utterances was manifest, the island folk decided, like the bosun of the *Starry Grace*, that only the devil could have had a hand in so untoward a happening. And the infatuated woman, so Sara Dack reported, insisted that it would be a boy." "Eleven bairns ha' I borne," she said; "Sux o' them lossies an' five o' them loddies. An' sunce there be balance un all thungs, so wull there be balance wuth me. Sux o' one an' half a dozen o' the other—there uz the balance, an' oz sure oz the sun rises un the marnun', that sure wull ut be a boy."

And boy it was, and a prodigy. Dr. Hall raved about its unblemished perfection and massive strength, and wrote a brochure on it for the Dublin Medical Society as the most interesting case of the sort in his long career. When Sara Dack gave the babe's unbelievable weight, Island McGill refused to believe and once again called her liar. But when Dr. Hall attested that he had himself weighed it and seen it tip that very notch, Island McGill held its breath and accepted whatever report Sara Dack made of the infant's progress or appetite. And once again Margaret Henan carried a babe to Belfast and had it christened Samuel.

"Oz good oz gold ut was," said Sara Dack to me.

Sara, at the time I met her, was a buxom, phlegmatic spinster of sixty, equipped with an experience so tragic and unusual that though her tongue ran on for decades its output would still be of imperishable interest to her cronies.

"Oz good oz gold," said Sara Dack. "Ut never fretted. Sut ut down un the sun by the hour an' never a sound ut would make oz long oz ut was no hungered. An' thot strong! The grup o' uts honds was like a mon's. I mind me, when ut was but hours old, ut grupped me so mighty thot I fetch't a scream, I was thot frighted. Ut was the punk o' health. Ut slept an' ate, an' grew. Ut never bothered. Never a night's sleep ut lost tull no one, nor ever a munut's, an' thot wuth cuttin' uts teeth an' all. An' Margaret would dandle ut on her knee an' ask was there ever so fine a loddie un the three kungdoms.

"The way ut grew! Ut was un keepun' wuth the way ut ate. Ot a year ut was the size o' a bairn o' two. Ut was slow tull walk an' talk. Exceptun' for gurgly noises un uts throat an' for creepun' on all fours, ut dudna monage much un the walkun' an' talkun' line. But that was tull be expected from the way ut grew. Ut all went tull growun' strong an' healthy. An' even old Tom Henan cheered up ot the might of ut an' said was there ever the like o' ut un the three kungdoms. Ut was Dr. Hall thot first suspicioned, I mind me well, though ut was luttle I dreamt when he was up tull ot the time. I see hum holdun' thungs un front o' luttle Sammy's eyes, an' a-makun' noises, loud an' soft, an' far an' near, un luttle Sammy's ears. An' then I see Dr. Hall go away, wrunklun' hus eyebrows an' shakun' hus head like the bairn was ailun'. But he was no ailun', oz I could swear tull, me a-seeun' hum eat an' grow. But Dr. Hall no said a word tull Margaret an' I was no for guessun' the why he was sore puzzled.

"I mind me when luttle Sammy first spoke. He was two years old an' the size of a child o' five, though he could no monage the walkun' yet but wen' around on all fours, happy an' contented-like an' makun' no trouble oz long oz he was fed promptly, whuch was onusual often. I was hangun' the wash on the line ot the time when out he comes, on all fours, hus bug head waggun' tull an' fro an' blunkun' un the sun. An' then, suddent, he talked. I was thot took a-back I near died o' fright, an' fine I knew ut then, the shakun' o' Dr. Hall's head. Talked? Never a bairn on Island McGill talked so loud an' tull such purpose. There was no mustakun' ut. I stood there all tremblun' an' shakun'. Little Sammy was brayun'. And I tell you, sir, he was brayun' like an ass—just like thot, loud an' long an' cheerful tull ut seemed hus lungs ud crack.

"He was a eediot—a great, awful, monster eediot. Ut was after he talked thot Dr. Hall told Margaret, but she would no believe. Ut would all come right, she said. Ut was growun' too fast for aught else. Guv ut time, said she, an' we would see. But old Tom Henan knew, an' he never held up hus head again. He could no abide the thung, an' would no brung humsel' tull touch ut, though I om no denyun' he was fair fascinated by ut. Mony the time I see hum watchun' of ut aroun' a corner, lookun' ot ut tull hus eyes fair bulged wuth the horror; an' when ut brayed old Tom ud stuck hus fungers tull hus ears an' look thot miserable I could a-puttied hum.

"An' bray ut could! Ut was the only thung ut could do besides eat an' grow. Whenever ut was hungry ut brayed, an' there was no stuppun' ut save wuth food. An' always of a marnun', when first ut crawled tull the kutchen door an' blunked out ot the sun ut brayed. An' ut was brayun' that brought about uts end.

"I mind me well. Ut was three years old an' oz bug oz a lod o' ten. Old Tom hed been goun' from bod tull worse, ploughun' up an' down the fields an' talkun' an' mutterun' tull humself. On the marnun' o' the day I mind me, he was suttun' on the bench outside the kutchen, a-futtun' the handled tull a puckax. Unbeknown, the monster eediot crawled tull the door an' brayed after hus fashion ot the sun. I see old Tom start up an' look. An' there was the monster eediot, waggun' uts bug head an' blunkun' an' brayun' like the great bug ass ut was. Ut was too much for Tom. Somethin' went wrong wuth him suddent-like. He jumped tull hus feet an' fetch't the puck handle down on the monster eediot's head. An' he hut ut again an' again like ut was a mod dog an' hum afear'd o' ut. An' he went straight tull the stable an' hung humsel' tull a rafter. An' I was no for stoppun' on after suchlike, an' I went tull stay along wuth me suster thot was married tull John Martin an' comfortable off."

I sat on the bench by the kitchen door and regarded Margaret Henan, while with her callused thumb she pressed down the live fire of her pipe and gazed out across the twilight-sombered fields. It was the very bench Tom Henan had sat upon that last sanguinary day of life. And Margaret sat in the doorway where the monster, blinking at the sun, had so often wagged its head and brayed. We had been talking for an hour, she with that slow certitude of eternity that so befitted her; and for the life of me I could lay no finger on the motives that ran through the tangled warp and woof of her. Was she a martyr to truth? Did she have it in her to worship at so abstract a shrine? Had she conceived abstract truth to be the one high goal of human endeavor on that day of long ago when she named her first-born Samuel? Or was hers the stubborn obstinacy of the ox? The fixity of purpose of the balky horse? The stolidity of the self-willed peasant mind? Was it whim or fancy—the one streak of lunacy in what was otherwise an eminently rational mind? Or, reverting, was hers the spirit of a Bruno? Was she convinced of the intellectual rightness of the stand she had taken? Was hers a steady, enlightened opposition to superstition? Or—and a subtler thought—was she mastered by some vaster, profounder superstition, a fetish worship of which the Alpha and the Omega was the cryptic *Samuel?*

"Wull ye be tellun' me," she said, "thot uf the second Samuel hod been named Larry thot he would no hov fell un the hot watter an' drownded? Atween you an' me, sir, an' ye are untellugent-lookun' tull the eye, would the name hov made ut onyways dufferent? Would the washun' no be done thot day uf he hod been Larry or Michael? Would hot watter no be hot, an' would hot watter no burn uf he hod hod ony other name but Samuel?"

I acknowledged the justice of her contention, and she went on.

"Do a wee but of a name change the plans o' God? Do the world run by hut or muss, an' be God a weak, shully-shallyun' creature thot ud alter the fate an' destiny o' thungs because the worm Margaret Henan seen fut tull name her bairn Samuel? There be my son Jamie. He wull no sign a Rooshan-Funn un hus crew because o' believun' thot Rooshan-Funns do be monajun' the wunds an' hove the makun' o' bod weather. Wull you be thunkun' so? Wull you be thunkun' thot God thot makes the wunds tull blow wull bend hus head from on high tull lussen tull the word o' a greasy Rooshan-Funn un some dirty shup's fo'c'sle?"

I said no, certainly not; but she was not to be set aside from pressing home the point of her argument.

"Then wull you be thunkun' thot God thot directs the stars un their courses, an' tull whose mighty foot the world us but a footstool, wull you be thunkun' thot he wull take a spite again' Margaret Henan an' send a bug wave off the cape tull wash her son un tull eternity, all because she was for namun' hum Samuel?"

"But why Samuel?" I asked.

"An' thot I dinna know. I wanted ut so."

"But *why* did you want it so?"

"An' uz ut me thot would be answerun' a suchlike question? Be there ony mon luvun' or dead thot can answer? Who can tell the *why* o' like? My Jamie was fair daft on buttermilk; he would drunk ut tull, oz he said himself, hus back teeeh was awash. But my Timothy could no abide buttermilk. I like tull lussen tull the thunder growlun' an' roarun' an' rampajun'. My Katie could no abide the noise of ut, but must scream an' flutter an' go runnun' for the mudmost o' a feather bed. Never yet hov' I heard the answer tull the *why* o' like. God alone hoz thot answer. You an' me be mortal an' we canna know. Enough for us tull know what we like an' what we duslike. I *like*—that uz the first word an' the last. An' behind thot *like* no mon can go an' find the *why* o' ut. I *like* Samuel, an' I like ut wull. Ut uz a sweet name, an' there be a rollun' wonder un the sound o' ut that passes onderstandun'."

The twilight deepened, and in the silence I gazed upon that splendid dome of a forehead which time could not mar, at the width between the eyes, and at the eyes themselves—clear, out-looking, and wide-seeing. She rose to her feet with an air of dismissing me, saying:

"Ut wull be a dark walk home, an' there wull be more than a sprunkle o' wet un the sky."

"Have you any regrets, Margaret Henan?" I asked, suddenly and without forethought.

She studied me a moment.

"Aye, thot I no ha' borne another son."

"And you would . . . ?" I faltered.

"Aye, thot I would," she answered. "Ut would ha' been hus name."

I went down the dark road between the hawthorn hedges puzzling over the why of like, repeating *Samuel* to myself and aloud and listening to the rolling wonder in its sound that had charmed her soul and led her life in tragic places. *Samuel!* There was a rolling wonder in the sound. Aye, there was!

1913

TOLD IN THE DROOLING WARD

Me? I'm not a drooler. I'm the assistant. I don't know what Miss Jones or Miss Kelsey could do without me. There are fifty-five low-grade droolers in this ward, and how could they ever all be fed if I wasn't around? I like to feed droolers. They don't make trouble. They can't. Something's wrong with most of their legs and arms, and they can't talk. They're very low-grade. I can walk, and talk, and do things. You must be careful with the droolers and not feed them too fast. Then they choke. Miss Jones says I'm an expert. When a new nurse comes I show her how to do it. It's funny watching a new nurse try to feed them. She goes at it so slow and careful that supper time would be around before she finished shoving down their breakfast. Then I show her, because I'm an expert. Doctor Dalrymple says I am, and he ought to know. A drooler can eat twice as fast if you know how to make him.

My name's Tom. I'm twenty-eight years old. Everybody knows me in the institution. This is an institution, you know. It belongs to the State of California and is run by politics. I know. I've been here a long time. Everybody trusts me. I run errands all over the place, when I'm not busy with the droolers. I like droolers. It makes me think how lucky I am that I ain't a drooler.

I like it here in the Home. I don't like the outside. I know. I've been around a bit, and run away, and adopted. Me for the Home, and for the drooling ward best of all. I don't look like a drooler, do I? You can tell the difference soon as you look at me. I'm an assistant, expert assistant. That's going some for a feeb. Feeb? Oh, that's feeble-minded. I thought you knew. We're all feebs in here.

But I'm a high-grade feeb. Doctor Dalrymple says I'm too smart to be in the Home, but I never let on. It's a pretty good place. And I don't throw fits like lots of the feebs. You see that house up there through the trees. The high-grade epilecs all live in it by themselves. They're stuck up because they ain't just ordinary feebs. They call it the club house, and they say they're just as good as anybody outside, only they're sick. I don't like them much. They laugh at me, when they ain't busy throwing fits. But I don't care. I never have to be scared about falling down and busting my head. Sometimes they run around in circles trying to find a place to sit down quick, only they don't. Low-grade epilecs are disgusting, and high-grade epilecs put on airs. I'm glad I ain't an epilec. There ain't anything to them. They just talk big, that's all.

Miss Kelsey says I talk too much. But I talk sense, and that's more than the other feebs do. Doctor Dalrymple says I have the gift of language. I know it. You ought to hear me talk when I'm by myself, or when I've got a drooler to listen. Sometimes I think I'd like to be a politician, only it's too much trouble. They're all great talkers; that's how they hold their jobs.

Nobody's crazy in this institution. They're just feeble in their minds. Let me tell you something funny. There's about a dozen high-grade girls that set the tables in the big dining room. Sometimes when they're done ahead of time, they all sit down in chairs in a circle and talk. I sneak up to the door and listen, and I nearly die to keep from laughing. Do you want to know what they talk? It's like this. They don't say a word for a long time. And then one says, "Thank God I'm not feeble-minded." And all the rest nod their heads and look pleased. And then nobody says anything for a time. After which the next girl in the circle says, "Thank God I'm not feeble-minded," and they nod their heads all over again. And it goes on around the circle, and they never say anything else. Now they're real feebs, ain't they? I leave it to you. I'm not that kind of a feeb, thank God.

Sometimes I don't think I'm a feeb at all. I play in the band and read music. We're all supposed to be feebs in the band except the leader. He's crazy. We know it, but we never talk about it except amongst ourselves. His job is politics, too, and we don't want him to lose it. I play the drum. They can't get along without me in this institution. I was sick once, so I know. It's a wonder the drooling ward didn't break down while I was in hospital.

I could get out of here if I wanted to. I'm not so feeble as some might think. But I don't let on. I have too good a time. Besides, everything would run down if I went away. I'm afraid some time they'll find out I'm not a feeb and send me out into the world to earn my own living. I know the world, and I don't like it. The Home is fine enough for me.

You see how I grin sometimes. I can't help that. But I can put it on a lot. I'm not bad, though. I look at myself in the glass. My mouth is funny, I know that, and it lops down, and my teeth are bad. You can tell a feeb anywhere by looking at his mouth and teeth. But that doesn't prove I'm a feeb. It's just because I'm lucky that I look like one.

I know a lot. If I told you all I know, you'd be surprised. But when I don't want to know, or when they want me to do something I don't want to do, I just let my mouth lop down and laugh and make foolish noises. I watch the foolish noises made by the low-grades, and I can fool anybody. And I know a lot of foolish noises. Miss Kelsey called me a fool the other day. She was very angry, and that was where I fooled her.

Miss Kelsey asked me once why I don't write a book about feebs. I was telling her what was the matter with little Albert. He's a drooler, you know, and I can always tell the way he twists his left eye what's the matter with him. So I was explaining it to Miss Kelsey, and, because she didn't know, it made her mad. But some day, mebbe, I'll write that book. Only it's so much trouble. Besides, I'd sooner talk.

Do you know what a micro is? It's the kind with the little heads no bigger than your fist. They're usually droolers, and they live a long time. The hydros don't drool. They have the big heads, and they're smarter. But they never grow up. They always die. I never look at one without thinking he's going to die. Sometimes, when I'm feeling lazy, or the nurse is mad at me, I wish I was a drooler with nothing to do and somebody to feed me. But I guess I'd sooner talk and be what I am.

Only yesterday Doctor Dalrymple said to me, "Tom," he said, "I just don't know what I'd do without you." And he ought to know, seeing as he's had the bossing of a thousand feebs for going on two years. Doctor Whatcomb was before him. They get appointed, you know. It's politics. I've seen a whole lot of doctors here in my time. I was here before any of them. I've been in this institution twenty-five years. No, I've got no complaints. The institution couldn't be run better.

It's a snap to be a high-grade feeb. Just look at Doctor Dalrymple. He has troubles. He holds his job by politics. You bet we high-graders talk politics. We know all about it, and it's bad. An institution like this oughtn't to be run on politics. Look at Doctor Dalrymple. He's been here two years and learned a lot. Then politics will come along and throw him out and send a new doctor who don't know anything about feebs.

I've been acquainted with just thousands of nurses in my time. Some of them are nice. But they come and go. Most of the women get married. Sometimes I think I'd like to get married. I spoke to Doctor Whatcomb about it once, but he told me he was very sorry, because feebs ain't allowed to get married. I've been in love. She was a nurse. I won't tell you her name. She had blue eyes, and yellow hair, and a kind voice, and she liked me. She told me so. And she always told me to be a good boy. And I was, too, until afterward, and then I ran away. You see, she went off and got married, and she didn't tell me about it.

I guess being married ain't what it's cracked up to be. Doctor Anglin and his wife used to fight. I've seen them. And once I heard her call him a feeb. Now nobody has a right to call anybody a feeb that ain't. Doctor Anglin got awful mad when she called him that. But he didn't last long. Politics drove him out, and Doctor Mandeville came. He didn't have a wife. I heard him talking one time with the engineer. The engineer and his wife fought like cats and dogs, and that day Doctor Mandeville told him he was damn glad he wasn't tied to no petticoats. A petticoat is a skirt. I knew what he meant, if I was a feeb. But I never let on. You hear lots when you don't let on.

I've seen a lot in my time. Once I was adopted, and went away on the railroad over forty miles to live with a man named Peter Bopp and his wife. They had a ranch. Doctor Anglin said I was strong and bright, and I said I was, too. That was because I wanted to be adopted. And Peter Bopp said he'd give me a good home, and the lawyers fixed up the papers.

But I soon made up my mind that a ranch was no place for me. Mrs. Bopp was scared to death of me and wouldn't let me sleep in the house. They fixed up the woodshed and made me sleep there. I had to get up at four o'clock and feed the horses, and milk cows, and carry the milk to the neighbours. They called it chores, but it kept me going all day. I chopped wood, and cleaned chicken houses, and weeded vegetables, and did most everything on the place. I never had any fun. I hadn't no time.

Let me tell you one thing. I'd sooner feed mush and milk to feebs than milk cows with the frost on the ground. Mrs. Bopp was scared to let me play with her children. And I was scared, too. They used to make faces at me when nobody was looking, and call me "Looney." Everybody called me Looney Tom. And the other boys in the neighbourhood threw rocks at me. You never see anything like that in the Home here. The feebs are better behaved.

Mrs. Bopp used to pinch me and pull my hair when she thought I was too slow, and I only made foolish noises and went slower. She said I'd be the death of her some day. I left the boards off the old well in the pasture, and the pretty new calf fell in and got drowned. Then Peter Bopp said he was going to give me a licking. He did, too. He took a strap halter and went at me. It was awful. I'd never had a licking in my life. They don't do such things in the Home, which is why I say the Home is the place for me.

I know the law, and I knew he had no right to lick me with a strap halter. That was being cruel, and the guardianship papers said he mustn't be cruel. I didn't say anything. I just waited, which shows you what kind of a feeb I am. I waited a long time, and got slower, and made more foolish noises; but he wouldn't send me back to the Home, which was what I wanted. But one day, it was the first of the month, Mrs. Brown gave me three dollars, which was for her milk bill with Peter Bopp. That was in the morning. When I brought the milk in the evening I was to bring back the receipt. But I didn't. I just walked down to the station, bought a ticket like any one, and rode on the train back to the Home. That's the kind of a feeb I am.

Doctor Anglin was gone then, and Doctor Mandeville had his place. I walked right into his office. He didn't know me. "Hello," he said, "this ain't visiting day." "I ain't a visitor," I said. "I'm Tom. I belong here." Then he whistled and showed he was surprised. I told him about it, and showed him the marks of the strap halter, and he got madder and madder all the time and said he'd attend to Mr. Peter Bopp's case.

And mebbe you think some of them little droolers weren't glad to see me.

I walked right into the ward. There was a new nurse feeding little Albert. "Hold on," I said. "That ain't the way. Don't you see how he's twisting that left eye? Let me show you." Mebbe she thought I was a new doctor, for she just gave me the spoon, and I guess I filled little Albert up with the most comfortable meal he'd had since I went away. Droolers ain't bad when you understand them. I heard Miss Jones tell Miss Kelsey once that I had an amazing gift in handling droolers.

Some day, mebbe, I'm going to talk with Doctor Dalrymple and get him to give me a declaration that I ain't a feeb. Then I'll get him to make me a real assistant in the drooling ward, with forty dollars a month and my board. And then I'll marry Miss Jones and live right on here. And if she won't have me, I'll marry Miss Kelsey or some other nurse. There's lots of them that want to get married. And I won't care if my wife gets mad and calls me a feeb. What's the good? And I guess when one's learned to put up with droolers a wife won't be much worse.

I didn't tell you about when I ran away. I hadn't no idea of such a thing, and it was Charley and Joe who put me up to it. They're high-grade epilecs, you know. I'd been up to Doctor Wilson's office with a message, and was going back to the drooling ward, when I saw Charley and Joe hiding around the corner of the gymnasium and making motions to me. I went over to them.

"Hello," Joe said. "How's droolers?"

"Fine," I said. "Had any fits lately?"

That made them mad, and I was going on, when Joe said, "We're running away. Come on."

"What for?" I said.

"We're going up over the top of the mountain," Joe said.

"And find a gold mine," said Charley. "We don't have fits any more. We're cured."

"All right," I said. And we sneaked around back of the gymnasium and in among the trees. Mebbe we walked along about ten minutes, when I stopped.

"What's the matter?" said Joe.

"Wait," I said. "I got to go back."

"What for?" said Joe.

And I said, "To get little Albert."

And they said I couldn't, and got mad. But I didn't care. I knew they'd wait. You see, I've been here twenty-five years, and I know the back trails that lead up the mountain, and Charley and Joe didn't know those trails. That's why they wanted me to come.

So I went back and got little Albert. He can't walk, or talk, or do anything except drool, and I had to carry him in my arms. We went on past the last hayfield, which was as far as I'd ever gone. Then the woods and brush got so thick, and me not finding any more trail, we followed the cow-path down to a big creek and crawled through the fence which showed where the Home land stopped.

We climbed up the big hill on the other side of the creek. It was all big trees, and no brush, but it was so steep and slippery with dead leaves we could hardly walk. By and by we came to a real bad place. It was forty feet across, and if you slipped you'd fall a thousand feet, or mebbe a hundred. Anyway, you wouldn't fall—just slide. I went across first, carrying little Albert. Joe came next. But Charley got scared right in the middle and sat down.

"I'm going to have a fit," he said.

"No, you're not," said Joe. "Because if you was you wouldn't 'a' sat down. You take all your fits standing."

"This is a different kind of a fit," said Charley, beginning to cry.

He shook and shook, but just because he wanted to he couldn't scare up the least kind of a fit.

Joe got mad and used awful language. But that didn't help none. So I talked soft and kind to Charley. That's the way to handle feebs. If you get mad, they get worse. I know. I'm that way myself. That's why I was almost the death of Mrs. Bopp. She got mad.

It was getting along in the afternoon, and I knew we had to be on our way, so I said to Joe:

"Here, stop your cussing and hold Albert. I'll go back and get him."

And I did, too; but he was so scared and dizzy he crawled along on hands and knees while I helped him. When I got him across and took Albert back in my arms, I heard somebody laugh and looked down. And there was a man and woman on horseback looking up at us. He had a gun on his saddle, and it was her who was laughing.

"Who in hell's that?" said Joe, getting scared. "Somebody to catch us?"

"Shut up your cussing," I said to him. "That is the man who owns this ranch and writes books."

"How do you do, Mr. Endicott," I said down to him.

"Hello," he said. "What are you doing here?"

"We're running away," I said.

And he said, "Good luck. But be sure and get back before dark."

"But this is a real running away," I said.

And then both he and his wife laughed.

"All right," he said. "Good luck just the same. But watch out the bears and mountain lions don't get you when it gets dark."

Then they rode away laughing, pleasant like; but I wished he hadn't said that about the bears and mountain lions.

After we got around the hill, I found a trail, and we went much faster. Charley didn't have any more signs of fits, and began laughing and talking about gold mines. The trouble was with little Albert. He was almost as big as me. You see, all the time I'd been calling him little Albert, he'd been growing up. He was so heavy I couldn't keep up with Joe and Charley. I was all out of breath. So I told them they'd have to take turns in carrying him, which they said they wouldn't. Then I said I'd leave them and they'd get lost, and the mountain lions and bears would eat them. Charley looked like he was going to have a fit right there, and Joe said, "Give him to me." And after that we carried him in turn.

We kept right on up that mountain. I don't think there was any gold mine, but we might 'a' got to the top and found it, if we hadn't lost the trail, and if it hadn't got dark, and if little Albert hadn't tired us all out carrying him. Lots of feebs are scared of the dark, and Joe said he was going to have a fit right there. Only he didn't. I never saw such an unlucky boy. He never could throw a fit when he wanted to. Some of the feebs can throw fits as quick as a wink.

By and by it got real black, and we were hungry, and we didn't have no fire. You see, they don't let feebs carry matches, and all we could do was just shiver. And we'd never thought about being hungry. You see, feebs always have their food ready for them, and that's why it's better to be a feeb than earning your living in the world.

And worse than everything was the quiet. There was only one thing worse, and it was the noises. There was all kinds of noises every once in a while, with quiet spells in between. I reckon they were rabbits, but they made noises in the brush like wild animals—you know, rustle rustle, thump, bump, crackle crackle, just like that. First Charley got a fit, a real one, and Joe threw a terrible one. I don't mind fits in the Home with everybody around. But out in the woods on a dark night is different. You listen to me, and never go hunting gold mines with epilecs, even if they are high-grade.

I never had such an awful night. When Joe and Charley weren't throwing fits they were making believe, and in the darkness the shivers from the cold which I couldn't see seemed like fits, too. And I shivered so hard I thought I was getting fits myself. And little Albert, with nothing to eat, just drooled and drooled. I never seen him as bad as that before. Why, he twisted that left eye of his until it ought to have dropped out. I couldn't see it, but I could tell from the movements he made. And Joe just lay and cussed and cussed, and Charley cried and wished he was back in the Home.

We didn't die, and next morning we went right back the way we'd come. And little Albert got awful heavy. Doctor Wilson was mad as could be, and said I was the worst feeb in the institution, along with Joe and Charley. But Miss Stricker, who was a nurse in the drooling ward then, just put her arms around me and cried, she was that happy I'd got back. I thought right there that mebbe I'd marry her. But only a month afterward she got married to the plumber that came up from the city to fix the gutter-pipes of the new hospital. And little Albert never twisted his eye for two days, it was that tired.

Next time I run away I'm going right over that mountain. But I ain't going to take epilecs along. They ain't never cured, and when they get scared or excited they throw fits to beat the band. But I'll take little Albert. Somehow I can't get along without him. And anyway, I ain't going to run away. The drooling ward's a better snap than gold mines, and I hear there's a new nurse coming. Besides, little Albert's bigger than I am now, and I could never carry him over a mountain. And he's growing bigger every day. It's astonishing.

1914

THE PRINCESS

A fire burned cheerfully in the jungle camp, and beside the fire lolled a cheerful-seeming though horrible-appearing man. This was a hobo jungle, pitched in a thin strip of woods that lay between a railroad embankment and the bank of a river. But no hobo was the man. So deep-sunk was he in the social abyss that a proper hobo would not sit by the same fire with him. A gay-cat, who is an ignorant new-comer on the "Road," might sit with such as he, but only long enough to learn better. Even low down bindle-stiffs and stew-bums, after a once-over, would have passed this man by. A genuine hobo, a couple of punks, or a bunch of tender-yeared road-kids might have gone through his rags for any stray pennies or nickels and kicked him out into the darkness. Even an alki-stiff would have reckoned himself immeasurably superior.

For this man was that hybrid of tramp-land, an alki-stiff that has degenerated into a stew-bum, with so little self-respect that he will never "boil-up," and with so little pride that he will eat out of a garbage can. He was truly horrible-appearing. He might have been sixty years of age; he might have been ninety. His garments might have been discarded by a rag-picker. Beside him, an unrolled bundle showed itself as consisting of a ragged overcoat and containing an empty and smoke-blackened tomato can, an empty and battered condensed milk can, some dog-meat partly wrapped in brown paper and evidently begged from some butcher-shop, a carrot that had been run over in the street by a wagon-wheel, three greenish-cankered and decayed potatoes, and a sugar-bun with a mouthful bitten from it and rescued from the gutter as was made patent by the gutter-filth that still encrusted it.

A prodigious growth of whiskers, grayish-dirty and untrimmed for years, sprouted from his face. This hirsute growth should have been white, but the season was summer and it had not been exposed to a rain-shower for some time. What was visible of the face looked as if at some period it had stopped a hand-grenade. The nose was so variously malformed in its healed brokenness that there was no bridge, while one nostril, the size of a pea, opened downward, and the other, the size of a robin's egg, tilted upward to the sky. One eye, of normal size, dim-brown and misty, bulged to the verge of popping out, and as if from senility wept copiously and continuously. The other eye, scarcely larger than a squirrel's and as uncannily bright, twisted up obliquely into the hairy scar of a bone-crushed eyebrow. And he had but one arm.

Yet was he cheerful. On his face, in mild degree, was depicted sensuous pleasure as he lethargically scratched his ribs with his one hand. He pawed over his food-scraps, debated, then drew a twelve-ounce druggist's bottle from his inside coat pocket. The bottle was full of a colorless liquid, the contemplation of which made his little eye burn brighter and quickened his movements. Picking up the tomato can, he arose, went down the short path to the river, and returned with the can filled with not-nice river water. In the condensed milk can he mixed one part of water with two parts of fluid from the bottle. This colorless fluid was druggist's alcohol, and as such is known in tramp-land as "alki."

Slow footsteps, coming down the side of the railroad embankment, alarmed him ere he could drink. Placing the can carefully upon the ground between his legs, he covered it with his hat and waited anxiously whatever impended.

Out of the darkness emerged a man as filthy ragged as he. The newcomer, who might have been fifty, and might have been sixty, was grotesquely fat. He bulged everywhere. He was composed of bulges. His bulbous nose was the size and shape of a turnip. His eyelids bulged and his blue eyes bulged in competition with them. In many places the seams of his garments had parted across the bulges of body. His calves grew into his feet, for the broken elastic sides of his Congress gaiters were swelled full with the fat of him. One arm only he sported, from the shoulder of which was suspended a small and tattered bindle with the mud caked dry on the outer covering from the last place he had pitched his doss. He advanced with tentative caution, made sure of the harmlessness of the man beside the fire, and joined him.

"Hello, grandpa," the newcomer greeted, then paused to stare at the other's flaring, sky-open nostril. "Say, Whiskers, how'd ye keep the night dew out of that nose o' yourn?"

Whiskers growled an incoherence deep in his throat and spat into the fire in token that he was not pleased by the question.

"For the love o' Mike," the fat man chuckled, "if you got caught out in a rainstorm without an umbrella you'd sure drown, wouldn't you?"

"Can it, Fatty, can it," Whiskers muttered wearily. "They ain't nothin' new in that line of chatter. Even the bulls hand it out to me."

"But you can still drink, I hope." Fatty at the same time mollified and invited, with his one hand deftly pulling the slip-knots that fastened his bindle.

From within the bindle he brought to light a twelve-ounce bottle of alki. Footsteps coming down the embankment alarmed him, and he hid the bottle under his hat on the ground between his legs.

But the next comer proved to be not merely one of their own ilk, but likewise to have only one arm. So forbidding of aspect was he that greetings consisted of no more than grunts. Huge-boned, tall, gaunt to cadaverousness, his face a dirty death's head, he was as repellant a nightmare of old age as ever Doré imagined. His toothless, thin-lipped mouth was a cruel and bitter slash under a great curved nose that almost met the chin and that was like a buzzard's beak. His one hand, lean and crooked, was a talon. The beady gray eyes, unblinking and unwavering, were bitter as death, as bleak as absolute zero and as merciless. His presence was a chill, and Whiskers and Fatty instinctively drew together for protection against the unguessed threat of him. Watching his chance, privily, Whiskers snuggled a chunk of rock several pounds in weight close to his hand if need for action should arise. Fatty duplicated the performance.

Then both sat licking their lips, guiltily embarrassed, while the unblinking eyes of the terrible one bored into them, now into one, now into another, and then down at the rock-chunks of their preparedness.

"Huh!" sneered the terrible one, with such dreadfulness of menace as to cause Whiskers and Fatty involuntarily to close their hands down on their cave-man's weapons.

"Huh!" the other repeated, reaching his one talon into his side coat pocket with swift definiteness. "A hell of a chance you two cheap bums 'd have with me."

The talon emerged, clutching ready for action a six-pound iron quoit.

"We ain't lookin' for trouble, Slim," Fatty quavered.

"Who in hell are you to call me 'Slim'?" came the snarling answer.

"Me? I'm just Fatty, an' seein' 's I never seen you before—"

"An' I suppose that's Whiskers, there, with the gay an' festive lamp tangoing into his eyebrow an' the God-forgive-us nose joy-riding all over his mug?"

"It'll do, it'll do," Whiskers muttered uncomfortably. "One monica's as good as another, I find, at my time of life. And everybody hands it out to me anyway. And I need an umbrella when it rains to keep from getting drowned, an' all the rest of it."

"I ain't used to company—don't like it," Slim growled. "So if you guys want to stick around, mind your step, that's all, mind your step."

He fished from his pocket a cigar stump, self-evidently shot from the gutter, and prepared to put it in his mouth to chew. Then he changed his mind, glared at his companions savagely, and unrolled his bindle. Appeared in his hand a druggist's bottle of alki.

"Well," he snarled, "I suppose I gotta give you cheap skates a drink when I ain't got more'n enough for a good petrification for myself."

Almost a softening flicker of light was imminent in his withered face as he beheld the others proudly lift their hats and exhibit their own supplies.

"Here's some water for the mixin's," Whiskers said, proffering his tomato-can of river slush. "Stockyards just above," he added apologetically. "But they say—"

"Huh!" Slim snapped short, mixing the drink. "I've drunk worse'n stockyards in my time."

Yet when all was ready, cans of alki in their solitary hands, the three things that had once been men hesitated, as if of old habit, and next betrayed shame as if at self-exposure.

Whiskers was the first to brazen it.

"I've sat in at many a finer drinking," he bragged.

"With the pewter," Slim sneered.

"With the silver," Whiskers corrected.

Slim turned a scorching eye-interrogation on Fatty.

Fatty nodded.

"Beneath the salt," said Slim.

"Above it," came Fatty's correction. "I was born above it, and I've never traveled second class. First or steerage, but no intermediate in mine."

"Yourself?" Whiskers queried of Slim.

"In broken glass to the Queen, God bless her," Slim answered, solemnly, without snarl or sneer.

"In the pantry?" Fatty insinuated.

Simultaneously Slim reached for his quoit, and Whiskers and Fatty for their rocks.

"Now don't let's get feverish," Fatty said, dropping his own weapon. "We aren't scum. We're gentlemen. Let's drink like gentlemen."

"Let it be a real drinking," Whiskers approved.

"Let's get petrified," Slim agreed. "Many a distillery's flowed under the bridge since we were gentlemen; but let's forget the long road we've traveled since, and hit our doss in the good old fashion in which every gentleman went to bed when we were young."

"My father done it—did it," Fatty concurred and corrected, as old recollections exploded long-sealed brain-cells of connotation and correct usage.

The other two nodded a descent from similar fathers and elevated their tin cans of alcohol.

By the time each had finished his own bottle and from his rags fished forth a second one, their brains were well-mellowed and a-glow, although they had not got around to telling their real names. But their English had improved. They spoke it correctly, while the argo of tramp-land ceased from their lips.

"It's my constitution," Whiskers was explaining. "Very few men could go through what I have and live to tell the tale. And I never took any care of myself. If what the moralists and the physiologists say were true, I'd have been dead long ago. And it's the same with you two. Look at us, at our advanced years, carousing as the young ones don't dare, sleeping out in the open on the ground, never sheltered from frost nor rain nor storm, never afraid of pneumonia or rheumatism that would put half the young ones on their backs in hospital."

He broke off to mix another drink, and Fatty took up the tale.

"And we've had our fun," he boasted. "And speaking of sweethearts and all," he cribbed from Kipling, " 'We've rouged and we've ranged—' "

" 'In our time,' " Slim completed the crib for him.

"I should say so, I should say so," Fatty confirmed. "And been loved by princesses —at least I have."

"Go on and tell us about it," Whiskers urged. "The night's young, and why shouldn't we remember back to the roofs of kings?"

Nothing loath, Fatty cleared his throat for the recital and cast about in his mind for the best way to begin.

"It must be known that I came of good family. Percival Delaney, let us say, yes, let us say Percival Delaney, was not unknown at Oxford once upon a time—not for scholarship, I am frank to admit; but the gay young dogs of that day, if any be yet alive, would remember him—"

"My people came over with the Conqueror," Whiskers interrupted, extending his hand to Fatty's in acknowledgment of the introduction.

"What name?" Fatty queried. "I did not seem quite to catch it."

"Delarouse, Chauncey Delarouse. The name will serve as well as any."

Both completed the handshake and glanced to Slim.

"Oh, well, while we're about it . . ." Fatty urged.

"Bruce Cadogan Cavendish," Slim growled morosely. "Go on, Percival, with your princesses and the roofs of kings."

"Oh, I was a rare young devil," Percival obliged, "after I played ducks and drakes at home and sported out over the world. And I was some figure of a man before I lost my shape—polo, steeple-chasing, boxing, wrestling, swimming. I won medals at buckjumping in Australia, and I held more than several swimming records from the quarter of a mile up. Women turned their heads to look when I went by. The women! God bless them!"

And Fatty, alias Percival Delaney, a grotesque of manhood, put his bulgy hand to his puffed lips and kissed audibly into the starry vault of the sky.

"And the Princess!" he resumed, with another kiss to the stars. "She was as fine a figure of a woman as I was a man, as high-spirited and courageous, as reckless and dare-devilish. Lord, Lord, in the water she was a mermaid, a sea-goddess. And when it came to blood, beside her I was parvenu. Her royal line traced back into the mists of antiquity.

"She was not a daughter of a fair-skinned folk. Tawny golden was she, with golden-brown eyes, and her hair that fell to her knees was blue-black and straight, with just the curly tendrilly tendency that gives to woman's hair its charm. Oh, there were no kinks in it, any more than were there kinks in the hair of her entire genealogy. For she was Polynesian, glowing, golden, lovely and lovable, royal Polynesian."

Again he paused to kiss his hand to the memory of her, and Slim, alias Bruce Cadogan Cavendish took advantage to interject:

"Huh! Maybe you didn't shine in scholarship, but at least you gleaned a vocabulary out of Oxford."

"And in the South Seas garnered a better vocabulary from the lexicon of Love," Percival was quick on the uptake.

"It was the island of Talofa," he went on, "meaning love, the Isle of Love, and it was her island. Her father, the king, an old man, sat on his mats with paralyzed knees and drank square-face gin all day and most of the night, out of grief, sheer grief. She, my princess, was the only issue, her brothers having been lost in their double canoe in a hurricane while coming up from a voyage to Samoa. And among the Polynesians the royal women have equal right with the men to rule. In fact, they trace their genealogies always by the female line."

To this both Chauncey Delarouse and Bruce Cadogan Cavendish nodded prompt affirmation.

"Ah," said Percival, "I perceive you both know the South Seas, wherefore, without undue expenditure of verbiage on my part, I am assured that you will appreciate the charm of my princess, the Princess Tui-nui of Talofa, the Princess of the Isle of Love."

He kissed his hand to her, sipped from his condensed milk can a man-size drink of druggist's alcohol, and to her again kissed his hand.

"But she was coy, and ever she fluttered near to me but never near enough. When my arm went out to her to girdle her, presto, she was not there. I knew, as never before, nor since, the thousand dear and delightful anguishes of love frustrate but ever resilient and beckoned on by the very goddess of love."

"Some vocabulary," Bruce Cadogan Cavendish muttered in aside to Chauncey Delarouse. But Percival Delaney was not to be deterred. He kissed his pudgy hand aloft into the night and held warmly on.

"No fond agonies of rapture deferred that were not lavished upon me by my dear Princess, herself ever a luring delight of promise flitting just beyond my reach. Every sweet lover's inferno unguessed of by Dante she led me through. Ah! Those tropic nights! Those swooning tropic nights, under our palm trees, the distant surf a languorous murmur as from some vast sea shell of mystery, when she, my Princess, all but melted to my yearning, and with her laughter, that was as silver strings by buds and blossoms smitten, all but made lunacy of my lover's ardency.

"It was by my wrestling with the champions of Talofa that I first interested her. It was by my prowess at swimming that I awoke her. And it was by a certain swimming deed that I won from her more than coquettish smiles and shy timidities of feigned retreat.

"We were squidding that day, out on the reef—you know how, undoubtedly, diving down the face of the wall of the reef, five fathoms, ten fathoms, any depth within reason, and shoving our squid-sticks into the likely holes and crannies of the coral where squid might be lairing. With the squid-stick, bluntly sharp at both ends, perhaps a foot long, and held crosswise in the hand, the trick was to gouge any lazying squid until he closed his tentacles around fist, stick, and arm. Then you had him, and came to the surface with him, and bit him in the head which is in the center of him, and peeled him off into the waiting canoe. . . . And to think I used to do that!"

Percival Delaney paused a moment, a glimmer of awe on his rotund face, as he contemplated the mighty picture of his youth.

"Why, I've pulled out a squid, with tentacles eight feet long, and done it under fifty feet of water. I could stay down four minutes. I've gone down, with a coral-rock to sink me, in a hundred and ten feet to clear a fouled anchor. And I could back-dive with a once-over and go in feet-first from eighty feet above the surface—"

"Quit it, delete it, cease it," Chauncey Delarouse admonished testily. "Tell of the Princess. That's what makes old blood leap again. Almost can I see her. Was she very wonderful?"

Percival Delaney kissed unutterable affirmation.

"I have said she was a mermaid. She was. I know she swam thirty-six hours before being rescued, after her schooner was capsized in a double-squall. I have seen her do ninety feet and bring up pearl shell in each hand. She *was* wonderful. As a woman she was ravishing, sublime. I have said she was a sea-goddess. She was. Oh, for a Phidias or a Praxiteles to have made the wonder of her body immortal!

"And that day, out for squid on the reef, I was almost sick for her. Mad—I know I was mad for her. We would step over the side from the big canoe, and swim down, side by side, into the delicious depths of cool and color, and she would look at me, as we swam, and with her eyes tantalize me to further madness. And at last, down, far down, I lost myself and reached for her. She eluded me like the mermaid she was, and I saw the laughter on her face as she fled. She fled deeper, and I knew I had her for I was between her and the surface; but in the muck coral sand of the bottom she made a churning with her squid-stick. It was the old trick to escape a shark. And she worked it on me, rolling the water so that I could not see her. And when I came up, she was there ahead of me, clinging to the side of the canoe and laughing.

"Almost I would not be denied. But not for nothing was she a princess. She rested her hand on my arm and compelled me to listen. We should play a game, she said, enter into a competition for which should get the more squid, the biggest squid, and the smallest squid. Since the wagers were kisses, you can well imagine I went down on the first next dive with soul aflame.

"I got no squid. Never again in all my life have I dived for squid. Perhaps we were five fathoms down and exploring the face of the reef-wall for lurking places of our prey, when it happened. I had found a likely lair and just proved it empty, when I felt or sensed the nearness of something inimical. I turned. There it was, alongside of me, and no mere fish-shark. Fully a dozen feet in length, with the unmistakable phosphorescent cat's eye gleaming like a drowning star, I knew it for what it was, a tiger shark.

"Not ten feet to the right, probing a coral fissure with her squid-stick, was the Princess, and the tiger shark was heading directly for her. My totality of thought was precipitated to consciousness in a single all-embracing flash. The man-eater must be deflected from her, and what was I, except a mad lover who would gladly fight and die, or more gladly fight and live, for his beloved? Remember, she was the woman wonderful, and I was aflame for her.

"Knowing fully the peril of my act, I thrust the blunt-sharp end of my squid-stick into the side of the shark, much as one would attract a passing acquaintance with a thumb-nudge in the ribs. And the man-eater turned on me. You know the South Seas, and you know that the tiger shark, like the bald-face grizzly of Alaska, never gives trail. The combat, fathoms deep under the sea, was on—if by combat may be named such a one-sided struggle.

"The Princess, unaware, caught her squid and rose to the surface. The man-eater rushed me. I fended him off with both hands on his nose above his thousand-toothed open mouth, so that he backed me against the sharp coral. The scars are there to this day. Whenever I tried to rise, he rushed me, and I could not remain down there indefinitely without air. Whenever he rushed me, I fended off with my hands on his nose. And I would have escaped unharmed, except for the slip of my right hand. Into his mouth it went to the elbow. His jaws closed, just below the elbow. You know how a shark's teeth are. Once in they cannot be released. They must go through to complete the bite, but they cannot go through heavy bone. So, from just below the elbow he stripped the bone clean to the articulation of the wrist-joint, where his teeth met and my good right hand became his for an appetizer.

"But while he was doing this, I drove the thumb of my left hand, to the hilt, into his eye-orifice and popped out his eye. This did not stop him. The meat had maddened him. He pursued the gushing stump of my wrist. Half a dozen times I fended with my intact arm. Then he got the poor mangled arm again, closed down, and stripped the meat off the bone from the shoulder down to the elbow-joint, where his teeth met and he was free of his second mouthful of me. But, at the same time, with my good arm, I thumbed out his remaining eye."

Percival Delaney shrugged his shoulders, ere he resumed.

"From above, those in the canoe had beheld the entire happening and were loud in praise of my deed. To this day they still sing the song of me, and tell the tale of me. And the Princess." His pause was brief but significant. "The Princess married me. . . . Oh, well-a-day and lack-a-day, the whirligig of time and fortune, the topsy-turviness of luck, the wooden shoe going up and the polished heel descending, a French gunboat, a conquered island-kingdom of Oceania, to-day ruled over by a peasant-born, unlettered, colonial gendarme, and . . ."

He completed the sentence and the tale by burying his face in the down-tilted mouth of the condensed milk can and by gurgling the corrosive drink down his throat in thirsty gulps.

After an appropriate pause, Chauncey Delarouse, otherwise Whiskers, took up the tale.

"Far be it from me to boast of no matter what place of birth I have descended from to sit here by this fire with such as . . . as chance along. I may say, however, that I, too, was once a considerable figure of a man. I may add that it was horses, plus parents too indulgent, that exiled me out over the world. I may still wonder to query: 'Are Dover's cliffs still white?' "

"Huh!" Bruce Cadogan Cavendish sneered. "Next you'll be asking 'how fares the old Lord Warden?' "

"And I took every liberty, and vainly, with a constitution that was iron," Whiskers hurried on. "Here I am with my three score and ten behind me, and back on that long road have I buried many a youngster that was as rare and devilish as I but who could not stand the pace. I knew the worst too young. And now I know the worst too old. But there was a time, alas all too short, when I knew the best.

"I, too, kiss my hand to the Princess of my heart. She was truly a princess, Polynesian, a thousand miles and more away to the eastward and the south from Delaney's Isle of Love. The natives of all around that part of the South Seas called it the Jolly Island. Their own name, the name of the people who dwelt thereon, translates delicately and justly into 'The Island of Tranquil Laughter.' On the chart you will find the erroneous name given to it by the old navigators to be Manatomana. The seafaring gentry the round ocean around called it the Adamless Eden. And the missionaries for a time called it God's Witness—so great had been their success at converting the inhabitants. As for me, it was, and ever shall be, Paradise.

"It was *my* Paradise, for it was there my Princess lived. John Asibeli Tungi was king. He was full-blooded native, descended out of the oldest and highest chief-stock that traced back to Manua which was the primeval sea home of the race. Also was he known as John the Apostate. He lived a long life and apostasized frequently. First converted by the Catholics, he threw down the idols, broke the tabus, cleaned out the native priests, executed a few of the recalcitrant ones, and sent all his subjects to church.

"Next he fell for the traders, who developed in him a champagne thirst, and he shipped off the Catholic priests to New Zealand. The great majority of his subjects always followed his lead, and, having no religion at all, ensued the time of the Great Licentiousness, when by all South Seas Missionaries his island, in sermons, was spoken of as Babylon.

"But the traders ruined his digestion with too much champagne, and after several years he fell for the Gospel according to the Methodists, sent his people to church, and cleaned up the beach and the trading crowd so spick and span that he would not permit them to smoke a pipe out of doors on Sunday, and fined one of the chief traders one hundred gold sovereigns for washing his schooner's decks on the Sabbath morn.

"That was the time of the Blue Laws, but perhaps it was too rigorous for King John. Off he packed the Methodists, one fine day, exiled several hundred of his people to Samoa for sticking to Methodism, and, of all things, invented a religion of his own, with himself the figurehead of worship. In this he was aided and abetted by a renegade Fijian. This lasted five years. Maybe he grew tired of being God, or maybe it was because the Fijian decamped with the six thousand pounds in the royal treasury; but at any rate the Second Reformed Wesleyans got him, and his entire kingdom went Wesleyan. The pioneer Wesleyan missionary he actually made prime minister, and what he did to the trading crowd was a caution. Why, in the end, King John's kingdom was blacklisted and boycotted by the traders till the revenues dimished to zero, the people went bankrupt, and King John couldn't borrow a shilling from his most powerful chief.

"By this time he was getting old, and philosophic, and tolerant, and spiritually atavistic. He fired out the Second Reformed Wesleyans, called back the exiles from Samoa, invited in the traders, held a general love-fest, took the lid off, proclaimed religious liberty and high tariff, and as for himself went back to the worship of his ancestors, dug up the idols, reinstated a few octogenarian priests, and observed the tabus. All of which was lovely for the traders, and prosperity reigned. Of course, most of his subjects followed him back into the heathen worship. Yet quite a sprinkling of Catholics, Methodists and Wesleyans remained true to their beliefs and managed to maintain a few squalid, one-horse churches. But King John didn't mind, any more than did he the high times of the traders along the beach. Everything went, so long as the taxes were paid. Even when his wife, Queen Mamare, elected to become a Baptist, and invited in a little, weazened, sweet-spirited, club-footed Baptist missionary, King John did not object. All he insisted on was that these wandering religions should be self-supporting and not feed a pennyworth's out of the royal coffers.

"And now the threads of my recital draw together in the paragon of female exquisiteness—my Princess."

Whiskers paused, placed carefully on the round his half-full condensed milk can with which he had been absently toying, and kissed the fingers of his one hand audibly aloft.

"She was the daughter of Queen Mamare. She was the woman wonderful. Unlike the Diana type of Polynesian, she was almost ethereal. She *was* ethereal, sublimated by purity, as shy and modest as a violet, as fragile-slender as a lily, and her eyes, luminous and shrinking tender, were as asphodels on the sward of heaven. She was all flower, and fire, and dew. Hers was the sweetness of the mountain rose, the gentleness of the dove. And she was all of good as well as all of beauty, devout in her belief in her mother's worship, which was the worship introduced by Ebenezer Naismith, the Baptist missionary. But make no mistake. She was no mere sweet spirit ripe for the bosom of Abraham. All of exquisite deliciousness of woman was she. She was woman, all woman, to the last sensitive, quivering atom of her—

"And I? I was a wastrel of the beach. The wildest was not so wild as I, the keenest not so keen, of all that wild, keen trading crowd. It was esteemed I played the stiffest hand of poker. I was the only living man, white, brown, or black, who dared run the Kuni-kuni Passage in the dark. And on a black night I have done it under reefs in a gale of wind. Well, anyway, I had a bad reputation on a beach where there were no good reputations. I was reckless, dangerous, stopped at nothing in fight or frolic; and the trading captains used to bring boiler-sheeted prodigies from the vilest holes of the South Pacific to try and drink me under the table. I remember one, a calcined Scotchman from the New Hebrides. It was a great drinking. He died of it, and we laded him aboard ship, pickled in a cask of trade rum, and sent him back to his own place. A sample, a fair sample, of the antic tricks we cut up on the beach of Manatomana.

"And of all unthinkable things, what did I up and do, one day, but look upon the Princess to find her good and to fall in love with her. It was the real thing. I was as mad as a March hare, and after that I got only madder. I reformed. Think of that! Think of what a slip of a woman can do to a lusty, roving man! By the Lord Harry, it's true. I reformed. I went to church. Hear me! I became converted. I cleared my soul before God and kept my hands—I had two then—off the ribald crew of the beach when it laughed at this, my latest antic, and wanted to know what was my game.

"I tell you I reformed, and gave myself in passion and sincerity to a religious experience that has made me tolerant of all religion ever since. I discharged my best captain for immorality. So did I my cook, and a better never boiled water in Manatomana. For the same reason I discharged my chief clerk. And for the first time in the history of trading my schooners to the westward carried Bibles in their stock. I built a little anchorite bungalow up town on a mango-lined street squarely alongside the little house occupied by Ebenezer Naismith. And I made him my pal and comrade, and found him a veritable honey pot of sweetnesses and goodnesses. And he was a man, through and through a man. And he died long after like a man, which I would like to tell you about, were the tale of it not so deservedly long.

"It was the Princess, more than the missionary, who was responsible for my expressing my faith in works, and especially in that crowning work, the New Church, Our Church, the Queen-mother's church.

" 'Our poor church,' she said to me, one night after prayer-meeting. I had been converted only a fortnight. 'It is so small, its congregation can never grow. And the roof leaks. And King John, my hard-hearted father, will not contribute a penny. Yet he has a big balance in the treasury. And Manatomana is not poor. Much money is made and squandered. I know. I hear the gossip of the wild ways of the beach. Less than a month ago you lost more in one night, gambling at cards, than the cost of the upkeep of our poor church for a year.'

"And I told her it was true, but that it was before I had seen the light. (I'd had an infernal run of bad luck.) I told her I had not tasted liquor since, nor turned a card. I told her that the roof would be repaired at once, by Christian carpenters selected by her from the congregation. But she was filled with the thought of a great revival that Ebenezer Naismith could preach—she was a dear saint; and she spoke of a great church, saying:

" 'You are rich. You have many schooners, and traders in far islands, and I have heard of a great contract you have signed to recruit labor for the German plantations of Upolu. They say, next to Sweitzer, you are the richest trader here. I should love to see some use of all this money placed to the glory of God. It would be a noble thing to do, and I should be proud to know the man who would do it.'

"I told her that Ebenezer Naismith would preach the revival, and that I would build a church great enough in which to house it.

" 'As big as the Catholic church?' she asked.

"This was the ruined cathedral, built at the time when the entire population was converted, and it was a large order; but I was afire with love, and I told her that the church I would build would be even bigger.

" 'But it will take money,' I explained. 'And it takes time to make money.'

" 'You have much,' she said. 'Some say you have more money than my father, the King.'

" 'I have more credit,' I explained. 'But you do not understand money. It takes money to have credit. So, with the money I have, and the credit I have, I will work to make more money and credit, and the church shall be built.'

"Work! I was a surprise to myself. It is an amazement, the amount of time a man finds on his hands after he's given up carousing, and gambling, and all the time-eating diversions of the beach. And I didn't waste a second of all my new-found time. Instead I worked it overtime. I did the work of half a dozen men. I became a driver. My captains made faster runs than ever and earned bigger bonuses, as did my supercargoes, who saw to it that my schooners did not loaf and dawdle along the way. And I saw to it that my supercargoes did see to it.

"And good! By the Lord Harry, I was so good it hurt. My conscience got so expansive and fine-strung it lamed me across the shoulders to carry it around with me. Why, I even went back over my accounts and paid Sweitzer fifty quid I'd jiggered him out of in a deal in Fiji three years before. And I compounded the interest as well.

"Work! I planted sugar cane—the first commercial planting on Manatomana. I ran in cargoes of kinky-heads from Malaita, which is in the Solomons, till I had twelve hundred of the blackbirds putting in cane. And I sent a schooner clear to Hawaii to bring back a dismantled sugar mill and a German who said he knew the field end of cane. And he did, and he charged me three hundred dollars screw a month, and I took hold of the mill-end. I installed the mill myself, with the help of several mechanics I brought up from Queensland.

"Of course there was a rival. His name was Motomoe. He was the very highest chief blood next to King John's. He was full native, a strapping, handsome man, with a glowering way of showing his dislikes. He certainly glowered at me when I began hanging around the palace. He went back in my history and circulated the blackest tales about me. The worst of it was that most of them were true. He even made a voyage to Apia to find things out—as if he couldn't find aplenty right there on the beach of Manatomana! And he sneered at my falling for religion, and at my going to prayer-meeting, and, most of all, at my sugar-planting. He challenged me to fight, and I kept off of him. He threatened me, and I learned in the nick of time of his plan to have me knocked on the head. You see, he wanted the Princess just as much as I did, and I wanted her more.

"She used to play the piano. So did I, once. But I never let her know after I'd heard her play the first time. And she thought her playing was wonderful, the dear, fond girl! You know the sort, the mechanical one-two-three, tum-tum-tum school-girl stuff. And now I'll tell you something funnier. Her playing *was* wonderful, to me. The gates of heaven opened to me when she played. I can see myself now, worn out and dog-tired after the long day, lying on the mats of the palace veranda and gazing upon her at the piano, myself in a perfect idiocy of bliss. Why, this idea she had of her fine playing was the one flaw in her deliciousness of perfection, and I loved her for it. It kind of brought her within my human reach. Why, when she played her one-two-three, tum-tum-tum, I was in the seventh heaven of bliss. My weariness fell from me. I loved her, and my love for her was clean as flame, clean as my love for God. And do you know, into my fond lover's fancy continually intruded the thought that God in most ways must look like her.

"—That's right, Bruce Cadogan Cavendish, sneer as you like. But I tell you that's love that I've been describing. That's all. It's love. It's the realest, purest, finest thing that can happen to a man. And I know what I'm talking about. It happened to me."

Whiskers, his beady squirrel's eye glittering from out his ruined eyebrow like a live coal in a jungle ambush, broke off long enough to down a sedative draught from his condensed milk can and to mix another.

"The cane," he resumed, wiping his prodigious mat of face hair with the back of his hand. "It matured in sixteen months in that climate, and I was ready, just ready and no more, with the mill for the grinding. Naturally, it did not all mature at once, but I had planted in such succession that I could grind for nine months steadily, while more was being planted and the ratoons were springing up.

"I had my troubles the first several days. If it wasn't one thing the matter with the mill, it was another. On the fourth day, Ferguson, my engineer, had to shut down several hours in order to remedy his own troubles. I was bothered by the feeder. After having the niggers (who had been feeding the cane) pour cream of lime on the rollers to keep everything sweet, I sent them out to join the cane-cutting squads. So I was all alone at that end, just as Ferguson started up the mill, just as I discovered what was the matter with the feed-rollers, and just as Motomoe strolled up.

"He stood there, in Norfolk jacket, pigskin puttees, and all the rest of the fashionable get-up out of a bandbox, sneering at me covered with filth and grease to the eyebrows and looking like a navvy. And, the rollers now white from the lime, I'd just seen what was wrong. The rollers were not in plumb. One side crushed the cane well, but the other side was too open. I shoved my fingers in on that side. The big, toothed cogs on the rollers did not touch my fingers. And yet, suddenly, they did. With the grip of ten thousand devils, my finger-tips were caught, drawn in, and pulped to—well, just pulp. And, like a stick of cane, I had started on my way. There was no stopping me. Ten thousand horses could not have pulled me back. There was nothing to stop me. Hand, arm, shoulder, head, and chest, down to the toes of me, I was doomed to feed through.

"It did hurt. It hurt so much it did not hurt at all. Quite detached, almost may I say, I looked on my hand being ground up, knuckle by knuckle, joint by joint, the back of the hand, the wrist, the forearm, all in order slowly and inevitably feeding in. O engineer hoist by thine own petard! O sugar-maker crushed by thine own cane-crusher!

"Motomoe sprang forward involuntarily, and the sneer was chased from his face by an expression of solicitude. Then the beauty of the situation dawned on him, and he chuckled and grinned. No, I didn't expect anything of him. Hadn't he tried to knock me on the head? What could he do anyway? He didn't know anything about engines.

"I yelled at the top of my lungs to Ferguson to shut off the engine, but the roar of the machinery drowned my voice. And there I stood, up to the elbow and feeding right on in. Yes, it did hurt. There were some astonishing twinges when special nerves were shredded and dragged out by the roots. But I remember that I was surprised at the time that it did not hurt worse.

"Motomoe made a movement that attracted my attention. At the same time he growled out loud, as if he hated himself, 'I'm a fool.' What he had done was to pick up a cane-knife—you know the kind, as big as a machete and as heavy. And I was grateful to him in advance for putting me out of my misery. There wasn't any sense in slowly feeding in till my head was crushed, and already my arm was pulped half way from elbow to shoulder, and the pulping was going right on. So I was grateful, as I bent my head to the blow.

" 'Get your head out of the way, you idiot!' he barked at me.

"And then I understood and obeyed. I was a big man, and he took two hacks to do it; but he hacked my arm off just outside the shoulder and dragged me back and laid me down on the cane.

"Yes, the sugar paid—enormously; and I built for the Princess the church of her saintly dream, and . . . she married me."

He partly assuaged his thirst, and uttered his final word.

"Alackaday! Shuttlecock and battledore. And this at the end of it all, lined with boiler plate that even alcohol will not corrode and that only alcohol will tickle. Yet have I lived, and I kiss my hand to the dear dust of my Princess long asleep in the great mausoleum of King John that looks across the Vale of Manona to the alien flag that floats over the bungalow of the British Government House. . . ."

Fatty pledged him sympathetically, and sympathetically drank out of his own small can. Bruce Cadogan Cavendish glared into the fire with implacable bitterness. He was a man who preferred to drink by himself. Across the thin lips that composed the cruel slash of his mouth played twitches of mockery that caught Fatty's eye. And Fatty, making sure first that his rock-chunk was within reach, challenged.

"Well, how about yourself, Bruce Cadogan Cavendish? It's your turn."

The other lifted bleak eyes that bored into Fatty's until he physically betrayed uncomfortableness.

"I've lived a hard life," Slim grated harshly. "What do I know about love passages?"

"No man of your build and make-up could have escaped them," Fatty wheedled.

"And what of it?" Slim snarled. "It's no reason for a gentleman to boast of amorous triumphs."

"Oh, go on, be a good fellow," Fatty urged. "The night's still young. We've still some drink left. Delarouse and I have contributed our share. It isn't often that three real ones like us get together for a telling. Surely you've got at least one adventure in love you aren't ashamed to tell about—"

Bruce Cadogan Cavendish pulled forth his iron quoit and seemed to debate whether or not he should brain the other. He sighed, and put back the quoit.

"Very well, if you will have it," he surrendered with manifest reluctance. "Like you two, I have had a remarkable constitution. And right now, speaking of armor-plate lining, I could drink the both of you down when you were at your prime. Like you two, my beginnings were far distant and different. That I am marked with the hall-mark of gentlehood there is no discussion . . . unless either of you cares to discuss the matter now . . ."

His one hand slipped into his pocket and clutched the quoit. Neither of his auditors spoke nor betrayed any awareness of his menace.

"It occurred a thousand miles to the westward of Manatomana, on the island of Tagalag," he continued abruptly, with an air of saturnine disappointment in that there had been no discussion. "But first I must tell you of how I got to Tagalag. For reasons I shall not mention, by paths of descent I shall not describe, in the crown of my manhood and the prime of my devilishness in which Oxford renegades and racing younger sons had nothing on me. I found myself master and owner of a schooner so well known that she shall remain historically nameless. I was running blackbird labor from the West South Pacific and the Coral Sea to the plantations of Hawaii and the nitrate mines of Chili—"

"It was you who cleaned out the entire population of—" Fatty exploded, ere he could check his speech.

The one hand of Bruce Cadogan Cavendish flashed pocketward and flashed back with the quoit balanced ripe for business.

"Proceed," Fatty sighed. "I . . . I have quite forgotten what I was going to say."

"Beastly funny country over that way," the narrator drawled with perfect casualness. "You've read this Sea Wolf stuff—"

"You weren't the Sea Wolf," Whiskers broke in with involuntary positiveness.

"No, sir," was the snarling answer. "The Sea Wolf's dead, isn't he? And I'm still alive, aren't I?"

"Of course, of course," Whiskers conceded. "He suffocated head-first in the mud off a wharf in Victoria a couple of years back."

"As I was saying—and I don't like interruptions," Bruce Cadogan Cavendish proceeded, "it's a beastly funny country over that way. I was at Taki-Tiki, a low island that politically belongs to the Solomons, but that geologically doesn't at all, for the Solomons are high islands. Ethnographically it belongs to Polynesia, Melanesia, and Micronesia, because all the breeds of the South Pacific have gravitated to it by canoe-drift and intricately, degeneratively, and amazingly interbred. The scum of the scrapings of the bottom of the human pit, biologically speaking, resides in Taki-Tiki. And I know the bottom and whereof I speak.

"It was a beastly funny time of it I had, diving out shell, fishing beche-de-mer, trading hoop-iron and hatchets for copra and ivory-nuts, running niggers and all the rest of it. Why, even in Fiji the Lotu was having a hard time of it and the chiefs still eating long-pig. To the westward it was fierce—funny little black kinky-heads, man-eaters the last Jack of them, and the jack pot fat and spilling over with wealth—"

"Jack pots?" Fatty queried. At sight of an irritable movement, he added: "You see, I never got over to the West like Delarouse and you."

"They're all head-hunters. Heads are valuable, especially a whiteman's head. They decorate the canoe-houses and devil-devil houses with them. Each village runs a jack pot, and everybody antes. Whoever brings in a whiteman's head takes the pot. If there aren't openers for a long time, the pot grows to tremendous proportions. Beastly funny, isn't it?

"I know. Didn't a Holland mate die on me of blackwater? And didn't I win a pot myself? It was this way. We were lying at Lango-lui at the time. I never let on, and arranged the affair with Johnny, my boat-steerer. He was a kinky-head himself from Port Moresby. He cut the dead mate's head off and sneaked ashore in the night, while I whanged away with my rifle as if I were trying to get him. He opened the pot with the mate's head, and got it, too. Of course, next day I sent in a landing boat, with two covering boats, and fetched him off with the loot."

"How big was the pot?" Whiskers asked. "I heard of a pot at Orla worth eighty quid."

"To commence with," Slim answered, "there were forty fat pigs, each worth a fathom of prime shell-money, and shell-money worth a quid a fathom. That was two hundred dollars right there. There were ninety-eight fathoms of shell-money, which is pretty close to five hundred in itself. And there were twenty-two gold sovereigns. I split it four ways: one-fourth to Johnny, one-fourth to the ship, one-fourth to me as owner, and one-fourth to me as skipper. Johnny never complained. He'd never had so much wealth all at one time in his life. Besides, I gave him a couple of the mate's old shirts. And I fancy the mate's head is still there decorating the canoe-house."

"Not exactly Christian burial of a Christian," Whiskers observed.

"But a lucrative burial," Slim retorted. "I had to feed the rest of the mate overside to the sharks for nothing. Think of feeding an eight-hundred-dollar head along with it. It would have been criminal waste and stark lunacy.

"Well, anyway, it was all beastly funny, over there to the westward. And, without telling you the scrape I got into at Taki-Tiki, except that I sailed away with two hundred kinky-heads for Queensland labor, and for my manner of collecting them had two British ships of war combing the Pacific for me, I changed my course and ran to the westward thinking to dispose of the lot to the Spanish plantations on Bangar.

"Typhoon season. We caught it. The *Merry Mist* was my schooner's name, and I had thought she was stoutly built until she hit that typhoon. I never saw such seas. They pounded that stout craft to pieces, literally so. The sticks were jerked out of her, deckhouses splintered to matchwood, rails ripped off, and, after the worst had passed, the covering boards began to go. We just managed to repair what was left of one boat and keep the schooner afloat only till the sea went down barely enough to get away. And we outfitted that boat in a hurry. The carpenter and I were the last, and we had to jump for it as she went down. There were only four of us—"

"Lost all the niggers?" Whiskers inquired.

"Some of them swam for some time," Slim replied. "But I don't fancy they made the land. We were ten days in doing it. And we had a spanking breeze most of the way. And what do you think we had in the boat with us? Cases of square-face gin and cases of dynamite. Funny, wasn't it? Well, it got funnier later on. Oh, there was a small breaker of water, a little salt horse, and some salt-water-soaked sea biscuit—enough to keep us alive to Tagalag.

"Now Tagalag is the disappointingest island I've ever beheld. It shows up out of the sea so as you can make its fall twenty miles off. It is a volcano cone thrust up out of deep sea, with a segment of the crater wall broken out. This gives sea entrance to the crater itself, and makes a fine sheltered harbor. And that's all. Nothing lives there. The outside and the inside of the crater are too steep. At one place, inside, is a patch of about a thousand coconut palms. And that's all, as I said, saving a few insects. No four-legged thing, even a rat, inhabits the place. And it's funny, most awful funny, with all those coconuts, not even a coconut crab. The only meat-food living was schools of mullet in the harbor—fattest, finest, biggest mullet I ever laid eyes on.

"And the four of us landed on the little beach and set up housekeeping among the coconuts with a larder full of dynamite and square-face. Why don't you laugh? It's funny, I tell you. Try it some time—Holland gin and straight coconut diet. I've never been able to look a confectioner's window in the face since. Now I'm not strong on religion like Chauncey Delarouse there, but I have some primitive ideas; and my concept of hell is an illimitable coconut plantation, stocked with cases of square-face and populated by shipwrecked mariners. Funny? It must make the devil scream.

"You know, straight coconut is what the agriculturalists call an unbalanced ration. It certainly unbalanced our digestions. We got so that whenever hunger took an extra bite at us, we took another drink of gin. After a couple of weeks of it, Olaf, a squarehead sailor, got an idea. It came when he was full of gin, and we, being in the same fix, just watched him shove a cap and short fuse into a stick of dynamite and stroll down toward the boat.

"It dawned on me that he was going to shoot fish if there were any about; but the sun was beastly hot, and I just reclined there and hoped he'd have luck.

"About half an hour after he disappeared, we heard the explosion. But he didn't come back. We waited till the cool of sunset, and down on the beach found what had become of him. The boat was there all right, grounded by the prevailing breeze, but there was no Olaf. He would never have to eat coconut again. We went back, shakier than ever, and cracked another square-face.

"The next day the cook announced that he would rather take his chance with dynamite than continue trying to exist on coconut, and that, though he didn't know anything about dynamite, he knew a sight too much about coconut. So we bit the detonator down for him, shoved in a fuse, and picked him a good fire-stick, while he jolted up with a couple more stiff ones of gin.

"It was the same program as the day before. After a while we heard the explosion and at twilight went down to the boat, from which we scraped enough of the cook for a funeral.

"The carpenter and I stuck it out two days more, then we drew straws for it and it was his turn. We parted with harsh words; for he wanted to take a square-face along to refresh himself by the way, while I was set against running any chance of wasting the gin. Besides, he had more than he could carry then, and he wobbled and staggered as he walked.

"Same thing, only there was a whole lot of him left for me to bury, because he'd prepared only half a stick. I managed to last it out till next day, when, after duly fortifying myself, I got sufficient courage to tackle the dynamite. I used only a third of a stick—you know, short fuse, with the end split so as to hold the head of a safety match. That's where I mended my predecessors' methods. Not using the match-head, they'd too-long fuses. Therefore, when they spotted a school of mullet and lighted the fuse, they had to hold the dynamite till the fuse burned short before they threw it. If they threw it too soon, it wouldn't go off the instant it hit the water, while the splash of it would frighten the mullet away. Funny stuff dynamite. At any rate, I still maintain mine was the safer method.

"I picked up a school of mullet before I'd been rowing five minutes. Fine big fat ones they were, and I could smell them over the fire. When I stood up, fire-stick in one hand, dynamite stick in the other, my knees were knocking together. Maybe it was the gin, or the anxiousness, or the weakness and the hunger, and maybe it was the result of all of them, but at any rate I was all of a shake. Twice I failed to touch the fire-stick to the dynamite. Then I did, heard the match-head splutter, and let her go.

"Now I don't know what happened to the others, but I know what I did. I got turned about. Did you ever stem a strawberry and throw the strawberry away and pop the stem into your mouth? That's what I did. I threw the fire-stick into the water after the mullet amd held onto the dynamite. And my arm went off with the stick when it went off. . . ."

Slim investigated the tomato-can for water to mix himself a drink, but found it empty. He stood up.

"Heigh ho," he yawned, and started down the path to the river.

In several minutes he was back. He mixed the due quantity of river slush with the alcohol, took a long, solitary drink, and stared with bitter moodiness into the fire.

"Yes, but . . ." Fatty suggested. "What happened then?"

"Oh," said Slim. "Then the princess married me, of course."

"But you were the only person left, and there wasn't any princess . . ." Whiskers cried out abruptly, and then let his voice trail away to embarrassed silence.

Slim stared unblinkingly into the fire.

Percival Delaney and Chauncey Delarouse looked at each other. Quietly, in solemn silence, each with his one arm aided the one arm of the other in rolling and tying his bindle. And in silence, bindles slung on shoulders, they went away out of the circle of fire-light. Not until they reached the top of the railroad embankment did they speak.

"No gentleman would have done it," said Whiskers.

"No gentleman would have done it," Fatty agreed.

1918